Call of Brindelier

By Missy Sheldrake

For James and Wesley,
my two true loves

Table of Contents

Map of the Known Lands

Map of Cerion City

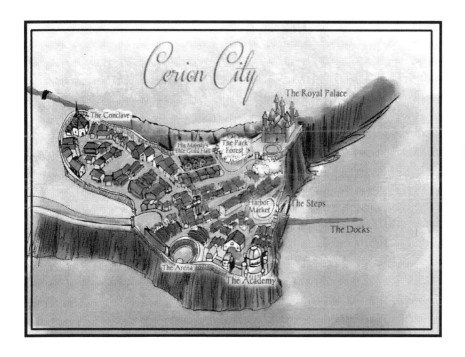

Map of The Hammerfel Residence

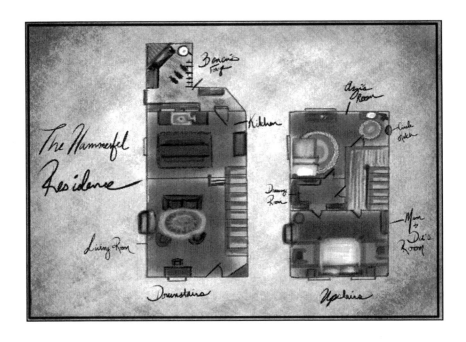

Map of His Majesty's Elite Guild Hall

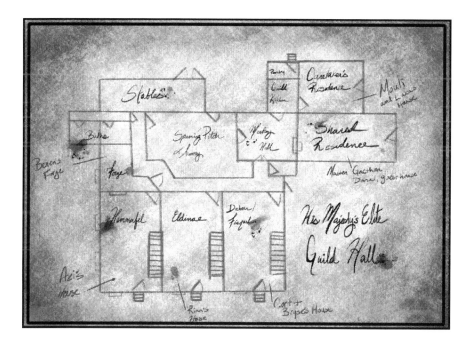

Chapter One

THE SORCERERS' LAIR

Celli

I lie still, too afraid to open my eyes as the Sorceress finishes her spell. I can feel the heat from her hands as they hover over my face. Her bracelets jingle softly as she moves. I don't have a lot of time to take stock of things. She knows I'm awake. My breathing is too fast. My heart is racing. Still, I pretend to be asleep.

"Take your time," the woman soothes. Her voice is deep and unfamiliar. The power behind it makes my skin prickle.

Her soft footsteps leave the bedside, but her scent lingers behind: roses, spice, and incense. Carefully, quietly, I let my fingers graze the bed. It's cloud-soft. Silky, like a fine gown. Not like my pallet at home, where straw and feathers poke through the rough burlap. I want to burrow into it and forget my whole life until now, or at least forget how I failed.

That island boy was so weak. I don't care if he was a Mage. I shouldn't have let Tib interrupt me or distract me. I should have just taken the satchel and ran with it like I was supposed to, but I was afraid of the spells. I knew he'd do it if he had to, that satchel boy. He'd cast something on me.

"I should have just killed him," I whisper.

The Sorceress jingles closer. Her hand scoops mine gently from the bed. *Stupid, Celli.* I tell myself. *Be quiet.* I squeeze my eyes shut even tighter. I don't know how I got here, or why. I don't know who this woman is. I don't want to give her a reason to hurt me.

"First blood, though thrilling, is not to be taken lightly," she murmurs. Something traces along my palm, tickling my skin. I remember the swirls there from whatever was in that satchel. Mage Mark, but red. The pain is gone now. I wonder whether the Mark is, too, but I don't dare look. If I keep quiet and still enough, maybe she can forgive me. Maybe they'll go easy on me for failing the task. It seemed like such a simple job at the time, to steal a satchel from a boy.

Thieving has always come easy to me. It started when I was much younger and things were different in Cerion. Everyone was cheerful then, always smiling. Da had regular work then, and he'd come home tired from a long day with a sack full from the market. A toy for me and my brother, Hew. A flower for Mum. He'd kiss her and whisper into her soft golden hair and her cheeks would go rosy as the soft petals brushed her nose.

I used to go out even then, into the city. It was so crowded that it was easy to take a coin from a belt or two and never be noticed. I didn't need it. We weren't starved or anything. I did it for the thrill. I would pick out the richest looking ones. Lords and ladies in finery. People who wouldn't miss a silver or two. Some of them even had guards with them. Those were the most challenging. I tried to best my take every day. Sometimes, my own purse would be so heavy with coin that I'd have to go home and empty it by midday.

I got a reputation. The boys on the street noticed. They started trying to steal my earnings. That's when I had to learn how to fight. The younger ones started following along so I taught them how to steal and fight, too. Among the kids in Redstone Row, I was either looked up to or feared. That was fine by me. I mostly stashed the coin I stole, but I'd always come home with something for Hew.

The Sorceress lowers my hand to the bed and jingles away again. She doesn't say anything more to me, but I can hear her quill scratching across the parchment as she makes notes nearby. I swallow the lump that forms in my throat when I think about my brother. His adorable drooling smile swims in my memory, but then his face changes. Blue. Blotched. His tiny bundled body on the mattress nestled between me and Mum, unmoving. My eyes fly open with my mother's screams still ringing in my ears. That's the only way I can remember him anymore. Stiff. Lifeless.

I look around, trying desperately to push the image out of my mind. The first thing I notice is all of the red. Red canopy and curtains on the bed, red silk coverlet, red tapestries. Even the Sorceress at the desk across the room is draped in the color, like camouflage.

I've never seen a place so rich before. The furniture is carved and polished to a high shine. A table at the bedside holds a silver pitcher and a goblet that sparkle in the sunlight beaming through the high windows. The glass is stained with colorful pictures of men and women in strange poses with their robes fluttering around them.

"Are we in the palace?" I ask. As soon as the words leave my lips I feel foolish. *Of course we're not in the palace, stupid,* I think to myself.

She doesn't answer. Maybe she knows I feel ashamed for asking. I imagine they can tell those sort of things. Anyway, she keeps writing. I glance at the pitcher and goblet again. I'm so thirsty, but whatever's inside could be anything. A potion, maybe, put there to kill me. I close my eyes again and see my brother's face lingering, leering at me.

Da started drinking after the baby died. Mum was never the same, either. When the work stopped coming, things got much worse. I spent all my stashed coin on food, and when that was gone I stole to eat. The thrill made me want to steal more, so I just kept doing it. Coin, trinkets, food, fighting. What did it matter, when Da was barely able to get up most days and Mum was too sick with grief to notice me anymore? Maybe if they'd paid better attention, I wouldn't be stuck here now. Or maybe they noticed I'm gone. Maybe they're worried about me. I wonder how long I was out. A sleep spell can go on for days. The ones they put on prisoners in Cerion can stay on for months.

"Am I a prisoner?" I ask the woman across the room.

"Do you feel like one?" she replies without even looking up from her desk.

I run my hand over the soft bed covers and think about it. They're so rich and fine, like the robes of the man whose purse I tried to slip a coin from just days ago. Or maybe it was longer. I'm not sure.

He was just standing there at Cerion's harbor wall, tucked to the side near the Academy. I knew he was a Mage right away. The robes were a dead giveaway.

I had been less interested in the coin than the challenge. Mages are tricky to pick from. They have too many protections. But, stupid Celli, I keep trying to figure out a way. Just to see if I can do it. Being able to steal from a Mage could make me famous, I had thought. I imagined there were people out there who'd pay heaps to have something filched from one of them. So I kept trying.

I almost did it, too. I had the coin in my hand. It was a strange one. Silver, with little prongs around the outside. One side was smooth, and the flip side had clouds on it. He probably wouldn't have caught me if I wasn't dumb enough to stand there in the open gaping at it, but the next thing I knew, his gloved hand was clamped around my wrist and I was being pulled into an alley.

As soon as I looked into his face, I knew my mistake. Even through the black veil I could see the blue-black Mark curling over his cheeks and nose. Nobody is Marked in Cerion. The Mages here are all too careful. Too good. If they end up with the Mark, they work hard to

3

make it fade. If not, they face getting stripped of their magic. This man was no Mage. He hadn't been for a long time, judging by the amount of skin the Mark covered. No, he was a Sorcerer.

"Yes, you see now," he said. I can still see his grin beneath the cover and his cold, dark eyes like they've been imprinted on my soul. "Clever girl."

I remember feeling anything but clever in that moment. Terror, shame, and a strong desire to run, maybe. Not clever at all.

"What will you do to me?" I whispered as his spell shimmered around us, concealing us from those walking in the street nearby.

His eyes bored into me. He looked at me for so long that I finally had to look away.

"You need not fear me," he said. His voice was gentle and smooth. It made my heart race. I looked back into his face. He was handsome, I could tell, underneath the veil. The Mark gave him an air of mystery and danger that made me want to please him. "I shall forgive this transgression. Look there." His hand on my shoulder sent a warmth spreading through me as he turned me toward the street. "Do you see that boy in the yellow?"

The memory fades away, snuffed out by the lingering weight of my failure. I sigh and prop myself on my elbows cautiously. The Sorceress doesn't say anything. I wonder if he's here; the Sorcerer who pulled me into the shadows, who let me keep the strange coin in exchange for the satchel I promised to get for him. I wonder if he knows I failed yet.

The thought of failing him sends me to a dark and desperate place. I don't know why. I don't even know his name. I try to remember what happened after I touched the thing in the satchel, but there's nothing but pain and darkness.

"Where are we? What is this place?" I ask as the woman at the desk blots her writing and sets down her quill. She's very pretty, with long, wavy brown hair and deep brown eyes. Her Mark is not as prominent as the Sorcerer's. The blue-black swirls of it have only begin to curl up to her chin.

"Far from any place you've been, girl," she drawls, like she's already growing bored of me.

Her words and her tone draw out my anger and make it bubble inside of me. I want to argue that I'm not just a girl. A child. I want to shout at her for assuming I haven't been anywhere, even though it's true. She crosses to me again, and the soft jingling and the swish of her gown soothe me. I'm entranced by the Mark that curls across her elegant neck and up behind her ear.

When I was very young, I longed to be a Mage, but our family could never afford it. Instead, my mum taught me a healthy fear of the Arcane, just like every dutiful mother in Cerion does. It's forbidden to even try to dabble in magic without proper instruction. We're taught early that a Mark is treason and wickedness. It shows the greed for power plain on your skin, for all to see. Watching this Sorceress as she nears me, though, makes me curious. Envious. I want to look like her. I want to be powerful, like she is.

She comes to sit beside me and takes my red-Marked hand again.

"What matters more than where you are is where you're going," she says. "Quenson has seen promise in you. Even though you failed him, he wishes to speak with you."

"Quenson? Is that his name?" I blush, remembering the Sorcerer's handsome face. He sees something in me. The thought makes me grin. Nobody's said that about me before, especially not someone like him.

"It is," she smiles knowingly. "And I am Sybel. I'm to look after you while you're here." Her eyes drift to my hand in hers. From the way she fixates on it and how much she's been writing, I figure she's more interested in the red Mark than anything else.

"What is it?" I ask, turning my hand over to look at it. Some of the curls are already fading.

"Inquisitive," she says, but doesn't bother to answer my question. "We must make you presentable. Come, stand up."

I slide from the bed with her help. I'm still a little dizzy from the sleep spell. She circles around me, looking me up and down. After a moment she points at my feet and they start to tingle. I fight the urge to scream and run as her spell creeps over me. It weaves through the fibers in my clothing, changing them slowly. The spell changes me, too, a little. It gives me courage.

"There," she says when her work is through. "You shall not forget this small kindness, nor shall you forget it is my spell which afforded it to you."

I look down at myself in disbelief at the change. When I do, my usually stringy, sticky hair slinks forward freely. I turn my head and it swings and bounces perfectly. My skin is clean and soft. Even my knuckles are free of the ever-present bruises and scrapes from fighting with my fists. The old Celli is gone. I feel like a noble.

My clothes have changed, too. Soft gray suede trimmed in red and silver. The new tunic and leggings are finer than anything I've owned in my life. They cling to me and move with me as comfortably as a second skin. A rich black cloak drapes my shoulders, mocking the summer heat. It drifts behind me like a veil. I can feel the magic in it. When Sybel flicks a finger and the hood settles on my slicked-back hair, I feel the same shift I felt when Quenson concealed us in the alley.

"If you prove yourself," Sybel rests her hands on my shoulders and whispers, "Quenson will offer you more than this in exchange for your allegiance. But should anything happen to me, you shall lose my gifts."

"Why would something happen to you? Is he your enemy?" I whisper, pushing my hood back.

"My dear girl," she chuckles, "among our group, allies and enemies are one and the same. You would do well to remember that. Come."

I've never been inside of a palace before. If this isn't one, I can't imagine what it is. Even in the corridors the ceilings are so high they disappear into darkness. There are so many details that if I wasn't concentrating so hard on following Sybel I'd probably get lost just from fixating on them.

Da was a stone carver before the king stopped ordering work and the drink ruined him. I've spent long afternoons outside of the conclave and other buildings around Cerion admiring his craftsmanship. None of it can compare to this, though. Patterns and mazes and swirls and filigree cover every surface. I'm so busy taking it all in that I forget to pay attention to where we've been and how we got there.

When Sybel leaves me to wait alone in a circular room, I suddenly realize that was probably the whole point of all of those patterns. To distract me from knowing where I was. The realization makes me feel angry and foolish all over again.

This room is strange. It's dark, and the floor is covered with gold tiles in the shape of a sunburst that starts in the center and goes out toward the walls. Each point of the sunburst creeps up to an alcove in the wall, and each alcove holds an empty pedestal. I think about going to look at one closer, but before I can move, Quenson appears in the doorway.

He's flanked by two guards: a woman and a man both wearing heavy chain mail. They post themselves just inside and eye me with caution while the Sorcerer approaches me. I don't let them intimidate me. With him standing as close to me now as we were in the alley, they don't matter, anyway. He's even more handsome than I remembered.

"Sybel has outdone herself," he says as he circles around me, looking me over.

His tone makes my cheeks go hot. He's dangerous, I know, but that excites me. All I want is his approval. I want him to admire me. I want to always be close to him. I want to show him that I can do anything for him. Whatever he needs me to do. I watch him come around to face me again, where he stands and looks at me without a word. He's not wearing his veil here. His face seems older than it did in the street, wiser and more impressive. With his eyes on me, suddenly I feel like a child about to be scolded.

"I'm sorry," I blurt out. "I won't fail you again."

"I believe you," he says. "You will begin by never speaking unless spoken to."

I nod my agreement and he smiles at me. I want him to keep smiling. I want to be his favorite. I never want to make him scowl.

"This is Dub," he says after a long pause. It takes me a moment to realize there's someone else here. He's been lurking against the wall all this time. He steps out of the shadows as Quenson introduces him.

He's in his twenties, maybe, lean and strong, and dressed all in leathers like me, except they're black. His face is coarse with whiskers, and one eye is covered with a patch. The most remarkable thing about him, though, are all the knives. I can count at least a dozen strapped to his torso, his belt, his arms, and his legs. I wonder how many others he's concealing.

His one good eye looks me over like Quenson did. Except when he does it, it makes me uncomfortable. I square my shoulders and cross my arms and raise my chin, trying to seem bigger. Tougher. He smirks, but doesn't say a word.

"Go." Quenson says.

Before I have time to think, Dub leaps at me, his knives flashing. He swings and I duck and roll away. He throws a blade, and I somersault and narrowly dodge the attack. His knife clatters and skids across the floor. I tumble to grab it and another one of his blades slices my sleeve as it whizzes past. I don't know why, but this guy is serious. He means to kill me.

With Dub's knife tight in my grip, I charge him. He's nearly twice my size but I don't care. If he wants to kill me, I'm going to make it difficult. He's ready for my attack though. As I swing to stab him, he sheaths a knife and grabs my arm, twisting it painfully behind my back. He's strong, but I'm a fighter. I elbow him hard in the ribs and kick him between the legs until he doubles over. That makes him loosen his grip on my arm, so I spin and punch him hard in the face. His nose cracks and he curses.

Quenson's laughter somewhere to the side of the room is a musical sound that echoes up to the high-domed ceiling and back down again. It reminds me of how much I want to please him. It makes me fight harder.

Dub is furious. I punch his jaw and he growls and grabs my wrist again. With his free hand, he draws another knife from his endless supply. He overpowers me and shoves me against the wall, pressing my hand against the stone. His good eye is dark with madness. He raises the knife. He's going to drive it through my hand, pin me to the stone with it.

I struggle to break free. I kick and swing and squirm, but he's too strong. He thrusts the blade forward. I can't escape him. He's won. I brace myself for the strike and gasp as his empty fist smashes into my hand.

"Enough," Quenson says.

Dub growls in frustration and throws my hand down. I open my eyes in disbelief to see the Sorcerer standing several paces away, holding Dub's knife between his thumb and forefinger with a look of disgust.

"Such rudimentary, primitive things," Quenson scoffs as Dub retrieves the weapon and shoves it into a sheath at his thigh. He wipes at the blood that trickles from his lip and sneers at me.

"She has proven herself a worthy fighter," Quenson goes on. "The moment has come. The day of the verdict," he says darkly, and turns to me. "You and Dub have a common goal now: That of redemption. You see, he has also failed us. More than once." Quenson's voice darkens, and Dub looks away from us both. "You shall work together. He will teach you. Fill you in. Not too much," the Sorcerer raises a finger. "Slowly, slowly. Take your time with the girl. Leave me now. When I see you again, I hope for both of your sakes that you will not have disappointed me again."

With a hateful glare, Dub jerks his head at me and I know I'm meant to follow him. As disappointed as I am to have to leave the Sorcerer's presence, I don't dare argue or ask why. I agreed not to speak, and I won't go back on my word. Even though my heart is still racing from the fight and my thoughts are full of questions, I do as I'm told and I follow Dub from the room.

We walk for a long time, and just when I worry that maybe he's lost, Dub stops outside the open door to the bedroom where I woke up.

"You have to change," he says to me. "Back into the clothes you came in."

"But—" I start, and he's on me in a flash, pinning my shoulders to the wall.

"You listen to me. This isn't a game, little girl, nor do I have the patience for you. If I had my way, I would have ended you in there. I don't need an accomplice, nor do I want one. You will do as you're told." His voice deepens. "Go in there and change. Now." His face is so close to mine that his bloody spit peppers my face when he talks. I press my mouth closed and wrinkle my nose and look right into his one good eye.

"You don't scare me," I say with surprisingly more courage than I feel, even as he presses so hard that my shoulders feel like the bones will snap. "I nearly won that fight."

"That wasn't a fight, it was a demonstration," he smirks. "And nearly won is the same as dead in my book. You're sloppy. A street brawler. I've seen it before. Too cocky for your own good. It'll get you killed."

"You didn't kill me," I say defiantly. He presses closer.

"Only because I was under orders not to," his good eye flashes with a crazed hunger that makes me look away. I focus on the leather patch. I wonder what's underneath it.

"You don't scare me," I repeat, more for my own benefit than for his.

"I should," he sneers. "Don't you know who I am?"

I shake my head.

"Good," he growls. "That means I do my job well. How many famous assassins have you heard of? Not a single one worth his salt." He shoves me toward the door. "Now, do as you're told or Quenson will hear of it."

"I can't," I rub my sore shoulders. "These are my clothes. Sybel changed them with a spell."

His fist flies faster than I can react. It hits the door jamb next to my head with a such a force that the carved wood splinters and cracks.

"Sorcerers," he hisses a curse through clenched teeth. "Damn showoffs. Let's go, then. We'll find you something on the way. You can't go back to Cerion wearing that. It doesn't fit with the plan."

"What is the plan?" I ask as I trail behind him through the

corridors.

"Tib," he replies, stalking ahead.

"Tib?"

"You lure him, I bag him," Dub says simply, and his words thrill me. It won't be easy, but I'm glad he's the target. Tib's been on his high horse for long enough. He's got it coming.

Chapter Two
PROMISES

Azi
Two Days Earlier

"Twenty-ninth Midsummer?" Rian suggests.

I stroke his hair, deep in thought as he rests his head in my lap and gazes up at me. It's been two years since we defeated Jacek. Two years since Rian stood beside the golden pool and bent his knee to ask me to be his bride. I try to imagine myself on our wedding day, dressed in finery, standing before the entire kingdom, promising to be his forever. The notion is as abstract as ever. I feel as though I'm imagining someone else instead. Being a wife always seemed like such a distant prospect and yet here I am, looking into Rian's hazel eyes, certain that he's the only one I'll ever love. He wants to move from imagining to planning. I should want it, too.

A sunbeam dances through the leaves above and splashes across his neatly trimmed beard. He looks far more Mage-like with it. More handsome, if that's even possible.

"Are you really keeping this?" I ask as I tickle his coarse chin hair with my fingers.

"Are you really changing the subject again?" Rian smirks up at me and covers my hand with his.

"You can't answer a question with a question," I tease, smiling through the pang in my heart at the reminder of Flitt's question game.

Rian laughs and starts to sit up, but I push him down gently, kiss him, and try not to think about Flitt. It's too perfect here in the forest park outside of the castle walls, where we've hidden ourselves since mid-morning in the shadiest grove, on the greenest patch of grass. We don't get many moments like this anymore, just the two of us, quiet together.

"You're heavy on the distraction tactics today, Azi," he murmurs between kisses. I sigh. He's right. I can't avoid the subject forever, and I don't mean to.

"The twenty-ninth?" I ask, trying to place the date. I go back to stroking his auburn hair. It, too, is growing long. In the past months he's really begun to embrace the Mage style. Soon he'll be able to tie it back like Uncle does. I'm still getting used to it. It makes him look much older. But that could be a result of the weight on his shoulders lately, too. Rian has been through much more than most Mages in their Twentieth Circle.

It's been two years of quiet since the worst of it. Two years on edge. Even now when I think of Jacek's last words I get chills.

It has only begun. The wheels are in motion. The Order lurks, waiting to strike. You feared me? You have no idea. Bask in your cursed victory. May it forever blind you to the truth.

The image of his blackened, crumbling form is etched in my mind. Jacek was the Dreamwalker, a Sorcerer in the Dreaming who terrorized us and tried to turn us all against each other. He haunts my memories daily. Worse than him is the memory of Rian's cold, limp hand in mine as the battle was nearly lost against him.

"Do you remember that date?" Rian's question jerks me back to the present. He meets my eyes and pulls me down to kiss him again. Soon we're rolling around playfully in the soft grass, breathless. The cool ground beneath me and his loving arms around me push away the dark memories until they're nothing but wisps.

"Of course," I fib and giggle as we tumble to a stop. He props himself on his elbows and brushes his thumb across my cheek. His long auburn forelocks tickle my neck as his smiling gaze meets mine.

"Look," he says. His eyes sparkle golden, green, and orange. Inviting and warm, they pull me in until I feel the rush of my Mentalism, which allows me to tumble through his gaze into his thoughts and memories.

In the training square of the hall of our guild, His Majesty's Elite, I see a slightly younger version of myself. I'm surprised by how much I've changed since then. I look tired and worried, but there's also a gleam of hope in my eyes. That, and determination. I wonder if I've lost that now, after everything that's happened.

It's strange to see myself from Rian's perspective. Looking through his eyes into this memory, I can feel his emotions strongly: Love and nerves that tie his insides up. I feel his thoughts linger on the younger Azi's long blond braid.

Back in the forest park, I laugh and pull myself out of his mind.

"Are you trying to tell me something?" I ask.

"What?" Rian winks and runs his fingers through my newer, short-cropped haircut.

"You said you liked it," I say a little self-consciously. It was a hasty decision to chop off the braid. After a long, hot day of training I was sick of dealing with it.

"I do," he says, but I'm not convinced. "Now hush, and stop distracting. Look."

I tumble back into his eyes and into the memory, back to the Elite's training pitch where Rian and I stand face to face among the various weapons littered on the dirt floor around us. It had been a grueling day of research trying to figure out the workings of the curse that had befallen me and my father after Da's encounter with the Guardians at the eastern border of Kythshire. The awful curse prevented both me and Da from wielding any weapon, and left Da in the grips of madness.

We seemed so young then, Rian and I, so oblivious to the obvious attraction between us. I can see it now, when I look into the memory, plain as day.

Rian takes my hands and poses them a certain way, and I feel his own hands go warm and tingly when he touches me. He casts a spell and a slash of ice appears in my younger self's grip. An ice sword to replace my own. Rian's magical creation somehow circumvented the restrictions of the curse.

I watch it play out from his perspective: My excitement at this new discovery and the knowledge that I won't be completely useless under the curse, my concern for his use of magic he's not yet ready for, our kiss. Our first kiss. I feel it the same way he does, a flutter of excitement and a rush of warmth so deep and pure that I never want to pull away. I want to be there forever with him in that moment.

It's perfect and beautiful, until Flitt bursts in and interrupts us.

Immediately I pull back to the Forest Park. Back to myself again. I wasn't expecting her there. The image of the bright little fae in my mind is too much to bear. My heart aches for her, and with that ache comes the rush of guilt and worry that has been plaguing me for weeks now.

I roll away from Rian and sit up with my knees tucked to my chest. As the rush from Mentalism drains away, the emptiness which takes its place is deeper than normal. Wielding magic is a powerful experience. It fills you up with euphoria. The down side is when I stop, I feel miserable, exhausted, and empty. It isn't just the magic that leaves me feeling drained, though. The memory of Flitt and her recent absence sends tears spilling down my cheeks. Rian wraps his arms around me and I feel a little better, but I can't help the tears. I miss her so much.

"I'm sorry," he whispers, rocking me. "I forgot about that part. I forgot she had been there."

"Distractions," I try to laugh, but my throat is too thick with tears. Flitt's silence happened slowly over the course of months. First a day would go between visits, then a week, then several weeks. It's been two months, three weeks, and four days since she's been to see me. Rian and I have even gone to her grotto to seek her out whenever we could steal a moment in between hearings, but she's never there.

"She's always interrupting our moments," he jokes weakly. It does little to cheer me. I reach for the pouch that never leaves my chest and touch the diamond that tethers her to me.

"What if she's angry with me?" I ask him. "What if I said something to insult her, or slighted her somehow? You know how she is. They can certainly hold a grudge. You know her temper. Or Rian, what if something's happened to her?"

"Azi," his breath is warm on my skin as he brushes his lips across my cheek. "If something happened, I'm sure you'd know it. You'd be able to feel it. I'm sure she's safe. It's just…they're on a different schedule than we are, that's all. They have a completely abstract concept of time. She probably thinks it's only been hours."

"The last time she came," I say as I wipe the tears from my cheeks, "I was so dismissive. I had been called up to the palace, remember?"

"She can't be angry with you for that," Rian says. "She understands the importance of the trial."

"I suppose," I say. I take in a shaky breath and tuck my head into the crook of his arm. "I just wish it was over."

"Everyone does," Rian says as he looks off to the east, where the palace towers stretch up over the treetops. "It has certainly dragged on longer than any of us expected."

I press myself closer to him as my thoughts turn to darker matters. Prince Eron's trials have been going on for nearly two years now. Everyone knows that the end of them will most certainly mean the prince's death. Wishing for such a thing to happen faster always makes me feel guilty, but the memories of his crimes haunt my waking hours. At night while I dream, they play over and over in my mind.

So much more has come to light through the trials. The prince's conspiracies stretched deep through the kingdom and beyond. His hunger for his father's throne and his ruthlessness to gain it have been a shock to everyone.

It doesn't help to have to attend the daily Waking ceremony that frees the prince from his sleep to allow him to watch his trial. It doesn't help to have to sit before much of the Kingdom and recount my side of it time and time again with the prince's eyes on me, cold and distant, knowing that if there's any justice, my testimony will eventually lead to his death.

And the king. I can't begin to understand His Majesty's suffering, but somehow he doesn't see that all he's doing by ordering appeal after appeal is prolonging the inevitable. His son has committed crimes against the throne. He will never be fit to rule Cerion. Traitors and murderers are to be put to death, and that's exactly what Eron is.

The prolonged trial has settled over our usually cheerful, peaceful kingdom like a lingering storm. The certainty of Prince Eron's sentence circles within it; a darkness waiting to strike. Midsummer passed this year with no festival, no squire trials in the arena. No celebrations of any kind have been held. There is no place for joy during these times. We are a kingdom in mourning for an heir who's not yet dead.

"Mum says she can't remember a year without Cerion Day," I trace the gold trim of Rian's vest with my fingertips.

"My mum sang at the first one," he says. His chest rises and falls beneath my hand as he sighs. "This year would have been the thirtieth anniversary."

"She was young," I say, glad to turn the conversation away from our gloomy present and into the past.

"Thirteen," he says. "Can you imagine?"

"I can't imagine performing in front of so many people at any age." I laugh softly. Rian's mum, Mya, is a bard. She's easily the most sought-after performer in Cerion. Her concerts have drawn a crowd for as long as I've been alive. She's also our guild's leader and a friend of my family since before I was born. My earliest memory is of Rian chasing me through the crowds at the Arena, the two of us laughing and squealing over the cheers of her adoring audience, and each of us being scooped up by our fathers and scolded for running off.

'So, twenty-ninth Midsummer?" he asks again after a sweet, lingering kiss. Together with those early memories, it works well to lift my spirits.

I try hard to focus on the present. Here in the woods there are no trials, no absent fairies, no forgotten suits of magical armor collecting dust in corners of closets. There are no awkward, silent hours sitting with our guild family, waiting for the order to adventure that never comes. There is just Rian and me, past, present and future: a tiny beam of hope shimmering beyond that dark cloud, waiting to burst out. Twenty-ninth Midsummer is just under a year away. Long enough to plan. Long enough to allow the Royal family a period of mourning once the trials are finally through.

"It's the perfect date for our wedding," I say, and the kiss he gives me warms me from my cheeks all the way to my toes.

A shrill whistle interrupts our intimate moment. Rian and I hasten to sit up just as my squire appears between two trees near the path to our secret clearing. Saesa is one of the only people who knows where to find us when Rian and I sneak away. Today in particular I'm grateful for her discretion which gives me just enough time straighten my clothes and maintain some semblance of innocence.

"Sorry to disturb you, My Lady Knight," Saesa says, her cheeks going red. She curtsies and graciously averts her eyes.

"It's all right, Saesa," I laugh and hop to my feet and offer Rian a hand up. "Is it that time already?" I eye my squire, whose red curls float wildly around her face instead of being tied back for training. She's dressed in a late summer split skirt and sleeveless tunic instead of her sparring leathers. Still, her sword, as always, is strapped to her belt.

"No'M," she says. "Well it is, almost, but that's not why I've come."

She crosses to me and hands me a folded note. It's sealed with purple wax pressed with the image of a tiny winged lady.

"Princess Margary?" I glance at Rian. My heart races. Since the trials began, our only contact with the royal family has been summonses to testify. I've worried about Margary through all of it. She and her older sister and I used to be much closer, but then Sarabel married and left with her prince to Sunteri, and it's no wonder Margy hasn't wanted to see me since I began testifying against her brother.

On the first day of the trials, I was shocked to see the youngest princess in attendance. Since then she's been a fixture there, stoic in her little throne. She never acknowledges anyone, not even with a glance. She only listens and watches her brother, never daring to show emotion, not even while her mother is crying. Not even when the king's jaw is set so tight I fear he might crack his teeth. She's suffered so much through it all and remained so strong, but Margy has always seemed somehow wiser than her twelve years.

I pull the wax away and open the note, but my hands are shaking so hard I can't focus on the words written there. Aside from the trials, the last time I saw the princess I was sitting in her father's treaty room, fighting my newly-acquired Mentalism skills to keep from delving into the king's mind. Margy knew that somehow. She saw what I could do and she forbade me silently. Since then I've wondered about that night. I've agonized over it. I never wanted to lose her trust. I never meant to put her father in danger. Rian covers my hand with his to steady it.

"Her Highness Princess Margary," he reads aloud over my

shoulder, "requests the grace of your company tomorrow noon, for High Lunch. Sir Azaeli Hammerfel and one guest. Please present this invitation at the gate, et cetera..." he murmurs the last.

"Don't joke, Rian," I say, dubious that the princess would invite me to lunch after all of my testimony against her brother. Long gone are the days when these invitations were a regular event I would roll my eyes at and begrudgingly attend. Now that I've fallen out of favor of the younger princess, I'm both thrilled and intrigued by her summons. I read it over myself and shake my head in disbelief.

"I got one, too," Saesa says as the three of us make our way down the path toward the city together. "By your leave, Lady Knight, I thought I'd bring Tib if I can pin him down long enough."

"I saw him near the shipyard yesterday on my way to the Academy," Rian says as I look over the identical invitation and hand it back to her. "He was watching the lifts again."

"Of course, Saesa, if you can lure him away from that invention of his. He's really determined, isn't he?" I laugh and shake my head as I tuck my note away.

"He says he's almost finished," Saesa shrugs. "Though with what, I have no idea. He's tried to explain it to me before, but it's over my head. I believe he can do it, though."

"If he can he'll be a rich man," Rian takes my hand as we step out onto the cobbles and head toward the guild hall. The familiar sound of Da's hammer at the forge rings out to welcome us as we near.

"Go on and change," I say to Saesa. "I'll meet you in the sparring square."

She gives me a quick bow and rushes off, leaving me and Rian alone at my doorstep. I pull him to me.

"I should get back," he says. "That tome isn't going to scribe itself. Well, it could, actually, but that would fall under Unnecessary and Frivolous Use of Magic." His voice takes on a mocking tone and he grins at me.

"We can't have that," I hold him closer and tip my head back for another kiss. He doesn't deny me and we linger for a long while on the doorstep together.

"See, this is the sort of thing that makes leaving that much harder, Azi," he says. He kisses the top of my head and tries to extract himself.

"How many pages do you have left?" I squeeze him tighter as he tries to pull away. It's no use. I'm stronger than he is, and he knows it.

"Three hundred and seventy-two. Then I move on to the Dorane

Tomes," he wiggles one arm out of my grip and then the other before he gives up with an exaggerated sigh. "Shipment leaves in two days. The longer you keep me in your clutches, the longer it'll take me to finish."

"All right, all right." I pout and give him one last squeeze and a reluctant kiss farewell, and we part ways.

The clanging at my father's forge fills our otherwise quiet house. I follow the sound through the kitchen and out back to find Da busy with his back to me, working a strangely shaped strip of iron. Tib is perched on the wall nearby, stroking the fur of a thickly-tufted orange and black cat while he oversees Da's work.

"Hey, Azi," he says, and hops down to land lightly beside me. The cat stays on the wall.

"Good to see you, Tib," I give him a squeeze around the shoulder and he quickly pats my back and pulls away. "Saesa's looking for you. She'll be back to train soon."

"All right," he says, already distracted. He leans toward Da, examining the iron strip. "Narrower there, please," he says, pointing to the end. "Then flaring out this way."

He draws a shape in the soot with his finger. Da nods to Tib and then winks at me and taps his cheek. I give him a quick peck and he turns away to plunge the iron into the coals.

If Cerion has favored any one of us these past two years, it's Tib. No longer the tortured, skinny slave-boy he was when first we met, Tib has grown from a timid, angry boy to a confident young man. His fringe of straight black hair still hangs to cover his slanted eyes, and he's never without his dagger. With my fighter's eye I can pick out at least three others hidden on him, which is impressive considering his summer short-pants don't leave him many places to stash them.

Since our return to Cerion, Tib has earned himself an impressive reputation for lurking. Throughout the city, many are wary to speak openly about their enemies in public for fear that Tib has been hired to follow them and spy. Apparently he makes quite a stack of coin at the dangerous profession. He keeps it honest, though. He's settled happily into Nessa Ganvent's crew of orphans, and whisperings of his mysterious project follow quickly behind nearly every mention of his name.

"Zeze looks better," I point to the cat.

"Yeah. She just needed some scraps, didn't you, Ze?" Tib smiles. He pats her affectionately, and she meows in reply. "No, stay up there or Mouli will have your hide. You remember last time?" The cat mews and curls up near the warmth of the forge vent. "Good girl," he says, and turns back to me.

"Are you traveling any time soon?" he asks secretly under the cover of Da's hammer clangs. I know he's referring to Kythshire, the land of fairies where his sister guards the North border with the Spirit of the Shadow Crag, Iren.

"Maybe," I say, and the familiar pang of guilt over Flitt's absence strikes me again. Perhaps another trip is in order after all. I could go now, quickly, while everyone else is busy. No, I can't bear to go without Rian. We could go tonight when he gets back from scribing, but no, I don't want to go and possibly get caught up in something that will make me miss the Princess's invitation. And then, of course, tomorrow I must see the Princess. I sigh. No wonder Flitt is angry with me, the way I prioritize her.

"Day after tomorrow, I think," I say, pushing away the guilt. "Will you join me?"

"I think so. Thanks," he leans toward Da, already distracted again by the iron. "Sharper there, please, sir," he wiggles his finger, "and then a curve."

I leave the two of them to their work and head up to my room to change into my training leathers. Saesa will be here soon, and the weight of my sword in my hands always makes me feel better, even if it's only practice.

In the quiet of my room, my thoughts wander. With no orders from the king since the trials have started, most of the Elite have gone off on their own to keep busy. This has left the guild hall feeling empty and lonesome. A certain melancholy has settled in. None of us likes being idle. We all have a taste for adventure, and as long as the trial continues there'll be no hint of a quest on the horizon. The glory of His Majesty's Elite along with the glory of Cerion itself, is fading.

A glint of light reflecting off of my armor catches my eye. The helm has recently been polished, perhaps just this morning. I think of Saesa, my eager squire, and smile as I pick up the glossy, shimmering piece. A gift from the fairies, my armor is unlike anything made by man. The material is smooth like polished stone. Its color is deep blue flecked with tiny golden crystals. It shimmers as it catches the light, and holding it quickens my heart and makes me feel braver and more daring. Wearing it makes me feel safe. Bolstered. I cross to the mirror, pull the helm on, and slide down the face guard.

The young woman looking back at me is startling. She's strong, confident, and determined. She has the look of a true Knight, complete with that distant hint of mystery in her eyes. Something that says she's seen tragedy and risen above it. A stirring that makes me want to follow her, to rally behind her.

"Eh, it looks wrong," a squeaky voice pipes up outside my helm. At my shoulder, rainbow-colored light twinkles and splashes off of the armor to dance across the low eaves of my ceiling.

"Flitt?" I whisper. She responds with a sharp tug of my hair.

"Azi! What were you thinking?" the fairy cries.

"Ow!" I exclaim. My scalp starts to tingle. I pull my helm off and a long blonde braid tumbles down over my shoulder.

"That's better," Flitt emerges from the light and grins at me. "Hello!"

"Oh, Flitt!" I reach out to her.

In a flash she's my size. She throws her arms around me, and I can't help but squeeze her to make sure she's real. I'm so happy to see her that I really have to keep myself in check to avoid crushing her with my embrace.

"Wings, wings," she warns.

"Sorry!" I sniffle. I had forgotten how she smells like dew and sunshine, how bright her hair is with its multi-colored ponytails, how brilliantly her light sparkles from every pore of her skin. "Where have you been?" I ask as she pops back to fairy-size again.

"Ugh, I don't know how you stand being so enormous," she says, wrinkling her nose. She brushes at her ribbon skirt with disgust. "I've always said it. Humans are simply too ridiculously large. Don't you consider those around you? I mean, you could very easily step on something and kill it, and you wouldn't even know. A beetle, or an ant. Or a small chicken. You should really consider, as a race, smalling yourselves down a little. For the sake of those around you."

"Flitt," I laugh. "Honestly, where have you been? I've been so worried."

"Oh, wait 'til you hear," she says with a grin as she settles on the handle of my hairbrush. "I know, let's play!"

Chapter Three

THE SATCHEL

Tib

A brush of cobwebs against my skin. I step into the unseen. Into the shadows. Mevyn's gift. Valenor's lesson. A gift is not a trick. They taught me that. Sometimes, a gift is necessary. Sometimes it's the last hope for something better. This time, it's for something nobody else has dreamed up yet. I adjust the blade strapped to my back. It's longer. It stretches up over my head farther than I can reach. Flatter, too. Twisted. Perfectly worked by Sir Benen.

Zeze walks in front. Gets people to jump away or risk tripping over her. Some of them kick at her. I make a mental note of them for later. We travel this way for a while. Slinking on foot. Sticking to shadows. Out of the tucked-away street where Azi's guild keeps their hall, past the castle, through the market. Past the lifts to the docks. I pause here. Watch the Mage at the wall as he raises his arms. Bulky muscled men crank the cranks. The lift creaks and squeals and bumps along the cliff face. Crates jostle and threaten to fall, but the Mage keeps them safe. His spell is a powerful one. It makes the load lighter. It keeps it protected. It's necessary. Even the Princess thinks so.

This goes on all day into the dusk. Mage spells. Crates. Boxes. People. Animals. Up and down, never stopping. Workers working. Ships loaded and unloaded. Cargo in. Cargo out. In the summer, the Mages keep things light and safe. They protect from wind and rain and sea salt. In the winter, they melt the ice. Every spell drains a drop from Kythshire's Wellspring. A drop, a stream, it doesn't matter to them. The port gets busier. Their work needs to be done. Nobody thinks of the fairies. Why should they? To them, the fae don't exist. Legends. Stories. Mention them and they call you a simpleton. A liar. A tall tale-teller.

I slip away from the port. When I'm done, they won't need magic anymore for that task. My way will be better. My way will preserve the Wellsprings. Kythshire's and Sunteri's, too. I'll sell my machine to them, then I'll find another need to fill. Rian says we'll always have a need for magic. He says the arts are getting more popular by the season. It's harder to get into the school now. The Academy. They're very careful about who's allowed to learn its secrets. I'm glad. Magic is selfish and dangerous. It ruins people. It destroys things too easily. They shouldn't trust just anyone with it.

Zeze knows the way to Redstone. I follow her without thinking past the bright white walls of the Academy. Past the dorms and the stables and the rows of merchants in the main square. Through to the poorer places. The places you don't really notice when you first come to Cerion. The places you walk by without looking too hard. The places you try to avoid. When I first came to Cerion, I didn't think anyone here was poor. In Zhaghen, they're everywhere. Spread out through the city, right in the open. Begging. Coughing. Crying.

It's different here. They have their place, neatly tucked away. Dark, stinking rows of red-brick houses. Houses so old and ignored that they might crumble to dust with one careless bump of a cart. Redstone Row. It used to be a small part of the city, but now it's growing. The king is too distracted to pay his people the attention they need right now. Everyone's talking about it. They say he doesn't care. He doesn't see them like he used to. The people aren't important anymore. He's too focused on his son. On the trials.

Whispers that Cerion's age of peace is coming to an end echo from the shadows here. through the filth of these forgotten streets I understand why. I slip from the shadows. Stop in the usual places. Unload my pockets slowly into outstretched hands. Coins. Rolls. Fruit. Trade them for smiles, for thanks. For information. Dreiya talks to me with a baby on each hip. Her husband is at a meeting. A secret rally. He's a master stone carver. Worked for the Royal builders. They stopped working last year. Nothing left to build, they said. No orders from His Majesty for new construction.

Lots on this row are in the same boat. No work because Cerion is fading. It's happening slowly, just like it did in Zhaghen. Just like there, the poor are the first to see it. Just like there, powerful men sit in their towers, too caught up in their own problems to care. While things are getting worse in Cerion, in Sunteri things are getting better. The new princess is helping her prince. They're working to rebuild the kingdom. Their first step was to make strong rules against magic. Guiding the royal treasury away from the Mage scholars and into the hands of the poor.

Maybe Princess Sarabel should come back. Maybe she'd see what's happening. Tell her father. Snap him out of his selfish misery. Show him how skinny everyone's getting down here.

I turn the corner, straight into a gang of boys. Their backs are turned to me. Some older than I am, some younger. All dirty. Scrappy. Grouped around something. Their arms are linked together to keep whatever's inside from getting out. I step closer and peer in. A fray. A fistfight. A girl dressed in tatters fighting a dark-skinned boy in fine clothes. He doesn't know how to fight. He's grabbing at her hair. Kicking. Thrashing a lot and missing. She's better at it. She lands a punch to his gut. A kick to his hip.

"Give it back!" The rich boy huffs, grabbing at a bag slung across the girl's chest. It doesn't match the rest of her. It's finer. Cleaner. Something's inside that I can feel, but not see. Something magical. Powerful. Dangerous. Definitely not hers. The boy lunges at her and she swings up with bloodied knuckles. Uppercut to his jaw. He's thrown back. She laughs. The circle of boys cheers. To them it's a game. To the boy, that bag is important. He wipes blood from his lip onto his yellow silk sleeve. Pushes himself up. The rest of the boys charge him. Push him down. Kick. The girl joins in.

He doesn't give in. He keeps trying to get up, even when the flash of a blade catches the sun. That's when I step in. Zeze goes first. Saunters up to them. The boys in the back of the pack freeze when they see her. They tug at the others. Point. The fight dies down as nudges travel through them into the center. One of the boys tugs the girl's arm. She shoves him away but Zeze catches her eye. She turns. Lowers the knife.

Cowered against the wall, the rich boy peeks around his upraised arms. Glances at all of them, standing with their backs to him. Staring at me. Waiting.

"What's the word, Celli?" I ask. Casual. Like I didn't just interrupt her almost murdering someone. She shrugs. Rolls her eyes a little. She's my age. Fourteen, maybe fifteen. Cold eyes. Thin mouth. Broad shoulders. The look of someone who's been fighting for a long time. The other boys step back a little. Watch between us.

"What's that?" she points to the iron slung to my back.

"Later," I say. "What's that?" I point to the bag. She shrugs again.

"It's my lord's bag, and she stole it right out of his hands!" the rich boy cries. His accent is thick. He starts to get up, but Celli turns a fist to him and he cowers away.

"That true?" I ask her.

"Nope. This stupid clod left it lying on a stool," Celli sneers. "So it walked. What's in here that's so important?" she asks. Folds open the flap. Reaches a hand inside. The rich boy jumps up. Grabs at it. She shoves him away.

"Give it back!" he shouts. "Don't touch it!"

"Celli, no!" I try to warn her.

She doesn't listen. She touches whatever is in there. When she does, she screams. Pulls her hand out. It's red. Bright red, like the petals of the flowers I used to pick. The color creeps up along her arm, swirling and curling like Mage Mark. She scrambles with the bag. Yanks it from her shoulder. Throws it at the rich boy. The curls don't stop. They stretch over the skin of her chest, sizzling. She screams. Claws at it.

The boy doesn't hesitate. He grabs the bag and runs. Fast. I'm caught. Do I chase him down? Find out what that was? Or help Celli? I glance at her. The other boys are already surrounding her. Lifting her. Arguing over whether to go to the Academy or the Conclave. I let them. I turn and chase. I'm fast in a footrace. Known for it now. Made a few silver off it, racing.

The rich boy is easy to spot. A streak of yellow silk against the dingy gray. He's fast, too. I trail him through narrow alleys and past sagging shop stalls. Zeze darts ahead in a blur of orange and black fur. The boy ducks around a corner and I follow. I skid to a stop in the crowded sea market street. It's midafternoon. The lifts have been emptied. New wares are on display. Silks of green and red and gold that billow out from their hangings. Banners that snap against the salty wind. People. Crowds of people so thick I can barely squeeze through them.

"Young Master Tib," Averie, the apothecary merchant, calls out from his booth nearby. He's always pestering me to buy from him ever since Saesa told him about my vials. I brush him off as I catch a glimpse of yellow ahead. The rich boy ducks into a tavern. I know that one well. It's not a good place for a kid like him.

"Later," I say. I tug my sleeve from Averie's grip and he fumbles with the lavender vial he'd been holding up to me as I run off.

Seabird's Swoop is the name of this place. It used to be nice when I first came to Cerion. Now it's a little more run down on the outside and the inside smells like fish, sweat, and ale. That doesn't matter much to its patrons, though. Thirsty sailors don't care what it looks or smells like, as long as there's cheap drink and pretty women. This place has both.

Zeze slinks around my ankles as my eyes adjust to the dark. The fire is just coals and the candles aren't lit yet, but I still see him in the corner, bright like a beacon. I take a step. Feel the cobwebs brush my face just before he glances to the door. He'll see it as empty, even though I'm still here. Watching. I creep forward, past a bunch of men gambling at a long table. Past a few other men occupied with the tavern's ladies. The barkeep looks up. Winks at Zeze. He lets her stay. He knows I'm here. We have an agreement.

I sneak up to the boy, who's hunched at a small table with his back to the wall. He doesn't look like he just got in a fight. His yellow silks are spotless. The blood on his face is cleaned away. Even his bruises are fading as he sips from a cup and sets it down with a shaking hand. Mage. He's got to be.

With his other hand he's got the bag under the table where I can't see it. He peers into it. I try to come around for a better angle, but I can't get one. He's too tucked into the corner. His lips are moving like he's whispering, but as close as I am I can't hear anything. Saesa is teaching me to read lips, but I can't make anything out. It's a different language. A Mage spell, or Islandic, considering his dark skin and stubbly shaved head. He's definitely an islander from Stepstone. Or Vermina.

An ocean-blue glow splashes the front of his silks. He snaps the bag shut and looks hurriedly around to see if anyone's noticed. Nobody has, though. They're all half drunk. None of them cares about the rich boy in the corner. His leg bounces nervously. He glances at the door again. I follow his gaze to the man who's just entered.

He's broad-shouldered with a respectably trimmed beard, dressed in well-fitted plain clothes. A short sword is belted to his waist. It takes me some time to place him. I'm not used to seeing him out of his royal armor. He's one of Princess Margy's guards. His name is Finn. I lean back against the wall and watch. To my surprise, he crosses straight to the rich boy. Nods. Sits. Eyes the strap of the bag showing above the table.

"Loren," he says in greeting.

"Sir Finn," the boy nods.

"You have it, then?" Finn asks.

"Right here," Loren pats the bag under the table carefully. "You'll take it to the princess?"

Finn leans across the table. His lips press into a thin line. He drums his fingers. Leans back again. Never takes his eyes from the boy's.

"You're certain of this?" Finn asks. Turns his hand over and beckons.

"My master swears by it," Loren pushes the bag across the table into Finn's outstretched hand. Finn scowls. Peeks inside. The same splash of sea-blue light spills over his face.

"How does it work?" he murmurs and shakes his head slightly. His expression is wary. Reluctant. He presses the flap closed to shut out the light.

"By touch," Loren says simply. I think of Celli's arm, covered in the red Mark. How she screamed. The magic in that bag is strong and strange. I can't figure it out, and that worries me.

"You will remain here until it is done," Finn says sternly. The boy smiles. Bows his head.

"Of course," he says. "That was my master's agreement. We of Stepstone keep our word."

"Very well, then. Our business is done for now." Finn stands up with the bag. Glares at it. Tucks it under his arm.

"I have this, too." The boy stands. He hesitates and watches Finn warily.

"Course you do. What is it?" The princess's guard holds out his free hand and huffs impatiently.

"A letter for Her Highness," Loren produces a fold of parchment sealed with an aqua ribbon and a red seal. Finn nods and tucks the parchment away.

"That'll be all, then." It's a statement, not a question. Finn is done with this business.

Loren gives a humble nod. He watches Finn cross through the noisy, crowded tavern and out the door. Then he sinks back into his chair, closes his eyes, and lets out a long sigh of relief.

"It's done," he whispers. I stare out the door and into the street in disbelief. What business was that? Why would Finn come here to collect such an object from a strange island boy and bring it to the princess? "No, master," Loren whispers. He rests his head in his hands. His lips are moving again. Whispering strange words. I watch, unsure what to do.

Finn has sworn to protect Princess Margary. He's her truest, most noble guard. He loves her like his own daughter. That much is plain. He would never put her in danger by delivering such an object to her. Princess Margary loves him, too. She trusts him. If he told her to touch that thing, whatever it was, she'd do it. But why would he? Does he know what it could do?

I watch the boy, Loren. He's relieved, but still shaking. I can feel his fear like a blanket around him. He glances at the sailors and ducks his head again. His lips are still moving. He presses his forehead into his hand. A tavern maid comes over. Asks him to order something. He does. Good. He'll be here for a while. I leave him to go chase down Finn. As curious as I am about the boy, I need to warn the princess.

I slip out of hiding among the crowded market patrons and run to the palace. I catch up to Finn just before the side gate. He's hidden the bag away. Tucked it in the back of his belt and pulled his tunic free to cover it.

"Finn!" I call to him. He hesitates before turning to face me.

"Well, Master Tib," he offers me a kind smile. Natural. Like he wasn't just lurking in a low-class tavern conspiring with strangers. "Good to see you."

"You too," I cross my arms. Look him in the eye. There's determination there. Urgency. No regret. No sign that what he's about to do could be dangerous. He's a soldier, though. He's trained to be stoic. I glance past him at the guards at the gate, who are close enough to hear us. Choose my next words carefully.

"Nice day for a drink," I say. Narrow my eyes. He scowls.

"I don't partake on duty, Tib," he says.

"But you're not on duty," I reply, pointing to his clothes.

"Not so," he pats his sword. Chuckles. Tries to brush me off. "Why the sudden suspicion, boy? You have your sights set on old Finn?"

Zeze slinks around Finn's ankles, purring and rubbing. He glances down at her and smiles. Doesn't kick her away like most would. Looks back at me again.

"It's dangerous," I say. "I saw what it can do."

With that, he glances over his shoulder. Puts a hand on my back. Guides me out of earshot of the guards.

"Best put it out of your mind," he says to me as we stop along the low wall overlooking the sea. "It's not your concern."

"It is my concern. She's my friend, and I won't let anything happen to her." I clench my fists at my side. His casual attitude about all of this really bothers me. If he had seen what that thing had done to Celli, he would have second thoughts about bringing it into the palace. He doesn't care, though. He shakes his head. Looks like he's going to say something, then thinks the better of it and turns back toward the guards.

"Don't, Finn!" I shout as he starts to walk away. There's nothing else for it. I dive at him. Grab the bag from his belt before he can react. He spins, giving me just enough time to reach in and close my hand around the object before he yanks the bag away. I have it though. It's small. Soft. A baby doll's vest woven of silver and gold and encrusted with sparkling jewels. Fit for a prince. It emanates magic. I can feel it tingling in my hand and trying to stretch along my arm like it did to Celli. It can't, though. I'm protected. Magic doesn't affect me.

Finn's eyes go wide. He stalks toward me, seething. Yanks the thing away. Shoves it in the bag even as the red curls sizzle across his hand. Pushes me against the wall and holds me there.

"Go home, Tib," he hisses between his teeth. "Go home before I change my mind and have you arrested for thieving. Go!"

I don't think. I turn and run. Back through the market toward home. Back to Nessa, who keeps me safe. Past the market stalls. Past Seabird's Swoop. I pause. The boy would still be inside. I slip into hiding again and step to the door. He is. Just there, tucked in the corner, finishing his supper.

Chapter Four
REUNIONS

Azi

"So you asked first: Where have I been? Answer: Kythshire. My turn!" Flitt giggles.

Flitt's game verges on annoying on a good day, when I've had practice and I'm not teeming with questions that have been floating through my mind for months. Today, I have little patience for it and I'm out of practice, but I try hard anyway. I don't want to do anything to upset her and make her go away again. She darts around curiously as I sit cross-legged on my bedroom floor and watch her. Her light dances over me, lifting my spirits. Despite the dark mood in the kingdom, I'm grinning like a fool and I don't even care.

"My question is," she rests on the windowsill, "how much longer do you think the trials will go?"

I'm not surprised that this would be the first thing she asks, since Flitt reports most of what goes on here to the Ring in Kythshire. The fairies there have a personal grudge against Prince Eron. They're as eager for a verdict as any of us.

"I'd say weeks. Two, maybe three," I sigh. "I've said that before, though, and then the appeals come, so who knows?"

"Nobody knows, apparently!" Flitt answers. "My turn again."

I groan. My question wasn't really a question, but it counts as one.

"Do you think they're right to go through with it, if he's guilty?" she asks. I'm thrown off by the question. She seems more interested in my opinion of the situation than the actual decision. My thoughts drift to Eron and my own experience of his wickedness. His plots with the Sorceress Viala. The way he used to look at me with hunger and desire to force his power over me. The coldness in his eyes when he ran his blade through Ki to end her life. His vow that he would rule not only Cerion, but Kythshire and every land he could conquer. Slowly, I nod.

"I do," I reply. "I'm not usually quick to cry death, but Eron is too far gone. There are things that have come out in the trial beyond what we knew. There's no hope for redemption. His heart is black. He wants only power, and he doesn't care who he hurts to get it. He would see his own father dead to help him claim the throne. If he was ever able to be king, not only would Cerion be ruined, but he wouldn't stop. His selfishness would destroy everything that the Plethores have worked so hard to build. I don't see any way he could be allowed to live if we're to preserve Cerion's peace."

Flitt nods thoughtfully and stretches out onto her belly in a beam of sunlight, facing me. She plucks a sugar cube from the dish I always keep full there, and takes a bite. Her wings slowly open and close, like a butterfly happily sipping at nectar.

"Your question," she says, resting her chin in her hand.

"You were gone for a long time. I was worried and I missed you so much," I say as I move closer to kneel at the windowsill. "Why were you gone for so long?"

"Lots of reasons," she says, grinning impishly.

"Flitt! That's not a real answer. Come on, don't be so tricky," I force a laugh, but my eyes brim with tears. I want to know. I need to know.

"Aw, Azi. I missed you, too," she floats up to pat my cheek. "I'll tell you, but you can't tell anyone else, okay? Promise."

"I promise, but, not even Rian?" I press my fingertips to the spot that she touched, which tingles warmly as they stick to the sugar she left behind.

"Oh, don't be stupid. Of course you'll tell Stinky. I'm not completely brainless, am I?" She rolls her eyes and settles again on the windowsill.

"I never said you were. We're back to Stinky again, are we?" I ask. Poor Rian. Flitt loves to tease and torment him, and he tolerates it because he knows I adore her.

"Yup," she replies, grinning. "This has to do with him anyway, sort of. So are you going to ask me again?"

"Okay. What kept you away for so long?" I glance out the window and see Saesa's red hair bouncing along toward us. She'll be headed to the training square. She'll wait for me there.

"New titles," Flitt says excitedly. "You're looking at Flitter. Felicity Lumine Instacia Tenacity Teeming Elite Reformer. Can you believe it?" She jumps up and does a little celebratory spin in the air.

"Wow, two new names," I exclaim, genuinely pleased for her. "Well done, Flitt!" Fairies earn new names as rewards and recognition for impressive deeds. The longer a fairy's name, the higher her esteem. When I met her, she was Flit. Since then, she's earned three names. She giggles and straightens up a little, her chin raised proudly. "Elite Reformer," I repeat. "That sounds rather important. How did you get those?"

"Oh, that's the interesting part. I had some ideas about fairy relations. Old fashioned ideas. From the old days, you know. Way back when. I was just sitting in my grotto one morning listening to the chimes and it came to me. We should go back to it. The way things were. Once Prince Creepy is gone, I mean. Not 'til then, because it would mean exposing ourselves a little, and we'd have to really make sure Cerion was on our side first. But your kingdom has respected our treaty for a long time, now, and we've been safe. The elves do it, you know. They do it in other places, too. And with Princess Margary how she is, Twig says she'll be Queen. She won't let bad things happen. And if it works, it's like built-in protection. So that would make sense.

"But then I brought it up at the Ring, you know. And Crocus and Scree were wary. Shush was for it. Ember of course wasn't. Twig was. There was a vote. There was lots of arguing, too. I almost got kicked out of the Circle for it, if you can believe it. There was so much dancing. Dancing for weeks and weeks. Some of them still hate me for bringing it up. I won't be putting myself alone with Ember any time soon, if you know what I mean."

I understand some of her rambling. The Ring is where decisions are made among the fairies of Kythshire. Crocus and Scree are the leaders, and Ember and Shush are members of the High Council, along with several other fairies I haven't formally been introduced to. When there's an argument or an issue that's particularly difficult to discuss, the whole assembly dances wildly until their emotions about the issue at hand are as exhausted as their little bodies are.

"In the end," Flitter goes on, "mostly everyone agreed on it. But Crocus and Scree wouldn't pass an edict. They say it's beyond them. They agreed to send me to the Palace of the Dawn to present it. You know, where our Queen is. I thought it might help if you came, too, so I can show them how good you are. Will you?"

"Will I...?" I trail off, thinking over her words, trying to make more sense of what she's said. I can't, though. Other than the customs at the Ring, I have no idea what she's going on about. "Flitter, of course if you need my help, I'll do what I can. But I don't understand. What exactly did you propose? What do the elves do that you want to do, too?"

"Ah, ah!" she wiggles her finger. "One question at a time. Well, those were sort of the same question, so I'll let it go this once. Oh, and by the way, you can just call me Flitt like always. Unless we're in front of someone important. So: What did I propose? We'll go with that question."

I nod, a little bemused. Once she gets on a roll, she tends to be a little more lax about the rules of the game.

"Just this," she floats up again and comes to settle on my shoulder so she can whisper. "Pairings. The elves call it *Ili'luvrie*. We fairies didn't used to hide away all the time, you know. We were part of life with people. We paired up. Like you and me. Or like Princess Margary and Twig. Like Tib and Mevyn. Well, not really like them, actually. That was a little twisted and over the line. It's supposed to be mutual, and Mevyn made it creepy."

I start to say something, but she holds up her hand to stop me. It's not my turn yet. Not until she asks a question.

"It was a good system. Fairies would find a friend. Someone they had things in common with. Someone they trusted. They'd help each other out. Learn from each other. Share magic. Protect each other. Give insight. It was mostly done with Mages, but every once in a while a fairy would find a child, or someone who was particularly pure and valiant. They'd get a tether, like you have, and they'd be good friends. And if one of them ever needed the other, they'd help each other out. Like you and me, see?"

"So," I say thoughtfully, "you're saying that if this goes through, if it's approved by the Queen, then fairies wouldn't be a secret anymore in Cerion. Isn't that dangerous for all of you, though? It took so long for you to make yourselves forgotten."

"That's the big argument," Flitt sighs. "Some of them think just that. They said I'm an idealist. They don't want to expose us, no matter what. But they've been talking about something else at the Ring for a long time. Ever since the attack on the North. Your battle with the Sorcerers wasn't the end of it. Something big is coming, Azi. Something we can't handle on our own, no matter how much they convince themselves that we can. A threat we've seen for a long time on the horizon is moving closer, and the ones against the pairings are turning a blind eye to it. They don't realize it could mean the end of us. All of us."

She flies down to the long-forgotten silver pitcher that Margy fixed up for her so long ago. It's the same as it was then, turned on its dented side and adorned with fringes of lace and piles of old satin. She rummages in the dusty scraps for a little while and then curls up and looks at me expectedly. We sit in silence, staring at each other. It's her turn to ask, so I wait even though I'm dying to know more about this threat.

"Oh. My question. So, what do you think of that?" she asks broadly.

"A lot," I reply with a teasing grin. She rolls her eyes and shakes her head.

"Come on," she says.

"I think a threat is always a good reason to make alliances, but you have to make sure that the allies are trustworthy. Are the fairies who agree to it really willing to pair with our Mages after all this time?"

"Well," she grins. "There's one who is. And he knows exactly who he wants, too. Can you guess who?"

"Rian," I say without hesitation. As far as I'm aware, he's the only Mage they know well enough to trust. "But which fairy?"

"Shush," she replies. "He sent this with me. He said he hopes Rian accepts." She reaches into her belt pouch and pulls out the tip of a quill. She keeps pulling and pulling and the object keeps coming, impossibly growing out of the tiny pouch. It's a beautiful sleek bluehawk's feather: royal blue edged with aqua, and with creamy spots speckling it from top to bottom. It isn't the sort normally used for writing. It's too fine and rare. She smoothes out the vane and hands it to me. "Fitting for a Wind fairy, don't you think?"

"Definitely. It's beautiful…" I turn it in my fingers and feel its silky fronds between them. "Rian will be honored, Flitt. I'm sure of it."

"Eh, we'll see. Stinky hasn't really shown me a lot of patience," she yawns. I consider reminding her that he's probably impatient because of the way she constantly torments him, but I decide against it. This is a huge step for relations between our people. One that Flitt has apparently fought hard for, based on her relationship with me. I can't help but feel a little pride at that. All this time she's been away, she's been fighting for us to be closer. I smile.

"Your question," she says. I think for a while.

"Something big is coming, you said. The threat. What do you know about it?" I ask as I tuck the feather reverently into my vest.

"It's complicated. It has to do with the…" she peeks out of the pitcher and looks around cautiously. "You know. The things where the stuff comes from." I know what she means. The Wellsprings. I thought the only one was in Kythshire, but we learned that there was another in

Sunteri that had been drained by its surrounding Sorcerers. Tib and Mevyn had something to do with restoring it. I thought I had been there to see it, but my memories when I try to recall it are too foggy. Perhaps because it was around the same time Rian proposed to me. I get too distracted by memories of that wonderful time when I try too hard to remember.

I nod to Flitt. "Go on."

"Well, ours has been giving portents for a while. Since before you and I met. Warnings of dark magic all around. They're linked, you see. All of them. They know what's going on with each other, everywhere. And the threat is just that. Bad people trying to reach the link. Trying to learn what's known. Oh, it's too difficult to explain here where I have to be so secret. Give the feather to Rian and then come see us in Kythshire, okay? I have to go. I'll try to come tomorrow again if there's not as much dancing."

"Wait, Flitt—" I cry and snatch up the pitcher but I'm too late. She disappears, leaving me staring into the bundle of silks in confusion and disbelief.

It's a lot of information all at once, and it's just like her to leave me so abruptly to try and sort it out without her help. I set the pitcher down and gaze off toward the Academy spires, pristine white against the distant blue sky. Most of Cerion's Mages are trustworthy. It's rare to see the Mark on any of them. Uncle makes sure of that, as do the King's highest Mage advisers.

We've shown our respect for Kythshire's Wellspring for generations now. But could it go on this way if the fairies revealed themselves, or would it go awry? I myself have felt the power of magic before. When I attempt to use Mentalism, it's intoxicating. I avoid it at all costs because of that. I don't like the out-of-control feelings it gives me. Would the pairings help curb that desire, or feed into it? I imagine it would depend on the partner. Still, I'm excited for Rian that Shush would choose him. The two seem like a perfect match for one another.

I find Saesa waiting in the sparring square as I expected, sharpening my sword with a whetstone.

"Again?" I laugh. "Thank you, Saesa, but if you keep sharpening it, I fear there will be nothing left."

Her reply is a respectful bow after she slides it back into its sheath and hands it to me, hilt-first.

This session I have Saesa try a similar blade to mine: a great sword, long, wide, and heavy enough that it must be wielded with two hands.

It's a drastic change from Feat, her beloved short sword, but the glint in her eye when I offer her this one tells me I've made the right choice. She takes the weapon with reverence, and I'm surprised when she holds it with her hands spaced properly right at the start. She knows the grip already, and she has the stance well-practiced.

My own sword gleams in the light that splashes through the open ceiling and my heart quickens as it does every time I hold it. This sword is the one Da forged for me and gifted me on my sixteenth birthday. It was lost in the Battle of the Keep at Kythshire, sucked into a Sorcerous vortex. I had thought it gone forever until I found it again in the throne room of Jacek, the Dreamwalker who had stolen the mantle of Valenor, the true Dreamwalker. He used it to lure me to him, then he used it against me, enchanting Saesa and goading her to fight me with it. In the end, he was defeated. In the end, the sword is mine again, as it should be.

All of it flashes back at me in the reflection of my eyes on the blade. Quick moments, there and gone. As trying as it had been, as threatening and dangerous, I want it again. My whole body aches for adventure. I anchor my feet into the dirt and raise my sword to Saesa. We bow, and the bout begins.

She's been practicing, I can tell. Her swings are more graceful and her thrusts more powerful. Over the two years she's been my squire, Saesa has grown almost a hands-width taller. Her body is filling out its womanly curves, and her arms are long and leanly muscled. She didn't bother to tie her hair back today. Her thick red nest of curls barely moves when she does.

"Hey, your hair!" she says, echoing my thoughts as she swings a long downward arc. "How did you—?"

"Check your grip." I say sternly as I meet her blade with a hard parry, knocking her off center. "Hands apart. Plow stance, elbows in, pommel at your hip. Elbows, Saesa!"

"Elbows, elbows," she chastises herself with a murmur and tucks them in.

"Someday, Saesa, you'll be on the field. Someone will see those elbows poking out from a league away," I thrust my blade close to her rib and she spins away, "and take them right off. Below the hip, strong arms stay close."

"Yes, my lady," she says, "strong arms stay close." She tries again with the proper stance, and I jump back as the blade glances my leather training vest.

"See? That's better," I grin.

"But your braid," she tries some elaborate footwork and fails miserably, stumbling under the weight of her weapon.

"You can do that with a short sword, Saesa, but it won't work with a great sword. Left foot back, anchor yourself. Greatswords rely on strength over speed. Let the weight of the blade guide your strike." I show her a strong forward thrust and she repeats it fairly easily. "Good, let's practice that one."

"It was Flitt, wasn't it?" she asks as she tries the move again. "I thought I saw her in your window."

"Anchor that left foot. Watch your arms, Saesa. Elbows!" I arc my sword upward and knock her right elbow hard with the flat of my blade.

"Sorry!" she yelps. "Ah," she says under her breath and skips backward with the tip of her sword dragging in the dust. She tries to put on a brave face, but I know that had to hurt. I felt the crack.

"Take a breath," I say, but she shakes her head.

"I'm fine, m'lady," she says, and comes at me again but I sidestep the attack. Her blade wobbles dangerously as her injured arm fights to keep it steady.

"Take a break, Saesa." I slip my sword back into its scabbard at the bench and beckon to her. "Let me see it."

She comes as beckoned, and I unbuckle the clasp at her shoulder and pull the leather sleeve down. A dark bruise, blooms around her already swelling elbow. I take her arm gingerly and bend it, and she gasps and winces.

"Conclave," I say. "You need healing. It's a break."

"But we just got started..." Saesa groans in frustration.

"Conclave." I repeat. "Put it on the guild's tally. Next time don't be lazy with your elbows."

"Yes, Lady Knight," she sighs and stows her weapon at the wall, then bows respectfully and rushes out.

It's hours before Rian finally returns from the Academy. He finds me in the meeting hall helping Mouli, our cook and housekeeper, clear away the dinner that's gone cold. She clucks her tongue at the nearly untouched food and hurries off to the kitchen with it to see what can be salvaged.

"Nobody turned up again?" Rian grabs a roll and bites into it.

"Everyone's off on their own," I say as I slip my arms around him. "Mouli can warm the fish for you. It was a good catch."

"That's all right," he shrugs.

"Well, well, nice of you to turn up!" Mouli says shrilly as she comes back to the table. "I'll make you a plate before you disappear to nothing, Rian! Honestly, you've got to eat. Books and ink will not sustain you!"

"Yes, Mouli," Rian grins. "Thank you for that sage advice. Such a revelation, coming from you. Never before have I heard such wisdom escape your lips."

"Don't be cheeky," she flicks her apron at him and rushes back to the kitchen.

"Hey," Rian says after she leaves. He reaches up and tugs my braid with a questioning tilt of his head.

"Flitt didn't like my new style," I laugh softly.

"She was here?" he asks as he takes my hand. "Where has she been? What did she say?"

Between visits from Mouli, I fill Rian in on my conversation with Flitt. His expression seems to darken slowly the entire time, until he's finally fully scowling when I get to the part with Shush and the feather. I pull it out and set it on the table beside his plate.

"What's wrong?" I ask as his whole demeanor changes. His body goes rigid, his jaw and fists clench. This is the way he gets when he goes to Kythshire. Measured. Careful. Slightly terrified. "I thought you'd be honored."

"It's too dangerous," he replies, staring at the feather with distaste.

"How is it dangerous?" I stroke the soft, spotted fronds thoughtfully with my fingertip. "It's exciting. A chance to strengthen our alliance. And Shush is amazing. It'd be fun to get to know him better, wouldn't it?"

"No," he pushes the feather back toward me with the end of his spoon. "It crosses the line. It's too much power for us, Azi. Too much risk for him. For all of them."

"But Flitt said—" I start, but he interrupts me.

"Flitt is young. I bet the others argued against it. The older ones. The ones who were there during the darker times. She's an idealist. She doesn't realize what could happen."

"That's what they said, too," I sigh. "But don't you think we've changed since then?" I rest a hand on his arm. "Don't you think our Mages can be trusted? Don't you think you can be?"

Rian stares thoughtfully at the feather for a long time, pondering the question. He presses his palms into the bench and stays silent through Mouli's return. She fills his plate again and Rian makes a show of eating it until she goes out again.

"In the end," he says quietly as Mouli slips out to the kitchen again, "no, I don't. I don't even trust myself, Azi. Not with that. Not with the life of a fae. The way I could drain him, use his power to feed my own, it would be a constant temptation. A constant battle. A distraction and a danger. I won't risk it."

"That's why he chose you," I take his hands in mine. "He's seen how restrained you are. He knows you're respectful and cautious. He trusts you. They all do."

"Well," Rian says, his hands shaking in mine, "they shouldn't. I'm not arguing anymore. That's my final decision. If you respect me, you'll accept it."

"Very noble," a whisper from the feather itself startles us. The sound is quick and soft, like a brisk wind through the leaves of trees. "But you left out the important part, Azi. Remember? The threat. The reason why all of it is necessary."

The air shimmers over the feather and the form of a fairy emerges slowly. He's dressed in shining leaf-green plates that mimic a mantis shell. His body is long and lean, giving the appearance that he's been stretched out, and his yellow hair is blown straight back to a point. He pushes his beetle-like eye-scopes up to rest on his forehead and squints at us.

"Well! It's been a while, hasn't it?" Shush whispers hurriedly. "Good to see you again, both of you!"

Chapter Five

WHISPERINGS OF WARNING

Tib

"Suppertime Ze," I whisper to the cat as I slink to the doorway. She meows at me a little reluctantly. "Go on," I say, and she saunters away off toward the south. Toward Nessa's. I don't want her spotted in the tavern again so soon. Someone might get suspicious.

I sneak along the tables. The rich boy is still there. Spooning cobbler into his mouth. Staring at the fire. The crowd's gotten louder in here since I left. Thicker, too. There's barely a place to sit. I take a deep breath. I slip between two larger men who are busy with their dice and come out visible on the other side. Loren doesn't notice me. He's in a daze. Thinking. Probably thinking about the horrible things that are about to happen to the princess.

"This seat taken?" I drop onto the bench beside him. Put a hand on my dagger hilt. He's observant. He notices the threat right away. Nothing he can do, though. He's got me on one side and the wall on the other. His eyes slide slowly away. Back to his bowl. He shrugs. Tries to act calm. He can't fool me. He's scared.

"Tib!" the shrill voice makes me wince. Gemma, a young barmaid, swoops in on me in a flurry of skirts and perfume. Her face is painted crazy pink and red and blue. Some men love it. I've seen the way they eye her. Not me. It makes her look much older than when I met her at the fishmonger. Not my age anymore, definitely. She leans down so we're eye to eye. Looks me over. Flutters her eyelashes. "Something to eat?" she asks with an inviting smile.

"Uh," I swallow. Slide away, toward Loren. Nod. "Whatever he has, Gemma." I point to the bowl.

She moves closer. Purrs at me like Zeze. "Anything else?" she whispers.

"No. Thanks." I try not to let my gaze stray to her bare shoulders or the low cut of her shirt as she hovers. When I shake my head again, her smile falters a little.

"All right, Sweeting. If you change your mind, you let me know," she taps my shoulder playfully and goes off to get my cobbler. Loren turns to me.

"Are you friends with her?" he asks. The way he watches her leave makes it obvious he likes her paint and perfume.

"I've known her for a while," I say.

"That girl in the alley. You stopped her. You stopped all of them. They were afraid of you or something." He leans back against the wall. Tries to look taller. "I could have, you know. They would have all been sorry. Except..."

"Except you weren't supposed to use magic," I finish for him.

"How did you...?" he asks. Stares at me. Shakes his head. "Anyway, thanks for stopping them," he says after a while. He glances past me, like he's trying to figure out his escape.

"What was it? In the bag?" I rest my arm on the table. Make it clear he's not getting past me until I have answers.

"I *can* use it. Magic. I can if I need to. I could use it now." He reaches toward me. His fingertips crackle.

"Go on," I laugh. "Try it."

He tilts his head. Watches me. Moves his crackling hand closer. Blue sparks. A lightning bolt is painful, even at a small scale. It would jolt through me. Burn my flesh. Well, not me. Someone else, maybe. When I don't flinch, he drops his hand to his lap, looking puzzled.

"I can't tell you," he says.

"Can't you?" I scowl and drum my fingers on the hilt of my dagger. "I'm surrounded by friends here. They'd look the other way, you know."

Loren swallows. Pushes his cobbler around in his bowl. "I really can't. I swore a Binding Oath to my master."

"Oh," I say. My heart sinks. I know about those magical oaths. Even if he wanted to tell me what it was, he couldn't. He's not lying, either. He really took one. I can tell. Gemma comes back with my bowl. She tries again to get my attention but I'm too caught up with Loren and the vest. After a while, she gets tired of being ignored and wanders off again.

"Tell me this. Will it hurt the princess?" I ask. It's really all I need to know.

Loren's eyes go wide. He looks shocked and disgusted I'd even think to ask him that. He shakes his head. "Never," he says. That's good enough for me. I start to get up.

"You're going?" he asks. "That's it?"

"That's all I needed to know," I say. I look at him. Slowly start to see him differently. He's only a kid my age. He tries hard to look confident, but he's out of place here. Alone in a dirty tavern full of sailors. An islander in a strange land. A boy in a country not his own. Like I was, when Mevyn lured me out of Sunteri. When he made me do things and then made me forget.

I look at Loren. Really look. He's scared. He ought to be. What kind of master sends a boy dressed like that into a place like this? He should have at least disguised his clothes. It's stupid of them both. Strange, too. And if he had a delivery for the princess, why not go straight to the castle with it instead of meeting her guard here? It doesn't add up.

Loren shifts uncomfortably while I think all of this over. Doesn't say anything. Waits for me to speak first. He's smart.

"How'd you get to Cerion?" I ask. "Ship?"

"Sure," he nods.

"A charter? By yourself?"

He nods again.

When I ask him, "What about your master?" he winces.

"He's not here," he says vaguely.

"Yeah, figured that one out. If that thing's so special, why didn't he bring it himself?" I ask.

"He's working on something more important," Loren replies. He's relaxing a little. Warming up to me, maybe.

"I don't know, a delivery to Cerion's palace seems pretty important to me." I say.

Loren shakes his head slowly. "Some things are more pressing," he looks around carefully. Looks down. "Threats."

"Threats?" I ask. "What kind of threats?" I sink back to the bench. The iron at my back scrapes against the wall. I had almost forgotten about it. The sound draws the attention of a nearby table. They eye us curiously. Eventually, they look away. I adjust the straps. Lean closer to him. "Threats against Cerion? Or Stepstone?"

"Threats," he whispers. "Painted in the stars. Threats against everything. The Known Lands and beyond. Master sees them. Watches for them. He knows what will start it coming. He's wise. He couldn't leave observation. He had to stay. He's the only one who can see clearly."

"Start what coming? What threats?" I whisper. When he doesn't answer, I press on. "Sorcery? Something worse?"

"Sorcery!" he laughs. "If only it was so simple as that. No, this is like nothing anyone has seen. And not something I'll talk about anymore. Master says mention of it gives it power. It feeds on fear and belief. It grows as it feeds. It consumes. Better to put it out of your mind."

"If that's true, then why'd you just tell me about it?" I ask. "Didn't you just make it worse? You're helping it, whatever it is."

Loren's eyes go wide. He shakes his head slowly. "You asked. I didn't think..."

I cross my arms and lean back. Either he's lying or he's not very bright. Since he's a Mage, I choose the first option. Lying. I think of what Nessa always says. Keep close to the ones you don't trust. Keep them in your sights. That makes it difficult for them to hide their secrets.

"You staying here at the Swoop?" I ask.

He looks around a little distastefully. "I imagine," he says.

"I know a better place," I offer. He looks at me. Thinks I'm trying to trick him, I bet.

"I have to wait here for that guard to come back," he says.

"Suit yourself. It's on Overlook," I say. "Out of here, turn right. The Ganvents. They're my family. Ask for them. Nessa takes kids in. She'll be happy to have another even for a short stay. We've got a Mage girl there. Name's Lilen. You two will have a lot to talk about. Tell them Tib sent you. I've got to take care of this anyway." I gesture to the iron at my back. "I'll be home before sundown."

"What is it?" he asks, pointing to the iron.

"Later," I reply. Before he can ask me anything else, I put a silver on the table and slide from the bench. I disappear into the rowdy crowd and out into the market.

The sun is low in the sky, but it's still so hot that sweat runs down my back. I shift the metal again and wipe my brow. I don't have a lot of time if I'm going to get back to Nessa's by supper. I hope Loren decides to show up. If not, he'll be one more thing on my daily list to track down. I duck into alleys and jog along twisting, lesser-traveled routes until I reach the shack. Goosebumps prickle my arms and neck. The first time I came here, I was attacked by mercenaries, and then the Dreamwalker. I almost died. If Saesa and Raefe hadn't found me and brought a healer to me, I would have.

It was Mevyn who forced me here, I think to myself like I do every time I climb down this ladder. Into darkness. Into the cool underground. I think about Mevyn every time I come down here. I wonder if I'd have fought harder against him if I knew what we'd end up accomplishing together. No, I would have chosen it. Chosen to help him revive Valenor and restore Sunteri's Wellspring and its fae. He was the last of them, after all. He should have trusted me with the truth from the beginning. Still, as difficult and controlling as he was, I miss him sometimes.

I close my eyes as I climb down. Remember the fight above, when Mevyn drove my attacker away with a spear to the eye. Remember the vision Jacek, the Dreamwalker, created for me as I tried to escape him. Zhilee running through the red blooms. My little sister, happy and alive. My older sister, Viala, buried in the pages of her book. Red petals floating in the air. My foot finds the dusty bottom too soon. I hop down. Back to reality. At least I still have Viala. She's changed, but she's still alive. Her name is Ki now. She lives with the fae in Kythshire. In service to Iren, the Guardian of the North.

It's different down here since I've been working. I light the torches with my flint and unbuckle the iron from my back. It falls to the ground with a clatter. I roll my sore shoulders with relief. Look over my work. Chains. Gears. Cranks. Fins. Wings. Bellows. Bladders. This iron will be the brace for the left. Tomorrow I'll track down another strip and have Benen shape the right for me.

I get started attaching it with thick cords and screws. I'm too absorbed in my work to notice the shadows stretching longer. Thicker. My eyelids droop. It's been a long day. I could sleep. Just a nap, a short one. My head bobs forward. My eyes close. I snap them open again.

"Very funny," I mumble. Tie a knot. Burnish the leather. The shadows laugh. I'm not afraid. I know very well who it is. A friend. Out of the corner of my eye I glimpse his billowing cloak. His bright grin against deep brown skin. His long, silver beard. Valenor. The rightful Dreamwalker, who reclaimed his position after Jacek's defeat.

"Don't make me regret that I allowed you to help me sleep, Valenor," I chuckle. When I turn to look at him properly, he's gone.

"You're making progress," his amused voice echoes around me. "Have you thought of how you'll be getting it out of here?"

"I have to find a new place," I say. "Soon. I'll carry it up in pieces to wherever. I think I found a spot. An old stable out of business."

"Rather out in the open, wouldn't that be?" Valenor asks.

"I'm going to have to show it to people eventually," I shrug.

"Why not ask the Princess for a place to work? Certainly she'd provide," his voice is far away and back again. Dreamy. Unreal. His shadows creep around my work, inspecting.

"If I asked Margy," I say as I work a screw through the wood, "then there'd be paperwork and contracts and check-ins by men who'd think they could do a better job than me. I don't need the headache. And I don't want help. I want to do it on my own."

"There's always…" he starts, but I shake my head.

"Thanks, but you know I don't want to build it in the Dreaming," I say. "I want to do it without magic. Make sure it really works without help."

"Very well," Valenor sighs. "What you've already done is extraordinary, Tib. What is this?" His cloak flicks at a thick pile of waxed silk.

"Air bladder," I reply. Squat back on my heels. Shake out my arm, sore from twisting screws.

"Air bladder, hm. So it would go above?"

"No, below. This long one goes below. One on both side. Then it gets pumped up through here, through sealed holes in the bulwark. Five men, five pumps. That blows up. Lifts the ship up above. See? Meanwhile this other one," I scoot across the dirt and pat a larger pile of silks, "goes above, and that gets the hot air. These are stabilizers. They'll keep things level once it's airborne. And these are for steering."

"I have to say it is quite ambitious, Tib. Quite." Valenor's cloak swirls and glitters just beside me. It's amazing, I think, how differently the mantle suits him than it did Jacek. On Valenor's shoulders, it doesn't feel like a threat. It feels friendly. Welcoming Familiar. His shadows are a comfort. Always balanced by the light. Always sparkling with stars. Just like his kingdom, the Dreaming. Pleasant again. There are still nightmares, and there are still pleasant dreams. Most importantly, there's balance.

"Is something wrong?" I ask him as I take a wide step over fins to reach the brace again. "It's nice to see you, but…" I let myself trail off.

"No, no, nothing pressing," he says.

"Nothing pressing? That's reassuring." I snort and adjust the wood against the iron. Two more screws. I flex my sore fingers and then set to work again. Valenor stays silent. Watches. Waits. When I finish my work and he still hasn't said anything, I look up. The shadows are still again. Unmoving.

"Valenor?" I whisper. "What do you mean, nothing pressing? Valenor?"

"Keep an ear to the darkness and shadows, Tib. Listen to

whisperings, especially at dusk. Do not dismiss that which strikes you as unusual. Keep working. Keep thinking. Be vigilant." His voice echoes softly as it fades away, leaving my arms prickling with chills again.

"Thanks for that!" I call out to the empty room, a little annoyed. No use trying to get more information out of him. He's gone. I toss my turnscrew into the toolbox and douse the torches. Climb up the ladder. Bar the door. Weave through the routes again. Back to the rich part of town. Back to Nessa's, all the while thinking of Valenor's warning and Loren and the vest and Celli. It's not like her to steal. Not that way, anyway. A loaf of bread, maybe. A handful of coin. Anything to get by. Not a rich man's bag. Or a rich boy's, for that matter. *Do not dismiss that which strikes you as unusual.*

The Ganvent manse stands sturdy and welcoming in front of me. Cool stone, rosy with the sunset. Ruben is outside, tossing a ball up the stoop and catching it as it rolls down. He's ten now, and always wants to do whatever I'm doing, only better. He doesn't notice me yet. I pause. My mouth waters as the smoky aroma of roast meat wafts past. Supper. Nessa worries if I miss it. It's really all she asks of us in exchange for her kindness. Make sure you're home for supper. But these new thoughts about Celli are weighing on me. Valenor's words ring in my ears with Loren's. Something's coming. Listen.

I take off at a jog. Past Ruben. Past the manse.

"Where you going?" Ruben calls after me. "It's grouse tonight! Raefe caught 'em! If you're late, someone'll eat yours! Tib! Can I have it then?"

"Go home, Rube," I shout, waving him off. "And don't you dare eat my grouse!"

He keeps following.

"Go home or Saesa will eat yours," I shout over my shoulder. His footsteps stop. Go back the other way. My mouth is still watering. I'd much rather be at the table right now, but I have to find out about Celli. Why she stole that bag. The real reason. I pick up my pace. Run fast. Think about the red swirls. Celli's screaming. Did they take her to the conclave, I wonder, or the Academy? Did the Mark keep growing?

My feet pound across uneven cobbles. Pebbles. Dirt. Mud. I leap over the filthy gutter and skid to a stop. The street that runs through the crooked houses of Redstone Row is empty. Too empty for this time of day. Usually at supper there are people wandering around, chatting. Looking for an open place at the table of a generous friend or neighbor. Either that or standing in their own door, calling out they have extra. Not tonight. All the doors are closed. Everything is quiet.

I step back over the gutter and pull the cobwebs around me to sink out of view. I press against the crumbling wall of Old Ven's house. Listen harder. Hear low voices. Whispers. Urgent. Frightened. I follow the sound along the wall. Four houses down are the Deshtals. Celli's family. Their small house is full of people. The door is closed tight. The shutters, too. I press my eye to the crack. Try to see. It's too dark to make anything out, though, and the whispers are all jumbled together.

I turn to press my ear to the shutter. When I do I catch a glimpse of something even more strange. Two boys across the way, slipping into an alley. One looks back over his shoulder. His glance is full of fear and secrets. I step lightly into the street. Follow them to where they're huddled together in the narrow space between crooked buildings. They don't notice me as they stand close together, whispering. I know these two. Griff is twelve, skinny and scrappy. The son of a woodcarver. Mikken is eight. Rounder. Son of a butcher. Both are thought to be good boys by the adults, but I know better. They're almost always up to some scheme.

I step closer. They smell strange. Like Averie's apothecary booth. Old, odd things. Dead things. Not just that. Magic. Strange magic. I feel it around them. It lingers like perfume. Powerful. Quiet. Forbidding. *These boys are mine*, it seems to say. *Don't touch.*

"What are we going to do?" Mikken, the younger of the two, hisses. He's terrified. Breathless. He's got Griff by the arm. Griff's not doing much better. He's shaking. His eyes dart around. He tries to catch his breath.

"We gotta tell someone," Griff mouths. His voice is too weak, too scared to make a sound.

"We can't. He said—" Mikken starts, but Griff cuts him off.

"Shh!! Don't mention him! You remember? Don't dare, Mik. Don't, or he'll…" Griff trails off. Shudders.

"But Celli," Mik whines under his breath. Glances toward her house. "Everyone's looking for her."

"She didn't listen. They told her to get it and not to touch it, and she didn't listen," Griff clings to Mik, too. Keeps looking around, like the shadows will pop out and grab him.

"That doesn't mean she deserves what they—" Mikken starts again, but Griff claps a hand over his mouth.

"You can't. You can't talk about them. Mik, remember what they

49

said. Anyone could hear. Shadows have ears. Remember?" Griff slides his hand away as Mikken nods, wide-eyed.

"But Celli," Mik says again. "What do we do?"

"She failed," Griff whispers. "She failed, and she's got to pay. We can't do anything. You heard them. We have to do what they say or they'll take us, too."

"But how?" Mik whines again. "It's impossible."

"We gotta find that kid in the yellow. Track down that bag," Griff says hopelessly.

"What if it's already in the palace? What if he delivered it?" Mikken asks.

"Then we find someone to get it. We have to," Griff whispers.

"But who? How?" Mik snaps his head up to a sound at the mouth of the alley. I look, too. A rat scurries past in the twilight.

"Tib. He goes sometimes. To visit the princess. We could ask him to get it. To find it," Griff suggests.

"How do we even ask him that?" Mik shivers. "We're not supposed to talk about it. Not to anyone."

"Maybe he could get us inside, then." Griff shrugs.

"No way. They'd never let us in the palace, it doesn't matter who we're with. We're peasants! Look at us," Mik grabs a handful of his filthy threadbare tunic. Griff looks at him.

"If Eron were king," he whispers, "things would be different. He wouldn't keep his people out, no matter what they looked like."

"Yeah," says Mikken. "He'd be a better king. I hope the appeals work. Hope he gets to be king soon."

"Me too," whispers Griff. "Things might get better, then."

"Yeah," Mikken says. He shakes his head. Neither of them has anything else to say.

I stand there, right next to them, my hands balled into fists. I have my own opinions about what should happen to Eron, and apparently we're on complete opposite sides.

Still, whoever is behind this, whoever is so desperate that they would terrify children to recover that vest, must be wicked. Evil. Sorcerers. Why, though? Why is that object so important? What do they need it for? Who are they? I think about showing myself to them. Offering help. Asking all of these questions.

They won't answer, though. I'm sure of it. If Sorcery is behind it, and I'm sure it is, they wouldn't be able to tell me, anyway. I know how it works. I've seen it before.

"We'll track him," Griff says. "The rich boy. That's the best first thing. Maybe he still has it. If he does, we can get it."

"Yeah," Mikken cracks his knuckles. "We can get it from him. He wasn't so strong, anyway."

"Let's go," Griff squares his shoulders. Tries to look brave. Mikken lets go of him and tries to feign bravery, too. They hurry off together. I follow them out of the alley, out of Redstone Row, and into the streets of Cerion. If they won't ask for help, I'll stick close to them. Try my best to keep them safe while I figure out exactly who they're working for, and what they're up to.

Chapter Six
RIAN'S STRIFE

Azi

"Imagine," Rian paces the length of the meeting hall with Shush drifting close behind, "a constant, nagging—"

"Nagging?" Shush interrupts with a hiss of a whisper.

"All right," Rian pauses and rubs the back of his neck, looking up to the ceiling. "Persistently enticing?" He glances at Shush, who nods his approval.

"Imagine a constant, persistently enticing, luscious, divine little personal source of power. You know how it feels, Azi, to use it. To cast a spell. That sensation of the magic coursing through you. The euphoria. The…" he sighs, his eyes half-closed.

"I know," I cross to him and take his hands. I do know. When I was lured into the Dreaming by Jacek and tricked into using Mentalism, I abused it. I let it tempt me just like Rian is describing now. It filled me with such ecstasy, such rapture that I lost myself. I forgot who I was and why I was there. I only wanted more. I wanted to feel nothing but that, forever. I shiver, and Rian pulls me close. "But you're trained. You're tempered to it, Rian. You've been tested and tried since you were a child. You know your limits. You're in control."

"Never," Rian murmurs into my hair. "I'm never in control, Azi. I'm on constant guard. After a while it becomes second nature, but it's still there. The conscious effort I have to make to keep myself in check. To keep from losing myself to Sorcery."

"But you'd never let it go that far," I say, stroking his arm reassuringly. "You wouldn't turn to that."

"Do you think," he pulls away from me and starts pacing again, "a Mage just wakes up one day and says oh, I think I'll be a Sorcerer? No. It happens gradually. Slowly. It inks its way into your heart when the Marks curl. A little bit here, a little bit there. That's what makes it so dangerous. The more you allow, the more you want, the more you justify, until you're black as coals."

I glance at Shush while Rian keeps pacing. He seems to have lost interest in the conversation in favor of a dish of sugared summer fruits

Mouli left out on the table. He picks up a morsel and sniffs it, pokes it, nibbles it.

"Human logic," he sprays juice and sugar as he whispers through a mouthful. "You think I'd just give it to you, hm? Just let you take my power? Let you leech it out? Just like that?"

Rian pauses and turns to the fae. "Couldn't I?" he asks.

"You'd have to make a conscious effort, first. Break down my barriers. Wards, you call them. Unweave the winds." He snaps his sticky fingers and a tiny dervish of a breeze whips around him, scattering the sugar crystals at his feet and swooping his hair into a sharper point. "I wouldn't offer myself for this pairing without taking precautions. Nor would I if I didn't trust you. Even so," he beckons Rian closer, "try it."

"What?" Rian spins to fully face him, and slowly backs away.

"Come, now. Try it," Shush beckons again. "I'll show you, you can't just sap me. Not anymore. We've learned things since the Battle of the North."

I think back to all that time ago, two years to the month, almost, when Sorcerers attacked the Northern Border of Kythshire. Their combined power was terrifying. They moved mountains, literally, to gain the upper hand. When their keep was in place, they captured wind fairies, Shush's charges, and used them to restore their own power. I remember clear as day, the cages filled with tiny white bodies. Sapped fairies. Drained and wasted.

Rian closes his eyes and pinches the bridge of his nose. The invitation obviously disturbs him. Slowly, he shakes his head and pushes his hand up across his forehead and through his hair. He looks at Shush squarely.

"I understand what you're offering me is a great honor. An unbelievable gesture of trust. I am truly humbled, Shush," he says quietly.

Shush looks up from his fruit. He gives me a glance and a little nod. He's hopeful that Rian will accept. I'm not, though. I know him. In matters like this, he'll always be stubborn.

"But until I see an honest, pressing need for such a partnership, I'm afraid I have to decline," Rian crosses to the table and leans down so he's eye-to-eye with the fae. "I'm sorry," he whispers, "I think you should leave now."

"I see. Well." Shush looks wide-eyed from Rian to me. When I shrug apologetically, he stuffs his pouches full of fruit, gives us both a swift salute, and disappears in a blink.

I take Rian's shaking hand and pull him to the group of squashy armchairs arranged around the hearth. He's silent for a long time, his eyes covered with one long, slender hand. I take in everything about him: the slump of his shoulders, the way his robes pool around him in the chair, the way the firelight turns his auburn hair to fiery orange, the smoky scent of incense that lingers in the air around him.

I collect these things and tuck them into my memory for some dark moment in the future, when they may be all I have to cling to. I find myself doing this often since my time with Jacek in the dreaming. I have lots of little collections stashed away. Mum, Da, Flitt, plenty of Rian. Even Mouli.

Rian slumps back, still covering his eyes. I don't realize he's crying until he sniffles softly.

"Rian?" I reach for his free hand and he slips it into mine. He's not shaking anymore, but his hand is cold and stained with ink. I rub it between mine and kiss his knuckles one by one while he weeps quietly in the chair beside me.

"Do you want to talk about it?" I whisper, pressing his hand to my cheek. There's something more weighing on him. Not just the fairies. It isn't like Rian to succumb to tears. He's one of the strongest people I know. For him to cry here, in the guild hall where anyone could walk in, something else must be going on.

"Can't," he whispers and draws in a deep breath. He rubs his eyes and wipes them dry. After a moment, he strokes my cheek and guides my chin to face him. "Look," he says.

I feel it well in my heart, the warm desire that comes from his invitation. Look. All I have to do is gaze into his eyes and let myself tumble. Let the magic of Mentalism course through me. Allow myself to walk in his memories. Be him. Feel the bliss of it. *The more you allow, the more you want.* His words from moments before ring in my ears. Maybe it's because I want to help or maybe it's because I'm not as strong as he is. Maybe he's trying to prove a point. I don't know. I don't care. The lure of the thrill pulls me until it's nearly impossible to resist.

I gaze into his red-rimmed eyes and feel the swell of magic rush through me. My body tingles as I lose myself in the hazel flecks of his eyes: gold and copper and green. I fall away from the room, away from myself, and into his mind.

The Academy walls stretch up overhead to an elegant domed ceiling. He's in the entry hall, which is stark white and completely unadorned. I remember this place in my own mind. I've been here once before, but now I'm Rian. His own memories and emotions leak into mine. He's nervous. Afraid. He walks at a brisk pace through the entry, avoiding eye contact with the other students. They whisper to each other behind their hands as he passes by. Some of them raise their chins disdainfully, or glare. It's obvious they have little respect for him here. It's almost as though they're afraid of him.

He pushes open a door that leads to a passageway of rich wood walls lined with shelves of various artifacts and instruments. As he walks through it, Rian works to calm himself. There is something very unnerving about this passage, as though these things were placed here to intimidate. He tries not to look at them, focusing instead on the gray door at the far end. When he finally reaches it, his heart is racing even faster. Despite his efforts his nerves are on edge. He rests his shaking hand on the latch and takes a deep breath before pushing the door open.

Inside is a cramped triangular room, all gray and dark. It's the size of a dressing room or a closet. The shape of the room is unnerving, too. Stepping inside makes one feel off balance. He looks down at his feet. The floor is polished stone, white with circles of red, and slightly slanted. He takes a deliberate, measured step into a red circle, and magical light from an unseen source beams down around him. Within it are orbs of brighter light that cling to him in places. I remember these. They are used to identify any enchanted objects he might be carrying.

"Mentor Rian Eldinae," a voice booms through the small room. The light goes dim again. "Step to the center."

Rian does so, but the slant of the polished floor requires a constant effort to keep him from sliding. In the short time waiting for the voice to speak again, the muscles of his calves and ankles already burn.

"Mentor Rian Eldinae," the voice booms again, "you are charged with six counts of Sorcery and Unknown Dealings, two counts of Trespassing at the Source, and one count of Intentional Harm to a Fellow Student. This trial will determine your motives for these actions and deem them necessary or unnecessary. If they are found to be willful and unnecessary, you will be stripped of your Title and Circles. Is this clear?"

"Yes, Master. I agree to answer all questions willingly and truthfully," Rian replies to the empty walls with a shift of his feet.

Later, hours later, he's still standing. His legs ache from the effort but he refuses to lean or sit. His hands are clasped behind his back as he answers question after question. They grill him about every noted instance of Mage Mark recorded in the time leading up to the Battle of Kythshire. He answers everything truthfully. Their questions turn to Viala, the student turned Sorceress. They ask him how he found out about her. Why he didn't report her to a Master or Advisor. Why he chose to strip her without ceremony or permission. Most importantly, they ask him how he managed, as a Mentor-level student, do to it on his own. At that, Rian pauses.

"Answer the question," the voice booms. I've counted several different voices throughout the interrogation. This one makes my skin prickle. I'm certain it's Gaethon, the Headmaster of the Academy. My uncle. My own anger charges through me, overclouding Rian's fear and nervousness. Uncle had been at the border for much of the battle. He saw things firsthand. How could he put Rian through this?

"I . . ." Rian's heartbeat thunders in his ears. He reaches up and scrapes his fingernails through his short-cropped hair. This happened some time ago, I realize then. They must have questioned him right after Kythshire.

"I drew it into me. Her knowledge and power. I drained it from her, all of it, until it was mine and she had no memory of it." This is true. I remember it well. But not entirely true. Shush was there, and Ember as well. The two fairies were sent with us to put a stop to Viala and her plots. Rian is careful to protect them, though.

"Impossible," another Master barks after a long pause. "A Sixteenth-Circle Mage simply cannot, on his own, perform a full and complete stripping. We do not accept your answer as the entire truth."

Rian shifts again. His feet are pounding, his knees ache. His toes are curled and cramped by his effort to keep from sliding. He wants nothing more than to relieve the pain, but he knows that's precisely what this room is meant for; to demonstrate his conviction and his discipline. He could do any number of things: sit, float, even tilt the floor to level it. He could, but any of those actions would incriminate him as weak-minded and ruled too much by his physical needs. He visited this place many times as a child for counts of mischief and learned the rules quickly. This time is different, though. These accusations are far more serious.

"To protect the Wellspring and its Keepers, I regret that I'm unable to answer to your satisfaction," he says clearly. To my surprise, they seem to accept this reply. They move on to the next round of questioning. This one focuses on Kythshire itself, how he was able to enter, what sort of things he saw. He answers each one in turn with the same calm reply: "To protect the Wellspring and its Keepers, I regret that I'm unable to answer to your satisfaction."

The scene changes slowly as those words repeat over and over.

Now, he's sitting in a dim room at a broad desk stacked with tomes and thick sheaves of parchment. Other desks line the room in neat rows, each holding its own stack of books, each employing a student hard at work.

Rian's long hair tumbles into his face while he works and I understand that this is the present. Today, possibly. His finger traces across the ancient page as he transcribes its words to the stack of paper before him. His writing is neat and clear, not at all like I've seen it in the assignments he works on at home. Here, he's careful and deliberate with each stroke of the quill. I understand these are books being copied to replenish Sunteri's burned libraries.

I look closer at Rian's book. The drawings on the page are disturbing: Men with skin peeled away to reveal the muscle and bone beneath. Their faces are twisted and tortured. While he copies, Rian seems to be in a state of deep meditation. His stomach is twisted in knots. He tries hard not pay attention to the words he copies, which are dark and wicked. Not many are trusted to transcribe this content. Rian's high Circle and his restraint have earned him the privilege. At first he was proud to be given the honor, but the deeper he gets into these dark volumes, the sicker he feels.

Around him, the other students whisper to each other. They joke and laugh. No one seems to acknowledge Rian, though. Instead they make an effort to actively avoid him.

He finishes the page, places it on top of the neat stack at the edge of his desk, and starts another. At the table beside him, a younger student whoops and tucks his work into a leather binding.

"Did my three," he whispers across to a blond haired girl. "You finished, Lilen?"

She nods and they both pick up their bindings and get up to leave. The boy, only a year or two Rian's junior, brushes past his neat stack of pages and they go tumbling to the floor. He doesn't pause to pick them up or apologize. Instead he smirks at the high tower of tomes on Rian's desk. Lilen freezes and stares pale-faced at Rian, who sets his quill down with measured patience.

"Come on, Lil," the boy tugs her sleeve as he tramples over the pages. "He can handle it. He's got friends, you know." He chuckles and Lilen gapes, wide-eyed.

"S-sorry," she breathes at Rian as she's tugged away. She whispers a spell and wriggles her fingers and the pages float up and settle back onto his desk. At first I think it was kind of her and then I realize the truth. She's terrified of him. Several of the others stare over their shoulders at the scene. A score of faces younger than his and a few who are older watch and wait to see what he'll do. Whether this will be the moment Mentor Rian finally loses his temper.

He doesn't, though. He offers Lilen a smile and a thank-you, he nods cordially to those who stare, and he tucks back into his meditative scribing.

"At first it was a thrill, the way they looked at me with fear. The way they saw me as this mysterious figure with secrets. Unapproachable." Rian's voice in my ear jars me back to the present. I blink my eyes rapidly and feel myself plummet back to the guild hall. At some point I must have crawled into his lap, because now I'm curled there with my forehead pressed to his. His arms tighten around me and soothe me as despair and emptiness quickly replace the magical euphoria.

I break my gaze from his and look down to my hands in my lap. They're covered again with golden swirls; evidence of my craft printed plain for everyone to see. For once I don't care about that, though. I knew things had been difficult for Rian, but I had no idea of the details until now. Before Kythshire, everyone had looked up to him. Everyone wanted to be him. He was the first seventeen-year-old from Cerion in decades to reach Seventeenth Circle and be named Mentor. He had a promising life ahead of him. He was the favorite of Headmaster Gaethon. Everyone wanted to know what Rian the Protégé would become. He was at the brink of fame, not only in the Academy but also throughout the kingdom.

Now he's nineteen, treading carefully, and reduced to copying dark tomes in the library.

"What was that book?" I whisper.

Rian shakes his head wearily. "Never mind."

"Has it occurred to you," I ask after a long time thinking, "that maybe your path doesn't lie here in the Academy, or even in Cerion? Maybe you belong somewhere else." It breaks my heart to say it. I can barely speak through the lump in my throat. But Rian is a talented Mage, and he isn't like the others. He's not proud or haughty. He's got a better sense of humor and a kinder heart than any other Mages I've ever known.

Although I'm grateful for Uncle, who I know must have spoken on his behalf countless times, I'm furious that the Academy and its council would treat him this way after all he's done for Cerion and for Kythshire. He doesn't deserve to be scorned and feared. "If only they knew…" I whisper.

"They don't, and they never will," he says. "No one will ever know the truth of it and that's fine by me. But you see now why I can't accept Shush. I'm already thought of as an outsider. Few of them trust me, and those who do suspect I'm losing my mind. It'd be a torturous secret to keep, and if they ever found out, if they knew, they'd…" he trails off and sighs and kisses the top of my head as I burrow closer.

"They'd have you stripped and thrown out," I say.

"That's not what worries me most," he says in a hushed tone, barely loud enough for me to hear. "I fear what would become of the fairies, Azi. Many of the Mages are on the brink. They corner me in dark hallways and offer me bribes and promises. They want to know what I know about Kythshire. They want me to tell them what I know about the Wellspring. They try to get me to break its secrets. The Academy is not as disciplined as they'd have you think. Just like everywhere else, there's corruption and games of power. You never hear tell of it because it's too covered up. I couldn't even be telling you about it now if you weren't already marked as my apprentice. But it's there."

"Does Uncle know?" I whisper, watching the fire light catch my gold swirls.

"Oh, yes," Rian sighs wearily. "Yes, indeed. He keeps a close eye on those who seem to be edging toward Sorcery. I've seen his stern counsel. I'm just glad he's on my side."

THE COIN

Tib

Griff and Mik are not very good at searching. They don't even have a plan. Maybe it's because I know the two places he's most likely to be, but their method of trying to find him almost makes me laugh. They ask around a while for a boy dressed in yellow carrying a satchel. Nobody gives them any answers. Why should they? The boys have no motivation to offer. No reason to make anyone talk.

They don't go near the sea wall at all. Not even a thought for Seabird's Swoop. Instead, they stay in the richer part of the city. Peek in windows. Ask maids and servants doing the night rounds. Their methods make no sense to me. He's obviously an islander, not a native to Cerion. Why bother asking the richer locals? It's getting dark. Dusk. They're running out of light to search in. People have gone inside. The boys don't even try to knock on doors.

Griff slips around a corner. Mikken follows, whispering warnings. I feel it before I see it. Magic, forceful and cruel. I pick up my pace to catch up with them. I rush around the bend expecting to see some dark figure waiting. Instead, I find nothing but an empty alley. I run to the end of it. There's no other way out. The boys came this way, there was magic, and now they're gone. I slap my hands against the rough stone wall. Solid. Around me I can still feel it. Smell it. The dregs of magic, thick in the air. It can't affect me. I know if it could I'd be gone, too.

"Griff!" I call, "Mikken!"

No answer.

"I know you took them!" I yell. "Come and face me!" I draw my dagger. It's ended more than one Sorcerer in my hands. I'm ready, always ready, to run it through another. Eager, even. Maybe they know, and that's why they don't come out. "Cowards!" I growl.

I slide my hands over every brick I can reach along the alley, hoping to find some secret passage. Something to show me that the boys are safe. That they weren't actually swallowed up by a Sorcerer's spell. I find nothing to comfort me. The only strange thing is a small circle carved into the stone at the far wall. It still tingles with magic, but nothing I do to it changes that sensation. I sigh and go to the end of the alley. Lean against the wall. Keep watch. Wait and see if anyone else comes around.

At dawn, ships' bells wake me. I push myself to my feet and stretch, sore from sleeping all night against hard stone. The alley has changed. It's bright, washed with pink from the sunrise. Empty. Lighter. I walk to the end again. The magic is gone. Something glints in the far corner, catching my eye. A coin, silver and small. I crouch to look closer. Nudge it with my fingernail. Feel nothing. Its edges are little spikes with balls on the end. Its face is blank. I flip it over. This side shows a symbol. A cloud with a single spire piercing through the top of it. On top of the spire, a hand with fingers spread wide.

There's no magic to it, but the symbol captures me somehow. I can't stop looking. Thinking about what it might mean. I pick it up. Feel its weight. It's just an ordinary coin with an unfamiliar design. It doesn't hold any magic or enchantments that I can tell. I turn it to the blank side. Think for a while. There's nothing else I can do now. The portal is gone. The danger has passed. I tuck the coin into my bandolier and decide to head home.

At the steps of the manse, my stomach growls. Breakfast. I can smell it. Biscuits. Eggs. Fish and potatoes. Stewed fruit. The meals are always hearty at Nessa's, but today, it's even more so. Today, the Admiral is home. When her husband dines with us, every meal becomes a feast. I push open the door. Inside, it feels like a holiday. It's early, but everyone is already up. Their laughter and playful chatter drifts out from the sitting room. Saesa's on the stairs when I step inside. She's still in her dressing gown. When she sees me, she dashes across the foyer in a blur of red hair and bright blue flapping silk. She skids to a stop in front of me. She throws her arms around me and hugs me. Before I can wriggle free, she shoves me and then punches me in the arm, hard.

"Ow," I wince and back away. "What's that for?"

"Where were you, Tib?" she asks, her fists clenched at her sides. She looks tired. Like she didn't sleep much. "Ruben said you'd be home for supper. He said you were running off but you said to save you grouse. And then you didn't turn up all night!" She punches my other arm.

"Ow," I rub both spots. Glare at her. "Stop punching me."

"Don't be a baby," she scowls. "Are you going to tell me where you were or not?"

I can see it through her frown. The worry being pushed out by relief. She was up all night, probably. I take her hand and link it through my arm. Lead her into the empty dining room, where the table is set with glistening silver. Some of the serving trays are already covered with steaming domes. Others sit empty. Saesa's green eyes flash at me as I tuck her into the corner. She crosses her arms and tries to seem angry, but her cheeks are rose pink under her freckles. Her gaze flicks to my lips and back to my eyes again.

I tell her about everything, from Celli and Loren all the way to the disappearing boys in the alley. About the magic that lingered there. About how I stayed to keep watch. By the time I'm finished, her eyes are wide. Her hand covers her mouth.

"Then I found this," I say. I reach into my bandolier and pull out the coin. She looks it over. Stares at it, like I did, unable to look away for some time.

"What does it mean?" she whispers.

"Don't know," I say. "Never saw it before. What about Loren?" I ask as she rubs her thumb across the symbol. "Did he show up?"

"No," she whispers. "It was a quiet night." She looks up at me again, scowling pointedly. "Too quiet."

"Sorry, sorry," I rub my arms. "Don't punch me again."

"I can ask Rian today. Maybe he knows what it means," she says. "A hand and... What is it? A floating city?"

"Take it with you," I reply and press it into her hand. "I don't know if it's a whole city. It looks like just a tower to me."

"Actually," she says, "I was going to ask you to come to the palace with me today. I was invited to luncheon with the Princess. Me and a guest. She invited Lady Azaeli, too."

My heart starts to race. If I can get into the palace, maybe I can find that doll vest, or at least warn Margy about it.

"Sure," I say. "I'll come."

Saesa grins at me and starts to say something, but she's interrupted by Bette, the cook, who comes in holding a tray of hot biscuits.

"Look at you two, skulking in corners! If you're coming to breakfast you'd better go dress properly. Saesa, in your dressing gown." She clicks her tongue and turns to me. "And Master Tib, you look as though you've slept in the street. Off with you both! I won't have you ruining the Admiral's breakfast. Go on!"

Saesa grabs my hand and we run up the stairs together. She giggles all the way until she flings me into my room.

"See you at breakfast!" she calls.

Admiral Ganvent is a broad-shouldered man with a stern brow. His face is always red from too much sun. The first time I saw him, I was sure he was a harsh man. He is sometimes, I imagine, but not now. At the breakfast table with Nessa beside him and the children gathered around, he's relaxed. Amused. There are eight children for breakfast, and not one of them is his. They've all been taken in by Nessa, who can't have children of her own. We don't know why. Nobody has ever dared to ask.

It's different today than it was the first time I sat at this table. Saesa's brother Raefe is gone. He's off at the barracks, training for the navy. He wants to work on the Admiral's ship but Ganvent said he's going to need a lot of training and some ranks for that. Lilen and Ruben are still here, but Maisie married off last year and took her baby, Errie, with her. Emmie is older now, maybe eight. She's a glass blower's apprentice. Garsi is only five and she wants to join the Academy already. There's Jeshan, who's eleven. He's studying woodcarving for ships. The newest is Hett. He doesn't talk much. We're still trying to figure out where he fits. Nessa says he'd better speak up soon. He's older. Fourteen, maybe. The same age I was when she took me in.

It's only a little less noisy today with the Admiral here than it usually is. Lots of chatter and gossip from around the city. Nessa's kids are taught early how to gather information, and all of them are good at it. None of what anyone shares really interests me until Lilen speaks up.

"I overheard something curious yesterday while I was scribing for Master Gaethon," she says in her usual haughty tone. "You know, the Headmaster?"

"Yes, Lilen," Saesa rolls her eyes. "I think we might have heard of him."

"Never mind, then." Lilen huffs. "If you're going to be rude, I won't tell you."

"Go on, Lilen," Nessa says, leaning toward the girl. "Saesa, stop teasing."

"Well," Lilen pointedly looks away from Saesa to Nessa. "Master Gaethon was having an argument with Cari, the bookbinder. It seems that six of the books we scribed have somehow gone missing between when they were dropped off to be bound and when the order was returned to us. Cari insisted they were finished and returned, but Master Gaethon was certain they were never returned. Master Gaethon was shouting. I've never seen him so mad."

"But the books are bound right in the Academy, aren't they?" Nessa asks.

"Yes, they've all been done there, in the workshop," Lilen takes a tiny bite of stewed fruit.

"Did he ever figure out what happened to them?" Nessa asks.

"No," Lilen replies. "He's furious. Six books missing from the library. It's unheard of."

"Which books?" I ask out of curiosity.

"Tib, you know I can't tell you that. Academy secrets," she says primly. Dabs her lips with the corner of her serviette. She lowers her eyes to her plate and then looks up at me again. Smiles.

Next to me, Saesa huffs impatiently.

"Well, either Cari is in on it or someone stole them," Saesa says.

"Don't be ridiculous, Saesa," Lilen rolls her eyes dramatically. "Nobody steals from Cerion's Academy. It's impossible. And Cari is a wrinkled old failed Mage. What would he want with a bunch of old tomes that he can't even use?"

"He could sell them," Saesa suggests.

"Even more ridiculous," Lilen chides. "Who'd buy them? Only Mages have an interest in such writings, and everyone knows it's illegal to trade in the Arcane, especially in Cerion."

"That's what the Undermarket is for," Saesa glares at her. "Or hadn't you thought of that in your brilliance?"

"Enough, you two," Nessa laughs softly at the tension between the two girls. She glances at me quickly and looks away, still smiling.

"I hope they're found before tomorrow," Admiral Ganvent says thoughtfully. "We can't delay the shipment any further. The council at Zhaghen is getting restless to finish its library now that the towers are rebuilt."

Saesa and I exchange a quick, knowing look. Suddenly I find my own breakfast very interesting. She's the only one here who knows what happened. Why Zhaghen had to rebuild their Mage towers. Mevyn and I burned them to thwart the Sorcerers. To keep them from draining Sunteri's Wellspring. To distract them so we could work to restore it and hide it away.

It's still a secret. Especially the Wellspring. Even Saesa doesn't remember that it's been restored, or where it is. They were all there. His Majesty's Elite. Azi, Rian, everyone. I'm the only one who remembers it today, though. Mevyn swore to me that he wouldn't tamper with my memories any more, and he kept his promise. The rest of them weren't so lucky.

The table goes quiet except for the clink of silver on china. Everyone's deep in their own thoughts about the missing tomes, or other things.

"Will you bring me back a silk robe, like Saesa's, Pabie?" Garsi asks.

"If you'd like. In lavender, I imagine?" The admiral leans back in his chair and grins. Nessa gets up to fetch his pipe for him. She kisses him as the table erupts into requests.

"A brush and ink!" cries Jeshan.

"A spyglass like Raefe's," Ruben bobs up and down excitedly.

"You had one," Admiral Ganvent says to him. "I brought it last time."

"Yes, but I was climbing and it fell out and smashed," Ruben whines.

"All right," the admiral laughs, "but what happens to the scout in the crow's nest who drops his spyglass?"

"Throw him overboard!" Everyone shouts.

The rest of breakfast is lighthearted as they talk about the adventures in store for the Admiral. Even Saesa and Lilen seem to forget to hate each other.

After breakfast, everyone goes their own way as usual. The children head out to the streets to gossip and collect secrets. Admiral Ganvent goes to check on the readiness of his fleet. Nessa calls me into the sitting room. Saesa comes, too.

Nessa sits on the chaise and smoothes the ruffles of her dress. She looks perfect, like a trinket that belongs in this bright, rich room. Like a doll, set in place. Her eyes are brown, wide, and a little sad when she looks at me.

"We held supper for you last night," she says quietly. Pats the cushion beside her. I cross and sit there. Take her hand. I've missed supper before. I know the routine. She won't shout. She'll be kind and gentle, so I can't help but feel guilty. I consider lying about where I was, but I know Nessa. She gets information from everywhere. She might even know the meaning of the coin. Saesa perches on the arm of the chaise beside me. I chew my lip. Look up at Nessa, considering.

I start telling her little bits, starting with the fight in the alley. I tell her about Loren and Finn and the vest. I tell her about Celli's disappearance, and the secret meeting of peasants in Redstone Row. I tell her how I tracked Mikken and Griff and how they vanished in the alley. I have Saesa show her the coin. She turns it in her hand thoughtfully. After a long time, she tears her gaze from it and looks at me.

"Go and close the door, Saesa," she says. "Make sure no one is snooping."

Saesa does what she's told. She comes back to us again looking both excited and intrigued. When Nessa says close the door, it's obvious she's about to trust you with a secret. I lean closer as she hands the coin back to me and tucks a brown curl behind her ear.

"There are whisperings," she starts so quietly that I almost have to read her lips to make out what she's saying. "Whisperings of conspiracies within the city. His Majesty's guard is down. He is distracted, we all know. Some sympathize with the prince.

"This makes room for shadows to seep into the cracks of doubt among the people. Dark magic. Dark dealings. Some whisper that Prince Eron was in their grips all along. That their spell was weaved around him like fine clothing, all in a plot to take him from us, to break the king, to open the way, ever so slowly, to allow them to infiltrate the city. You see it working even now. Their actions are rallying some in the kingdom to consider taking action against the throne."

"Who?" Saesa whispers. She leans across me, taken in by Nessa's words.

"No one knows their true name. They're cloaked in mystery. Rumor is the only source of information on them. Many don't dare speak of them at all. Some simply call them the Order. I've heard tell that they call themselves Circle of Spires. That seems likely to me now, given your coin. It is an old order. Ancient, even. Its members were scarce and few. But now, based on what you've told me, Tib, they have grown bold. Perhaps they are stronger. Perhaps they're simply desperate." She looks at both of us and shakes her head. Gives me back the coin.

"I'm not foolish enough to forbid you to pursue this," she sighs. "I know you'll do what you will regardless of what I say. Nor do I doubt your capabilities. You two are both very strong-willed. You have powerful friends: the princess, Azi and the Elite. Trust in them. I beg you, though, to be careful. Please. And don't speak of this around your brothers and sisters. I won't have them frightened or involved."

She grips my hand tightly until I nod in agreement. Beside me, Saesa nods too.

"We're invited to the palace today," Saesa says, "for luncheon. We'll talk to the princess and warn her. We'll see if she's ever heard about this Circle of Spires. Right, Tib?"

"Yeah, of course," I agree absently, thinking over the last few weeks since I started working on my project. Circle of Spires. I look at the coin. At the cloud and the spire. Could it be coincidence? Did I know on some level that my invention would be needed? Not for Cerion's ships, but for something else? Something more important?

Out of nowhere, Zeze hops up onto my lap. She mews and kneads and purrs. She pushes her head against my hand as I curl my fingers around the coin.

"Well," Saesa reaches to stroke Zeze's back, "shall we go to My Lady Knight's?"

"You go on," I say, still thinking about air bladders and propellers. "I have to check on something first."

"All right." Saesa says. We both get up. Kiss Nessa's cheek as she reaches for her book.

"Be careful," Nessa calls after us. Zeze weaves around my ankles all the way out into the street. Saesa and I hug, agree to meet up later at the palace, and go our separate ways.

Chapter Eight
UNSAVORY ORDERS

Azi

I rap softly on the circle hatch that connects my room to Rian's and slide it open as quietly as I can. The sun is barely up, so I'm not surprised when I peer across his room and the nest of blankets on his bed groans back at me.

"Rian," I whisper, and am answered with a loud snore. "All right, then," I say a little louder. "I'm going down without you." I leave the hatch open as a signal to him that I've gone.

Our visit from Flitt and Shush along with Rian's confessions had me up all night worrying and thinking. Something has been off lately. I've felt it lurking beneath the somber mood of the city. Not just the trial, but something else. A hint of foreboding. Their arrival yesterday and the memories Rian shared only reinforce this nagging feeling. I wish I could pinpoint it. I try to convince myself that it's in my mind. Maybe it's boredom or a desire to be out righting wrongs, fighting the wicked. It has been too long since I've tasted adventure. I miss it.

Mum and Da aren't in their bedroom or downstairs. I step out into the open corridor that connects our house with the rest of the guild complex and am greeted right away by the distant chatter of the guild gathered in the hall beyond. My heart races as I pick out the voices one by one: Mya, Mum, Da, Donal. It's been a long time since they were all together in the hall, talking. Their urgent discussion is interrupted by a deep, booming voice that overwhelms the rest of them. I quicken my pace to a jog and reach the gathering just as Bryse finishes his tirade.

"Damn straight it's wrong! That's what we've been trying to say!" Bryse slams his fist on the table. Out of habit, everyone reaches to steady their goblets as the silverware clatters. Bryse is huge. Twice as broad as my da and nearly twice as tall, with stony gray skin and a glare filled with temper. Beside him, the much shorter, slender, brown-skinned Cort looks just as annoyed, which is out of character for him.

"All we're saying is be careful." Despite his scowl, Cort is much more soft-spoken. "The things we saw out there were far from natural. There's something happening. Something strange. It could all be linked."

"I don't think it's an unreasonable command, considering," Mum says. I can feel her power drifting out from her center: a quiet peace that works to comfort and soothe those gathered around the table. "Nor does Benen. After all, no one expects His Majesty to carry out the sentence himself. Not this time."

"Still, we must be careful," Mya says, her melodic voice doing its own work to calm the group. "The command comes from His Majesty himself, yet once carried out, even the most reasonable man would have bitter feelings as a result. We could easily fall out of his favor."

"Morning, Azi," everyone says as I slide into the bench beside Da.

"Good morning," I reply. I reach for a hot roll and pause as I spy the letter lying on the table. His Majesty's seal is cracked open and his own hand fills the page. "What happened?" I ask, my heart racing. "Have they reached a verdict?"

"Not yet," Mum says quietly, "but His Majesty is making arrangements."

"Seems he's finally seeing where it's going," Bryse says gruffly.

"He's known it all along. He's just coming to terms now." Cort pushes the parchment across to me. "We got back just after midnight. There was a Page waiting outside the hall. He gave this to us and asked us to use discretion."

I slide the letter close and turn it over. Three initials grace the outside: H.M.E.

"His Majesty's Elite," I whisper and flip it again to read the letter. Unlike the tight, neatly formed letters usually written to us by his scribes, the king's hand is broad and loose. It's more personal and intimate this way. I can almost hear his anguished voice echoing in my mind as I read the words on the page.

> *My dear, most trusted friends,*
> *It is with a heavy heart that I write you this night. The verdict for my son is all but officially declared, and there is no question in my mind at this time that the judgment of my High Court will be just and fair. To my lament, I know it to mean that his remaining days are few.*
> *As custom and law demand, it is the King's duty to carry out executions by his own hand for treasonous charges. If he cannot fulfill this duty himself for any reason, he is permitted to name a Champion to do so in his stead.*

*I have spent many sleepless nights in distress thinking
of my son, my wife, and my daughters. Perhaps I am weak.
Perhaps a stronger man could carry out such a deed himself. I
fear carrying out this sentence with my own hands would break
our already broken family.*

*So I turn to you, yet again, my Elite, to do the
unthinkable. To right a wrong that I cannot bear to face.*

*Thus I inform you that when the time comes, I shall
name Sir Benen Hammerfel as my Champion. Benen, your
arm is strong. I pray that your strength does not fail you. I
pray that your ax flies swiftly, cleanly, and effortlessly. If I
must lose my son, I pray it be done without his suffering.*

Yours in deepest faith and confidence,
Tirnon

I don't realize my hand is shaking until Da covers it with his own. I look at it over mine, broad and strong, scarred and calloused. The veins of his arm bulge out over his thick muscles. I understand immediately why His Majesty has made the choice he made. Da has been there throughout the trial. He has listened to my testimony, the prince's, and that of countless others. He knows every fact, every accusation, and every bit of proof. Despite that, he has always remained calm within the gallery, even when others have been prone to outbursts. Sir Benen Hammerfel is known for his mercy, and for his loyalty to the king.

"Will you?" I break the long silence and look into his gray-blue eyes. He closes them slowly and nods.

"I will do as His Majesty bids. Always," he says firmly as he looks across to the others. "I would bear this burden for him."

I try to imagine my father swinging his ax against the prince, defenseless at the block. Unarmed and unable to fight back. I try to think of him as an executioner. A killer outside of battle. I wonder if it would change him, or change the way I look at him. Or the way others do. The thought turns my stomach.

None of us says a word about how much Eron deserves it. We don't need to. We know we're in agreement there. He has plotted against the king. His selfish lust for power has blinded him to any semblance of compassion or sense of right. He is lecherous, cruel, and twisted. He has no concern or love for his wife or his heir, and he never has. He has shown no loyalty to throne or his father. He would speed the king's death so he could rise up and take his crown. All of this has been proved time and again in the trials. Eron is wicked. He threatens the peace of the Kingdom. He has no respect or reverence for his family's line. He is a danger for the Plethores and for the future of Cerion itself. He is a murderer. He must be put to death.

"Eggs and sausages," Mouli sings brightly as she bustles into the room with a steaming tray. Da quickly folds the letter as she sets down the food. "Sweet rolls for you, my dear. I know you've been hungry for them these few days," she says to Bryse, who beams a smile at her.

"Rightly spoiled we are by you, Mouli," he laughs. "I dreamed of your cooking every day out in the caves and mists."

Bryse scoops a half-dozen of the large rolls onto his plate with his bare hand and Mouli smacks him lightly.

"Use the servers," she clicks her tongue. "By the stars, you're gone for a week and basic table manners are all but forgotten! I hope you at least washed!"

"Shorry," Bryse says around a mouthful of bread and icing. Mouli rolls her eyes and rushes out again as the others laugh.

"What did you find?" I ask Cort and Bryse, turning the conversation away from the prince for now.

"Wraiths." Cort says simply as he loads his plate with potatoes and sausages.

"Wraiths and Undead. Skeletons. Imps. You know, the usual dungeon fare," Bryse mumbles through another mouthful of sweet roll.

"Except not in a dungeon, that's what was strange. They were just out in the village, terrorizing everyone. People were barricaded in. They had been for days. They were half-starved when we got there."

"In the daylight?" Mya asks in surprise.

"Sort of," Bryse replies.

"It was day, but dark. Mists all over. They had cover," Cort says.

"Like it was put there, just for them," Bryse nods.

"What did you do?" I ask, my heart pumping as though I'm there with them on the adventure.

"Chased 'em out. Killed what we could," Bryse spears a sausage with his knife.

"Yeah," Cort nods. "Deep into the woods along the ravine. Far away from the village. It was dark. We think we tracked them all down. In the morning when the sun came out, the village was clear. No more mist. People were out and about. We called it a job done."

"They tried to pay us, but this one refused," Bryse elbows Cort.

"They needed it more than we do," Cort shrugs, "they've been hit hard by the drought out there. Fields all dried up. Cows not milking. A day's walk to the nearest working well."

"That makes no sense," Rian says from the doorway. "You said it was misty enough to provide cover for the wraiths. Mist brings moisture with it." He crosses and rubs my shoulder and I make room for him to slide in beside me.

"Unnatural, like I was saying. Something's off. I told you," Cort says. "We were going to talk to Gaethon about it after a rest."

"Something else," Bryse says. "Tell 'em," he nudges Cort.

"Missing people," Cort nods. "The villagers were telling us that when the mists came, they lost a few of their own. Vanished, they said. One moment they were there, and the next they were gone. Taken."

"Taken?" Rian rubs his eyes and pours himself a strong cup of tea.

"That's what they said," Bryse nods. "We looked for them, but you know, we're fighters, not trackers."

"Maybe Elliot could sniff them out," Mya suggests. "He should be back from his map scouting later today. In the meantime, Rian, please let Gaethon know we need his aid in the hall at supper. We haven't seen him here in nearly a week."

"Of course," Rian says, sipping his tea. I try to catch his eye, but he avoids mine.

"Will you come with me to the palace at lunch?" I ask him. When the others look at me questioningly, I explain about the princess's invitation.

"Odd timing," Brother Donal, who has been unusually quiet, offers.

"I'll try," Rian replies. He drains his cup and takes a roll. "But I should go now if I'm going to make my escape later."

"Have a plate first, Rian," Mya says with a hint of worry as she eyes the way her son's robes hang on his frame.

"Good lad. Listen to your mum," Bryse says, "or you'll be the next to disappear, from the looks of you."

***

My reception at the palace gates is not as warm as it once had been. There was a time I would have had a friendly chat with the gate guards while waiting for Rian to meet me. Now they eye me with a hint of dislike, as though it's my fault that their prince is being tried for treason and murder, and not his own. I find myself longing for Kythshire, for some reason. Unlike here, I always feel happy and welcome there. Thankfully, Saesa is her usual punctual self, and she arrives just in time to save me from the downward spiral my thoughts have begun to take.

Dressed in soft, airy green silk, she looks very different than I'm used to seeing her in the training square. By the look on her face I can tell she feels the same about my own choice of clothes. It didn't seem like official guild business to me, so I opted for a simple sleeveless summer dress in yellow, with long slits and billowing white pants beneath.

Tib is the next to arrive, looking much the same as usual. His clothes are dark as always, but at least they're clean today. He smiles his greeting and Saesa rubs a smudge of dirt from his cheek with the heel of her hand.

"Go in if you'd like," I say. "I'm waiting for Rian." I crane my neck to look for him along the road in the direction of the Academy, but there's no sign of his blue robes among the crowds that bustle past.

"We'll wait," Saesa says.

"Sure," Tib shrugs.

"Hello!" Flitt's voice pops into my thoughts, and I feel a tickle at my earlobe.

"Flitt!" I push to her mind, *"I wasn't expecting you back so soon. What a wonderful surprise."*

"I was invited, too. By Twig," she replies. I grin and nod. Twig is a fairy who has befriended Princess Margary. He and the princess have been inseparable for as long as I've known Flitt. They were the first to discover Eron's plots and send me with Rian to investigate the threat of Sorcery against Kythshire. Two years ago feels like ages. That was a better time. A time when my visits with the princess were lighthearted and carefree and didn't turn my stomach to knots.

"Perhaps he isn't coming," I say as I search the streets again. My heart sinks. It isn't like Rian to miss something like this. When he tells me he'll be there, he's there. "We should go in," I try hard to mask my disappointment, "or we'll be late."

"Typical. Mages." Flitt tisks as she settles on my shoulder. No one else notices her, not even the gate guard as I hand him my invitation. She keeps herself well-hidden from humans, for her own protection.

"It isn't typical," I push to her as a Page greets us. *"It's worrisome. It's not like him."*

"Don't worry," she giggles, *"he probably got caught up reading some old tome*

or something."

We follow the Page through burnished walkways where tall windows spill bright sunlight over polished stone floors. Colorful tapestries line the walls opposite the windows, stretching up to the impossibly high arched ceiling. Despite the summer heat outside, the air in the palace is much cooler and more crisp. So much so that I find myself wishing I'd brought a wrap or at least worn sleeves.

We pass through the indoor gardens, which are only slightly warmer, and up a winding staircase that leads to a long, low corridor. Here, the doors are carved with intricate reliefs of vines, flowers, mushrooms, and fairies. Guards stand at attention on either side of a double set of doors. I recognize one of them as Finn, Her Highness's personal detail. He offers a slight nod as the other guard, who I don't recognize, looks us over and the Page raps lightly on the wood.

"Strange," I push to Flitt as Saesa and I glance at each other with worry, *"High Lunch in the princess's private rooms?"*

The door opens a crack and the princess's nurse greets the Page.

"Sir Azaeli Hammerfel of His Majesty's Elite, Squire Saesa Coltori of House Ganvent, Young Master Tibreseli Nullen of House Ganvent," the Page announces. The nurse nods. Instead of allowing us in, she steps out and closes the door behind her.

"That will be all, thank you, Elan," she says to the Page, who gives a respectful bow and rushes off. She waits until his footsteps fade at the bottom of the stairs and then turns to us. "You will do nothing to excite or upset Her Highness. You will not discuss the trial. You will not discuss any distressing news of incidents outside of the palace, including any untoward actions or rumors regarding the peasantry. You will not address her condition. This is to be a friendly, lighthearted visit to lift the princess's spirits. Do we have an understanding?"

"Her condition?" Tib crosses his arms over his chest and gives Finn such a glare that I fear he might lose his temper and throw a punch. Finn raises his chin ever so slightly as if to dare Tib into action. Saesa is busy staring at the door, her face pale with worry at the nurse's list of restrictions. I reach past her to Tib and rest a hand on his shoulder.

"Of course we agree," I say, tightening my grip on his shoulder. "Right, Tib?"

"Sure," he says, and wriggles free of my hand. "Whatever you say, m'lady," he murmurs, still glaring at Finn.

"What's got into you?" Saesa whispers to him as the nurse pushes the door open to allow us in. He only shakes his head in reply, and at once our attention is drawn to the canopy bed at the end of the ornately painted room, where the princess sits propped on pillows of satin and silk.

I try to think of the last time I saw Her Highness. It was a trial day just a week ago. She looked well then, if not tired. Small, but as the baby of the Royal Family, that's expected. Despite her youth, she has always had an unexpected wisdom about her; an understanding of the world that many twice her age have not yet grasped. Still, she looked well then. Even now she seems well enough, like a little cherub almost swallowed up by the rich, billowing silk robes that spill over the bedside in pools of shimmering lavender.

"My friends!" she cries and holds her arms out to us. "You came."

"Now, princess—" the nurse starts, but Saesa rushes across to the bed and gingerly accepts the princess's hug.

"I must insist—" the nurse starts, but Princess Margy interrupts her.

"Thank you, Tirie," she says dismissively, her arms still tight around Saesa.

"But Your Highness," Tirie wrings her hands.

"Thank you, I said," Margy's tone is firmer this time, and Tirie huffs.

"I'll be just outside," the nurse gives a reluctant curtsy.

"Very good," Margy nods. She waits for the woman to show herself out and then rolls her eyes at the rest of us. "I'm twelve years old and they still think I need a nurse. I ought to have ladies in waiting by now. Sara did, at my age." She shakes her head and scowls. "Oh! It's safe now, Twig."

"Find me!" A tiny voice calls out from the wall near the window. Margy giggles and slides off of the bed. She takes Saesa's hand and pulls her toward the voice.

"Are you sure you should get up?" I ask the princess, but she and Saesa are too busy in their search. Tib is looking, too, but it's obvious his focus is not on finding the fairy. He goes to the opposite side of the room where the princess's dolls are neatly arranged around mushroom-shaped pillows. As I follow him, I feel Flitt push off of my shoulder.

"Come out, Twig!" she calls in a sing-song voice.

"Oh, Flitt! You came, too!" Margy claps. "Help us find him. Sometimes he's up in the branches." She points up at the trees painted across her ceiling, and I turn my attention back to Tib.

"Tib," I whisper as he starts rooting through the princess's collection, "what are you doing?"

Chapter Nine
THE PRINCESS'S TALE

Tib

I don't spare Azi a glance. I have to find it quickly, before anyone realizes I'm looking. Before Finn comes in and sees me and stops me. It must be here. That's what's making her sick. I look for a glint of silver, a flash of jewels, but all the princess's dolls are silver and gold and glitter.

"Looking for something," I finally mutter in response. I kneel at the center of the mushrooms and close my eyes. Maybe if I can't see it, I can feel it. Maybe it will reveal itself to me.

"For what?" Azi whispers with concern, "What's the matter?"

"A vest." I say, still searching. "A vest with magic. It's silver and jeweled and powerful. I saw Finn bring it into the palace yesterday. It's dangerous. I saw what it could do." I don't feel anything, though. No magic in here except for the fairies. And the princess.

"Found you!" Flitt cries from across the room. "That was tricky!"

I keep searching. I'm running out of time.

"Help me," I hiss at her, "I think it's what's making her sick."

"Think of what you're saying," Azi whispers as she crouches to look through the dolls, "Finn would never endanger the princess." Still, she doesn't stop her search.

"I know what I saw," I say under my breath. I don't care if she believes me. I only care about finding it.

"Princess," Tirie calls through the door, "you aren't out of bed, are you?"

"No, Tirie," Margy fibs. Her robes and gown trail behind her as she crosses the room to me and Azi. Twig flies beside her. He's a dirt-covered fairy, with ragged green clothes and messy black hair. He smiles at me as the princess sits down and I slump back against a mushroom, defeated. It isn't here.

"Why are you supposed to stay in bed?" I ask the princess.

"Tib, we're not supposed to talk about that," Saesa whispers.

"Because Tirie forbade you?" Margy raises her chin. "Don't listen to her. She's got too many rules."

"To keep you safe," Azi says quietly.

"To shelter me," Margy scowls. "I'm not a baby. I'm growing up, and they refuse to let me."

"Are you sick?" I press. I want an answer. She looks okay. A little dark around the eyes, maybe, but not too sick. Just tired.

"Tib!" Saesa gasps.

"It's all right," Margy says.

"No, it's disrespectful," Saesa turns to me. "She's our princess."

"She's my friend first," I say.

"That's right," Margy beams at me. "You see, that's why I asked you here. You three are my most trusted friends. Two of you know my secret." She nods at me and Saesa. "Now it's time for me to tell Azi."

She turns to Azi, who looks very confused. Their eyes lock for a while, and at first I think Azi might be doing Mentalism, but there are no tendrils of gold between them. They're just looking at each other. Like Margy is deciding whether it's really safe to say something.

"When you came to the palace that night," she says to Azi quietly, "you were different. You learned to do something. It was dangerous. I knew it. I could tell you were trying to fight it and that it was a danger to Paba. I didn't understand at the time, and I was angry with you."

"But how did you…" Azi shakes her head. "How could you know?"

"I sensed it. I could feel it. Strange magic. Not a magic I was used to. Not a magic I knew." The princess watches her carefully. I know the secret she's planning to tell. It's a dangerous one. She has magic within her, Princess Margary. I saw her use it once to revive Mevyn and restore his power. If it was discovered, she'd be severely punished. Perhaps put to death. Twig helps her curb it. Helps her hide it.

In Cerion it's forbidden for royalty to learn magic. Something to do with a Sorcerer King generations ago, who nearly destroyed everything because of his greed. When the Plethore Dynasty took over after that, they swore they'd never use magic. They've kept their promise for generations. This isn't Margy's fault, though. Magic wasn't taught to her. She didn't seek it out. She was born with it. She's fought it her whole life. Kept it secret. She knows it could start a war. A revolution. Especially now, when the peasants are already rallying. She's smart to keep it to herself. Nobody else knows. Not even the king.

"Maybe it would be better," Twig says to the princess gently, "if you read the story first." He hovers in front of Margy, his stick-like wings moving so fast they're almost invisible. After a little thought, the princess nods. Inside the circle of mushrooms, everyone settles in on their pillows. Saesa sits beside me. Across from us, Margy slides a book from beneath a pillow. It's old-looking. The cover is embossed with patterns of vines and leaves. It reminds me of a place I've been. Ceras'lain. The White Wall, where the elves guard their lands against outsiders. Saesa and I exchange a glance. She recognizes it, too.

"It's in Elvish, so forgive me if I'm slow to translate," Margy says.

"You speak Elvish?" Saesa gasps.

"Of course," Margy smiles. "Paba insists all of his children learn the languages of his allies." She looks a little sad at the mention of her father. A little more tired. Probably because of her brother, I think. It's only a matter of days before he's found guilty. Margy looks at each of us and smiles. She opens the book and starts to read.

"There is a place of legend and lore, a tale passed from mother to son and father to daughter and written here for the eyes of innocents. Once carried in whispers on the wind, it speaks of a city like no other. It is the tale of Brindelier, a kingdom obscured by mist and cloud. A palace out of reach, golden and bright. A land of promise and peace, where no wish goes ignored, and no desire is unfulfilled.

"Within walls of sparkling gold and silver, tucked away in their tower, the heirs to the city wait. Prince and Princess, brother and sister, hand in hand they abide, wrapped in enchanted sleep until they are woken by one worthy to rule beside them. Of royal blood the suitor must be. Their kingdoms shall unite, and none shall divide them. They will be a beacon of power, where magic flows freely and all manner of creatures are welcome as equals. Only those with true intent may enter the hidden gates, for Brindelier is a place well-guarded by enchantments and strong magics.

"If you are capable of reading these pages without difficulty, or if you are listening to the tale and words do not fail the storyteller, then you have already proved yourself worthy. The gates of Brindelier shall open to you, should you seek the kingdom in the clouds, and marvels beyond measure shall be yours to delight in for all time."

The princess strokes the page with her fingertips. Caresses the words written there. The rest of us sit quietly, waiting for more. I glance at Saesa again, but she's distracted. Watching Margy. Thinking. I reach into my vest pocket and find the coin. Feel the strange bumps along the edge of it. Think of the image carved in its face, the tower in the clouds. Brindelier.

"Eron," Margary says, startling all of us, "read this to me once many years ago. Before…" she sighs. Shakes her head. Squares her shoulders. "I remembered it and asked him to read it to me again just a few years ago, but he couldn't find the page. I tried to remind him of the story, but whenever I spoke of it I would lose the words." She blinks tearfully. "Now I understand why. I used to look through its pages, but I could never find the tale. It revealed itself to me again days ago, and now I can only think of the twin heirs in their castle, sleeping. Waiting for their worthy suitor. It calls to me."

"Princess," Azi offers gently, "you can't mean that you wish to seek out this place? It's a legend. A story."

"Typical," says Flitt from her perch on Azi's shoulder. "Weren't we the same to you once? Just a story? A tale for children? We proved that wrong."

"It isn't that I simply wish to, Azi. I must," Margy says tearfully. "I must. I belong there. I feel it calling to my heart. If I remain here, as I am now…" she trails off. Looks at Twig. He gives her a nod of encouragement.

"What do you mean, as you are? You're beloved in Cerion, Margy. You're the sweetheart of the kingdom. Everyone adores you," Azi says.

"I won't be. Not for long. Not if they find out, and they will someday, because I can't hide it forever," Margy sighs.

"Princess," Azi says with a mix of worry and amusement, "what could you possibly have to hide?"

"This," Margy says. She stands up and lifts her hands, palms up.

At first nothing happens except a soft, warm breeze. It rustles our hair and clothes. Glints of light sparkle at Margy's palms and drift away to settle around the room. Slowly, the branches of painted trees along the walls shift. The carpet beneath our feet becomes grass. The leaves wave playfully in the breeze. The lights become stars, sparkling in the sky. Birds chirp and sing all around us. I can even smell it: the damp soil, the tree bark. It's as real as any forest could be. It's more than a simple Mage spell. This is magic at its purest. Raw and perfect.

Azi stands and walks slowly to the wall. The yellow silk of her dress trails out behind her. She rests a hand on a tree. Looks up along the trunk, up into the leaves. Into the sky. The stars drift down. They collect on her arms, her legs, her body like a suit of shimmering armor. In her hand they form a sword, long and elegant. She raises it like a golden statue. A statue of a perfect Knight. The princess stands up and goes to her. Takes her free hand.

"Be my Champion, Sir Azaeli," Margary says. "Please. I could think of no one more worthy than you. Seek out Brindelier. I know in my heart it is real. Find it for me. Please."

The lights begin to fall away. The trees flatten to the walls again. The princess slumps a little, but Azi catches her as the magic fades away. She's different, Azi. The Princess's spell weaves around her, unseen. Azi lifts the princess easily and carries her to her bed.

"I'm sorry," Margy whispers. "It drains me."

"I'll go," Azi says. "If it exists, I'll find it for you, Princess. I promise."

Margy looks so small as Azi tucks the blankets around her. Like a child again. The princess nods. Closes her eyes. Azi bends close. Whispers something. Flitt and Twig hover at the pillows. Beside me, Saesa leans close so her shoulder touches mine. I turn to her.

"Will you show the coin to Azi?" she whispers. "It's got to be linked."

I nod and give it to her. When Azi comes back to us there's a glow around her. I can feel it more than see it. A protection, an excitement. A sense of purpose. It's not just a feeling. It's some sort of power she carries now. The promise of a quest.

"My lady," Saesa whispers. "Tib found this this morning." I hand the coin to Azi just as the door opens.

"Ah, as I thought," says Tirie a little smugly. "This visit was too much for the little dear. Come, luncheon is set for you on the East Terrace. Leave the princess to her rest."

"This way," the page calls to us from the hallway. When we file out, the fairies follow us. Twig, too. That surprises me. He isn't known to leave Margary's side. I glance at Azi. Her gaze is distant as we follow the page. Full of concentration. Twig sits on her left shoulder, Flitt on her right. She looks down at her hand, closed around the coin.

"*Why has no one ever mentioned such a place before?*" I hear Azi's words form slowly. See them in my own mind. Ideas, tinged in gold. "*A city in the clouds. Certainly there would be legends. Bardsongs.*" This is how they talk to each other sometimes, she and the fairies. Through the Half-Realm. Into each other's thoughts. It's a different sort of magic, but I can still detect it.

I can't help eavesdropping. I'm too curious.

"*I can't believe you're still doubting after everything you've seen and done,*" Flitt pushes to her.

"*I'm not doubting,*" Azi says. "*Just...I don't know,*" she sighs and hands the coin back to me as we're shown to the terrace. A table is set here, shaded from the hot sun by a canopy. Bright silks flutter in the sea breeze. The rest of them keep talking, but I'm too distracted by the view of the ocean. The ships. The port. I go to the stone rail and watch the lifts. Watch the comings and goings of captains and cargo. Think of my contraption, nearly finished, waiting in its dark hiding place. Think of Valenor, my friend. Dreamwalker. The one who gave me the idea. Who planted it like a seed in my mind. Did he know, somehow, about the city the princess would seek?

At the corner of my eye, I see a flash of silver. I'm torn from my thoughts, suddenly aware of the woman standing quietly beside me. Tall and slender, with dark, rich skin that glows in the sunlight. She's dressed all in silks and veils of purple so deep they're almost black. A crown of silver gleams in her black curls, but that's not the silver that caught my attention. No, that silver is lower. It flashes again. A vest. A boy at her hip.

"Princess Amei," Saesa says from beside me. She nudges my rib hard. Ducks into a low curtsy. I bow, but I can't look away. It's unmistakable. Loren's vest fits perfectly on the young prince. Its jewels sparkle brightly as he giggles and reaches for me. I remember Celli. The red swirls. The screaming. The Mark. The prince's skin is smooth and tan. No Mark. He leans closer, nearly tipping out of Amei's arms. I reach to catch him and feel it, same as I did when I tried to take it from Finn. A tingling in my arm. A powerful magic. Amei pulls him back. Holds him closer.

"Stay with mama, my little prince," she whispers to the boy. Glances at me with suspicion. Confusion. Mistrust. Turns to Azi.

"Lady Knight," she nods, and Azi comes up out of her curtsy.

"Your Highness," Azi says. "You look well, and how the little prince has grown!" she smiles, but I can see the truth between them plain as day. Anyone could. The awkwardness. The unspoken apology. The concern.

"Yes, he's quite healthy," Amei says quietly. "Strong and bold, as a prince ought to be, aren't you, my little one?" She bounces him on her hip. He giggles happily.

No one knows what will happen to Prince Eron's wife and son after the trials are over. Some think they'll be sent back to her homeland, to Stepstone Isles. Others say she should be executed with him. Those are the ones who don't know the princess. Anyone who has met her realizes she's too kindhearted, too gentle. She never had anything to do with the prince's dealings. And there's the boy to think about. The young prince, who would have been heir. Except what about heirs of traitors? I eye the vest, sparkling gold and silver. The princess is smart. She's already planning for the worst. Finn's helping her, too. Arranging protections. I feel a little bad now. I shouldn't have accused him of trying to hurt Margary. I should have known it'd be something like this.

"Please don't let me keep you from your meal," the Princess says. "We just came out for some sea air," she offers a wistful smile and looks out to the ocean again. Maybe she'll get to go home after it's over. I hope they let her.

"Be well, Your Highness," Azi says to her. Curtsies low again. Saesa does, too. I bow.

"And you," Princess Amei says. Her silks trail behind her with the prince's giggles as she goes to leave, but she's stopped at the door by a man leading two others. He's dressed in court formals. A clerk. Behind him, two guards. He surveys us all. Nods.

"Good to find you here together," he says sternly. "Princess Amei. Sir Hammerfel. A verdict has been reached. It will be read at High Court in one hour's time. If you would please pass word to His Majesty's Elite," he says to Azi, then turns to Amei. "Your Highness, please come with me."

Azi and Amei exchange a glance. The princess seems to hold her son tighter. Without a word she rushes out after the clerk.

At first Azi seems shocked. Quiet. Distant as the fairies chatter at her shoulder.

"Typical it took so long," Flitt says.

"They had to be sure," Twig offers. "It'll be over soon."

"Well," Flitt rolls her eyes. "It's about time."

"It isn't over," Azi says so quietly I can barely hear her over the rush of the sea breeze. She offers me the coin, and I take it. "This will leave us without a prince to become King. You've heard the whisperings. Whatever the verdict, our kingdom will be torn in two." She looks toward the door. "This could be the beginning of the end of peace in Cerion."

Nobody says anything. We know she's right. Before the end of the day, the Prince will be free or the ax will fall. Either way, the kingdom will be divided. Either way, it's bound to cause trouble.

"Saesa," this time when she speaks, Azi's voice is stronger. I've seen that change in her before. The one where she switches instantly to a fighter. Battle ready. Commanding. Like a Knight should be. "Run to the Academy. See if you can find Rian and let him know to meet me at the Court."

"Yes, my lady," Saesa bows. She grabs my hand and pulls me with her. Azi follows behind us until we reach the main gate. There's already a crowd here, waiting. We have to push through them to get out. Most are calm, but I can feel it as Saesa pulls me through. Tension. Threat. Unrest. Bubbling, waiting. Seeping through each of them like a shroud. Like a spell. I glance back at Azi. Catch a glimpse of her yellow silk as she rushes toward the guild hall. Grip Saesa tighter as we spill out from the crowd.

It's not just unrest. Something else is at work here. Something bigger. Something nobody else notices, somehow. As much as I hate Mages, I'm glad we're going to the Academy. Rian will know what to do. As Saesa and I break into a run, Zeze joins us. She jots alongside, looking just as determined as I feel as the Academy's sparkling white walls stretch out before us.

Chapter Ten
HIGH COURT

Azi

This vast room is imprinted in my mind. I could close my eyes while sitting here and still see every detail in the frames around the narrow, bright windows. Every unusual pit in the stone of the walls, every carving of past judges engraved in the massive columns is etched into my memory. Their faces, young and smooth or rough and wrinkled gaze across the vast hall, stern and sober, the weight of justice as heavy on their shoulders as it is on my own.

I've spent so many endless hours here on my feet, testifying and listening to others' testimonies against the Prince, but I've never seen these intimidating halls as full as they are today. Rows of benches line the Walk of Justice like the aisle of a cathedral. The closer one sits to the front, the more important their rank in the trial at hand. I sit on the first bench. Right behind me I feel the presence of my guild: Mum and Da, Mya, Bryse, Cort, Donal, even Elliot has come in from his trek in the woods to witness the verdict.

Thankfully, I'm not alone on my bench. Rian is by my side along with Uncle Gaethon. A dozen others are seated beside them, all of whom have been key to the Prince's trial. Cousins, generals, guards and attendants all look around, seemingly as on edge as I am to have this affair come to an end.

The High Court is an annex of the palace, kept apart from the main building by a series of corridors and courtyards. There is a separate entrance for commoners and guests which, right now, is flooded with people trying to get in to watch the verdict being read. I peer over my shoulder at the unusually loud crowd. Since the start of the trials there has been interest in the Prince's fate, but the mood from the lower sections is usually quiet and respectful. Today is different. The kingdom is on edge. The guards lining the walls beneath the high stained-glass windows feel it. They are much more tense and watchful than usual. I'm sure they fear the worst if the commoners don't hear the verdict they want. I do, too.

Still, Cerion is a place of transparency and justice. Its people have a right to be here to witness the fate of their prince and their city. Sitting in my full armor with my sword laid beside me I find myself hoping fervently that they choose to accept the judgment of the court with grace and composure. I know if they don't, my duties would force me into action against them.

My worries aren't eased much when the High Justiciar enters the platform with his attendants and the crowd begins to hiss and shout. A fight breaks out between a group of men with opposing views, and they are promptly ushered from the court at spearpoint.

"Let it be stated," the Justiciar's voice booms through the lofty arches, hushing the crowd once more, "before we begin, that there will be no tolerance for disruption of any kind for the duration of these proceedings." He raises his arms and nods to the great doors, and a score of additional city guard march in. They stand at attention in the aisles at the ends of the rows, their chain mail glinting in the afternoon light that streams through the high windows.

A crier in royal livery steps forward on the platform and surveys the hall as the back rows settle down. When it is quiet enough, he squares his shoulders and announces clearly:

"His Royal Majesty, King Tirnon, Her Royal Majesty, Queen Naelle, Her Royal Highness, Princess Margary, Her Royal Highness, Princess Amei." The crowd goes silent and all of us stand as the royal family takes their place in the box on the far right of the platform. I can't keep my eyes off of Princess Margary, who looks well-rested despite the exhausted state we left her in only an hour ago. A glint of green flashes at her shoulder and I know that Twig is with her.

"He gave her too much," Flitt murmurs from my shoulder. "Guess he had to. Be right back." I watch her dart away from me in a streak of light. Beside Margy in the place where Twig had dimly bobbed, Flitt's colorful prisms twinkle. She comes back to me and I glance around. No one seems to have noticed the fairies, and that's as it should be. They remain safely hidden in the Half-Realm. Only Rian raises a brow at me as the officers of the High Court take their places in a box opposite the Royal family. A slight breeze rustles Rian's hair and in my mind's eye I catch a glimpse of Shush.

"How many fairies are here exactly, Flitt?" I push to her silently.

"Oh, are we playing?" she giggles and claps as she settles into her usual place tucked into the collar of my pauldron. *"Three as far as I can tell. Maybe more. I'm not the Keeper of the Fae, you know."*

The High Justiciar takes his place at center, in a box against the wall.

"Begin," he says as the gallery takes its seats.

"Anod Bental, High Master of the Academy of Cerion," the crier announces, and then, "Yorid Gauntry, Mage General of Incarceration, bearing His Royal Highness Prince Eron."

We all stand again and turn toward the back of the hall, where another set of doors swing open beside the main doors. These lead below to the catacombs and network of dungeons carved into the cliff stone beneath the city.

"*They keep the Prince down there?*" Flitt asks as those around us crane to get a glimpse of the procession. The thick crowd makes it impossible to see anything but Master Anod's red pointed cap as it bobs along the Walk of Justice.

"*Everyone awaiting justice is kept below in the Catacombs, in sleep chambers,*" I explain. Already, the low pulse of pain that comes from sending thoughts this way is nagging at me.

"*It seems too kind, just letting him sleep,*" she says.

"*It's for his own safety and the safety of those guarding. Sleeping prisoners can't conspire. They don't eat anything, they don't bother anyone. They don't try to trick the guards or smuggle things in and out. They can't try to escape,*" I push to her. Beside me, Rian shifts his feet. The procession is nearing. I can see Master Anod in his white robes now, with Master Yorid several paces behind him. Between them, Prince Eron floats motionless as if being carried on a litter, except there isn't one. He drifts, sound asleep, by means of a levitation spell. The three are followed by a procession of a dozen Mages in robes of red to mark their high stations.

As Eron drifts past us I'm startled as I always am by how serene he looks. His sand-blond curls are perfectly arranged, his fine embroidered jacket neatly buttoned over his chest. Even his boots are polished to a high shine. He looks every bit the part of a Prince, even as the Mages guide him up to the platform.

"*Did you feel the shift?*" I push to Flitt, knowing it's my turn for a question and curious as to how attuned she is to the Mages who fan out along the steps between the platform and the gallery. They make no motion, they don't even whisper, but I know their protections have been cast like an invisible wall between the platform and the people. Wards meant to protect Cerion's highest ranking lawkeepers and wisest men.

"*Wards. Typical,*" Flitt pushes to me. We watch in silence as the Prince is eerily turned upright in front of his own bench: a single seat that faces the gallery. He sinks into it and Master Yorid waits for the Justiciar's signal before he whispers the words that will break the Prince's sleep.

As he blinks awake the crowd grows restless again. Some of them shout obscenities as Eron looks around, disoriented.

"Your Highness. You sit before your judge and jury accused of treason, murder, and conspiracy. You have stated your case and it has been argued a record long time. Eighteen months you have had, and now the scales of Justice have weighed your words and deeds," the Justiciar goes on in his booming voice while Flitt needles her way into my thoughts again.

"Will he do it here? Your da, I mean? In the hall in front of everyone? If he's guilty?" she asks, her tone a mix of excitement and distaste. My heart starts to race. I glance behind me at my father, who watches the proceedings with little show of emotion, the blade of his great axe gleaming at his shoulder. Behind him, Saesa's red curls catch my eye. Tib sits beside her with daggers in his eyes for the Prince. Beyond them I scan the faces of eager onlookers and my stomach churns with nerves. I turn back and look past the prince.

"Do you see that block?" I nod slightly toward the platform, where just before the Justiciar's bench, built into the stone, is a raised block set with an overlay of fresh pine.

"Azi!" says Flitt, exasperated. *"How many times do I have to remind you? You can't answer a question with a question! Honestly, it's like your head is a beehive and the rules are the honey and everything's gone and dripped out of the comb. Every time!"*

"It's all set up to happen today," I turn my attention back to the Officers' box, where the High Court has risen to its feet. *"Why do you think so many people have come?"*

"They came to watch him die?" Flitt gasps. I think to chide her about forgetting her own rules, but my head is pounding from the conversation. *"That's revolting!"*

"Well, why'd you come?" I ask pointedly.

"That's different!" she sputters. *"I know Prince Creepy on a personal level! I have a right and a responsibility to—"*

"Shh!" my hand flies to my shoulder as the Justiciar's ruling echoes over the hall.

"…in these matters, after much deliberation, we find Eron Plethore guilty on all counts. There be no special consideration in sentencing due to station, and as we have exhausted all avenues there will be no further deliberation on the matter. Execution of the prisoner will be dealt by the hand of His Majesty King Tirnon or a declared Champion forthwith."

The gallery, surprisingly, is so quiet that I can hear Rian breathing beside me as the king slowly stands. His Majesty's face is pale as his hand grips the pommel of the ceremonial sword that hangs at his waist. He stares at his son, who still seems to be trying to clear his head from the effects of the sleep spell. After a long pause, Tirnon leaves the booth to a spattering of applause from the gallery. Behind me, Mum whispers something to Da. He doesn't reply to her.

"*Is the king going to do it himself?*" Flitt asks. "*I thought you said he named your Da.*"

"I don't know," I whisper. A glance at Rian shows him not to be focused on the prince at all. Instead his attention is fixed on one of the towering windows of the High Court. He leans to Uncle and whispers something, and Gaethon follows his gaze. When I look up and see nothing, I can't help but feel a pang of annoyance. The two of them have been very mysterious this afternoon. In the short time we had to talk while getting ready to come here, Rian was very vague in answering my questions. I couldn't get much out of him through our hatch other than a quick and hushed murmur about stolen books at the Academy.

At the center of the platform, the king stands beside his son looking weary and downtrodden as Eron pleads with him.

"Father," he implores as though suddenly realizing the gravity of the situation. He seems so sincere, so innocent.

"*How can he act so meek,*" Flitt pushes to me, "*after everything he's done? Can you believe it? Typical human.*"

His Majesty's jaw clenches as he turns away. His eyes search the rows and come to rest on Da behind me.

"As has been arranged," the King's voice rings steady across the great room, quieting even the slightest whisper, "I name Sir Benen Hammerfel for this grievous task."

"Coward!" someone cries at the rear of the gallery, but I'm too taken by the scene unfolding before me to turn and watch the scuffle that follows. On the platform Eron's eyes go wide as my father stands and approaches the steps. The axe at Da's back is nearly as broad as his shoulders, its blade so well-honed it seems to slice the very air with every step he takes. The wards shift as he nears the dais, allowing him to pass through them.

"Father," Eron says again, white-lipped, "please." When the King gives no response but to clasp hands with my father, Eron changes his tactic. "My wife!" he cries, looking over his shoulder.

In the royal box, Princess Margary sits between the Queen and Princess Amei. One tiny white-gloved hand grips her mother's hand, and the other squeezes Princess Amei's. At the sound of the Prince calling for her, Amei shifts in her seat. A pained expression crosses her face but she quickly squares her shoulders and checks herself.

"Please, I would have my wife beside me and I would say a word to the kingdom," Eron begs King Tirnon, whose eyes slide to look at his son and then to the Justiciar, who nods slightly.

"If the Princess will consent to it," King Tirnon turns to her. Slowly, bravely, Amei allows herself to be escorted from the box. Through it all, Da stands at attention, his plate armor burnished to such a high gleam that it's nearly blinding as it reflects the sun beaming through the windows.

"*Be on guard*," Rian pushes to me. His voice in my mind is sharp and quick, and I have to catch myself to keep from gasping with surprise. I turn and look over my shoulder at the crowd, which is settled again as they watch the events on the platform with morbid fascination.

"My lady," Eron says as the Princess comes to stand beside him. He whispers to her so quietly I can't hear, and he leans toward her as if asking to be kissed, but she dismisses him with a graceful turn of her head. The back rows jeer and catcall, and many of them start to shout to get on with the execution.

Eron is led to the block and as the Judiciar forces him to kneel and press his head to it, Eron stares across the platform. His eyes meet mine and lock onto them. I feel the pull toward him as my father raises his ax blade.

"Sparrow and fox, boar and perch," Eron's shout echoes over the arches. "high in the clouds and into the depths, foreshine, forewarn, induct, destroy." His eyes narrow and flash with wild excitement. "*They come*," he mouths to me, and I feel myself pulled closer.

"Azi." Rian's voice is far away. I feel him shaking my shoulder, but I've already tumbled too far from myself. Eron is still speaking, his words sometimes in my head and other times echoing aloud in a garbled form of Mage tongue. I'm in his mind, looking out at the gallery from his perspective. I'm him. I see myself, Azi, sitting beside Rian, my eyes casting a strange golden glow. From Eron's perspective, I glance up and see the glint of the ax blade overhead. It slams down to the cheers of the crowd. Everything goes black, and everyone screams.

Chaos erupts around me. I don't know at first where I am or even who I am. Men are shouting all around me: "Princess! Princess!"

I panic. I can't move. I can't see. My head is heavy and the room is black. People trample past me, crashing over my legs and arms with little concern.

"Princess, here! Secure the queen, I've got Margary!" This voice is familiar. Finn, Margy's guard. Good. She's safe.

"Azaeli!" Margary screams as she's ushered past. Something in her panicked tone startles me out of my daze. I'm aware again of where I am, back on the bench. Myself again. Azi, beside Rian. Still, I can't see. Spells fly past me, bursting into powerful explosions. Crowds of people surge from everywhere, screaming for each other in the darkness. Rian's hand grips my arm and pulls me to the side just in time to dodge a spell flying right toward us.

"What's happening? I can't see!" I cry out.

"Blindness spell," Rian says. I don't need to see him to know that his teeth are clenched. "Powerful one. Flitt," he cries, "Take Azi out of here. Go!"

Someone slams into me and I grab my sword as another burst of magic blasts past us. Flitt's hand presses to my cheek and my skin starts to tingle.

"Don't you dare!" I shout at her. "I'm staying to fight!"

"Nope, not this one!" she says in a singsong voice.

"Go!" Rian shouts again as magic surges around us, crackling in my ears. "Go!"

"Okay, okay," Flitt says. Before I can argue or pull free of her tiny hand, I feel the ground shift beneath me. I'm falling fast, soaring, spinning through the unknown into the Half-Realm. The light that sparkles from Flitt's tiny form is blinding after the darkness. It burns my eyes and washes everything in a strange blue glow. We hit the ground so hard that the breath is knocked out of me. As I lie gasping for air, a strange sensation pulses through me, as if I'm being sucked into myself. My eyes adjust slowly to the bright surroundings until I'm aware of someone else lying very still beside me in the cushion of grass.

"Flitt!" I whisper frantically, patting the ground beside my head and shoulder. She isn't anywhere. "Flitt?" I ask again with the sudden dreadful thought that I might have landed on her and crushed her. I roll to one side frantically and comb through the enormous blades of grass. "Oh, Flitt, please, where are you?"

When she giggles, I'm taken by how much louder her voice seems to be. It fills the bright space with such a powerfully pleasant feeling that I almost forget to be angry with her.

"Cut it out," I grumble. "No more games! How could you take me away like that? I have to go back!" I push myself to my feet and nearly trip over the strange figure my eyes are still having trouble focusing on through Flitt's blinding light.

"I'm not playing games," Flitt says. The figure stands up and moves toward me and I reach for my sword. "Really, Azi, are you that thick?" she giggles again. It's not until she steps forward and places her hands on my shoulders that I realize the figure is her.

"You're my size," I blink and shield my eyes.

"Nope, guess again!"

"I'm your size?" I shake my head. "But why?"

"So you won't try going back. Nobody's going to be threatened by a tiny Azi with a tiny sword." She giggles again, as if this is nothing more than an amusing game.

"Nobody?" I raise my sword to her.

"Oh, please." Flitt laughs again, this time a little nervously. "You wouldn't." Her light flashes a little brighter, and through it I catch a glimpse of her multi-colored ponytails.

"Wouldn't I?" I stalk closer to her, gripping my sword tightly.

"Nope!" she says airily. She's right. Frustrated, I turn away and start to pace. My eyes are still blurred and partially blinded. I shake my head to try and clear my vision and then it dawns on me.

"Do you think you could tone it down a little?" I spin to face her again.

"Huh? Oh, sorry," she chuckles and dims the light she casts.

It helps. Slowly the blindness fades until I can see the towering green fronds of grass waving overhead against the crisp blue sky. The beauty of the scene does little to calm me. The more I think about what just happened, the more agitated I get until I find myself fighting to breathe through the grips of panic.

"What—" I try to calm myself, but it's too difficult as the gravity of the situation crashes over me. "What *was* that?"

"Uh," Flitt lifts herself with her wings and floats beside me as I pace frantically. "A Mage battle, I think. At least that's what it felt like."

"But," I grasp for the right words, but I can barely form a thought let alone a sentence. Rian. Eron. King Tirnon. Da. Margy. Mum. Saesa. All that darkness. All that chaos. The Mages, they were there to prevent that. They were supposed to be protecting the High Court. "How?" I manage dumbly.

"Who knows? Rian saw it coming, though. He warned me. Told me to get you out of there if something happened." She pauses behind me as I turn to face her, seething. Her glittering wings flutter to keep her aloft, and her eyes shift from blue to green to yellow as they widen. "Azi, calm down!" she cries, half annoyed, half frightened.

"How could you? How could you listen to him? You made me leave all of them there to fight without me! Whatever it is, it's powerful enough to get through all of those defenses. And now they're there facing that danger, and I'm here hiding away like a coward! I don't care how small I am. I can't stay here knowing what's happening there. I'm going back." I close my eyes and think of Rian and start to feel the shift in the air around me, but Flitt shoves me back, breaking my concentration.

"You can't," she says. "You can't risk it."

"Oh, I can't, but everyone else can? What sense does that make, Flitt? In case you hadn't noticed, I'm a Knight. It's my job to put myself between others and the threat. It's my duty to protect those who are too weak to fend for themselves, and you pull me here, away from them. All of those innocents, just left there…" I sink into the grass and press my eyes with the palms of my hands, trying hard not to let my emotions overwhelm me. Crying won't help. It'll only make me feel weaker and more helpless than I already do.

"Azi…" Flitt comes to my side and rests her arm across my shoulders. Peace and joy flow from her in waves, and even with my eyes covered I know her light is shining bright around us in her effort to change my mood. "I had to get you out of there. You're too important. Rian knows that. Everyone else knows it, too. Even Eron knew it as the ax fell. It's the honey dripping from the comb all over again. You have a rare purpose. You're special. Why is it everyone else can see that except you?"

Chapter Eleven

THE DUSK

Tib

I'm here for my sister. That's what I keep telling myself. I didn't really think much of the trial at first. Didn't bother coming to watch. Then Ruben came home for luncheon one day. Said they were questioning Eron about Viala. Ruben didn't know she was my sister. Nobody in the house does, except Saesa. Once I heard some of the trial was about her, I started coming to listen. I guess I was curious about what she was like before. I wanted to hear the story of her and the prince. Try to figure out how it all went so wrong.

They never used her new name. The one she's known by now. Ki. They don't know about how she was given a second chance. Nobody does. Only Iren and the fairies of Kythshire. And Saesa and the Elite.

Azi struggled with that for a while. With not telling the king. We talked it over for a long time. She felt torn, since really Ki is still alive. Like maybe she should tell them. Maybe Eron shouldn't be tried for that part of it. In the end I helped her see reason. Second chance or not, Eron killed her. I saw what happened when I wore Valenor's cloak. Saw what he did. How he held her, looked into her eyes, and drove his sword through her. How he dropped her on the floor like refuse and waited for her to die. Watched her last breath leave her. He was cold. Wicked. Whatever he gets, he deserves it.

I think of all that while I sit here, watching. Think of Azi's pain and her struggle to do the right thing. The good thing. Think of my sister and the choice she made, too. To stay true to her new life. To keep her promise to Iren, even in the face of death.

Saesa's knee is bobbing up and down. The soft heel of her boot tap, tap, taps on the stone floor. She does that when she's nervous or excited. It bugs me. I nudge her with my elbow and she shrugs an apology and goes still.

Sir Benen is called to the platform. He was a good choice by the king. A strong arm, a sharp blade. More mercy than the prince deserves. I wish he had chosen me. I'd have done it really slow. Made him think about every horrible thing he did. Made him repeat it back to everyone here. Made him sorry.

He isn't, though. Eron tries to play helpless and innocent. He tries to make the king feel sorry for him. Tries for sympathy. It's hard for me to hear a lot of what's said. Hard to concentrate. The wards are strong in here. Magic is so thick in the air that I have trouble thinking. It presses down on me. Blocks too much out.

"Oh no," Saesa whispers as Eron calls for Amei. "Oh, Tib."

I can't concentrate on what's going on up there. Something else is nagging at me. A warning feeling I can't pinpoint. A draw. A pull. A scent. Something foul, like death. Something that stings my senses. It's hard to describe. A screen over the light. The point of a needle peeking up through the weave of fabric. I have to leave. I have to run. I try to get up but Saesa stops me with a hand across my chest.

"What are you doing?" she hisses.

"Something's wrong," I say, and my words somehow make me more aware. Something *is* wrong. The window. I look up and see it too late. A figure shrouded in blue against the blue sky. It shifts slightly. Raises a hand. That's when Eron starts talking. Shouting strange words.

"Move," I whisper to Saesa, shoving her. "Get out of here, now!"

She swats me away. Doesn't hear me. She's too caught up in the Prince's execution. Everyone else is, too. Nobody else seems to notice what I notice. Except Rian. Up ahead in the front row he's watching the figure, too. So is Gaethon. Rian turns to Azi. He looks at her, scared. Shakes her. The ax rings out. Thuds to the block. Everyone starts screaming. Even Saesa. They get up and start trampling around. Along the front, the Mages start casting.

"Tib?" Saesa gasps and jumps to her feet beside me, flailing at the air. Her eyes are wide. Searching. I don't understand it. It's bright as day in here. Then I realize what's happened. A spell. Darkness. No one else can see. I grab Saesa by the shoulders and pull her out of the path of the surging, panicked crowd.

"Outta the way!" Someone swings a fist and I shove Saesa to the side just in time to avoid it. Another wave of magic washes over the gallery and half the people scream. The crowd rushes the aisles, trying to get out. I glimpse Bryse and Cort pushing ahead, clearing the way for the terrorized victims of the fear spell.

"What's happening?" Saesa cries. "I can't see!"

At the front I hear them calling for the princess and my attention snaps back to the platform. Spells are flying everywhere without a target. The Mages are on high defense. They're just as blind as everyone else, though. It's idiotic in a crowd like this. Bolts of fire crash into peasants. Lightning crackles out over the gallery. People are screaming. Crawling over each other. Beyond the Mages, palace guards are ushering the royal family to safety. I take Saesa's hand and pull her against the chaos. Tuck her into an alcove beside a column.

"Stay here," I say. "I'll be right back."

"Tib, no! I need to find my Lady Knight!" she cries. Her helplessness only drives my anger more.

"You can't see, Saesa. No one can. Stay here or they'll trample you. Or hit you with some bolt. The Mages are casting blindly. People are falling everywhere. Just wait here until they all get out or they'll plow right over you. I'll come back when it's safe. Promise." That seems to calm her a little.

"Did you wear it?" she asks me.

"Course I did," I lie. I know she's talking about my bandolier. The one Mevyn gave me, all decked with throwing daggers and vials of potions. I was stupid to take it off before I came. To tuck it safely in my drawer at home. I didn't think I'd need it. I have some daggers, though. Like always. One in my boot. One in my belt. One in my sleeve.

I look up at the window where I first saw the figure. The glass is gone. Strange I didn't hear it break. Odd there's no shards on the floor.

The hall is clearing now. The stone floor is littered with people. I don't know if they're injured or dead. I don't want to know. Up near the platform, a fight has broken out. Yellow and blue. The Elite are battling something I can't see. Palace guards are trying in vain to pull the King to safety. I rush toward them and skid to a stop.

Red everywhere. Blood. Swords clashing. Something purple in the center. Purple like the Prince's doublet. It doesn't make sense. Their opponent swings and steps and turns to avoid them. His blade glances off of Benen's armor. For a blind fight, it's impressive. Six on one. Their opponent is a fair warrior.

Even King Tirnon has his sword out. When he refuses to leave the fight, his guards try to step to shield him. Their eyes blankly search the space before them. None of them can see what I can. If they could, they'd stop.

I creep closer. Watch in disbelief. My stomach twists in knots. The Prince. That's who they're fighting. He's wounded, though. His doublet is stained crimson from the neck to the belt. I creep closer. I realize why. The sight is enough to send me to my knees. The Prince, fighting boldly. The Prince, stepping surely. The Prince, swinging his sword. Strong. Spry. Headless.

I try to stay on my feet but I can't. My legs shake like jelly on a spoon. I fall to my knees. I scream for them to stop fighting. They don't listen.

"Tib?" Rian calls out. A soft breeze rustles my hair. A streak of green. Shush hovers in front of my face.

"Over here! Left, okay right, wait. Step over that Mage. Right. You made it." Shush pushes to Rian, guiding him through the fallen and around the battle. When he reaches me, Rian puts a hand on my shoulder. He crouches beside me.

"What do you see, Tib?" he whispers.

"The battle. They're fighting the Prince. But he's...he's dead already." I can't say more. Rian tightens his grip on my shoulder.

"What else? Mages? Sorcerers?" he asks.

I put the Prince out of my mind. Turn my attention to the rest of the Court. The spells have stopped, mostly.

"Some of the Mages have fled," I whisper. "Others are lying on the steps. The gallery has cleared out. Everyone has run away. Master Gaethon is stalking someone on the platform. He's pressed against the wall, whispering something. He doesn't see—Master Gaethon, look out!" I shout, but too late.

A bolt of red shoots toward him. He's blind to it. Can't defend himself. It goes right through his wards like they're not even there. He's thrown against the wall and tumbles down like one of Margy's rag dolls.

The scent comes again. It barrages me. Death. The needle. The sting. Laughter, deep and wicked. I follow it to the block, to the source of the blast.

"Tib," Rian hisses, "what do you see? Tell me!"

"Master Gaethon is struck. The man from the window is standing by the block," I hope Rian can hear me. My throat is dry with fear. My voice too shaky even at a whisper. "He's got a sack tucked neatly under his arm. The fabric is already soaked red. It drips onto the blue of his robes. He's smiling, like this is all a joke. Raising his hand toward the fight. Casting a spell. Eron's fighting harder. The guards are still trying to pull His Majesty away."

Rian thrusts his hand toward the block, releasing a crackling bolt of light that the Sorcerer dodges easily. The Sorcerer glares and turns toward Rian.

"Missed," I whisper. "He sees us."

I jump to my feet. Put myself between the two of them. Scream something foul at him. He smirks at me. I draw two of my daggers.

"Tib, don't!" Rian tries to grab my arm but I'm too fast. I charge up the stairs. Raise my daggers to fling them at the Sorcerer.

He leers at me. The white of his eyes and teeth seem to almost glow against the black curls of the Mark that cover his skin.

"*That's the one. Get a good look. Mark him in your memory,*" his voice drifts through the space between us. His words aren't meant for me. He's pushing his thoughts to someone nearby. Someone small. More than one someone.

"*Black hair.*"

"*Black and straight. Skinny.*"

"*Sunteri boy.*"

"*'Course he's a Sunteri boy! You remember the story. Idiot.*"

"*He's weak. Small.*"

"*Knobbly fingers.*"

"*Slanty eyes.*"

They dive out of thin air. Small creatures, like fairies. Three of them. They aren't fairies, though. These are twisted and dark like tree roots. Their skin is scaly like a snake's. Their wings are leathery and lined with veins. One of them hovers in front of my face. Hisses at me. Bares sharp teeth that drip with poison. A foul puff of air wafts over my face.

"*That won't work, fool! Pay attention!*" another of them pushes.

"Get away from me," I shout with a slash of my dagger. A breeze blows from behind me. Brushes the creature's breath away. Pushes them back a little. Shush hovers just behind my shoulder. Rian stays close, ready to cast.

"The Dawn," the smallest of the scaly fairies sneers at him. "Far from home, aren't you?"

"The Dusk," Shush replies. "You have no place here."

"No more than you do. Who broke the rules first, eh?" the small one shivers and glares.

"Yeah, who opened the door?" this one is a little larger, with a rounder face. Shush clenches his jaw. Doesn't say anything.

"*Enough banter. Fetch the Prince,*" the Sorcerer commands.

"*Stop ordering us. You're not in charge,*" the third creature taunts.

"*Well, he can hear us maybe, and he doesn't know who's what. Except now maybe he does, witless!"* says the round-faced one.

"*Yes, fetch the Prince,*" says the smallest. "*Now. But let them see him first.*" The dark fairies dart off toward the battle. The Prince is still fighting. The King is still there.

The Sorcerer laughs, deep and cruel. He raises his hand with a swift motion. The clashing of swords stops. I feel the blindness lift from them and know what they must be seeing. A few of them scream. The king cries out in anguish.

"Oh, no," Lisabella gasps, "no, it's the Prince! Oh, your Majesty, I'm so sorry!"

I don't let them distract me. I know better than to turn my back on a Sorcerer. I fling a blade at him, breaking his wards. I throw my second as Rian sends a streak of energy over my shoulder. It doesn't meet its mark. The Sorcerer vanishes before it reaches him. Rian races past me to tend to his fallen master.

I scream in frustration. Draw my last dagger. Spin to find a target. Anyone, anything to take my rage out on. The dark fairies are on the Prince. Cloaked by the Half-Realm. Shush streaks toward them. I try to aim, but I don't have a clean shot. The dark fae grab the Prince's lifeless body. The king drops to his knees. His sword clatters to the floor. The white fur of his robe soaks up the pool of red. He reaches toward the Prince as the guards try to pull him away. Just as His Majesty's fingers brush the purple doublet, the dark fae laugh. They vanish. So does Eron's corpse.

"No!" His Majesty bellows. He claws at the stone where his son lay just a moment before. Lisabella kneels beside him. She whispers to him. I can see the pulse of her peace ebb and flow. It soothes him. Keeps him calm.

I turn away. Many of the court Mages are crumpled on the stairs. Some are dead, some wounded. People lie everywhere. Slumped over benches, sprawled on the floor. I scan the great hall and my eyes rest on Saesa, still pressed against the column where I left her. Pale. Wide-eyed. I nod to her and she pushes away from it and runs to me. Throws her arms around me. Turns to the others.

"My Lady Knight?" she asks, shaken. Lisabella looks up from the King. Rian calls to her from beside Master Gaethon, who's slowly coming to.

"Azi's safe," he says. "I saw to it in the beginning."

"My son," the king whispers.

"I know, Tirnon. I know," Lisabella continues to soothe him.

"Come, Majesty," one of his guards offers gently. Helps him to stand.

"My son," the king says again. He's in shock. Lisabella and Benen and what's left of the Royal Guard usher him through the palace doors. Back to the safety of the palace. Rian helps Gaethon up. I think they'll follow the others, but instead they close the doors and start setting wards on them.

"How could this happen?" Saesa whispers to me as the rest of the Elite get to work. Donal is kneeling beside Mya, who was knocked out early on. Elliot holds her hand. Dacva is making his way from one Mage to the next, waking the sleeping. "How could one Sorcerer do all this?"

"It wasn't just one. There was something else, too," I say.

"Not here," Rian warns as he jogs down the steps. Shush follows just above his head, tucked safely out of sight in the Half-Realm. Rian passes us by. Goes to check on his mother.

"How, indeed?" Master Gaethon looms on the steps, scowling. Pale. His eyes scan the destruction. "Everything we thought we knew has been disproved with a single act. A single, unthinkable, horrific act. Our King has been traumatized, and all of it performed masterfully before an audience of innocent men and women. This was a brazen flaunting of the worst kind of magic. Wicked, arcane, and destructive to the core."

"I pray that His Majesty will keep a level head," Mya says weakly as Donal leaves her to tend to more of the injured. "I fear his actions in the wake of this if he does not."

"Nevertheless," Gaethon's gaze flicks to the West. Toward the Academy. "We must ensure the rest of the city was spared their wrath." He looks to surviving Mages. Some of them are just now waking up. "You three, stay and clean up. The rest of you, with me. And you, Rian." He flicks a finger and they all file out together, some leaning on others for support.

"Tib, Saesa," Brother Donal calls wearily as he delivers healing to a man with a gash on his head. "If you would, please run to the Conclave and tell them what's happened. We shall need more healers."

"Yes, of course," Saesa says a little distantly. "Come on, Tib."

"The rest of the city," I mumble once we're outside. "You know what Gaethon meant. He needs to check on his precious Academy. Mages." I huff.

"I know how you feel about them," she clings to my arm. She's still shaking.

"Not just them," I start, and she finishes for me.

"Magic in general. Yes, I know," she scowls. Goes quiet as we weave through forlorn-looking crowds still milling around outside of the Court. "Race you," she says suddenly, and lets go of my arm and takes off. I chase after her. The rhythm of my feet pounding the cobbles clears my head. Running frees me. Keeps me from focusing on the faces of people lingering in the streets. More people who were probably inside when it happened. People who are scared, but don't even know half of the truth of what went on.

The wind in my face reminds me of Shush. The Dawn. The Dusk. What did it mean? Who were those dark fae? How did that one Sorcerer cause so much havoc? When we finally reach the Conclave I'm out of breath and overwhelmed with questions. Saesa's faster. I find her leaning against the white stone wall, panting with her head on her arm.

"Saesa?" I step closer. She's not resting after all. She's crying.

"We'll figure it out," I say.

"She left us," she whispers through her tears. "Just left. Ran away and left everyone else to fight. Why? How could she?"

"I don't know. It's not like her," I say, trying to comfort her. I think of Azi. Remember what Rian said in the gallery. *She's safe. I saw to it.* "Maybe it wasn't her choice. Maybe she was forced. Rian said he saw to her being safe. You know Mages."

Chapter Twelve
A RARE PURPOSE

Azi

"A rare purpose? What does that even mean?" I ask.

I give in to the light a little and let myself lean into Flitt. I'm surprised by how strong and solid she feels now that we're nearly the same size. Her magic drifts over me effortlessly, taking away my anxiety bit by bit, allowing me to focus on what she's saying. "And how can I think to fulfill whatever it is without my friends beside me? I need them, Flitt. Rian and Saesa, Mum and Da, the Elite."

"Honeycomb! Honestly, Azi! Every time! I ask a question, then you—"

"Flitt!" I growl.

"All right, all right," she says, and gives the shoulder of my armor a placating pat. "I'll answer your last one first, then. You won't be without them. They're all a part of this. You're going to need them. All of them."

"A part of—" I stop myself midway through asking and groan. "You know, just once I'd love to have a conversation with you without playing this game. It's your question. Go, then."

"Doesn't it smell wonderful here? Like ripe berries and roses."

"I…" I lean back in the grass and look at her curiously. Her purple ponytail slides lazily over her shoulder as she tilts her head to the side and widens her eyes. She waves her hand to try to hurry me to answer. "Yes, it's lovely," I say.

"Good, your turn. Ask that first question again," she nods excitedly.

"You can't tell me what to ask."

"Azi!" she whines.

"What did you mean when you said I have a rare purpose?" I sit up again and watch her as she thinks on it. She sighs, looks up at the sky, and crosses her arms.

"I meant that there's something only you can do, that we really need you to do. Well, I guess someone else could do it, strictly speaking, but it's really unlikely that we'd ever find someone who's so well suited for it. I mean, it's not every day you find a human with your gifts who's so trustworthy and not very selfish. And has friends like your friends. Well, sometimes you're selfish, but it's usually because you're worried about other people. Like with the High Court. Oh, never mind I said that. You had almost forgotten about all of that and then I had to go and bring it up again. Sorry."

She chews her lip and glances sidelong at me while I stare at her in disbelief. She didn't really even answer the question.

"Thank you for the definition, but that's not really what I meant," I say.

"Well, that's what you asked," she huffs. "It's not my fault you didn't ask the question you wanted the answer to."

"It's your turn," I hiss through my teeth at her.

"Don't get all snaky," she scolds. "You're just out of practice, that's all. Remember the first time we played?" She twirls a finger around her yellow ponytail.

"I do remember. It was just as frustrating," I push myself to my feet and start pacing again.

"You got the hang of it after a while, though. Your turn again," she stretches her legs out in front of her and taps her feet together excitedly. "Make it a good one."

"What is it exactly," I pause and think hard, making every word count, "you really need me to do in regards to this rare purpose, which is so important you'd whisk me here against my will in the midst of a battle that could very well mean the end of peace in my kingdom and possibly the deaths of people I'm sworn to protect?"

"Whoa," her eyes go wide as I come to a stop right in front of her. "That was brilliant. Really brilliant. Excellent question. See, you just had to focus, that's all."

"Flitt." I press my hand to my brow. My head is starting to ache from frustration.

"Don't hate me. I can't answer it," she says with a cute little shrug and an impish smile.

"What?" I can't help it. I lunge at her. She's too fast, though. She pushes off from the grass and flies up out of my reach. "So help me!" I shout up at her. "You'd better stay up there, I swear!" I glare up at her and then realize her mistake in putting distance between us. Instantly I think of Rian. I start to feel the shimmer around me and then she dives into me, pinning me to the ground.

"Don't," she pleads as she straddles my chest. She's surprisingly heavy for a fairy. "I was just playing. Don't go. I can't answer it, but I can show you something else."

"Get," I shove at her, "off!"

"Uh uh," she shakes her head. "You have to promise to stay. It's important, Azi. Really important. World changing important. Things are happening that never should happen. Bad things. Wicked things. Worse than Sorcerers. Worse than Jacek. Really bad." She leans over me with her hands on my shoulders and her rainbow-colored ponytails spill forward, tickling my face. "Really, really bad. Please. Do you promise?"

"Worse than Jacek?" I look up at her.

"You can't answer a question with a—" she stops herself at my death glare. "Worse than Jacek," she whispers. Her eyes sparkle with tears and change from blue to red to silver. This close I can see she has no pupils, just orbs of ever-changing light that shimmers softly and unpredictably. I've never seen them so clearly, never been so drawn to them.

"I promise," I say, tempted by the familiar tingle of magic rising inside me. I want to see what she's seen; I want to know what's in a fairy's mind. I let it fill me: the desire, the rise of elation that comes when I let go and allow the magic to take over.

With it comes the guilt. I think of Rian and his hard fight for restraint. I shouldn't let it entice me so much. I should shield myself from desiring it. It isn't Flitt I feel threatened by, it's the magic itself. The power. The thrill of it. I want it and I don't. I've let it consume me before. It's dangerous to let it call to me this way. I don't want to give in, but at the same time, I ache for it. "Show me," I say finally.

Flitt tips her head closer until her forehead rests against mine. Being this close to her is strange and wonderful. Her bangs brush my forehead, framing her round face in a rainbow halo. Flecks of light spill from every pore of her skin, which is smooth and fresh, pure and pale.

"Look, then," she giggles, and I realize my eyes have been wandering everywhere but where they need to be. "Go on," she whispers, sensing my hesitation.

My eyes meet hers and I'm immediately captivated by the shifting hues that ebb and flow there: green, blue, yellow, orange, then gold, everywhere gold. I tumble away from myself to drift in a shifting sea of color and light. It's the most beautiful thing I've ever seen. The most special, perfect, dazzling sight. My heart swells and races as I float weightless in the vast beauty of Flitt's mind. It's like no place I've ever been before, and unlike anything I've felt.

Floating here, I lose track of time. I lose track of everything. My own mind is soothed. Something vague and distant reminds me of some past danger, some lost opportunity, but right now it doesn't matter. This is where I need to be. I hear a voice: a woman singing, beautiful and sweet. I'm drawn to it immediately. The song is more lovely than anything Mya has sung. It has no words, just emotion. It tells of light and dark, of good and evil, of wicked and righteous. One voice sings in harmony with itself, to describe the weak and frail and the constant battle between those who swear to keep them safe and those who might exploit them.

"Memi, what is The Dusk?" a child's voice interrupts the song. The voice is Flitt's but younger.

"The Dusk is the beginning of darkness," the singing woman replies with a patient, nurturing tone.

"But who are they, really?" the child presses.

"Ask me again when you've found your place," the woman says softly.

"I want to bring light where there isn't any." The child says eagerly. "I want to help the weak ones."

"Perhaps you shall one day, my little Sunbeam," the woman replies kindly, and begins her song again.

She sings of the darkest places, where shadows lurk to pounce on the light. Thieves and ambushes, assassins and murders, Sorcerers and dark magic. The dusk that steals away the light.

"Why must they be so wicked?" Flitt asks. She sounds a little older now. I try to drift closer to get to a place where I can see her. "If I ever met a thief or a Sorcerer, I'd force them to change. I could go all around and make them good. Then there'd be no darkness. No cruelty."

"What good is the light," the woman's voice is filled with amusement, "without the shadow? Balance in all things, my little Sunbeam."

"That's wicked to think that," young Flitt says. "If there was light always, then everything would be good. There wouldn't be darkness to lurk in. There'd be no cover for the evil ones. They're foolish to think they can push us out. They can't exist without us."

I see them now: Two figures silhouetted in front of a shimmering pool. It sparkles and glitters with colorful light like a larger version of Flitt's eyes. Young Flitt sits on her Memi's lap, gazing up into her face.

"If there is light, there is shadow," the woman explains. "Light casts it, you see. There is no way around that. Dawn and Dusk, little one. Light and shadow. Do you understand? One without the other is impossible." She combs her fingers through Flitt's long pastel hair.

"But who are, they, The Dusk?" she asks. "Zilliandin says they're growing stronger. He says they're coming. They could defeat us."

"Zilliandin is wise, but that is a question for another time. Ask me again when you've found your place," the woman says softly.

"One day," Flitt sighs as she rests against the woman, "I'll travel the known lands. I'll bring my light where it's needed. Anywhere it's needed. I'll keep the shadows away. I'll stop them from ever harming this world."

"So you shall, my little Sunbeam, if you wish it. Goodnight," the woman kisses Flitt's brow tenderly. The scene changes slowly, filling me with a sense of sadness. A pending farewell.

Upon a pristine ivory pedestal, Flitt's Memi gazes down with a wistful smile. She wears a glistening silver crown of spider silk and dewdrops. Her throne stretches high over her head like sea coral or stag's antlers, white and intricate and so tall that it disappears into the ceiling. Her gown of flower petals and dandelion fluff cascades around her, its train trailing down at least a hundred steps to where Flitt kneels before her.

Flitt is quiet, a little sad, but determined. As she looks up, other fairies begin to emerge to stand beside the throne of the queen, lining the pedestal on either side of her. Most give off the same light as Flitt and the Queen, but some are not as brilliant.

"So it is, then," the queen says, her voice just as tender as it had been in the previous memories.

"Yes, Memi," Flitt replies with pride. She looks down the rows of fairy children and back at the queen again. "I mean yes, Your Majesty," she says gravely. The queen laughs softly.

"You shall always be my little Sunbeam, and I shall always be Memi to you, no matter where you go. But when you leave this place, you shall no longer be afforded the luxuries and care that is lavished upon you here, do you understand? Your status will be lost, and you shall have to find your own way in the Light. If you are determined to leave, then once you have declared it, what's done is done."

Slowly I'm aware of more than just the children. The palace, once a globe of pure white light, begins to fill with a countless number of fairies.

"I saw it in her from the moment she was born," a knobbly-looking male fairy speaks up. "She is not suited for the palace life. She is destined for distant places and greater challenges."

"Thank you, Zilliandin," the Queen nods gracefully, "as have so many others. And so, my Sunbeam, we must perform the ceremony. Come," she gestures to Flitt who looks so small as she climbs the ivory staircase all the way up to the throne. When she reaches the top, the Queen embraces her.

"Do you intend to leave the Palace of the Dawn?" she asks a little tearfully.

"I do," Flitt replies.

"Will you keep your allegiance to the Light?" the Queen asks.

"Always," Flitt says. When the queen stands, tiny white petals flutter from her gown like snowflakes. They catch the light and drift lazily through the vast hall. Some of the watching fae giggle and chase after them, but most remain quiet, still, and watchful.

"Then go, my child, and find your place." She smiles at Flitt and then turns to the others. "Today, we say farewell to our little one, who leaves us for places unknown. May her light shine even in her darkest hour. May she ever be a beacon for the Dawn."

"A beacon for the Dawn!" everyone calls out in unison.

"Say farewell to your sisters and brothers, my Sunbeam, and go to the Ring at Kythshire, where my cousin presides. You will find a home there, and perhaps one day, your place." She kisses Flitt on the forehead and hugs her, and Flitt turns to the line of fairies beside the throne. As she goes to each giving hugs and kisses, the scene fades away.

I feel myself falling, and with it comes the sensation of magic quickly draining away. The dread that always follows hits me hard as I slowly become aware of my own body again. My arms and legs are heavy. My body is like a stone. I jolt back to the present and Flitt looks away first to break the connection.

"Here," she says, and starts shoving something into my mouth. Sugar cubes, one after another. Her light glows brightly, but it doesn't help much with the desolation that feels like it'll swallow me up. Between having to leave such a beautiful place and ceasing my Mentalism so quickly, I feel like I want to curl into a ball and sink into the earth. Flitt is still perched on my chest, though, so instead I just lie there and sob.

"It'll pass," she says thickly through her own mouthful of sugar. "Eat." She pushes another cube into my mouth.

"Stop that," I protest, but the sugar is sweet and comforting. It distracts me from my misery. I let it dissolve on my tongue and give in to more of them.

"Stop crying, you'll get all blotchy," she says.

"Why did you show me that?" I ask after I calm down a little. "I thought you were going to show me whatever it is that's worse than Jacek."

"I can't show you *that*," she mumbles around her sugar and scoots back to sit on my legs. "Can I see your hands?" Confused, I take off my gloves and hold my hands out to her.

"What do you mean, you can't show me that? That was the whole point of looking in the first place."

"I can't show you what I haven't seen. And no, that wasn't the point. The point was this." She holds my hand up to my face and turns it, showing me the golden Mark that creeps over my skin in intricate spirals.

My heart pangs with anger and shame. I shiver and tug my glove on securely to cover it up.

"Why do you hide it away?" Flitt asks. I realize we've fallen into the rhythm of the game again and shake my head.

"It frightens me, seeing the Marks," I say honestly. "I've had nightmares about the Justiciar spotting them and making me use my magic in the trials. Or people kidnapping me and forcing me to delve into the minds of others, to find out their secrets and make them do things. I don't like how I got it. It came from evil, from deception. I don't like how it makes me feel. If people saw it, they wouldn't trust me anymore."

"Stubs isn't evil," Flitt laughs. "He's just a tuffet. He gave you a gift to help you fight Jacek. Imagine if he hadn't, where we'd all be now. It's part of what you can do. Part of who you are, Azi, and you're not wicked. You don't need to be ashamed of it. Not here, at least," she says.

"Wait, you're distracting me," I shake my head. "I'm confused. The point was my Mark?"

"Yup," she grins. "Oh, good! It's on your face, too. Look."

She flutters up, pulls me to my feet, and guides me through the enormous grass. The tall fronds part slowly to reveal a mirror, and my own reflection.

She's right. The gold Mark curls elegantly across my cheek. I step back and shake my head in protest. It's never gotten that bad before. Now, everyone will see. Everyone will know. My heart pounds in my chest.

"Look at yourself," Flitt says. Her tone is gentle and calming. "Look at yourself like you're a stranger. Like you've never seen yourself before. Really look."

I try my best to stay calm and do as she says. At first I can only fixate on the golden Mark. Eventually, I tear my eyes away and I look at the woman in the mirror.

Her midnight blue armor gleams in the sunlight. Her blonde hair falls over her shoulder in a long braid that coordinates perfectly with the swirling Mark and the gold trim of her white cloak. Her sword is sheathed at her back, its handle highly polished steel. The name Hammerfel is etched in the hand guard, which is inlaid with blue enamel to go with the armor. Scale and plate armor, but made of something else, not metal. Stony, with flecks of gold and black and lighter blue that echoes in her eyes. Even while she looks herself over with curiosity, she has an air of determination, of strength and righteousness.

Not only is she a knight, she could be a Paladin. The golden Mark gives her an air of power and mystery. She's impressive. Stirring.

Flitt hovers beside me in my reflection, her usual tiny self. After a moment, she tucks herself into her niche in my collar where my pauldron meets my neck guard. When she does, her light bursts across the crystals in my armor and shines over the golden swirls so brilliantly that I have to shield my eyes.

"This," she beams, "is what I meant to show you." She leans back in the tiny space and looks very much at home there. A Paladin's companion. Ili'luvrie. A perfect duo.

"You've found your place," I breathe.

"I've found my place," she grins. "Now, let's go see the Queen."

Chapter Thirteen

DOORWAY TO CERION

Celli

More maze-like passages. We weave through them for ages, and the harder I try to keep track of the lefts and rights, the dizzier and sicker I feel. By the time Dub stops in front of a huge red door, I have to lean on the wall to keep myself steady. The swirling design carved into the frame of it press into my shoulder. It reminds me of the beautiful Mark on Quenson's face, and I can't help but daydream a little.

"Don't lean," Dub orders, but I have to. Everything's spinning. I'm too dizzy to stand on my own. I might tip over or even faint. "You want me to tell Quenson you can't follow a simple direction?" he growls, grabs my arm, and yanks me roughly away from the wall.

I can't help it. I cling to him. As much as I hate him and as cruel as he is, I don't want to disappoint Quenson and I can't stand on my own.

"What's wrong with me?" I ask him. "I feel so strange."

"Wards," he says with a smirk. "You're too close. You'll get used to it if they keep you around."

"Wards on the door?" I ask. He doesn't answer. Instead he holds out his hand.

"Give me your coin," he says.

"My coin?" I try to play stupid. The coin Quenson gave me is mine. It's the only thing he's given me. I'm not about to give it to Dub or anyone else.

"I swear to…" his gruff oath trails off and he grasps me hard by the shoulders and turns me to face the door. "Look. What do you see?"

"A door," I say, and when his grip tightens painfully I look harder. "It's red, with Mage Mark swirls. It's got no handle, but carvings all over."

He doesn't say anything, but reaches past me and presses a coin into a circle in the door that's carved to fit it perfectly. His coin's just like mine, with prongs around the outside and a picture of a spire in the clouds on one side.

"Do yours there," he says, and points to another carved circle beside it. I get my coin out of my pouch and press it into the space where it's meant to go. A spark jolts my fingertip when I do and I jump back. His laugh infuriates me, and I have all I can do to keep from punching him. "Now, press your finger to it," he demonstrates with his own fingertip, "and repeat after me."

"Sparrow and fox," he says. I press my finger to my coin in the door.

"Sparrow and fox," I say, and the coin crackles under my touch.

"Boar and perch," he whispers, and the wooden surface starts to shimmer.

"Boar and perch," I say, and feel the coin give under my touch.

"Foreshine, forewarn," he says, and the Mage-Mark swirls on his side of the door start to dance and curl across the red.

"Foreshine, forewarn," I repeat, and my side does the same. I push my finger harder against the coin and it moves forward. The surface is soft now, like a piece of fabric stretched across an embroidery ring.

"Induct, destroy," Dub says, his expression darkening.

"Induct, destroy," I repeat, and the Mark expands until it covers every bit of the red with thick black spirals.

"Cerion," Dub says, and the curling lines flick out and grab him. Before I can react, they pull him through the door and I'm left alone in the corridor, watching the tendrils swirl and slither like a pit full of black serpents.

My finger slips on the coin. My hands are shaking. I know what I have to do, but the black swirls are terrifying. I try to have courage. Dub's words ring over and over in my mind: *You want me to tell Quenson you can't follow a simple direction? Quenson will hear of this.*

"Cerion," I manage to croak, and the swirls lash out, binding my arms, creeping over my waist, my legs, my face until I'm completely enclosed in darkness. I can't think, I can't see, I can't breathe. The coin nearly falls, but I catch it as I'm pulled forward into the space where the door once stood. My stomach lurches as I race forward under the force of the shadowy tendrils, and just as suddenly as they grabbed me, they deposit me on the other side.

I fall to my knees at Dub's feet, panting for breath. The floor is rotted wood and dust. The musty smell of it combined with the violent speed of my journey makes me gag.

"You'll get used to that, too," Dub says gruffly. He lifts me onto my feet by my collar. He's still smirking, like my confusion and fear is entertaining to him. Amusing. I try hard to hide it. I don't want to give him that satisfaction.

"I'm fine," I say, and shove my coin back into my pocket. "What was that?" I ask, still trying to catch my breath.

"You're not here to ask questions," he says.

He makes me wait while he goes to get me something to change into. He tells me to stay away from the windows and keep out of sight. I obey him not because I want to, but because I'm afraid to walk across the rotting wood floor that seems like one misstep will send me crashing through it.

While he's away I shuffle carefully around to look at the wall we came through. That's all it is. Bricks and mortar. I look closer and make out a half dozen coin-sized circles stamped into the crumbling faces of the bricks. High above the circles, stamped on another brick, is a strange symbol. A circle slashed in half with a straight line. It could be a horizon, I think. A reflection of the sun on the water. Sunrise or sunset. Dawn or dusk.

"Put these on," Dub calls to me from the door. The clothes he's scrounged up hit me in the back before I can turn around. He goes back out without waiting for a reply, and when I gather the clothes from the dust I realize they're mine. He must have stolen them from my house. The thought makes me shiver. I think of Mum and Da. I wonder if they're safe.

Once I'm dressed, Dub comes back inside.

"You know this kid, then?" he asks me.

"Ti—" I start, but he clamps his gloved hand over my mouth.

"Don't say his name," he hisses and takes his hand away. "You're friends?"

"Not really," I say, "he's kind of a jerk. He thinks he's better than everyone. Most of the others either stay out of his way or idolize him. I can't stand him."

"You're going to turn that around," Dub says. "You two are going to become best friends."

"Why do they want him?" I ask, but his only reply is to jerk his head toward the street to order me outside. I'm not here to ask questions.

Chapter Fourteen

AFTERMATH

Tib

It doesn't take Saesa long to gather herself. She's a warrior in training, after all. We follow the wall around to the open gate. There's already a crowd here. Injured. Bleeding. Healers dressed in brown robes weave through the wounded, casting and curing. This kind of magic is different to me. Soothing. I can sense it the same as the arcane, and if I want to, I can allow it to affect me.

Beside me, Saesa steels herself. I try not to look, but I can't help it. I've never seen so much blood, so much pain and fear in one place. Dozens of people crying, pleading. There isn't much we can do for them aside from keeping out of the healers' way.

We make our way slowly through the gates. I've never been inside the Conclave before. Never needed to, thankfully. No one is here to greet us. The gate is open, just like always. Cerion's arms are always open to the suffering. In a peaceful kingdom, there's no need to shut out the sick and hurting.

Saesa takes the lead. She's been here before. The halls are empty, though. The healers gone. It's so clean. White. Stark. Open. Peaceful, compared to the outside. Quiet, except for the shuffle of boots on stone and the soft trickle of water. Ahead, the ceiling arches up to the sky. Light pours through the ceiling onto the sculpture of a woman as tall as Nessa's house.

She's a round woman with a kind, smiling face. Water spills from her eyes like tears. It trickles into the folds of her robes that pool at her feet. In one hand she holds a bundle to her chest. The other one is stretched out over us in a healing gesture.

I forget Saesa and move closer. I feel drawn to her, the statue. She reminds me of my mother somehow. The mother I lost when I was much younger.

"Isn't she beautiful?" Saesa asks with awe. "She reminds me of my mother," she echoes my thoughts.

"Mother of Peace. Lady of Solace," a pensive voice comes from the other side of the statue. A hunched old man peers around the Mother's

116

feet at the two of us. He beckons us closer.

"Come for a healing?" he asks, reaching for us with knobby, wrinkled hands. Saesa takes them in hers. His milky gray eyes smile.

"Saesa Coltori," he says with kindness and warmth. "Your heart is heavy, as it should be at the decline of the Age of Peace. You have come to ask for help, but help has already been granted to those at the High Court. Most of our numbers are there now, undoing the evil that has befallen our great city. Dark times. Dark times, indeed."

"How do you know me?" Saesa asks, "And what do you mean, the decline of the Age of Peace?"

"I know what the Lady tells me," the man says, his voice less feeble as he goes on. "She sees you. She cries for a future rent with suffering, not unlike that which you have seen today. Our source of healing is finite, Saesa. It cannot withstand this much pain, this much destruction, at once. She weeps for the loss of it. She weeps for the children. She weeps for Cerion, the great city. The fallen city."

"You shouldn't say such things," Saesa says, dropping his hands. "It's not true. One attack doesn't mean that the city is falling, and if you go around telling people that, they'll start to believe it and it *will* become true. There's truth in untruths, Nessa says."

"The Lady of Solace does not lie," he replies, and reaches out to me. I hesitate and give him one hand.

"Tibreseli," he smiles. "Key to the Skies."

His words make my heart race. I think of my invention, tucked deep underground. Almost finished. Almost ready.

"Do not tarry in your work," he says. "It will be needed soon, but not for the purpose you envisioned. Go now. I will not waste any more of your precious time. Work in the Light. Carry Peace with you." He lets go of my hand. Gestures back toward the gate dismissively.

Saesa stands beside me, staring at the man with a mix of awe and distaste. I take her arm and she blinks rapidly, like she's clearing something from her eyes.

"Come on, Saesa. We have to go," I say urgently. She looks reluctant, but she nods slowly and the two of us turn and dash out.

"Who was that?" she asks as we reach the gates and pick up speed.

"I don't know," I say. "I thought you knew, the way you took to him."

"No, I—" she skids to a stop in the street. Looks around. "Tib, where is everyone?"

She's right. We're in the middle of market street at midday, and it's empty. Stalls are set with wares, banners flap in the breeze, fires at food carts crackle low, and yet the place is completely empty. Abandoned.

"It's so eerie," Saesa whispers. She clings to my arm.

The urgency I felt in the Conclave has faded. The thought of checking on my contraption now seems silly and pointless. This is all wrong. Something is off. Not just the absence of people. I feel it. The presence of magic. I edge forward cautiously.

"What is it, Tib?" Saesa whispers, refusing to let go of me.

"Magic," I reply, approaching a cart. "Wards. They're everywhere."

"That's not unexpected," Saesa says. "Lots of merchants pay to have wards set on their wares. Look-aways, mostly, when they're away from them."

"There's something else," I say. I crouch low and keep moving forward. "Something powerful. Threatening. Waiting." My free hand rests on the knife at my belt. I focus on the source of it and hone in. Averie's stall. The apothecary. It's a mess. Torn up, herbs scattered everywhere, bottles of powders smashed and spilled.

"I feel it too," Saesa whispers, her own hand gripping her sword, ready to draw. A wave of magic pulses over us. It's weak, but I recognize it right away.

"We should go," Saesa hisses urgently, and starts pulling me back. "Come on," she whimpers. "Turn around, Tib."

"Fear spell," I murmur to Saesa, unaffected. That seems to snap her out of it. She shakes her head, scowling, while I press closer to the source. The inside of the stall is cramped and cluttered. Puddles of potions glow and steam and bubble on the cobbles. "Watch your step," I point to them and Saesa nods. I'm getting closer now. The only thing between me and the source of the fear spell is a tattered curtain. I reach to it. Draw a dagger. Pull it back.

"A bucket of water?" Saesa's tone is somewhere between relief and disappointment. We crane forward over the bucket.

"This is where the spell came from," I say, not bothering to whisper anymore.

That's when I see it. A glimpse of yellow silk. I don't have time to place it. The bucket sloshes on its own. A globe of water pools up out of it. Not a globe, a head. A shoulder. Another. Arms. A torso. The water bubbles and swirls within the form of a man. It splashes and gurgles and sloshes out of the bucket with watery feet.

"Water golem!" Saesa shouts. She draws her sword and slashes it through the middle. It doesn't do much aside from angering the golem.

The water simply reforms around the wound. In response, it raises its fist to smash her in the face. Saesa reacts quickly, though. She swings upward, blocking the attack with her blade. Water sprays over her like sea mist, soaking her. The golem shrinks a little.

Its back is to me. I take the advantage. With a dagger in each hand, I plunge the blades into it and pull my hands outward. Water splashes out with the motion, spraying the silks draped around the tent. It shrinks a little more.

"Keep making it splash," Saesa says, hitting the creature's fist again as it drives toward her. She's drenched to the waist now, her hair limp and dripping. "It's weakening it!"

That gives me an idea. I sheath my weapons and grab the bucket. Saesa blocks another punch with a swing of her sword and a wet fan of droplets.

I dive at the golem with the bucket. Scoop as much of its torso as I can away. Toss the water out into the street. The golem stumbles. It's smaller now. A little shorter than I am. I do it again and it shrinks to my chest height.

"It's working!" Saesa whoops. She's too quick to celebrate, though. The golem dives at her with all of its might, hitting her with the full force of an ocean wave. It crashes down over her, sacrificing itself for one last powerful attack. Saesa is thrown back against a shelf. She hits it hard and the remaining bottles and powders tumble over her as she sputters and coughs, half-drowned.

"Saesa!" I leap toward her. Her face is covered with green powder. Something purple and jelly-like oozes across her chest.

"It's all right, Tib," she says cheerfully, pulling herself up out of the multi-colored puddle. "We did it! Wow, I feel great. Nothing like a good fight to get the blood moving. Let's go do something daring. I feel like I could take on the world." She takes my hand. Instantly, something changes in her. She turns to me slowly. Gazes into my eyes.

"I have something to tell you," she whispers, her expression serious, her eyes wide. She moves closer. Leans against me. Keeps staring. Her face is splashed with pink potions. The green powder is soaking up the water, crackling. Her hair is caked with something black that smells like tar. I look away from her to the shelf of smashed potions. She could be under the effect of any of them. Or all of them.

"What?" I ask a little reluctantly. She moves closer. Tilts her head down to look down at me. Her eyelids droop a little. I have no idea why she's looking at me that way. Dreamily. Maybe one of them was a sleep potion.

"Tib, I can't hide my feelings anymore," she leans closer until our noses are almost touching. Tilts her head to the side. Closes her eyes. Her lips brush mine. I lean back and look over her shoulder where Zeze has just jumped up onto the railing above where the bucket of water had attacked us.

The stall banners rustle behind her. I glimpse that same flash of yellow silk and it finally dawns on me. I step around Saesa and squint past the curtain.

"Loren!" I shout, and the Mage jumps up from his hiding place.

"I didn't know it was you!" Loren cries. He backs up against the silks. Zeze saunters along the rail behind him, flicking her tail into his face. "It could have been anyone!"

Saesa leans heavily against my arm. At first I think she's crying. Her forehead rests on my shoulder. Her body shakes. I pat her awkwardly.

"Come out of there," I call to him. "Tell us what happened. Where is everyone?"

Loren hesitates, but he does as he's asked. As he moves closer I feel the wards heavy on him. Look-aways. Anyone else would have surely passed him by without a second glance.

Beside me Saesa snorts, and I realize she isn't crying after all. She's laughing. The snort makes her laugh harder. She doubles over in a fit of giggles. Loren watches her, wide-eyed.

"See what you did?" I scowl and rest a hand on Saesa's back.

"It was just a water golem. I had to protect myself," Loren says. He does look regretful, though. "Looks like she got a pleasure potion almost full on. That's the green powder," he says, bending to examine Saesa. His assessment makes her laugh even harder. She's down on one knee now, gasping for breath between peals of it. "You're only supposed to use a pinch."

"All right, Saesa, hang on. We'll fix this," I say, looking around. Zeze has moved to the side rail of the stall now. She sits there, watching us patiently. Beneath her is a barrel of rainwater. She stands and paces again, mewling softly.

"Will it help if we wash her off?" I ask Loren. He follows my gaze to the barrel and nods.

"It should," he says.

"Help me, then."

Together we lift Saesa up by the elbows with some difficulty. She's laughing so hard we can barely keep a grip on her, and she's fairly heavy in her wet studded leather.

"Sorry about this," I murmur to her as we reach the barrel. We struggle to lift her up, and then plunge her in headfirst. Zeze hops down to avoid getting splashed.

Saesa comes up instantly, coughing and swinging. I dodge her fist easily, but Loren is right beside me. Before I can pull him away, she makes contact and knocks him out cold.

"Saesa!" I cry and grab her hand. "Stop!"

She shakes her head and wipes the water from her eyes. When she sees Loren passed out on the wet cobbles, she gasps.

"Was that me? Oh, I'm sorry!" she exclaims. She sinks to her knees and pats his face with her palm gently, trying to wake him.

I try hard not to be annoyed with her. I haven't always been immune to the effects of magic. I know what it's like to act under the influence of it. To have no control over yourself or your actions. Still, between the man at the conclave and the way she acted after the potion took hold, I know she's vulnerable. Whatever is happening here in Cerion, Saesa doesn't have the same protections I do. She needs to be shielded from it. She's better off at home.

"Come on," I say to her. "Help me carry him. We'll take him to Nessa's."

Thankfully, she doesn't argue. She hefts him under his arms and I get his feet, and we hurry along the deserted market street. When we arrive at the manse, it seems just as quiet. Just as deserted, except for Zeze who is there waiting for us. She licks her paw casually on the stoop as Saesa and I struggle to get Loren up the steps.

We stop at the door and Saesa looks at me hesitantly. I know what she's thinking. What if no one is inside? What then?

"I'll go in first," I say, setting Loren's feet down on the stone gently. Saesa nods her agreement and I push the door open slowly.

I'm greeted by a blade at my throat. As soon as he recognizes me, the admiral takes his sword away and pulls me inside.

"Tib," he lets out a sigh of relief. "My apologies. Come in, quickly."

"It's okay, Saesa," I say, and the Admiral peers out at her. His eyes drift to Loren, who's just starting to stir.

"Who is that?" he asks with an unusually stern tone.

"His name's Loren," I say.

"He's a Mage. Do you trust him?" the Admiral asks.

"Who is it, darling?" Nessa asks, coming out from the sitting room. In the doorway, Lilen and Emmie poke their heads out to see.

"Tib!" Nessa gasps. "Saesa! Thank goodness! We were so worried. Don't linger in the doorway. Come in, quickly!"

"Not the Mage," the Admiral says as Saesa starts to drag Loren over the threshold.

"Oh, but Tristan, he's just a boy," Nessa says, rushing to help Saesa. "He's been hurt. What happened?"

"I punched him," Saesa says, wincing. "It's a long story." Nessa clicks her tongue in disapproval.

"Lilen," Nessa says, "come look. Do you recognize him?"

"Close the door," the Admiral orders again, shaking his head in defeat. Everyone knows it's useless to argue with Nessa where stray children are concerned. Zeze slips in as I shut the door. Inside, the others crowd around Loren.

"I've never seen him before," Lilen says. "He's not from the Academy."

"He's an islander," I explain. "From Stepstone. He was delivering something for the Prince, to protect him."

"Prince Eron?" the Admiral asks darkly.

"No, his son," I reply. "He brought something for Amei so the young prince would be safe."

"Well, if he is an ally of the princess, then he's certainly welcome," Nessa says decisively. "Settle him upstairs in the spare room. Put a sleep on him, Lilen, for now. Just to be safe."

The admiral takes Loren from Saesa and carries him upstairs, and Lilen follows behind looking smug. When they reach the top, Nessa turns and throws her arms around the both of us. I know better than to squirm away. I just let her hug me.

"We were so worried," she says.

"Can't breathe," Saesa gasps.

"Why are you soaking wet?" Nessa asks, holding her at arm's length. She draws her in for a hug again. "Never mind. I'm just glad you're safe. When you didn't come home, we feared the worst. Raefe insisted on going to look for you. Then the decree went out and Tristan refused to let anyone else leave the house."

"Decree?" I ask.

"His Majesty has issued a decree," Nessa explains as the admiral and Lilen come back down the stairs. Emmie clings to her waist and Ruben stands with his arms crossed, listening. "That any citizen loyal to the throne should seek shelter until the threat has been assessed. Anyone found wandering streets will be considered suspicious, and held for questioning. All business within the kingdom has been halted."

"For how long?" Saesa asks. She tries to extricate herself from Nessa, but it's no use. She's got us both in a tight hug, as though she's afraid she'll lose us again if she lets go.

"As long as it takes, I imagine, to find whoever was responsible for the attack on the High Court," Admiral Ganvent says.

I think of the man in blue robes peering through the tall windows, then standing on the platform with the bag holding Eron's bloody head. I remember the black fairies with their scaly skin and skin-like wings. How they all vanished. I shake my head.

"They can't keep the city closed up that way," I say. "It could take weeks to find that Sorcerer. Months. It could take forever." I think of the empty market streets. The people walled up in their houses. What the man in the Conclave said about Cerion. "The city will die if people are made to stay inside. People will starve." Saesa and I exchange worried looks.

Emmie looks up from Nessa's skirts, her eyes brimming with tears. Ruben leans to her. Puts his arms around her.

"It's all right, Emmie," he whispers. "Don't be scared."

"Oh, Emmie," Nessa offers soothingly, "come, let's find a game to play."

She gives us one last squeeze and then ushers Emmie into the parlor. When they're out of sight, Saesa looks from me to the admiral.

"Raefe's out there looking for me," she says with concern.

"I know where this is going," Ganvent says. "There's too much of a risk. Raefe can hold his own. Even if he's brought in, he's innocent. They'll escort him here. He'll be fine." The firmness of his tone leaves little room for discussion. "Go upstairs and dry off, Saesa."

"Surely you could go looking for him," I say to the admiral. "Couldn't you?"

"And directly disobey explicit orders from His Majesty?" he shakes his head. "Absolutely not. My place is here, keeping the rest of my family safe. Don't you get any ideas either, Tib."

Saesa stomps upstairs, glancing once over her shoulder at me. I know that look. I nod to the admiral and trail behind her, taking the steps two at a time.

We duck into my room, where Zeze is curled on my pillow. She opens one eye as I shut the door, then closes it and goes back to her nap.

"Tib," Saesa says pleadingly, her voice thick with tears.

"Tell them I'm napping," I say, and go to the window.

"What? No, you can't!"

"That's what you were going to say, isn't it?" I ask as I shove the shutters open. "Raefe's out there somewhere. I'll find him and bring him back here. Don't worry. If I see any guards I can hide."

"Actually, I..." she trails off. Whatever she was going to say, apparently she decides against it. "All right. I'll cover for you." She crosses to me. Kisses my cheek. "Be careful," she whispers.

On the bed, Zeze stretches. She pads across the mattress to me.

"Stay here with Saesa, Zeze," I say as I climb out onto the trellis. "Watch out for each other. I'll be back soon."

I climb down and press myself to the wall outside the kitchen door to listen to the street beyond. I've never heard the city so quiet. I can even hear the distant crash of ocean waves far below the sea wall.

I try to think of where Raefe might have gone to look for Saesa. The clear choice is obvious. I keep to the shadows and make my way through alley. Pick my way cautiously across the city. East, and then north, toward His Majesty's Elite's guild hall.

A couple of streets over from the hall, in the alley behind a baker's shop, my ears pick up a sound. A whimpering. A shuffle, very slight, just before the street. I turn my head quickly and peer in the direction of it. There's a crate there, and a pile of burlap sacks. I creep closer and sense it before I see it.

Someone's hiding in the sacks. Crying. Sounds like a girl. I move even closer. She's covered almost all the way with the sacks, except for a tuft of white-blonde hair sticking out. She hears me approach and she goes quiet.

"Please don't hurt me," she whispers as I reach her. I crouch down. Pull the sack away. Her face is bruised. Her eyes swollen with tears.

"Celli?" I whisper in disbelief. "What's going on? What happened? Where have you been? Are you all right?"

"They were chasing me, but I lost them. I hid here, but now I can't leave. If I do, they'll find me. They'll hurt me again, Tib," she whispers, and the fear in her eyes is plain.

I don't hear the man creeping up behind me. I don't notice the shadow he casts over me until it's too late to react. Celli claps her hands over her mouth, covering her scream. Something strikes me hard on the side of the head, and I black out.

124

Chapter Fifteen

AZI'S TEST

Azi

"The Queen? Right now?" I ask in disbelief.

"Yes. She'll be able to tell me about the Dusk now. I mean us, of course," Flitt says hopefully. Her light twinkles brightly as she lifts from my shoulder and grows to my size again. The mirror fades away. "Are you ready?" she asks, grinning. "You look perfect. Come on."

As she pulls me along through the thick grass, I'm taken by the beauty of this place. All the colors are vastly more brilliant here than they are in Cerion. Even the gray mossy tree trunks and the earth under our feet radiate with a sparkling, perfect beauty. Perhaps it's because I haven't been to Kythshire in some time, but it feels different to me. Calmer but also more powerful.

"It's less wild, somehow," I say to Flitt as we make our way through the grass.

"Less wild than what?" Her wings glitter in the sun as she drifts ahead of me.

"Than it used to be," I say. "Before whenever I came to Kythshire, I could feel the constant pull of magic. It seemed to always be testing me, changing my emotions. It's quieter now," I sigh. "I don't know how to describe it. Maybe it's me that's changed. Maybe I know to expect it now, so it isn't so difficult to keep it at bay."

Flitt raises a pink-tinted eyebrow. She shakes her head and giggles softly.

"What?" I ask.

"Azi," she grins, "it feels different from Kythshire because it isn't Kythshire at all." With a gentle tug she pulls me into the air with her until we're able to see above the grass. "See?"

I gasp at the landscape that sprawls before us. The grass is a simple meadow dotted with delicate flowers of red, orange, white, and purple. Their sweet fragrance is carried past me on the breeze in a swirl of petals that brush my cheeks. Blue and yellow songbirds dart playfully in and out of the grass. Beyond them a towering forest stretches high overhead, with ancient trees that watch over us with silent curiosity.

"There," Flitt points in the opposite direction, where the sun is just cresting over the horizon. Squinting into it, I can just make out an enormous white flower bud like a spire against the bright sphere, its petals twisted tightly closed. "Come on, we're so close!" She tugs me again and I drift along behind her with the tips of my toes brushing the tall grass.

"It's stunning, Flitt. Where are we, if not Kythshire?" I ask.

"Someplace else," she answers vaguely as she flies faster into the rising sun. "That's the Palace of the Dawn."

When she says it, it occurs to me that the sun is bright overhead, yet it looks like it's rising against the horizon. It's an odd realization. "There are two suns," I say, trying hard to follow the rules of the game we still seem to be playing by not actually asking a question. I can tell she notices by the way she looks back at me and grins.

"At the Palace, it's always Dawn. Even after the sun goes down everywhere else. The start of the light, where the Queen keeps her throne," she says. "It's a safe place where all fae can find solace. Oh, it's even lovelier than I remember. Have you ever seen anything so perfect?"

The petals fall open ever so slowly to welcome us as we approach, and a golden path of glittering pebbles leads our way.

"I've never seen anything like it," I whisper as she sets us down on the path. "But why not just appear inside?"

"Ha!" Her laughter echoes through the blades of grass. Towering overhead, giant mushrooms of yellow, orange, and red line the golden path. Upon each of them stands a fairy sentry in full battle gear. Some wield spears, others swords, and still others bows. Their sharp eyes watch us sternly as we stand at the edge of the path. "That would be rich! 'Just pop in,' she says. No invitation, no tests. Just appear in front of the Queen! Hello, Your Majesty! Can you imagine?" she looks up at the sentries and laughs. When they don't react, she rubs her neck sheepishly and looks at me. "Heh," she chuckles. "Guess I lost the game. I answered a question with a question. It was a good one, though. Nice and long," she glances at the guards again.

"It was," I agree with a reassuring smile.

"Well," Flitt says, her tone that of forced cheerfulness, "see you on the other side, then. Be careful!" Before I can stop her, she vanishes.

"Very funny, Flitt!" I say, crossing my arms. Above me, the first two sentries shift slightly. "Flitt?" I wait a little while, expecting her to appear again, laughing at her little joke. When she doesn't, I look up at the mushroom sentry to my right.

"Excuse me," I call to him, "do you happen to know where my friend went?"

He turns his head very deliberately and looks down his nose at me. His polished armor glares in the sunlight. His eyes, dark and wide, seem to bore through me, straight into my heart.

"She must follow her own path," he declares, "And you, yours."

I peer ahead at the trail of golden pebbles and up at the sentries. There are at least a dozen of them on each side. For some reason, their presence reminds me of Iren, the Guardian of the North in Kythshire. I understand immediately what that means. If I tried to walk this path without their permission, the results could be deadly for me.

"Azaeli Hammerfel," the sentries announce in unison with a resounding, eerie echo. "The Temperate, Pure of Heart, Reviver of Iren, The Great Protector, Cerion's Ambassador to Kythshire."

As always, I feel my cheeks go warm at the recitation of my titles. I bow my head as the echoing voices fade, slightly embarrassed. These titles were given to me by Crocus in Kythshire two years ago, and I find them a little pretentious.

I look up, ready to move past the titles and get onto the path, but the sentries keep going.

"Knight of His Majesty's Elite, Champion of Princess Margary of Cerion, Ally of Valenor of the Dreaming, Vanquisher of the Prince, The Betrothed of Rian Eldinae: Oathkeeper, Windsaver, Arcane Guardian, Steward of the Wellspring. The Mentalist. The Paladin."

"No," I say, "I…those last ones, they aren't—"

"Do you deny that you are Azaeli Hammerfel, Knight of Cerion?" They interrupt. The two closest to me turn to face me.

"Yes! I mean no, I don't deny that's who I am, but those titles aren't mine. The Mentalist, The Paladin, Vanquisher of the Prince."

"They have been bestowed upon you in this place," they explain, and turn to face each other again.

I close my eyes and try to calm myself. My hands are shaking. Titles are important to the fae. I don't accept them lightly. I didn't vanquish Eron. I'm not a paladin, nor can I call my meager skills of looking into people's minds full-fledged Mentalism. I think of Flitt and her insistence that I embrace that side of me. I wish she was here to guide me. Thinking of her reminds me of the game. The sentries are still once more, and I realize it's my turn to ask a question. I think for a moment and formulate a good one.

"Please, good sentries, will you grant me passage down this path, so that I can join my companion and present myself to the queen?" I venture.

The rest of the sentries turn to face me. They stomp their feet in unison and stand at attention.

"To prove your worth, you must first pass through the Three," the two before me announce. The others join in. "The Gauntlet. The Challenge. The Gateway. State your consent, and we shall begin."

"I agree," I nod. As soon as the words leave my lips, the sentries charge me. A score of them at least, wielding spears or swords. They make a line in front of me and form a wall of wings and armor that stretches several fairies high. The higher ones draw bows, notch gleaming arrows, and aim them at me.

My instincts kick in. I clap my visor over my face and draw my sword. They offer a bow, as is the custom in duels, and I respond with the same. As soon as I straighten, it begins. The first line rushes in as arrows glance off of my armor from above with the unnerving thud of stone on stone.

It feels like a dream. The sentries bear down on me. They surround me on all sides. I start out cautious, but when they don't hold back, I understand quickly this is a serious duel. A matter of survival. I don't have time to wish for Rian's wards or Flitt's light or Mya's song. I understand the test. I'm meant to prove my mettle alone, without the aid of those who usually stand beside me.

The two before me are shield-bearing. They arc their elegant long swords with grace and power. I've trained for this. I know the most effective counters and attacks. Still, their strange fighting style makes it difficult to fall into a rhythm.

These aren't the fairies from children's stories. These fae are fierce warriors, steadfast in their duties. More of them close in on me, and I position myself with my back to a mushroom for cover.

They encroach on me with a wild hunger. I see it in their eyes. This is no test to them. They won't relent. They'll finish me. A shower of arrows rains down on me. One of them flies straight into my visor, glancing my temple. Swords and spears flash, and I count six in melee with me as I press back against the mushroom.

More arrows shoot toward me, but none meet their mark. The blade of my great sword catches on a spear. I twist it up and fling it away, disarming that opponent. I have no time to celebrate the small victory. Blood from my temple drips into my right eye, obscuring my vision. The fairies close in. Their small weapons give them even more of an advantage. My own sword is heavy and difficult to maneuver in such a closed space. The mushroom serves to protect my back, but it also prevents me from using my attacks to my full advantage.

While I do my best to hold my position, a hint of a thought creeps into my mind. I have other abilities I could use to make them stop. I could easily force them to give me passage. I push the thought away as the thin blade of a rapier pierces into my shoulder beneath my pauldron. They aren't using magic. Mentalism would give me an unfair advantage. It'd be uneven.

More uneven than this? I think as I finally defeat one of the sentries with a longsword. It's a short victory. His companion heals him completely, and he comes at me again with even more enthusiasm.

My shoulder is bleeding. I can feel it sticky and warm under my armor. I swing my sword again, but I'm too distracted by my thoughts and I miss the parry.

"Wait," I say breathlessly, "is the object of this duel that I'm meant to defeat all of you?"

I'm answered by laughter and another shower of arrows.

"Of course not. That would be nigh impossible. You must simply reach the other side," the second sentry says as he slams me with his shield.

"She didn't know? That would explain why she hasn't been moving much!" one of the archers giggles. She's dressed in glittering strips of grass that only barely cover her for modesty.

"I was starting to wonder if she wasn't a little thick," chuckles a blue-haired one. She notches an arrow and aims it at me, one eye closed.

"My friend Windy says she is," another one chimes in. She's twice as tall as the other two and looks as though her skinny limbs have been pulled and stretched. "She said," she whispers something to the others, and they float higher in fits of giggles.

A blow to my knees jars me back to the fight. I swing my sword hard and slice through three of my closest attackers. They hardly seem bothered by the wounds. My blade leaves a thin trail of red blood behind, but the gashes it leaves on their skin close as quickly as they open. I growl in frustration.

As much as I hate to admit it, I know I have to run from this fight. I'm outnumbered and outmatched. If the object of this battle is to get to the end of the path, I'm not going to get there by fighting my way through. Again, I consider using my Mentalism, and the idea thrills me. I feel the rush of it, the pull which is so much stronger in this place that's already so full of magic. I don't let it take hold of me, though. Instead, I simply stop fighting.

"I concede," I say. I drive the point of my sword into the earth in front of me and raise my hands to the group of them.

"Maybe she's not stupid after all," one of the archers whispers. I don't spare them a glance. I keep my attention on the first two sentries, who lower their swords looking slightly disappointed. For a moment I fear that they won't accept my yield, but the score of other guards drift back to their mushrooms to stand at attention, and the archers settle back into the leaves above them.

"Very well. We accept your offering," the first sentry to address me nods to the second, who pulls my sword from the earth. The other steps to me and pulls the arrow from my visor. My temple and shoulder tingle with a soft, refreshing sensation as he heals me. "You are a formidable fighter, and your concession has demonstrated that you are wise enough for self-preservation. Walk the path, Azaeli. The Challenge awaits you."

"Thank you," I say with relief. I turn to the second sentry and hold my hand out for my sword. He looks at me with a bemused expression.

"Yes?" he asks, and it dawns on me. Your offering, he'd said. I look at my sword with longing. It has been with me since my sixteenth birthday. We've been through so much together. It isn't just a weapon. It's a part of me. Who am I, without it?

I look from one to the next of them, and my heart starts to race again. They won't give it back to me freely, I'm sure of that. I could force them to with my magic, or I could grapple it away and run. I'm fair in a fist fight…I shake my head. *What is the matter with you?* I ask myself, and memories of the ways that weapon has lead me into distress flood into my memory. I hold too much attachment to it. It's an object, just an object. The thought gives me a pang of guilt. It feels like a betrayal to Cerion, to my father. Still, I've given that weapon too much importance, and it's gotten me in trouble time and again.

The moment I make the decision to let go of it for certain, relief washes over me. I bow to the two remaining sentries.

"Thank you," I whisper. Without a glance behind me, I turn to walk the golden path.

Leaving my sword behind is easier than I would have thought. With every step away from it, I feel lighter. The path ahead is dappled with sunlight that dances over the stones, making me feel as though I'm walking across a golden pool. It reminds me of the glimpse of Kythshire's wellspring that I caught years ago. The familiarity of it soothes me. I don't worry about being weaponless. For some reason, I'm at peace with that now.

The path ends at a curtain of vines bearing fragrant blooms of white and yellow. I take a deep breath and gently push them aside to step through.

The air here is much thicker with magic. Towering in the distance is the closed bud of the queen's palace. The ever-rising sun casts a sharp shadow of it across the forest ahead and tumbles onto soft, green grass. The scene would be lovely were it not for the rocky chasm which slices the earth at my toes, barring my access to the other side.

I yelp and jump back, clinging to the vines to steady myself as vertigo sets in from being so close to the cliff's edge.

"Flitt?" I venture, remembering her promise to meet me on the other side. My heart sinks when I'm met with silence. I'm not finished yet. I need to face this alone, too.

There is no bridge across, that I can see. Thinking I could possibly climb down the cliff face, I hold tight to the vines and lean forward. I can't see the bottom due to a thick, swirling mist quite a way down. The rock face of the chasm is sheer, with no place to grip and climb. If there's water beneath the mist, I think, that presents another problem.

I remember my first trip to Kythshire with Rian. When he realized anything was possible there, he was able to soar through the air.

"Always with the flying," I murmur, my heart racing. Reluctantly, I let go of the vines and edge myself to the lip of the chasm. I close my eyes and imagine myself floating up.

"Huh," I say with a hint of relief when nothing happens. I don't relish the thought of flying, anyway.

I pace along the edge, looking for anything that might help me cross. It's certainly too far to jump it, even if I had a pole for leverage. I peer across to the other side, and that's when I see the lever. Standing beside it is a squat, round old man with shiny red cheeks and a beard that grows to his toes.

"Hello, sir!" I call across to him, but he doesn't seem to hear me. He just stands by the lever, his hand ready to pull it. I run until I'm directly across from him, and wave my arms. His gaze is set straight ahead. He doesn't seem to see me, either. "Good day!" I shout louder. His only reply is to rock back on his feet and whistle merrily.

"Could you pull that lever, please?" I shout.

He cocks his head to the side and cups a hand around his ear.

"I said could you pull the lever?" I yell as loud as I can.

His only reply is to shrug and start up again with the whistling. I groan in annoyance and shake my head. I know where this is going. They've been pushing me to it since I arrived here.

I focus on the man and reach my thoughts out to him. In my mind, I conjure the idea of golden strings. The rush of magic floods through me and bursts forth easily. The strings loop around the man's hand. His eyes go even more vacant than they had been. He grips the lever, guided by my golden threads, and pulls it up.

The ground beneath my feet starts to rumble. I fall back against the vines and hold them tightly as a massive bridge scrapes and thunders up the chasm wall. The golden threads break. Across the way, the man shakes his head in confusion. The rush of magic fades, leaving me feeling empty and tired.

The bridge looks sturdy enough as it settles into place, but there are no rails or ropes along the side. It's simply a slab of stone just wide enough for one person to cross over. I hesitate only for a moment before I step carefully onto its smooth, slippery surface.

I take my time in my effort to keep from slipping into the endless chasm below. I'm so busy concentrating on not falling that I don't notice when the man across the way scowls and slams the lever down again. The bridge beneath me shifts and rumbles and starts its descent. I drop onto my stomach and try hard to cling to the stone, but there's no place to grip the wet, smooth surface.

"Stop!" I scream. On the edge of the chasm, the man rocks casually back and forth on his heels. I reach out again with the golden strings and grasp his hand. The lever goes up. The bridge reverses. When it stops at the top again, I get to my feet. I brush my fear aside and sprint the rest of the way. The golden strings break, and the man scowls and pushes the lever down one last time. The bridge rumbles and quakes. I close my eyes, leap from several paces away, and land with a thud in the cushion of soft grass on the other side.

The bridge disappears into the mist of the chasm, and I roll onto my side, gasping for breath. Beside me, the man continues to rock and whistle as though nothing has happened. I glare up at him.

"You could have killed me," I yell. He tilts his head just slightly and stops whistling.

"Someone there?" he asks vaguely.

"This is nonsense," I grumble. "What kind of place has an old man who can't see or hear guard their only means of entry?"

"Best keep your temper if you're off to see the Queen," the man snickers.

"Can you hear me or not?" I push myself to my feet.

"What's that?" he asks. He looks away from me, grinning. I get the sense that he can hear just fine, he's just being difficult.

"If you can hear me, why didn't you push the lever when I asked you to?"

"You'll find the gate through the trees there," he says without bothering to acknowledge my question. "Best hurry up now, mustn't keep them waiting. Good day," he says merrily, and promptly vanishes.

Chapter Sixteen
THE LAIR

Tib

Mold and filth. Rot. Decay. Waste. Blood.

The stench is overwhelming. My nose comes to before the rest of me. My stomach follows, churning. Next, the pain. My head is ready to split. My ears are ringing. My heart is racing. I want to jump up and run, but I don't. I lie still. I take stock of myself, one bit at a time. Head throbbing. Shoulders sore, but working. Arms? Muscles twitching. Hands? Bound. Legs? Bound. Feet? Seem okay. I take a deep breath and something scratches my lips. A bag over my head. Rough, like burlap.

I force myself not to panic or move. Instead I try to figure out where I am.

It's dark, but that could be the burlap.

I'm lying on something hard. The floor. It's cold. Wet.

I'm not alone. Nearby, someone sobs. A girl.

Celli. My stomach churns again, this time with anger. He got her, too.

"He's awake. Get him up," a deep voice orders.

I try to fight, but the men that lift me by my arms are too strong. They set me on my feet. They pull off the burlap and my eyes sting as I blink into the sudden torch light. The first thing I notice when my eyes adjust is Celli, tied up just like me, slumped against a wall. Her head's bagged up, too. The same type of bag the Sorcerer put Eron's in. I shiver when I remember the blood dripping from it as he held it, watching the fight. Celli's shivering, too. It's cold in here.

There's something else. A void. I can't feel Celli or the men holding me. It's like they don't exist. The room is strange. A cell, with walls of dark, hammered metal. The floor is metal, too, and slick with water mixed with blood. My blood, probably. Some of Celli's too, I'd bet.

A shift in the shadows beside me catches my eye. A man, all dressed in black. Handles of knives glint along his torso. One eye is covered with a patch. Visions of my past flash in my memory. This man, throwing knives into a post, guarding a place I needed to get into.

This man, chasing me into the shack, closing in on me, screaming as Mevyn's spear plunged into his eye. I remember him from that night. Dub.

His lip curls into a sneer as he sees the recognition cross my face. He grabs me by the front of the collar and lifts my feet from the floor.

"Been waiting to see you for some time, Tib Nullen. We've got a score to settle," he growls through clenched teeth. "What's it they say? An eye for an eye?"

I hear his knife sliding from its sheath. With his free hand, he presses its sharp point to my lower eyelid. I don't dare fight. If it were to move even the slightest bit...

I glance at Celli as Dub bears down with his blade and the other two men tighten their hold on me. I could slip into the half-realm and grab her. I don't have the ability to move from place to place like Azi and Rian do, but I could at least hide us both until we could figure out a way out of here.

The problem is the step. I always step into it, like Mevyn taught me to. A step through the cobwebs, into hiding. I wonder, as Dub presses harder and a bead of blood drips down my cheek, whether I could do it without actually stepping.

I squeeze my eyes shut and try, but nothing happens. No shift. No cobwebs. It's empty. Like it doesn't exist. I think of Mevyn in Sunteri. Of Valenor in the dreaming. I have always felt like they were nearby, like they would come if I ever needed them. Like I had their protection, somehow. If I called out to them, would they hear me? Could they help? Do I dare try it and risk them coming to this place?

"Enough," a different voice barks from outside.

Dub lowers his blade with a grunt of annoyance and we both look toward the door.

The man there is a Sorcerer, obviously. The Mark creeping across his forehead announces that proudly. He's very tall and thin, and his gray robes hang on his frame. His skin is white. His hair is white. When he turns his head slightly, I see the point of his ear. Elf.

I swallow the lump in my throat. All the elves I've met have been peaceful, gentle, and kind. They respect magic. They're good. This Sorcerer is a walking contradiction. It's disturbing. Confusing. My breath catches. I can't stop staring at him. He notices. His lips curve into a graceful, terrible smile.

Through the bars of the cell he watches me with a mix of curiosity, fear, and something else. A need to own. To control. It makes me feel like an animal in a cage. Right away I know what he's after. He wants to keep me. Tame me. I'll die before I let him.

"Bring him," he orders, "and the girl."

Dub crosses and hefts Celli up. He doesn't let her walk. Instead, he slings her over his shoulder. She doesn't squirm or fight. She must be scared or hurt, because that's not the Celli I know. The two holding me lift me up too, so my toes drag along the floor as they carry me into the hallway.

As soon as I cross the threshold I feel the shift. The magic assaults me so much that I can't breathe. It seeps in from every crevice of this place, strong and powerful. Wards. Spells. Shadows. Power. Darkness. Death. Waking. Desire. Manipulation. Sorcery. I feel all of it pressing in around me, taking up the air, drowning out the sound. I'm sure nobody else notices the sudden flood of arcane power. Celli doesn't. She just lies limp.

I try hard to catch my breath and notice the Sorcerer watching me again with that same curiosity. He sees how it affects me. I can almost hear him thinking about how he can use my abilities for his own twisted cause, whatever that might be.

It makes me furious. If my arms weren't tied, I'd fight them all. I'd wring his skinny white neck. They try to drag me forward, but I refuse to be meek like Celli. I don't care that my legs are tied. I squirm and kick and swing my bound hands. With my heels I bash one guy in the kneecap. With my fists clenched together I slam the other in the nose.

They both curse and throw me onto the floor. One of them presses his knee to the back of my neck.

"Try that again," he barks into my ear, "and I'll gut you."

"Now, now, Jin, no need to be barbaric. Yet." The Sorcerer laughs softly. Jin presses his knee harder into my neck. The elf steps closer. His soft boots come to rest right at the tip of my nose. I look past them, into the cell across from the one I was just dragged from. A dozen terrified faces stare back at me. Two of them I recognize. Griff. Mikken. So this is where they ended up.

"Come now," the Sorcerer's tone is quiet and dark, "Tib, if you will agree to come peacefully, I shall allow your bindings removed."

"Back off," I scream and spit on his boot. "I don't bargain with Sorcerers!"

"Have it your way," he laughs and walks away. Jin, or at least I assume it's Jin, grabs me by the hair and whacks my head hard on the stone floor.

When I wake up again, I'm propped against a wall in a room like the first one. Another cell, except this one has stone walls instead of metal. It's empty except for the mirror in the center of it, and Celli next to me. Her head rests on my shoulder. The bag's off her now. We're all tied up together. Her left wrist is tied to my right wrist, and my right ankle is tied to her left one. Our other arms and legs are shackled to chains that attach to a ring in the floor in front of us.

I'm not sure if she's awake until I hear her sniffle. My shoulder is wet. I wonder how long we've been here. How long she's been crying.

"Celli?" I whisper. She shakes her head slightly.

"Don't," she warns, "they'll hear."

Now that she knows I'm awake, she sits up and moves away from me as far as the chains will allow.

"Who are they?" I ask her. She shakes her head again.

"Just do what they say," she says wearily. "Whatever they say. Please. They said if you don't do what they want, they'll kill me."

Her eyes meet mine and the fear in them makes me look away, to the mirror in the center of the room.

It's magical. I can feel the flow of it shimmering on the surface of the glass. It feels like a portal, or a way of seeing more than what there is. As I watch it, the reflection of the stone wall across from it changes. I nudge Celli and point.

"Look," I whisper. "It's Nessa's house."

She and I crawl closer and peer in at the scene that unfolds. It's sunset. Nearly dusk. A dark form passes by in the street. A gloved hand emerges from dark robes and conjures a ball of fire. With a flick of a wrist, the fire bursts forth. It smashes through the windowpane into the Ganvents' dining room. The figure vanishes as the fire catches. Black smoke billows from the window. The fire spreads through the first floor quickly. The windows of the sitting room shatter into the streets.

"It's a trick," I whisper. "It has to be. It can't be real." I watch in horror. I can almost smell the smoke. That's when I see her in the upstairs window. Saesa. She throws the shutters open and looks down into the street. Emmie is beside her, crying. Saesa shakes her head. Scoops up Emmie. Ducks back inside.

"Saesa!" I scream and fight the chains that hold me back. It's really happening, I'm sure of it. It isn't a spell or an illusion. I'd know it if it was. That mirror is a portal. If I can get through it, I can save them. "Help me, Celli!" I shout and yank at the chains with all of my strength. Celli does her best, but we aren't strong enough to break the bonds.

The flames lick higher in the Ganvent manse. The fire brigade comes, but they're close to useless with their buckets and pumps.

"Where are the Mages?" Celli grunts as we try again to pull the chain link from the loop in the floor. "They're always there to stop a fire."

I don't answer. I'm too caught up in the scene in the mirror, where some of the brigade rescue emerges from the house. Two of them carry Nessa. Her dress is black and burnt, her skin covered in soot. They wrap her in blankets and run off with her. Probably to the Conclave. More of them come out. They get Ruben, Garsi… both are coughing and black as coal. Both get wrapped up and raced off to the healers. I wait and watch, but two more men come out empty-handed. One shakes his head at the other. The house crumbles into itself.

"No!" I scream again, "Saesa!"

I charge at the mirror until my wrist and ankle are bloody and raw, until Celli finally pulls me back and shakes some sense into me.

"She's fine, she got out. I'm sure she got out, Tib. There's a back door, right?" She forces me to look away from the mirror, to look at her instead. "Right?" she whispers again.

"Right," I say hoarsely. "She got out. She had to."

I look again at the mirror and see something curious. Zeze, just her face, just a flash, looking right at me. Our eyes meet, and the mirror goes black.

"Curious," the voice of the Sorcerer hisses around us. "He is not immune to visions of what might come to pass."

The elf Sorcerer steps through the mirror. He's dressed the same as the figure that sent the fireball through Nessa's window.

"No bargains with Sorcerers, you say?" he laughs. "Did my little scene convince you, perhaps, that it might be prudent to consider a slight exception to your policy, Dreamstalker Tib? Who knows what may happen, if you refuse."

Chapter Seventeen

PALACE OF THE DAWN

Azi

"Flitt?" I call out to the light beaming through the white birch trunks. It shines with the purity and intensity I've come to recognize with her tiny, perfect radiance. There are no motes of dust or swirls of smoke to obscure it. I rush forward, wanting to be closer to it, knowing that the hard part is over and on the other side of these trees is where I'll find her. Just through the trees is the gate we'll go through together to get to the palace.

I shield my eyes when I finally come through the forest to stand before what I can only assume are the sweeping gates. I can't see a thing. Everything is dancing light and color.

"Flitt?" I call again, and the light beams so intensely that I have to squeeze my eyes shut. It glares and pulses with a strange warmth that draws me in and pushes me away all at once.

"Azi!" Flitt's sudden squeaky voice makes me jump. "You did it!"

She emerges from the light the same size as I am and I rush to her and throw my arms around her. I feel as though I've been alone for days, and I'm exhausted by the thought of it. I'm so relieved to see her that I don't bother to hide my tears.

"Wings, ow," Flitt winces and shrugs and tries to wiggle away but I hug her tighter, afraid if I let go she'll leave me alone to fend for myself again in this strange fairy proving ground.

"*Azi*," she whispers to my mind and flicks her eyes toward the gate. "*You're embarrassing me. They're watching, you know.*"

The gate of the palace tower over us, gilt and shining. Its lace-like design sparkles with drops of dew like a spider's web. Beyond it, the white rosebud towers of the palace stretch up to the sky, washed in the ever-present lavender and pink glow of the rising sun.

They're watching. Two shining sentries flank the gates on either side. They tower over us like giants standing at full attention, their dark hazel eyes fixed on us both. Their ornate spears are crossed over the threshold, barring our entry.

"Ow," Flitt whines and wiggles again and I let go reluctantly.

"Sorry," I murmur as she reaches back and rubs her wings.

"You nearly crushed them," she pouts.

"No I didn't, I was careful," I say, a little annoyed.

"Well, you could have let go when I said," she crosses her arms. "Typical."

"Sorry!" I scoff in disbelief. "Excuse me for being relieved to see you after all that!"

"Funny way of showing it, smashing my wings." She looks behind her and waves her glittering wings slowly as if checking for damage. I don't know what to say to her sudden annoyance of me, so I just stand and wait.

Just as I'm about to ask her what comes next, the soft sound of chimes dances through the air around us. It's so soothing and peaceful that I nearly forget why I'm standing here. The sentries raise their spears and drive the ends of them into the mossy green earth before them. They give us an abrupt nod of approval.

"No harm done!" Flitt chirps, grabs my hand, and tugs me forward. Her sudden change in spirit makes my head spin.

As we approach, the sparkling doors swing open to reveal the entry hall of the palace. I gasp at its grandeur as I peer inside. The hall is so vast and splendid that I find myself pausing on the threshold. Flitt does, too. Even with the permission of the sentries and the invitation of the open doors, I can't bring myself to step from the earthy moss to the glossy white stone. I don't want to taint the perfection of it with my presence.

It's magic, I know it is, yet I can't help but obey its command. I stand together with Flitt, entranced by the endless pure ivory arches that stretch up into the pink sky and the lines and lines of carved pillars that seem to go on to infinity, each one flanked by two fairy guards dressed in silver and gold. The light of this place washes over me and I drink it in slowly, savoring the feeling as it seeps into every pore of my skin.

Power, light, love, peace, beauty, compassion. This magic, these wards encompass everything that is good. As drawn to it as I am, I still can't bring myself to spoil it by entering.

"Enter," a voice drifts from within, so sweet it brings tears to my eyes.

I lean forward and will my foot to raise and step, but I stop with my knee in mid-air. The guards closest to us snicker softly, and their chuckling invites more of the same from within the great hall. Soon, the sound of fairy laughter echoes across the arches and columns, flooding my ears, further enchanting me with the magic of this place.

Beside me, Flitt giggles and takes my hand again. The moment she does, all goes quiet. I feel something change between us, something I can't describe. It's as though the bond between us just in that simple gesture has solidified.

"*What was that?*" I push to her as the command of the warding magic fades away.

"You know fairies," she replies aloud. "They had to be sure we were the right fit. Come on."

I look down at my raised foot and this time when I try to step forward it comes easy to me. Flitt's hand squeezes mine and the unseen fairies inside the palace applaud. The guards each stomp a single foot and point within, toward the endlessness of the great hall. Flitt bobs along beside me, still tugging my hand as she goes. I want to ask her to explain, but I get the distinct sense that I should remain quiet, so I do.

We walk for what seems like ages, until when I look behind me I can no longer see the gate, and when I look ahead there is nothing but pillars and arches and splashes of the pink light of dawn. After a while, the peace and grandeur of this place begins to fade, and I find myself growing annoyed as my thoughts drift back to Cerion and the plight I was torn from.

The sensation of my mind inside of the prince's is the first thought that comes to me. As I walk hand in hand with Flitt, I remember the feeling of the ax on the back of his neck. I relive the darkness that followed. The fear, the panic of the people. I recall Rian's command to Flitt to escape with me.

Despite the peaceful magic of this palace, my heart is racing. I feel the anger rising in me, the shame of running, the worry, the fear. Sorcery has returned to Cerion, after generations of peace. The existence of dark magic so powerful, with such little concern for our common people, is terrifying. That they would be so bold as to attack such an important gathering with the Royal family present is even more so.

I remember the faces of the common folk during the trial. Men and women, hardworking, loyal to His Majesty the King. Commoners and their children who live kindly and honestly. People who give to one another and care for those less fortunate. I remember their terror in the quick moments before Flitt whisked me away. I remember the prince and his strange words. I remember Rian, standing ready with his spells, commanding Flitt to take me. Rian, who always stands beside me. Rian.

I can't bear to think of the outcome of the attack. We had our Mages there, but they ought to have been able to prevent whatever evil that was. Their wards alone should have kept it out. I think of Rian again and how on edge he's been. I think of the visions he showed me of his life at the Academy since the battle of the keep at Kythshire. I think of his face, how it's changed since then. How young he was before, and how much older now. But still he has that glint in his eye, that mischief, that self-assured smirk. It's rarer these days, but still it makes my heart skip to think of it.

I don't realize that I've reached the end of the hall, or that the steps to the throne of the Fairy Queen stretch out before me. I don't notice the mass of onlooking fairies who line the pillars and hover in groups all the way up to the ceiling. I don't hear them whisper or see the twinkle of pink light that glances off of their wings. I'm unaware of Flitt's hand holding mine tightly, or the queen who watches from her throne high above.

I don't feel my feet on the steps or know that I am nearing Her Majesty. I walk in a trance, my thoughts still on Cerion, on the High Court, on Rian, my memories telling the story of my recent past.

I don't notice that her steel-gray eyes are fixed on mine, or see the golden tendrils that drift between us, pulling these scenes to her. Showing her everything she wishes to see about Cerion and its people.

Rian and I are together again, lying in the soft, cool grass of the Forest Park, our noses touching as we gaze at one another. I feel his arms around me warm and soothing. I fall into his eyes and see things he never showed me. The Academy and its workings shuffle between us like cards in a deck. Secrets I never would have asked to know, rules and mandates and policies strictly adhered to by the Mages of Cerion. Regulations put in place for the safety of the fairies, for the preservation of the Wellspring of Kythshire.

I see the Mages who value these rules like a sacred canon, and I see the others who treat the rules as loose guidelines. Faces of men and women who have dedicated their lives to their work. Most of them are familiar to me simply as acquaintances of my uncle. I see the Mark on a few, covered by their high collars, a sign of their overreaching, a brand of their thirst for power that is not theirs to take. These faces imprint on my mind and linger.

I slowly become aware of Her Majesty the Queen as the face of a

Mage fades between us to be replaced by her own. As the golden tendrils linger, I take in the perfect line of her lightly blushed high cheekbones and the way the light catches on her white-painted eyelashes. Her rosy lips smile playfully as slowly she closes her eyes and breaks the connection between us.

I don't feel angry or violated. The knowledge she sought was her right, her claim. Not an imposition, for the knowledge of Cerion's Mages was borrowed from her people, and therefore hers to own.

I'm left with a sense of serenity so delicious that I can do nothing but stand in awe of the woman on the throne. Her gown is white petals and birch bark and dove feathers that cascade to the floor like a waterfall. Her crown is diamond and ivory and dew-kissed twig and lacewing held by loose, flyaway locks of spun-gold hair. Curls of the same tumble down her bare shoulders and reflect in the shimmer of her wings, which are as delicate as a dragonfly's. I have never seen wings as impressive as hers. They dance with a light even more colorful and bright than Flitt's and they're twice as broad as her arm's reach.

"My Sunbeam," the queen's voice is the whisper of a sweet spring breeze and the tinkle of a chime. She holds her arms out to Flitt, and I'm surprised when my fairy companion doesn't dive into them. Instead, Flitt looks at the queen with a hint of caution and something else I can't place. Actually I can, but I'm so shocked by it that I can't believe Flitt could have the audacity to show it. Defiance.

All around us the fairies in the hall hover silently, leaning in, waiting. They sense it, too, this tension between Flitt and the queen.

"Why, little one," the queen tilts her head to the side, causing her crown to jingle and glitter. "Long has it been since we held you in our arms. Why do you deny us your embrace?"

Flitt tightens her grip on my hand. She tugs me along with her as she leans in and allows the queen to hug her. This close to the queen, I can feel her power like the beams of the sun itself. I fear if I linger too long, I might be burned by it. The palace erupts into applause and sighs of approval as the queen hugs Flitt closer.

"I missed you, Memi," Flitt whispers only loud enough for the three of us to hear. "But you shouldn't have done that to Azi. She didn't even know it was happening. People have different rules than we do. You've been away from them too long to remember."

"Indeed, but there were things we needed to see," the queen says. "No matter. One who has more vast knowledge than she is being tested even as we speak. This one has been well-trained in the human ways of magic." She gazes past Flitt to the great hall for a moment, and then turns her attention back to the colorful fairy. "We are proud of you, our little one. We have heard tell of your accomplishments." She lets Flitt go after one more squeeze, and right away Flitt takes a step back and pulls me with her.

"Yet," the queen says with a hint of sadness, "there is little time for happy reunions. The Mage approaches."

She makes a graceful motion with her hand, and Flitt and I turn toward the sweeping hall to watch. At the queen's command, the air shimmers before us to form a portal or a looking glass. It is large enough to show the reflection of much of the throne and of the queen, myself, and Flitt, and it hovers in mid-air for all to see. After a moment, its surface ripples like the waves of a pool and our reflections give way to a completely different scene.

I gasp as the image shifts to that of a familiar figure: Auburn hair and blue Mage robes which hang on his narrow frame. At his shoulder, a fairy in glinting green armor whispers to him. The figure turns to face us, and Rian's eyes meet mine through the fairy portal.

"Rian!" I whisper, tears springing to my eyes. I rush toward his image, dragging Flitt along with me. I know it's only a spell, a vision, but I need to be close to him. I need feel his arms around me. I take in every detail of him. His robes are torn at the shoulder and one bell sleeve is splattered with blood. His face has been singed on the left side, and he walks with a slight limp as he hurries forward.

"What now?" Rian asks Shush, his tone urgent and hushed.

"Now we part ways, my friend, and meet on the other side," the fairy whispers. "Take heed. I'll see you there."

Rian's tests are vastly different from my own. Rather than a path guarded by sentries, he's faced with a single, ragged-looking old man with a long white beard.

"Circle and stone, flat and yet round, I speak with no voice, yet knowledge abounds," the man says to him, without any formal greeting at all. "What am I?"

"You are a scroll," Rian answers.

"I fall with a flutter, I rise with the wind, yet I can do nothing without flesh and skin," the man watches him through narrowed eyes. "What am I?"

"You are a feather," Rian answers.

"A golden pool, a blackened heart, a bruis-ed fool, a stolen spark," the man tugs his beard and leans in. "What am I?"

"You are Mage Mark," Rian answers.

They go on this way for what seems like hours, the man offering a riddle and Rian answering, until his head dips low and his eyes droop with exhaustion. Though most of the fairies watching from the palace are still engaged, several of them nod off in mid air, snoring softly. As the man recites yet another riddle, Rian dozes and stumbles to the side as he startles awake again.

"Please, sir," he interrupts, rubbing his temples. "I have answered your riddles time and again, and I don't think I've answered a single one incorrectly."

"That is so," the man replies.

"To what end?" Rian asks.

"What end do you seek?" the man rocks back on his heels, humming merrily. The grueling game of riddles doesn't seem to have affected him the same way has Rian.

"I was lead to believe this was some sort of test," Rian replies. "Have I passed it?"

"No indeed," the man chuckles. "But almost."

Around us in the gallery, the fairies are laughing. Some of them wake and chuckle with the others. Even Flitt grins with amusement as she watches the exchange in the portal.

"Almost?" I whisper. "How many more questions are there?"

"Just one," Flitt replies, "but it has to be the right one."

"I sing in the sunshine and the rain. I soothe in the summer. In winter I'm wicked again. What am I?" The man's eyes glint with mischief.

"You are the wind," Rian answers and pinches the bridge of his nose. His fingers spark and he yelps and shoves his balled fists into his robes.

"I follow behind you or I can lead you. My way can be washed by the sea or blown by the wind. I can remain for a year or a day. What am I?"

"You are a footprint," Rian scowls. "Now, wait!" he holds up a hand to interrupt. "No more. I've answered enough of your riddles."

"Perhaps," the man's laughter joins the mirth of the fairies among us in the palace. "And yet one question remains unanswered."

Rian takes a deep breath and stares at the man for a long time. He blows it out with an exasperated sigh.

"What end do I seek?" Rian repeats the riddler's earlier question.

"What end do you seek?" the man nods.

"I wish to gain passage to the palace," Rian replies. His hands inside his robes crackle. A bit of smoke puffs out from the edges of his vest. "Please, I seek my companions. The Lady Knight Azaeli and the fairy Flitt. If they passed this way, will you allow me to seek them out, please?"

"Indeed they have, and in asking to pass, you have earned the passage you seek." The man grins, steps aside, and bows.

"You mean to tell me all I had to do was ask for you to let me through?" Rian groans. "We've been at this for hours. How many riddles did I answer?"

"Four hundred and seventy-three," the bearded man replies. "Impressive."

"Impressive, but pointless," Rian shakes his head, "unless you meant to stall me and keep me from urgent matters."

"Not at all," the man shakes his head apologetically. "The point, my dear Mage, was for us to see you for who you are. You have shown us your wit and knowledge, yes. Your wisdom, indeed. But also your tolerance, your resolve, your restraint. Not once did you lose patience with my riddles. Not once did you think to blast me out of the way, which is well within your power. No. Instead you were respectful. You kept your head. And when it all stopped making sense, you questioned. We have seen all of you that we needed to, and now you may proceed to the gates. Hurry. They are waiting for you."

Rian hesitates just for a moment, slack-jawed, as the man waves him through. It isn't until the riddler vanishes from view that Rian shakes his head in exasperation and rushes off in the direction that he was motioned.

"Fairies," he murmurs under his breath as he jogs through a thicket of trees and is met with a wall of glass.

From our angle at the mirror, we can see the extent of the next test laid out before him: a series of walls of different make. There are glass walls, stone walls, walls made of towering trees, walls of ice and fire. Rian's fingertips crackle as he stands before the first one: a wall of glass. I understand it right away, even as Rian rushes along the length of the wall, looking for a door in or an end to go around. It's endless, though, just like my chasm was. He isn't meant to go over or around. He's meant to use his magic to make his way through.

I cling to Flitt beside me. Together we watch him grow more frantic as he stalks along the glass wall.

"He won't cast a spell here," I whisper to her. "He won't risk it."

He doesn't, either. Not for a long time. More hours. Finally, he turns his back to the glass and slides down it until he's sitting in the moss. He hugs his knees and presses his forehead to them. At his sides he flexes his fingers, which pulse and crackle with the magic that begs to burst forth.

"Oh, Rian," I call out with a sigh, my heart breaking for him.

In the forest, with the glass to his back, Rian raises his head. He looks around. He jumps to his feet.

"Azi?" he calls.

"Rian?" I cry out to the mirror. "Can you hear me?"

All around us, the fairies in the great hall murmur and whisper with excitement. The dozing fae pop up and look around. Most of them drift closer to the portal, gazing with great interest at the Mage within.

"He should not be able to," the queen says from behind us, "but true love has ways that are yet unknown, even to us. Tell him, Azaeli, that he is permitted to display his skill. I fear if you do not, we shall spend an eternity waiting."

"Rian!" I step forward. Flitt drifts alongside me, still gripping my hand. "Rian, it's all right. Show them your magic. They want to see."

At first I think he'll continue to restrain himself, but he steps forward to the glass and presses his palms to it, closing his eyes. The spell he whispers is slow and methodical, and soon the glass glows yellow and red and melts away leaving a hole just large enough for him to step through.

Next comes the stone, which he causes to quake and thunder until it cracks and crumbles to dust. He faces the wall of trees and casts another spell to guide the trunks to grow apart from each other just wide enough for him to step through. The fire he faces with water, the ice he faces with fire from the wall he'd just defeated. With each pass through a wall, the palace erupts into cheers and Rian seems to gain more confidence and control.

By the time he passes through the final wall, that of water, he is grinning from ear to ear. I don't realize he knows for certain he has an audience until he turns to face the gates and offers a bow with a flourish of both hands.

"Don't get show-offy," Shush gusts as he comes to Rian's side before the gates.

I gasp at the sight of the wind fairy, who has grown himself to Rian's size if not a little taller. Rian seems just as surprised to see him appear in such a way. As Shush moves closer to him, Rian's robes swirl around him in a cyclone and his hair whips into his face. He raises his hands to stop Shush's approach.

"Could you tone it down a little?" he asks him.

"Sorry," Shush whispers, "sure." He shrugs his carapace-clad shoulders and the wind dies down to a breeze.

"So what now?" Rian asks.

"Just step inside," Shush whispers as the sentries plant their spears and motion the two through.

The portal shimmers and fades, and beyond it at the far end of the endless hall I see a pinpoint of light as the gates open. He's so far away and so tiny that I could cover him from my view with the finest point of a quill, but his form is unmistakable.

"Rian," I gasp and take off down the stairs. At the end of the hallway I hear him running, too. Flitt's hand is still in mine, and rather than let go or try to stop me, she squeals with delight as she floats along beside and I throw myself into Rian's open arms in front of the audience of fairies.

"Azi," he whispers to me with both relief and hunger. His lips are on mine before I know what's happening, and his hands are in my hair. He kisses me urgently and gratefully, with little regard for the fairy audience that whoops and sings and cheers.

"Love, young and pure. Love at its most powerful," the queen's voice carries a hint of amusement over the hall. "Love, rising above all else. Love and light. To the Dawn."

"To the Dawn," the shouts of fairies is deafening. It rings out over us as Rian pulls me closer and deepens his kiss.

"*To the Dawn*," we reply in unison in each other's thoughts, refusing to let each other go. The moment is too sweet, too perfect, too filled with pleasure and relief. I could stay here locked in his embrace forever, bathed in the pink light of the palace, washed in fairy song and laughter until the end of our days.

Chapter Eighteen
SLATE SKY

Tib

"What do you want?" I growl at the elf as he stalks closer. I try to shuffle myself so I'm between him and Celli, but the shackles make it difficult.

The elves of Ceras'lain usually emanate peace and light. Not this one. He's the complete opposite. Chaos. Fear. Power. Even his presence makes Celli cower and shake. I don't feel it the way she does. I can sense it, but it doesn't affect me.

The closer he gets, the stronger his magic presses in on us. Celli whimpers and buries her face in her hands. I square my shoulders and glare at him. Think of ways I could overcome him. They took my knives, but I have chains. He's tall but he's skinny. Weaker than I am, probably, physically.

"Back off," I bark at him as he stoops closer to us both. Close enough for me to hit him. I ball my fist and swing hard. I hit him in the throat. He stumbles back, gasping.

"You filthy wretch!" he screams and thrusts his palm out toward us. Fingers bent like claws crackle. Lightning sparks from them and shoots across the room. It hits me like a soft breeze, a tingle. I start to laugh, but Celli's screams twist my stomach as she takes the full force of the spell. She writhes on the floor in pain, her skin singed and smoking, her eyes rolled back in her head. The smell of her burning flesh is sickening

"Celli!" I scoop her up, but she doesn't move. I shake her frantically and her head lolls back against my arm. "Please, wake up. I'm sorry!"

"Do not provoke me, Nullen," the elf sneers, rubbing his throat. He straightens to his full height again. Tries to regain some of his dignity. "You may be immune to our powers, but we have ways of convincing you all the same. I have already provided two such examples. Perhaps you require yet another?"

He stays away from me. Out of my reach. Even though it got Celli hurt, which I regret, I know I've had a small triumph. Sorcerers depend on their wards to protect them. They get so used to that power they take it for granted. I bet if I could get my hands on a weapon, if I could get out of these chains, I could take this elf out before he knew what was happening.

I could go through this fortress or whatever it is, and figure out what's going on here. So much darkness. So much power in one place. They've got to be planning something big. I remember what Valenor said, what Loren said, what the healer in the Conclave said. Predictions of some great threat. Darkness coming. This has to be the source of it, and now they have me. They must need me for something. If I can find out what it is, maybe I can stop them.

I look at Celli and she blinks up at me blankly and coughs. His spell could have killed her. I think of the fire at Nessa's. If I keep refusing, they'll just keep hurting everyone else around me. I lay her down gently onto the stone floor and push myself to my feet. I meet the eyes of the elf Sorcerer. His Mark has grown already since our first meeting in the metal room. The sight of it makes me sick with hate. I have too much of a history with Sorcerers. This could be my chance to put an end to them once and for all.

"Let Celli and those other kids go," I tell him, "and I'll do whatever you want."

"The spoken word in this hall is as good as a blood pact. Do you understand?" The elf eyes me hungrily. "Once you make such a bargain, it cannot be undone. You shall be compelled to keep it under any circumstance."

Beside me, Celli struggles to sit up. I crouch to prop her and she offers me a weak smile. I think on the Sorcerer's words and wonder whether that sort of magic would affect me. I think of Celli and Mikken and Griff. Getting them out of here would be a small triumph, but what if these Sorcerers want me to do something awful? Like kidnapping Margy? Or sneaking into Kythshire for them, or doing something to Sunteri's Wellspring? Or getting into the Dreaming? Or infiltrating His Majesty's Elite to spy? They probably know about all of these connections I have. That's why they want me.

I chew my lip thoughtfully. Are the lives of these three kids worth a promise like that? Is the chance to destroy them worth making a bargain with them? I narrow my eyes at this filth who calls himself an elf. He waits, watching me with that same hunger. That need to tame. To own.

"Show me," I say to him. "Show me what you want me to do. I

won't agree to anything until I know."

"*Do it.*" A hint of a voice echoes in the elf's mind and his eyes flick to mine as if wanting to know whether I heard. I try to seem like I didn't. That will be useful later, I bet.

"Come," he says to me. With a snap of his fingers, the shackles on my hands and feet fall away. I rub my wrist as I jump to my feet. My heart races as he turns his back to me to lead me out. I could tackle him. Overcome him. Choke the life out of him. I don't, though. I have a better idea.

The walls here aren't metal like the last room. They're stone, dark and polished. I close my eyes. I step forward through the cobwebs, into the shadows. Out of sight of the Sorcerer. He doesn't notice at first. He waves his hand and the door opens. A pair of guards flanking the door turn to face him. One of them glances inside.

"Sir?" she asks hesitantly. I glance behind me at Celli, who lies on the floor, breathing slowly.

"What?" the elf barks.

"The boy?" the guard points her gaunted finger into the cell.

The elf spins around. His eyes search the room. I creep along the wall and glance at the door. I could slip out and explore. I could find out what's going on here without having to risk making any pact.

Then the Sorcerer's fingers crackle again. His eyes glint wickedly. He points at Celli. She's still weak.

"Another spell would end this wretch, don't you agree, Nullen? Perhaps a bolt of ice this time. Or fire." His eyes dart around a little frantically, searching for me. "Tell me, girl. How would you like to die?"

I sigh and close my eyes. Step through the cobwebs, out of the shadows. It failed, but at least I can do it. I could use it in a pinch.

"Good lad," the Sorcerer grins. "You will follow me," he orders.

The passages are black stone blocks. The mortar sparkles with gold and silver. The Sorcerer leads the way and his guards march behind me. We leave the dungeons and climb a spiral staircase to the upper levels. The main levels. Here, it's not much different from below. No windows to the outside, just carved, polished stone and thick wooden doors. Some are flanked by guards. Others stand open.

I close my eyes and use all of my senses as we walk. I sniff the air. Incense. Wood smoke. Decay. Strangely familiar smells. Like the apothecary booth. I listen. It's quiet. Eerily quiet. I feel for the magic. The amount of it in this place is overwhelming. All different types.

Elemental. Mentalist. Destructive. Necromancy.

That one I feel the strongest. Necromancy. There's a frenzy about it. An excitement. A challenge. It's nearby, in one of these doors we're passing. Something fresh. Something new. Something special.

I think of Eron's bagged head dripping crimson. I remember the fight between the Elite and the fallen prince. I have no idea why these images are dawning on me right now. I don't realize what it means until the winged things appear all around us. Ahead, the Sorcerer stops abruptly. The creatures hover in front of him.

"What do you mean, walking him this way?" the sharp-toothed one sends to the Sorcerer.

"Always talking when you shouldn't, stupid! He might hear, remember?" The round-faced one hisses.

My heart races. These are the same three who were at the High Court. The one with poison breath, the small one, and the round-faced one. They knew about me. They knew, but not everything. I pretend I can't hear them. I try to hide that I'm listening.

"They're right, Osven. You shouldn't have come this way with the boy," the smallest one sends to the Sorcerer. Good. I know his name now. I peer around the Sorcerer at them. Try not to shiver at the sight of the wicked little things. Look away. Stay quiet. Nessa says you learn more sometimes if you don't say anything at all. Silence draws truth.

"Your graces," the elf, Osven, bows his head with deep respect.

"Foolish thoughtlessness," the smallest says, and the Sorcerer winces.

"A strip. A small one. Just for us," the round-faced one pushes.

"He saw nothing. We shall take another route to the cliffs," Osven's shoulders rise in a slow wince. I keep my head low, but raise my eyes to watch through black fringe of hair that covers them. The scene tells me a lot. The Sorcerer. He's actually afraid of them. They're in charge.

"Too risky to keep you on this task," the sharp-toothed one chides.

"We have a rapport," Osven argues. *"To put another in charge of the boy now would be the true risk. Do not lose your faith in me, Your Graces. I shan't fail you."*

"Take a little," the smallest says to the round-faced one. *"Remind him of the pain of failure."*

The round-faced one licks his lips and cackles greedily. He stretches a leathery webbed hand out to Osven. Tendrils, black and blue like the Mark, swirl away from the Sorcerer into the wicked thing's outstretched hand. Osven goes rigid. He gurgles and gasps in pain.

"That's enough," the small one says. *"Payment for your foolishness. Take*

another route. Do not fail us with this boy."

The greedy round one turns to look at me. I look away trying to seem oblivious to what's just happened. I don't know how convincing I am.

He drifts closer. Looks me over. He smells like blood and tar, like earth and rot. He's close enough to touch me. He tries to look into my eyes, to breach my thoughts, but he can't. His eyes narrow.

I think he might say something, do something, but he doesn't. Instead the three of them vanish as quickly as they appeared. Osven turns to face me. He grabs me by the arm and roughly guides me off down a different corridor. Away from the scent of death and the powers of Necromancy. Away from thoughts of the executed prince, and what they're likely doing with his stolen remains.

Fairies, but not like any I've seen. I'm sure that's what they are. Fairies. I think of Mevyn. He was good, mostly, and still he took what he needed from me. He made me do things for him. These are obviously wicked. Cruel. Evil. The Dusk.

Why, though? What do they want from me? And why did they take Celli and the others and lock them up?

Osven's stride grows more confident with each step. He's back in control. Ready to be as ruthless as he needs to be. We stop in front of an open tunnel. The air from inside licks toward us, damp and musty. Osven turns to our guard escorts.

"You will remain here. If I do not return by sunset, come looking." He waves a hand over the entrance. Whispers an incantation. The air from inside is closed off. The ward is set between the Sorcerer and me and the guards.

"Nullen," he drawls, jerking his head toward the inside of the passage.

I raise my chin. In casting the ward between us, I know what he's after. He wants to see me in action. Watch me go through. I oblige him. I step across it like it's not even there. He regards me with a smirk of triumph.

"That," he explains, flicking a bony black-Marked finger toward the space between us and the guards, "is a Master Ward. Used in Cerion by the highest ranking Mage guards of the king himself. I believe there, they would rank it forty-fifth circle. Yet you pass through it as though it is nothing at all. But how? What is the extent of your power? And how did you come by such a gift?"

He leans closer as he murmurs, his eyes wild with the need for answers. His breath is foul, like rotten teeth. I stand tall, even though he towers over me. I try to look braver than I feel. Defiant. I'm not telling him a thing. Not a word. I clear thoughts of Mevyn and Valenor from my mind as a precaution. Just in case.

He examines me like a scroll. As if my face is the page of a book that can just be read. I think about how much I hate him. I imagine wringing his skinny Marked neck. I wonder if he can read that.

On the other side of the wards, the guards watch the two of us. They couldn't stop me if I tried it. They couldn't do anything. I glance at them. Osven chuckles wickedly.

"Try it," he says. "And the girl dies." At first I think he means Celli, but then his grin twists cruelly. "What was her name? Saesa?"

I try to stay stoic but I'm sure I fail. I'm sure my concern for Saesa is plain on my face.

"Yes. The squire," his tone is low and hateful. "I know of her. We know much about you here, Tibreseli Nullen. Curious that no one has come to your aid yet, is it not? That Sunteri fae of yours, or Valenor? Or your sister, hm? They all have the means. They must be aware that you are being held here. Why have they not come? We should very much like to meet them. Any or all of them."

I try hard to hide my shock at his words. He's right. Almost all of them are able to slip through the Half-Realm. Valenor, Mevyn, even Ki, my sister, though she'd need the permission of Iren, her guardian. Everyone except Saesa. I'd just have to reach out to them, probably. I won't, though. I won't put them in danger.

"Curious," he says with that smirk that never seems to go away. "No matter. This way."

The passage is narrow, damp, and slick. The farther down we go, the clearer the air gets. It isn't long before I smell the sea. It reminds me of Cerion. Of Saesa and Margary. Of my invention, left to gather dust at the bottom of a pit. I wonder how long it will take for them to notice that I'm gone. Through all of it, the Sorcerer's words nag at me. He's right. Mevyn and Ki might not know I'm in trouble at all, but Valenor never seems far away. As much as I refuse to call him, to endanger him, he must know I'm in trouble. Why hasn't he tried to help me yet?

The passage twists and turns for hundreds of paces, until finally a dim light brushes the stony walls ahead. As we near the light, I can hear the rhythm of waves crashing on stone. The sound calms me. I close my eyes and I could be sitting at port, watching the lifts go up and

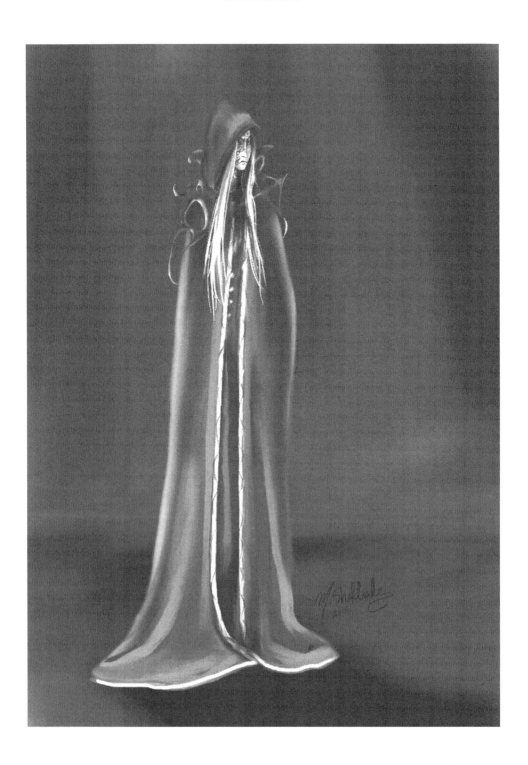

down.

When we finally get to the end, I can tell right away we're nowhere near Cerion.

Mist from the rough sea drenches us almost immediately. The waves that crash below are unforgiving. They smash the black rocks with relentless anger. The sky is cast with strange greenish clouds. On the horizon, a dark funnel plunges from them into the sea.

Osven grabs my arm and pulls me to the edge of the cliff. His gray robes whip and snap around us violently.

"What do you see?" he growls into my ear over the roar of the storm and jabs a finger to the sky.

I look up into the clouds as a spike of lightning cracks into the sea. At first I only see the storm. Then, as the clouds swirl above, a dark form emerges. A stone in the sky, black as the ones being pounded by the sea below. It's like the ground itself broke off in an enormous chunk and floated away. Looking at it leaves me with a slight feeling of unease. The idea of it is disturbing. Creepy.

Looking closer, I see a dark line like a jagged streak of ink across a page that stretches from the floating stone into the sea. A staircase, maybe.

I glance at Osven, who is staring intensely through narrowed eyes into the storm, searching for what he obviously can't see. He looks down at me and I understand right away. The floating stone is concealed with magic. The eerie feeling I get from it is just a hint of the real power it holds. Wards and enchantments so strong that it's invisible even to this braggart Sorcerer.

He looks down at me and I gaze into the sky, pointedly away from the floating stone. If this is what he needs from me, I refuse to give him any hint of it.

"What do you see?" he asks me again. His grip on my arm is strong. If I say the wrong thing I could anger him. Even without magic, he could throw me over. Into the angry sea. I take advantage of his desperation. If I can figure out where I am, maybe I could plan an escape. I turn slowly to look behind me. Up the black cliff face.

Perched high above us on the edge of the cliff is a fortress. Tattered banners flap angrily in the storm, scrabbling like red and orange wraiths against the slate sky. Its ramparts are half-crumbled but still a strong enough defense. Several of the windows glow with firelight, their colorful glass a bright contrast beside the pitted gray stone. I wonder how many Sorcerers are in there, bent over scrolls, reading tomes, preparing rituals. How many of those dark fae?

"My patience with you is threadbare," Osven hisses into my ear and shoves me toward the cliff's edge so my toes hang over and only my heels are keeping me from falling to my death.

"I see a storm," I say, peering up at the floating stone and then away. "A funnel cloud. Waves crashing on black stone. Green sky."

"Tell the truth," his shrieking voice stabs my ear.

"I am," I lie.

"If you see nothing but that, you are useless to us," he presses me closer. One of my heels slips from the edge. "Do you understand? Look again. What do you see?"

My heart races. If I told the truth, he would know about the stone in the sky. What harm could that do? What is that stone, anyway? Is it Margy's Brindelier? Is it the city on the coin? I squint up at it again as I try to scramble back from the ledge. It seems too small to hold a city. A house, maybe. A street, but not a whole city. There are no spires rising into the clouds. All I can make out is the thin black line that goes to the sea, and something like an archway at the top of it.

What harm could it do? It doesn't matter. If he can't see it, he isn't meant to. I don't bargain with Sorcerers.

"I see a storm. Clouds of green. An angry sea," I repeat.

"You," he spits into my ear, "are a filthy liar."

Before I can react, before I can think to fight, he shoves me from the edge. I scramble to keep from falling while Osven's wicked laughter pierces through the storm. It's no use. I claw at the stone. Rip my nails bloody as it streaks past. Tumble toward the sea like one of Margy's dolls. My elbow splinters painfully on the stone. My body thuds against the rock again and again. My hip smashes against the craggy cliff. The pain is unbearable. My head cracks. Before I reach the thundering sea, I black out.

Chapter Nineteen

CHAMPIONS OF LIGHT

Azi

"The Dusk and the Dawn," the queen says much later, after hours more of kissing, celebrating, dancing, and general merriment. For a while, Rian and I allowed ourselves to get lost in the revelry. He became the carefree boy I grew up with once more, happily slighting nearly every pretty fairy in the great hall as she vied for his attentions, only having eyes for me.

The two of us are still aglow with love even after the rest of the fairies have retired and left us and our companions alone with the queen and Zilliandin. I recognize the trusted advisor from Flitt's earlier memory. He has not once left the queen's side.

"Ever have the two factions met with conflict, as you might imagine," her Majesty explains quietly. Rian tucks me into his arms as we settle before her throne on cushions, content and exhausted as children in a nursery listening to a bedtime fairytale. Beside us on her own cushion, Flitt yawns and leans into Shush, whose eyes are half-closed and just as sleepy as hers.

"As long as the stars have been blotted out by morning sun, as long as the moon has shone in the dark sky of night, as long as light has cast a shadow, each of us has fought for the upper hand." While she talks, the waning sun beams across her throne, casting crimson light over the pure white of her gown. "It is the natural order of things, and one that we have come to accept. As long as there is light, there will be shadow.

"It is a boon to us that the Dawn holds the upper hand in this arrangement. Though there is balance, it nearly always tips in our favor. But from time to time the Dusk breaks through and darkness overcomes the light. Right now, we are on the precipice of such a time. A great treasure hangs in the balance. For over a century, it has been protected and hidden away. For hundreds of years, none knew of it.

"With the fall of the Wellspring of Sunteri came knowledge of places long undiscovered. Cities and villages. Flats of stone impossible to find. You have heard tell of one of these places. The Kingdom of Brindelier."

Flitt and I exchange a glance as the queen goes silent. Her Majesty lets the pause in her speech hang heavy between us. Even Zilliandin, who has been stoic and quiet all of this time, perks up. His eyes go wide and he gives an excited little squeak.

"Oh! Please excuse me, Majesty," the elder fairy's cheeks go rosy red.

"Indeed, Zilliandin," her Majesty smiles. "You are right to be so delighted. It is a surprise, is it not, that I could speak the name before these two humans? The Muses' songs took an interesting turn."

"And to think, I'm the one who found her! Can you believe it? But you must have known, Memi, when you sent me to Kythshire." Flitt bubbles.

"I'm not sure understand," Rian says slowly.

"I think I do," I venture. I tell Rian about Margy's storybook, and how she said she couldn't find the pages with the story about Brindelier until they revealed themselves to her.

"Yes!" Flitt chirps excitedly. "And she and Memi—I mean the queen— wouldn't have been able to tell you about Brindelier if you weren't worthy to be told. And not many are. You two are special, Azi and Rian. You two were meant for—"

"Now," the queen interrupts, raising a slender white hand in elegant protest. Everyone hushes. "No need to say too much, my little Sunbeam. Even here, the shadows listen as they are wont to do. But you are both correct. That I could say the name is proof enough that we may have found our Champions of Light."

"Champions of Light." Rian murmurs. His tone says he knows exactly what she's talking about. I look up at him, and he nods to the queen to indicate I should listen to her.

"Brindelier," the queen's lilting voice carries a melody that invokes a festival. "The lost city is a place of fellowship that has been hidden for ages past. It was closed away during the time of the Sorcerer King, but now it calls to the Dawn and the Dusk alike with promises of its power. It sings to us in sunshine and moonlight, asking us to see it, compelling us to open its gates once more.

"Ever have the Dark and the Light agreed to leave it lost and not seek it out, for Brindelier holds a great Source. The waters of its Wellspring are gold and red, blue and silver, green and copper. This Great Source feeds all others. To own it would be to own all of the magic of our lands."

She smiles a little sadly.

"Alas, such power cannot be entrusted to just any leader. Such power is a great responsibility. One must possess the qualities of restraint, of generosity, of understanding of the Balance. One side cannot be deprived over the other, and one side must not hold control over the other. And so it remains barred. The city lies in enchanted sleep, its twin heirs ever waiting for one worthy to rule with utter clarity and symmetry.

"Still, it does not keep those determined to wield its power from seeking its gates. The Dusk has built an alliance on this premise. It is called The Order, or the Circle of Spires. They have pooled their resources with Sorcerers who have been lying in wait for some years now, conspiring and plotting. Dark fae and darker men, who scour the lands for any clue which might lead them to the Great Source. What they do not know is this: The more determined they are, the more selfish and ruthless they become in their efforts, the further they skew the balance, and therefore the more elusive the gates become to them. Still, their numbers are such that they stand at the precipice of victory. They could discover the gates at any time and take them by force."

"Many a quest such as this has begun with a choice, Azaeli and Rian," the queen tilts her head to the side gracefully. "Azaeli, you have sworn to seek this city for your princess. We see the seal of the promise between you plain as the Light. Rian, you have given yourself to the fae time and again in the name of the Light, and time and again you have shown us a selfless restraint which rivals that of any living Mage. Knowing so, your choice is this: Walk away from this place and the quest set before you and forget all connections and dealings with our people, or take up this quest to thwart the Circle of Spires, open the gates of Brindelier for the Dawn, and set a worthy ruler upon its throne."

Rian's arms tighten around me at the queen's proposal. None of us says anything in response, not even Flitt or Shush. I can feel them both holding their breath as they wait for our reply.

"It is the custom," Zilliandin pipes up with his finger raised, "to have a game at questions. I propose to Her Majesty that, in the interest of time and clarity, in consideration for the gravity of the quest set before them, we forgo this custom." He blinks and gives a nervous chuckle. "Just this once, of course."

"A fine proposal, and one that we shall grant. You may ask your questions freely, and we shall answer to the best of our abilities."

Beside me, Flitt's eyes go wide. She looks at Shush, whose

expression matches her own. "Wow," they both mouth to each other. The dismissal of the question game is apparently as big a deal as I would have expected.

"I have one," Rian says right away. "Actually, I have more than I can count, but a good one to start. How long do we have to find this worthy suitor you speak of, and how do we find the city ourselves if it's hidden to those who seek it?"

"That's two questions, Rian!" Flitt rolls her eyes and groans. "Typical."

"It is fine, my love," the queen chuckles. "Zilliandin?"

The queen's advisor pushes his spectacles up his long nose and drifts closer to the rest of us. He looks over his shoulder conspiratorially.

"You must remember what Her Majesty said earlier. The shadows listen. So anything I tell you here, anything we speak of, could be overheard by the Dusk. From this point on, you must assume they know everything you know. That being said, I'm happy to answer your questions, Mage. It is our belief that you have found the suitor already. You will find the answer to your second question in Orivosak."

Leaving Rian to ponder his answers, Zilliandrin turns to me.

"And you, my dear," he gives a little bow, "have you a question?"

I think long and hard on the ocean of information that's been revealed by the queen, and as always my thoughts go to Cerion. Obviously, Margy is the suitor, but she's also the last living heir to the throne of Cerion. Eron is dead, and Sarabel has married off to Sunteri. With no one to rule in His Majesty's wake, what will happen to the peace of our kingdom?

"I understand the importance of keeping the Dusk out of Brindelier," I start slowly, turning over my thoughts carefully before I speak them aloud. "But if the suitor is who I think it is, it will leave our kingdom in chaos. We will have no one to hold the throne, if our only remaining heir lays claim to another. If we were to accept this quest, how could we ensure the stability of Cerion?"

Rian turns his head slowly to look at me. His eyes are wide with disbelief, and his mouth opens slowly before he snaps it shut again.

"That...that's really an excellent question, Azi," he says in awe. I guess I should be flattered, but I'm a little annoyed that he'd be so surprised that I'd come up with it.

"It is difficult for us to understand the delicate balance of the governments of man," Her Majesty says with a patronizing smile.

"Though we know how important your peace is to our own survival. The Plethore Dynasty has kept our secret for over a century, and for this we are grateful. If your quest were to succeed, Azaeli Hammerfel and Rian Eldinae, it would be the start of a new age for all of us. An age of kinship. It is our hope that fae and folk could live in harmony after the gates of Brindelier are opened, and the time of Ili'luvrie could return once more.

"As such, your suitor would keep a throne both in Cerion and Brindelier, and all of the territories of both would fall under one ruler."

"You mean to say," I gape at the queen, "the suitor would rule over both, and have command of the Source of all of the Wellsprings, everywhere?"

"That's a lot of power," Rian says quietly. "Too much for one person."

"If it is meant to be, then the way will be open to you. If the right suitor is chosen, then your path will not be difficult. Brindelier will guide you," Zilliandin says with a smile. "The Great Source, the city, is a power in itself. It lies in wait for the proper alignment of the stars, for the Champions of Light to show themselves. If you are meant to succeed, you shall."

"Do not make it sound so simple, Zilliandin," the queen warns, "the Dusk encroaches. They will try to take the city by force, if they are able to find it. They will stop at nothing to keep you from your goal. Your quest shall not be as simple as my advisor makes it seem. But if you are true to the Light, the way will open to you."

"The first step," Zilliandin nods, "is to accept the quest."

"I have another question first," Rian says quietly. Behind his eyes I can see the cogs turning. His mind is racing already, and more answers will surely set his head spinning. "In recent months, there have been many portents of some great dark force. We at the Academy have seen these warnings come in many forms. Is it this Circle of Spires, this Dusk you speak of, or could there be some larger, darker force that threatens?"

"We, too, have seen the portents you speak of. We cannot say for certain, but if the Dusk is allowed to present its own suitor, and if this suitor is allowed to reign, then a darkness unlike any that has been seen will fall over the Known Lands. Light will become shadow, and good will be snuffed out forever. This faction of Dusk is ruthless and hungry for power. Long have they felt that the balance is too oppressive. They will crush the light for the sake of their own power. Hopelessness and cruelty will reign."

"Chosen heroes face the end of the world against all odds," Rian murmurs. "Light versus Dark. This is a tale I've read many times."

"The good news is the Light always wins, right?" Flitt tries to sound cheerful, but there's a hint of doubt she can't quite hide.

"We're certain you have more questions," the queen says, "but the sun sets now, and we're certain you're all quite spent. You must decide whether to accept the quest laid before you, or walk away and lose all memories of this place and those you have encountered within it. We shall give you the night to think it over. In the morning, we shall feast and hear your declaration. For now, go, and rest your weary heads."

Before we can protest, the queen makes an elegant gesture and the scene before us fades away. Flitt, Shush, Rian and I find ourselves in a room with glowing walls of rose petals. Four beds draped with gauzy white webbing and dressed with lavish silky coverlets line the wall, and opposite them a fire of blue and golden flames crackles merrily. There is a table set with fruits and wine and draped in sparkling cloth. Orbs of light drift lazily through the room, casting soft, soothing light.

The inviting coziness of the beds makes me realize how very tired I am, and the table of food makes my stomach growl.

"Typical," Rian sighs as he strides to the table. A whisper and a gesture of a spell ensures him that the food is safe to eat. He pulls out a chair for me and nods with a forced smile. Across the room, Flitt and Shush converse in secret whispers. Once in a while, they throw a glance our way. I sink into a velvety chair, and we both eat in thoughtful silence. The berries are plump and perfectly ripe, and the wine is the best I've ever tasted. Together we eat our fill, and eventually Shush and Flitt come to join us.

"Looks like it's okay to talk freely in here," Flitt says thickly around a mouthful.

"Oh, indeed," Shush whispers. "Thanks to the wisps." He nods to an orb that drifts past.

They're right. The fire at the hearth and the soft light of the orbs ensure there isn't a single shadow cast in this place. Flitt seems to be grateful for this reprieve. She allows her own light to dim a little as she tucks in to her plate of berries.

"How much of this did you two know about? And for how long?" Rian asks as he tips back on the two feet of his chair. "You," he points at Shush and narrows one accusing eye, "you said something way back at the battle of the keep at Kythshire."

Shush shrugs. He lets out a guilty sigh of wind which swirls across the table, nearly tipping my goblet.

"A while," he whispers.

"Well, we couldn't be sure, really, could we? And we did have to make sure. The princess taking to Twig was the first real sign, and then your Mum just happened to stumble back to Kythshire, didn't she, Azi? A while ago, they thought it might be her. But then she married that metal-pounding hothead and—"

"Hey!" I glare across at her. "Don't talk about my Da that way. He's a good man." Flitt shrugs.

"I guess he could be both, couldn't he?" Shush placates. "Hot-headed but a good man, too."

"Doesn't matter," Flitt waves her hand dismissively. "I was saying, they thought it could be her, but then she ended up with him and that wouldn't work. You know what the song says, Mage and Sword, Blade and Arcane, twixt the two, hmm, hmm…." She hums the rest, trailing off.

"Actually, no," Rian interrupts.

"What do you mean, no?" Flitt scowls. "They've sung it forever. I've heard it a million times and sung it myself another million. It gets stuck in your head, doesn't it? Can't really get the words wrong."

"I meant no, we don't know what the song says." Rian explains. "We haven't heard it."

Flitt's jaw drops, her open mouth revealing a half-chewed bite of berry.

"But, your mum's the most famous bard in Cerion. How could she not have sung that to you?" Flitt asks in disbelief.

"Why would my mum know a song sung by fairy muses?" Rian scowls, obviously annoyed by Flitt's criticism of his mother's knowledge of songs.

"Same way bards know most songs," Shush whispers. "They pluck them from the aether. They absorb them from inspiration."

"The aether?" I ask.

"Aether, Dreaming, inspiration, Source, Half-Realm…" Flitt shrugs. "Lots of names for the same general thing. Magic. You humans think of Magic as a thing that's molded and wielded and bent to your will. Fairies know it's more than that. It's a thing, sure, but it's also a place. It has lots of locations. Lots of ways to access it."

We stay up talking late into the night until we can barely keep our heads from nodding and our eyes from drifting closed. Once we have our answer for the queen and our general plan mapped out, we retire to the welcoming clouds of our beds and drift into the most perfectly comfortable slumber any of us has ever had the luxury to enjoy.

In the morning when we're ready, the room fades as easily as it had appeared the night before, and we find ourselves standing at the base of the long staircase to the throne.

The queen sits regal and commanding in a gown of butterflies and spider silk that twinkles in the morning light like drops of molten gold. Hundreds of fairies have come to listen to our declaration. They line the open spaces between the columns all the way up to the open ceiling where the fragile tips of the palace's petal walls fall open to the soft pink sky above.

Rian is caught mid-yawn beside me through the transformation. He blinks sleepily and goes wide-eyed at the scene, then takes my hand as if to check and see if we're still dreaming. Flitt and Shush don't seem at all surprised. Rather, to my surprise and slight embarrassment, Flitt soars up the stairs and gives the queen a sweet, dainty kiss on the cheek.

"A bright morning to you, my little Sunbeam," she says with a smile. Flitt grins and squeezes the queen's hand before floating slowly to my side again. "And to all assembled here."

"Bright morning!" The wish surges through the crowd. Perhaps it's my imagination, but the light of dawn seems to shine stronger as their chorus echoes through the ivory pillars.

The queen nods to Zilliandin, and the elder fairy drifts forward to address the crowd.

"Today our champions stand before us," he declares. "From Kythshire: Felicity Lumine Instacia Tenacity Teeming Elite Reformer." He nods to Flitt, and she darts to the first step.

Her wings close and open slowly, catching the golden light and splashing it across the crowd in a dazzling, blinding display of rainbow prisms. The crowd erupts into applause and cheers.

"From Kythshire," Zillandin's call hushes the crowd, "Soren Hasten Udi Swiftish Haven Illustrious Noble General."

Shush towers beside Rian. His iridescent green armor shimmers with flecks of blue and magenta. He raises his long spear as he stalks forward on mantis-like legs to take the step beside Flitt. Turning to the crowd, he lowers his bug-like goggles over his eyes and draws in a deep breath. All around us, the crowd pauses. The smart ones cling to pillars. Rian steps closer to me and takes me in his arms.

Shush blows out and his wind rushes through the palace, rattling the pillars, shaking the fragile petals, and sending tiny dervishes to dance across the white stone. The assembled fairies giggle as they cling to anything they can, even each other. Those who weren't prepared tumble away through the wind, whooping and laughing. Rian's robes and my cloak lash around us like whips, and my feet slip on the polished stone as we're pushed back by the force of it. When the windstorm finally dies down, Shush grins and bows, and the crowd erupts into applause the same as they had for Flitt.

"From Cerion," Zilliandin announces, and the crowd hushes once more. "Rian Eldinae, Mentor of the Academy of Cerion, Mage of His Majesty's Elite, Windsaver, Oathkeeper, Arcane Guardian, Steward of the Wellspring." Rian's arms tighten around me nervously and then drop away. He stands silent as the hushed whispers of the crowd echo around us.

"*Do something impressive,*" Shush pushes to him.

At his sides, Rian's hands flex and relax. He takes a calming breath and steps to the stairs. My heart races nervously as he gazes out over the mass of fairies. I'm not sure if my anxiety is sympathy for him or my own apprehension about what I'll do when it's my turn. His eyes scan the hall thoughtfully, and he raises his hands in an elegant gesture.

He starts to speak the incantation of a spell and the magic in the air around him is tangible. It gathers on his fingertips like clusters of pollen, white-hot and bright. It seeps into the pores of his skin and radiates outward. His fingers curl with the intensity of the power that flows through him. His eyes go wild and vacant. All around us, fairies cower behind the shelter of the pillars. Even I take a step back, surprised by my own fear of the devastating arcane power he's about to wield.

All of the light in the hall gathers around him, poised to unleash itself by his command. His eyes flash with terrible might. He raises his hands straight up as though he'll thrust them forward. Then slowly, with measured restraint, he closes his fists, lowers his hands, and closes his eyes. The gathered magic dissipates. Rian bows his head, and I understand. His power, his talent, is restraint.

The fairies break into cheers twice as loud as their show of appreciation for Flitt and Shush. In time, they finally quiet down and my stomach twists into knots. It's my turn, now.

"From Cerion," Zilliandin's voice seems louder to me this time, "Azaeli Hammerfel, Knight of His Majesty's Elite, The Temperate,

Pure at Heart, Reviver of Iren, The Great Protector, Cerion's Ambassador to Kythshire, Vanquisher of the Prince, The Mentalist, The Paladin."

I stand rooted to the spot as the fairies stare at me and whisper amongst each other with great anticipation. My heart pounds. I can't think of what to do. My new titles ring over and over in my head. I try to push them away and think of something to do, but I have no idea what it could be. My sword was given up. That's my only true talent. That's what I'm known for. Without it, what proof can I give of my worthiness for this quest?

Their eyes are steady on me. It seems like Rian has only just noticed my weapon is gone. I will my feet to move. I hope when I reach the step and take it, I'll be able to prove myself somehow. My feet are heavy as I trudge forward to stand beside my companions.

I turn to face the hundreds staring at me, waiting for my demonstration. The pull of their thoughts entrances me. Tendrils of gold hang thick in the air between us. So many minds, so much power to behold. Still, my heart aches for my sword. If I hadn't given it up, I could show them. I could impress them with skills honed over years of training. Instead I stand before them feeling foolish and unprepared.

"*Do something,*" Flitt pushes to me desperately, and my desire for my sword fills me up. My hands raise as though curled around a sword's hilt. I don't know what comes over me, but I imagine the most impressive weapon I can. With the tendrils of thoughts that reach out from the fairy crowd, I begin to weave my vision.

I imagine a shining, heavy broadsword with a serrated blade as sharp as a surgeon's knife. The tendrils of fairy minds collaborate with my own memories of my father and the sword he honed perfectly for me out of love. The sword I lost. The intertwined thoughts curl into place like the Mark, floating in gold filigree in midair before me. They form solidly in my hands, forging a sword of the perfect weight and balance. Its hilt and hand guard are spirals and curls. Elegant script bears the name Hammerfel, glinting and pulsing with magic. Its blade glows with shimmering light as it shifts from imagined to real.

I venture a swing that feels as though it could slice away at the very shadows, and a streak of light follows in the wake of it. The entranced crowd breaks into thunderous applause and wild dancing.

"*Whoa,*" Flitt pushes to me, staring at my new sword, "*how did you do that? I've seen a lot of things, but I've never seen anything like* that!"

Grinning, I glance at Rian. His reaction is the complete opposite of the rest of them. His face is pale and flushed. He looks at me in a way he never has before. Not with admiration as always, or with pride and impressed, like the others. Beyond the blade of my raised golden sword, he regards me with uneasy awe, tinged with fear.

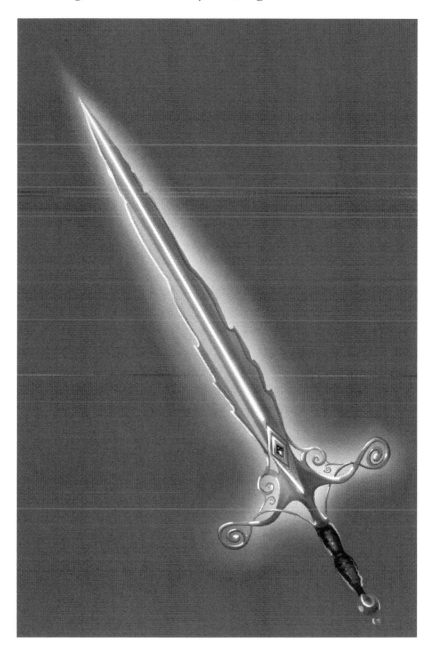

Chapter Twenty
BELONGING

Celli

I don't know how long I've been lying here on the unforgiving stone floor, feeling like I'll die. My thoughts are jumbled and scattered. My mind races sometimes, and other times it's completely empty. Those times are the worst, when I remember the Sorcerer raising his hands toward me. The crackle of hot blue light. The pain. Pain so strong it swallows me up. Pain to the breaking point.

Once, Da and I sat under an awning at the sea market during a lightning storm. We saw a gull get struck in midair.

"Cooks you from the inside out, lightning does," he had said to me. It certainly feels like it. I've gotten used to the stench of my burnt flesh. I don't smell it anymore. But then thinking about it, about that gull lying on the cobbles smoking, puts me in a panic again.

I can't move my left leg at all. My arms don't hear my commands. I start to pant in fear. My breath comes in short gasps. When the attack is at its worst, I stop breathing altogether. My lips go numb first, and my vision closes in. I'm going to die here. I want to die. Just please, let me die. Let it be over.

Of course, my body wins out over my panicked mind. My lungs burn. I gasp for breath. I sob. My tears tickle the side of my nose as they roll down. I want to swipe them away, but my arms refuse to move. The panic starts again but I hold it back this time. I think over how everything went so terribly wrong.

I vaguely remember them taking Tib out and parading him away. Leaving me here, alone. Of course it was his fault. His stupid, selfish fault. It wasn't supposed to be like this. I was supposed to be part of it. I was going to make something of myself. I was going to impress Quenson.

Even now, thinking about Quenson quickens my heart. Does he know what the other one did to me? Why hasn't he come for me yet? And Dub. As much as I hate him, where is he? How could they just leave me here?

The answer feels like a stone in my stomach. *Stupid Celli. They have*

Tib. They don't need you anymore. You're worthless. Unimportant.

The pain of that thought is worse than the feeling of my cooked insides. I let out a sob that echoes through the cell.

"Unlock it at once," a muffled voice blends with my cries. I work to quiet myself. At first I think it's my scrambled brain making things up, but when the door creaks open, my breath catches.

His soft boots come into view first, gray and graceful. Perfect. The red lining of his black robes flicks in and out of view as he walks toward me. Quenson. I try desperately to look up into his beautiful face, but the pain in my neck is too much. I start to cry again. I need to see him. I ache for him. *Don't be a baby,* I scold myself.

"My, my," Quenson clicks his tongue, "Osven, it seems, was a little heavy-handed with you, my dear."

His whisper of a spell strips the stone floor of filth and liquid. When it's suitably dry and clean, Quenson kneels by my head. Relief washes over me. I can finally see his face. I'm filled with a sense of peace, like looking at him is essential to my survival. He called me *my dear.* He's my air and my pulse. He's all that matters. His lips curl into a smirk and I'm sure I'll die happy in this moment, his smile the last thing I see.

"You amuse me so, girl," he laughs softly. "It is not your time to die." He produces a corked vial of shockingly pink liquid from his robes and pulls out the stopper. "Drink," he says, and presses it to my lips.

The acrid potion tastes like blood and fire. It burns my tongue and throat and creeps into my stomach like molten lead, and it doesn't stop there.

"Hold her," Quenson's voice is drowned out by the ringing in my ears. Someone holds me down. The touch of their hands sears my flesh. I writhe in pain as the potion works its way through me, down my arms into my fingertips, down my legs into my feet and toes until every fiber is swathed in burning pain. I feel myself convulsing. My legs kick out, my arms thrash. My mouth fills with foam. More men come. More pin me. Their hands are red-hot clamps of iron.

My screams echo through the cell, but they're distant. Not really mine. I'm separate from the girl on the floor, pinned and burning. I'm outside. Quenson is even more handsome from this point of view. I drift toward him. I want to be him, not her. I ache to be close to him. He looks from the writhing girl to me. Something shifts, and I understand.

I'm his. Fully his, now. His blood in the potion links us. The pain is necessary. It strengthens the bond. He flicks his eyes toward the girl, whose convulsing is starting to calm. He commands me with a single look. Return.

I sink back into her without a second thought. The burning is welcome. It means we'll be together. I slow my breath. I wear the pain. I drift to sleep.

I wake in luxury. Silks and satins. Clouds of pillows. Sweet incense. It feels like a dream. I don't want to open my eyes.

"Dress," Quenson's command is velvety smooth and thrilling.

My eyes fly open. I slide from the bed in sheer excitement. My clothes are laid out for me, the ones that were gifted by Sybel. The ones Dub made me change out of. I put them on in a rush and spin to search the room for Quenson. He was here. I felt him. I heard him. But I'm alone.

"Come outside," Quenson orders. It's his voice, I'm sure. But I don't hear it. Not outside or in my head. It's more of a feeling. A compelling. Something I want to do, even though it wasn't my own idea.

It puzzles me, but when I reach the door and pull it open, it doesn't matter anymore. He's there, waiting. Smiling again. Looking me over with appreciation. He's everything. Everything.

I follow him not knowing or caring why or where. It doesn't matter. We're together. We pass others, other Sorcerers. Some of them greet him, some don't. I want to punch those who ignore him. Kick them. Make them hurt. Make them see how amazing he is.

"All in good time, my dear," he murmurs, and his words placate me.

He brings me to a room that's small and cluttered. The walls are stacked with books and scrolls and shelves lined with bottles of herbs and solutions floating with bits of flesh or preserved animals. A small desk is stuffed to the side. Scraps of parchment are tacked to the wall above it, with scratchy reminders I can't read scrawled all over them. Torn pages of books, showing drawings of men with their skin pulled back to show their muscles and bones.

He takes the chair there and gestures for me to sit in the only other one, a ruby velvet footrest. The door closes as I sit, and he whispers a spell over it. As always, his voice thrills me like I can feel his whisper on my bare skin.

"You have proven your loyalty," he leans toward me in his chair and presses his fingertips together. "I will entertain your questions."

I stare at him blankly. I should have questions. Lots of them. The truth is, none of them matter. I'm here with him. We're together. As long as that's so, I don't care. My past life is a distant memory. Another girl. A child who died in that cell. My new life is here, with him.

"Can I stay with you?" I ask. "Always?"

His laugh is more of a scoff. A perfect, wonderful scoff that warms me. I lean forward, too. I need to be closer to him. His eyes glint with amusement and power.

"If you behave," he says. "Have you no other questions? No pondering about this Order or this place?"

"Who were those who ignored you in the corridor?" I ask. I want their names. I want to be able to track them down later. Quenson grins again. I'm drunk with the beauty of his white teeth against the blue-black Mark.

"Sorcerers like me, my dear," he starts to elaborate, but my scowl interrupts him. He raises a questioning brow.

"Not like you," I say. "There's no one like you."

"Truly," he laughs softly, "you delight me. Perhaps so. Not exactly like me. We all have our talents here, but work toward the same end, you see. Domination of the Sources. Still, though our goal is the same, we spend much time watching our own backs. As you would imagine, our ilk does not value loyalty highly, nor are we adept at maintaining our alliances. We work together because we must."

"But," he leans in even closer. I watch his lips as he speaks. I barely hear what he's saying. "The fewer of us there are in the end, the more powerful the ones who remain. Do you see, my lovely? We make our alliances on false pretenses, each of us knowing the other will most likely try to kill us in the end. It is not, as you would imagine, a hospitable environment. Still, it is necessary. And so you see why your loyal companionship is such an amusement."

I grin stupidly. He called me a companion. I amuse him.

"I must ask you to do something for me," he reaches for my hand, and his touch jolts me with warmth.

"Anything," I say.

An insistent pounding on the door interrupts us.

"What?" Quenson's irritated shout makes me jump. His anger becomes my anger. He curses under his breath and waves a hand. The silence ward on the door fades. "What?" he yells louder this time.

"I got it," Dub's quiet reply is muffled by the thick wood.

"Open the door, Celli," Quenson commands, and I'm on my feet and opening it before I can even think.

Dub glowers at me with his one good eye. His face is covered in scratches. He looks past me at Quenson and scowls, and that's enough for me. I lunge at him, swinging my fists.

"How dare you?" I scream in rage. To come here, to scowl at my master? I swing hard and my fist cracks his jaw. Dub curses and grabs me by the throat. Behind us, Quenson laughs heartily.

"What in the black shadow?" Dub growls and shoves me back.

"Enough, Celli. Close the door," Quenson says, and I do. Dub takes my seat. That's fine with me. I stand next to Quenson. Close enough that my arm brushes his shoulder. That's when I notice the squirming black sack in Dub's grip. It's covered in shed fur: black, white, orange. White claws poke out from the fibers as whatever's inside struggles. Dub holds it away from himself, still scowling.

Without any command from Quenson, I think of what to do. I turn around and fetch a small iron cage that's stuffed among some old scroll cases. I open the door and hold it out to Dub, and he shoves the sack inside. It squirms and fights and yowls as I close the door and hand it to Quenson.

"Now we'll see what's so special about you, won't we?" Quenson murmurs. The creature inside frees itself from the sack with a great, yowling thrash.

"You got Zeze," I whisper, and the cat in the cage turns to me and hisses.

Chapter Twenty-One

SAILS AND PEARLS

Tib

"Will he live, Valenor?"

"If he allows their magic."

"Sorcerers' healers? He won't. You know Tib."

"Sometimes we must make difficult choices in order to survive, my dear Ki. You know this better than most."

"Why won't he wake? It's been hours…"

"He is only now becoming aware."

I am. Aware, I mean. Of soft sunlight on my face. Of a calloused hand in each of mine. Of the voices of people who care about me. I've been aware of them for a while, actually. I've just been afraid to open my eyes. Afraid if I do, I'll lose the dream.

"Your sister is here, Tib. As am I," Valenor says. "You are safe for the moment, but your time is waning. Will you join us?"

I squeeze one hand. Ki's hand. Then I squeeze the other. She cries silently. She doesn't speak. I don't need her to, though. I know who she is.

"Saesa?" I whisper.

"Tib," she gives a choked sob and presses my hand to her wet cheek.

"I don't want to wake up," I murmur.

"It is nigh impossible that you would wake against your will, my friend," Valenor says mournfully, "under the circumstances."

His words swim in my thoughts. The face of the jagged cliff side streaks through my mind. I remember the pain as each bone broke. That pain is gone now. I feel nothing. I understand. I'm in the Dreaming. I trust Valenor if he says I won't wake up. I open my eyes. Slowly. Carefully.

The first thing I see are sails stretched tight by a rush of wind. I hear the creak of wood. Masts. The crow's nest towers over me. Soft white clouds drift above. Sunlight gleams on Saesa's orange curls. Her eyes are red and puffy. She leans over me. Gives a reassuring smile. A fan of shimmering black hair tickles my face as Ki does the same.

"Sister," I grin, and she scoops me into her arms. Beside me, Saesa sniffles again. "Why are we on a ship?" I ponder.

"We should ask you the same, my friend," Valenor's voice drifts on the wind. "After all, this dream is of your making."

I peer over my sister's shoulder. Through the black locks of her hair that whip in the breeze, I look into the distance, expecting to see the familiar line of sea meeting sky. I don't, though. There's no sea. Just sky. I jump to my feet and nearly knock Ki over as I sprint to the port side. I lean over, way over.

The ship's belly rounds out below me. Beyond that, a bladder of air. Just like in my drawings. Just like in my designs, wings of varying shapes and sizes stretch out, bracketed to the bulwarks. They reach forward and back like a great, graceful bird, pushing us forward with ease. I whoop and run to the bow, where I lean so far over that Ki has to catch my ankles to keep me from teetering over, into the sky.

The ground below is patches of dark and light green. Golden fields. Gray stone mountains. We're so high up that it doesn't even feel like we're moving. A flock of geese fall in beside us. They keep time with the strokes of the ship's great wings, honking their greetings.

"It's unbelievable!" I shout into the wind. I race aft, to the quarterdeck, to the captain's wheel. I stare at it for a moment in disbelief. I put my hand on it. Give it just a small turn. The ship responds smoothly, listing to port. "It's impossible!" I laugh and spin on my heels and climb up to look over the aft, where four enormous blades spin lazily. Benen's blades.

"They work!" I whoop. "It works!" I spin back to face the others. Valenor's cloak flaps into view first, and the rest of him follows. He stands between Saesa and Ki. My chest feels like it could burst with joy.

"You did it, didn't you? You finished it." I jog down the steps and hug all three of them at once. "I'm not even mad that you did it without me. It's amazing! How did you know what to do? Did you use magic? Was it difficult to get the ship floating?"

When no one replies, I pull away from them and catch them giving each other worried glances.

"What?" I ask, confused but still beaming with triumph. My invention works. I can fly anywhere now. The port at Cerion will never be the same. Ships. Floating ships!

"It's a dream, Tib," Saesa says gently. "It's your dream. It's not real. You haven't finished it yet."

I look at Ki. She nods apologetically. My heart plummets. The ship fades from beneath us. I'm falling again. The cliffs rise up beside me. The jagged rocks rush past, sharp and cruel. Saesa tumbles past. Ki grabs my wrist. Reaches for Saesa, too. Valenor's cloak stretches out and gathers us up. The blur of the rocks slows. We settle into darkness. It's night. The sea is calm. Its black waters swirl, licking at my body. I'm alone. Broken. Lying on a rock.

A figure drifts close to me. Tall and slender, dark and wicked, he flicks his hand out in haste. I feel the spell settle over me. Levitation. It does nothing. I can't be touched by spells.

"Ki," I scream. "Saesa!"

I can't move. Broken back, broken legs, broken hip, broken arms. I shouldn't have survived. I should be dead. My mouth is filled with blood but I can't swallow. Can't even choke.

"Valenor!" Wait. How can I scream for them if I can't even swallow? Is this real? Is it a dream? A memory?

Osven sneers at my broken body with disgust. He hovers a hand over me. Detection spell. I'm alive. He lands beside me. He's outwardly annoyed. He looks far above at the fortress. Maybe thinking about asking for help. In the end, he decides not to. He picks me up. My body is limp. I dribble blood down the front his perfect gray robe.

A different place, now. A room. A stone slab like an altar in the center. I'm lying on it, neatly arranged. My hands are clasped over my chest like a corpse at a viewing. It's strange. I'm lying there, but I'm standing watching, too. Somewhere nearby, Saesa sniffles.

A woman in brown robes stands beside me. Her fingertips glow pink. Healing magic flows from them, bathing me in its glow. Her hand begins to shake. She's been here for hours. She takes her hand away. Presses her palms to the stone and leans, exhausted.

"Next!" Osven bellows. The healer steps back, only to be replaced by another.

"You," Osven growls at the spent woman and grabs her arm as she rushes past. "You have failed. Explain."

"He resists it," the woman offers wearily. "I might as well have been healing the stone itself. It would have done as much good."

Osven glances at her replacement. This healer bows his head. He whispers a fervent, faithful prayer and presses both hands to the sides of my head. The pink energy glows.

My awareness shifts. Someone else is here with me. Someone familiar. Someone comforting. I search the room for her. She's difficult to find at first. Hidden by iron. Bars. A cage. A cat.

"Zeze!" I rush to her and reach for the cage, but I'm not really here. My hands go right through the bars. Right through her. She sits watching, though. She sees me. Both of me. Her eyes meet mine. Calm. Trusting. Waiting.

I spin on my heels. Run straight through the healer. Straight through myself on the dais. Fling myself at Osven. I want to claw his eyes out. I want to choke him. Feel his life leaving him. Watch him bleed out.

"I hate you," I scream at him, "I hate all of you!" I lash at him wildly. Swing through him. My fists are clouds. Apparitions. He doesn't even feel my energy. Some Sorcerer.

"Valenor," I cry, confused. I feel him beside me before he appears. His cloak flutters around me, offering peace. Offering comfort. I welcome it. I let it close around me. I let it calm me. I let him take me away from here.

We're on his terms now. Valenor. The Dreamwalker. My friend. The darkness is pushed out by light. Forms swim before me, silhouetted. Saesa. Ki.

We settle in the grass at the base of a great castle. He lets me sit for a while, in between Ki and Saesa, drinking in the sun. When he knows I'm calm enough, he speaks.

"Do you understand what you have seen, Tib?" he asks.

"I think so. This isn't real. The real me is in that fortress, about to die," I say. "And they have Zeze." My heart pangs with the last, and my anger starts to bubble again. "They're trying to heal me, but they can't."

"Two days they've tried, Tib," Valenor says with a disapproving shake of his head. "Why do you deny them?"

"Deny them? What are you talking about? I'm unconscious! Besides, what difference does it make? I've been healed before without having to give anyone permission!"

"People you were familiar with," Valenor explains. "You welcomed their healing. These are strangers. They cannot touch you with magic, good or bad."

While I turn his words over in my mind I note something else. Something different about him. No, not something. Someone. A familiar pulse. Golden wings and armor of the same. A gold fleck in his eyes, peering out at me.

"Mevyn?" I whisper and push myself to my feet. Ki and Saesa follow me silently, like they're afraid I'll stray too far. "Is that you?"

"It is," Valenor says, and Mevyn's voice echoes within his.

I reach out to him, to Valenor, shocked by my reaction to our reunion. Tears roll down my cheeks. I missed him. Mevyn's presence fills a hole I didn't even realize I had.

"This reaction is quite normal," Mevyn explains. "I assure you, there is no magic between us, my old friend. What you are feeling is the bond we had. It is still present, despite the distance between us. It always will be. I would explain further, but there are far more urgent matters at hand."

"Why do you speak through Valenor?" I ask him, disappointed. "I'd like to see you."

"I cannot leave the Wellspring for the Dreaming. Not now. We are on the precipice of Dusk. Tib, you must listen."

I don't know how to respond. I have too many questions. I remember what Nessa says. Silence draws truth. I wait.

"Your title, Dreamstalker, still stands. As such, you cannot be touched by magic. You cannot be swayed by Mentalism. You cannot be harmed by Sorcery. You cannot be healed by Mending. None of the Arcane can touch you, unless you will it so. Unless you consent to it. Do you understand?"

"What if I don't consent?" I ask. "What if I let myself die? What happens to me then?"

"Death is the Great Mystery, Tib. We only know that if you die, you will be gone from our reach. Only your shell will remain on the worldly plain, and it is an evil act to pluck you back from wherever the rest of you goes," Valenor's voice is stronger during this explanation. The corner of his eyes crinkle with a smile even through his light scowl. "We hope this is not the end you wish. Especially not in the grips of Sorcerers who are capable of raising you and manipulating you. For, once you are dead, your titles die with you."

"Of course I don't want that," I say impatiently. "And I won't leave Zeze in their hands. I want to stop them. They need to be stopped. Do you know what they're doing? They're raising the prince! I felt him there. I felt them doing it. If what you're saying is true, then they can do that to him, can't they? They can bring him back. Manipulate him."

"One of many sinister plots, Tib." Valenor says. "One of many. But you must understand what you face, should you allow them to heal you. We cannot reach you in that place. It is too protected. If you are to return, once you do, I cannot stand beside you."

"But we were just there together! I don't understand."

"I was able to reach you at the cliffs, my friend." Valenor explains.

"Their wards and iron walls protect the fortress, but not the grounds surrounding it. And I was your guest in the Dreaming in the room with the dais. Once you awake, I shan't be able to reach you there. But you will not be alone. Zeze will be with you."

"You need to be calm about it, Tib," Saesa offers quietly. "When you wake up, don't lose your temper."

"You need to outsmart them and get out of there," Ki says. "You can do it."

I look from one of them to the other. My sister. My best friend. It makes sense that Ki would be here. She can travel easily to the Dreaming from Kythshire, as long as she has Iren's permission. We've met here lots of times before. Saesa is another story, though. The Dreaming is vast. Infinite.

"How did you find us, Saesa?" I ask.

Saesa's eyes flick to the air beside her head.

"Are you going to come out now?" she asks. "I think he's agreed. You're going to let them heal you, right, Tib? You're going to go back?"

"Do not answer yet," Mevyn's echo rings out. "As soon as you agree, their healing will wake you."

"Who are you talking to?" I ask Saesa.

The air shimmers beside her, revealing a slender, stick-like form.

"Afternoon," Twig bows merrily. "Glad to see you up and about, Tib, so to speak."

I look from him to Saesa. Shake my head.

"I don't understand," I say. "Why aren't you with the princess? Is she all right? Did something happen?"

"I'll be happy to explain later," Twig says cheerfully. "Once you wake up."

"But, how…" I'm so confused, I can't even form a question.

"Like I said," Twig grins, "all questions will be answered at a later point in time. What you need to do is get Zeze, okay? Get the cat, and have them bring you outside. Someplace calm, if you can. A place with trees would definitely help. Or even just a little grass. And Tib? It's really important that you succeed. Really, really important."

"First things first," Valenor says. "You must consent to their healing. When you are ready."

Ki steps forward. Her hair shines bright and slick in the sunlight. The studs on her gray leather armor twinkle and shine. The last time I saw her, it was winter. She has since shed her long sleeves and leggings for something that shows off the muscles in her arms and legs. She looks good. Healthy. She adjusts her bow on her shoulder and offers her outstretched arms to hug me. I let her.

"I'm not sure when you'll see me again," she says, "but I'll be watching you from here. From the Dreaming, okay? I believe in you."

I bury my face in her shoulder. Stay there for a while. Feel Iren's hold on her, the magic deftly woven between her and the Guardian of the North. Take in the scent of her: crisp mountain air and pine. Save this feeling, the love of my sister. Even though the magic of that fortress can't touch me, it's still heavy with despair and hopelessness. I'll need this to help me through.

Next to us, Saesa's sniffling again. She doesn't wait for Ki to let go. She flings her arms around the both of us.

"I'm glad we found you," she whispers. "Be careful."

"I'm glad you're safe," I say. "Stay that way. I'll see you in Cerion."

I don't let go of any of them. I keep hugging. Valenor's cloak settles around us, poking us with starry pinpoints of hope. I think of myself back on the dais. The man with his hands on me. In my mind I agree to it. I allow it. I let him heal me.

There's no gentle shift. It happens suddenly. Pain. Agony. Suffocation. The blood in my mouth sputters out as I gasp and choke on it. His hands are rough over my ears. His fingertips jab into my temples and skull. I open my eyes to pink light. Healing magic pulses through me, ripping through my bones, binding and fixing splinters and shards. It isn't the soothing healing I'm used to. This is forceful. Powerful. Fast and hard. Excruciating.

I scream and gasp and scream again. My own voice echoes back at me. The pain is too much. I need it to stop, but no. It must continue. I remember Ki's arms around me, and Saesa's. The sun-splashed deck of a flying ship. I focus on the scent of mountain air and pine. They help me through, just like I thought they would.

Through a cloud of pink and pain, his face hovers over me. Narrow and haughty, with slits of eyes that turn up as he grins. Triumph. The boy is awake. The boy he flung over a cliff for not seeing what he needed him to see. For refusing to tell. I have never hated anyone more than I hate him.

As the sensation returns to my arms and fingers, I fight the urge to reach up and strangle him. My back, my legs, my feet and toes mend, but I lie still. Unmoving. I don't want him to know the extent of my healing. I bide my time.

All I reveal is a slight turn of my head to look for Zeze. She's still there in the cage across the room. Watching intently.

"You've done it, Prent. Go," Osven says, peering over me. The healer removes his hands and leaves the room.

"Zeze," I whisper with difficulty around the crust in my mouth. "I need Zeze."

"Fetch his familiar, girl," Osven commands.

In my mind I chuckle. Of course this is a term the Sorcerer would fall back on. Familiars are pets. Old magic. Once someone is bonded to a familiar, they have an empathic link. Anything that happens to it, happens to them. They're not a custom in Cerion. They used to be, in Sunteri. Before the really powerful Sorcerers snuffed out the Mages and weaker Sorcerers. Nan used to tell me fables about them.

Anyway, Zeze is definitely not a familiar. She's not even really a pet. She's a cat. We have a bond. Sometimes it feels like something more. Sometimes I wonder about her. I used to think she was Ki, like Elliot can dreamwalk in the form of a fox, but it was wishful thinking. I asked her about it once when Zeze first came around, and she denied it. She said Iren wouldn't let her just wander around the city that way. It's too risky.

"My master said—" the girl's voice sends chills through me. Celli. I whip my head in her direction. Her hand rests on the cage latch, ready to open it.

"Do you defy me?" Osven hisses. "You were ordered to assist me, were you not? If you wish to disappoint Quenson, then by all means, ignore my request."

"But I'm not supposed to—" she starts again, and Osven growls.

"What," he demands through clenched teeth, "exactly were your master's orders?"

"To do as you say, and not to let the cat out of my sight," she answers. "And to fetch him if there's any change."

"And will the cat," he over-enunciates every word with utter annoyance, "be leaving your sight if you bring her to Nullen?"

"N-no, sir," Celli answers with a wince.

"Then do as you are told, whelp," Osven jeers wickedly, "or I shall remind you of the taste of lightning."

"You can't," Celli raises her chin, "my master protects me."

"If you wish to test me," Osven huffs, "I'm happy to oblige. THE CAT!" he shouts.

Celli jumps and fumbles with the cage latch. She reaches in to grab

Zeze, but the cat hisses and lashes out with her claws and she pulls her hand away fearfully. I chuckle.

"Bring the cage, witless," Osven sneers. "Dump her there," he points to the crook of my arm.

Celli tips the cage and Zeze slides out. Her soft fur brushes my skin. She looks calmly at me, licks my cheek, and curls into a ball with the top of her head pressing on my neck. The comfort she brings me is quickly dampened as I look past her at Celli.

She's a completely different person, standing there. Dressed in assassin's clothes, hair slicked back, eyes flecked with malice. A spell hangs heavy over her, woven through her blood. Allegiance. Loyalty. Bound to another. A Sorcerer. Quenson. His name pulses through her veins with every beat of her heart. The magic is so strong my breath catches. She revels in it. Embraces it. It's who she is now. No turning back. If I get out of here, even if I wanted to try and take her with me, she wouldn't come.

She slams the cage shut and stalks away, never taking her eyes from me. She won't. Quenson ordered her not to. She'd die before she'd allow Zeze to leave her sight. Despite the furry warmth that nestles my neck, I shiver at the utter, evil power of it. Irreversible. Celli's gone.

"You have your pet now, boy. But to what end? What powers does she afford you?" Osven leans closer, his eyes wild with his hunger for knowledge.

"You," I think of how he lost his temper with me, how he shoved me from the cliff. I remember every single crack of a bone as I struck the wall. "You saved my life," I utter. The deception is sour on my tongue. I swallow bile as his eyes flash with triumph.

"Fetch your master," he waves behind him at Celli, who hesitates only for a moment before rushing off.

I close my eyes, pretending to be tired. Really, I've never felt stronger. The healing they gave me pulses through me, energizing my bones and muscles. I want to jump up. I want to run. I have a plan to get them to take us outside. I curl my arm around Zeze and she purrs happily.

It doesn't take long for Quenson to arrive. I feel him without even opening my eyes. Feel his power. His wards. His link to Celli. I don't want to look at him. He's awful. Wicked. Cold.

"You saved my life," I whisper again, and the Sorcerers hover closer to me. "I'll try again. With Zeze. She helps me. I'll look again. I'll tell you what I can see. Just don't hurt her. Let her stay with me."

"Well done, Osven," Quenson murmurs, impressed.

I pretend to struggle from the dais. They walk with me, Osven ahead, Celli and Quenson behind. Guards all around us, of course, but just like last time the guards stop at the wards to the tunnel. I step through with Zeze in my arms. At our ease of passage through the wards, Quenson gasps.

"Remarkable," he whispers. "Remain here, Celli, with the guards."

The Sorcerers guide me hastily through the tunnel that leads to the cliffs, and my heart starts racing. What if this doesn't work? What if Osven throws me off again? Zeze nuzzles my arm. It'll be okay, she seems to say.

I stroke her neck absently as we go, and something odd grazes my fingers. A collar? But, Zeze doesn't have a collar. I never got her one. I stroke again and feel the smooth, hard beads buried in her thick fur. Feel the faint magic in them. Fairy magic. A flash of a memory surges through me. A pearl bracelet, offered to Crocus and Scree. The same bracelet later, slung over Twig's shoulder. A tether, ready to be taken to its owner.

My feet slip on the slick stone as we reach the edge of the tunnel. My hands are numb. My whole body tingles. I can't believe it. Zeze, all this time. All this time, and she never told me. I cling hard to her. Nothing else matters. I need to get her home. Back to Cerion. I don't dare think her name. I don't dare think of her at all. I clear my head of my memories of her. I can't risk her safety.

My feet touch the grass, and Twig's voice rings out bright and clear in my mind.

"Hello!" he says.

My eyes snap to Osven ahead of me. He's already looking out into the sky. The black stone hovers there. The inky staircase leading to it glints in the sunlight. The storm is done. The air is fresh and crisp. Quenson slips out from behind me to join him. Both of them are too focused on the sky. They haven't noticed Twig at all. Thankfully, he's hidden safely in the half-realm. He settles on the crook of my arm next to Zeze and makes sure he's got a hand on both of us.

"Ready?" he asks. I understand. He needs my consent.

"Get us out of here," I whisper.

I grin at the look of surprise and fury on the Sorcerers' faces as they spin to face us, and wave farewell as we fade away into the Half-Realm.

Chapter Twenty-Two

SECRETS SQUANDERED

Azi

The breakfast feast promised by the queen is spectacular. They adorn us with necklaces of live flowers that open and close with the sound of our laughter, and set dishes before us so delectable that even Mouli would be impressed.

The quest is set aside as we eat our fill, and though when I sat down I was rather impatient, by the time my belly is full I'm lulled into a quiet calm that eases my nerves. We have time, the mood of the place seems to say. Live in the moment. Enjoy life while you can.

Rian is very affectionate through the meal. His hand rests on my shoulder, his fingers play with the end of my braid. Once in a while I catch him watching me, just looking, taking me in.

"It is not every day we see love in its purest form between humans," Zilliandin is saying to Flitt. "You know, in days past, it was not unusual for the queen to perform the maritals. Ah, yes, humans would come from countries wide to seek her bonding ceremony. And then the wedding night! Heheh! One could not imagine a more romantic place to spend it. Something to think about, you two." He gives us a wry grin.

Rian catches my eye and winks, and I blush and look down into my lap.

"Something to think about," he murmurs to me. I nod.

"Yet now, the time has come," the queen declares at the head of the table, "for us to hear your decision."

With a nod of her head, the table fades away. Flitt grabs for one last berry and shoves it into her mouth before it vanishes completely. With a shift of light, the queen is on her throne again, high above us up the stairs. The rest of us stand on the landing halfway up with throngs of fairies looking down on us, waiting.

"Azaeli Hammerfel, Rian Eldinae," the queen calls out, "what is your declaration?"

Rian takes my hand as we turn to face the queen. Flitt and Shush float to stand beside us. I let Rian do the talking for us. I'm suddenly too nervous to speak.

"We accept your quest, Your Majesty," he says.

The fairies erupt into deafening cheers of approval so loud that my ears ring with the noise. The queen rises from her throne. Her gown of white butterflies moves with her, their wings opening and closing in unison. She raises her scepter and holds it over us, and the crowd hushes.

"Then I officially bestow upon you, Rian Eldinae and Azaeli Hammerfel, Flitter of Kythshire and Shushing of Kythshire, a title: Champion of Light. Wear it with pride. Take it with you where you go. You shall find this blessing of Light quite useful against the darkness."

She bows her head and closes her eyes, and four white orbs emerge from the scepter. They glide down the staircase and hover before us. Then, one by one, they touch our foreheads and fade away.

The sensation is that of a mother's warm kiss. It tingles softly and then grows until I feel a buzz through my whole body. I close my eyes. When I open them again, I find myself standing in the dim passage that connects the guild hall to our houses. My father's hammer rings a steady tempo from his forge. The orange glow of sunset spills through the louvered slats of the door at the end of the hallway. It's disorienting, since a moment ago, we were facing a new day in the throne room of the fairy royal court. It feels like we've lost a whole day.

"*Azi,*" Flitt pushes to me. "*Shush and I have to go home and tell the Ring. We'll be back in the morning.*"

I nod silently. "*See you soon,*" I push back.

I look from one direction to the other and find myself alone in the hallway.

"Rian?" I call tentatively.

"Yeah," he answers from right in front of me. I jump as he emerges from the Half-Realm.

"Why do you always do that?" I move to smack him playfully, but he takes my hand and pulls me secretively to him.

"I know how much it amuses you," he laughs, then hushes me. He draws me closer and strokes a soft thumb across my cheek. I close my eyes and sigh.

"Why are we still hiding?" I whisper. His fingertips trace across the bridge of my nose.

"We need to for now," he says vaguely. I look at him and see myself reflected in his eyes. The golden Mark swirls across my cheek and nose. It glows brightly, reflecting off his chiseled cheekbones. "I

187

don't want them to know we're back yet. I have to find something first."

"Liar," I scowl and scratch at the brightest part of my cheek where the gold Mark shines. I imagine what I must look like, covered in the gold Mark, and I'm grateful to him for hiding me.

"I'm only half a liar," he retorts with a shrug and a grin. "I really do need to find something. It's a book. Sort of a directory. In there." He points toward the meeting hall.

"Oh," I whisper.

"I might have to reveal us, though, so you'd better keep your helm on if you're still keeping it secret," he says. As he takes my hand and leads me up the hall, I clap my face guard down and hope it covers what it needs to.

A fire crackles merrily in the hearth and Mya sits in one of the stuffed chairs beside it with her mandolin poised to play. She's dressed in her performance clothes with her hair done up in the spiked style she usually wears for a show. Her fingers slide silently over the strings as she stares at the spacing of them as though in deep meditation.

Elliot dozes curled up in the chair beside her. The firelight dances on the feathers in his hair and casts shadows over his eyes. The scene is so peaceful I'm glad Rian chose to sneak in to keep from disturbing them. He leaves me, goes to a shelf in the far corner, and glances over his shoulder at his parents.

When he's sure they haven't seen him, he pulls a tome from the shelf and tucks it under his robes. He doesn't make a sound. Behind us, Mya starts to play.

It's a new song I haven't heard from her before. Her fingers pluck the strings softly, her lips move with the words, her voice testing the melody.

"*She's learning it,*" Rian pushes to me. "*The Muses' song. The one the queen and Flitt mentioned.*"

I barely acknowledge what he's saying. My attention is drawn to a scattering of scrolls on the meeting table bearing the royal seal and the king's signature. I see my name on one and lean over it to read:

Six Summerswan

Attention: His Majesty's Elite

His Majesty King Tirnon Plethore requests the presence of Azaeli Hammerfel, Knight of His Majesty's Elite, Ambassador to Kythshire to discuss the events of Two Summerswan in the High Court of Cerion.

Failure to respond to this request immediately shall be considered an act of willful defiance and treachery.

I feel the color drain from my face as I read the words twice more. My head starts to spin at the seriousness of the notice and the severity of the wording. My eyes dart around the table. In addition to the summons and several canceled quest decrees, there are two small scraps in my mother's handwriting that look like traveling notes.

"Six Summerswan?" I push to Rian as he grips my shoulder. *"How long have we been gone?"*

"You were gone for two days before Shush convinced me to go with him. That was the fourth," he replies.

"I have to go," I say aloud and spin toward the door.

"I'll—" Rian starts, but the soft padding trot of paws in the corridor beyond interrupts him.

We watch together as the fox comes up the hallway sniffing, stops in the doorway, and looks right at us. With a huff, it saunters to Elliot, hops up onto his chest, and fades.

Elliot yawns and stretches and blinks a few times. He tips his head to Mya.

"So much for that," Rian mutters.

"Found them," Elliot says around another thick yawn.

Mya stops playing.

"Are they safe? Where are they?" she asks with a hint of urgency.

Elliot stretches his arms up over his head and then points in our general direction. Rian sighs and whispers the Revealer, and the two of us step together out of the Half-Realm into view.

"Where have you two been?" Mya scowls. "And why are you skulking around the guild hall?"

"I'll get Benen," Elliot says. His eyes linger for a moment on my face. Only the bridge of my nose and my eyes show through the slit in the face guard, but it's enough, apparently. I turn slightly away from the fire, hoping the shadows will hide the Mark. Elliot shakes his head and slips off down the hallway.

"We were just…we just got back," Rian says, a little flustered. "We didn't want to interrupt you learning a new song."

"I used to know it. It's just coming back to me," Mya glances at her mandolin with a sort of dreamy longing. She starts to play again as though she can't resist the draw of it, and then shakes her head and sets the instrument aside.

"Where have you been?" she asks, focusing on the two of us again. "You could have at least sent a note! It was utterly irresponsible of you,

Rian Dustin Eldinae!" She stalks toward him. Though the tips of her red-spiked hair add to her height, she only comes to Rian's chest. Even so, he shrinks away from her warily. "Your father has been sleeping for days searching for you!"

"And your mother," she turns to me, jabbing a finger into the chestplate of my armor, "took off to Kythshire searching for *you*!"

"What?" I gasp and glance at Rian.

"That's right. She took Donal with her two days ago." Mya stalks past Rian and picks up my summons. "She's terrified you'll be the next on trial."

Her eyes linger on my face the same way Elliot's did, and I duck as she reaches a graceful hand to my helm.

"What?" she whispers with wonder. I turn away, my heart racing.

My father's boots clomp loudly toward us, and I cower closer to Rian as Da emerges from the hallway. His face is red, I can't tell whether from the forge or from anger. Probably both. At first he seems relieved to see me, but then his eyes narrow and his lips purse.

"Our house. Now," he orders me.

"Da," I take the scroll from Mya and hold it up, "I need to go to the palace."

"Now." His nostrils flare out and his eyes narrow to angry slits. I don't dare argue any more. Fairies and quests aside, I'm his daughter, and I'm in trouble. I risk a glance over my shoulder at Rian, Mya, and Elliot as I follow my father out. From the looks of it, he's in for it, too.

"*Stay strong*," he sends to me.

"*You too*," I reply.

"Six days," my father paces across our kitchen. As his anger builds, his voice gets louder. It's been a long time since he's shouted at me. Usually Mum keeps him calm. She's not here, though. She's out looking for me.

"Six days, and no note! No sign! Nothing! Your mother's worried sick, crying day and night. Then the king sends this!" He snatches the scroll from my hands. "And she goes off back to *that place* to find you."

"But why didn't Uncle just—" I start, and his eyes go wide. He turns away and leans on the counter, breathing heavily.

"Don't talk to me about that man," he growls. "He showed his loyalty straight away. Hasn't left the Academy once since the attack. Always sending excuses."

"But I'm here, now, right? I can go get Mum and tell her—"

"Absolutely not!" he shouts, shaking. "You're not going anywhere.

190

None of us are. We're under orders to stay in the city."

"Why?" I whisper. Through the hallway to the guild hall, I can hear Rian getting much of the same from both of his parents. Shouting. Scolding. I swallow the lump in my throat hard and focus on my father.

"Things have changed since the execution," he explains, making an obvious effort to keep his voice steady. "Cerion is divided. Suspicion is everywhere." He clomps to the window and motions me over. I follow and peer outside as he opens the shutter a crack for me. A city guard stands on our front stoop, keeping watch. Farther down the street, another group of them marches past.

Da closes the shutters silently and faces me. The way he looks at me frightens me more than his anger had. His love for me is pushed to the background. In its place I see only hesitation. Fear.

"You changed," he says. "You're different."

My eyes well with tears. I don't know how to reply. I start to turn away and he catches my shoulder.

"Take your helm off when I'm talking to you, Azi," he says sternly. The way his voice goes quiet is unnerving. I'd much prefer the shouting. I reach up with shaking hands to obey, and to my relief he gets distracted as the hilt of my new sword catches his eye.

"What's that?" he growls. "Where's your other sword?" My heart sinks at his pained expression. "I made that for you, Azi. For your birthday. With my own hands. What did you do? Trade it in? Did you give it to *them*?"

"Da, I..." my throat closes around the lump that rises in it.

"Let me see it," he holds out his hand, scowling.

Reluctantly I loosen my scabbard from my shoulder and pull the sword free. Its golden blade glows with a soft, white light. I hold it between us and Da looks it over. Despite his anger, his awe of the weapon is plain on his face.

"It was," I start, but I can't finish. "I had to," I try again, but the words don't come. The scene is sharp in my memory, but try as I might, I can't form an explanation. I can't tell my father why I gave up the sword he forged for me and how I ended up with this one. I understand he's not meant to know, but it still hurts me to be forced to keep such a thing from him. Instead I offer it to him, hoping somehow it'll mend this sudden rift between us.

He reaches to take the handle and his hand goes straight through it. His eyes snap to mine and narrow. He tries again. The pommel is solid and perfectly weighted in my palms. As real as any sword can be. But when Da reaches for it again, it's like an apparition. Any hope of quelling his mood is destroyed as he looms over me, absolutely seething.

"What's the meaning of this?" he growls. "What are you playing at, Azi?"

"Da," I try hard to choose the right words to explain. "You know that I'm pulled between two places. I'm not like you. Cerion is my home, but I have responsibilities elsewhere, too." I try to sound calm, but my voice is shaken.

"You are a Knight of His Majesty's Elite," his fierce tone makes me shy away. "Your allegiance is to Cerion and King Tirnon first, Azaeli. His Majesty is wracked with grief over Eron. Over the son I executed. He's wild with rage over the attack on the High Court. He's got twenty different edicts about what should be done to stop it from ever happening again. One moment, he wants to ban magic and close the Academy. The next, he's looking for someone to blame so he can start a war. Nobody can talk any sense into him. Not his advisors. Not even Mya.

"Meantime, the kingdom is losing faith in the throne. Murmuring about an uprising. Half of them don't think he's fit to rule anymore, you see? He lost too much control. Strange happenings outside the city gates, and no orders to investigate them. The guild, we're on edge. Ready to jump up at any command. Ready to defend the palace, if we need to. Meantime, we have to be guarded! From what? Don't ask me. I have no idea what's going through his head. Then he sends that summons for you! And you come strolling into the hall, oblivious to all of it, waving around this shiny new f— f— fai— Argh!" he bellows in frustration and slams his fist on the table, rattling the vase of flowers set upon it. I jump. He goes on.

"You belong here, Azi. In service to His Majesty. You are sworn to him. Not some foppish nuts who lure you with magical swords." His knuckles go white as his fists clench. "First your mother, now you. At least she's strong enough to resist their sway. You have to do the same, Azi. Stay away from them, or they'll draw you in. Stay away, or you'll end up belonging to them. Remember your oaths to Cerion. People are talking about you, Azi. They're suspicious. I'm starting to wonder if they have something there. Where is your allegiance? Is it where it should be?"

"Da," his words shock me. I ought to have realized it sooner, really. I should have seen his side. The fairies tried to steal his wife away, they cursed us, they lured me. He could even argue that their influence tainted the prince he was ordered to execute. When I look into his eyes, I see it plainly there. He hates the fairies. He hates everything about them. He despises them, and he sees them in me.

I want to tell him why I was gone. I want to tell him everything I've seen. I want to tell him about Margy and her powers, and how much she needs me to do this for her. I want to explain to him my fealty isn't only to Cerion or only to Kythshire. It's to both. To the Light. To the Dawn. He can hate the fairies all he wants, but there's no way to avoid our alliance with them. We have to stand together against the Dusk. If we don't, everything we know will be overcome with darkness.

I want to convince him I wasn't being irresponsible. That I didn't leave him and our guild for nothing. That my allegiance hasn't changed. I was so sure, in the Palace of the Queen, of my path. Now that I'm home again, my allegiance to Cerion seems more important. Between the two, I feel as though I'm being torn in half. I want to tell him all of this, but the words fail me.

Silently and slowly, I sheath my sword again and shrug into the straps of my scabbard. I try hard to come up with some explanation that will help him see my side.

"The world is bigger than Cerion," I start carefully. I try to keep my voice calm, like Mum does when Da loses his temper. "And because of that, there is always the risk of a threat. My friends," I gesture over my shoulder to the hilt of my sword, "have sent me a warning. That Sorcerer in the High Court was just the beginning, Da. There's a scourge of them waiting, poised to strike." I close my eyes and press my hand to my helm. A hundred sentences run through my mind before I find the one that I can speak. "If they find what they seek, Cerion will fall."

"They're threatening us now? Is that it?" Da starts pacing again. "Of course they would, with the king as he is. They'd swoop in, right when he's at his weakest. They set all of this up, didn't they?" His eyes grow more wild with every word. It reminds me of how he was years ago, right after he crossed the border into Kythshire without permission and went mad. I take a step back toward the door.

"You're scaring me, Da," I whisper. "I never said they were threatening us, I said there were others. Sorcerers."

"And where do you think the Sorcerers get their magic, Azi? THEY give it to them!" Da shouts. He takes me by the arms and pulls me close, searching my eyes with his. He truly believes what he's saying. He hates the fae. He's justified it. Good or bad, it doesn't matter. I can't change his mind.

"I said take off your helm when you're talking to me," he whispers fiercely. Already I can see the glow of the Mark reflected in his eyes. I'm certain he's seen it. There's no way to explain so that he'll understand. No way I can argue without him going off on another tirade. No way, except one. With my hands still shaking, I reach up and push my visor back.

I gaze into his wild eyes, gray as steel, flecked with amber and blue as they take in my face. In them I see his pain and confusion over the Mark. I sink deeper into them, and the connection between us takes hold.

The rush of magic fills me up. His breathing slows and calms as our gazes lock together. When I'm sure I've made the link, I send my own memories to him. I start at the beginning, when I stood vigil over him during the time he was cursed. I show him Flitt's light dancing on the wall of our upstairs hallway, drawing me out of his room and into mine.

He tries to move away from me, but I won't let him. I hold him with gold threads. He can't go yet. I'm desperate to show him. He has to understand how important my work is with the fae. I show him Flitt. Her games, her aid. I show him the Ring and the fairies dancing. I show him Margy and Twig in the palace, reading me the first story about the warrior who came to Kythshire. Revealing the prince's treachery to me.

Da squeezes his eyes closed, breaking the connection. He shoves me away from him and stumbles back against the kitchen basin, panting. I realize my mistake too late.

"The palace. They're in the palace," he murmurs. "They're in the palace, and they've got the princess." His knuckles go white as he grips the edge of the basin. He spins to face me. "How could you know this and never say a word? That was nearly three years ago, Azi! Are they still there? Are they still spying?"

He crashes toward me and grabs my arms again. He shakes me frantically. I see my own face in the reflection of his wide eyes. The golden mark glows sharply as it curls around my left eye.

"Are they still there?" he yells and shakes me.

"Da, please!" I cry, terrified by his reaction. "It's not like that..."

Someone's hand slips into mine. Rian. I grip it hard as my father bears down on me.

Rian thrusts his free hand out whispers a spell that settles thick and pink over Da. His eyelids grow heavy and drift closed. His grip on my arms loosens and his hands slide down. He starts to droop to the floor and I catch him.

"Good thinking, Rian," Mya says as she rushes in. "That was getting out of hand." Bryse fills up the rest of the doorway behind her.

"I heard yelling," he says. "Hey, when'd you get back?"

"Just now," Mya answers for me. "Good that you're here, Bryse. Get Benen to bed, please."

Bryse stoops through the kitchen door and comes to my side.

"Thanks," I whisper shakily to him as I heft Da up.

"I got 'im.' Bryse loops an arm around Da's chest and picks him up with ease. His eyes linger on my face for a moment and he shakes his head and averts them, but not before I notice a flash of the same confusion Da looked at me with just moments before. Tears spill down my cheeks and I wipe at them angrily, wishing with all my heart that I could push away the Mark just as easily.

"Thank you Bryse," I try to whisper, but nothing comes out.

"Rian," Mya orders, "go to Lisabella and Donal. Tell them to ride home. Azi, come with me."

"*See you soon*," Rian pushes to me, and I feel a kiss on my cheek as his hand leaves mine.

"Quickly," Mya says, and guides me through the back door.

We slip into the corridor and pass by Mya's house. I assume we'll be heading to the palace so I reach up and close my visor again to keep anyone in the street from noticing. To my surprise, instead of leaving the guild hall, Mya stops at Cort and Bryse's door and knocks.

"Cort," she calls with an urgency that makes the hair on my arms prickle. The door opens and Cort peers out at the two of us. He's dressed in a plain sleeveless tunic, short trousers, and bare feet, and his braids are swept back from his face and piled on top of his head.

Without a word, he ushers us inside and closes the door behind him. He kicks aside several unmatched, discarded boots and sandals and leads us to the small sitting area. The only sofa is piled with pillaged sacks, crumpled maps, weapons and empty drinking skins. Cort shoves them to the floor to make room for us to sit, and perches on the arm beside me.

"What's going on?" I whisper. I can count on one hand the number of times I've been inside this house. It hasn't changed much over the years, aside from gathering more clutter.

"I'd ask you the same," Mya says in a hushed tone. "Show Cort your face."

Cort's dark brow furrows as I consider it. I don't want a repeat of Da's reaction, but it's not right to keep a secret like this from the guild. Reluctantly, with my heart racing, I sigh and shove my visor up yet again.

As soon as the sight registers, Cort gasps. He stumbles from his seat and rushes to the laundry-ridden stairs, taking them two at a time. We hear him rummaging around upstairs for a while, and then he slides back down the banister, barely touching a step on the way down.

"Where's Bryse?" he asks.

"Tending to Benen," Mya replies vaguely.

"What happened to Benen?" Cort asks.

"Later," says Mya. "Do you have it?"

Cort tucks himself between me and Mya on the sofa. He rests his closed fist on his knee and turns to look at the Mark on my face again.

"All this time," he says to Mya with a grin of awe, "it was her."

"Are you really surprised?" Mya laughs softly.

"What?" I sputter, completely confused by the two of them. "What was me?"

"This," Cort opens his hand to reveal a note that has been folded several times. The tattered parchment seems to glow brightly against his deep brown skin even as worn as it is.

"An old master approached me in Stepstone almost two decades ago. Said he'd pay me well to go to Cerion," he explains, "for a job. I was happy to take the work and get away from ah," he glances at Mya, "being a deckhand for a while."

Mya shakes her head and smiles, but doesn't say anything to that. We both know the truth. Before he came to Cerion, Cort was a mercenary pirate. That's why he's never been knighted even after all of his years in the Elite.

"He gave me this," he continues. "He told me when the time was right, the golden one would reveal herself to me here. When she did, I was to give it to her." He nods to the folded note, offering it to me. "Longest job of my life."

"Me?" I whisper. They both nod, and I take it with trembling hands and unfold it gingerly. Even that small act seems to impress the two of them.

"She opened it," Mya whispers.

"Can you read it to us?" Cort sits up and leans closer to me.

The words on the page are scrawled in the flowery hand of a Mage. The ink glistens freshly, as though it was written just moments ago. It takes me some time to stop the words from swimming. When they finally seem to settle on the page, I read aloud.

"Champion of Light," I croak, and the place where the fairy queen's orb met my forehead tingles softly. "Long have we awaited this moment…"

Chapter Twenty-Three
CONFRONTATIONS

Tib

Zeze gives a little meow and leaps gracefully from my arms as I hit the green carpet hard and roll into the corner. Margy's dolls and mushroom pillows cushion me from slamming hard into the wall.

Across the room, Zeze saunters casually to the bed. Hops up. Fades into Margy. Twig hovers over her. The princess sighs and stretches and pushes herself up on her silky purple pillows. She blinks sleepily and looks around the room.

My heart pounds with fury. All this time, she was Zeze. She put herself in danger. Why didn't she tell me? I would have protected her more. I never would have let her wander around like that. I push myself to my feet and stalk across the room toward her, ready to tell her so. Twig sees me coming. He darts across and puts both hands on my lips. Shakes his head frantically. Points to an armchair beside the bed. Tirie's there. Sound asleep. I take a step. Hide myself in the Half-Realm.

"Hum," Margy says softly, and Tirie's eyes fly open.

"Princess! You're awake! How do you feel? Do you feel ill?" she whispers frantically as she rushes to Margy's side and presses a hand to her forehead.

Margy sinks back into her pillows. She lets Tirie flutter around her. She looks like she's trying hard not to be impatient. She steals a glance at me and looks away quickly.

She can see me, but Tirie can't. I test it. I walk up beside the older woman. She goes on fussing over Margy. Doesn't notice me at all. It scares me. If I wanted to, I could kill them both. I wonder how easy would be for one of them to get in here. The Dusk.

I glance at the windows. It's night, almost. I move closer to them. Feel the wards there. They're strong. Layered. Dozens of protections, one over the other. Days old, months old. Years. Decades.

"She's safe," Twig murmurs to me. "See? No one is getting through that."

"You did," I whisper.

"I couldn't until she brought me in from the garden," he explains.

"Azi and Rian could," I keep my voice low, so Tirie doesn't hear.

"They were already welcome in the palace, before they could travel through the Half-Realm," Twig says. "Men's spells are complicated. They have lots of rules and contingencies."

"Complicated means there could be holes," I scowl. "They could still get her."

"I'm hungry," the princess sighs softly. She looks up at Tirie with wide, innocent eyes. She could be seven years old again. A little girl, tucked in her enormous bed.

"I'll fetch the physician first. He'll need to check you. And Their Majesties wanted to know the moment you woke," Tirie pats Margy's cheek tenderly.

"Don't bother them at supper," Margy pushes the blankets away and Tirie puts them back on.

"Nonsense," Tirie scoffs. "Princess, you've been sleeping over a day. Nearly two, now. They'll want to know you're up." She tucks the fluffy blanket around Margy's body. When Margy goes to protest again, Tirie puts her hands firmly on her hips. "I won't hear another word. I have my instructions. Would you have me lose my position?"

"All right. I'm sorry," Margy yawns. Her eyes flick toward me again and away.

Tirie rushes to the door and opens it. A small group is waiting in the hall. Two pages, three royal guards, and a Mage. Tirie goes out and closes the door behind her, and I press my hands into the velvet coverlet and lean closer to Margy.

"What were you thinking?" I hiss at her. "How could you do that?"

"I had to find you," she whispers and leans closer to me. She looks me right in the eyes. Hers are brown, flecked with gold and green. Just like Zeze's. She's not afraid at all. Not regretful. No, she's charged with excitement. "We had to get you out of there."

"You could have been killed!" I shout, and she grabs my hand and shushes me.

"You, too," she whispers. Her hand on mine sends a rush through me. Like a spell, except spells can't touch me. I try to resist. To make the feeling go away. It doesn't, though. It's not a spell. It's a warm feeling. A wanting. Margy leans closer. Her face is so smooth. So soft and perfect. I want to pull her close. Tell her it'll be okay. Then she speaks again, and I remember why I was so angry. "Don't be mad," she pleads. "I had to be Zeze."

"But, why? How? I don't understand. How long?" I yank my hand away. I can't think straight with her touching me. She looks a little sad when I do. I don't care. I'm too agitated. I move away from the bed and start pacing.

"A few months," she whispers. "Think of the first time you saw Zeze. There was so much talk here in the palace. Rumors of an uprising. Fear of unknown magic. Even Master Gaethon, even Master Anod, didn't know the source. Or what exactly it was. I was worried for the people. I was afraid. I had to see for myself what was happening in the kingdom. I had to know. Twig understood. He helped me."

I glance at Twig, who has settled beside the princess in a fold of her blanket. His knobby knees poke up, brown and earthy against the pale lavender. He doesn't look regretful. Not at all.

"This will be my kingdom someday, Tib," Margy goes on. "I can't have it fall apart before then. I won't have the Plethore peace threatened."

I close my eyes. What she's saying is too sensible. It's the way a queen would think. This is Margy. She's young. Too young to have worries like that.

"I'm a princess," she says, almost like she can read my thoughts. "This kingdom is my responsibility now just as much as it will be when I'm queen. Tib," she whispers desperately, and I turn to face her. She looks older now than the little girl who was buried in her bed with Tirie hovering over her. She motions me closer. I stalk back to her bedside.

"I know what's coming," she says with a tone so hushed I have to lean close to hear. "I saw it before you were taken. In the High Court. The Sorcerers. My brother," her voice cracks. Her eyes are rimmed with tears. "You've seen it, too. Firsthand. The Dusk. Paba is trying to ban magic," she whispers in a rush as Tirie opens the door to come back in. "If he does, it'll just leave us more vulnerable." Her eyes flick to the windows, toward the wards.

I shrink against the wall as Tirie rushes in with a stern-looking man beside her. He's got a leather sack which jingles mysteriously. He leans over the princess and presses a glass circle to his eye.

"The physician," Twig whispers at my shoulder. I spin and snatch him out of the air.

"You," I snarl. He doesn't squirm. He rests his tiny elbows calmly on the crook of my thumb. Looks up at me dubiously. No, not dubious. Patient. Like he's ready to ride out my anger. His skinny body pokes my hand like a stick. Like his name. Twig. I could snap him. "How could you let her do that?"

"Let her?" Twig chuckles. "You say that like you don't know the princess at all, Tib. How could I have stopped her? Margy is quite capable. If not for me, she would have tried the Half-Realm, maybe. That would have far more dangerous. This way, as Zeze, is much safer. There are protections--"

He stops talking and shies away as Tirie and the physician creep closer to us and farther from the princess to whisper.

"Is it serious?" Tirie clings to his arm. Like he'll have to steady her because whatever he's going to say will make her faint.

"*Is it serious?*" Twig pushes to Margy, who sits with her hands folded in her lap and her eyes closed. The bed is at least twenty paces away. Far enough that the nursemaid and the physician think they can't be overheard. I smirk and shake my head while Twig goes on repeating everything they say. Nice trick.

"My lady," the physician murmurs, "as I have insisted many times before, there is nothing wrong with the princess. There are no physical ailments or illnesses present. She is the prime example of a perfectly healthy young lady. A testament to your fine care, if you will."

"But the sleeping!" Tirie hisses. "You cannot assure me that it's healthy for a normal child her age to sleep for days, sir!"

"Perhaps not," the physician says thoughtfully, and Tirie gives him a smug nod. "But I would not presume to put Her Highness firmly in the category of 'normal'."

His words send a rush through me. He knows. He knows about Margy and her powers. Twig freezes. We both hold our breath. Even Margy leans forward in her bed, trying to hear.

"No?" Tirie's eyes go wide. Her grip tightens on his arm. "And why not?"

"Think of what she's been through," he explains. "The girl just watched her brother executed. She's no one to confide in who could possibly understand."

"Nonsense. She can talk to me!" Tirie scowls.

"With all due respect," he bows his head to her honestly, "she is a growing girl. She requires peers. Others her age who can keep her spirits up. If anything, her constant sleeping is an indication of low spirits. Let her be frivolous. Give her some small freedoms. That is my advice to you, as a physician, and that is what I shall advise His Majesty in my report."

Tirie's not as relieved by his solution as I'd think. Her lips purse into a scowl. Her eyes narrow just a little. She leaves the room with him and closes the door behind them.

Together, Twig and I let out the breath we'd been holding. He darts to Margy's side.

"Maybe now she won't hover so much," she sighs. "And maybe it won't be so hard for me to convince her to let you and Saesa come to call."

"I thought maybe she suspected," I whisper.

"I think she knows something's different about Margy," Twig replies. "I just think she's trying to catch a gnat with too wide a web."

"Tib," Margy scoots closer to me. "What did you see in that place? What was there? Are they the ones who attacked the High Court?"

Her change in the subject sets my heart racing. Right away I'm back there, looking up at the Sorcerers' keep. Walking through tunnels. Being confronted by dark, scaly fairies. I remember what I felt. Eron. Their prize. Their intentions. My eyes go wide.

"Yes," I whisper. "It was definitely them."

"Can you remember anything about it?" she asks. "Where it was? I was in a sack, so I couldn't see when they brought me there. But the man who carried me said the same words Brother did before Sir Benen…" She swallows hard and looks away.

I describe the keep to her from what I saw of the outside. It's not much to go on. She asks me all kinds of questions. Where the sun was, where the storm was. I tell her everything. Even the part about the floating chunk of stone.

"I have to tell Paba," she says quietly. "I think I know where it is. We have to stop them from doing what they're going to do. We can't let them bring him back."

She avoids saying Eron's name, but I know who she means. I shake my head.

"How?" I ask. "How can you tell him any of this without telling him what you can do and what you've been up to?"

"I can't," she replies with a long, shuddering breath. "Which means it's time for him to know. I have to tell him everything and hope he understands. He needs to know the truth. All of the truth. It's time for the plan, Twig."

Twig nods. He looks conflicted. Sad, but excited, too.

"I think you're right, princess," he says. "I'll make the arrangements."

He floats up and gives her a kiss on the cheek. She smiles at him and he pops away.

"What plan?" I ask. "What arrangements?"

"Tomorrow at dawn," she whispers to me, "you'll see."

The latch on the door clicks, signaling that Tirie's about to come back in. Margy slides to the edge of the bed and looks at me.

"That man," Margy says darkly, "the one-eyed one. The one who got us both. He's still out there, Tib. They'll send him back to find you, and Zeze. Maybe even Saesa. Watch out for him. Be careful. You should go before she comes back in. Nessa's really worried about you. Stay hidden, though. Paba has guards everywhere, and they're suspicious of everyone."

She gives me a hug and I feel that same warmth from before when she touched me. I don't want to let go of her, but when Tirie opens the door, I take my chance and slip out.

What she said to me about Dub goes through my head over and over while I sneak out of the palace. The king and queen rush past with a score of guards and I have to press myself to the wall to avoid bumping anyone. I watch them pass. Feel the wards on them. Strong magic seeps out from each of them. Protective. Guarding.

I think of Margy alone in her room. Without Twig. I follow the entourage for a few paces, trying to make sense of the wards. When I'm sure they won't reveal Margy's magic, I rush away again. Toward the gates. Into the streets.

Leaving the palace feels just like leaving the Sorcerers' keep to go into the tunnel. The sudden absence of magic as I step into the streets takes some adjusting to. My feet freeze on the cobbles. I'm torn. Margy's right. I should go tell Nessa I'm safe. Saesa's probably worried, too. But Dub is out there. He's dangerous. Not just to me. I think of Celli. What happened to her. The dark shadow of a man behind me while she cried. Griff and Mikken in the cell. He's ruthless. How many more kids will he steal? How many more do they need? And what for?

The more I think about it, the more Margy's words seem like an order to me. Stop him. Find him, and make him pay. I bet he expects it, too. I bet he knows just where I'd go looking for him. I glance toward the sea wall, toward Nessa's. I look the other way, toward Redstone where my shack is. Where my invention is almost finished.

I'm just about to turn in that direction when a flash of orange hair catches my eye. She's rushing in my direction with a guard escort beside her.

"Saesa!" I dash toward her. When I get a little closer I see it's not a guard at all. It's Raefe, all dressed up in a royal navy uniform. His hand is on the handle of his rapier. He looks stern. Serious. Proud.

I fall into step beside them, on Saesa's side. Her eyes are rimmed with red, but determined. She's dressed for battle. Her gloved hand rests on the pommel of Feat, her sword.

I stay hidden as I fall into place beside her.

"How can you be sure they'll know anything about it?" Raefe asks her in a hushed tone.

"I just have a feeling," she says. "Besides, I needed an excuse to see if she's back yet."

"You know the rumors," Raefe huffs. "She's got it in with those Kythshire folk. Half of the guild does. She fled, Saesa. She probably had something to do with it. You should play it safe. Find a new Knight. Keep your reputation clean."

Saesa grabs his arm. Skids to a stop. If looks could kill, Raefe would be obliterated. He knows it, too. He shies away from her.

"Don't you ever," she looms toward her older brother. She's much shorter than he is. It'd almost be funny if she wasn't so livid. "Ever—!"

"Everything all right there?" an approaching pair of guards calls from a nearby cross-street.

"Fine," Raefe takes Saesa by the elbow. "Just escorting this one to her duties."

"Carry on," one of them says, and they wave him along.

We keep going. The streets are empty except for the city guard. I never knew Cerion had such a large force of them. Everywhere we turn there's groups of them, watching. It makes me shiver even in the heat. It feels more like Zhaghen to me. Oppressive. Frightening. Cerion's changing.

I keep close to Raefe and Saesa. When we finally reach the hall of His Majesty's Elite, no one answers any of the doors they knock on until they reach the kitchens.

"The sight of you both, lurking in the night!" Mouli gasps and waves them inside. "Look at you, Saesa! Raw with tears. Come have a cup. You too, Raefe."

I follow them in, still hidden. Pass through the wards undetected. Mouli closes the door firmly behind us.

"Is she back?" Saesa asks as soon as she steps inside. Mouli glances through the kitchen toward the meeting hall.

"You know, Miss Saesa, even if she was, I wouldn't say unless I was cleared to," Mouli replies. "Hard times, these."

"I have to see her or Rian," Saesa says. "I found something important."

"Well, if you're determined, you can wait in the hall. I'll bring you a tray. You, on the other hand," she says to Raefe, "can't go farther than the kitchen, I'm sorry to say."

"Of course. I understand," Raefe says with a nod.

"Good lad," says Mouli. "I'll fix you something."

"What was that about?" I whisper to Saesa later as she takes a chair in front of the huge fireplace. She jumps and yelps and whips around looking for me.

"Tib?" she gasps.

As soon as I step out of hiding, she throws her arms around me. Starts crying again. Doesn't stop for a while. I stand there awkwardly patting her shoulder. It doesn't help much. Just makes her squeeze me tighter and sob harder.

"I thought," she whispers once she starts to calm down. "I didn't think I'd ever see you again. And it was all my fault. Can you forgive me?"

I scowl as she leans back to look at me. She searches my face. I think she thinks I'm angry, but I'm not. I'm confused. There's nothing to forgive her for. Her eyes rest on my lips. She looks away fast.

"Forgive you for what?" I ask.

"If you hadn't gone looking for Raefe, they never would have gotten you," she sniffles and wipes her eyes, but she keeps one hand on me like she's afraid I'll disappear again if she lets go.

"What? That's stupid, Saesa. It wasn't your fault. That guy was after me. He would have gotten me either way. He…" I let myself trail off as I remember that moment in the alley. How Celli was crying. How he crept up behind me. "It was a trap," I whisper. "She was part of it."

"Who?" Saesa asks.

"Celli. She's with them now. If you see her, stay away, okay?" I think again about my contraption. The hut. The pit. I know he's got to be there waiting for me. I'll get my knives. I'll put a stop to him. Margy's warning echoes in my mind. "I have to go." I start to leave, but Saesa tightens her grip on me.

"Wait, Tib. Not yet. I found something," she says.

She reaches into her vest and pulls out a small, rounded wand. Right away I feel the magic in it. It's about the length of my hand. She offers it to me and I take it cautiously.

"Loren had it. That Mage from Stepstone, remember? When the decree against magic came out, the admiral thought to turn him in. Nessa convinced him to let him stay under Lilen's sleep spell. He's only a boy, after all, she said. But the admiral had us search him, just to be safe. That's when I found this. Look what's inscribed on it."

I turn it over and over in my hands, but there's nothing on it at all. It's a smooth wand, nicely polished, completely blank.

"See there?" Saesa whispers. "H. M. E. R. E. His Majesty's Elite. Rian Eldinae. What else could it mean?"

I turn it again and again, trying to see what she sees. I can't, though. It just looks blank to me. It must be a spell.

"I can't see it," I say. "It feels good, though." I weigh it in my hands. Sense the magic in it. "It's bright. Light magic. It feels like...I don't know how to describe it. Like it's meant to be here. Like it belongs."

I hear Mouli before I see her, so I hand the wand back to Saesa and slip into hiding again as she comes in with a tray.

"Well, you were right," Mouli says with a hint of annoyance. "Don't know how you managed to find out before I did, but apparently Azi returned a moment ago. She's visiting with Master Cort and Lady Mya right now, and they're not to be disturbed. I'll tell her you're waiting once they're through."

"Thank you, Mouli," Saesa says brightly. My stomach growls at the sight of hot iced rolls and chilled tea.

"You have them," Saesa whispers to me as Mouli rushes out again. She pushes the tray over. "I bet you're starved. There's nothing else to do but wait, now, anyway."

Chapter Twenty-Four
THE LETTER

Azi

"My name," I pause and smooth the note over my knees with trembling hands, "is Kaso Viro. I am a Muse of the Six and a Master Mage of the Stepstone Isles." I stop again and scan the rest of the note, and the sofa creaks loudly as Mya and Cort shift to lean in closer. Certain words catch my eye: Kythshire. Dawn. Wellsprings. Fae. My heart races.

I glance at Mya first and then Cort. These are things I've kept secret for quite a long time. Mya has never had more than a vague understanding of the relationship Rian and I have with Kythshire. She has never pressed us for information. Having a son who was schooled at the Academy, she's used to secrets. Secrets designed to protect the Wellsprings that she doesn't even know exist.

"Go on," Cort prods with obvious interest. "What does it say?"

"Perhaps she shouldn't, Cort," Mya says with quiet understanding. "Perhaps it's not meant for us."

I think of what Flitt told me before we went to see the Fairy Queen: "They're all a part of this. You're going to need them. All of them." I remember Margy reading the story of Brindelier. If it wasn't meant for them, I wouldn't be able to share it. I take a chance, take a deep breath, and go on reading.

"If this note has reached you, then the pieces have fallen into place. The Dusk is growing stronger. It threatens that which you hold dear: Your country, your peace, your allies in the fairies of Kythshire. Even the Wellsprings are endangered by this dark force. Already, your city has been a victim of the Dusk. You must give His Majesty a warning. You must tell him to protect the sons of the prince or risk the fall of Cerion. You must convince him to strengthen his alliance with Kythshire. You must make him aware of his daughter's talents. I tell you this, Azaeli Hammerfel, because your name is written in the stars. You and you alone can show His Majesty the truth of all things. Once you have, seek me. Oh, and a small favor. Do kindly return my apprentice to his master. He's a good lad, and my tower has not been swept in weeks. Yours in Light, K.V."

Mya laughs softly at the last, and Cort shakes his head.

"Mages," he says. "All that, and he's worried about his tower being swept."

"Right," Mya says pensively. "Right."

None of us says anything else. We simply sit, taking it all in. I'm the first to break the long stretch of silence.

"Protect the sons of the prince," I whisper. "Sons?" Mya and I exchange a glance.

"It doesn't surprise me," she offers quietly, "considering Eron."

"And what about that other part?" Cort asks. "About his daughter's talents?"

His question brings me back to Margy's room, surrounded by the live forest created with her own magic. I keep my eyes fixed on the note, afraid that my memories might leak into one of them if I dared look up. Who is this Kaso Viro, I wonder? How can he know all of this? Why should I trust him? Should I risk Margy's trust by revealing what she told me in confidence? Is it safe?

"I know what he's referring to," I say cautiously, "but I'm not sure it's the place or time to tell you."

Between the Queen's quest, Da's earlier outburst, the summons from the King, and now this letter, I have no idea what to do. It's all chaos and emotion in my head, keeping me from being able to think logically. I wish Rian was here. He'd be able to sort through it. He'd know where we should start.

"Maybe I should answer the summons first," I suggest. "Then, when I return, we can hold a meeting and go from there."

The thought of going to the palace to face the king makes my stomach flip. Da was right, though. My duty is to Cerion above all, and I'm already two days past the date of his royal command. I slowly fold the note and tuck it away as I stand up.

"No, Azi," Mya says to my relief. "I think we should meet first. All of us. In case..." she trails off and glances at Cort, and he nods mournfully.

"In case what?" I frown.

"We don't know why you've been summoned," Mya says. "You heard your father. He's not the only one with prejudices. There are whisperings about you. About your alliances. The king is at his wit's end. He's looking everywhere for someone to blame for the High Court attack. And the fact that you disappeared right in the middle of it, well, it's…"

"Suspicious," Cort rolls his eyes.

I don't say anything. I don't know what to say. I feel as if my world is spinning out of control. I'd almost prefer the idle, unsure quiet of two days ago—no, eight days, apparently--to this chaos.

I stand shaking until Mya takes my hand and guides me out of Cort's house and across the passageway into the meeting hall. She tells Cort to go get Bryse and Elliot. I'm so dazed I don't even notice Saesa is in the meeting hall until she jumps up from her seat and hugs me.

"I knew it!" she cries. "My Lady Knight, I knew what they were saying wasn't true. I knew you would come back."

She remembers herself quickly and tries to step back, but her closeness and her trust in me is a comfort. I hug her tighter.

"Thank you," I push to her. Two weeks ago, I never would have done it. Saesa has no idea of the extent of my abilities. She's been a devoted squire, and yet I never trusted fully her with the knowledge of who I really am.

When I finally let her go, Saesa looks at me with the same awe and respect as always. I know she can see the Mark, but she doesn't react to it. It doesn't frighten her. I'm still Azi. Her Knight.

Before I can wrap my head around her unconditional acceptance, Rian appears beside her with Mum's arm looped through his. It takes Mum a moment to get her bearings and then she throws herself at me and lifts me off of the ground with her embrace.

"Oh, my sweeting," she whispers into my hair. Our armor scrapes together as she squeezes me, and I find myself crying yet again as her peace soothes me.

"Rian told me," she murmurs only loud enough for me to hear. Her thumb brushes the Mark on my cheek. At first I'm afraid to look at her and see the same fear in her eyes that the others held, but when I finally force myself to, I'm so relieved. There is no fear or hesitation in her eyes. It's like she expected it. Like it was something she's been waiting for. They shine bright and blue with love for me, and with pride that seems to burst forth and wash over me along with her peace. The way she looks at me seems to give me permission to accept myself for who I really am.

The Mentalist. The Paladin. Between Saesa and Mum's reactions and Kaso Viro's letter, my perspective is beginning to change. Maybe it's time for me to be open about it. To stop hiding and being afraid of what I can do. I don't fit here like I used to because I'm not who I was before. Da is right. I've changed. I'm different now, but my abilities are a part of me They're not something I should ashamed of or hide away. I reach up and take off my helm completely. It's time to stop being afraid.

"I'll talk to Da," she says, "don't worry." I don't want her to leave, but I'm eager to see Da again after she's had a chance to calm him, so I don't protest when Rian whisks her away to wake him.

As they leave, a shift in the Half-Realm draws my attention. A figure nearby. A boy.

"Tib?" I whisper out of range of Mya, who has gone to the meeting table to sort through the piles of parchment there.

Tib nods in greeting and I glance from him to Saesa, who looks a little guilty. Da's forge is one thing, but Tib isn't an official member of the Elite or a squire. He's not permitted in the meeting hall. He's usually respectful of our rules and boundaries, so his disregard disturbs me a little. I slide my eyes toward Mya and nod to him.

Cort returns with Bryse and Elliot just as Tib reveals himself. Bryse twitches a hand to his sword but relaxes as soon as he recognizes the boy. Mya scowls.

"Tib," she says. "Where did you come from?"

"Sorry, Mya," Tib offers an apologetic shrug as the two of them rush off. "I followed Saesa in. I just got back from…someplace, and I wanted her to know I was safe."

Saesa reaches for Tib's hand, but he doesn't notice. Instead he leans against the back of a chair and shoves his hands in his pockets as Mya assesses him carefully.

"I'm afraid I'll have to ask you to leave," she says as she taps a stack of parchments on the table to straighten them. "The guild has some things to discuss which are not meant for a wider audience."

Saesa scoffs and looks from Tib to Mya. She claps a hand over her mouth and looks at me with wide, apologetic eyes. Mya raises a brow.

"Do you have something to say, Saesa?" she asks with a stern tone which is very firmly meant to remind the squire of her place.

"I'm so sorry," Saesa replies, "it's just…I think you'll be interested in what Tib has to offer. He's been places recently. He's seen things that you should know about."

"Nah, it's fine, Saesa," Tib broods and walks toward the door. "She's right. I have my own things to do, anyway."

"Wait," Mya holds up a hand to stop him as he starts to leave. "Where have you been, Tib?" she asks.

"A keep," he replies with a shrug. "Full of Sorcerers. They kidnapped me. Same ones who attacked the High Court." He looks at me like he wants to say more, but is holding back. "They're planning things. They're not through with the prince."

"You can stay," Mya says as Mum and Da return. "We'll need you to tell us everything you remember." Da looks a little sleepy-eyed, but much calmer than he had been. He looks at me, shakes his head, and offers me a one-armed hug.

"We'll get through it," he says. His tone is gruff, but his words are a small comfort. As he goes to take a seat at the table with the others, I look to the door expecting to see Rian. Mum notices.

"Rian's going to see if he can convince Gaethon to come," she explains.

"Good luck with that," Bryse grumbles. "Haven't seen hide or hair of him for the better part of a week."

"He's doing what he must, Bryse," Mya says. "These are trying times. His priorities are the Academy, and Mage relations with the Palace. We accept that. What about Donal?" she looks to Mum.

"He offered to bring the horses back," Mum replies. "We were just past the Forest Wall and he wanted to take a moment with the White Line."

"Inquiring about Dacva, I imagine," Mya shakes her head.

"What about Dacva?" I ask with a shiver.

"He disappeared after the attack," Elliot explains as he curls up in his armchair by the fire and yawns. "Just like you did."

"What do you mean, disappeared?" I ask.

"Donal sent him out to Redstone to offer healing," Mya explains. "He never returned. Donal's been inquiring about him since then. Elliot even took some time to search."

"Suspicious if you ask me," Bryse grunts and pours himself a tankard of wine. "Never did fit in, that one." He looks at me seeking support for his sentiment. Bryse knows Dacva and I have a history, and he's always been abrasive toward Dacva because of it. Dacva used to be my rival, and spent the better part of our growing years tormenting me. When his guild, Redemption, betrayed the King, he became a healer under Donal and made an effort to join us. Mya is the one to make membership decisions, and she has continued to hold Dacva at arm's length. He isn't even permitted in the guild hall like Saesa is, even though her seniority is lower than his.

"So he just disappeared?" Tib asks with a scowl. "From Redstone?"

"At the risk of sounding callous," Mya sighs, "his whereabouts is the least of our worries right now. The Conclave has assured us they're doing their best to search for him. In the meantime, we have bigger fish in the net."

When everyone nods their agreement with varying degrees of reluctance, Mya continues.

"We'll have to make do with those of you who are here, for now." Her gaze lingers across the room at her lute before it comes to rest on the stack of papers spread across the table. She gestures to the benches, and everyone takes a seat.

"As those of us who have been in Cerion know well," she begins thoughtfully, "His Majesty is grieving. He is fighting with his conscience over the loss of his son. Justice was served by the courts, indeed, and the king is pleased, but the father is stricken with grief," she sighs, "and fear." She glances toward the door to make sure no one is eavesdropping.

"In the wake of the attacks and the horrific nature of them, he is enraged. He seeks to blame and to avenge. He looks everywhere he can for some inkling of explanation, for some relief for what's happened. These are dangerous emotions for a king. It's trying enough to rule a kingdom fairly in times of peace. The greater challenge is presented when times are difficult. When emotions are raw."

The room is silent save for the crackling of the fire as Mya goes on. Even Bryse and Da, who are usually rather vocal, sip from their tankards quietly as they listen.

"We must remember who we are in such times. Each of us joined this group as a trusted friend of the man, Tirnon. His Majesty's Elite is not just an honorable title bestowed upon us. It is the meat of our existence. The essence of who we are. We stand beside our king in easy times and in difficult times. We are not soldiers who unflinchingly follow his orders. His Majesty has his generals and his fleets and armies. He has his city guard. We are not those. We are a trusted fellowship with the responsibility to Tirnon, the man. He is our king first, and very closely behind that, he is our friend. We cannot forget Tirnon the man in these difficult times. It is to him that we owe our fealty."

"None of us argues against that, Mya," Mum says. "But when he accuses our daughter—"

"We aren't getting into that again," Mya raises her hand and interrupts Mum. "We all agree that we trust Azi and there's no basis for him to be suspicious of her. Some new information has come to light that complicates things, but we need to organize ourselves before we go to His Majesty with it. Thankfully, I think Tib here has some knowledge that will help. He's been in the attackers' stronghold, apparently, so His Majesty will have a proper focus."

"What? Why didn't you say so sooner?" Bryse slaps his hands on the table. "How'd you manage that? What did you see, boy?"

"Where is it?" Elliot asks.

"How many are in there?" Da leans toward Tib.

"I don't know how many, or where it is," he replies. "I know there are at least a few Sorcerers, and some guards. The Sorcerers aren't the ones in charge, though. I don't think so, anyway. They answered to creatures. Like fairies, only black. With black skin and wings. They could talk in the Sorcerers' minds, but I could hear them. They're the ones who took the prince. I could feel him."

"Feel him?" Mya leans across the table to Tib. "What do you mean?"

"The magic was thick there," Tib explains. "It was all over. Heavy and strong. Cruel. I felt an excitement around the prince. Like they were doing something to his remains. Planning something. The Sorcerer that held me got yelled at for bringing me too close to that place."

"Necromancy," a deep voice in the doorway makes us all jump. Uncle Gaethon shakes his head darkly as he ushers Rian in and whispers stronger wards across the door. "They mean to raise him."

The two Mages, Master and Mentor, cross the room together. Rian takes a seat beside me, but Uncle chooses to pace while thoughtfully stroking his beard.

"Just before the attack," he explains, "we noticed that several transcribed titles from our libraries had gone missing. Tomes which had been copied to send to Sunteri, to replenish their libraries. They shared a common theme: that of the afterlife. Necromancy. Restoring that which has perished. These tomes were highly protected, deeply secret, and only permitted for study by the highest ranking Mages of the Academy. Within our walls, they were never to be practiced. Their knowledge was only meant to be gleaned in order to educate those who might seek to fight against it.

"There were many arguments against transcribing these tomes for Sunteri's library. In the end, those who argued for them were the winning voice." He stops behind Rian and squeezes his shoulder reassuringly.

"My most trusted student was given the task of copying those tomes," he says, and Rian pales a little. "Several wards of protection were placed upon them before they were taken to the binder, and yet they still managed to escape our watchful eyes."

He turns and for the first time faces me. When he does, his brow rises so high that it nearly gets lost in his arched hairline.

"Niece," he says, and when he speaks, I'm surprised his voice is filled with relief rather than scolding. "Rian has explained to me the manner of your recent travels. It did not take long to conclude that your journeys have been orchestrated in an effort to balance out this recent darkness. This threat."

He turns to the others, who are listening with rapt attention.

"I urge us all to rally behind our new Paladin in the quest which has been bestowed upon her. The balance of all things is in jeopardy, and I believe she and Rian and their relations with Kythshire will be the only hope of restoring order and peace to our great city, and comfort to our king. We at the Academy have been watching the approach of a great convergence for some time now. That event is growing near, and we must do what we can to guide it to the Light."

"Azi," Mya says in a hushed tone, "perhaps you ought to read the letter again, now that we're all here."

Chapter Twenty-Five
SONS OF THE PRINCE

Tib

Everything's quiet while Azi reads the letter aloud. As soon as she finishes, Saesa gasps and clings to my arm. Azi looks up at her. Everyone else does, too.

"Errie," Saesa whispers and glances at me. She looks back at the table of Elite. "Sorry," she says, "it's just…"

"You know of a son other than the young prince?" Master Gaethon asks Saesa. He's been pacing all this time, but he stops in front of her and his jaw clenches. "Other than Amei's child?"

"We never spoke of it, sir, but a palace maid came to live with us in the manse nearly three years ago," Saesa explains. "She was forced to leave her position due to her condition." She whispers the last. "Her name is Maisie. She named her son Errie."

"Bold of her," Cort smirks.

"Where is she now?" Master Gaethon asks.

"She married a kind old merchant," Saesa replies. "They live on Ansten Row, near the center market."

"Rian," Master Gaethon leans over his student. Rian doesn't hear at first. He's busy writing something down. He slides it to Azi. I don't bother looking. Someday I'll get around to learning to read.

"You'll find the answer you seek in Orivosak," Rian says, like a quote of something only the two of them know.

"Orivosak," Azi murmurs. "Kaso Viro." She looks a little relieved at the discovery, but the rest of us are puzzled.

"When we were away," Rian pauses like he's trying to find the right words, "we were given a quest. To find a hidden city and claim it for the Dawn, to keep the Dusk from doing so. If we succeed, the city will belong to Cerion. We were told to look for instructions on how to reach it in Orivosak. I thought it was a place." He takes a book from the folds of his robes and puts it on the table. "It's not, though. It's a person. Orivosak is Kaso Viro, backwards."

"Indeed," Master Gaethon says. "But the letter explicitly lists that which must be done before you seek Kaso Viro."

"Right," Mya says, "the first of which is ensuring the safety of the sons of the prince."

"If they get their hands on a relative of Eron," Rian says with fear, "especially a descendant, they'll succeed. They'll raise him, and he'll be theirs to command."

"It's unthinkable," Mya shivers. "Imagine what His Majesty would do at the sight of it."

"Precisely," Gaethon agrees. "Amei's son is safe enough. He's quite well protected by the wards of the palace, and in addition he has come into possession of a powerful item gifted by the princess's homeland. It seems they had the foresight to bestow extra protections on the lad."

"The vest," I nod, remembering Loren's satchel. "Loren brought it." I explain to Saesa.

"Loren?" Master Gaethon asks.

"He's an apprentice," I explain. "From Stepstone. His master sent him with it, for the prince." I explain to them about the fight with Celli in the alley, and how when Loren delivered the vest to Finn, I was suspicious.

"Interesting," Gaethon says. "I should like to meet this apprentice."

"Where is he now?" Azi asks as her eyes scan the page again.

"Sleeping," Saesa whispers, "At Nessa's. We weren't sure whether he was trustworthy, but Nessa didn't want to turn him out." She avoids Master Gaethon's gaze as she explains. "Lilen put a sleep spell on him. He's been resting in the spare room ever since."

"Lilen," Master Gaethon mutters, "is that so?"

"Yes, sir," Saesa whispers, a little pale.

"Remarkable," is all he says. He scratches his beard and turns back to the others.

"One son protected," Mya says with a satisfied nod. "And another located. We'll offer them wards for now until we can break the news to Tirnon."

"What if there are more?" Azi asks. "More than two sons?"

"There is a way to find out," Gaethon sighs, "though it means dabbling further than our reach permits."

"What do you mean, Gaethon?" Mya asks.

"Blood magic," he answers darkly. "A drop of blood from any of the royal family would guide us to others of their line."

I think of Quenson standing on the dais at the front of the High Court, holding a dripping burlap bag.

"How long does it take?" I ask. "That spell?"

Gaethon turns to me.

"It is fairly immediate," he says.

"They already know about Errie, then," I scowl.

"Most likely," Gaethon nods.

"So why are we standing here?" I start for the door. Rian gets up, too. Azi joins him, but Mya shakes her head.

"Azi, we need you here. Rian and Tib, go ahead," she says. "Outfit yourself first, Tib." She points to a door that's unfamiliar to me. "Hurry. Offer them a place here, if they need it."

"Wait," Saesa calls. At first I think she's going to want to come, too, but instead she holds out the wand to Rian. "This is why I came here tonight. Loren had it on him. I think it was meant for you."

Gaethon cranes his neck to watch as Rian takes the wand from Saesa. As soon as it touches his fingertips, I feel a change. A charge. A melding. It binds to Rian. He rolls the ivory between his fingers. The room goes silent.

"*Greetings, Rian,*" a woman's voice echoes in his mind. One that only he and I can hear. "*It's a pleasure to meet you. I am Aster. I belong to Kaso Viro. I'm here to help, but you must return me when our work is finished.*"

"Thanks, Saesa," Rian nods to her. He tucks the wand into his pocket and bends to kiss Azi.

"Wait," Mya says just as we're about to leave. "Tib, before you go, tell us about the keep. Could you tell where it was?"

"Not really," I say with a shake of my head. I'm too concerned about Maisie and Errie to focus on her question, but I try to. "I was only outside for a short time, and I could only see it from a cliff below. It was a stout keep. Short. It had colored glass windows. The south wall looked crumbled. Like ruins. The rest of it was all right, though. There were flags flapping from some of the towers. Red and orange and all torn up."

If it was quiet before, it's even quieter now.

"Impossible," Bryse growls eventually.

"It's a coincidence. It has to be," Mya whispers. "Elliot."

"I'm halfway there already," Elliot murmurs in his sleep.

"What?" I look from them to Saesa, who seems just as shocked as the rest of them.

"Orange and red," she whispers, "are Redemption's colors."

"Don't," Mya scowls. "We've got enough on our plate already. We have to go with the facts."

"It'd make sense," Lisabella ventures. "They were always close with the prince. When was the last report from the Outlands?"

"Go, you two," Mya says with a little more urgency. "Quickly."

With a gesture to me, Rian leads the way through the door Mya gestured to. He closes it behind us and whispers a spell for light. It glints off of rows and rows of weapons that hang on the walls of an otherwise empty room. The training square. I've never been allowed in here.

"Take what you need," Rian says with a hushed tone.

"What's with the orange and red?" I ask him as I walk along the racks. There are lots of different knives and sheathes available. I take five of them. Wish I had my bandolier, but the straps and belts they have work well enough.

"They're Redemption's colors. That's right, you're fairly new to Cerion," he explains as he helps me into a shoulder harness that holds three knives. "They were our rival guild for many years. Favorites of the prince. They betrayed the throne the year Azi became a squire. They worked with Viala before…"

"Before she became Ki," I whisper.

"Mm," Rian says. "They were officially disbanded after that, and most of them were banished to the Outlands. Forgotten, or so we thought."

"The Outlands?" I ask as I tuck a sheath into my boot.

"They're part of Cerion, but separated by mountains. It's a harsh land, and difficult to survive. The only way in is a keep heavily guarded by His Majesty's forces. The rest of the borders are natural. Cliffs and sea, and mountains too high to climb."

"So they betrayed the king, and he sent them off to live together instead of executing them?" I shake my head.

"His Majesty tries to be merciful when he can, but I think his leniency with them is what made it so easy for the courts to convince him to do otherwise with Eron in the end." He looks me over. "Ready?" he asks. I nod.

"From your description, it sounds as though the keep was breached again," Rian whispers as he slips into the Half-Realm and nods to me to do the same. I close my eyes and let the cobwebs brush my face.

"Lead the way, Tib," he says, "but be careful."

"How can you be sure it's the same keep?" I whisper as we make our way through the darkness of the streets. "And why haven't there been any reports of a breach? They seemed like they had been there for a while."

"It doesn't take long for Sorcerers to make themselves at home," Rian whispers. "And it's easy enough to forge communications, especially if Necromancy is involved."

We make our way safely hidden in the Half-realm. After a while, Rian pushes his thoughts to the wand.

"*So, Aster, what's your purpose? And why all the secrecy?*" he asks.

"*Communication, mostly,*" the wand replies.

"*So I can talk to Kaso Viro through you?*" Rian asks.

"*Not precisely.*"

"*What, then?*"

"*I know what needs to be done, and I can give you guidance. You and only you. And Tib, I guess, apparently. He can hear us, you know. He's an odd boy.*"

Rian glances at me as we creep past a small troop of city guard that marches past. He takes his hand out of his pocket, which breaks his connection with the talking wand, thankfully.

"That could get annoying fast," he whispers to me with a grin. "A sentient wand."

"Yeah. There's Maisie's," I point at the house I know to be hers. There's no light in the windows. No candles burning. Rian and I exchange worried looks. We creep up to the wall beside the front door.

"You feel anything?" he asks me.

I press myself to the stone and close my eyes. Listen. Try to feel.

"Someone's crying inside," I whisper.

"I hear it, too," Rian takes my wrist and pulls me deeper into the alley between Maisie's house and the next. He presses his fingertips to the wall and whispers a spell, and the stone fades just long enough for us to slip through.

Inside is the kitchen. The crying is coming from the front room. Now that we're inside, I feel something else. It makes my breath catch. Binding. Blood magic.

"Celli's here," I whisper. Together, Rian and I creep to the doorway. We see the source of the crying, first. Maisie. She's lying in a heap on the floor. Next to her is someone else. A man. Her husband. Completely still. Silent. I move closer and see that her hands and feet are bound to his. Anger pulses through me. They left her alive, but her husband wasn't so lucky.

I move to cut her free, but Rian's hand on my shoulder stops me.

"She might scream if you free her. Let's get the boy first," he whispers and nods toward the stairs.

I hate to leave her, but Rian is right. If we helped her now, it would give us away. Errie is more important.

We climb the staircase together and I feel us nearing Celli. There's something else, too. Some other magic. A protection. I lead Rian closer to it. To the door that leads to our waiting enemy. Even though she can't see us, we're careful. We peek together inside the room. She's there, leaning against the wall. Her face is covered with a hood, and even though it's a hot evening, she's got her cloak wrapped around her like a cocoon. Beside her is a low cradle, swathed in magic. Errie's there, kneeling with his chin resting on the end of it, watching the door where we stand.

"Odd," Rian whispers. His eyes scan the room. He starts to go in. That's when I realize why Celli's all wrapped up. Her cloak. It hides her, and Rian can't see.

"She's there," I whisper, and point in Celli's direction. Usually when I'm hidden in the Half-Realm I can't be heard, but Celli's eyes snap to the door where we're standing as soon as I speak.

She pushes off from the wall and slinks nearer. Makes sure she stays covered by the cloak. Her eyes don't leave the doorway, but they never focus on us. Not even when she's close enough for me to feel her breath. Without a sound, I draw a knife from my sheath. I glance at Rian. He doesn't see her. She doesn't see us. I think about Zeze her arms. About Celli's deception that got me captured. About the Sorcerer's name that pulses in her veins. Quenson. I pull back my knife hand and thrust it forward, into her side.

"They're here!" she screams out and doubles over.

"Tib, no!" Rian hisses. I don't hear. There's too much rage. I raise my knife to strike again and he catches my wrist.

"Errie," Rian says to me. I snap back to my senses.

Celli's revealed now, her cloak forgotten. She stumbles forward and swings a fist hard at Rian. It bounces off his wards. She kicks, she punches. Her wound doesn't seem to weaken her. Her eyes flash red and cruel as she dives to claw at him.

I run to the cradle and reach through the wards for Errie.

"Mumumum!" he screams when I pick him up. The wards break. He's exposed. The cobwebs brush away from me. I can't take anyone into hiding with me, so I'm exposed now, too.

"Errie!" Maisie cries downstairs.

In the doorway, Celli finally gets through Rian's wards. She's got him pinned by the throat. She fumbles for the dagger at her belt. His fingertips spark with a spell. He thrusts his hand to her face and chokes over the words. The spell fails.

"You!" Celli sneers at me. Lets go of Rian. Her eyes light up when she sees my prize: Errie, squirming in my arms.

"Stop wiggling," I whisper to the boy. Try hard to calm him, but he's too scared. "Remember me? Tib?"

"Mumumum!" he screams again.

Celli dives at us and grabs for him, but I dodge her easily. Rian coughs and tries his spell again. This time it works. It hits Celli square between the shoulder blades. She's flung forward into the wall. She tumbles to the floor and rolls over to face us. Her eyes are open. At first I think he's killed her, but she looks around in a panic and breathes with quick gasps.

"Stun," Rian says. "It won't last long. Get him out of here."

"That's right," a familiar voice calls up from downstairs. Dub. "Bring him down here, and nobody gets hurt."

Rian reaches for me. Grabs my arm. At the bottom of the stairs, Dub peers up at us. He's cut Maisie free and he's holding her up. He's got a knife to her throat. When she sees Errie, she sobs and calls his name.

"Mum!" Errie screams. He squirms and wriggles and fights to get to her.

"We have no choice, Tib," Rian glances at me. He's right. There's no way we can rescue them both. It's one or the other.

"Come on, Nullen. Be smart," Dub presses the knife harder. Maisie sobs and pleads.

"Go," I say to Rian. I can't help but fix my sights on Dub.

I'm filled with rage. I don't think straight. I just want to see him bleed. I want to watch his life leave him.

When I feel Rian start to shift, I pull away from his grasp and shove Errie into his arms. I charge down the stairs. Reach for my knives. Hit Dub so hard that he's knocked prone and the knives in my hands clatter away. His blade leaves a trail of red across Maisie's throat. She falls to the floor.

I realize in that moment what a horrible mistake I made by giving into my rage. It would have worked if Errie had cooperated. He didn't, though. At the last moment, he squirmed out of Rian's grasp. Now Rian's gone, and Errie's there, scrambling down the stairs, trying to get to his mum. Before I can react, Celli appears in the upstairs doorway. It won't last long, Rian had said, but I didn't realize how short the span of the spell would actually be.

Celli's eyes light up at the sight of the retreating boy. She runs down the stairs and grabs him roughly by the arm.

I fight to get to her, but Dub is on me. He yanks me up by the collar and throws me hard against the steps. I tumble for my knives, any of them, but they're in unfamiliar places. My instinct is thrown off.

"Get out," he bellows at Celli. She runs past us with Errie screaming and kicking at her hip.

"Sparrow and fox," I hear her say downstairs.

Above me on the steps, Rian reappears. Dub doesn't notice. He's crazed, hovering over me. His knife flashes in my vision and then my left eye goes dark with searing pain.

"Eye for an eye," he hisses as I scream. Above me, Rian's hands crackle with energy.

"Induct, destroy," I hear Celli say in between Errie's screams. I feel the change. Something is shifting. A way is opening.

"Downstairs!" I holler at Rian. "She's getting away!"

The blast of magic Rian releases throws Dub back hard. The knife he was holding slides from its mark and I scream at the pain of it and clap my hands over my eye. At the base of the stairs, Dub shudders and convulses as the spell's energy crackles around him. Maisie lies beneath him, completely still.

I try to scramble to my feet but the pain is too much. The room spins and I stumble to my knees as Rian races past me.

"Asio," Celli announces. Instantly, Errie's screaming stops.

"No!" Rian's defeated cry breaks the silence. I crawl to look with my limited vision and see him kneeling on the floor staring at his hands in disbelief. "No," he whispers.

The edges of the steps press into my spine as I drop onto them. I let my head fall back. I press my eye to stop the bleeding. My stomach churns and I try hard to keep Mouli's sweet rolls down.

"Tib," Rian's voice is distant. It moves in and out. "Hold on."

"We failed," I whisper. It's my fault. They knew I'd come looking. They were waiting for me to get Errie free of the wards. I can't hold it back. I roll to the side and get sick all over Maisie's stairs. Maisie. Did she survive? Someone scoops me up. Rian, I'd guess.

"Hold on," he says again. "Take my hand," his voice echoes in the distance. Maisie sobs. The ground beneath us falls away and we spin, back to the Half-Realm. Back to the meeting hall. I close my good eye. I let myself pass out.

Chapter Twenty-Six
TRIUMPHANT RETURN

Celli

The wood beneath my knees shifts and I close my eyes and cling to the wriggling boy with one arm. With my other hand I fumble the coin from the hasty carving and snatch it up just before the floor swallows us. Tib's screams are the last thing I hear as we start to plummet. Then the floor goes solid above, shutting out what little light there was. My side throbs as the boy screams and struggles against the spot where Tib stabbed me. I curse at him and clamp my arm around his neck.

The pumping of my blood pulses loudly in my ears. With every pulse I feel my need for Quenson. I did it. I got the boy. He'll be so proud. I'll be the most important to him. I need to see him. I need to show him.

We hit the stone floor hard. The pain in my side spikes. I push it away. *Quenson. Where is he?* The boy has stopped struggling. I shift my hold on him so he can breathe again now that he's out. I don't move him, though. He's good where he is. Keeping me from bleeding.

I know this room where we appear. It's the circular one they brought me to that first day. The day Dub attacked me and Quenson watched. That day, the six alcoves were empty. Now, two of them hold a decorative glass bottle. Inside of each bottle is a glowing liquid. I'm drawn to their light right away. It mesmerizes me. I almost forget the boy. My wound. Quenson.

"You were told to bring him alive." His anger jolts me. Spikes through my heart. I spin and face him, my everything. My lord. My master.

"He's alive," I rush to Quenson, ignoring my dizziness. I hold the boy out like an offering to him. His eyes light up. I could survive on his smile alone.

"Well done, Celli," he says, velvety smooth. His elation is my elation.

He takes the limp child from my arms and looks him over. I didn't realize until now how it must look, but the smears of red all over him are mine, not his. From how I was carrying him.

Quenson holds him up like he's trying to figure out where it's coming from. Then he looks at me.

"Dar," he says, and a hulking guard clomps forward. He passes the boy to him.

With the rush of my triumph fading, it's hard to stand. I stumble to the side. Quenson catches me. His arms slide around me. Hold me up. I could die happy this way.

"He did this to you," he says to me. His breath is soft on my face. "Nullen."

His mention of Tib sets my insides on fire. He did this to me.

"And Dub?" Quenson asks.

"I left them fighting. He told me to get out," I explain. My vision is closing in. Darkening. I focus on his face. His beautiful, perfect white teeth. The pulse of the Mark that slithers across the surface of his skin.

"You did well, Celli," he purrs. "The healers are coming. Rest."

I close my eyes, and smile.

Chapter Twenty-Seven
SWORD OF LIGHT

Azi

"Is it even possible that Outland Stronghold was breached again?" Mya asks as she flattens a large, worn strategy map across the table. The holdings and territories of Cerion's armies are marked upon it with blue ink.

"It's unlikely," Mum says. Da nods from over her shoulder.

"Since the battle at Kythshire," he explains, "watches have been set in place. New towers with signal fires on the outlying roads here." He points to several places along the road leading to Outland Stronghold.

"But they could have been taken," Cort leans over the table. "Or circumvented."

"Nah, not easily. It's all mountain around there," Bryse argues. "Rocks and cliffs."

"Anything is possible," Uncle says. "Do not forget, we are dealing with Sorcery, not armies of men on foot."

Across the room, Elliot slides from his chair and yawns. He trots to the table and nudges in between me and Mum. With him he carries the scent of sea air and elm trees. If I closed my eyes, I might feel a rush of wind in the leaves. I don't, though. Instead I watch him as he slides his finger across the worn surface of the map. His eyes flash beneath his fringe of red-orange hair. His nose twitches slightly.

"There," he says, and his finger rests on an inlet across the Outlands from the border keep, right on the edge of the coastline.

I breathe a sigh of relief along with everyone else. Mya marks the spot with a stick of charcoal, and Elliot shake his head.

"No, not on land. It's an island." He smudges her mark away and makes another one beside it in the water.

"Outside of the borders of the Outlands?" she asks.

"Mm hmm," Elliot affirms as he takes a seat beside me. "I didn't actually see it. It's too well protected. They've got it covered in dozens of wards. I couldn't get close. I could sense it, though, just like Tib described."

"Indeed," Uncle agrees. "But if it can be so hidden from you, my friend, with your keen senses, then this is no small foe. Such wards require time and numbers."

"How much time?" Mya asks. "How many numbers are we talking, Gaethon?"

"It's difficult to say for certain without having seen it for myself," Uncle replies. "But, to give you an example, a single one of the palace wards would take a month to set, and at least three master Mages."

"Wouldn't the patrols have noticed activity like that?" Da asks. "They travel the coastline regularly. They take their duties seriously."

"We heard rumors," Bryse says darkly, "of goings-on in Outlands. Remember, Cort? When we were out in the mists?"

"Aye," Cort scratches the thin line of his beard that traces his chin. "We put it in our report, but didn't think much of it. Just peasant talk, it seemed. Now I wonder if there was some truth to it."

"What sort of rumors?" I ask with a shiver.

"Uprisings," Cort replies. "Talk of revolution among the banished."

"It's not saying much, is it?" Bryse grunts. "You banish a bunch of criminals and put 'em in the same place, of course there's going to be rebellions and threats."

"That's why the stronghold and its battalions are so important—" Da starts, but he's interrupted by a loud curse from across the room. Everyone is on their feet before we can think. Swords flash. We start to charge. Rian's form shimmers in space and before he even comes into focus, he's gone again.

"Rian!" Mya and I shout in unison. We exchange a worried glance.

"Why was he alone?" Saesa, who has remained quietly in the background since Tib left, whispers.

"I'll go," I say, and close my eyes. *Rian*, I think clearly, and feel myself being pulled away from the hall.

The first thing I notice as my feet meet the floor is the darkness. The second is the metallic smell of blood that hangs heavy in the air. Rian vanishes again before he even notices me. Two others go with him.

The journey through the Half-Realm sends a rush of magic through me. At my shoulder, my sword glows and the shadows retreat. I'm just about to follow Rian through again when something on the landing of the stairs shifts. My eyes adjust to the darkness and I make out the figure of a man.

He groans and holds his head as he struggles to his knees. Slowly, quietly, I move to draw my sword. Normally, this means unclasping the scabbard from my back and sliding the great blade free, but before I can even reach back the hilt is in my hands, as though the very thought of it has summoned it to me.

I gasp at the sight of it. The blade shines with a light so brilliant that I have to look away for a moment. The man on the landing scrambles backward and shields his eyes, too. I blink rapidly and squint past the angle of my sword at my cowering opponent. The handles of countless knives glint in their sheathes across his chest. They glow a golden warning that I understand is meant for my eyes only.

He reaches to draw one and I take a step closer.

"I wouldn't," I say, and the power in my voice surprises me.

"You're too late," he says with a simpering tone that holds none of the confidence I'd expect from such a heavily armed assassin. "They have what they sent us for. Your men failed."

"Who?" I demand. "Who has him?"

He scrambles backwards as I take another step toward him. The light from my sword is so searingly bright it washes out the black of his leather armor completely. I try not to let myself be distracted by it as he scrambles back against the wall and gasps for breath. His mouth opens and closes like a suffocating fish plucked from the sea. I recognize the struggle in him. He wants to tell me, but he can't.

I move closer and his one good eye goes wild with panic.

"Please," he whispers, "mercy. Please."

"Calm down," I say softly. His terror of me is confusing and disconcerting. He slides along the wall in an attempt to escape, but I put my shoulder to it to block him. "You don't need to say anything." I try to keep my voice from sounding overwhelming or powerful. The light of my sword dims slightly. "Just look."

The words are more of a command than I intended. My scalp tingles as the excitement of magic surges through me. Golden tendrils stretch between us, catching his one good eye, holding it so I can see. More stretch around him, lulling him into a sense of safety.

This is unfamiliar territory for me. I don't trust his mind, so I don't allow myself fall into it as I usually do. Instead I pull his memories away from him to play between us, like Iren did at the Northern Border all that time ago. I keep myself alert to our surroundings as the moments of his recent memories rise and fade. I watch the fight between him and Tib. I watch the girl race away with a boy who looks so much like Eron.

I look deeper. Past tonight, into an earlier moment. A Sorcerer on an ill-tempered rampage, pacing across the floor of a round room. Alcoves line the walls. Two of them hold bottles of glowing liquid. The assassin's gaze lingers on them. They're a surprise to him. A small triumph.

"Quenson," he says to the Sorcerer, "we can get him back. We'll use the boy."

I'm so drawn into the scene that I'm unaware at first of the subtle shift around me. The light of my sword has dimmed further. Its glow is nearly snuffed out by shadows. I pull away from the one-eyed man and raise my weapon. A cloaked figure steps out of the shadows of the living room. He raises his hand toward me and whispers.

At the end of his incantation I reach out with the threads of my thoughts and wind them around his wrists. With a nod of my head I give them a tug and his hand flings to the side. He looses his spell and it hits the assassin full on.

Amid a string of curses, the Sorcerer summons his shadows. They creep through the room and stretch into the light like bent henchmen to stalk me. A dozen or more of them attack, and I raise my sword to face them.

I swing at one close to me and a beam of light trails behind my blade, slicing the shadow into oblivion effortlessly. The room fills with earsplitting screams as the shadows are painfully slashed by the light of my sword. Again and again I fight away the approaching darkness. My arms never tire, my resolve never fades. They descend on me, clawing at my arms and face with slender, pointed fingers and gnashing fangs at me that seem to drip with shadowy poison.

Beyond the crowd of darkness, I hear strange words strung together. They're oddly familiar, though I can't seem to place them. Sparrow. Perch.

My arms are strong and capable, but my mind is slowing. I'm exhausted from using magic. The absence of it drains me from the inside. I move on reflexes, but there is no strategy to my attacks. My capacity to think has been spent.

The shadows thin gradually. I swing a dozen times or more, and each time I do their screams shatter my eardrums. When the last one finally falls I find myself standing by myself in the dark, empty living room. The Sorcerer and the assassin have escaped somehow. I trudge to a nearby sofa and sink into it, exhausted. I lay my sword across my knees. My gaze rests on the shimmering blade with wonder. It's like it knew. It knew exactly what needed to be done and it acted like an extension of me. Like my arm, or my finger.

"Thank you," I whisper, and right away I feel foolish. After all, it's a weapon of my own making, not something to be spoken to. Still, Saesa's sword has a name. Perhaps mine should, too. I pick it up again and think of the time I've had with it so far. How it eluded my father's grasp and inspired fear and awe in the assassin. How it garnered his respect so I wasn't forced to fight him. I close my eyes and let its peaceful light tingle on my fingertips.

"Mercy," I whisper, and the sword pulses softly in acceptance.

Our strange conversation is interrupted by a sudden rumbling and quaking coming from a room deeper within the house. I get to my feet and creep toward it with the light of my sword guiding the way.

I'm greeted in what I expect is the kitchen by a sharp cracking sound as the stone wall splits and crumbles apart. Just when I'm about to charge, Rian pokes his head through the opening.

"You're here," he says with a sigh of relief. He clambers unsteadily through the wall and we crash into each other's arms.

"What happened?" he asks. "Are you all right? I tried to get back but I was blocked somehow. I couldn't get to you."

I cling to him and nod into his chest. In the sudden, complete quiet, I tell him everything that happened.

"The floor," he says when I'm through, and takes my hand to guide me back. For a moment he looks confused as we stand together in the living room.

"What is it?" I ask him.

"When we arrived there was a man here. Maisie's husband. He didn't make it. Did you see him?"

I think back and shake my head. When I arrived, there was definitely no one in this room aside from myself and the assassin.

"He must have been drawn into the portal," Rian says thoughtfully. He sinks to his knees and finds the carving on the floor.

"This is how they get in and out," he whispers. "Sigils."

"Sigils?" I ask. "Like teleportation?"

"A little, but these are less complicated, and they're only meant to travel to a fixed point that's already been prepared." He brushes his fingers over the carving. "You put a marker in here. That's what holds the spell. It activates the runes." He points to the black swirls of charcoal. "This one's temporary."

"A marker?" I think back. "Like a coin?"

"Sure. A coin would do nicely." He taps the carving again. "If only we had one."

"Tib does," I whisper, suddenly remembering. "He showed it to me before the attack on the High Court."

Rian raises a brow curiously. He flicks his wrist and the sofa and rug slide across the floor and skid to a stop to hide the markings.

"That'll have to do for now," he says and takes my hand again. "We have to get back. Tib's in bad shape, but he refuses healing until he's sure Maisie and the boy are safe. Maisie's getting healing. She'll be fine, but Errie is another story. We can't recover him. Not yet. Master Gaethon estimates there are at least a dozen master Sorcerers barricaded in that keep. Probably more. The Dusk is an ancient order, just like the Dawn is. We have to be cautious."

I nod. "Let's go home. It's probably not safe to talk about it here."

He folds his arms around me and I bury my face in his chest. I breathe in the warmth of his embrace and the smoky scent of incense on his robes as the ground falls away beneath us and we spin into the Half-Realm.

When we arrive at the guild hall again, we're greeted by a strange sight.

At the center of the meeting room, seated on a tufted footrest, is a young woman dressed in a shimmering white cloak emblazoned with the crest of Kythshire. Her hood is pulled low to cover her face. The Elite stand in a semi-circle around her, their expressions a mix of curiosity, awe, and confusion.

"She says she's here for you, Azi," Mya whispers. "She says you know her."

At Mya's words, the figure stands gracefully. She reaches to her hood and carefully pushes it back. Multi-colored locks tumble over her shoulders and she reaches up to smooth her rainbow bangs with a slender, pale hand that shimmers in the firelight. Her pink lips curve into a smile as she turns to face me. At first I'm confused. I know those eyes, that hair, but it can't be. As she turns her attention to me, I'm overcome by a powerful feeling of awe and honor. It's as though I'm in the presence of something legendary. Something to be revered.

Hesitantly, I move close to her as the others watch in fascination.

"Whoa," Rian breathes.

"Flitt?" I whisper. It isn't like the other times when she grew herself to my size to look me in the eye or give me a quick hug. This time is different. It's difficult to describe. Somehow, she's more solid, more present, more visible and important.

I glance back at the others. Mum and Da. Mya, Elliot, Cort, Bryse. They're all looking at her. Not only can they see her, but they all seem utterly enchanted by her. Even Uncle is agape.

I shake my head slowly and walk around her, taking her in. As a fairy, Flitt has always been a little on the full side, probably due to all of the sugar cubes. Her round cheeks and soft shoulders gave her a child-like quality. As a human, she's more slender and dainty. Her face is slightly narrower. It's pleasing, but also strange to me. Something I can't quite put my finger on proclaims her very un-human.

"What did you do?" I whisper and bend to peek beneath her cloak. At first I thought it was meant to conceal them, but they would never fit under there. "Where are your wings?"

"Oh, it's only temporary, thank the Light," she chuckles and looks over her shoulder at me. "I know how you all are with appearances. Imagine if I went to meet the king looking the way I usually do. Could you imagine? Though it does feel strange. You really are all so very hulking. I don't see why my feet must be as large as a mountain troll's nose. No offense of course, Bryse," she says and blinks up at Bryse with a sheepish grin.

"What?" Bryse huffs. "I'm no mountain troll! And how do you know my name?" he scowls.

"Oh, of course not! No, no. Mountain *giant*. Forgive me." Flitt laughs nervously. "Not that there's much difference," she utters under her breath.

"Stone giant," Bryse grumbles.

Flitt shrugs apologetically and reaches for the tip of a wing that isn't there. Her hand then drops to her skirts. Her skirts. That's something else that's changed. The frayed ribbon scraps are gone, replaced by a gown of shimmering iridescent fabric that floats around her legs in a mesmerizing shift of color.

"Perhaps introductions are in order?" Mya's voice cracks at the suggestion as she eyes the crest of Kythshire. Everyone else nods, wide-eyed. Even Da stands speechless.

"Not really," Flitt says with a dismissive wave of her hand. "I already know everyone."

"Perhaps, then," Uncle clears his throat and looks at me, "for our benefit?"

"This is Flitt," I say a little uneasily. "She's…"

I glance at her for guidance. I have no idea what's going on or how much I'm supposed to say.

"*Help?*" I push to her.

Flitt rolls her eyes impatiently.

"Honestly, so typical. Always needing to over-explain everything."

She does a little hop like she's about to lift off, and then seems to remember that she can't do that, so she just bounces a bit. "I'm Flitt. I'm from Kythshire. Azi's known me for a while. Lisabella, too. And I've been around all of you, so no need to tell me who you are. I was sent ahead to let His Majesty know there's going to be a procession in the morning. Lots more are coming. Mostly my kind, but elves from Ceras'lain, too. At dawn." She gives me a meaningful look.

Everyone continues to stare in disbelief. I can understand why. Though Cerion has long opened its gates to people of all nations, this is unheard of. Only the Academy's occasional secretive contact keeps the fairies from fading into legend. Even then, many have lost faith that they exist. So, to have a woman show up at the hall proclaiming herself a representative of Kythshire is quite a lot to wrap one's head around. It's undeniable, though. The magic that twinkles from every pore of her skin is proof enough. Flitt, who is obviously tiring of being stared at, crosses her arms impatiently.

"I heard Tib got hurt," she says. "Is he around? I told Ki I'd check on him for her. Then I'm to go to the palace. You know, to let them know we're coming, so they can make all those important preparations that you people seem to feel are so necessary."

Rian is the first to speak. His voice seems to jolt everyone out of their dazes.

"He's in the guest house," he says. "Azi, could you show her? I need a word with Master Gaethon."

His voice is shaken, and it's not from Flitt's transformation or her presence in the hall. I don't need to read his thoughts to know his mind is on the boy he failed to rescue.

"Of course," I say quietly. Flitt rests a hand on my shoulder, right on the spot where she usually perches.

"*See if he'll give you the coin,*" Rian pushes to me.

As I lead Flitt out of the hall, I look back over my shoulder at Da, who stands shaking his head in disbelief.

I don't need to look at his mind, either. I'm just as shocked and amazed. I don't think any of us would have imagined our lifetime would be the one in which fairies would return publicly to Cerion. It feels unreal. Like a dream.

"Ugh," Flitt says as she stumbles in the hallway over her own feet. She leans heavily on my shoulder. "Really. I just don't see the point of it. Being this humongous. Walking everywhere. And I honestly didn't think it was possible for this place to smell even *worse.*"

She wrinkles her big human nose and pinches it closed with a scowl. "How do you live like dis?" she asks with a high-pitched nasal whine.

Chapter Twenty-Eight

FAILURE AND REGRET

Tib

Pink light splashes the wall. Across the room, Maisie moans. I try to sit up and look, but Saesa pushes me down gently. I hold in a groan as my head pounds. Don't want to draw attention to my own pain. Even with the potion Mya gave me to take the edge off, it hurts. I feel strange, too. Like I'm floating. Without thinking, I reach for the bandage over my eye. I test it gently with my fingertips.

"Don't touch," Saesa whispers and pulls my hand away. She's being annoying. Really annoying. She has been ever since Rian brought me back. Raefe even had to go get the healer because she wouldn't leave my side. I kept telling her don't worry about me. Worry about Maisie. Worry about Errie, who we failed. The thought of him in that place makes me seethe. I want to jump up out of this bed and run to free him. To get back to that keep and finish every last one of them.

"He's almost done," Saesa murmurs in my ear as she watches the healer work. "You'd better rethink things, Tib. What good will you be getting Errie back with one eye? If he can fix it, you should let him."

I swear, sometimes Saesa acts more like a mother than a friend. She's right, though. If I'm going to fight against the Dusk, then I'll need both eyes wide open. I make my mind up to agree with her. I'll let him heal me.

Across the room, Maisie gasps and screams and cries out, "Errie!"

I want to go to her and swear I'll get him back, but my head is too heavy. Saesa's hand on my shoulder is like a pile of bricks. The healer murmurs something. A rest spell. Like Lisabella's peace pulse, but stronger. Maisie quiets.

"She lost a lot of blood," he says to Saesa. "She'll rest for the night and feel much better in the morning."

No she won't, I think to myself as he comes to my side. *Not without her son.* Even with my good eye closed I feel him near. He's a powerful healer. One of the best at the Conclave, I bet. They know the Elite there. They respect them. I wonder if he'd be so willing to help me, knowing I'm the reason Maisie's heart is broken. Knowing I let an innocent boy get taken. Maybe I won't let him heal me after all. I deserve the pain.

"Tibreseli Nullen," he sighs and his hand rests on my chest. I open my good eye and look him over. "Turn your head this way." My jaw clenches and I scowl. "Come, now. You are not the first to try to martyr himself for his mistakes, my child. By the Lady, I urge you to use reason."

He leans over me like he's looking into me. I can feel the insistence in him. I remember the pure white conclave. The statue of the weeping mother. The words the old man said: *Key to the Skies. Do not tarry in your work.*

My heart quickens. My contraption. If I can get it working, we can fly there. To the keep. I imagine the look on Dub's face when he sees me. How shocked he'll be when I glare at him with both eyes as I throw my knives right into his filthy heart. The thought fills me with urgency.

"Hurry," I say, pulling at the bandages. "Please. I have things to do." Saesa takes my hands away and holds them. The healer unwraps the bandage and lets his magic flow into my wound and I allow it.

It's a strange sensation. Not at all like the healing I got in the Sorcerers' keep. This time it's much more pleasant. I focus on it. I feel the bone and muscle pulse and knit back together. My eye mends itself slowly, filling up round and cool to fit perfectly in the socket. I blink and roll it from side to side, testing it as the pink light fills the darkness.

"Will the color come back?" Saesa asks as she leans over me, watching.

"Curious," the healer peers at me.

"It's a nice gray-blue," Saesa offers.

"Look around, Tibreseli," the healer says. "How does it seem?"

I scoot up in the bed with ease. My healed right eye seems quicker than my left one. It flicks around eagerly. I glance to the far wall next to the door. Outside, there's a hallway. In the hallway, I can see beyond the wall, the shape of two figures coming closer. Women. I see their outlines like they're painted on the wall. One in armor, one in a gown. That one stumbles a little and bumps the frame of the passage.

"Oof! Wall," she says. Her voice is familiar. Like Flitt's, but not as squeaky. "Really! Why does it need to be so closed up and twisty in here? If you're going to insist on being so big, you should make everything more open so you can get around without—ouch!"

The woman trips on the runner rug just outside the door. I see her outline stumble into the armored woman.

"I can see," I whisper to the healer. "How can I see them? Two women?"

"Sometimes," he answers as he turns toward the door. "The Lady of Peace bestows gifts through healing as a way of rewarding us, or preparing us."

"What?" Saesa whispers. "You can see them? It sounds like..."

"It is," I say quietly. Flitt. I always know when she's around. She's got that bright magic that tries to creep in and make you feel better. Happier. Lighter. This time, it's a little different. It has some influence to it. Like it's trying to make her instant friends with everyone.

"Oh, hello," Flitt's strangely deeper voice comes out of the woman in the doorway.

Beside her, Azi looks at the group of us with relief.

"Victer!" she strides across and offers the healer a hug. "Thank you so much."

"Of course," the healer hugs her back. "This one was stubborn, but we convinced him in the end, hm?"

He smiles and pats me on the shoulder. I try to look grateful, but all I can think about is getting out of here. Unfortunately, the sudden appearance of Lady Flitt and Azi tells me that's not going to happen any time soon.

"I'll be on my way," Victer says. "Unless you have something more?"

"No, thank you, Victer. Mya will settle up with you." Azi turns to look at me while Flitt wanders around the room and Victer shows himself out. Her brow furrows as her eyes meet mine.

"Can you see well?" Azi asks me.

"Oh, your eye!" Flitt gasps. She tries to skip over to me but her feet get tangled and she stumbles into Azi again. "Honestly!" she groans.

"What happened to you?" I ask her.

"Well, I grew myself up," Flitt whispers conspiratorially, "but I think I got the feet wrong."

"Flitt has come to talk to His Majesty," Azi explains.

"Right!" Flitt agrees as she scowls down at her feet. She screws her eyes tightly shut and we all watch as they shrink a size or two. "That's better, I hope," she murmurs. Then she sniffs her shoulder and wrinkles her nose. "Can't do much about the smell, though, I guess."

Azi gapes at her for a moment, blinks, and then turns to me again.

"Apparently there's going to be a visit in the morning from an assembly of them…" she trails off and looks to Flitt again.

"Yes. The Ring chose a whole group to come. They'll be arriving at dawn to meet with His Majesty. I was sent ahead to give some notice. I just wanted to check on you first. I promised Ki," Flitt nods. "So if you're okay, I'll be on my way."

"Yeah," I push myself up. Test my feet on the floor. Stand up. I feel amazing. Not just healed, but like I could do anything. I glance across at Maisie. I know exactly what that anything's going to be.

"There's something else," Azi says. "That coin. Do you still have it? Rian was asking after it."

I shove my hand into the pocket of my crusted, tattered short pants and pull out the coin. It glints in the light that Flitt gives off. I inspect the tower in the cloud design and remember the floating land in the clouds.

"I'll give it to him," I say to Azi. "If that's all right. I need to ask him something."

She looks at me like she's trying to determine something.

"Do you know what it's for?" she asks. I shake my head.

"Well," she glances at Flitt, who shrugs at her. "All right. We left Rian in the hall. We'll take you there, and then Flitt and I will go to the palace. Saesa?"

"Lady Knight?" Saesa perks up after being mostly forgotten.

"Will you please let Mouli know to check in on Maisie? Then meet us in the hall. I'll need you by my side at the palace."

Saesa's eyes flash with excitement. She gives me a quick hug and then rushes out looking proud and excited.

When she's gone, Azi turns to me.

"Rian," she says quietly, "is just as distraught as you are about letting the boy slip through his fingers." She glances at the coin. "While Flitt and I are at the palace, I hope you two don't do anything reckless."

She waits for me to agree, and then we go off together to the meeting hall.

When we get there, Cort and Bryse are gone and everyone else is just mulling around. Mya's strumming her lute, Elliot's sleeping. Lisabella's tucked in a corner with Benen. Her peace pulses over him. Toward the back, at the table, Rian and Master Gaethon are bent over that wand. Everyone looks up when Flitt comes in. They all smile softly. Like they're relieved she came back. Flitt doesn't seem to notice.

Azi crosses to Rian and bends to kiss him.

"You have a stinky Mage stuck to your face again, Azi," Flitt giggles. Everyone else laughs, too.

"We're back to Stinky, are we?" Rian teases her without looking away from Azi.

"Oh, so much more so, now that my sniffer is the size of a burrowing mole," Flitt pinches her nose shut.

Rian smirks and rolls his eyes.

"*I see her charming personality grew with her,*" he pushes to Azi, who laughs and shakes her head.

"There's nothing left but to go to the palace, now," Azi says quietly. She turns to the others, looking nervous.

"We've discussed it," Mya says with a nod. "Gaethon and I will escort you. If His Majesty intends to question you, I think it's best if I'm there. And if they hold you for some reason, Flitt will need another escort."

Gaethon smiles warmly at Flitt. She pretends not to notice. Instead she clings to Azi's arm, looking impatient. She only lets go when Azi and her parents exchange hugs. Benen looks like he's definitely unhappy with the plan. Lisabella looks worried. So does Azi. Nobody argues, though. It must have been some discussion they had.

Saesa comes back while Azi and her parents and Rian and Gaethon are whispering conversations. With nothing else to do, she comes over and hugs me. Really tight. I pat her arm with one hand and wriggle free as she kisses my cheek.

"Don't do anything stupid," she whispers.

"Don't do anything rash," Gaethon's words to Rian echo Saesa's.

I watch Saesa go with the group. She looks small beside the rest of them, except for Flitt. Small, but determined. Beside me, Rian chuckles.

"What?" I ask him with a scowl. He shrugs and grins.

"She's pretty, don't you think? Saesa?" His brow goes up. When I don't reply, he grins and shakes his head. "Don't look at me like I have two heads, Tib."

"What's that got to do with anything?" My fingers curl around the coin in my pocket. "She's Saesa."

"Aha. All right then."

Beyond him, Lisabella and Benen laugh. I don't get the joke.

"We'll be off as well," Lisabella says quietly. She stands up and offers Benen her hand. I wonder if he knows how much power she has over him with that pulse of hers. Wonder how much his temper would control him if she let it.

After they leave, Rian glances at Elliot, who's been asleep this whole time. I know why. He's the same as Margy and Zeze, except for him, he's a fox. I wonder if she told the king yet. I wonder if she's safe.

Beside me, Rian clears his throat. He leans down and looks me in the eye.

"That's new," he says.

"Yeah," I rub my eyelid absently.

"The healer did a good job. Not even a scar," he looks harder. "So what's it do?"

"Is it obvious it does something?" I ask. He shrugs, and I tell him how I could see Azi and Flitt through the wall.

"That'll come in handy," he exclaims.

"I'm going back to the keep," I whisper. "I have to get him back."

To my surprise, he gives me a slight nod, then tips his head toward Elliot.

"Now, Tib," he says loudly for Elliot's benefit, "you heard what Master Gaethon said. We mustn't act rashly. We must go about this with caution. I'm to interview you about what you saw in there. I'm to write it all down so there's a reference for later. Then we'll go to Nessa's and fetch Loren and wait for Master Gaethon to return. Those are my orders. Do you feel up to it?" He glances again at Elliot.

I nod. I get it. He's got to do this first. We huddle at the table together. I tell him as much as I can remember about the keep. Everything I saw, both inside and out. He asks good questions and gets more out of me than I thought I knew. It doesn't take long.

"Well," Rian leans back against the wall and takes a deep breath while he looks over the notes. "This should be enough." He looks at me with a glint of mischief, then glances at Elliot and leans closer. "Do you have the coin?" he mouths.

I pull it out and show it to him. He nods.

"Let's hurry to get Loren," he says loudly again. "I hope it's not too late to call."

"Nah," I say. "Nessa stays up reading, and she'll be glad to see me, I think."

We slip out into the street together. As we pass by a column of guards, he straightens up and looks confident. Like he's doing exactly what he's supposed to be doing and there's no reason for them to be suspicious.

"Rian," I say when they pass. "What about Errie?"

"Loren first," he whispers. "We'll get him back to the hall. After that, I have a plan to get us to the stronghold."

"Just you and me?" I ask. My heart's racing. "How?"

"That coin. I figured out what it does," he says. "It opens a portal. It'll bring us right there."

"But you could do that anyway," I whisper. "Couldn't you? Through the Half-Realm?"

"Not this time," he says. "From what Da said, it's too well-protected. It's risky as it is, since I've never been there myself. If we use their portal, it'd be easier."

"But they'd know, wouldn't they? They'd be able to tell someone used it." I think of the keep. All the magic. All those Sorcerers. Rian is a powerful Mage, but he's only a Mentor. There's no way he can stand up against forces like that on his own. "We need a better plan. There's too many of them not to have one. Even if we do get there and manage to stay in the Half-Realm, it's dangerous."

"That's true," he nods thoughtfully. "I'm impressed, Tib. You're usually a lot less cautious."

I clench my jaw and scowl. He's right. I usually just jump into these things. "That's what got Errie taken. I won't risk him again by getting us killed before we can get him out of there."

"The good news," Rian says, "is we have time."

"What do you mean?" I ask as we reach Nessa's street. It's late. Nearly midnight. Moonlight glances off the cobbles. The face of the manse is washed in blue from the moon and yellow from the lamplight.

"It's complicated," Rian rakes his fingers through his hair. "The ritual they'll be performing. The spell. It requires Errie to be in perfect health. They'll take some time to pamper him. To heal him up. Get him fed and happy. Then there's a period of waiting. Acclimation, they call it, where they'll put him in close to Eron."

He pauses and closes his eyes, like he's trying to push the mental image of it away. I picture it, too. Maisie's son, in that dark place.

"So, what? They put him in a room with a corpse?" The thought of it makes my stomach churn with anger again. "That's disgusting."

"Our hope is we'll have him out of there before they get to that part," Rian closes his eyes and shakes his head.

The Ganvent Manse is mostly dark, except for a single light in the sitting room window. Nessa's waiting up. I feel a pang of guilt. I've been gone a while. I think of how happy she'll be to see me. How relieved. I'm glad I have Nessa to come home to, no matter what. I'm so excited to see her that I take the steps two at a time, throw the door open, and rush inside.

"Nessa!" I call eagerly. Rian closes the door behind me. Maybe it's because I'm not expecting it. Probably because I never would have thought of it. The sight of the Sorcerer bowls me over. Osven. Here. The foyer spins. I stumble backward into Rian, who is quick to utter a spell. I feel the wards settle over us. I allow them to protect me.

"Nessa!" I scream. My heart thuds in my throat. If he did something to her, if something happened, I swear I'll make him suffer. I'll make him bleed.

"Don't worry," Osven purrs to me. "Lady Ganvent and I have become quite well acquainted, though her current accommodations are not quite as lavish as these. Pity the admiral couldn't be here to see her go, but, as you know, he had an important shipment of books to oversee. They, too, should be making their way into our hands soon. They will make for quite a library. It is really rather remarkable how well crates of books can float when the ship carrying them has been obliterated."

"No," I whisper.

"Foolish of you," he takes a couple of steps forward. Picks up a dainty figurine of two playing children from Nessa's hall table, "not to ensure the safety of this place. I was surprised to find it left so utterly vulnerable. Quite an unfortunate misstep, to be certain. I did, after all, offer some warning that we were aware of the manse and your association with it. It would have been prudent to send a warning to the Lady Ganvent and her husband."

He's right. I should have warned Nessa and the others. I should have made sure there were wards. Guards. I was careless. I took this place for granted. I push the thought away. Try to think rationally. What he's saying can't be true. Admiral Ganvent is smart. Strong. He'd have protections, himself. He'd be prepared for an attack. There's no way his ship was attacked. Osven's just trying to get a rise out of me.

"What about the others? What did you do to them?" I growl at him. Reach for a knife from my belt. Behind me, I feel Rian's energy building. The wand is pulsing with it. I sense his hand around it even though my back is to him. He's ready to cast. When he does, it'll be devastating.

"A little drain is all," Osven waves his hand dismissively. "They're comfortably nestled in their beds. I'll spare them and return their mother," his eyes darken, "if you agree to come with me."

Behind me, Rian's unspoken spell reaches its peak. It's ready to be unleashed. He moves, just slightly. Osven's eyes flick to him. The figurine in his hand bursts into flames.

"Do not be a fool, Eldinae," he says calmly and moves to set the flaming statue back onto the wooden table.

I look upstairs, toward the bedrooms. Just like before with Azi and Flitt, I can see them through the walls. Not in detail, just in outlines. The kids are up there, asleep. Loren, too. If it's like he said, if he drained them, they have no chance of waking, even in a fire. They'll die. Osven follows my gaze. While he's distracted, I reach into my pocket for the coin. I sneak it back to Rian.

"Find me," I mutter, and then I step out of the wards.

"*Don't*," he pushes to me, "*there's got to be another way.*" There isn't, though. We both know it.

"Let's go," I say to Osven. "Before I change my mind."

"*Impressive. Though…there's brave and selfless, and then there's just plain foolhardy,*" Aster pushes to Rian. Her words make me pause.

Osven eyes me with that same hunger he did the first time we met. This time, though, there's something else there. Triumph. Ownership. I feel my healed eye pulse. My attention is drawn away. In the closed pantry behind the Sorcerer, I see her. A woman, tied up. I try hard not to react, not to let him see what I've discovered. He's a liar. He never took Nessa. She's been here this whole time.

"Come, now," the Sorcerer beckons me greedily. He knows he can't force me. I can only go willingly.

He doesn't expect me to attack him. He's so haughty with his own power and distracted by Rian's threat of a spell that he forgets me, again. My lips curl back and I charge him before he can even think. I crash through his wards like they're nothing and hit him with the full force of my weight. He flies backward with a very un-elflike grunt and skids across the floor with me straddling his bony chest.

His crackling hands claw for my throat. The charge of lightning coming from them would kill me if I was anyone else. If I couldn't do what I can do. He's too weak to even strangle me. His hands are too frail. They're trained for spells, not for combat. I claw them away from my throat easily. Raise my fist. Punch his filthy, lying mouth.

"Who's a fool now?" I spit at him. "Coming here with no guards, thinking you can lie and get me to do what you want? Did you forget the last time I attacked you? Did you think I wouldn't do it again?"

He lies stunned. Wide-eyed. Panting. Shocked that I'd dare touch him. I swing again and his head snaps to the side. That gets him going again. His eyes flash with rage. He raises his hands. Whispers. Behind me, something crashes and sizzles. I grab his hand and bite his wrist until I taste blood and feel bones crunch. He screams. Claws at me with his free hand. Gasps in pain.

Rian shouts something behind me. Sleep spell. The pink cloud settles over us. Osven's eyes don't even close. He just laughs.

"What are you?" he growls with a sneer past me at Rian. "Fifteenth Circle? Sixteenth? And not even a hint of the Mark. Not a shadow of it. Your spells cannot touch me, Eldinae. You're too weak. Too Light."

I feel the power behind his words. They're entwined with a spell that streaks past me. It sways Rian. Fills him with doubt.

Osven thrusts his uninjured hand upward. The ceiling cracks and crumbles. Chunks of plaster break free and crash down. I raise my arm to shield myself and fight the urge to roll off of him. I won't let him get away.

I brace myself for the barrage of plaster, but just before it strikes us a heavy wind gusts through the foyer and sends it spinning away.

"Sorry I'm late," comes a whisper from Rian's general area.

"*Not at all, Shush,*" Rian pushes.

Osven whispers. I don't have time to react. All around me, the wood of the floorboards splinters and crackles. Spikes of wood poke up, writhing. They shift and change and slither. A dozen of them. A score. White fangs drip with sickly poison. The serpents eye me hungrily.

"I'll call them off," Osven hisses much like the snakes. "It's not too late to agree to my terms, Nullen."

I have no idea what sort of spell it is. I've never seen one like it. I know it's very possible if these are actual serpents, they could kill me with a bite. I catch myself actually considering his terms, until a conversation between Rian and Shush interrupts my train of thought.

"*Yes, they're certainly real serpents. Very impressive.*"

"*Impressive and easy enough to…*" Rian's voice trails off.

The pink cloud forms and settles again. The snakes coil up and go still, sound asleep.

"*I'll distract him,*" Shush pushes.

He sends another gust of wind that catches my breath. Osven screws his eyes shut and turns his head away from the blast. It's so strong my skin ripples under the force of it. My hair feels like it'll tear out by the roots. Osven and I start skidding away across the floor. Out of the range of the snakes. Onto Nessa's flower rug the admiral brought from Elespen. The vines on it pulse and grow plump and alive. The green tendrils wind around Osven's mouth first. They bind his arms. Twist around his fingers and squeeze his hands closed. I jump off as they curl across his body like a hundred leafy ropes.

Osven struggles against the bindings but he's too weak, and with his hands and mouth tied up and his eyes blindfolded by the carpet-vines, he can't cast a spell. I hope.

"*Bring me closer,*" Aster begs from inside Rian's pocket.

Rian creeps near the Sorcerer and draws the wand. It's almost impossible to tell that Osven's in there now. The ropes are so thick he looks like a giant basket tipped over.

Aster twitches in Rian's hand as they get closer. Dark energy seeps out from between the spaces in the bindings. As it streams toward the wand, it shifts from shadow to light. Draining him. Stripping him.

Rian's hand shakes as he realizes what's happening, but he allows it.

"That's enough, wand, don't you think?" Shush whispers.

"*Just a little more,*" Aster's reply echoes eerily through the house.

Chapter Twenty-Nine
APPEALING TO THE KING

Azi

At the palace, it's all very strict. Rather than a cheerful Page to guide us to a room to wait, we're flanked by palace guards who march us to an annex of the throne room. They stand at attention at four points around us, allowing us very little freedom while we wait for His Majesty.

Mya and Uncle stand in front of me and occasionally exchange a nervous word or two. Saesa, Flitt, and I stand behind them. Saesa makes me proud. She remains respectful and patient while we're made to wait. Flitt is exactly the opposite. She fidgets and bounces on her toes and looks around the richly decorated room impatiently.

"Rather empty," she declares, and her loud voice echoes through the vast hall. "And quiet." Beside me, Saesa winces.

"Shh," I whisper. "It isn't usually so empty, but it's late, Flitt. Everyone's gone to bed."

"I thought there'd at least be dancing like we have," she announces, not bothering to lower her voice at all. "And music. You know. Mya, you should play something and I'll dance. Oh," she sighs with a scowl, "maybe I shouldn't. I still haven't sorted out my feet yet. Ow. How do you manage to stand for so very long? I feel like the flesh on my soles is going to hurt right off."

Mya, Uncle, and the front flank guards slowly turn to look at Flitt. Uncle seems amused, but Mya presses a finger to her lips.

"We've been waiting an awfully long time, haven't we?" Flitt huffs. "Is it normal to wait so very long in such a dreadfully boring room?" she tugs on one of the guards. "Are you sure you told His Majesty we were here?"

When he doesn't answer, she wrinkles her nose. "Rude," she mutters under her breath. "Typical."

"Flitt," I hiss between my teeth, mortified by her impatience, "he knows we're here. They said they'd announce us, remember? Just try to keep quiet."

"What's the point of having to be quiet?" she asks innocently. "It just seems to make the wait longer. I bet he's making us wait on purpose."

Her eyes wander around the room and slowly her feet begin to wander, too. She drifts away only a little, and the palace guards put a gentle hand up to stop her.

"Please remain with us," one of them says.

"Oh, so you do talk!" Flitt pats his arm condescendingly and then quickly pulls her hand away, sniffs her fingers, makes a face, and wipes them on my cloak.

"Sorry," I whisper to the scowling guard as I tuck Flitt behind me. "She's not from here."

"Aye," the guard grumbles and looks down his nose at the two of us. His eyes linger on my Mark and I slide my visor down self-consciously.

"Indeed, it must all seem very strange to you. Come," Uncle offers brightly. To my surprise, he smiles at her and offers her his arm. Flitt scowls and looks at me.

"*Link your hand through his elbow,*" I push to her.

"*Do I have to? He's worse than Stinky Rian,*" she pushes back.

"*He's trying to be nice to you,*" I give Flitt an insistent look, and she rolls her eyes and reluctantly links her hand through Uncle's offered arm. The guards allow him past after a short exchange, and he guides her across the vast room to stand before a portrait of His Majesty's father. There, he goes into great detail, describing the importance of painters and their patrons throughout the history of Cerion.

"*He's torturing me,*" she pushes the thought to me without even looking over her shoulder. Uncle gestures across the canvas, explaining away. "*You see him torturing me, right?*"

I suppress a chuckle and shake my head. With the two of them occupied across the room, my stomach starts to twist with nerves. Saesa's quiet presence centers me. I settle into attention beside her and stare ahead, alert and still. It's been such a long time since I've taken this stance, I'm surprised by how much it calms me. It's almost meditative.

I'm reminded of Cerion Day all those years ago, when I was a hopeful squire waiting for her trials to start. So much has happened since then. I don't even feel like the same person anymore. Da saw it. I wonder if His Majesty will, too. Am I too different now from the Azaeli who used to come and amuse the princesses in the gardens? Will he think me too changed from the girl who dreamed of serving them one day the way my parents have served him?

"His Majesty will see you now."

The announcement jolts me. My stomach knots up. Before us, the doors to the throne room swing open. Uncle leads Flitt to my side again, and the guards march us in.

King Tirnon is on his feet as soon as we enter. He jogs down the steps of his throne and strides toward us. His fists are clenched at his sides, the veins at his temples pulse with anger. As he approaches, we all drop to one knee out of respect. Except for Flitt, of course. She stands oblivious at my side as the king weaves between the others to stop before me.

"What is the meaning of this?" His Majesty bellows. My heart races at his fury. I pray he'll spare me rather than placing me under arrest. The summons in my shaking hand crinkles loudly. I duck my head to hide the Mark behind my helm for fear that the sight of it will have me sent straight to sleep.

"*Get down*," I push to Flitt. To my surprise, she does.

"Stand down," he snaps at the guards in front. "And you. Go." He jabs his finger toward the two behind us. "Completely unnecessary," he growls. "Kristan, what is the meaning of this?"

"Sire, it is just a precautionary—" the palace guard behind him starts to explain, but His Majesty holds his hand up to silence him.

"Paranoia," he says darkly. "I will not have my kingdom ruled in fear. Do you understand me, Kristan? These," he gestures to the group of us, "are my most trusted. My Elite. They rank above even you in my eyes, General. I will not have them treated this way."

"Of course, sire. We only meant to—" he stops again, mid-sentence, as His Majesty slowly turns to face him.

"I have been patient with your precautions and your overzealous protections until now," he says in a tone so low I can barely hear him, "but I grow steadily wearier of your dissenting tone toward me. I am your king."

"Yes, sire," Kristan bows.

"Go." His Majesty says.

Kristan glances at us as though he might argue against it, but when his Majesty narrows his eyes at him, the general nods and marches off with our escort.

When the door closes with a heavy thud behind them, His Majesty turns to us. His dismissal of the guards doesn't seem to have lifted his mood much.

"This way," he commands, and ushers us into a smaller side room where a merry fire crackles in the hearth. The room is otherwise empty, save for a round table at the center. Two guards flank the door at attention. Flitt pauses between them and looks them over.

"Are these people, or just suits?" she asks aloud and flicks at his burnished metal forearm with her finger making a *plink, plink, plink* sound. The guard remains absolutely still.

"They're real," Saesa whispers and takes her by the shoulders as I follow Mya and Uncle to the hearth with His Majesty. "Sorry," she mutters to the guard.

"But they're so still," Flitt says with awe as Saesa guides her away. "*No chairs again?*" she whines in my head. "*My poor, gigantic feet.*"

Thankfully, His Majesty doesn't even look at me as we approach him. Instead he broods into the fire. "I expected to see you much sooner, Azaeli," he says with a tone I can only take for disappointment.

"Yes, Your Majesty," I try with difficulty to keep my voice steady as I bow to him. "Please forgive me. I wasn't in Cerion when your summons arrived."

"Summons?"

He scowls and flicks his fingers toward me, his eyes on the parchment in my hand. I hand it to him. When he looks it over, his frown deepens. "These are not—" he looks up and his gaze darts from my closed visor to Flitt's colorful presence beside me. He takes her in a bit at a time: her strangely colored hair, her changing eyes, the crest of her cloak.

"Not what?" Flitt asks, blinking innocently as the firelight sparkles across her pale skin.

"It isn't the message I requested to be sent. Those aren't my words." His Majesty shakes his head slowly and hands the note back without even looking at me. He's mesmerized by the sight of Flitt. He steps closer to her as though he can't believe what he's seeing. "Who is this enchanting creature?" he whispers.

As he approaches her, Flitt's light grows brighter and brighter. She opens her hands at her sides and a score of luminous orbs drift from them and add their own light to the small room until all of the shadows are washed away. She raises a shoulder to her cheek and grins at His Majesty with adorably flirtatious giggle.

"My name is Flitter," she says once the peaceful glow has settled. A bright yellow orb drifts between her and the king. "Felicity Lumine Instacia Tenacity Teeming Elite Reformer. I'm supposed to be just a traveler, but things change, you know. They made me a messenger, too. Not one like those you've been dreaming about. Those are different. I'm an actual, in-person messenger."

"How do you know my dreams?" Tirnon whispers in awe.

"They were sent to you on purpose," Flitt replies matter-of-factly. "So you'd be expecting me."

We all stand in complete silence, watching the exchange between the two of them. I remember when Flitt and I first met in person, how disorienting it had been. I, too, had had several dreams before she showed herself to me. Dreams of dancing with fairies at the Ring and fighting shadow cyclones in a golden field. Dreams of lying in that same field and becoming one with the landscape. Dreams of a fairy, giving me the gift of Flitt's diamond tether which allowed her to travel to me.

"I thought I was going mad," His Majesty says, shaking his head, "dreaming of fairies in such a time."

"You never spoke of it, Your Majesty," Uncle ventures.

"Would you have, Gaethon?" His Majesty asks. "Considering?" His eyes never leave Flitt, as though daring to look away might cause her disappear.

"Most likely not," Uncle agrees quietly. "Considering."

"So, they're coming?" King Tirnon asks. "It's true? In my lifetime? I never would have expected it."

His voice is tinged with excitement and pride. "All these years we've protected our alliance. Decades. A century and more, and always I have wondered whether you even existed to begin with. Whether any of it was truly real, or just fairy tales."

"Of course it's real," Flitt says with a huff. "What a silly thing to think. Absolutely typical that you'd doubt it, though."

"But why have you remained so hidden all of this time?" His Majesty asks.

"Azi," Flitt says with a roll of her eyes, "I think we're going to have to teach His Majesty the proper way to play."

"Play?" Mya asks curiously.

"A question game. It's the custom," I explain. "Or is it a rule?"

Flitt shrugs and wriggles her pink eyebrows beneath her colorful bangs at the king. I go on.

"How it's played is," I explain, "you ask a question, Your Majesty, then Flitt will answer, and then she can ask hers, and you answer. It goes on that way until someone breaks the chain."

"Right," Flitt nods. "You can go first, since you're the king."

"Ah, thank you," His Majesty says, still quite in a daze. "Thank you, my dear. My first question is this: What manner of visit do they intend? Is it merely a friendly introduction? Or should we perhaps be prepared to make diplomatic negotiations?"

Flitt groans and rolls her eyes. Beside her, Saesa takes a step away from her and closer to me, as if to disassociate herself from Flitt.

"That was three questions, Your Highness," Flitt huffs.

"Of course," he nods. "Then I'll start with the basics. The royal staff will need to know how many to accommodate for. How many should we expect to be staying, and for how long?"

"Oh, not very long, and how many doesn't really matter," Flitt smiles. "My turn. Why aren't there any chairs in here?" She shifts her weight from one foot to another with a wince. "I'm not used to standing on my feet for so long, you see."

"This is a planning room," His Majesty replies. "My men and I think better on our feet. It allows us to circle around the table. Gaethon, if you would?"

"Hm?" Uncle, who has been staring with a mix of thinly-veiled amusement and fascination at Flitt this whole time, snaps his attention to the king. "Oh, indeed, Sire," he says.

With a sweep of Uncle's hand, the tabletop shifts. The illusion of a city emerges from it, growing and shaping itself into a perfect model of Cerion cast in moonlight. Everything is represented, from the crumbling blocks of Redstone Row and the golden dome of the Academy to the pristine white towers of the Royal Palace.

Flitt walks around it, gazing at the little buildings with mild interest.

"It isn't very useful," she says after a moment, and Uncle looks very put-down. Flitt notices.

"Sorry," she says. "I just think it would be better if it wasn't so empty, that's all."

"Empty?" Uncle frowns. "This model is the collaborative work of no less than four Master Mages, my dear. It shows the ever-changing city just as it is in this precise moment. See? This ship is docked now, whereas earlier it was just arriving."

He points to the docks beside the empty market, where the cliffs plunge to the sea.

"But a city is made up of people," Flitt says as she leans over the model. "That's what makes it a city."

She holds her hand out over the palace and casually wiggles her fingers, and tiny points of light drift from them to settle into place throughout the palace. The lights split from each other and scatter across the table model to settle in houses and on streets. Some of the lights stay still, while others drift lazily from one place to the next.

"There," she smiles. "That's my present to you, Your Majesty. In return, I would really very much like a chair."

"Of course, a chair." King Tirnon murmurs. He shakes his head in fascination at the sight of all of the now-populated model. "Would you be so kind, Haris?" he says over his shoulder, and one of the guards steps out.

"It's your turn, Your Majesty," Flitt says sweetly. Tirnon tears his attention away from the model.

"Ah, yes. What is the manner of this visit? I'm afraid I must know so that I can be certain to summon the proper subjects to greet and entertain."

"It isn't really my place to tell you that," Flitt glances at the door, hopeful for the guard to return with a seat for her. "But I will say that it should be a pleasant time, and that we of Kythshire are ready to make a stronger alliance. You've proved over decades that you respect us and our Source, so we feel it's time to strengthen our bond."

She looks over her shoulder at me and giggles. I know she means that much more literally than His Majesty can imagine. The guard returns with a comfortable-looking chair and Flitt scoots back in it gratefully, leaving her feet to dangle just above the floor.

"Ahh," she says with eyes half-closed. "All right. Thank you, armor suit, sir." The guard inside the suit nods. "My next question," Flitt turns her attention back to the king, "is this. Do you know it was The Dusk who was responsible for the attack at your High Court?"

"We have been searching for any clue that would lead us to the attacker, and as of yet have found nothing. I have been at my wit's end trying to seek answers, to take action. In the meantime, my kingdom doubts me. They accuse me of tyranny in one moment, and of leniency in the next. The Dusk, you say." His Majesty strides to the chair and stoops to Flitt's level.

"You must understand," he says as he searches her eyes, "I am convinced the loss of my son was due to the workings of evil the likes of which Cerion has not seen since the age of Diovicus. I beg you, my dear. If you have knowledge that would aid us in seeking out this threat and putting an end to it, tell me. Too long have there been secrets between our people. It is time to join together, to combine our

knowledge and fight this darkness. Flitter, please. Tell me what you know."

Flitt leans closer to him, her ever-changing eyes wide and pensive. She and the king stare at each other for a long, thoughtful moment. The others lean in, expecting whatever she's about to say to be profound and meaningful. To my embarrassment but not at all to my surprise, she finally whispers quite seriously, "That's not a proper question, Your Majesty. I win!"

"Flitt!" I gasp.

His Majesty lets out a bellowing laugh. "You are perhaps the most enchanting creature I've met in all my years. Is she not enchanting?"

"If you say so," Flitt grumbles. "But I'm not a creature. Anyway, Azi'd be better suited to tell you what she knows," Flitt says with a shrug and a bob of her head in my direction. "Since she can show you rather than tell you. Isn't that right, Azi?"

I feel the color drain from my face at Flitt's proclamation. I had hoped our meeting with the king wouldn't come to this. My heart pounds and my stomach twists into knots again as His Majesty straightens and turns to me. For the first time, he really looks at me. I push my visor up. His gaze lingers on the Mark on my face. There's no hiding it now. No bending my head away or allowing him to be distracted by his fairy visitor.

"Sir Hammerfel," he asks with a measured tone. "You are Marked. What is the meaning of this? What does she mean, show me?"

The silence grows deafening as everyone's attention turns to me. Uncle and Mya, Saesa and Flitt, even His Majesty and the guards stare, waiting for my reply.

"Your Majesty," I start. I glance at him and look away when, as soon as our eyes meet, the spark of magic threatens to burst forth. "As you know, my journeys to Kythshire have helped me form unlikely alliances," I nod my head to Flitt. "With them, I've also received many gifts. My armor, for example, and my sword as well. But not all of what I've received has been physical, Sire. In my dealings with Jacek, I stumbled on the ability to see into people's memories, and show them my own."

"Mentalism," Uncle offers quietly from across the room, to my relief. "It is a rare school of magic indeed, Tirnon. I know of only two others living who have been granted the key to this path, and neither is a subject of this kingdom. This gift to Azaeli is a gift to Cerion itself. And to you, Sire, for you are her liege."

"She's a Paladin, now, Your Majesty. Our queen says so herself," Flitt beams at me, but I have trouble sharing in her pride. The way the king looks at me with such trepidation makes me feel guilty and ashamed. Why should I be so favored by the fae when his son was so ruined by them?

"If it has been gifted by our allies and approved by the Academy, then I have no quarrel. What can you do with it, exactly, Azaeli?" His Majesty asks me.

"I can see through one's eyes into their memories, Sire, and I can show them mine as well," I explain. It isn't the whole truth. I'm not sure I'm ready to tell him about the golden threads that can control people. If there was one part of this ability that I could forget forever, that would be it. It's too powerful and underhanded. I glance at Uncle, and his nod tells me I've said enough.

"Show me," His Majesty says.

I'm comforted by his trust in me, though I don't know why. He has always put his trust in us, through the trials and everything else. He has come to my family for aid time and again. I don't know what I've done to earn it, but the reminder of our close relationship and the relief that he still trusts me makes me so emotional I have to close my eyes and take a long, deep breath to keep myself from crying.

The simple act of centering myself somehow reminds me of Iren. I think of the way my memories played in the space between us whenever we visited with each other. I feel the same way with him that I did with the assassin in Maisie's house, though for different reasons.

I don't want to look into His Majesty's eyes and invite him into my head. It's too personal, too intimate and powerful. It could be construed as a threat. Besides, what I would show him is something I'd want the rest of them to see, too. I'm just unsure whether I know how to do it that way. Show my memories outside of myself the way I pulled them out of that man.

"*Go on*," Flitt's gentle push is just the encouragement I need. I take a cautious step toward Tirnon and hold my hands out to him. To my surprise, he accepts them without hesitation. His touch is different than I would have expected a King's to be. The skin of his palms is warm and rough with callouses.

"Azaeli," Uncle warns, "perhaps you should explain first what you will do, in order to put us all at ease."

"Of course," my voice comes out weaker than I expected it to, and I clear my throat before I go on. "If you look to our hands, Your

Majesty, what I hope you'll see are my own memories. I'll show them to you, like actors on a stage, so you can see them as I have."

He nods and follows my gaze as I focus once more on my hands in his and allow the sensation of magic to fill me up. My vision is framed with sparkling golden energy and I breathe and send it forward into His Majesty's upturned palms. Scenes from my past fill the space between us, not as clearly as Iren was able to show, but still mostly visible. Flitt's diamond at the cord around my neck bursts forth with colorful light, and immediately I'm aware that the fairies are guiding me to show him what he needs to see.

Blurred images flecked with gold become more crisp. I show him the Ring at Kythshire, the dancing. I show him Iren and the crumbled keep at the Northern Border. The skeleton sentries. Rian's battle with the Sorcerers. I show him Jacek in the Dreaming and the moments with Eron beneath the water at Kordelya Keep.

His hands begin to shake at that scene, but when I glance at him he nods to me to go on.

I'm not sure how long we remain this way. I show him so many more memories of the fae and my dealings with them. The images flow, sometimes without my bidding them to, until he knows nearly as much as I do. In this way, he's seen everything from our battle with Jacek to the tests at the Palace of Dawn and the Fairy Queen's tale of the Dawn and the Dusk. The only thing that I fail to share is the Princess and her secret. I understand it isn't time for that, yet.

When the final images begin to fade, the rush of magic goes with it, leaving me completely drained. The gold flecks that encroached on my vision are replaced with nothing but with prickles of black. Exhaustion takes me quickly, and I grip His Majesty's hands to keep from collapsing to the floor. Mya starts to hum a restoring melody and Saesa catches me as I stumble back. Flitt shines her light, but it barely helps. I went too far for too long.

"Rest, Niece," Uncle's whisper is the permission I need. I allow my eyes to close, just for a moment.

Chapter Thirty
INTO THE SEA

Tib

I scramble to my feet while Rian and Shush argue about how long to let the wand do what it's doing. I don't care. If I had my way, I'd kill him and be done with it. My concern right now is for Nessa, and for the rest of our family upstairs.

I pick my way across the twisted vines of the carpet toward the pantry and wrench the door open. Nessa gasps and pants. Her terrified eyes search me and then the others.

"It's all right Nessa," I assure her as I squat and offer her my hand. She's not tied up after all. She's just curled with her back against the wall, hugging her knees to her chest. The ripped ruffles of her dress are piled all around her in strips. She doesn't move to take my hand. She just sits there, shaking and staring. "Really, it's safe now," I grab her hand and try to pull her up, but she still doesn't move. When I let go, her hand drops to the floor beside her.

"What's wrong?" I whisper. She doesn't answer. It's like she's paralyzed. I take her hand again and that's when I feel it. The spell, binding her. "Rian, help!" I call over my shoulder.

Aster mumbles its protest as Rian rushes to my side. As soon as he sees Nessa, he nods matter-of-factly.

"Immobility," he says with a frown. "It can only be undone by the caster."

"*Use me,*" Aster's voice echoes between us. Rian and Shush exchange a reluctant glance.

"What?" I growl. "Do it! Look at her!"

Rian raises the wand. I can tell he's hesitating. Trying to think of another way. It makes me furious.

"Do it, Rian," I glare at him. "She doesn't deserve this."

Rian points the wand at her and closes his eyes. I can feel him searching for the right spell. Inside the wand, the energy shifts. Light streaks out of the tip of it. Midway to Nessa, it turns dark and inky. I gather her close as it winds around her, pulls the spell away, and releases her from the magical bindings. She slumps against me and takes a long, shuddering sob. I prepare myself for a long, awkward time in the cupboard holding Nessa while she cries. To my surprise, though, she immediately growls and pushes herself to her feet.

At first I think her sudden rage is some new spell, but I can't feel anything on her. She stalks to the table with the figurine and yanks open the drawer. The dagger she pulls out is long, sharp, and elegant. The shredded bits of her dress flare out as she spins to the pile of rug roots that keep Osven bound.

She purses her lips, drops to her knees, and plunges the dagger into the lump of vines where I imagine Osven's throat to be. Along with it, she releases a shocking string of curses and oaths against the Sorcerer that I'd never imagine coming from sweet Nessa. Her attack is a frantic, brutal flurry that leaves me and Rian staring slack-jawed and shocked by the sight of it.

"So much for keeping him to question," Rian utters, looking sickened.

"Something tells me," Nessa pulls the dagger free one last time and wipes it on her ruined ruffles, "there'll be more." She turns to Rian. "Can you wake the others? He got to me first. I could hear them screaming the whole time." She tightens her grip on the dagger and glares at the carpet like she's thinking a few more stabs might be good. I take her elbow gently and lead her to the stairs. She's still shaking, really hard.

"Of course," Rian shoves Aster back into his pocket, like he wants to spend the least time holding it possible. He skirts around the mess that was once Osven. So much for Nessa's rug.

All of us run up the stairs together. Shush keeps hidden over Rian's head. Nessa bunches her dress up to her chest. First room is mine. I dash in and grab my bandolier, just in case. Everything's where it should be. Knives, vials. I buckle it on and catch up to the rest of them outside Lilen's room. Lilen's right at the threshold, flat on her back with her arms stretched toward the ceiling. Her nightgown and hair are burnt. Her eyes are shot through with red. She tries to scramble away when she sees us, but her arms and legs only flop around weakly.

"Lilen!" Nessa chokes and stoops beside her.

"What happened to her?" I whisper.

"She's been stripped," Rian whispers. This time it's his turn to curse. He kneels next to her and puts a hand on her head.

"Can she be un-stripped?" I ask while Nessa utters an oath and strokes her charred hair.

"Maybe. It hasn't been that long. Shush," he whispers, and Shush lands next to her ear. Rian pulls out Aster again, and the three of them—Rian, Aster, and Shush—restore her.

As soon as she's back to herself, she pushes past everyone else and throws her arms around me. "Oh, Tib," she sobs, "I heard everything. You were going to go with him to keep us safe!"

She clings to me for a long time, even after the others file out, until I decide that the only way I can follow is to drag her along. The next room is Ruben's, which he shares with the new boys. The next room is Emmie's. Rian helps them up. Nessa stays with them while the rest of us move on to Loren's room. That's not easy, since I've still got Lilen's face buried in my chest.

"Where's Saesa?" she gulps for breath between sobs and Rian looks at the two of us with a bemused smile.

"With her Lady Knight," I reply.

"Oh good," Lilen wails and holds me tighter.

"Ah, Lilen, you put the sleep spell on Loren, correct?" Rian asks as he rubs his neck, still amused by the sight of Lilen clinging to me.

"What?" she blinks at Rian. "Oh, I suppose I did. I imagine it's time to wake him now."

I wriggle free from her hold and she sniffles and wipes her eyes. She gives me an odd look before she goes to Loren's bedside. Like she's sorry to leave.

"Fighting them off, I see," Rian mutters to me under his breath while Lilen whispers the spell to wake the apprentice. He tucks the wand into his pocket again.

I scowl up at him. "Huh?"

He doesn't answer. Just shrugs and gives that same half-grin like he did earlier with Saesa. Strangely, all of it makes me think of Margy. I push the thought aside as Loren sits up. It takes him a little time to focus. We let him get oriented. He looks from Lilen to me and then Rian, and his eyes go wide.

"Is that a fairy?" he whispers hoarsely. "Is he your Ili'luvrie?" he asks Shush, not Rian.

"Not yet, friend," Shush replies with a whispered chuckle. "Soon. Perhaps after dawn."

"Where?" Lilen squints at Rian curiously.

"Lilen," Rian says, "as the resident Mage of this house, I'm putting you in charge. Please go check on Nessa and the others. Make a plan to report the mess downstairs to the Academy. Use caution."

"Of, of course, Mentor," Lilen bobs a quick curtsy. She squares her shoulders with haughty pride and rushes out, ready to take charge.

As soon as the door closes behind her, Loren doesn't waste time. He rushes to Rian. "Dusk. It's coming. I saw it in the Dreaming. You have Aster?"

Rian nods and offers the wand to Loren. Looks like he's glad he'll be rid of it.

"*Ah, ah ah,*" Aster chides as Loren reaches to take it. "*I like this one better. He actually lets me do things.*"

"Oh," Loren promptly drops his hand and sighs. "She's yours now." He reaches for the wand again anyway, then shakes his head like he's coming back to his senses. "We've got to go. Quickly. They have two. They only need four more. Master says we need to see him, and then be off again."

"Slow down, please." Rian crosses to the boy. "What do you mean, they have two?"

"Two. Two offerings." Loren gets up and starts pacing. "I dreamed it. Two."

"Two of what?" Rian asks again, patiently.

"I can't speak of it. But it means two more than we have. We've got to hurry. Please. To my Master. He'll be able to explain. Do you have a way to get us to Stepstone tonight?"

"Stepstone?" Rian asks. He looks at Shush. "I don't know," he says hesitantly.

"What about Errie?" I ask. "We've got to save him."

"Listen," Loren comes to face me. He's a lot more confident than he was in the tavern. Urgent. Determined. "If they get any more, they'll have half. Then they could start it. We have to catch up."

"Half of WHAT?" I shout. I'm through with Mages and their secrets. After this, no more Mages in my life. Ever.

Rian crosses to the door. Starts to set wards of silence. Loren shakes his head. Shush scowls.

"The shadows are listening," Loren whispers.

"No they're not," I argue. "There's no one else in here. I'd feel it. Believe me. Tell us what you know."

"I already told you," Loren shouts, "as much as I know, Tib! Listen to me!" He spins to Rian, like he's waiting for him to agree that I'm being stupid.

"All right, you two," Rian stands between us and puts a hand on each of our shoulders. I shrug it off. I don't need him placating me. His eyes flash with secrets when he turns to Loren. Seems like he already knows what the other Mage is talking about. Figures. "Calm down," he says, and the steadiness of his voice only makes me angrier.

"I don't care what you two are up to," I growl. "We let them take Errie, Rian. We have to get him back. You said we'd fetch Loren and then we'd go, so I'm going. With or without you."

"You think you're invincible, don't you?" Loren glares. "You think you can do anything. You can't, Tib. Not without help. This is important. You have to believe me."

I cross my arms and scowl until Rian takes me aside.

"We'll be quick," he says. "A step to Kaso Viro, and then a step back here, or straight to the stronghold. I want to get him back as much as you do, Tib. But what that Mage has to tell is, well, I have a feeling it's all going to lead us there, anyway. He's got answers we don't have."

"And more problems to solve, seems like," I sigh. "Let's go, then."

"Good," Rian turns to Loren. "Now, think of your Master. Think hard on him. I'm going to take you into the Half-Realm. It's your job to get us to Stepstone from there. Tib?"

"Yeah."

"All right?"

"All right."

Rian puts a hand on my shoulder again, and his other one on Loren's. Shush clings to his sleeve. The air shifts around us. The cobwebs brush my face. Loren calls out his Master's name, and the floor beneath our feet drops away. I reach up. Cling to Rian's arm as we spin through the space between dreaming and awake.

We hit the shore of the beach with a spray of sand. The rush of ocean waves crashing nearby summons terror in me as I remember my fall from the cliff. At first I think it's a trick, but then Rian gasps.

"Remarkable," he breathes.

Loren straightens and motions across his yellow robes. The wrinkles and sand fall away. He follows Rian's gaze and grins up into the night sky behind me.

The light of a million stars sparkles across the water. The moon shines so brightly it turns everything blue. From the dark, glittering water, a great tower pierces the sky. It's ten stories high at least, and reminds me of the towers of Zhagen. This one is different, though. It's like a sculpture of stone and metal that shines in the moonlight. The top of it is domed, and the dome has a slit in it that's open to the sky.

When Loren starts into the crashing waves, he stretches his hands toward the water. He doesn't stop, even when he's drenched up to the knees. A surge of magic rumbles the sand beneath our feet.

"This way," he calls over his shoulder. Rian grins over at me, obviously impressed as Loren trudges through the water.

The rumbling keeps on until a narrow walkway finally emerges from the sea, leading straight to the tower. Loren does another spell to dry his robes off, and Rian and I follow him along the stone walkway to the tower.

I want to be annoyed by the magic. I want to hate the excess of it. There's no reason for it except to show off. I can't help but admit it, though. It's kind of impressive.

When we reach the tower, the stone wall shifts and opens magically. Of course there aren't any doors. Why would there be? Rian brushes his fingers along the stone as we go in. He's really impressed. I bet he's going to write it all down when this is over. Make a book of it for their ridiculous libraries.

Inside it's dry and warm. The walls are adorned with colorful silks and tapestries. The circular entry is larger than I expected. It's a little confusing. The energy is bright and overwhelming. It's embedded in the stone. It pulses in the air. Power. Might. Majesty. Protection. Knowledge.

Otherwise, the place is dusty and full of cobwebs. Shelves and shelves of moldy books line the walls behind the coverings. Books and tubes and glass vials and stacked clay pots teeter and lean against each other. I sniff. Sea air. Must. Incense. Behind Rian, Shush blows out a wisp of fresh air that sends the white smoke swirling away.

"Master's downstairs," Loren says. His voice echoes up into the rafters and a passage opens up across the entryway. It glows with a merry orange light to welcome us.

The stairway down is lined with glass walls as thick as my arm. Loren takes this for granted. He jogs off down the steps without a glance, but Rian and I can't help but stop and stare. Through the glass, a world stretches out before us. The depths of the ocean. The surf plunges above, bubbling and churning.

Waves scoop up the sandy seaweed bottom and push it down again. It's like a field. A drifting, rhythmic meadow. Colorful fish swim past in schools of red, orange, and yellow. Creatures like I've never seen cling to bright pink and green stones. They wave long tendrils with the motion of the sea. Shells of every color catch the light of the spiral staircase which shines through the glass.

I've never seen anything like it. It's simple. Pure. Beautiful. I had no idea there was a world like this under the ocean. I can't tear my eyes away. I press my hand to the glass as a dolphin races past us, chasing a group of purple fish with long, flowing fins. It's not just the sight of it that interests me. It's the simplicity of it. There's no magic out there. Not in the sense I've known it. It's perfect all on its own.

"Rian! Tib! He's coming!" Loren's shouts echo from below.

Rian pulls at my elbow as he rushes downward, but I'm still entranced by the scene. In the distance, a creature emerges from the depths. It's fast, huge, and coming right for us. It doesn't slow as it gets closer. Instead, it seems to speed up. I grab the edge of Rian's vest to stop him. "Look," I say and jab my finger to the glass.

"It's fast," Shush whispers. "Like the wind."

"Come down," Loren calls again.

"We should greet the Master," Rian says. He doesn't look away, though. He's just as held by the sight as I am. I don't even notice Loren until he's standing right next to me.

"Stop gaping and come on," he nudges me just enough to snap me out of it. We all jog down the rest of the stairs together.

The stairway opens up into a circular chamber. The walls here are glass, just like the stairway. There's a wide walkway of pebbles arranged in mosaics of crabs and fish and mermaids with sharp teeth and flowing hair. It's lined with high arches of pearls and shells, and it goes around the edge of a deep pool of water which takes up the whole center of the chamber.

In the pool, a dark-skinned man lounges with his eyes closed and his elbows propped on the side. He's sleeping, or meditating. His curly white beard ripples down his chest like seafoam. Blue and turquoise and yellow silks drift around him in the water, covering his legs. His chest and arms are puckered in places with strange markings. Like the mosaic pebbles. Or fish scales. Aside from the scales, he looks a lot like Valenor.

Rian clears his throat, but the Mage doesn't stir. Past the pool, past the glass, the creature from before is getting closer. Rian moves closer to me. Shush huddles near him.

"What is that?" Rian asks Loren. His voice is shaky. Nervous. "It looks like a..."

"Sea serpent," Loren grins.

Beside me, Rian stiffens. He grabs my arm, like he's ready to run. I'm with him. I didn't sign up for dragons.

"It's not slowing. It's going to crash…" Rian trails off as the enormous creature bears down on us. Its markings somehow remind me of the man in the pool. Elegant, flowing fins of turquoise and yellow, like silk. Long, streaming wisps of tendrils streak from its face. Its mouth is open, gaping wide to show sharp, needle-like glistening white fangs.

It's so close now I can see the reflection of the wall in its gleaming yellow eyes. I imagine it crashing into the glass, sending shards over us, making the tower crumble above us. I focus on the needle sharp teeth. What they could do. I don't know whether to cower or run. I'm frozen to the spot. Terrified.

Then, something dawns on me. A feeling. A reminder. I think of Zeze and Margy, and the fox and Elliot. Just as the wall magically opens and the dragon plunges through it, I know. It's him. The Mage in the pool is the sea dragon.

It sweeps gracefully through the opening like a dancing serpent, sending a spray of salty water over all of us. With a swirl of colorful trailing fins, it plunges straight into the Mage's chest. The glass wall closes up. Kaso Viro sits up and opens his eyes, which are as bright and yellow as the dragon's.

"Well, well," he says with a curious glance at the four of us, "you certainly took your time getting back, Apprentice."

"Yes, Master. Forgive me. I was held."

As Kaso Viro leaves the water, his silks are already dry. No spell, no magic. It's like the water wasn't wet. Loren summons a robe and drapes it over his master's shoulders.

The Mage grunts his thanks to the apprentice and draws the robe around himself. He looks at Shush first, and offers a cordial nod to the fae while Rian stands gaping.

"I have seen you, Soren Hasten Udi Swiftish Haven, and your unclaimed Ili'luvrie, Rian Eldinae," he says with a glint in his eye and a half-smile to Rian. Then he turns to me. "And I have seen you, Tibreseli Ganvent. The Dreamstalker. The Untouched."

"Nullen," I cross my arms over my chest. Some muse. "Not Ganvent."

"No?" he asks with a grin. "Are you certain?"

Behind him, Loren looks scandalized that I'd think to argue with his master. I don't care. He's just a man.

"Well," I mumble, "not officially."

"I see what is there, Tibreseli," he points to my chest. "Come. I have much to show you. All of you."

We follow him to the first level and the Mage stops and turns to his apprentice.

"Rather a lot of work you have, don't you?" he asks, and gestures to the dusty shelves. "You'd best get to it."

I'd have scowled. I'd have protested, if I was Loren. Or at least seemed disappointed to be dismissed so easily. He doesn't do any of that. He just nods and gets to work. Magically, of course. Uses spells and magic on the lower shelves to clear away the dust, while Kaso Viro leads the rest of us into another stairway.

This one goes up. No glass walls here. Instead, they're made of sandstone and carved with charts of stars and maps of places. Rian seems even more interested in these than he was in the sea. To me, they don't make much sense. Kaso Viro is patient with him. He doesn't rush him. He seems to understand why Rian would be so interested.

It takes us a while to get to the top, with Rian stopping every few steps to stare. When we finally do, the slit of the dome is perfectly angled to show the bright, full moon. It streams into a crystal in the center of the room, and the crystal casts its beams all around so there's no shadow in sight.

Otherwise, the room is empty. No chairs, no tables or shelves or instruments. Kaso Viro beckons us close to the crystal.

"Forgive me for being so blunt and informal," he says with urgency. "There is little time to lose. The son of the prince has been lost, as you both know, and this misstep affords our enemy a great advantage. In addition, they have Two of the Six. One more, and they shall be able to open the way. As you well know, we have none." He gestures to the walls, and six empty pedestals appear against them.

"We can get one," Shush whispers, "possibly two, if Sunteri is willing."

"Three, if the elves will agree. Then," Kaso Viro nods, "the Dawn shall have the upper hand."

"Forgive me," Rian says slowly. "Three what?"

"Offerings, Rian Eldinae." Kaso Viro whispers. "You see, in order to seek the gates of Brindelier, in order to be granted entry, one must bear proof of the approval of three of the Six."

"Six what?" I ask, not bothering to hide my annoyance at the cryptic manner of Mages.

"Six Keepers, Tibreseli," the Mage replies. "Keepers of the Wellsprings."

Chapter Thirty-One

MARGY'S GIFT

Azi

The sweet, distant sound of lutes and harps drifts in with the breeze of the late summer morning, its song so lovely that I lie in my bed for a long while simply listening. I feel more rested than I have in some time, and I revel in the pleasant sensation that everything is right with the world, and we are all at peace. I smile and hum off-tune to the melody. It's familiar, somehow. A song I heard long ago. The drums join in slowly with their deep, steady rhythm. A heartbeat, strong and true.

"Up, up, up!" Mouli's voice from my doorway jolts me. "Get up, dear! They'll be coming through this way, Flitt said, to collect you." I hear the clink of a tray on my bedside table, and I groan and burrow deeper into my bed. Mouli swats at me.

"Get up and eat something. It's no wonder you fainted last night. No sleep and no food!" She clicks her tongue and tugs the covers away with surprising strength for an old woman

"Ahh!" I groan, "All right, all right—wait. Did you say Flitt?"

"Aye," Mouli practically shoves a hot roll into my mouth. "She said last night when they brought you in to have you ready at Dawn for the procession. Eat! The others have already gone to the palace to receive them. Luca's saddling your horse now."

"Shadling mah…" I say around the enormous, hot mouthful. The events of the previous day come back to me slowly. No wonder why I'm so out of sorts. If it's dawn, I must have only gotten a quarter night's sleep.

"Don't," Mouli swats at me again, "talk with your mouth full. Honestly."

I nod and swallow, and the hot bread burns my throat all the way down. "Why is Luca saddling my horse?"

"Aren't you listening? You're to ride in with the procession from Kythshire," she explains as she makes another attempt to feed me. I grab the roll from her and bite it dramatically.

"I'm eating, all right?" I mumble. "Why do they want me to ride my horse two blocks? It seems a waste." I take another bite and crane my neck toward her while I chew, and she rolls her eyes at me in a fluster.

"Appearances, I imagine. Knights ride horses, Azi."

The fairy song grows louder as it nears.

"Oh," Mouli whines and snatches the tray up. "No more time for that. I'll get Saesa to help with your armor."

She rushes out, and I pad across the floor in my bare feet and slide open the circle hatch. I nibble on the last bit of roll as I peer inside. Rian's bed is still made.

"Rian?" I call, not at all surprised to be met with silence. I start to worry as I wipe my sticky fingers on my nightshift and begin working the straps of my hauberk to pull it from the stand. If he didn't sleep here, did he rush off someplace foolish?

"Lady Knight," Saesa bows in my doorway and I wave her inside. She gets to work right away getting me into my leggings and padding. While she works, she tells me in hushed tones about the goings-on at the Ganvent manse the night before. Her story blends oddly with the fairy song, and by the time I'm dressed, my skin prickles with chills.

"They didn't come back?" I whisper to her. She shakes her head, looking just as worried as I feel.

"They're nearing!" Mouli shouts, and Saesa and I rush out to the street where Luca is waiting with my horse. I mount up just in time to turn and see the start of the procession nearing on the main road. Saesa jogs alongside as I ride to meet them.

The first to appear are the banner bearers, carrying flags of green silk embroidered with golden threads in the pattern of tree branches. The three are triplets; female fae with flowing black hair and striking eyes of bright silver. Their high cheekbones sweep up to the line of their ears, which point elegantly at the crowns of their heads. Their limbs are long and slender, and they are dressed in billowing, airy silks the color of crisp blue sky. Colorful birds and butterflies soar behind them in the folds of the silk, diving in and out of it in an enchanting display. As they pass, the sound of rushing wind mixes with the fairy song.

The flag bearers offer me a low, respectful bow when they see me. All around, crowds of people crane and gawk and point at the procession and at me, too. I keep my horse steady and peer ahead for a glimpse of Flitt's rainbow hair, but the entire spectacle is filled with so much color and life that I'm sure I wouldn't be able to pick her out from it.

The flag bearers are followed by dancers dressed in a shade of pink that I've only ever seen in a sunrise. Their wings glitter and sway with their graceful movement, and their skirts release a sweet floral perfume as they twirl. The dancers are followed by jugglers who toss enormous flower buds up to the sky which bloom as they rise and close as they fall again. The jugglers are followed by a wave of winged fairies who rise and soar in a perfectly synchronized dance.

After the fairies comes a carriage of crystal and gold. A team of six white horses leads it and, I blink. They aren't horses, and they aren't leading the carriage. Each has a gleaming white horn on its head, and none of them wear reins or tack to pull the coach. It simply follows behind them magically. The coachman at the driver's seat bobs his head to the beat of the drum and grins and waves to everyone as he passes as though they're dear old friends. I have seen him many times before at the Ring, but never learned his name.

As the coach nears, I finally see the colorful head of hair I've been so eager to spot. Seated in the carriage, grinning from ear to ear, is Flitt. She waves excitedly to me, then points to herself as though she's shocked she's there. She's wearing the same gown as last night, and her hair drifts out behind her like a banner as the carriage glides along.

Twig sits towering beside her. I can't help but chuckle at the sight of him. He's human-sized and has no wings, but otherwise he hasn't changed. His tunic is of moss and dandelion petals, and his earth-crusted short pants are frayed at the hem. His bony knees are pressed to his chest in the small space. Even the fringe of black and green hair that covers his forehead is the same as always: matted with mud and sticks. He raises his skinny arm to wave to me, and leans to whisper to Flitt.

As they pass, she points at the empty spot behind her, and then to me, and I guide my horse into place behind them. Saesa walks beside me on foot.

The procession slows a little when I join, as if to show me off to the crowds. It works. Rows of sleepy-eyed men, women, and children have gathered in the streets to watch us pass. Some of the children laugh and rush in to dance with the fairies ahead of us. To my surprise the fairies encourage it, and our numbers grow as we pass through the streets. Behind us it sounds like a festival day. The music blends with cheers and sounds of revelry so merry that I can't help but turn in my saddle to gape.

The line behind me seems to go on forever, with one spectacle after another lined up on display. There are spinning dervishes of pixies and enormous walking trees, and prancing doe-like fae with long spotted blonde hair who toss glittering gems into the crowds. There are fairies who play the locks of their beards with a bow like fiddles, and fairies of flame and light who are so breathtakingly beautiful that I have to tear my attention away to keep from being mesmerized by them.

Among all of this, brightly colored fairy orbs drift and bob in time to the music. At the end, far in the back, is one final coach. This one is covered in grass and soft white blooms which sway with the jostle of the cobbles. It resembles a hillock of earth. Standing at the very top of it is the most beautiful, pristine white crocus bud.

If this dazzling show wasn't enough, a half-dozen Cygnets soar overhead on the sea breeze, announcing the arrival of the elves with their low, whistle-like calls. I strain to see the riders, but the mounts are so swift and so high that I can't make out who's driving.

The palace gates stand open in anticipation of our procession, guiding us onto the washed white sandstone of the promenade which sparkles brightly in the emerging light of morning. The way is lined with palace guards in highly burnished armor, standing straight and proud. Each bears a flag of blue and purple marked with the crest of Cerion's Plethore dynasty. It's such an impressive and rare display that I find myself grinning with pride. I had nearly forgotten the might of Cerion's battalions. It isn't something we have much of an occasion to show off on normal days.

As we make our way deeper into the palace grounds, the fairies' song grows louder, wilder and more joyous. A few ahead of us try to entice the guards to join them, but they won't be moved.

We reach the inner courtyard to the sound of Cerion's trumpets. His Majesty stands on the steps, his eyes twinkling with amusement as he watches the procession. Beside him, Queen Naelle is magnificently dressed in fine brocade of lavender and blue. Princess Margary stands between the two of them, holding each of their hands and grinning. She, too, is in her finest gown of deep purple dripping with crystals which catch the pre-dawn light and toss it away again to dance playfully on the creamy white stone of the staircase.

A dozen palace guards flank the Royal Family on either side. His Majesty's Elite, resplendent in their gold and blue, stand at perfect attention a few steps behind them. Everyone except for Rian is there in rank order: Mya, Uncle, Da, Brother Donal, Mum, Elliot, Cort, and even Bryse.

As the procession fills the courtyard with those from both Kythshire and Cerion, the cygnets circle overhead gracefully.

I watch in wonder at the marvel of allies of a century converging in one place, finally meeting without secrets or fear. It feels like a perfect, impossible dream.

With that thought, my heart sinks. I have had dreams like this before. Ones that felt as real as any other moment, like this one does. Terrifying dreams and wonderful dreams. The fairy music rises and echoes from the castle walls, and the dancing grows so infectious that even the king begins to tap his feet. My pulse quickens with the tempo of it. *What if it is just a dream?* I wonder, and I reach out carefully with my thoughts.

"*Valenor?*"

My mind is somewhat eased when he doesn't reply. Had this been a dream, I'm sure he would have answered.

Saesa's hand on my boot draws my attention. She moves closer to me and points into a shadowy alcove at the edge of the courtyard. A figure dressed in murky leathers stands in the cover of shadow. His bow is nocked with an arrow that drips inky black. I don't need to check his aim to know it's pointed directly at His Majesty.

I glance around in fear, but no guards seem to see him. Dancing fairies and silky banners swirl between us. My ears ring with the threat of sudden danger. There is no way, no time to warn the king. The archer's fingers twitch on the string, prepared to let the poisoned arrow loose. I know what I must do. I summon my powers, let the magic fill me, imagine golden strings which weave around his arms. He lowers his bow. I make his arms heavier, and he tips to the ground with his arms splayed over his head.

"Fetch the guards," I say calmly to Saesa without breaking my concentration on the golden threads. "Quietly."

Her red head bobs away through the crowd, and moments later she appears with two guards at the alcove. I don't look away until they drag him away, into the dungeons.

The threat weighs heavy on me as the spectacle of the procession finally begins to quiet. The carriage bearing Twig and Flitt and the second one, the hillock of earth, come to a halt at the steps. Twig is the first to stand, and Flitt hops to her feet beside him. I glance up at the crocus bud, but it remains closed. When the music finally fades away, Twig is the one to address the crowd. His strong, gentle voice carries with it the promise of friendship and light.

"Your Majesty, King Tirnon, Your Highness, Queen Naelle, Your Highness, Princess Margary," he pauses at the last and gives Margary a reassuring nod. Margy beams up at him, her shining eyes filled with pride. "Royal subjects of Cerion, Riders of Ceras'lain, and commoners, the people of Kythshire greet you."

This of course invites an eruption of cheers from fairies and humans alike. As exciting as it is, I'm still shaken by the archer. I find myself peering beyond the ceremony into all of the shadowy places within the courtyard, watching. Saesa returns to my side and I notice her doing the same. Thankfully, the threat has prompted a heavier presence of palace guards. They line the wall where they hadn't been before. This comforts me enough to turn my attention back to Twig and the others.

Twig offers Flitt a hand down from the carriage. Even on the ground, he towers above most of those gathered. When they come to stand before the king, despite the fact that His Majesty is a half-dozen steps up, Twig meets him eye to eye. They all bow to each other, and when Twig straightens up he seems to realize his mistake. He's made himself far too tall. To the collective gasps of the crowd he shrinks himself down, just a little bit.

"People of Kythshire," His Majesty's voice rings strong through the courtyard, "we are honored by your presence and delighted by the spectacle of your arrival. We offer a most heartfelt welcome to each of you."

High above on the hillock of earth, the crocus bud giggles softly. The sweet, child-like sound echoes playfully through the courtyard. Everyone turns their attention toward the flower, and a hush falls over the crowd. The petals of the bud open one by one to reveal a dainty fairy inside. The flower becomes her skirt, and she stretches fragile arms toward the sky with a sweet, soft yawn.

Crocus, the leader of the Ring in Kythshire, has not bothered to grow herself larger. Instead she has chosen to remain her fairy size, a tiny, perfect figure high above everyone else. Barely covered by the rich green moss at her feet, I spy the shiny black stone known as Scree. I'm as surprised as everyone else is to see the two of them here.

"May I present Chantelle Rejune Cordelia Unphasei Seren," Twig sweeps his hand toward her. "Crocus. And with her as always is Subter Crag Rever Enstil Evrest. Scree."

At his introductions, the carriage beneath Crocus rumbles slightly, just enough to hint at Scree's presence.

King Tirnon offers a respectful nod of his head.

"Welcome, friends," he says. He invites them inside to break their fast, and Crocus giggles once more.

"We very much appreciate your kind hospitality, Your Majesty," Crocus smiles dreamily. "I am afraid our time here is too short for such libations." She gestures to the east, where the sun is just beginning to peek over the horizon. "You see, when the sun has risen completely we shall be gone, save for a chosen few. The Dawn is waning."

"I see," says the king. "Then please, tell me why you've honored us with this visit."

"First, to bear a warning," Crocus dips her head mournfully, and Scree rumbles beneath her as if to emphasize the point. "The Dusk, our enemy, is encroaching. You have seen evidence of this, Your Majesty, as have your people. Take heed. Be ever watchful of Shadow and Darkness. My stewards shall speak to you at length on this matter after we have gone."

King Tirnon nods. "Very well," he says.

"Second, to reveal a secret," Crocus smiles sweetly. "But before we do, we shall praise you for your dedication to the promise your family made us generations ago, when Asio Plethore struck down Sorcerer King Diovicus, whose wicked and selfish actions nearly destroyed all of Kythshire. You remember the oath, Your Majesty. That no member of the Plethore line shall seek to wield the Arcane. No royal heir shall be schooled in the ways of the Mage."

"I do," he nods. "I have lived my life in chaste awareness of that oath, my dear Crocus, and have taught my children the same."

Between the king and queen, Margy shifts nervously. She looks so small and helpless between them that I want to rush to her and protect her.

"Yet," Crocus sighs, "sometimes it finds its way on its own, Sire. Sometimes, despite one's fervent wish, despite one's conviction and strength, despite one's respect for the rules set in place, the Arcane chooses for itself. Sometimes, it finds the purest, most balanced heart, and seats itself firmly within such a welcoming home. A perfect host. A promise of things to come. A light that forever shines with truth, justice, compassion, and understanding."

She offers a slow, deliberate nod of her head in the direction of the royal family, and Margy stands a little taller. On the horizon, the sun is half-obscured by the sea. The dawn is giving way to sunrise.

"We do not fault such occurrences, Your Majesty. Instead, we celebrate them. We nurture them. We infuse them with Light."

"I do not understand," the king says, his brow slightly furrowed. Crocus holds up a delicate, pale hand and smiles.

"Long has she lived with this secret, and long has it tormented her. When she reveals herself, I ask you, please do not feel scandalized or betrayed. Her secret was part of her trial, and she has earned our protections and our welcome with her earnest concern for our ways. And now I ask her to step forward and receive the Gift of Light, that she might let it guide her heart in moments to come, known and unknown."

Crocus reaches to the crown of dew that rests on her hair and plucks a round, sparkling drop from it. She gives it a gentle kiss and pushes it off to drift over the crowd. As it makes its way toward the steps, other fairies send beams of their own light to join with it.

"Step forward," Crocus whispers with gentle encouragement. The courtyard is so silent it feels like a spell has been cast over it. No one dares cough, we barely dare to breathe. I realize suddenly that many of the commoners' eyes are on me. Even the king and queen seem to be expecting the shining dewdrop to be intended for me, so when it drifts past me and continues on toward the steps, a hushed whisper rustles through the crowd.

Finally, it reaches Twig, who plucks it carefully from the air and kneels before the princess.

"Your Highness," he says with reverence.

Princess Margary looks up at her father and then her mother, as though asking for their approval. Queen Naelle, looking shocked, shakes her head in confusion and looks at the king. On her other side, His Majesty simply stares in disbelief. He looks up at Crocus.

"My daughter?" he asks. She nods slowly.

After a moment, His Majesty looks down at Margary again. He offers a hint of a nod. Instead of accepting the gift, Margy throws her arms around her father and he drops to one knee to hold her.

"I so wanted to tell you, Paba," her muffled cry is clearly audible in the stunned silence. "I wished dearly to show you."

The king whispers something to her that I can't hear, and she nods and hugs him tighter. I glance at the sun, which is nearly fully risen. Only a flat sliver of it remains beneath the horizon.

Back on the steps, His Majesty stands and squeezes his daughter's shoulder. Margy raises her hands. The crystals on her dress twinkle pink and gold in the brilliant sunrise with every movement. She looks at the dewdrop in Twig's outstretched hand.

"If it pleases you, Crocus of Kythshire," she says sweetly, "I wish to share this gift with my countrymen, should they accept it."

"It is yours to do with as you choose, Princess," Crocus replies. "We must say farewell now, until another Dawn, but we ask you to welcome the Elves to guide you. They have long fostered their own alliance with our kind."

She turns toward the courtyard gate and nods, and six elves file in to a chorus of gasps from the human crowd. They stand tall, shoulders above even the tallest man in the gathering. All dressed in white armor and white cloaks, they march in unison to the front and bow to the king. Their white hair slides across their intricate leaf-etched armor as they do. If I hadn't just witnessed a procession of fairies through Cerion, I'd say it was the most perfect display I've seen in this courtyard.

I recognize two of the group from our previous journeys to Ceras'lain: Julini and Shoel. The others are unknown to me. As they straighten from their bow and His Majesty offers them a hearty welcome, the gathered fairies begin to call out.

"Farewell! Farewell!" most of the entourage cheers and waves as the last sliver of sun is exposed. In a single burst of yellow-gold sunbeams, the majority of the figures fade away. Just like that, Crocus' mound and Flitt's carriage and unicorns vanish, and the dancers and performers disappear as though they never were. All that remains are Flitt and Twig flanked by the elves and Crocus's dewdrop, which Margy guides to hover over the crowd.

"Share this with me, if you care to," she says to the gathered crowd, and the dewdrop bursts into hundreds of specks of light which fall like a summer sun shower over the commoners.

I reach out for one and it drifts to me and settles in my palm. As soon as it touches me, I'm filled with a sense of peace and ease. All around me others do the same, until the golden drops have dissipated and we're all left standing in bliss, watching the Princess and the others at the steps.

"My people," King Tirnon's voice is slightly shaken as he addresses the crowd. "This news comes as just as much of a surprise to me as it does to you. I would take this day to speak with my daughter and our newly made acquaintances from Kythshire," he nods at Flitt and Twig. "As well as our allies from Ceras'lain. I ask your patience, please. As

275

honesty fosters peace, I shall offer you a truthful address again before the setting of the sun tonight. Until then, be well."

He raises a hand and waves to the crowd, and they erupt into a chant that brings tears to my eyes.

"Long live the king," they cry, "long live Princess Margary!"

Their cheers stir a new fire in me; a need to make sure my king and his family remains safe. I catch myself grinding my teeth, seething at the thought of the archer in the shadows.

"Saesa," I say, leaning down so only she can hear me. "Take Pearl back home, and come find me in the dungeons."

"Lady Knight?" she asks wide-eyed as she takes my horse's reins and helps me dismount.

"I'm going to get some answers," I reply, surprised by the threat in my tone.

Chapter Thirty-Two
ALLIES IN DREAMING

Tib

Sleep and dreaming. Rest. At first, I fight it. My thoughts are too scrambled. Too filled with new information. New, urgent things. Worries of home. Even with all of that, I guess I'm still tired, because I fall asleep quickly.

Valenor is waiting for me. I see him clearly, floating in the blue sky above. Drifting with the clouds. Nearby, sails snap and billow and catch the wind. Calming wind. Cool, refreshing wind. My palms press into rough wood worn smooth. A ship deck. My heart races.

"We're here again, are we?" I call up to him. "My ship. My invention."

"As ever, this is a dream of your making, Tibreseli. And as ever, I am delighted you would invite me to it," he says. "You have gained knowledge since last we met."

As I sit up, Valenor floats down to the deck of the ship and sits cross-legged in front of me. His eyes dance with amusement and kindness. After all I've been through, I'm surprised to feel comforted by his amusement rather than annoyed. He doesn't say anything else. Just sits there, looking me over. Waiting for me to be ready to talk.

My thoughts are jumbled, though, and I'm distracted. Something about him is different. Or maybe he's the same. I can't place it. His dark skin, his white beard, the curly gray hair that brushes his shoulders.

"You look like him," I say thoughtfully.

"Him?" Valenor quirks a brow.

"Kaso Viro," I reply. "You look just like him."

"Ah. Such is often the way with brothers, my friend," Valenor winks.

"He's your brother?" I scowl and think back. The harder I do, the more I see it. There's no way they couldn't be. "But how? I mean, why? If you're brothers, why didn't he help you when Jacek took over here? Why didn't he stop him, or come rescue you in the caves?"

"He is bound to his realm, as I am bound to mine," Valenor

explains. "He cannot leave the sea. But this is a concept better left until later to discuss, friend. There are more urgent matters at hand."

"Right…" I scratch my head and stand up to look over the side of the ship. It's not like the last time, when we were simply floating along aimlessly. This time, the ship is moving much more swiftly. In my heart, I feel a sense of urgency. "Where are we going?" I ask.

"Once again," Valenor smiles, "I have no way of knowing where your dreams might take you."

I look up at the sky and off into the distance. With the position of the sun, it's easy to see we're going south. South of Cerion is Elespen, and then farther on is Sunteri. I remember what Kaso Viro said about the Keepers of the Wellsprings.

"Mevyn," I whisper. "We're going to Sunteri."

"Ah, yes. That would fit well."

"But, last time in the dreaming, I was able to talk to him through you."

"Indeed."

"Can I again?" I ask.

"I imagine," Valenor replies thoughtfully. "Though if you seek him for the reason I expect, a simple conversation will not do, will it?"

"No," I scowl and rush up to the ship's wheel. Valenor follows.

"Shall I make him aware of your imminent arrival?" he asks.

"You can do that?" I ask.

"Of course," Valenor peers out over the dreaming. The wind rustles his hair and bright cloak. "He and I are ever linked, from the moment we became one in the caverns of the North. Though we have since gone our own way, we shall always have this connection. A thread that binds us through leagues and through realms. A bonding, just as the one he shares with you, Tibreseli."

"He's still linked with me?" I ask.

"Oh, indeed. If you wished to speak with him yourself, you have but to call on him. But doing so would invite him into your mind once more, and if I remember correctly, that is an imposition Mevyn swore he'd never make again."

"Right," to my surprise, I smile a little. Somehow, knowing there's still a link between me and Mevyn is more comforting than disturbing. As much as I used to hate him, I realize I have missed him these past years. I sort of wish he would be around sometimes. I scoff and push the feelings away. I'm just getting sentimental because so much is happening right now.

Still, it makes sense. I never could bring myself to get rid of the boots he gave me. His tether. In fact, I'm wearing them now. I always do, even in the summer. They feel lucky to me. Like even though he's gone, he's still watching. I didn't realize until now how much I really believed that.

"So, my friend," Valenor drifts to the port side. Below, the land stretches out in great patches of jungle green. Elespen. "Tell me. What have you learned since last we met?"

"Your brother," I start, feeling strange. I never thought of Valenor as a man with relations. He's always just been Valenor. Dreamwalker. "Your brother told Rian and me all about the Six. The offerings."

"Did he, now?" Valenor scowls. "Things must be getting quite urgent."

"He told us about the Keepers of the Wellsprings," I say. A shiver goes down my spine at the mention of it. Like I shouldn't say it. Like it's forbidden. "And then he said I should speak to you to learn more."

"That was wise of him. Do not fret," Valenor says. "It is safe to speak of such things here, for we are in your mind, Tib, and none can breach that. In fact, your mind in the dreaming, I might imagine, is the safest place one could find oneself."

I let the smooth wood of the ship's wheel slide over my fingertips as it unwinds. This feeling, the wind in my hair, the whole ship at my command, is one I could get used to. I don't say anything. I let myself enjoy it for a while. Let myself dream. Let us coast.

"Six offerings," I say after a while. "Three from Light and three from Dark."

"Yes," Valenor replies.

"Shush says the Light will be fairly easy. How will we get the Dark?" I ask.

"There are ways," Valenor replies. "Bindings to the earth. Origins. Rules that Light and Dark must both adhere to."

"Origins?" I ask.

"One's place of birth has power," he explains. "Going home."

"I was born in Sunteri," I say to him. "But it isn't my home."

"For some part of you, it will always be home, Tibreseli," Valenor says. "And so, receiving the offering from the Wellspring there shall prove very little challenge to you. Even less so because of your bond with Mevyn. Indeed. I daresay Sunteri and Kythshire will be the simplest of offerings for the Dawn to collect."

"What about the others?" I ask. "Shush says he can get Kythshire, but where are the rest of them?"

"That is where it becomes difficult, I'm afraid. You see, the elves are quite protective of their Source, and they hold the last of the Light. The Dark shall be hard-fought. One is hidden in the thickest jungles of Elespen. It is guarded as Kythshire, with wards of magic and totems and golems which will deny your entry. Only a child of Elespen may gain entry, and whoever it is must be determined, persuasive, and strong-willed.

"If you are fortunate enough to gain entry and collect the offering from Elespen, you must then travel to the frigid north, to lands which are so harsh they go unnamed even now. Not even the giants who reside there dare wander into these frozen peaks. Those who do become lost in endless squalls and jagged stone and ice. You have been near to there before, my friend. It is close to where I was held, though my prison was in a far less treacherous setting. As you might have imagined, that place is the home of the giants, and only one of Giant blood might convince the dervishes that protect it to allow him passage.

"Then there is Hywilkin, Tibreseli. Do not be fooled by what you know of this place. Humans live there, indeed, but its Source is well hidden in the darkest cavern, in the heart of the deepest lake. No man has set foot within its borders for centuries. The last to do so painted cryptic and primitive messages upon the walls in the stone depths. Warnings to those who were unfortunate to find the place. Filled with the Risen, it is. A wicked, dark place that will leave any sensible man clutching for the last remnants of his sanity. As you might guess, it is more easily conquered by a man whose family line can be traced to Hywilkin soil. Though I would warn against any effort to seek it out."

"But we need all six, don't we? Eventually?" I ask. The air is becoming drier, now, and filled with sand. A glance over the side shows me what I suspected, desert as far as I can see. In the distance, the ground is covered in red blossoms. Sunteri. My stomach flips. I promised myself I wouldn't come back here. It's not a place I ever wanted to see again.

"My advice would be to begin with three, my friend. Begin with three, and pray you have no need to seek out the rest from their source. There is another way to seek the Dark offerings."

I remember what Loren said about the Dusk already having two. They must be Dark. They have to be. They couldn't have gotten into the Light places without word getting back to us. Valenor is right, and I can't help but smile. It's another excuse to go back to the stronghold. We'll get the one from Mevyn, and steal the other two from the Sorcerers. That will give us three. That will open the way. We'll get Errie, and maybe even save Griff and Mikken and maybe even the other kids.

"How does it work?" I ask him. My heart races with anticipation. Finally, a plan. A real direction. A way to stop them. "How does it open the way?"

"First," Valenor explains, "you must understand the way cannot be reached by magical means. The first gateway into Brindelier is said to be well-hidden. An archway in the sky.

"An archway in the sky? Valenor, I've seen it. I know where that is!" I whoop loudly and turn the wheel hard until we tip to the side and nearly fall out.

"Now, now," Valenor chuckles. Rather than tip to the side with the rest of the ship, he floats upright in place. "As exciting as that is, you must still have a way to reach it. As I said, Tibreseli, it cannot be reached by magical means." He watches me closely. Like he's waiting for something to dawn on me. "Do you see now, why I so encouraged you to continue work on your invention?"

"You knew," I whisper. "You knew we'd need it to get to Brindelier."

"Indeed," he nods.

"Why didn't you say so? You knew all of this the whole time and you never explained." I try not to look as annoyed as I feel. "Was it my idea after all, or did you give it to me?"

"Oh, no, no," he chuckles. "You are entitled to claim the idea as your own. Absolutely entitled. A strange coincidence, to be sure, but still, it was fully yours. As for why I did not explain things to you...I have found, in my time, that it is best to allow these things to unfurl as they will. Much like a sail to the wind, with as little interference as possible."

"Helpful of you," I mutter and spin the wheel. "Where am I going, exactly?" I ask.

"Surely you know the way," Valenor raises a brow. "You have been there before, after all."

I shake my head.

"All you need to do is think about him, of course," he nods.

"Why are we flying all over the place, then?"

"I should ask you the same. It is—"

"My dream. Right." I close my eyes and think hard about the last time I was there. Sunteri's Wellspring. When I watched Mevyn restore it. I remember the oasis in the desert, green and bright, with its red-gold pool. When I open my eyes again, I see it in the distance. My pulse quickens. I will the ship faster and it obeys my thoughts, skimming across the sand, sending a wake of dust billowing behind us. Valenor holds tight to the rigging, laughing heartily.

We crash through broad green ferns and leaves as big as I am. The ship teeters on the edge between desert and grass. Everything around us goes silent.

"Mevyn!" I call into the green depths. The ship fades from beneath us and we tumble into the ferns.

"Do not fear," Valenor says quietly. "You cannot be harmed here. As real as it may seem, we are still in the Dreaming."

As if summoned by his words, the vines above twist and snarl together in an enormous tangle of a creature. It ducks beneath the canopy to lower its head to me. Opens its mouth. Lets out a ferocious growl that covers me in musty, damp soil and bits of leaves.

"We are Gred. The Oasis embodied. The Vine Keepers. Revived from Dust. Esteemed Guardians of the Northern Border. Who calls the out the forbidden name? What human knows to speak it?"

It howls fiercely and lashes its vines out at me like whips. I jump back to avoid them and stumble into Valenor.

"Answer them," he whispers to me.

I try to look brave. Even with Valenor's assurance it's hard. Gred is huge. Horrible. The vines. The voice. It's a nightmare. I try to steady my wobbling knees. Try to keep from collapsing. Its vines swirl with wicked force. They weave around it like writhing, thorny snakes. I imagine them reaching out for me. Binding my arms, my legs, so I can't move. Pinning me to the hot, dry sand.

"T-t, T," I try to speak, but my voice won't work. The creature is terrifying. It's just like the roots that held me to the ground the last time I was in Sunteri. The vines. The trees that were my prison. I'm the boy I was two years ago. Confused. Distraught. Alone. I'd rather face a hundred Sorcerers than this.

"Speak your name," the creature rumbles and hisses. It lashes at my wrist. Thorns catch and rip my skin. I come to my senses. Dodge away from it. It chases. Lashes again. The sudden fight, the rush of battle, somehow helps me find my voice.

"Tibreseli Nullen," I shout as I draw my knives and slice at a tendril. I tumble beneath the ferns as the vines whip the broad leaves that shelter me. "House Ganvent, Steward of the Last, Knifethrower, Dreamstalker, Bearer of the Guardian, Slayer of Shadows, Liberator of Valenor!"

With each title, the vines slow and shrink until everything is still. Valenor stands on the edge of the oasis, silently watching. Wearing a smile of pride. The vine-beast pauses. Curls its tendrils tight to itself. Bows its head to me.

"Tibreseli Nullen," it thunders. "House Ganvent, Steward of the Last, Knifethrower, Dreamstalker, Bearer of the Guardian, Slayer of Shadows, Liberator of Valenor, you are welcome here. Enter."

I glance back at Valenor. He nods to me.

"Can Valenor come, too?" I ask Gred. It rolls its shoulders and its eyes flash blue.

"Proceed," it says with a bow, and we walk together into the oasis.

The desert is a memory in the span of a few steps, replaced by dripping green leaves. Green moss on the trees. Green grass thick and squishy beneath our feet. All around us, I feel them. Fairies, hidden. I don't need to know where the Wellspring is. I can feel it. Its power is a beacon. It pulls me closer and closer. Fairy orbs drift behind us as we go. Watching. Listening. Curious. Their giggles make my skin prickle. Like they're amused by some secret I don't know.

Sunteri's Wellspring is a fairly small pool. Maybe the size of Nessa's dining table. Big enough for a few people to sit in. Not very deep, either. Up to my waist, probably. Not impressive at all, except that it glows like molten gold. It reminds me of the red-hot end of the blade Sir Benen hammered for me. The magic of it shines so brightly that the leaves and trunks of trees around it are pure white. Once in a while, sparks of magic spray up out of it like embers.

Even though it's so small, the feeling of it is overwhelming. The power it holds is incredible. Like ten Sorcerer's keeps. Like twenty Academies. It feels infinite, even though I know it isn't. Not long ago, it was depleted. Drained completely. That's why Mevyn needed me. That's why he forced me to help him. I used to hate him so much.

"Mevyn," I fight the lump in my throat to call his name.

All around the pool, they wait. Watch. Whisper. Fairies. Eyes between the trees. Flashes of wings among the leaves. When I look closer, my healed eye can see their full forms. Hiding. Waiting. I feel like I know some of them. Like I must have carried them.

The surface of the pool ripples and glitters. The first thing to emerge is his spear tip. The tips of his golden wings. His golden hair. His face like a burnished statue. His armored shoulders, also gold. He drifts toward me through the pool until only his toes are grazing the surface of it, leaving a rippling wake behind him. He doesn't stop until he's right in front of my face, close enough to touch me.

"My friend," he says and opens his arms in a welcoming gesture. "What a relief to see you. I feared we might have lost you to the Dusk."

"It's good to see you, too, Mevyn," I smile. I never would have thought it, but it really is. It's a relief. Even if I am only dreaming. It's like a part of me was missing and now it's back again. He moves closer and stares into my healed eye.

"Something new," he says.

"It's a long story," I shrug.

"Dub," he says simply.

"How did you--?" I start, and he shakes his head.

"I see things. Glimpses. He is allied with the Dusk. He has a great hatred for you."

"I know," I scowl.

"No matter. I know why you have come, and I shan't waste your time. I cannot give you what you seek, my friend," he says. My heart sinks. The Sunteri offering was supposed to be the easy one.

"Why?" I ask.

"Because you could not bring it away with you through the dreaming," he says mournfully.

"Oh," I sigh.

"There is another way, my friend. But I would need to break my promise to you and to this Source."

"What way?" I ask.

"I can deliver it myself. In the waking. You still have the tether, I see," he smiles fondly and points to my feet.

I shrug. "I like them. They're good boots."

"Tib," Mevyn glances over my shoulder at Valenor, and back to me again. "This task you've set for yourself, this quest, is more dangerous than you might expect. It is more than just a race to the same destination as the Dusk. It will test your will, your Light. In desperate times and difficult choices, the truth of one's heart is revealed. Who you think you are becomes twisted."

"I have help. Friends. They want to see the Dusk stopped just as much as I do."

"Perhaps so, but be wary," he warns. "For they, too, will face their inner darkness."

"Right," I say, "because that's a real struggle for Lady Azaeli and Rian and the rest of the Elite."

"You have no idea," Mevyn shakes his head. "Do not take their Light for granted, Tib. Darkness hides in the most unlikely places."

"Maybe," I shrug. I don't know why his warning annoys me so much. Maybe I just don't want to believe him. "So what now?"

"Now you shall wake, and I shall deliver the offering to you myself," he says.

"I'm sleeping in Kaso Viro's tower. Do you know him?"

Mevyn glances again at Valenor with a glint of amusement.

"I have heard the name," he smirks. There's the Mevyn I remember. Secretive. Cocky. Obviously smarter than me.

"I'll wake up, then," I say. I guess I shouldn't be surprised that he's already on my nerves. Maybe it's all the magic here.

I don't wait for him to reply. I shift my thinking. I'm not here. I'm back at the tower, in the comfortable guest bed Kaso Viro offered me. Sleeping. Waking up. The oasis fades slowly. I feel myself inside my head. It's a strange feeling. Difficult to describe. It's the Half-Realm. The place between sleeping and awake, where Rian and Azi can go with a thought. The place I slip into that feels like walking through cobwebs.

Mevyn's already here when I wake up. Sitting on my knee, looking smug. In his hands, he holds a red glass bottle that shines with liquid from the golden pool.

"Quickly," he whispers to me. I take the offered bottle, and he disappears before I can think to utter goodbye.

Chapter Thirty-Three
PALACE SHADOWS

Azi

The passage to the dungeons is dank and quiet compared to the courtyard just outside. It's so silent my footsteps barely make a sound on the sand-worn stone as I rush down the steep slope. I imagine what it must be like to be led through here as a prisoner, as a criminal facing her sentence, and I shiver.

If it wasn't for the light from my sword, it would be too dark to even see my feet. There are no doorways or other passages that branch off this one. The further I go down the passage, the more determined I feel. I see the archer clearly in my mind, his arrow dripping with poison, and my heart thunders in my chest. I need to know everything about him. Who is he? Why would he do such a thing? I can know. I can find out. The lure of it entices me.

The dark passage leads directly to a cell-like room with a carved wooden desk and a shelf filled with scrolls. Two palace guards flank a broad door to the side of the desk. A fairly young Mage dressed in disturbingly bright orange robes and a strange pointed hat faces them with his back to me.

The three of them are so occupied with whatever the Mage is doing they fail to notice me. I creep up behind the Mage and watch over his shoulder while he performs a complicated sleight-of-hand that involves three glass marbles and a square of silk. When the trick is done, I give a single clap. The guards startle toward me, hands on hilts, and the Mage yelps and catches his hat as it tumbles from his head.

"What-Who-Ah!" the Mage sputters and jumps to his feet. His eyes linger on my face and go wide. "H-how can I help you? That is—wh-what are you? I mean," he musters a little courage and stands a little straighter. "What are you doing here, Lady Knight?"

"That's Sir Hammerfel," one of the guards gives me a nod and drops his hand from his hilt. "She's within her rights to be here."

His statement is as much of a surprise to me as it seems to be to the Mage. I've never had a reason to be here in the dungeons before, so naturally I didn't realize I'm allowed to be.

"L-lady, S-sir Hammerfel. Pleasure, pleasure," the Mage stammers, offers a hand to shake, and then pulls it away with uncertainty before I can reach for it. "Right. Name's Dumfrey. Willis Dumfrey. I've always admired you. I mean, your, Rian. Your guild! The Elite. Admired them. Yes." He folds his arms over his chest and rocks back on his heels as though he's really unsure what to do with himself. His gaze lingers on the Mark on my cheek. Behind him the guards watch us both, obviously amused by his nervousness. "Wh-what can I do for you?"

"I'd like to see the archer," I say.

"Uh, the archer, the archer," he murmurs and rifles through the messy pile of parchment on the desk.

"He just came through," I crane my neck to look at the papers and then glance at the guards.

"Aye, you just put a sleep on him, Dum," one of the guards says. "It's that one there you were just filling out."

"Right! Well! Here it is, yes. Charges: Trespassing, High Treason, Attempted Regicide," he scowls at the page. "Name: Unknown. Origin: Unknown. Motive: Unknown."

"I'd like to see him, please," I say, and the back of my neck prickles with excitement as Dumfrey gasps.

"Oh, no. I can't allow that, Lady Knight. Once a prisoner is held asleep, I can only wake him up for trial. That's the law. I am sorry."

I look up at the guards and down at the paper again.

"I understand," I nod thoughtfully. Perhaps it's best to leave the matter to the courts, after all. Then again, this isn't about justice. It's about preventing another attempt at the King's life. I turn to the guards.

"I'm concerned he won't be the last," I say to the one who knew me. "Surely, that man has information. He had a reason to do what he did."

I rub at my tingling forehead. Something in my heart is guiding me to this, something is insisting it's the proper course. The memory of Margy's dewdrop prickles my palm. The lure of magic entices me. This is right, I convince myself. In the name of the king, this is good.

"Your duty is the same as mine," I explain. It seems like I'm starting to sway them. "To protect the throne. To preserve peace in Cerion. All I ask is for a moment to look into his eyes," my words send a thrill through me. A hunger to experience that rush of magic again. It frightens me a little, but the fear is blotted out by the excitement of what's to come.

"I wouldn't dare to ask you to go against your oaths or break the law for me…" I trail off as Dumfrey screws his lips together thoughtfully.

"Don't see the harm in it, really," one guard shrugs at the other.

"You say you just want to look at him?" Dumfrey asks.

"Into his eyes," I nod. I don't know whether a person would need to be awake for me to see into their thoughts. I don't know if I need their consent, or if it's something I can just take. The idea of finding out makes me even more excited to try.

"If that's all, I imagine it's all right," Dumfrey glances at the guards, who shrug and nod.

"Wonderful. Thank you," I smile at the three of them. "If it goes well, I might even be able to help you fill out the rest of that form."

They unlock the door with a series of keys and usher me down a long stone passage lined with at least a dozen more locked doors. What strikes me here is the silence. There are no cries of innocence, no catcalls or screams of frustration. There is no noise from the prisoners at all. They're all fast asleep.

They bring me to the end of the passage and pull open a heavy reinforced door. Inside, six prisoners sleep on simple cots arranged against the walls.

I see him straight away: The archer from the alcove.

"A fighter, that one," one of the guards says to me as I walk toward him. "Took four palace guards to get him to Dumfrey. He's heavier than he looks, too. Must be all muscle."

"Thank you," I say quietly. I creep to the edge of the cot and peer down at the man. He's young. Early twenties, maybe. His hair is stringy and caked with something that looks like tar. His face bears the scar of a burn which stretches from his ear to his chin.

"Should we remain, Lady Knight?" The guards ask. I nod and crouch. Now that I'm here, I'm having doubts. I shouldn't. It's not right. But it is. If I can find out why, then we can keep it from happening again. We can keep the king safe. My hand shakes as I push the man's eyelid open. His unremarkable brown eye stares blankly back at me.

My heart races with the influx of magic. I don't have to make any effort at all. It swells through me and bursts out in strands of soft, glittering gold, seeping into his open eye. The release of it is such a relief that I let it flow unchecked. I tumble toward him much more quickly than I expected to, into his dreaming mind.

I'm greeted immediately by darkness and the whisper of a fervent oath.

"I do so swear fealty to you, my prince. My word is my bond," the archer says. In his mind, he is me, and I am him.

"You understand what it means, Wrett," Eron's voice startles me so much that I almost pull myself back from the memory. The archer's dark thoughts mix with mine. If I do this, I will earn his favor, he thinks. If I do this and the prince is the victor, I will rise from the filth of Redstone row and become someone worthy of respect.

"I do, Your Highness," I say.

"Tell me, then," Eron commands.

"I will be the one to clear the throne for you," I say. "I swear it. When you fall. When they think you lost forever. My arrow will end him."

"Join hands," a third voice orders in the darkness. A woman. I fumble to reach for Eron. I feel his hand grip mine. It's weaker than I expected. Softer. A third hand rests over ours. A slash of pain. Our blood mixes and the woman whispers a spell. Her words are foreign, but the meaning is clear. This oath is bound by blood. Even if I wanted to, I could not forsake the prince now. His death will be the king's own sentence.

It's too dark to see either of them, but I have dealt with this Sorceress before. She's a beauty, with curls of rich brown hair and eyes the color of amber ale. Sybel. One day, maybe, she will see me as more than a tool for her plots. One day, when the king is dead, I might be someone to her.

My thoughts—his thoughts shift away from the darkness. Dreams, fleeting and confusing. Dreams that, under the spell of holding sleep, will be forgotten once he wakes.

The laughter of children floats carelessly in the air as I drift through the streets of Cerion's Redstone Row. My attention is brought to a brick one-story, where the windows have been shuttered tight despite the warmth of the midsummer breeze. I step to the threshold and push the door open. Inside is far too small a gathering place for the number of tired-looking men who sit squeezed around a small, worn table. A woman in a dingy summer dress wears her worry plain on her face. Her eyes are red and swollen from tears as she fills the men's cups with cool water from a clay pitcher.

She pauses beside one of them and rests her hand on his shoulder, but he barely acknowledges her. His eyes are far away; bleary and defeated.

"You mean to tell us there's nothing to be done, then," the woman says. She takes a sip from her own cup, but it does little to wash away the hoarseness and exhaustion in her voice. "Our daughter is gone, Milvare, and there is nothing to be done? And what about Tru's boy, and Polfe's? Are they to be forgotten, too? Throwaways? Is this what Cerion has come to?"

"His Majesty has other matters on his mind," a tall man in Mage's robes

replies. "He hasn't opened court for reception since the attack on High Court. He hides himself away with his advisers and refuses to hear the petty grievances of his people."

"Petty grievances!" the woman shrieks. "Our daughter has disappeared, Milvare!"

"I don't disagree with you, Kasha," Milvare says as he raises a hand in surrender. "I am just telling you the truth of the matter."

They go on talking, shouting, and I feel myself tense. Not me. Wrett. His fists are clenched, his face is hot. His hand goes to his belt, where his quiver hangs. His fingers graze the fletching. The feel of the rough-cut feathers calms his fury.

First Celli, then Mikken and Griff.

How many more kids have to disappear before something's done? How long will that bastard sit on his throne feeling sorry for himself? Not much longer. The prince is dead. It's time. Time to fulfill the oath I made to my prince, just days ago. Time for the New Age to begin, and all by my hand.

"All right, Lady Knight?" one of the guards asks gently. His hands are on mine. I look down at them to get my bearings. My fingers dig like claws into the archer, Wrett's, forehead. His eye is rolled back so only the white is showing. I think of the oath, the blood bond, and hesitate.

"No," I whisper, "I'm not all right." Roughly, I push Wrett's eye open further. I reach into his thoughts again and sift through them for that one moment, that memory with the Prince. If I took it away, what then? The oath would stay, but he wouldn't know what it was. What could happen? Could he go mad from it?

He'd deserve no less, I think as I search. My head spins with the flood of magic. The rush makes me soar. I see the memory. It lingers in his mind like a dangling string. I pull at it and drag it along with me. I watch it unravel as I tumble away from his mind one last time. Again, I feel the guard's hand on mine and his warning tone. Beneath my fingertips, Wrett convulses and shudders on the cot. His mouth foams and gurgles as I pull the memory away and fling it into the darkness.

"What was that?" the guard asks.

"He was mad," I whisper as I watch the golden tendril fade into the shadows and disappear. "Irrational." I work to calm my breath.

"Could have told you that, my lady," the guard grunts.

I know it's not his intention, but his comment makes me feel foolish. The sudden absence of magic leaves me feeling utterly devastated and spent far beyond my capacity. The whole situation was a horrible idea. I went too far. I should have stayed with the others up in the courtyard. I don't know what I was thinking coming down here.

I try to stand, but I'm too weak. My hands are shaking. I don't even know what's just happened. Did I actually alter that man's memory? How could I do such a deplorable thing? What if they discover what I've done when they question him? What if they needed that information for his trial?

"*There you are!*" Flitt's squeaky voice makes me jump. "*What are you doing down here? It smells horrible. Ohh, are these criminals? Are they going to get their heads chopped off, too? Like Prince—*"

"Flitt!" I bark, and the guards stare at me wide-eyed.

"My lady?" the quieter of the two guards asks.

Across the room, the fairy, restored to her usual size--wings and all--bobs above the archer curiously.

"Sorry," I mutter to them. "*Get away from him,*" I push the command to her a little more harshly than I intended to. "*I'm weak. Help me.*"

"*Help you what?*" she scowls.

"I need a *boost,*" I push. "*Just a small one.*"

"*Nope, not if you're going to order me. Everyone's meeting with the king. You should be there instead of down here doing whatever you're doing. Bye, Azi.*"

Her sudden disappearance leaves me feeling even emptier and angrier. I push past the guards without a word, through the passage, and out into Dumfrey's small room.

"His name's Wrett," I toss over my shoulder at the Mage as I stalk past. I'm so angry, I could spit. Angry with Eron, with Wrett, with myself for daring to do what I just did, and most of all with Flitt for making me feel horrible about asking for her help. I know my sour mood is a direct result of the magic I used, and that fact makes me hate myself even more.

"Never again," I say under my breath as I shade my eyes from the sudden harsh sunlight in the courtyard. "I'm through with Mentalism."

I knew this would happen. It's why I've been so careful since I learned it. It's why I've refused to use it. I knew the moment I allowed myself to, it would change me. Why couldn't I be stronger, like Rian? Why couldn't I fight the urge? I know exactly why. Because I'm a swordswoman, not a Mage. I had no business in that man's head. It was reckless. Changing his memories was utterly unacceptable.

"Rian," I whisper to myself as I stand at the carved wooden doors that lead to the palace interior. More than anything, I wish he was here. I never would have been tempted if he had been by my side.

The guards at the door recognize me. They salute with their spears and nod me inside. I want to tell them they're fools for their courtesy. I'm completely undeserving of their respect. I think of how I treated Flitt. Images of Sorcerers in the keep at Kythshire burst into my memory. They're quickly followed by memories of pale, drained fairies in cages. If that was what I thought to do with her...what must she think of me?

Numbly, I follow a page through polished corridors and desperately fight back tears. I don't care what anyone says. If this is a gift, I don't want it.

I'm so absorbed in my thoughts that I nearly collide with Uncle Gaethon, who is waiting for me outside of the closed dining hall doors. The sounds that come from within are merry: lighthearted laughter and jovial conversation.

"Thank you, Nate," Uncle says dismissively, and the Page bows and rushes away.

Uncle takes my arm and ushers me further down the corridor to a quiet alcove where he knows he won't be overheard. With a flick of his fingers, he summons a mirror and holds it to my face. I don't need to look to know the gold Mark has grown. I turn my chin away.

"Look at yourself," he hisses.

Reluctantly, I flick my eyes toward the mirror. Along with the gold, there's something else. A single tendril, blue-black, peeks up from the edge of my collar.

"How...?" I croak. I don't know what else to say. I didn't think it was possible to feel more miserable.

"How what?" he spits the words at me. Suddenly I'm a child again, cowering from his wrath. I refuse to let him intimidate me, though, even after what I did. I made my own choices, and I know they were wrong.

"How did you know to wait out here for me?" I ask with a more defiant tone than I intended.

His eyes narrow angrily. I feel if he could breathe fire right now, he'd do it.

"I have ways of knowing the goings-on within the palace," he says. "Ways of seeing the influx of Arcane that passes through these walls. I am attuned to it." He hovers over me, seething. "Do you know what I did last night after they brought you home to your bed? I spent an hour assuring His Majesty that you were under control. That you can be trusted with this power. And now, this. Do you have any idea how this looks, Azaeli?"

"You're the one who encouraged me not to keep it secret anymore. It's a gift to Cerion. That's what you told His Majesty. You told me it was all right, and it's not. It's not all right! Do you know what I saw? I saw awful things, Uncle. I looked into the mind of a would-be killer. Do you have any idea what I did? What it caused me to do?" I think of Flitt and choke back a sob. "I don't want this." I look up at him pleadingly. "You can take it, can't you? Strip it," I whisper.

Something in my anguished tone finally strikes him. I see it plainly on his face. He recognizes what's happening to me. His brow smoothes, his eyes grow mournful. Slowly, he shakes his head and presses his fingertips to his temple.

"It isn't that sort of magic, my niece," he says with a sigh. "It cannot be stripped. Not by any Mage of Cerion, at least. Indeed, no. And," he rests a hand on my shoulder, "it is useful. Honestly, it is."

"Useful?" I shake my head and don't bother to wipe away the tears that roll down my cheeks and into my collar. "It's not. I don't want it," I say again. "I can't refuse the temptation. It's too difficult."

Uncle presses a hand to his forehead and closes his eyes. He takes a long, calming breath.

"I forget," he whispers, "you are my niece, and I have watched you grow. I know you well, and so I forget."

"Forget what?" I ask, and step closer to him, sniffling. The hollow feeling in my chest is deepening. It aches with such an emptiness that I don't know how much longer I can bear it.

"It takes years, Azaeli. Years of training for a Mage to become attuned to the balance of give and take. Years of conditioning. It is much like swordplay," he explains. "Were you to begin now, an untrained woman with a two-handed broadsword like the one you carry, could you bear the weight of it? Could you swing it with as much skill as you do? Of course not. You would lose control. You might injure yourself with the blade, or strain muscles which have not been trained and strengthened for that purpose. Magic is much the same, Azaeli, and yours was thrust upon you. To make matters worse, you chose to bottle it up within yourself. To keep it secret and hidden."

I shake my head and swallow my tears. "I was weak," I say. "I did something awful."

"You were untrained," he offers gently. "And I apologize for not intervening sooner. I should have anticipated this. In time, you will learn to wield it just as expertly as you do your sword. And as long as I breathe on this plane, I shall do my best to guide you. But I cannot, nor would I, take it from you."

The laughter from inside grows louder. Mya is singing some lighthearted song, and through the door the elves' voices mix with her song. I glance that way and Uncle sighs.

"I cannot permit you to go in, looking as you do," he says. "It would cause an uproar, especially with the elves."

This causes the tears to start flowing again, but I don't argue. He's right. I simply nod in agreement.

"I have to go find Flitt anyway," I say hoarsely. "I owe her an apology."

"She is within," Uncle says with a sigh. "Though she seems quite upset."

"I need to speak with her," I say, swallowing my tears. "Is there any way, Uncle? It's important."

"A way to remove the Mark?" he scowls with deep disapproval.

"No, no," I say. "I understand that I'm meant to bear it for now, until it fades on its own. But could you talk to her for me?"

He shakes his head slightly.

"She is only just warming up to me, my dear. I do not wish to jeopardize that."

"I understand," I whisper.

"Go and redeem yourself," Uncle takes my shoulders and kisses me on the forehead. "A small, heartfelt deed should cause the Mark to fade. I must go back in. Be vigilant, Azaeli. I would wager that, at least for now, you won't allow yourself to be enticed again."

"No, sir," I whisper and lower my head.

Uncle excuses himself and slips back inside, where Margy's voice sounds like perfect bells against the low strum of the lute. As soon as he's gone, I bury my face in my hands and try hard to compose myself.

"I'll go in," Saesa's voice echoes down the corridor, startling me.

"Saesa! How long have you been there?" I straighten, wipe my face and try to catch my breath. A squire needs her Knight to be strong. I try hard to keep that facade for her sake.

"I only just came in when I couldn't find you in the dungeons," she replies. "You told me to find you there, Lady Knight."

"Yes," I say, clearing my throat. "How much of that did you hear?"

"Enough, My Lady," Saesa replies. Her eyes trace the Mark on my cheek. "If you'd like," she says softly, "I'll talk to her for you."

Chapter Thirty-Four

UNSPEAKABLE MAGIC

Celli

Quenson. My heart beats his name. Quenson. My lord. My master. My everything.

"Get up," Sybel orders, and I push myself out of bed. She isn't him, but he told me to listen to her, so I do. "Something's happened," she whispers to me. "Your master needs you."

My heart jumps to my throat. If he needs me, why didn't he come for me himself?

"Was he hurt? Who did it? I'll kill them," I snarl.

"Foolish girl," Sybel warns and mutters something impatient about having to be a nursemaid. "Why is your first thought that he must be hurt? You should have more faith in him, Celli."

"You're right," I say, ashamed. I hope she doesn't tell him.

"Quite," Sybel scoffs. "Come."

Shame gives way to different emotions as Sybel leads me through the maze of passages. Excitement. Quenson needs me. He needs me. Something else. Anger. His, not mine. His anger. Our excitement. My skin tingles just thinking about it. Something's happened. Something big. Something that changes the plan.

The closer we get to him, the stronger our connection is. I wonder if he feels it, too. I wonder whether he longs for me the way I do him. It's as though being too far away weakens me. Like I could never reach my full potential unless I'm beside him.

She pushes a door open and I gasp to see him there, handsome as ever in robes of red so deep they're nearly black. His hood is down, his dark hair swept back. Torchlight writhes across the raised swirls of the Mark on his high cheekbones. We go in, and Sybel locks the door behind us and whispers wards.

"Ah, Celli," he says. When he smiles, his appreciation of me strikes me like a spear to my heart. My legs give way, and I fall to my knees.

"A little much, Quenson," Sybel mutters under her breath. She slinks past me to him and traces a finger across his shoulder. "Don't you think?"

Don't touch him. He's mine, I want to scream. *Mine*. I won't, though. He told me not to speak and so I hold my tongue. Instead I glare at her as ferociously as I can.

"She delights me so," he laughs softly. I feel a little better when he brushes her away. "Come, my dear," he says to me. I push past the butterflies in my stomach and force myself back to my feet.

He rests a cool, beautifully black-Marked hand on my shoulder. "Look around, Celli," he whispers, and I tear my gaze from the elegant curving lines on his fingers to take in the rest of the room.

It's a medium-sized chamber with three large windows stained with strange designs. Nude women pouring different colored liquid from pitchers into pools. All around them are creatures I've never seen before. Scaly, winged ones that look like fairies, but black. Horses with cracked leathery skin instead of hair. Dragons. Hairy men with tails pointed like arrow tips and horns sprouting from their heads.

Disturbed, I look around the rest of the room. It's like Quenson's, but bigger. There's a neat, highly polished desk of dark wood, shelves lined with books and jars, and endless rows of potion bottles. Fine chairs. A fireplace. A long table carved with writing I can't read. The room is rich and well-kept, except for a half-dozen wooden chests carved with elven writing that seem to have been pulled out from under the desk and away from the walls. Quenson guides me to them. Sybel hovers nearby.

"Osven," he explains to me in a hushed tone, "has met his well-deserved end. We of the Circle have an agreement. As he was working with me, what's his becomes mine, as long as I stake my claim before anyone else." His stunning robes pool around him as crouches beside a chest and traces his fingers across the carved wood.

"I need you," he says, his voice growing deeper, "to open these." He hands me a roll of leather. Inside is a set of locksmith tools. When I take it from him, he moves away to stand across the room and watch.

"Perhaps we should leave," Sybel whispers to him.

"Certainly not. The effects wouldn't reach this far," he murmurs.

I don't think about what they're saying. It doesn't concern me. His command takes hold of me and fills me with desperation. *I need you*, he'd said. *I need you*. I don't think about why. Why doesn't matter. My fingers are steady as I work the tools into the intricate lock. I focus on my task and the lock clicks open easily.

"Well done," he calls from across the room. "Now, open the lid."

I push it open to reveal thick folds of very fine silks and velvets. Robes and cloaks. Gloves. Across the room, the two Sorcerers sigh with relief. "Open the next," he commands, and his rush of anticipation mingles with my own.

The next four chests hold a variety of items. One of them is filled with silver and gold coin. One holds neat stacks of books and scrolls. Another, smaller one is filled with fine jewelry wrapped carefully in bundles of silk or leather. The fourth holds strange, finely carved stone statuettes.

With each creak of a lid, I feel Quenson grow more disappointed and enraged. He needs something he thought would be here. I'm desperate to find it for him.

Someone makes a noise in the corridor outside, and Sybel and Quenson snap their attention to the door.

"Quickly," Quenson hisses at me. "Quietly."

I barely notice the smoke-like, greenish threads that wind around my hands as my fingers work the next lock. They seep into my skin and make my hands burn, but I ignore the pain and twist the awl until I feel the familiar, satisfying click. I reach for the lid and push it open.

Immediately, a force lifts me up and throws me hard across the room. Pain cracks across my back as I crash into the wall. Quenson and Sybel start to cast something. All I can think of is quiet. Master said we had to be quiet. I stumble to my feet and turn to look, ready to charge whatever it was that attacked me. Ready to silence it.

Floating above the chest is a figure all in black. A shimmer of shadow radiates around him. An aura, evil and ruthless. An apparition. A ghost. Osven.

"You dare," he shrieks and raises a bony finger to point at my master. I don't wait for his spell. I charge the chest and slam the lid down. My actions have no effect on Osven's spirit, though, except to cause him to laugh mockingly.

"Move away, Celli," Quenson says, and I obey. I move to stand in front of him, to guard him.

"I'm not at all surprised by your lack of decency to simply depart this plane, Osven," my master says.

"My work is incomplete," Osven says.

"Ah," Quenson raises a slender, perfect finger. "Our work, which is now, upon your death, mine alone. But do not fret, my ally, for we have made arrangements which will allow you, rather, require you, to continue. Sybel?"

The Sorceress scowls. I can tell whatever she's about to do is something she's reluctant about. She reaches into a pouch at her belt and produces a simple silver bangle. Around the outside, it's inlaid with polished stone. Half of the stone looks like it could have been carved from the cliffs of Cerion, and the other half has a grain to it, like light-colored wood.

"Cerion and Ceras'lain," Sybel's plump lips curve into a smile. "A simple native binding."

Quenson's hand on my back gives me chills. He guides me closer to Osven. Sybel follows, her grin widening at the sight of the ghostly Sorcerer, who shrinks back at our approach.

"Fools," he says. "Do you think me simple? I have placed bindings and woven protections upon this chest, and you have opened it with your own hands. The wards are set. You can never own me. No Sorcerer can."

"Indeed," Quenson's tone is low and pleased. Like the purr of a cat who's cornered a mouse. "No Sorcerer can. Celli, give me your hand."

"You wouldn't dare," Osven's growl terrifies me, but Quenson's hand around mine is a comfort. "Even you are not so low."

"Oh, I think it quite fitting," Quenson says as he takes the bracelet from Sybel. "You will be thrall of my thrall."

"Be reasonable, Quenson," Osven's voice is weak, like a hint of a thought. "Have mercy."

"Mercy?" Quenson huffs. "Celli, do you think I ought to be merciful to him?"

I don't have to think. Whenever I close my eyes, I can still smell my own cooked insides and feel the agony of Osven's lightning crackling though me. I don't know what this is about, but I don't care. If Quenson wants him to suffer, I do, too.

"No, Master," I reply.

"Quite right," Quenson says, and slips the bracelet onto my wrist. "A gift to you, my dear," he whispers, and I close my eyes as the thrill courses through me. It starts at my wrist: A soft, tingling energy that snakes into my bones and up. It travels to my shoulders, into my chest, up into my head, across my left arm, down into my legs, to my toes. It changes my insides.

Right away, I understand. He's mine now. He belongs to me. Osven. I know him. Everything he knew, everything he was. This is Necromancy. Spirit binding. I kneel at the chest again and push it open. Inside is a miniature obelisk, no bigger than my arm. It's carved from a stack of polished stones fused together. This was his soul stone, meant to hold and protect his spirit in the event of his death. No Sorcerer could have opened the chest. There were too many protections.

He didn't think about me, though. Didn't even give me second thought. Celli. The throwaway girl from Cerion. He thought me a mindless, worthless slave. He didn't understand the bond Quenson and I have. He didn't expect it. When Master suggested seeking Tib out in his home, Osven rushed to do it without thinking. He wanted to be the one to finally get Tib. He wanted to steal the credit for it from my master.

I feel his rage, but it's distant. Far away. Outside of me. Not like how I feel Quenson's emotions. We're closer, me and Quenson. Almost one. Osven would never understand that, and that's why they were able to trick him. Now he belongs to me, and I belong to Quenson, so, by rights, he belongs to Quenson.

I open my eyes and look into the face of my brilliant master. No one else could have planned something so perfect. Now, we have him. Now Osven belongs to us.

"This reward for your service, my dear, is just the beginning," he places his hands on my shoulders and looks into my eyes. My mind is a swirl of memories. Osven's memories and my own. But when I look into Quenson's eyes, my focus changes. He guides me away from those thoughts with a single, steady gaze.

"Your retrieval of the son has impressed me. Your skills are fair enough, but I wish to help you grow. I have decided to train you in the Arcane. You shall learn the ways of Necromancy, so that you may tap into the power Osven holds. But first," he leans in close until I can feel his cool breath, "you will bring me Tib. Do not fail me in this, Celli. It is essential to our plan that we have him. Dub is waiting for you at the dais. Go now."

***

I never thought much about the realm of death. Not even after we lost Hew. Mum said it was the place spirits go. There are some dabblers in Cerion if you look hard enough, who say they can talk to the dead. Some of the kids used to tell stories about people, wicked people, Necromancers, who could pull you out of the spirit realm and control you even after you were dead. I never really believed in any of that. Now, here I am, slunk in the shadows with Osven hovering nearby. Next to me, Dub is silent. Brooding.

The shack is small. One room, dirt floor. A hatch in the center of the room. We locked the door behind us. We're in the open, other than the darkness. No wards, no magic. I don't even bother with my cloak. He'll feel it and know we're here. Dub's so angry I can almost hear his teeth grinding. He doesn't like this place. He's got something personal against it. I don't care, as long as he's quiet and does his job.

Now, there's nothing to do but wait.

"What's down there?" I whisper, pointing at the hatch.

"A pit," Dub says. "He's working on something down there. Rumors all over the city about it."

"What is it?" I ask him. "Maybe we can use it."

"Not in our orders," Dub grunts. "We can look into it later. Now shut up and wait. He's bound to come in sooner or later."

"Don't tell me what to do," I hiss at him. "I'm in charge now, remember?"

Chapter Thirty-Five
THE PLAN

Tib

The vials. Two more to get inside Brindelier, or five more if we want to beat The Dusk. The machine. I need one more propeller, and then just a ship. The sons. I sigh as I pace across the polished stone. Kaso Viro seems to think Errie is lost for good. That they used him already. I shiver and clench my fists. I can't accept that. I won't.

I glance at the heavy window drapes. The sun is coming up. It squeezes its way through the blue-green fabric and splashes the color onto the sandy stone. Outside, waves crash against the tower. I like the sound. It'd be soothing, I think, if I wasn't so distracted. I cross to Rian's bed. He's completely burrowed into his blankets. *Let him sleep,* Shush had said before he went off to Kythshire. *He'll need to be well-rested.*

I pace faster, tugging my fingers through the knots in my hair. We can get Kythshire's easily. Azi and Rian and the fae won't have a problem with that. That leaves four: Ceras'lain, Elespen, Hywilkin, and Northern Haigh. Valenor had explained to me that the last three are Dusk Wellsprings. Dangerous. Guarded, even more than the Dawn. I think of the guardians at Kythshire and Sunteri and scowl. If the Dusk's guardians are more difficult than that, we're in trouble.

Or not, I think to myself. A plan starts to form in my mind. Loren said they have two. The Dusk. They have two, and they have Errie. My heart starts to race. If I could get back to the stronghold, I'm sure I could find their offerings. Maybe I could find Errie, too. I glance at Rian again. Still sleeping. I wish I had a way to get there without him. I pause in my pacing and focus. I take a step into the shadows.

"The Sorcerer's Stronghold," I whisper, screwing my eyes tightly shut.

"What are you trying to do?" Shush's whisper brushes my cheek like a soft breeze. Even so, it makes me jump. "Ha!" he exclaims with a gust. "Sorry to startle you, Tib."

"Nothing, never mind," I say with a shrug and step out of hiding.

"Oh, I'm glad it was nothing. I thought you might be doing

something careless like trying to go to the Dusk all alone. And with the Sunteri offering right in your pocket, too. You're smarter than that, though," he whispers.

"Sure, I'm smarter than that," I mumble and look away. He's right. It would have been pretty dumb of me to bring the bottle right to them. I didn't even think of that. I shake my head and rub my neck. "Can we wake him now, please?"

"I think he's rested enough," Shush nods.

As soon as he's awake, I fill Rian in on my dream and the offering. Mevyn didn't want to see him, but apparently Rian remembers enough of what happened in Sunteri to know why it was so easy for me.

Our farewell to Kaso Viro is quicker than I expected. He doesn't even offer us breakfast. Just tells us to call on him if we need anything. Tells Rian to keep Aster, just in case. Rian doesn't look overly thrilled about that, but he thanks Kaso Viro anyway. Loren offers us a quick goodbye and goes back to his dusting. I hope becoming a Mage is worth all that boring work to him.

"Home to plan, and to Mouli's breakfast," Rian grins as he puts a hand on my shoulder. "Ready?"

I nod, and he closes his eyes and whisks us away.

We arrive in a house. Rian's, I think. Right away, I notice the difference. Cerion's brighter than it had been when we left it, and it's not just because it's daylight. There's some new magic here. Quiet, steady. Peaceful. Beautiful. It reminds me of Margy, somehow. Rian notices it, too. He goes to the window and pushes the shutters open. The summer sun beams in, nearly blinding us.

"Tib," he says, and beckons me. "Do you feel that?" he asks as I cross to the window.

Shush bobs between us and turns his face to the sun. I look away from him, out toward the palace. I do feel it. Hope. Protection. It stretches out from the palace strangely. A feeling. Like bunches of pinpoints of light all over the city. Some places, there's lots of it. Some places, there's hardly any. I wonder why.

"Yeah," I say. "I do."

"It's so perfect. So beautiful. What does it mean?" Rian whispers.

Our growling stomachs interrupt his musing.

"Right," he says. "Breakfast and planning. Come on, you'll be my guest."

He leads me through into the meeting hall and skids to a stop. The guild hall is quiet. Eerily quiet. Empty. No food on the table. The fire in the hearth is just embers. Rian doesn't say anything. He just stands there, dumbfounded. Like the empty table is some devastating revelation.

"What's wrong?" I ask.

"Mouli?" he croaks and sniffs the air.

I do, too. Nothing. No sweet rolls, no sausages. No fresh bread.

"No breakfast today?" I ask.

"Never," Rian says, going pale. "It'd never happen. Mouli!" he shouts, this time a little more urgently. He runs toward the kitchen and Shush and I exchange concerned glances and follow. Suddenly I think of Nessa, trapped in the closet, paralyzed.

"Mouli!" Rian calls again as he pushes open the door. The kitchen is empty. He looks over the block top, where empty trays are neatly stacked. Everything's put away.

"Definitely no breakfast," I say to Shush. "Maybe she took a day off."

"She wouldn't," Rian croaks. "She doesn't."

He creeps toward the open half-door that leads out into the street and peers outside. "Mouli?" he calls weakly.

"Rian!" the old woman's voice exclaims from a distance away. "What are you doing here? You should be at the palace with everyone else! Oh, dear! You haven't come for breakfast, have you? I knew I should have made something. I told you, Luca!"

She rushes into the kitchen and immediately starts pulling things out of cupboards and making up a platter. Rian's stomach growls again. He opens his mouth, closes it, and yanks Mouli into a tight hug.

"Thank the stars," he whispers. "I was so scared."

"Oh," Mouli chuckles and hugs him back. "Figures the one time I don't cook, you come looking. See this?" She touches her elbows around his waist. "If not for my own bosom, I could put my arms around you twice! Sit down, sit down. Tib, you too. Hm." She squints past Rian at me and her brow goes up.

"Well, well," she grins, "thought you were all at the palace! What'll it be for you, then, little one? If you're anything like Flitter, you'll want your sugar cubes."

Mouli slips out of Rian's embrace, leaving him gaping from her to Shush in disbelief.

"Oh, indeed," Shush darts closer to her to whisper. "I do enjoy those. Though, have you any more of those delightful sugared fruits that were out a few days ago? I very much liked those."

"Wh—" Rian stares at the two of them in disbelief as she opens a clay canister and tosses Shush a sugared cherry. "You...you can..."

"Oh, right. Should have told you. We all came in this morning. From Kythshire. It was a big event. Too bad you missed it," Shush whispers.

"Mmhm!" Mouli agrees cheerfully as she gathers up some cheese and bread. "It was quite a sight! That's where everyone is, of course. The palace. Having breakfast with the elves and fairies. I thought you had gone, too. Sit, sit!"

She practically shoves Rian onto a stool. I sit, too, before she gets pushy. Beside me, Rian seems to be in some kind of trance. Like it's too much for him to grasp. He's trying to make sense of it. Mouli sets a plate in front of him, and nudges him when he doesn't start eating.

"Eat!" she orders. "Before there's nothing left of you!"

"So that spell, all those little hopeful points," he says to Shush, "those were fairies?"

Shush laughs, "No, can you imagine? There aren't that many here now. They went back to Kythshire once dawn broke. Only Flitt and Twig and I are here now."

Rian takes a bite of bread and chews thoughtfully.

"So what is that spell, then?" Rian asks.

"That's the Princess," he says. "Margy's blessing."

Rian chokes on his bread. He sputters and gulps from his mug and coughs.

"What?" he asks weakly. "The Princess?"

"Sure," Shush whispers around a mouthful. "That's why they came. To let everyone know her magic is permitted. She's had it for a while now, poor child. That's a big secret to keep."

Rian's eyes slide to Mouli and back to Shush.

"Are you sure it's wise?" he whispers to the fairy.

"What? Oh, yes," Shush nods. "Everyone knows now. There need to be a lot fewer secrets if we're going to beat the Dusk. Speaking of which, weren't we going to make a plan?"

The churning of my stomach over this news doesn't trump my hunger. I keep shoving bread into my mouth while the other two talk. Margy's secret isn't a secret anymore. They're going to have to keep her safe now. There's bound to be people who'll fear her. Who'll try to hurt her. Who'll think it's too much power for a princess. I hope His Majesty realizes old Finn isn't going to be enough protection now. I hope the king forgives her for her secret.

Between that, the offerings, Errie, and the machine, I have too much to think about. Too much to do. I start to eat faster. That's when I notice their eyes on me.

"Whut?" I ask through a mouthful of cheese and melon.

"Rian asked if you'd be coming to the palace," Shush whispers.

"We need to get everyone together, on the same page, and work out a plan. The palace is the safest place to do that, and everyone's there already," Rian says.

"You're right," I reply with a nod and finish what's left on my plate in one mouthful. "Do you think you can start without me? I'm going to check on my contraption." I sigh. "I was going to try and get it done without magic, but I don't think that's possible now. I'll get Valenor to help."

"Good idea," Rian says. "We'll need that finished sooner rather than later."

"Take this," I say, and hand him the red bottle. He accepts it with a reverent bow of his head.

"I know just the place for it," he says quietly.

My walk from the Elite hall to the shed is strange without Zeze. I think of her, of Margy, as I make my way. Those days are gone. It makes me sad to think about it. I'll miss her company, but there's no way she'll ever be able to join me in the streets again, cat or not. It's too unsafe.

Redstone Row is quiet and pleasant this morning. People mill around in the streets in small crowds, excitedly talking about the Dawn procession. Margy's spell pulses from some of them, but not others. As I pass them by, I try to understand it. It's hard to at first, but the magic tells a story. Little pieces that put themselves together as I gather them. The spell was a choice. It fell on those who believed in her. Who would protect her. Who love her. If they wanted to, they could pass it on to others. I wonder whether they know that.

My shed is the same as ever on the outside. Chipped paint, barred door. I rest my hand on the latch. When I look at the door, something catches my healed eye. A figure inside. No, two. I see the outline of each of them. A man. A girl. Quietly, I take my hand away. Step back. Look harder. I can't make out any more details, but I know who it is already. The likeliest pair to be lying in wait for me, in my own shed.

My pulse quickens. My face goes red. Did they see my invention? Did they steal it? No, I think to myself. They don't care about that. They're here for me. Defeating Osven bought me a little time, but I'm still not safe. They still need my help. They need me to tell them where the entrance is. The floating island. The gateway.

My instinct is to turn and run. To get as far away as I can from them. To tell the others, or palace guards. Get them arrested. Get them put away. I take a few steps back. Think about it a moment. About Errie. About the offerings. I take a step. Hide myself away.

"Valenor," I whisper, closing my eyes. "Are you there?"

"As ever," he replies from all around me. "What can I do for you, Tib?"

"Can you look," I whisper, "and see whether my plans are down below?"

"They are," he replies.

"Can you send an idea to Ruben and Raefe?" I ask.

"I can," he replies. "Are you about to do something foolish, Tib?"

"I think so," I murmur with my hand on the latch. "Will you stay with me?"

"I shall," he says. "Though it might not seem so, I shall stand beside you."

"This is a really stupid idea, isn't it?" I ask him.

"One of your worst," he replies, "though inevitable. Still, it holds promise."

Inevitable is a good word, I think. I keep fighting these Sorcerers, this fortress. Fighting them, and being taunted by them. I know I'm supposed to go there again. Valenor knows it, too. Something inside me compels me to do it. Some little voice in the back of my mind knows I'll end up there eventually. If I'm going again, I want it to be on my terms. I won't let them trick me again. Won't let them hurt anyone else I love, or surprise me.

"They'll just think they did," I whisper to Valenor.

"Indeed," he replies.

I step out from hiding again and go back to the door. Look inside. See something else. Not just Celli and Dub. Something, or half of something. It shifts in and out, like a creature not quite there.

"Is that a Dusk fae?" I whisper.

"A spirit," Valenor replies. "Do not be alarmed, but I believe it to be Osven."

"Great," I mumble. "Just what I needed. Leave it to a Sorcerer not to stay dead."

I slip a knife from my bandolier and palm it. Not sure why. Dub has me beat with knives. Celli's probably stronger than I am now, after whatever they did to her. And who knows what kind of damage a Sorcerer's spirit can do. I hesitate with my hand on the latch. This is stupid. Brash. Even for me. I shake my head. Think of Errie. Unlock the bolt and push the door open. Step inside.

Nothing. I pull the door closed behind me. Hesitate. Wait for an attack. When it doesn't come, I start toward the hatch. Dub grabs me from behind around the shoulders. I grip my knife and raise it, then make a show of dropping it on the floor. It clatters in the dust. Celli comes and picks it up.

Dub chuckles. Presses one of his blades to my throat. "Don't. Move," he hisses.

Celli creeps into view, holding my knife. She looks me over.

"You made him bleed," she says quietly to Dub. "Master won't be happy with that. We're supposed to make friends, aren't we? A truce, Tib. How about that?"

"A truce?" I choke under Dub's grip.

"Loosen up a little, Dub," Celli says. "Just so he can talk."

He does, but not much.

"I'll come with you," I say. "I'm tired of being scared about who's next." I glance at the shimmer of a form beside her in the darkness. "When that Sorcerer showed up at Nessa's..." I shake my head. Hope I'm convincing. "I won't let that happen again. They're too powerful to fight. If they promise to leave my friends alone, I'll do what they want."

Celli narrows her eyes. She looks at me hard. Fingers the bracelet on her wrist. The shimmer whispers something. I can't really hear it. It's all jumbled.

"He's not lying," she scoffs. "That sounds exactly like the Tib I know. Self-righteous. Overprotective. The big hero." She waves Dub away, and he lowers his knife.

"You're in charge, Celli. If I had my way," he growls into my ear, "you'd be dead." He shoves me toward her.

"You take him back," he says. "I've got other orders."

"Master didn't say anything about other orders," Celli glares at him.

"They weren't for you to hear," Dub spits. His good eye looks me over. Bores into my healed one. He sneers angrily and utters a string of curses. Then he turns and yanks the door open and slams it behind him.

Celli grips my arm hard. Leads me to the far corner. Pulls something from her pocket. Presses her hand into a carving in the wall. A carving that wasn't there before. I can't really see what she's doing.

It's too dark.

"Repeat after me," she says. "Sparrow and fox, boar and perch, foreshine, forewarn, induct, destroy." She glances at me. "Asio."

I do as she says. Repeat the words. I have no time to react. Something creeps over me. Tendrils. Magic. It grabs me and pulls me into the wall, and then I'm falling like when Rian takes me through the Half-Realm, only faster. More violently. We crash to the floor before I can brace myself, and I gasp for the breath that was knocked out of me.

The room is circular, with a pinpoint window all the way at the top of a high dome. I roll to my side and pant as my ability to breathe comes back. Look around. The floor is a starburst, gold and black. The walls are alcoves. Three. Six. Two pedestals have bottles on them. Bottles of glowing liquid. Four are empty. My heart pounds. Of all the rooms she could have brought me to, what were the odds we'd end up in this one?

I try to be still, to act like I'm stunned, so I can take stock of the magic here. Wards like I've never felt. Tangled up all together. Pressing down. Swirling and spinning. Anyone, any enemy, who tried to come in here would be confused. They'd want to leave. To run. They'd be terrified. If they made it in, they'd go mad.

"Well, well," the Sorcerer's voice makes my skin crawl. I push myself to my feet. Try not to look too defiant. "Impressive, Celli."

He walks around me, looking me up and down. I recognize this one. Quenson.

"He came willingly, Master," she says.

"Is that so?" Quenson tilts his head to the side. Watches me like I'm prey.

"He says he wishes to cooperate, if we'll leave his friends alone," she says.

"Really?" Quenson snorts. "But you have deceived us before, Nullen. How can I be certain you won't do it again?"

"I thought we could come to an agreement," I say. "I'll show you the gate if you'll make a deal with me."

His eyes flash with that same greedy hope I saw in them the last time I made the same promise. Then they narrow.

"It's closer than you think," I lean toward him. Try to be enticing.

"And in exchange?" He licks his lips. It's working.

"The boys from Cerion. The ones you stole. Griff, Mikken, and Errie. Let them go," I say.

"Celli," Quenson says slowly, rubbing his chin. "Take him to Osven's chamber while I consult with the others. You shall treat him as our guest. And Tibreseli, I expect you to behave as such, as an act of good faith between us."

I nod to him in agreement, and watch him go.

"This way," Celli says. She's got no emotion in her voice at all. No wariness. No concern or question. She walks in silence, guided by the spirit of Osven.

So far, so good, I think. They trust me enough not to keep me tied or chained. They're treating me as a guest. Valenor knows I'm here, and Mevyn would aid me if I asked him to. I'm confident, but not over confident. The machine? Taken care of, I hope. The son? Soon to be released, maybe. The offerings? Mine, if I can figure out a way to slip from Celli's eye and back to that circle room without being seen. I'll have to show them the island first, though. There's no way around that, if Errie's going to be saved.

Chapter Thirty-Six:
DINING HALL

Azi

"She says she doesn't want to see you right now," Saesa whispers after having slipped out of the dining room door just a moment before. Merry sounds of revelry drift through the thick carved wood: laughter, song, and dance. "She said…" she looks away and takes a deep breath.

"What, Saesa? Tell me," I slump back against the wall, defeated.

"She said you're a bad Mentalist, and if you want to stay friends with her, you have to figure out a way to prove you're sorry." She winces. "Sorry, m'lady."

I rub my eyes and push myself from the wall to start pacing. "Prove it?" I whisper. "How, though?" I try to contain my anger at myself. We don't have time for this now. I should be in there doing my duty as Ambassador to Kythshire. Making plans to triumph over the Dusk. Keeping my promise to Princess Margy. Instead I'm cast out, and it's all my fault.

"Can you go back in," I say, "and just ask her what I can do? How I can make it up to her?"

"Of course," she says, and goes in again.

This time when she comes out, she looks very grave.

"She said…" she hesitates again.

"Saesa, it's all right."

"She said, 'Thick as always. Typical. I said figure out a way, didn't I? That means she has to think of it herself. Or maybe ask…'" Saesa shifts uncomfortably and clears her throat.

"Ask who?"

"…Stinky," she replies, and her cheeks burn red. "Sorry, Lady Knight, but that's what she said."

"This is the last thing I need right now," I say, clenching my fists. "How could I have been so careless?"

"*You? Careless? I don't believe it,*" Rian's voice echoes in my mind and I whirl around, searching for him. As soon as I spot him coming from the opposite end of the corridor, all of my anger drops away. I forget myself and break into a run through the palace hallway until we crash together in a tight, desperate embrace.

His soft kiss starts out sweet, but quickly grows deeper and more passionate. We forget our place for a moment until Saesa clears her throat softly from down the hall and we force ourselves to pull away from each other.

His eyes linger on my face, and his finger traces the Mark at my collar. I start to look away in shame, but he lifts my chin with a gentle touch and tilts his head with concern.

"What happened?" he asks, not with a judgmental or harsh tone, but out of concern. His tenderness causes the floodgate of tears to open once more, and I can't help myself. I bury my face into the chest of his soft robes and cry.

"We'll be back, Saesa. Wait here please," he says, and I feel the shift as he slips me into the Half-Realm.

"Azi, what happened?" he asks again after the torrent of tears settles down. I recount my entire morning to him, from the moment I woke up until the moment he appeared in the hallway. He's patient and quiet as he listens, which only makes me feel more awful. If I had his restraint, if I was able to control myself the way he does, I wouldn't be in this situation. When I'm finally through, he lets out a breath as though he'd been holding it the entire time I was talking.

"Why didn't you tell Master Gaethon about the archer?" he asks. His question throws me off.

"I did," I frown. "I thought I did."

"You didn't. If you had, he would have reacted differently. Look," he guides me to look at him again, his hazel eyes inviting and warm. "What you did was overreaching, Azi. Looking into a sleeping mind without consent. Stealing a memory that you shouldn't have taken. But the reason you did it was forgivable. You were concerned for the safety of the King. As for Flitt..." he sighs. "Shush?"

"It was a misunderstanding," Shush whispers as he slowly comes into view beside Rian. "Flitt's got a wren in a spider's web when it comes to you. One small move and the gossamer breaks. She's put a lot of faith in you through all this. She talked you up to everyone, even the Queen herself. She probably just feels like she has to keep you in check, that's all."

His effort to help me feel better only causes my heart to sink more. I shouldn't have let her down.

"We need to get this resolved and focus," Rian says matter-of-factly. "Too much is in the balance right now. The stakes are high. I'd show you," he looks at me, "but I don't think you'd better for a while."

"I won't," I say. "I don't want to, ever again."

"I'll tell you, then," he says, and he does. He recounts everything from his encounter at the Ganvent house to his journey to Kaso Viro to his nearly missed breakfast this morning. By the time he's through, my tears are dry and I feel a fresh determination to jump to action.

"Don't worry," he says to me. "I'll talk to the others. We'll make a plan."

"In the meantime," Shush says, "I'll help you figure out how to make it up to Flitt."

"Trust Shush," Rian says. He kisses me again, softly, and strokes my cheek. I nod, and he casts the revealer on himself and leaves me to go into the dining hall. As soon as the door clicks behind him, I feel horrible again.

"I can feel it," Shush whispers. "Your regret. Your shame. Fairies are empathic, you know. Most of us, anyway. Especially the ones who are close to humans. Flitt's like that, too, but it's even stronger between the two of you. She can feel it even when you're far away from each other."

"So she knows how terrible I feel," I shake my head.

"Can you think of something?" his whisper is a cool breeze in my ear. "Some selfless act, some way to show her how much her forgiveness means to you? You know her better than you think, Azi. What could you do to prove it to her?"

A hundred thoughts run through my mind. Gifts I could give. Things she enjoys. Mouli's sweets, or the sugar cubes she loves so much. She loves light, the stars, colorful, bright things like ribbons and gemstones. There's not enough time, though. I can't go off searching for the perfect present to show her what she means to me.

Peals of laughter ring out from inside the ballroom, and Mya's song mixes with that of the elves. I imagine Flitt in there, laughing along with them through her hurt feelings and her disdain for what I almost did. I imagine Uncle, whispering with Rian, starting to plan. I imagine His Majesty entertaining Twig and Margy and the elves.

"You're getting closer," Shush whispers as if he can follow my train of thought. "Think about what you know of her. What she's risked for you."

What she's risked for me. My thoughts go to the Ring and what she told me of her struggles there. How they almost cast her out. How she stood her ground and kept to her beliefs so that we could maybe someday be Ili'luvrie. She risked her place with her own kind because she believed so strongly in our partnership.

"Our kind worries all the time," Shush whispers, "that because we're small, we're considered inferior by humans. We're not as important. That's what many of us think you think. That's why Flitt's so harsh sometimes. So she can seem as important. As equal. When you did that, down there, you made her feel lesser. Like something to be used."

I reach up and press my hand to my neck, where the curl of the Mark peeks up over my collar. I look at the door. I know what I have to do. Something selfless. Something that will prove to her that her forgiveness matters to me. That she's my equal, and she deserves my respect.

"What are you going to do?" he whispers.

"I'm going in there," I say, "in front of everyone, and I'm going to apologize to her."

"What about what Gaethon said?" Shush whispers.

"He's right. It would be a scandal to show myself like this," I take a deep breath and gather my courage, "but it's worth it to me to lose face with all of them, even my king, if it means I'll gain her trust again."

"Ha. You're brighter than she gives you credit for, Azi," Shush chuckles. "I'll join you."

The air around him swirls into a dervish so strong that I squeeze my eyes and duck away. When it dies down, Shush is standing beside me, actually towering beside me, resplendent in his gleaming green armor. My head comes only to the top of his shoulder, making him taller than Rian. Perhaps as tall as Bryse, though not as broad. In fact, his narrow frame gives him a rather ethereal and imposing appearance, similar to an elf. He bends slightly and offers me his elbow.

"Shall we?" he asks, and I nod and let him step me out of the Half-Realm.

Saesa gasps at our sudden appearance. Her gaze lingers on Shush for a moment and then bows low to the two of us.

"We're going in, Saesa," I say, a little shakily. Shush gives my hand a reassuring pat and then lets go.

"I think it'd be best," he whispers, "if I go first."

The guards flanking the doors push them open to allow us to enter. The dining room drapes are open to the morning sunlight. Dozens of fairy orbs drift in and out of the beams, catching the light and casting it out to dance across the walls and high ceiling. The tables and chairs, arranged in a u-shape around the entertainers in the center, are adorned with rich garlands of fragrant flowers. The elves have arranged themselves in the center to sing a perfect, lilting harmony together. Their backs are facing me, so I can't be sure, but I think I recognize Julini and Shoel. Both helped us face Jacek in Ceras'lain two years ago.

We enter facing the king and royal family, who are of course seated at the very center of the center table. Margy sits at His Majesty's right hand, and Queen Naelle at his left. Twig is seated beside the princess, bobbing his head in time to the music. Beside him is Flitt, human-sized again, and looking as though she's making an effort to smile and seem joyous. His Majesty's Elite line the table beside her, in order of rank from Mya to Bryse. Across from them on the other side of the U, His Majesty's Royal Advisors have their place. At least half of them are Mages of the Academy. I feel their eyes on me as soon as I walk in.

The elves' song ends. No one applauds. They're all too fixated on Shush and me. The performers turn to see what's caught everyone's attention. Julini is the first to notice my Mark. She nudges Shoel, and his brow furrows.

The silence in the room is deafening. Every eye is on me. My heartbeat thumps so loudly I'm sure they can hear it. I gather my courage as the first scandalized whisper breaks out amongst the Mages, and I stride, as knightly as possible, to face His Majesty.

I drop to one knee before him and press my fist to my chest. Beside me, Shush does the same.

"Azaeli Hammerfel," His Majesty says. His words are barely laced with a question.

"Your Majesty," I reply.

"I believe most of our guests know you by name, Lady Knight," he says, a bit more coldly than he might, probably, had I not come bursting in covered in black Mark. "But I do not know your companion."

"This is Soren Hasten Udi Swiftish Haven Illustrious Noble General, Your Majesty," I say with a nod toward Shush, who has already stood up.

"Shush is good enough," he whispers.

"What's that?" King Tirnon asks, cupping a hand around his ear and leaning forward. "Could you speak a little louder, friend?"

"Shush," Shush says aloud, and a puff of wind rushes out from him, ruffling the fur of His Majesty's cloak and setting his crown askew. "Sorry," he whispers bashfully.

"He's a wind fae, Your Majesty," I explain.

"Ha! That explains it," King Tirnon laughs merrily and straightens his crown. "We have a place for both of you, of course. Come join the table."

I stand a little nervously, certain that most in the room have noticed my Mark. They're all still silent, even after the king's welcome. I feel their eyes on me, especially Uncle's. His glare of disapproval bores into me, and in my imagination the Mark burns my flesh where it curls under their gaze.

I try to ignore it. I expected as much when I made my decision. The Mages are well within their rights to take me in and strip me. I expected it, and I accepted the risk. All for her.

In the continued silence, with everyone's eyes on me, I turn and walk slowly along the richly set table to face Flitt, who sits with her arms crossed, glaring. When I stop before her, she looks pointedly away and scowls.

"Felicity Lumine Instacia Tenacity Teeming Elite Reformer," I say. "Flitt."

"Flitter," she says sternly.

"Flitter." I repeat with a nod. "I lost myself. I went too far. Before His Majesty and all those assembled here, I am humbly, deeply, and wholly sorry for the way I behaved. I will never," I swallow the lump in my throat, "never do that again. You are my dearest friend, and I should never have ordered you or thought to use you in such a way."

"Your dearest friend?" she asks dubiously.

"Without a doubt," I reply.

"Dearer than Rian?" she tilts her head slightly. Around us, a few of the onlookers chuckle softly.

"Rian is more than a friend to me," I reply after some careful thought.

Flitt purses her lips together and stares at me for a long, uncomfortable moment. All around us, the dining hall seems to have collectively held its breath in anticipation of her response. She chews her pink lip and leans forward.

"Tell them," she says to me quietly, "what you did. Tell them all of it."

I start hesitantly, but after a while the words begin to flow more easily. The others' reaction is much what I would have expected. Heated, but better than I had hoped. His Majesty's Advisors question me extensively on the archer. The Mages question me on my

Mentalism. This opens a conversation with the elves, who have known Mentalists in Ceras'lain, apparently, and offer reassuring explanations of its workings. This leads to talk of different schools of Magic, and Margary's gifts.

I take my seat between Mya and Flitt, who seems to have mostly accepted my apology, or is at least acting as though she has, for now.

"*Your Mark is gone,*" she pushes to me, tapping her own neck. I reach up and feel the place where the black Mark had crept. I glance at Rian, who sits between Elliot and Uncle Gaethon, and he breaks his thoughtful stare at the two of us to offer me a half-smile.

"*That was quick,*" I say. Flitt grins in reply.

"*That was tricky,*" Rian pushes to us both. "*Even for you, Flitt.*"

"*Don't know what you're talking about,*" Flitt pushes.

"*The Mark doesn't work that way,*" Rian scowls. "*You put it on her, didn't you?*"

"*Hush up, Stinky Mage,*" Flitt wrinkles her nose and sticks her cherry-red tongue out at Rian across the room.

I push my plate away and a Page comes to take it. What does he mean, she put it on me? Why would she do that? I think back to the sleeping archer. To her sudden appearance. How she told me I should be upstairs, with them. Being absent from the gathering was an insult to her after all her hard work getting everyone together. Not only had I hurt her feelings by ordering her and insinuating I'd use her to replenish myself, but I made her look foolish by not showing up in the dining hall when I ought to have been by her side.

"You *put the Mark on me? You made me go through all of that,*" I push to her in disbelief, "*just to save face?*"

Flitt shrugs apologetically. "*You've been wobbly since we came back to Cerion. Divided. I needed you to be sure, not just in the magic of the Queen's palace, but here, in front of your own king, of how important I am to you. It was the last test, I guess you'd say. Oh, don't look so angry. I did you a favor. Now you don't have to worry about those Mages looking at you that way. You don't have to worry about having to tell everyone what you can do, either. That part's over. Everyone knows. The elves even helped!*"

I try hard to compose myself. She's right. I don't like the way she did it, but what's done is done. I look across the table and catch Mum's eye. She's smiling at me with that same pride she showed when she first saw my gold Mark.

"Paba," Margy says quietly, and the rest of the conversation dies down as the young princess stands up.

"Yes, dear child?" His Majesty gazes at her much the same way Mum looked at me: With wonder, awe, and respect.

"Now that everyone knows of my secret, and now that you've been shown the path the Dawn must take, there's little time to lose," she offers, a little unsure.

"Quite so," King Tirnon rises from his seat to stand beside her. "The time for merriment is done, my friends. Now we must make a plan to push back against the scourge of Sorcery and their allies, the Dusk. We must work together to aid the Dawn in claiming the lost city," he squeezes Margy's shoulder. "I intend to address my kingdom before the sun sets this afternoon, so I hope we can agree on our course of action by then."

The way Margy looks up at him, with such love and admiration, makes my heart swell with pride and affection for the two of them. My king and his daughter. Together, the two will rule Cerion and Brindelier both. I can't think of a better pair of leaders. Margy, with her kind, gentle, steady heart, and His Majesty with his open mind and level head for justice and peace. The promise of the Light between them is strong. With the fairies and the elves by their side, the path of Cerion along with the Dawn is easily set.

Chapter Thirty-Seven
THE THIEF

Tib

The room where Celli brings me is just like the rest of the place. Dank. Shadowed. Heavy with wards and spells. The spells in this room are old. Elvish. Twisted. Like the spirits of a thousand trees. Wild. Like a wolf pinned in a trap, the energy thrashes around us when we enter. Set in place, but nowhere to go. Osven's ghost wavers like he's under the surface of a pool.

Celli closes the door behind us and just stands there. She doesn't say a word. If I concentrate, I can feel the Sorcerer's hold gripping her. Quenson. Quenson. I glance around and step closer to her. She presses herself back against the door. I need to get out of here. Back to that room we arrived in. Back to the bottles on the pedestals.

I look Celli over cautiously. She doesn't react. She's content. She's done what she was told. Brought me here. Kept me here.

"What did they do to you, Celli?" I ask her. "You're like a slave."

"I'm not a slave," she narrows her eyes. "My master honors me."

"That's what I mean. Your master? Since when?" I edge closer. "These are Sorcerers, Celli. They're wicked. Dangerous."

"My master strengthens and protects me," she replies, like she's bragging about it.

I sigh and turn away. Look around the room. It's been ransacked. Books from shelves lay open, scattered across the desk, their pages torn out. Chests are tipped over, their contents spilled across the carpet. I cross to a chest and kneel beside it. There was magic on it. Wards and poisons. They've been spent, though. Now it's just an ordinary, tipped over chest. No, not ordinary. Something's inside. I see it. Feel it. Bundled up in an old robe. A creature. Something sleeping.

"Don't touch anything," Celli barks at me.

I don't listen. I pinch the fine red silk between my fingertips and pull it aside. One of the black, leathery fairies lies sleeping there, curled into itself. It's not as black as the other three I've seen. It's less solid, somehow. Less here. This one has a different face, too. When I pull the last of the robe off of it, it startles awake and hisses at me.

"What are you doing here?" Celli demands angrily. She stalks close to the creature and crouches. "No one is to be in this room aside from my Master. These things are his now."

"Master," the creature whimpers. Its voice is strangely female. It eyes Celli's wrist. The bracelet. I understand right away. That's what's keeping Osven's ghost held to her.

The creature lunges and clings to Celli's wrist, trying desperately to pull the bracelet free. Celli cruelly flings her across the room and then chases after her as she smacks the wall. Before I can reach them, she starts kicking the thing brutally, repeatedly.

"Celli!" I shout and try to push her away from the pathetic, whimpering creature.

"I am nothing, I am nothing," the black fae whimpers. "Without him, nothing. Kill me. Let her kill me. If she doesn't, they will."

Celli fights against me, trying hard to land another kick. I shove her back.

"Is this how you treat a guest, Celli?" I ask, my voice strained with the effort. Her wild eyes flash. "That's what your master said, wasn't it? Treat me as a guest. I'm asking you, as a guest, stop. Stop it."

"She hates me. She knows, she knows. When her master dies, she'll be the same as me. Nothing, nothing," the pathetic creature curls up again and starts sobbing.

Celli's eyes fill with disgust and hatred for the creature. She shuffles her feet and fights against me, but I see the conflict in her. She wants to kill this thing. She hates it. But her Master's orders come first.

"Water, Celli?" I ask her. "I'm thirsty, and I need to wash my wound." I point to the shallow cut that Dub had left with his knife.

"Dub did that. You won't tell my lord, will you?" Celli asks, momentarily distracted from the simpering ball of scales and black fur.

"I won't, if you go and get me some water," I say, rubbing my neck.

"I shouldn't leave you," she replies.

"That's not what he said," I say slowly. "He said treat me as a guest, and he made me agree to behave like one. You heard me. I agreed. Right? Where am I going to go anyway, Celli? This place is too well protected."

"That doesn't matter to you," she says, pursing her lips. "Their spells can't stop you. You got away before. You tricked my master."

"Celli…" I sigh and scowl. "It's just water. Should a guest be made to beg?"

Her gaze flicks from me to the creature and back again. I can see the conflict in her. She despises that thing, that example of what might become of her. She wants to forget it. To snuff it out.

I cough dramatically and rub my throat. Celli narrows her eyes and glares at me.

"Fine," she says reluctantly. "You'd better not move from that spot, though."

I drop to the floor and sit cross legged. At my knee, the creature shivers.

"I swear," I say to Celli.

"I'll be right back," she says, and then, reluctantly, she slips out of the room.

"You should have let her end me," the creature whimpers. "I am nothing now. Master is gone. Stolen from me. I cannot reach him. Only through my own death. Into darkness. Do me this mercy. End me. I am nothing. Worthless."

I stare at the thing, ugly and mangled and spent. Her leathery wings are twisted and torn. The hair on her head is a shag of charred black moss. The rest of her is almost nothing, like she says. Bone and scales.

"What's your name?" I ask her.

"Nothing and no one," she says.

"My name is Tib," I offer. She doesn't say anything. "What was your name, before?" I ask. I'm thankful for Nessa and Saesa, who taught me how to get information. To gain trust. Make it about them, they'd say.

"Before the master?" she asks. I nod. She thinks a while. I don't interrupt. Silence speaks volumes.

"Vae. Vicious Arson Envious," she replies.

"Arson. Are you a fire fae?" I ask her. "Or, were you?"

"Cinders and soot. Burning coals. We change things. We destroy so there can be new birth. We meld and mold and make stronger." When she speaks, I see a flash of something beneath the edge of her wing. Orange, like flames. A vein, like red coals blackened over. I feel the heat coming from her. The fire inside being stoked. The memory of her former self is being kindled.

"But, they are gone. All taken. Lost. Dead. Destroyed. All I have, all I had, was Master. He helped me. Saved me. Kept me," she cries and curls herself tighter. "She'll see. One day, hers will be gone, too, and she'll be nothing. Nothing but memories of the things they made her do."

"Who's gone? Other fae? The Sorcerers killed them?"

"No, they are not fae. We are not fae. Fae are Dawn. We are Dusk."

"What are you, if not fae?"

"Imps. The dark reflection. Shadows in the mirror. Crag and stone. From deep within the mountain. Molten, cracked, reformed," she whispers, like what she's saying is forbidden. "Oshteveska furle drulevents. Kerevorna."

Her words have power. Ancient feelings. I sense them circling around her as she speaks them. Like runes and wards. Ancient spells, forgotten a long time ago.

"You have given me these recollections," she whispers.

"Crag and stone," I whisper. At first I think of Iren, but then I remember what Valenor said about the Wellsprings. My heart thumps in my chest. "Are you from Hywilkin?"

"Hywilkin. Master was to take me home," she whimpers. "He was, and I was bound to give him a gift most splendid. Most precious and perfect. I was his, and he was mine. Our secret. And now he is dead, and I am nothing. Nothing."

"Vae," I say to her carefully, "you are not. You're not nothing. You're very important. How many more are there here, from Hywilkin?"

"I..." she closes her huge black eyes. "Many. Many here, stolen from our homes. Children. But we are lost. Divided. No longer kin. They have sliced our bonds and ties. We live for the Dusk, now. The Great Source will belong to The Void, and we will be returned."

"Is that what your master told you?" I ask with a scowl. Her brow knits together. She curls her bony fists up under her chin. Across the room, the door latch clicks. Celli's coming back.

"He kept me safe," she cries. "Now he is dead, and I am nothing."

"Stay with me," I whisper hurriedly. "I have to go to Hywilkin, too. I'll protect you and I'll bring you home if you show me the way."

"Water," Celli barks. She drops the pitcher onto the desk with a loud clang. "Serve yourself."

She goes back to the door and leans against it. I eye her stance as I push myself to my feet and walk to the desk.

"I would have left already if I was going to," I say to her. "You don't have to guard me." I pour some water into a cup and sniff it. Smells fine. No magic. I take a sip. Seems all right.

"Master will be here in a moment. I won't have him disappointed in me," she sneers. Her eyes flick to the floor where she'd left Vae. "Where's the imp?" she asks.

I shrug and glance at the same spot. Vae is gone. My healed eye flicks around the room and spots her, surprisingly, just above my shoulder. Hidden away. When I think hard, I can feel her heat right at my earlobe.

"You scared her away, I guess," I say, covering for her.

"Good enough," Celli huffs. "Osven is mine now. He can't own anything. Especially not a filthy imp like her. If anything, she belongs to my master now."

I hear a low hiss and a pop beside my head, and I reach up to scratch my neck. I stick my little finger out, like an offering to the imp. To my surprise, she takes it. Her hands are like tiny searing irons, but I try not to flinch.

Beside Celli, the air wavers and shifts. I see the outline of Osven for just a moment before he fades from view. I wonder if Vae did, too. If she did, she's not reacting.

I sip my water and wait for Quenson, all the while thinking about what I've gotten myself into. Tricking my way into a keep full of Sorcerers is one thing. Sneaking around, befriending dusk imps was not part of my plan. How can I know she's to be trusted? What if she was planted here for me to find? What if the whole thing was a setup? The more I think about it, the more I realize my mistake. Maybe I shouldn't have talked to her at all. Maybe I should have let Celli kill her.

The door swings open, interrupting my thoughts. Quenson simply looks at Celli and she falls into place behind him. In his presence, Vae ducks behind me. I feel her fingers weave into the straps of my bandolier. She tucks herself safely to my back. The heat of her charcoal body feels like it'll burn through my shirt.

"You are fortunate, Tibreseli," Quenson says with a velvety tone. "My associates have agreed to see you. It isn't every day that a guest from outside is welcomed so eagerly. I hope you will show them your gratitude by offering, at the very least, your respect."

He ushers me out the door and walks beside me in the passage. Celli trails behind us both.

"You see," Quenson says in hushed tones, "the True Dusk is quite startling at first meeting. Such power, you will not encounter again in your lifetime. Some call it The Void, and it is a true and mighty wonder to behold."

"Why does he want to see me?" I ask with a smirk. If this Void is so powerful, I don't see where I fit into the picture.

"They, Tibreseli," Quenson says, and pauses. He turns. His eyes bore into me. "They. They are all the darkness, all the pain, all the fear and hatred ever mustered. Dusk is too weak a word for them, Tibreseli, for the power they hold is unending. Infinite. Omnipotent."

I don't say anything. Somehow, his words don't bother me. If this Void is so powerful, why does it need to hide away? Why does it care that I even exist? If it's so omnipotent, why doesn't it already hold Brindelier? Why does it need a simple boy like me to find it?

After an endless journey through winding passages, we finally reach a set of iron doors two stories high. All sorts of runes are molded into them. Runes and scenes that are horrible to look at. Meant to scare. To intimidate. They just make me shake my head. It's like they're trying too hard to make sure everyone here knows how wicked they are. I find it a little amusing, more than anything.

Clinging to the back of my bandolier, Vae trembles. I want to tell her to wait here, but I don't have a way to do it without the others hearing. Sometimes I wish I could push my thoughts, like Azi and Rian do. I only ever could accept them from Mevyn. Even if I could, though, I wouldn't trust her enough for that, yet.

The doors swing open and Quenson gestures for me to go in. He's staying outside. Celli is, too. So is Vae, apparently. I know why as soon as I step in. The power of magic in here is so overwhelming it feels like a hammer to my chest. If it's this strong to me, I can't imagine what it must be like for anyone else. I go in. As soon as I step over the threshold, the power abruptly ends.

The doors creak closed with a thundering boom. Inside, it's black as pitch. There's nothing. No one. I stand in silence, searching the darkness with my healed eye. Trying to see something. Anything. Anyone. There's no magic here. No power. It's just as Quenson said. A void. *The* Void.

Time passes. How much time, I don't know. I call out, but no one answers. I start to pace along the metal wall, measuring the room with my footsteps. There is nothing here. Nothing. No one. No sound. No sense. I count a hundred paces along the wall and still no corner. No turn. I count a hundred more. This place is vast. Unending. Empty of everything, even light. Even me. Three hundred paces. Four.

In the darkness, with the rhythm of my footsteps, I start to question myself. What purpose do I have here? Why did I bother coming? I start to think it must be some powerful spell, shifting my thoughts, but how could it be? I can't be affected by magic. I'm the Dreamstalker. But what does that mean, really? I'm nothing. No one important. Six hundred paces. Seven.

I start to forget why I've come. I start to forget who I am. I remember something recent. A ruined fae. An imp. "I'm nothing," she said to me. "No one." I understand now. I am, too. I stop counting steps. Eventually, I stop walking.

"*Are you?*" asks a voice in my head. "*Keep walking.*"

Yes, keep walking. I do. I keep going, dragging my fingertips along the wall. That one voice, that one question, lingers. *Are you?* Are you no one? No, I'm not. I'm someone. Important. I have a job to do. I have a plan. Nine hundred paces. One thousand.

"Will this room ever end?" I ask aloud.

"He speaks," comes the reply.

"All this time, yet he still speaks," says another.

The voices are high-pitched and low at the same time. Everywhere. Everything and nothing. They drown out my thoughts. Make me start to believe it again. That I'm not, after all, anything.

"Who's there?" I call out. Talking seems to help as much as counting my steps does. It keeps my mind busy. Shuts out the nothing. One-thousand two hundred forty paces.

"We are the Void," they say. "The True Dusk."

"True Dusk? No. There's still light at dusk. This place is completely dark," I reply, still walking. Still counting. One thousand six hundred paces.

I look up. Try to find the source of the voices. It's too dark. I look down to the floor. To the center. Something is there. Something larger than I would have expected. Not a creature. I can't make out limbs or a head with my healed eye. I can only see something in the nothing. Something indescribable. A fog. A cloud. Something vast and unfathomable. Something dark and eerie. The Void.

"Clever boy," the voices echo through me. Chills prickle my arms and shiver across the back of my neck. "We see you. You are nothing to us."

Their words try to affect me, but they can't. They lick at me and cower away, back to the Void.

"You can't control me. You can't have me and you never will," I growl and keep pacing. At the center of the void, I feel them gathering. More of them, whatever they are. Imps. Sorcerers. Minds. Single, terrible forces gathered into one.

"Resistant little pup," they say. Their voices weave in and out of space. Try to get into my head. I feel them testing me, looking for a weakness. For some way in. They won't find it. There isn't one. *Dreamstalker*, I think to myself. *The Untouched*.

My feet pause. I think back. This is the purpose of this place. To make you forget. To make you feel nothing. To mold you to their will. To convince you their thinking is the only way. I wonder if Celli was sent through here. If Errie or the other boys were.

I keep walking. Keep counting. The rhythm of my steps grounds me. Keeps me aware of myself. Why did they bring me here? What did they think to gain? They need the location of the archway. The entrance to Brindelier. They need my cooperation. Is that all, though? If I revealed it to them, what then? Would they want more? Is this it? This Void? Is this the driving force for the Sorcerers and the Dusk? If it was defeated, what then? Would the Dusk go on without it?

The questions make me pause in my step-counting. I turn to face the deep dark. The Void. My hand drifts to the knives at my chest. The vials. I think of Valenor, all that time ago. The shadows that held him. How I fought them. How I was the only one. How he told me the truth of it. The vials are nothing. The power is within me.

"What is he doing?" their whispers repeat and echo and pulse around me. I push away from the wall and step closer to center. The Void recedes. It fears me. I feel it. I take another step forward.

"He mustn't," the voices cry, eerie and drawn out. Ghostly. Wraith-like. Other-worldly. Hundreds of them. I imagine shadows like the ones that held Valenor, but all balled up together. Endless and eternal. How long can I fight them, I wonder, before I get tired? Before I have to rest? And what then?

My dagger slides easily from its sheath. It's odd they didn't take it this time. Maybe they believed me when I said I'd make a deal. Maybe they trusted me. They shouldn't have. I take another step toward the center. The shadows shrink further away.

"Are you afraid?" I ask them. "Afraid of the Slayer of Shadows? Afraid of the Dreamstalker?"

"We fear nothing," they hiss in whispers.

"Then why do you cower?" I ask.

The shadows swirl around me in a vortex. A cyclone of darkness that whips the air beside my face and rustles my hair. To me it's a soft breeze. They can't touch me. The thought gives me confidence. I lash out with my blade and slice at the force. A flash of light bursts from it, casting away the shadows. In that moment I see my adversaries.

Tendrils of gray-black. Cyclones spinning. Souls and spirits. Wicked minds collected and gathered in this place. They squeal and shrink away at my attack. I swing again and see again. The more I fight, the more they reveal. I see plans. People. Agents of Dusk. Inner workings. Feelings. Secrets.

Eron lies on a stone slab, stripped bare. His body is whole again, but he still looks dead. Errie plays happily on the floor beside him. Strands of energy drift between them, like pipe smoke in a sunbeam. A single Sorceress stands with them, watching. Guiding the energy.

The Void screeches in disbelief and frustration. It fights harder, but it can't touch me. It tries again to mold me to its will, but I'm immune. It tries to keep me from seeing, but I'm in too deep now.

Another vision, another plan. Agents of Dusk, lying in wait. Bonds and oaths to kill the king. To kill Margy. To weaken Cerion, their best competition for Brindelier. To end the peace of the kingdom. A dozen men, ready to take action. Waiting for the word.

A smaller plot. Dacva. Stolen away. Strapped down. A man with Marks of gold and black, tearing away at his thoughts. Ripping into his memories. Gleaning whatever useful information he can about the Elite.

More of the same. Men and women. Sorcerers, gathering and planning. Using children to blackmail and control. To feed anger and fear. Not just Griff and Mikken. More missing kids, from everywhere. Seeds of mistrust planted. Seeds of hatred for the throne. Plots against the Academy. Against the Elves. Against the Dawn. Destruction.

The more I see of them, the less intimidated I am. The more powerful I feel. They can't help but reveal these things to me. They can't stop me. Can't reach me. Can't break me. It infuriates them.

I strike out for Errie. For Griff and Mikken. Even for Celli, as gone as she is. I fight until they drive me back against the roughly molded metal. The doors swing open and I stumble backward through them. I lose my footing. My dagger flies away into the void. I fall to the floor at Quenson's feet.

"Kill him," the whispers of the Void drift eerily across the keep, mingled with the thunderous sound of slamming doors.

Quenson towers over me as I lie at his feet gasping for breath. He gazes down, his eyes narrowed. His fingers crackle with energy.

"Celli," he says.

Something grabs the cross of my bandolier. Yanks me to my feet.

Something hot. Too hot.

"Get up." Vae shouts and tugs me forward. "Run!"

I take off down the passage away from the doors. Into the twisting maze. A knife whizzes past my shoulder. Behind me, Celli screams in frustration. She throws two more. My feet pound the stone. Ahead of me, guards step out to block my way. I duck into the Half-Realm. The cobwebs brush my face. I run, hard. Weave between them. Dodge another knife. Just because they can't see me doesn't mean they can't hit me.

At my chest, Vae clings to me. Now that we're both in the Half-Realm, I can see her. Her wings are still broken, but somehow she's helping propel me forward.

"The dais," I say to her, breathing hard. "The room with the pedestals. Do you know where it is?"

"This way," she tugs me down a side hall. Something behind me shifts. A spirit. A ghost. Osven. I curse under my breath. Behind me, Celli's footsteps near. I push my legs until my calves burn. Dodge around guards who can't see me.

Vae guides me until I can see it ahead. The closed door. The one. I can feel it. The wards. The spells. The forces in place to keep everyone out. Beyond that, the offerings, glowing like beacons. The door is guarded by half a dozen sentries. When I get nearer, they turn in unison. Stomp their feet, just once. Look right at me. Inside their helms, their eyes are black and empty.

I feel it on them. Smell it. Death. Necromancy. Bones, animated. Dark, wicked magic. They raise their swords. March toward me. Behind me, Celli's footsteps skid to a stop.

"They can see you, Tib," she says. "Step out of hiding so I can watch you die."

"Keep running," Vae whispers. "Run through them."

I look past the approaching six. Into the dais room with my healed eye. It's empty, save for the bottles. No one is in there. I just need to get past these sentries and through the door. All I have are knives, though. Small ones. Knives that wouldn't do much damage to animated bones.

"Just run," Vae screams, and I take a deep breath and decide to trust her. If she wanted me defeated, she wouldn't have helped me up to begin with. I crash through the sentries who swing their weapons wildly. One of them has a club. I tear it from his grip and swing it hard, catching two of them with the brunt of my attack. Two arms fly off at me with surprising strength and spin across the floor.

My attack doesn't scare the others. They're mindless. Thoughtless. At my chest, Vae burns. She spits a ball of fire that catches one right in its empty eye. The sentry stumbles mid-swing and catches its partner. Bones clatter against stone. A tapestry nearby catches the spark and bursts into flame.

"Go," Vae yelps, and I crash through the remaining two with my club and bash the door in.

The door itself is weaker than I expected. I guess they figured the wards were strong enough to keep people out. They didn't need to have heavy doors or locks. Whatever the reason, I'm grateful. I race toward the pillars bearing the bottles.

Outside, I hear them. An army. A mass of men, encroaching. I close my hand around a bottle. The spell protecting it sparks and fizzles. I probably would have lost my hand if I'd been anyone else, but all I feel is a slight tingle.

I whirl toward the door. My healed eye searches the corridor outside as I run toward the next pillar. Outside, scores of guards march on us. Quenson lifts the wards. The men charge through, weapons raised. I have no time to reach the second pillar. No way out, except… I look at the space between two pillars. A towering window of colored glass. I glance over my shoulder as the guards spill inside. Turn back to the window. Throw the club. Hard.

The window smashes and I dive through it and start to plummet. I gather Vae and the bottle to my chest.

"Valenor," I scream as I tumble from the parapet. "Mevyn!"

Chapter Thirty-Eight
DUSK ENCROACHING

Azi

The sun hangs low in the sky, casting deep shadows across the throngs of people who have come to hear the king's speech. I scan them with a smile, noting how very many of them bear the Princess's Light. The Elite line the balcony beside me, waiting for His Majesty to make his appearance. Rian stands so close our shoulders touch. Shush hovers beside him, in plain sight of the crowd. Flitt's here, too, tucked into her place at my pauldron. Her prisms of light dance across the stone facade of the palace in brightly-colored rainbows.

Saesa stands on my other side, and out of the corner of my eye I catch her wiggle her fingers surreptitiously to the crowd. I follow her gaze to see the gathering of Ganvent children hopping up and down, waving up at us. Even Nessa is here. The only ones I don't see are Ruben and Raefe.

The sense of anticipation mixed with the flying of colorful banners gives the gathering an air of excitement. It feels like Cerion day, the festival we were forced to abandon in the middle of Eron's trials. Cerion is merry again, its people glad to have a reason to celebrate once more.

On the other side of the balcony, the elves stand regal as they look out over the crowd. They garner as much attention as we do, if not more. From time to time, garlands of flowers are thrown up over the railings, tied with bright ribbons of blue and gold and purple.

It was a long afternoon of discussion and planning, and by the end of it all of us left feeling uplifted and bolstered by each other's friendship.

A crier steps out onto the balcony, followed by a pair of trumpeters. They raise the long brass instruments to the sky and play a quick, bold fanfare. The crowd goes silent.

"His Majesty, King Tirnon Plethore," the crier shouts. "Her Highness, Queen Naelle Plethore, and Her Highness Princess Margary!"

The royal family emerges from within and the crowd erupts into cheers. More flowers are thrown, and Margy catches a nosegay tied with silver ribbon and waves her tiny, white-gloved hand. She holds it to Twig, who closes his eyes and sniffs their perfume with a smile.

"People of Cerion," His Majesty gestures toward the gathering, palms out in a peaceful stance. "I welcome you to the dawning of a new age for all of us. An age of renewed friendship and hope, and of rekindled alliances. Long have our ways been guided by agreements made in the distant past. Today, I stand before you to reassure you that these alliances still stand.

"My daughter," the king says, resting his hands on Margy's shoulders, "has been blessed with the Gift of the Fairies. The gift of Magic. Our allies to the far west assure me that this is more than permitted. It is welcome and encouraged. The Princess will guide us into a more meaningful alliance with the people of Kythshire, and open the doors of friendship wide, to promote a deeper understanding between our people and theirs.

"'To what end?', you might ask. I shall tell you as much as I know, for this a time for us to learn together, you and I. Cerion will grow stronger. Our stores will be plentiful, and word of our peace and prosperity will spread throughout the Known Lands. Our reach shall extend, and our territories shall grow.

"Between us, as you well know, the elves reside. They have ever been our allies, and they have come to show us their support in this rekindled friendship with Kythshire. They have agreed to tutor our princess in the ways of Ili'huvrie, the pairing between fairy and man. This practice is common in Ceras'lain, and beneficial to all.

"In time, you will find the presence of fairies, the people of Kythshire, commonplace in our kingdom and beyond. This is the beginning of an exciting time for all of us." His words cause an eruption of cheers, which slowly fade when he holds up his hand to speak again.

"As with all such agreements, there is give and take. The elves of Ceras'lain have asked for our aid in putting a stop to attacks upon their gates, and I have agreed to send troops to assist them. Any able-bodied citizen interested in rallying to the cause in my name and taking up arms can refer to postings at the palace gates which are being made as I speak to you."

"And now, one final word. To my daughter, the last of my children, who has grown from beloved child to the bud of a young woman," Tirnon looks to Margy and smiles warmly, and when the princess looks up to her father, she shows him the utmost affection and adoration. At her shoulder, Twig grins.

"You have shown your temperance, your strength, your sweet-natured kindness through every difficulty. You are a diligent and caring young woman, and your love of our kingdom and its people is plain to anyone who meets you. I can think of no one else I would trust as successor to my kingdom," he says with great tenderness, brushing a curl from her temple lovingly.

Everyone is so caught up in the sweet, perfect moment between king and princess, father and daughter, that no one notices the arrow until it's too late. It spikes through the air, aimed straight for the princess.

Thinking quickly, Twig lashes out with a vine that catches it by the shaft and tosses it away. Everything erupts into chaos. His Majesty steps between Margy and the crowd, shielding her as another arrow flies.

The Elite close in to protect them both, but not fast enough. This one meets its mark. As Tirnon straightens to usher Margy away, it strikes him square between the shoulderblades. The queen screams. Da raises his shield as another two arrows fly.

Somehow, they slip past his defenses. The sound as one of them plunges into his Majesty's neck is sickening. He crumples, and Bryse shields Margy from another torrent in one swift motion.

The elves leap from the balcony and dash across, chasing through the crowd. They disappear through the gates, obviously on someone's trail. Below, the people gathered scream and panic. Rian grabs my hand. We rush toward Margy as Bryse darts past with His Majesty in his arms.

"Paba!" Margy screams, and then her screams are silenced. Bryse's hulking form blocks the place where she stood. As he moves past, I hold my breath, expecting to see her lying on the stone, struck by arrows. But when I can see the spot again, she's gone. Disappeared.

"Princess!" I cry.

"*Twig*," Flitt pushes. That's all she needs to say. I understand. Twig took her. She's safe.

I run to the railing and look out, trying to spot the archers. The courtyard is chaos. People are running from one place to another, trampling each other, screaming. Guards and patrols are trying in vain to keep them calm and moving. Mum skids to a stop beside me. She closes her eyes, and I feel her push herself harder than she ever has before. I can see her peace spread out from her like a silver dome. It settles over the people in the courtyard, calming them. They slow themselves, help each other up, and walk calmly away through the gates.

"Wards should have been set!" Uncle Gaethon booms from inside. "Why were there no protections?"

"There were," someone replies. "The arrows broke through them."

"Impossible!" he shouts, and their argument is hushed by the healers.

"There," Rian points. Across the courtyard, up in the ramparts, a group of men are scuffling. Two of them have bows, and the other four are Royal Guards. Despite being outnumbered, the bowmen seem to have the upper hand. Two of the guards are stumbling around, the other two seem to be blinded. One of them crashes against the wall and plummets into the courtyard below.

"No!" Shush shouts, and at the last moment a gust of wind cushions the man's fall.

Rian grabs my arm and pulls me into the Half-Realm. I reach out for Saesa and take a firm hold of her wrist. We don't go far. I barely have time to catch my breath before we're standing across the courtyard, face to face with the two archers. Mercy is in my hands before I can think. I slash at the closest of the two. Crimson blood blooms across his chest and he falls.

Saesa takes the second one with Feat. She skillfully disarms him of his bow, and he slashes at her with his rapier. Beside me, Rian thrusts his hands forward. An arc of bright blue energy bursts forth from his hands and crashes into the second man, singeing his leather armor. He falls back, screaming.

"Sleep them!" one of the guards calls as he waves his hands in front of himself blindly. "They'll need to be questioned. Sleep them, and the Sorcerer, too!"

"Getting his wards," Rian shouts.

"I'll help!" Flitt shouts. She sends a beam of light into the shadows to reveal a crouched and blackened figure. He stretches a crooked finger out to us, and Rian doesn't give him time to do any more. His fingers crackle and flame loudly, and he shoots a powerful jet of fire mixed with lightning at the enemy.

With the archers down, I scramble past the blinded guards and raise my sword. I bring it down just as Rian's spell breaks the wards, and the Sorcerer cowers away. Rian casts his cloud of pink and the man slumps down the wall, sound asleep.

I spin on my heel and look at Rian, who's already turned to the archers to sleep them, too. Flitt helps the guards by pushing away the blindness spell, and they push themselves to their feet and start carting away the held prisoners. Rian's eyes meet mine.

"The king," he says. The two of us don't stop to think. I link my arm through Saesa's and Rian and I close our eyes and pop through the half-realm again, across the courtyard, into the doorway that leads to the balcony.

Queen Naelle kneels on the floor beside her husband. Mum kneels with her, holding her as she sobs. Four healers stand over them, Brother Donal among them. The arrows that struck His Majesty lie discarded at his side.

Mya plays her lute softy, her hands shaking. When she sees Rian and I step into view, her face pales further. She looks at the king and looks at us again, and shakes her head. Behind her, Da paces. Cort and Bryse stand guard at the door. Uncle is outside in the hallway, still shouting. Elliot leaves Mya's side and picks up an arrow. He sniffs the point of it and closes his eyes.

"Blackheart," he whispers, and Brother Donal looks up.

"Aye," the healer whispers and shakes his head.

"No," I choke, and drop to my knees beside Mum.

"*Blackheart?*" Flitt pushes. I can't reply. I'm too numb. Too shocked. His Majesty. Tirnon. Our friend. Our king. Our kind, just ruler.

"He can't," I whisper. Mum pulls me close with her free arm.

"*Blackheart,*" Rian pushes, "*is a poison, rare and deadly. Once in the bloodstream, it rushes straight to the heart. It turns it to stone.*"

The queen takes her husband's hand and kisses it tenderly, weeping. Beside her Mum bows her head as her own tears spill down her cheeks. She squeezes me tighter as the healers unleash every last bit of energy into their efforts.

Flitt pushes off from my shoulder and settles on His Majesty's chest. Her bright light sparkles over his brass buttons and splashes over his gray curls. She presses her tiny hands to his wound and screws her eyes shut tight. When all of her color is drained and there's nothing left, Shush lands beside her and gives her all of his own.

Still, His Majesty doesn't stir. The healing efforts are fruitless, even when the second wave of healers appears to relieve the exhausted first. The poison, as Rian said, is deadly.

"Flitt," I whisper around the lump in my throat, and reach to gather her up. White as snow, completely drained, she slumps over in my palms and closes her eyes.

"I'm sorry," she says. "I tried."

Slowly, the healers lower their hands. They turn slightly toward the queen and bow their heads mournfully.

"The king is dead," one of them declares. "Long live the princess."

"Long live Princess Margary," the others repeat. "Long live the queen."

"No," Queen Naelle whispers. She drapes herself across His Majesty's chest and gathers his vest in her hands and sobs his name over and over. Mum kneels beside her, offering what small comfort she can. Saesa leans against my arm. In my hands, Flitt takes a long, shuddering breath. I can't bear the scene any longer. Tears flood my vision and I close my eyes and let them spill over.

"Kythshire," I whisper, and the ground beneath me falls away. I feel Saesa cling to me as I go, and I'm grateful for her companionship.

The quiet chiming of Flitt's bauble trees and the colorful fronds of leaves dipping into the clear pool of her grotto soothe my grief immediately. I sink to my knees in the moss and hug her to my chest.

"*What do you need?*" I push to her. "*What can I do?*" If I keep my attention on Flitt, if I focus on helping her, then I don't have to think about what's happening in Cerion.

"*Twig,*" she pushes back, and the thought is enough to send the three of us spinning away again. Flitt shudders in my hands as I hold tight to her. "Ow, *wings,*" she sends, and I loosen my grip a little as we settle on a cushion of fallen leaves. They rustle and crunch beneath my feet, churning up the musty scent of damp earth.

Before us in a grove of stout oak trees, a domed bush of forsythia, wisteria, and morning glory blooms brightly with yellow, purple, and white blossoms. As we approach, the white blossoms seem to follow us, raising their fluted blooms to watch us come. The nearer we get, the more alert they seem, until I find myself standing before them and being, for no better way to describe it, sniffed by the delicate white trumpets. Saesa reaches a curious hand toward them, and one of them shies away while the other licks out with its stamen.

A collective whisper seems to hush through them, rustling their leaves like a breeze. Their sweet floral perfume drifts lazily over us. After a moment, the vines wind apart to reveal the inside of the bush. Twig is there to greet us, and he ushers us inside right away. The vines close and wind together as soon as we pass through them.

Inside is even more enchanting than the outside. The space seems as though it could be a child's secret hideout. The trunk of the bush winds through the center of the dirt-packed floor and creates a dome of branches just above my head which cascade to the ground. The pink light of sunset streaks between the variety of blossoms, dappling light of every color across the earth. At the far end of the cozy space, Margy sits in a chair of live branches, her knees hugged tightly to her chest, her chin resting on top of them.

As soon as she sees me, she gasps. Twig takes Flitt gently from my grasp and a tangle of green tendrils dips down from the ceiling to make a cozy hammock for her.

"Flitt?" Margy gasps and runs to her little hammock. Immediately she puts her hands over the broken, drained fairy, closes her eyes, and begins to pour her own energy into her.

"Careful now," Twig murmurs to her with an encouraging tone as he hovers at her shoulder. "Easy, not too quickly."

The princess guides her own energy: pink, purple, blue, yellow, orange, red, green, into Flitt. I watch in awe as Flitt grows more solid, as each ponytail bursts into color, as her skirts and skin and even her boots begin to sparkle with Flitt's own light again. Slowly, the fairy pushes herself up in the vines. She reaches out and cups the princess's fingertip to her cheek with two tiny hands.

"I'm so sorry," Flitt whispers, nuzzling Margy's fingertip to her soft cheek.

Margy looks up at me, her brown eyes so wide I could see the world in them if I let myself look.

"Paba?" she whispers.

Tears wet my cheeks as I bow my head and shake it mournfully. Margy pushes up from the dirt and launches herself into my arms. The light of sunset shifts from pink to lavender, cool and dim, and I stroke the princess's soft brown curls. I hold her safe and close and let her weep for the loss of her father until dusk blots out the light completely, leaving us in shadow.

Chapter Thirty-Nine
SUN GUZZLER

Tib

Falling. Plummeting. Salt air. Black sky. Sea spray. I close my eyes. I cling to Vae in my left hand and the bottle in my right. The glass is cool and smooth. I feel the magic in it. Pulsing. Vibrating, even now. "*North*", it sends to me over and over. "*Home. North. Haigh.*"

We tumble fast toward the sea. My stomach flips inside me.

"Valenor!" I scream again. "Mevyn!"

"*Let go of the Dusk fae,*" Mevyn's voice bursts into my mind. "*NOW!*"

"What? No! She saved me," I shout. Even as I do, Vae wriggles free from my grasp and I lose sight of her. "Vae!" I yell into the sting of sea spray, and suddenly I stop falling. Something catches me by my boot, just inches above the crashing waves. I bend and look up. Squint toward the dark sky. Mevyn is there, one hand grasping my foot. His other arm is raised to shield his face in the crook of his elbow from the spray.

He doesn't say anything. Just lets me hang there with the splash of every wave soaking the top of my head.

"What?" I grumble at him. "Aren't you going to put me down?"

"I will if you want me to," he teases, lowering me closer to the surf. "Why are you conspiring with the Dusk," he asks me, "after all I've done for you?"

"I am *not* Dusk," Vae's smoky voice rises above the rush of the sea from somewhere beside my hip. I look for her and find her struggling to hover there. Both broken wings are apparently still working. She winces as she flaps the right one harder than the left, struggling to keep steady in the sea wind. "Leave it to a southerner to assume such things."

"I don't know how I could be mistaken," Mevyn retorts. "Shall I count the ways I might have come to such a deduction? Living in the keep of the Circle of Spires? Thrall to a Sorcerer? Pit fae?"

"Don't you dare," she hisses at Mevyn, "call me pit fae, you sun guzzler!"

She darts toward him a little unsteadily, her fists clenched.

"Hey!" I shout. "Cut it out, you two! Mevyn, put me down!"

"That's twice you've ordered me to put you down, Tib," Mevyn huffs. "I'll do it, if you insist."

I glare up at him, then down into the inky swirl of waves. The sea is angry tonight. There could be sharp rocks. There could be sharks. Vae comes back to me. Clings to my belt. Mevyn hisses at her.

"Valenor!" I call again. I don't like Mevyn's terms or his attitude. I'm starting to realize why I hadn't really missed him until I'd almost forgotten him.

"He's busy," Mevyn drawls, like this whole business is boring him.

"Busy?" I sputter.

"Something about a ship," Mevyn replies.

I think of our agreement. Ruben. My invention.

"Can you take me to him?" I ask Mevyn. "Please?"

"Oh, now you're polite," Mevyn smirks. "I cannot. You know that, Tib. I can only travel between your tether and my Wellspring. That is my bond."

"Take me to Sunteri, then, I guess," I say. I don't really know how it'll help me to go there, but any place is better than here right now.

"Let go of that creature," he sneers in Vae's direction, "and I shall be glad to."

I look up at him. Beyond the toe of my boot I see them gathering at the parapets. Dark figures, cloaks flapping. Rows of sentries sweeping the rocks below the keep. Readying to chase, if they see us. A ray of light tints the waves beneath me sickly green. I see it quickly. A swirl of yellow just below the churning surface. Fins of turquoise. Two choices: Sunteri, without Vae, or the sea, with her. I look up at Mevyn.

"Drop me," I say as a flurry of arrows streaks past us.

"Are certain—?"

"DROP ME!" I shout. Mevyn lets go. I swipe my free hand to my belt to shelter Vae as I tumble. She wraps herself around my hand, and her tight grasp burns my fingers as she clings to me. I grip the bottle tightly in my other hand as we splash into the churning waves, and kick my feet hard to push myself back to the surface.

"Kaso Viro!" I scream, sending bubbles of my voice out into the dark water.

Something hits me, hard. Knocks the rest of my breath out of me before I can get to the top. It grabs my legs and speeds us through the deep. Yellow and turquoise fins. Kaso Viro. He heard me. My lungs burn. I'm out of air. I hug myself, tucking both the bottle and Vae close to me.

A yellow tendril flicks toward me as we speed through the depths of the sea. A trail of bubbles flows from it. It whips at my face and tickles my nose. Black pinpoints start to flood my vision. If I pass out, I'll let go of the bottle. I'll lose Vae. I need to breathe. I struggle against Kaso Viro's hold. The yellow tendril whips my face again. Vae climbs from my hand to my chest and clings to my bandolier as bubbles rush up my nose and it dawns on me. I grab the tendril and hold it to my mouth. Air rushes in and I cough and gasp for breath.

I don't know how long we travel. Not long, but long enough for me to wrap my head around things. We have two now. We can get two more, easily. They've got Errie, and I failed him again. Right now, Eron is taking his life from him. What will happen if they raise him? The Dusk is powerful. More than I thought. I was able to get free, but what if anyone else ended up in that keep? Azi, or Rian, or Margy? They wouldn't have a chance. The Void would destroy them. I wonder how far its reach is. How many people has it gotten already? How does The Void work, exactly?

We surface in the pool of Kaso Viro's tower. Loren stands at the edge and offers his master his robe again. He tries a drying spell on me as I climb the steps, dripping, and then shrugs apologetically when it doesn't work.

"Try it again," I say, shaking off the sea water. He does, and warm wind shivers over me, drying me and Vae completely. "Thanks."

"Tib has another," Kaso Viro says to Loren. "That means two. Three, if Kythshire is as willing as they say. The gates shall open for the Dawn soon. Ah, and he has brought a friend."

I raise the hand that Vae is still clinging to, and she scrambles up my arm to tuck herself at my shoulder.

"This is Vae," I say. "It's all right, Vae. These are my friends."

"How can you be sure?" she asks. "How can you say they're friends?"

"We're working together for the Dawn," I explain.

"So? Working together doesn't mean friends."

"Here," Kaso Viro reaches for her, but she shies away.

"Come, little one. Look at your poor wings. And the ocean did you further harm, I am afraid."

He lifts his hand with three fingers touching, pointing to the ceiling. A fountain of water trickles from his fingertips. He closes his eyes and the water starts to shift. It becomes red, like molten metal. Sparks of yellow crackle from it in sprays that seem to entice Vae very much. The flow of it slows. Globs of the molten stuff drip onto the damp floor and steam as they harden to stone.

Vae is drawn to it hungrily, but she's still unsure. I move a little closer and reach my hand nearer to his, and she slowly climbs down my arm to drink in the molten liquid like a hummingbird at nectar.

The glow of her veins seems to beam from her skin, red under black. Her wings straighten and fix themselves. They stretch out healthy and strong, lined with red and gold. Rays of flame burst from her stony bald head, creating a fiery line of hair from front to back.

"Wow, Vae," I whisper. "I didn't realize how sick you had been. You look so much better."

The little imp grins up at me and pats my hand, then pushes off to hover between me and Kaso Viro.

"Oshteveska furle drulevents. Kerevorna," she says to him.

"Oshteveska furle, jusktaviel," Kaso Viro bows to her.

"Friends, then," Vae says. "For now."

"You said that to me in Osven's room," I say. "What does it mean, that phrase? Those words?"

"She said," Kaso Viro explains, "'Fire burns within the mountain, Kerevorna.' And my reply was the proper one: 'May it burn forevermore.' It is an ancient greeting of the Under-folk. The dwellers within stone."

"Oh. Well, thank you," I say. "But now we need to get back to Cerion. Do you have a way there?"

"I do. I shall call to Rian via Aster," he says with a nod to Loren. Without a word, Loren rushes off upstairs, I imagine to greet Rian.

"Come and rest a moment, Tib," Kaso Viro offers. "Tell me what you have seen."

He leads me to an area that I hadn't noticed before, with drapes of velvet and mattresses and cushions. I settle into a green one. Vae sits on my knee as I describe the Void, the Keep, and Eron.

"You must show all that you have seen to Azaeli Hammerfel. This knowledge is essential to the cause, and shall be a great aid to the Champions of Light."

"Tib!" Rian's voice blends with his footsteps on the stone as he rushes into the room. Right away, his eyes go to the bottle still gripped in my hand. "You got another one."

"Two, Rian Eldinae. Two for the Dawn, now," Kaso Viro says

with a hint of pride. "It is my recommendation that you not keep them together in one place. We have seen the folly of that on the part of the Dusk."

"Right," Rian says. "Maybe you should keep that one here."

"I shan't," Kaso Viro replies matter-of-factly. "It would interfere with my work to have such power so close."

"We'll figure it out later, then," Rian says, turning to me. "We have to go quickly. Something terrible has happened."

"The fall of the king," Kaso Viro says. "I have seen it in the stars."

Rian doesn't say anything. He just looks at the Mage for a long time. Like he's really thinking about what he's said. Like he's trying to solve a puzzle.

"What?" I ask, finally breaking the silence.

"His Majesty was assassinated," Rian swallows hard. "Right at dusk."

"What?" I jump to my feet. "Margy. What about Margy? Is she safe?"

"She is," Rian says quietly. He and Kaso Viro exchange a strange look. Like my question confirmed something to the two of them. Mages and secrets. "I'll take you to her," he says.

"What about Vae?" I ask of the imp who has scooted up to my stomach since Rian arrived. His brow goes up and he looks from her to me.

"Do you trust her?" he asks me.

"Yeah," I reply. "We saved each other's lives."

Vae looks up at me and offers me a grateful smile.

"Perhaps," Kaso Viro interrupts cautiously, "she could remain and aid me here. I have many questions about the Dusk, and vast unanswered research regarding her home, the fire under the mountain."

"That might be best," Rian offers Vae an apologetic smile. "I trust Tib, and he trusts you, but I'm not sure it would be wise to bring a strange fae into another fae's territory."

"At home, such a breach would be punishable by death," Vae says, "no matter the reason."

"That settles it, then," Rian chuckles and ruffles the hair at the back of his head. "What about bringing an offering from one territory to another?" he asks Kaso Viro.

"That is permitted, so long as you keep a distance from their Wellspring and do not allow one to touch the other," Kaso Viro explains.

"Easy enough," Rian nods and gestures to me, and I hop up and grab hold of his sleeve. "Ready?" he asks.

I nod, and the cobwebs brush my face, and the floor drops away and we fall through the Half-Realm. The Dreaming calls to me while we travel. I see visions of a great ship, fashioned with my wings and bladders. Propellers spin and sputter. The ship lifts from the sea with a great rush of dripping water. Boys cheer. The sounds and images fade quickly.

We hit the ground hard and tumble right into a weird looking bush.

"Sorry," Rian murmurs after he rights himself. "I took that one a little too fast. Azi?" he calls softly, and the flowers on the bush bloom open and hiss at us.

"Rian?" Azi's whisper drifts from inside of the bush. "In here."

The branches open up and the flowers turn their faces toward the inside. There, Azi kneels beside Margy, who's sound asleep on a hammock of vines. Saesa is there, too, sleeping in her own hammock, and Flitt and Twig are snuggled together in a third. I shiver at the sight of it. Even though I know they're good vines, Twig's vines, it's still creepy to me. Margy wakes up when we go in. As soon as she sees me, the princess scrambles off of her hammock and throws her arms around me. She starts to cry and I look at Azi, who gives me an encouraging smile.

"Let's not wake the others," she whispers to Rian. "We can talk outside." She takes him by the hand and leads him away.

I don't say anything to Margy. My time in the Void and at the Keep has made me miss her too much for words. I had no idea how much I needed to see her, I'm just grateful that we're together, now. I let her cry with her head tucked into my chest. That feeling I got before, in her room, fills me up. Warm. Tingling. Fluttering.

I don't know how else to describe it. It's like a spell without being a spell. Like something I want. Something exciting, like a gift. Like Midwinter's Day. Like the moment I could finally breathe under the water. I want to protect her, to make her happy, to keep her close. She sighs and squeezes me harder, and I rest my cheek on the top of her head. Her hair is soft and silky. It smells like green leaves and sea salt. Holding her calms me. Helps me think more clearly.

"Margy," I whisper after her crying seems to have stopped. She pulls away just enough to look up at me. Her cheeks are stained with dirt and tears. Her wide eyes are rimmed with red. "We got two," I whisper to her. "We only need one more to open the gate."

She doesn't say anything. Just looks at me. Looks closely at my face. My cheeks burn. I think I should look away, but I don't. I can't. At first, I'm ashamed. Maybe it was insensitive. Maybe I shouldn't be talking about the offerings so soon after she lost her father.

"Can I see?" she whispers without looking away. I pull the bottle from my pouch and hold it between us. Its light spills over us both as she reaches to touch it. I hesitate, remembering the shock it sent through me in the keep, but it has no reaction as she puts her hand over it. That spell has been spent. Her fingers graze mine, warm and soft. "It's beautiful," she says. "Can you feel it?"

I look away from the bottle back to her, and it's like I'm seeing her for the first time. Not as Margy, my friend, but as the princess. The young woman who will be queen. One day, she'll be the most beautiful woman in the Known Lands. To me, she already is. I try to explain it to myself. Try to feel the magic or the spell that's making me think this way. There isn't one, though. She's not doing anything. Neither is the bottle. These are my own, true feelings. I try hard to make sense of them. Slowly, I nod.

"I do," I say quietly. "I've never felt anything like it."

"Stay with me," she whispers. "When I go back to Cerion, through the Rites of Vigil. Please? Stay with me."

"The Rites of Vigil?" I ask, and she hushes me and pulls me to the far side of the bush, away from the others who are still sleeping.

"In Cerion, the Rites last one day for each year of reign. Paba was in his twenty-sixth year. As his successor, it's my duty to keep vigil over his pyre for twenty-six days, to honor his reign. Mum will be there sometimes, and Sara toward the end, but I'm allowed to choose someone to stay with me. Someone who supports me. It would mean so much if it was you, Tib," she whispers tearfully.

"Twenty-six days?" I murmur in disbelief. I think about the Dusk, the offerings, the archway that only I can see. I think of the Sorcerers and the Void. They have one now. They need two more, and they need to be able to see where to go. It might take them that long to get what they need. But then, there's Eron. He'll be ready by then, for sure. I wouldn't be able to try to save Errie again. I'd have to sit and wait and do nothing and trust that Azi and Rian can do it without me.

"Tib?" Margy whispers, looking up at me again. She takes her hand away from the offering. "Never mind. I shouldn't have asked you that. It was selfish of me." She tries to move away, but I hold her closer.

"Of course I will," I whisper. "I'll stay with you, Princess."

"Margy," she whispers.

"Margy," I sigh into her brown curls.

Chapter Forty
KYTHSHIRE'S OFFERING

Azi

"The elves came back," Rian says quietly. "They caught three of them, but they swear there was a fourth. They said the one who got away was dressed in black, and had a patch over his right eye."

"That assassin from Maisie's house," I whisper. Rian nods. "So it was definitely the Dusk. What else?"

"His Majesty," Rian clears his throat, closes his eyes, and takes a deep breath. "They're readying him for the Rites. We need to get Her Highness back to Cerion."

I nod, and we stand in silence for a long time. A soft breeze whispers through the leaves of the forest. Fairy orbs drift past, just like any other night in Kythshire. Nothing has changed for them. For us, our world is collapsing. My mind is swirling with thoughts of what will happen to His Majesty's Elite now that His Majesty is gone. I can't fathom Cerion without Tirnon's steady hand to guide it. I can't shake the feeling that with his death, a golden age has ended. All of these thoughts were coursing through my mind when others went to bed, and they're the reason why I kept watch instead of trying to sleep.

Rian moves closer to me and takes me in his arms, and I rest my head on his chest and listen to his heartbeat.

"Tib got the second offering," Rian says softly. "We just need one more for entry."

"It's not the time," I start, but Rian stops me with a hand on my cheek.

"It is the time, Azi. If what's coming is as bad as they say, then we need to press on and secure Brindelier for Cerion. Because if the Dusk claims it first, there won't be a Cerion anymore." I know he's right.

"Where's Shush?" I ask, eager to change the subject. I already know the stakes, and I can't bear to dwell on them.

"He stayed in Cerion," Rian replies. "He's shown me a new skill. A link. It's weak now, but it'll be stronger when we become Ili'luvrie."

"When?" Not if?" I ask, surprised by his change of heart.

"Most likely it's a 'when', yeah," he sighs. "Anyway, this link is remarkable. If I focus on him, I can see through his eyes and hear through his ears. So it's like I'm in two places at once. Sort of like Da, when he's the fox. It's very useful, but has to be done with respect and caution."

"That's amazing," I whisper, and wonder why Flitt has never mentioned it to me. A bright blue orb drifts past. It pauses near my face and giggles softly.

"Hello," I say to it with a forced smile.

"*Hello, gold-face,*" it replies in my mind. "*Paladin.*"

Another orb, a yellow one, comes to bob beside it.

"*Champion of Light,*" it giggles.

I nod, "hello, little ones," I say softly. Their presence soothes me and entrances me. "Are you simply light, or are there little fairies in there?" I ask, raising my hand to cup it under the blue one. To my surprise it settles in my palm, soft as a puff of cotton. Within the blue glow, a sweet little face smiles up at me.

"*We are the wisps,*" she says. "*Messengers of the In-Between. Dreams and tales and song and poetry. Thoughts and cares. Wishes and comforts.*"

"*Messengers?*" I ask.

"*Messengers, oh, yes. Sometimes. And I bear a wish for you. Courage. Courage and clarity for the Champion of Light. For the Ambassador of Kythshire.*"

"*Thank you,*" I smile gently.

"*But there is more,*" the blue wisp dims slightly. "*A message: 'My trusted friend, Daughter of the Elite, watch over my daughter. Keep her safe. Keep your promise. Honor my reign by ensuring hers. Set her upon the throne.'*"

"Is that," I ask thickly around the lump in my throat, "is that from the king? From Tirnon?" I glance at Rian, but he's too engrossed in his own conversation with the yellow wisp to notice.

The blue wisp giggles again and lifts off from my palm to float beside its yellow companion. Together, they swirl away and shoot off toward the stars.

Rian and I tip our heads up to the sky to watch them go, and then he turns to me again with such a look of wonder that I can't help the chuckle that bubbles inside of me.

"I'd tell you how incredibly rare it is to be spoken to by a wisp," he shakes his head and scoffs with amusement, "but honestly, I think this sort of thing is starting to just be routine for us."

"What did yours say?" I ask.

"Have confidence," he says. "Have confidence before your masters. Be assertive. Advocate for the Princess. Open the gate.

Yours?"

I tell him what my wisp said, and he nods. "She's the key to all of this. We have to make sure this doesn't change her."

"She's been through so much," I say.

Beside us, the branches of Twig's home rustle softly, and Tib peers out at us.

"Azi?" he says. "I need to show you some things, and then we need to get Margy home before they start to think she's lost."

"Right," I say, and follow him back inside where the princess is sitting in a whispered conversation with Twig, and Saesa and Flitt are still sound asleep. We look for a place to sit, and tendrils from the walls spring forward to make seats for us. Tib looks at his seat with distaste and decides to stand rather than sit. He leans close to me, and the rush of magic beckons me. Here in Kythshire, it's even more powerful and enticing. It fills me to every pore of my skin. I fight it at first, remembering the archer, but shake my head and clear my thoughts to allow it. This time is different. This time I have permission, and it's necessary.

Tib shows me everything he's seen. The Keep, the floating island, the Sorcerers, Eron, the Void, Kaso Viro, he and Margy holding each other. The torrent of memories rushes over me, bombarding me with too much information, too fast. Tib's mind is quick and abrupt. He doesn't linger. He shows me exactly what I have to see, and then he cuts himself off so abruptly that my head spins and I cling to the vines of my chair to stop the room from tipping.

"Whoa," I whisper, and take a deep breath to calm my churning stomach and spinning head.

"Okay, let's go," Tib says to Rian.

"Azi?" Rian asks. I can't do much more than close my eyes and hold my hand up to show I'm all right.

"Oh! Sugar!" Flitt chirps from her hammock and darts across to me. She pulls some sticky cubes from her pouch and starts shoving them into my mouth like she did before we went to see the Fairy Queen. "You went too fast, Tib," she says to him. "Azi's not ready for that yet." She pats my cheek stickily as the sweets melt on my tongue, and I slowly start to feel better.

"It's fine," I smile, "but Tib is right. It's time to go back."

"Not yet for you, though, Azi," Flitt says quietly. "We have to pick something up first." She winks at me.

Rian gives me a kiss farewell that I'm sure I'll remember for weeks to come. All around us, the others ready themselves to leave. Finally, Tib clears his throat, obviously uncomfortable with our display.

"You have a—" Flitt starts.

"Mage stuck to my face, I know," I say as I gaze into Rian's loving eyes. "I don't mind it so much."

"If you see Ki," Tib says, "Can you tell her I'm sorry I missed her this time?"

"I will. I'm sure she'll understand," I say.

"Ready?" Tib asks. He reaches for Margy and they clasp hands.

"Ready," Rian says, reluctantly pulling away from me. He puts a hand on Margy's shoulder and she clings to Tib. Twig tucks himself into the crook of Margy's arm.

"Should I wake Saesa?" I ask of my squire, who is still sound asleep in her hammock.

"She can come with us," Flitt says merrily.

"See you soon, then," Rian gives me a winning smile before he fades away into the Half-Realm with the others in tow.

"Okay!" Flitt says cheerfully as soon as they're gone. "Here's what we have to do."

"Wait a moment, Flitt. Please," I hold up my hand and sink back into my vine chair.

"Are you all right?" she asks.

"I will be," I reply. "The sugar helped, but my head is still spinning. I need a little time to sort through everything Tib showed me."

"Can you show me what he showed you?" she asks. My stomach churns at the thought of more Mentalism, but I don't feel like I can deny Flitt after she almost gave her life to try and save the king. I press my fingertips to my pounding forehead and nod.

"Look," I say, and she comes closer and gazes into my eyes.

To my surprise, sharing this information with her is not at all draining. In fact, it helps me to sort through it all at a much slower pace and make sense of most of it. By the time I'm through, my headache is gone, my stomach has settled, and I feel much better.

"That's grave," Flitt says. "All of it. Scary. I told you it was something big. Worse than Jacek. But I never actually saw it. I never knew the details. I can't believe Tib did that. Wow. But, oh! We have two now!"

"We do," I say. I can't help but smile at Flitt. Back to her colorful self, she's absolutely adorable. My heart swells with love for her. I reach out my hand, and when she settles onto it I can tell the feeling is mutual.

"Lots has happened," she says. Her light dapples the canopy above us cheerfully.

"Mm," I nod my agreement. "Lots."

"Lots more is coming," she says with an air of excitement.

"Are you ready?" I ask her.

"Are you?" she winks.

"You can't answer a question with a question," I laugh.

"Ha! You're right!" she snickers and pushes off from my palm, and I watch with affection as she flies to Saesa and tickles her nose. "Hey, Squire," she chirps, and Saesa bolts upright.

"I'm here! I'm ready!" Saesa gasps and tumbles clumsily out of the hammock. Her sword is out in a flash, and she crouches as if ready for a fight.

"Jumpy!" Flitt squeaks. "Put that thing away. We're going on an adventure."

"What kind of adventure?" Saesa asks as she sheathes Feat. She comes to my side and checks my sword and armor over. Finding little out of place, she busies herself fussing with the drape of my cloak.

"To the Wellspring," Flitt grins.

"What?" I ask. "You mean, all of us?"

"That's right," she darts around excitedly. "To get the third offering. Are you ready?"

"I think so," I scowl thoughtfully, "but, will they even let us close to it? I thought we were forbidden. I thought you would have to collect it."

"Oh, no, silly! I can't. I'm not a Keeper. You have to present yourself, and you have to ask for it. If the Keepers find you worthy, then they'll give you access. All right?"

"All right," I sigh. These things are never as straightforward as one would expect. "So, what do we have to do, then?"

"Well," Flitt tucks herself into her spot at the crook of my neck. "we have to go on foot. You have to be guided to it. Feel it in your heart. If you can find it, then you're almost sure to be allowed to collect from it. Cross your fingers, and follow the Light."

Outside of Twig's strange home, the sky is just beginning to turn from black to lighter blue. A hint of the sun. A hint of dawn. The grass is wet with dew that clings to my boots as I begin to make my way. Saesa keeps close by my side, and Flitt stays quiet in the crook of my pauldron. The beauty of Kythshire surrounds us. Even in this dim light, it's easy to be enchanted by the trees and flowers and perfumes lining our path. Nestled between fronds of grass and fern, the ground glitters with scattered gems. My ginger steps make every effort not to disturb any sleeping fairies or other creatures as we walk, and I can tell that beside me, Saesa is just as aware of how destructive the two of us might be.

"Flitt," I whisper softly, "could you light our way, please?"

"Sorry, Azi," she replies. "I can't make it look like I helped you. I'm only here to watch."

"I understand," I say, and think about drawing my sword. Mercy's light could guide me, but I don't want to seem like a threat. Instead, I pause to close my eyes and search with my heart. I have never seen a map of Kythshire. I have no idea where Twig's bush is, or where Flitt's Grotto is, or The Ring, or The Crag, where Iren watches over the North. I've been to all of these places before, but I could always just think of them and close my eyes and appear there. This time, I have to center myself and listen. The forest is rich with life, even before the light of dawn. Birds are just beginning to sing, and crickets chirp sweetly. Nearby, a trickling stream babbles past.

I try to center myself in the moment and feel everything around me. The ground beneath my feet is soft grass and damp earth and roots. The earthy scent of the forest is sweet and familiar. It reminds me of my escapes with Rian in the Forest Park and the journey with my parents to escort Amei and Eron. Pleasant memories. I begin to walk again, this time keeping my eyes closed. A glimmer of a sunbeam flashes across the red insides of my eyelids like a beacon. I turn my face toward it and see the light clearly, but when I open my eyes again, it's just as dim as it had been. Still, I'm sure of what I saw. I pick my way carefully through the dewy grass and wildflowers and head straight in that direction. At my shoulder, Flitt snores softly.

We walk through the dawn into early morning and stop only briefly to drink from a gem-strewn brook. We pluck ripe summer strawberries from blooming vines along the bank and find they're the sweetest we've ever tasted. Saesa asks me about the evening before, and I tell her about Tib's visit. She tries to seem like she doesn't care that he didn't think to wake her and say hello, but I know her well enough to see her heartbreak. I decide it would be best not to tell her about how close he seemed to Margy in the memories he showed me. Something is developing between him and the princess, but it will pass. It has to. Margy is destined for Brindelier, for the twin prince in the story who lies in enchanted sleep, waiting for her. Tib knows it as well as any of us do. He's smart. It will occur to him eventually that he and the princess aren't meant to be. Maybe he'll realize he and Saesa are a better match. Either way, I decide to stay out of it.

We keep walking through the afternoon and into dusk. The stars come out one by one, shining down upon us, and still I follow the light behind my eyes which guides me, I'm sure, to the Wellspring. Saesa never complains or asks to rest. She is a diligent squire, quiet and true. Sometimes Flitt drifts behind us on our trek, and other times she rests at my shoulder. The path is winding and treacherous in places, up hills and down again. Parts of it are covered in glittering, sheer crystals of quartz which catch the light like Flitt's diamond, other parts have us wading through thick fields of fragrant blossoms. My armor, dew-soaked as it is, never seems to hinder me. In fact, at times I feel it's helping to guide and energize me.

Night is washed away by dawn, and dawn gives way to morning, and still we walk. The landscape of Kythshire is more beautiful than I ever could have dreamed. My journey heals my grief over the loss of the king and soothes my fears about the future of Cerion. With every step I feel closer to this place, more a part of it. I understand this is why I was meant to walk and not travel with my wishes, with my mind. So I could see the vast, true beauty of this land. So I could learn about it and appreciate it. Everything here is a wonder. Every knot on a tree tells a story. Every blade of grass is an honored inhabitant. And everywhere, the fairies linger. Some of them are bold and friendly and rush to greet us and sing to us as we pass. Others hide behind leaves and bark and peer with curious, wide eyes.

I lose count of the days as Saesa and I travel in silence. Time passes differently here, I've been told before by both Rian and Flitt. I never worry for what's happening in Cerion. I know this is where I'm meant to be now. This is my part in the song. I have the King's blessing. I do this to honor him.

Several days pass, possibly even a week before the Wellspring reveals itself to us. It happens suddenly, as Saesa and I pick our way down a steep embankment into a lush ravine of ferns and bright purple blossoms. I feel it before I see it: The promise of something sacred, something special. Treasure of the most valuable kind. Power beyond imagining. I stop at the base of the ravine and take a moment to sit on a cropping of pink quartz that pokes through the greenery. The pull of the Wellspring is strong and powerful, and I feel the need to wait and just allow myself to attune to it before I rush in. I remember what the wisp said about the king's wish for me to have clarity, and I wonder if this is why.

"We're close," I whisper to Saesa, who stands beside me with her hand on her sword. "No need for that," I nod to the pommel and she lets her hand fall.

"Won't you keep going?" Flitt asks.

"Not just yet," I reply. "I need a moment."

Though I feel right in my decision to wait, I realize quickly that sitting was a mistake. The exhaustion I've been ignoring over the past many days finally sinks in. I lean back against the stone, close my eyes, and drift to sleep for the first time after many days of travel.

Sometime later, a strange noise wakes me. It sounds like the rush of a wave, but more forceful. It's difficult to describe. A spark of golden light bursts through the trees only paces away and up into the sky. Saesa dozes beside me, and I shake her awake. Around us, everything shifts. The trees seem to glow with their own energy. The leaves sing perfect harmonies with the wind.

"What's happening?" Saesa whispers. "I feel amazing."

"So do I," I grin and shiver as my skin tingles with the palpable magic that hangs heavy around us. The air glitters with gold like dust in a sunbeam. I reach out and wave my hand through it, and a streak of blue trails behind my gloved hand like a wake behind a ship. In my mind and in the air around us, the low, sweet melody of fairy song rises, welcoming us.

"Go on," Flitt giggles and taps her tiny hands on my neck as if to push me forward.

We take only a few steps before the lush green leaves of the thicket parts to reveal the Wellspring bright as a pool of molten gold surrounded by a lush copse of forest. I pause as my heart quickens. Its shape is a perfect, measured circle lined with moss-covered stones that sparkle with dew. Fronds of fern and willow dip lazily into the edge of the sun-dappled pool. I step closer and feel the contented energy of these plants as they drink in the power of the spring. Its surface is still and smooth, like highly polished glass. This place is peace embodied. Peace and power in perfect balance. I remember the first time I came here with Rian. Our first visit was accidental and forbidden. That time, I could feel only its power and my need for it. This time, it's different. I understand what it is I'm seeing. I respect it. My desire to rush to the Wellspring, to touch it, is quelled by my need to maintain the serenity that seems to echo from every tree trunk, flower petal, and gold-splashed leaf.

Flitt pushes on my neck again, though, and so I take a few steps until the toes of my boots touch the mossy stones. The fairy song ebbs and flows on the soft breeze. We stand for I don't know how long. It doesn't matter. All that matters are the beauty of this place and the peace and joy it brings me to stand before it. My life could be happily wasted, just standing here.

The golden pool ripples at the center. A pair of glassy wing tips emerge, followed slowly by the point of a spear, then golden hair, then the smoothest, most perfect bronzed forehead, bright yellow eyes, high chiseled cheekbones, perfect lips, smooth, muscular shoulders. The fairy drifts closer through the pool until he is revealed completely. Dressed in burnished golden armor and bearing a spear of glass to match his wings, he stops only inches from me with the tips of his toes still dipping into the pool. This close, I can see that his golden skin bears the Mark of Mentalism, much the same way a Sorcerer eventually goes all blue-black with the Mark.

"Felicity Lumine Instacia Tenacity Teeming Elite Reformer," he speaks into our minds at the same time his powerful voice echoes from the trees. Behind him, a jet of magic streaks from the pool into the sky. "Flitter."

"Subtle Acumen Patyr Illumine Ethereal Naiad Crystal Everwatch." Flitt lifts from my shoulder and sinks into a mid-air bow before him. "Sapience."

"You disturb the Source with your presence," he scowls, looking down his nose at me. "Why have you brought these humans," he gestures to me and Saesa with distaste, "to this sacred place?"

"Sapience, surely in your great wisdom," Flitt offers a tentative smile, "you know who stands before you. This is my link. My human. Azaeli Hammerfel. The Temperate, Pure of Heart, Reviver of Iren, The Great Protector, Cerion's Ambassador to Kythshire, Knight of His Majesty's Elite, The Mentalist. The Paladin, Champion of Light. And with her is her squire, Saesa. And I haven't brought them. Azi found her own way. She has been tested many times over. Look and see for yourself."

Sapience raises his chin even further. His eyes drift lazily from me to Saesa, and back to Flitt. "Champion of Light, you say. Of course I know of whom you speak. Yes, I shall look. Tell her to move closer, and gaze into my eyes."

I look from Flitt to Sapience, confused as to why he seems to be talking to her and not me. "Of course. I'm happy to——"

"Sh!" Flitt hisses into my ear. "Do what he says, and for goodness sake, don't speak to him!"

"She is quiet lovely," Sapience utters as he moves even closer and his eyes lock to mine, "for a human."

His last words echo in my ears as he delves into my mind and I tumble, in turn, into his.

Chapter Forty-One
THE RITES

Tib

To the east of the castle, there's a narrow path which squeezes between the palace wall and the sea wall. It's always quiet there. Somber. Secluded. Abandoned. The path winds along the edge of the wall and passes under the arches of the aqueduct. Past it, there's a carved stone bridge. The river beneath it rushes past and plunges off the cliffs into the sea far below.

The king's litter leads us, carried by a dozen unarmed soldiers dressed in white. A mound of flowers and rushes are piled so thickly over him I can't even see the rich purple silk they wrapped him in this morning.

Behind them, Margy and the queen walk arm in arm. Both of them are dressed in white, too. No fancy beading or lace decorates their robes. This isn't the time to show off riches. Even their crowns are left behind. The ocean winds whip their loose hair around them as they walk.

If it wasn't for the wind, the heat of the late summer sun would be oppressive. As it is, I'm already sweating through the gauzy white fabric they made me wear. I'm an escort, they said, and everyone who walks at the head with the royal family must wear the same plain white robes they do.

The pace is painfully slow. One step, pause. Another step, pause. I walk just behind the princess. Beside me, behind the queen, is Anod Bental, High Master and Advisor to His Majesty. Behind us are the queen's ladies, then Princess Amei and her attendants. Behind them, His Majesty's Elite. The line which follows them goes on and on.

We cross the bridge and follow the dusty path upward over rough-cut stone. The Royal Army lines the ridge above. Watching. Guarding. A constant reminder of the danger threatening everyone the king left behind. Anger pushes against my grief. The queen lost her husband. The princess lost her father. The people lost their ruler. They shouldn't have to be vigilant. They shouldn't have to be afraid, but they are. The threat is real. They almost didn't hold these Rites. This time is critical.

Cerion is at its most vulnerable. If something happens to Margy or the queen, the only Plethores left will be Sarabel, married to a Sunteri prince, or Amei's boy, the son of a traitor who won't be fit to rule for fifteen years at least.

At the guards' feet, withering shrubs cling to cracks in the stone. Gripping the cliff side. Half-dead in their desperation to fight the sun and the wind and keep their place. Twig, who hasn't left the princess's side, sweeps a hand out toward a cluster of them. Their branches plump up. Broad, green leaves unfurl. Buds burst into color. Purple blossoms fall open and their perfume clings to the breeze. The green catches like fire across the rock face, from the king's litter back to Margy. Tendrils of green and purple rush along the cracks and burst into thick green shrubs of their own. It spreads along past the princess, past us and to the crowd behind.

The soldiers carrying the litter raise the king higher. Their pace picks up slightly. With every step they take, the bushes bloom beside them. Margy turns her face to Twig and smiles. The sun catches on the tears that roll down her cheeks.

The path winds for hundreds of paces until it reaches a gateway of stone pillars surrounded by a low wall. Inside, a circular slab of stone has been adorned with garlands and banners. A gap in the wall opens up to the cliff below. Beside it, the pyre waits, piled with driftwood. They bring the litter in slowly. Set it on the pyre. The procession stops. The queen goes in after the king, held steady by Master Anod. She kneels beside the pyre and bows her head. The wind whips through and sends rushes and flowers tumbling away into the sea. After a long, silent vigil, she reaches into her white robes and tucks a folded note into the driftwood. Then she stands, kisses the silks over the king's face, and nods to Master Anod. He offers his arm. She leans heavily on him and they step back from the pyre. They're careful not to turn their back on the king as he leads her to stand at a seat carved into the stone. Neither of them sits. Instead, they watch the princess

Margy waits for me to come to her side. When I step forward, she links her hand through my elbow. She hides her trembling by gripping my white sleeve in her fist. Together, we make the slow walk to the king. Even though I just want to hold her and comfort her, I stand two paces behind her as she goes to her father's side. Like I'm supposed to. Like I was instructed by the experts on royal etiquette. My stomach is tied up and twisted. For Margy's sake, I don't want to make a mistake. This is important to her. She loved her father so much.

She and I kneel at the same time, and beside me Twig sinks to the stone and kneels, too.

The princess's reflection is twice as long as the queen's was, and her part in the vigil is different. She nestles her own note into the driftwood and then stands. She reaches to the silk coverings and gently pulls them aside to reveal the king's gray face. According to the Royal Historians, this represents honesty. A sovereign must be open to his or her people. The face of the departed king must only be revealed by the heir to the throne. I understand, but all I see is Margy, my friend, looking into the face of her dead father for the last time. She's brave, though. Her hand barely shakes as she presses her fingertips to her lips and then grazes them across his cheek and into his beard.

The moment the princess turns away, she's the only one in the kingdom with her back to the king. Everyone, everywhere, sinks to their knees and bows to Margy. It's a mark of their agreement that she is the rightful successor. She takes a step toward me, and while everyone is still kneeling I lead her to the seat closest to the pyre. The queen is the first to stand, and the rest follow. The princess hugs her mother and takes her place. My place is between her and queen. A chair of my own is set back some from theirs. Chairs don't matter, though. None of us sits, anyway. The next part is the longest. The princess and the queen must receive everyone who comes to the pyre to pay their respects.

Princess Amei comes next. She follows the same steps we did. Kneels, tucks in her note, stands, comes to the Princess. They hug, and Amei looks just as sad as the rest of the family. She nods to her ladies behind her, and one of them offers a cushion for Margy's chair. Another one offers an ornate scarf from Stepstone. I can feel the magic sewn into each thread. Music. Strength. They move on and take their places.

This is the custom in Cerion. Not just for kings, but for anyone who dies. I've seen it before. Long lines of people wait silently. Patiently. Respectfully. There are no speeches. No words, except what's written on the notes each person brings. Everyone also brings a gift of comfort for the vigil. Blankets. Pillows. Food. Drink. Symbolic gifts. The strangest part of the custom, to me, is what happens next. The items are not just for the family of the dead. They become everyone's. Mya demonstrates it well. When she comes to hug Margy, she takes the scarf offered by Princess Amei's lady and drapes it over her arm. In its place, she offers her own lute. She kisses the neck of it, rests it against the arm of the queen's chair, and moves on.

Beside me, Margy sniffles softly. The rest of the Elite follow. They bring all sorts of things. Lisabella offers her formal, embroidered guild cloak. Benen spends almost as long as Margy did at the king's side until Lisabella urges him on. He doesn't tuck a note into the pyre. Instead he weeps as he leans the axe he used in the High Court against the driftwood. Elliot brings a strange-looking tree branch which he sets a safe distance from the unlit pyre. Gaethon and Rian weave a spell and create a canopy over the chairs. Bryse and Cort offer a respectable pile of gold. Brother Donal performs a whispered prayer of healing to the princess and the queen.

The king's advisors come next. They bring all sorts of things that seem to mean a lot to the queen. She and Margy inch closer together and hold hands. I edge away behind them and try to stay out of the way as the great circle slowly fills with people. They sit on benches facing the pyre and the sea. This is the Day of Silence. They'll keep vigil here until the fire is lit at midnight.

The entire time, I'm distracted by the safety of the princess. The space is well-fortified. It's the highest point of the cliffs past the city. Guards stand shoulder-to-shoulder around the outside of the low wall. Wards and shields and protections blanket the circle thickly. Some of them are ancient, while others are recently placed by the group of Mages just now taking their seats on the benches. Still, I feel on edge. Watchful. So many people coming in, getting so close to Margy. From up here I can see the line of them that stretches back over the waterfall and disappears past the palace, into the city. Hundreds of people, and each of them will get closer to the princess today than most of them ever will again in their lifetime. Many of them carry her light with them. I can see and feel it plainly. Her loving subjects. Mostly. There are definite pockets of shadow in the line.

The risk is inherent. That's what the Historians said. Vulnerability is part of the ceremony. Twenty-six days of it. At the end, she'll have proved she's worthy of the throne. Not just by her own strength, but by the dedication and generosity of the people in the line. Not just people who will be her subjects and allies. People who will oppose her. It's a proving ground for the kingdom. Cerion will stand together through the rites. If they make it through, they'll be stronger for it. Love and respect between subjects and royals will be tested, and will carry them through.

It makes sense, I guess. Considering how the king died, though, I think it's stupid to parade Margy around and put her on display. But I'm just a kid, and not even from Cerion. So I don't bother to argue. It's not like I'm going to change centuries of tradition with my one opinion. Instead, I keep my guard up. I watch every single person who steps through the pillars. Every one of them who kneels before the princess or offers her their hand for comfort. Nobles, Mages, and commoners alike.

The sun sinks low, and the line keeps coming. Nessa and the kids come through. It's strange to see her out of the house. She looks very out of place as she leaves a book for Margy. Uncomfortable. Her hands shake as she reaches for Raefe and he offers her his arm. The rest of the kids leave something of their own. Ruben looks at me like he really wants to tell me something, but he keeps the Silence and stays quiet. He rests a spyglass at the princess's feet. Lilen, surprisingly, leaves my bandolier with all its knives and vials. They all leave the vigil after that except for Lilen, who sits on alone on a bench to watch the line. Margy slides my bandolier along the stone with her foot until it's out of reach of the line and easy enough for me to grab. Having it there makes me feel a lot better.

It doesn't last long, though. The closer we get to Dusk, the more on edge I am. The more concerned I am for Margy. There's no rest for the princess. She's been on her feet since this morning. Even when the advisors gesture for her to sit, she refuses. I know why. She told me this morning before it started, that she intends to greet the last mourner just the same way she greeted the first one. On her feet. In honor of her father, who did the same when his father died. In honor of all of the kings and queens before her.

The line starts to dwindle past sunset. The darker it gets, the fewer mourners arrive. Eventually there are gaps in the groups long enough that she lets herself rest. Her stone-carved chair is so covered with pillows and cushions and draperies that she doesn't even bother trying to find it. She just sinks onto the pile of them and closes her eyes. The stars twinkle overhead. The moon reflects on the black ocean below. The elves swoop overhead on their cygnets at regular spans, as they have been all day.

At midnight, the Day of Silence is over. The torchbearers come and pass the flames to the queen and Margy and Amei. They light the pyre together. The escorts give them time, and then we go to collect them. Anod reaches for a lidded basket that Mouli left for her offering. I know what's inside. My stomach growls. We kneel side-by side and nibble the sweet rolls together. From time to time, someone comes from the benches to take a loaf of bread or a morsel left by another mourner and bring it back to share. Even though the Day of Silence is over now, nobody says anything. We're too exhausted. Too moved. Too sad. Margy leans against my shoulder and holds her half-eaten roll in her lap. The tears in her eyes reflect the firelight. Beside her, the queen watches the smoke billow into the sky.

Five days of honor come next, during which it's Margy's duty to stoke the fire. After that, it'll be left to smolder until the sea wind carries the last of the smoke away and all that's left is ash. Then the main part of the vigil will be over. People will start to go back to their lives. Back to normal. Visits, even from the Elite, will be sporadic. The queen herself will return to the palace to act as Regent until Margy takes the throne. Margy will stay for the entire Successor's Vigil. A few Mages and two score guards will, too, to keep watch.

With the pyre lit, many of the visitors leave. The benches at the far end of the circle almost clear out. Even half of the Elite go home. Margy and the queen lie back against the pillows and close their eyes to rest.

It stays like this for a couple of days. Mourners come, many from faraway places. Elespen and Stepstone and the far north. The queen goes home in the evenings to rest, but the princess stays watchful and reverent. She stays gracious and true to her father and her people. There is a quiet rhythm to the vigil. Guards change out every few hours. Mages from the Academy come and go, setting and resetting wards. People bring gifts and take gifts. We eat the food that's offered to us.

On the third night, I can't sleep. I watch the fire. It reminds me of the towers. Of Sunteri. Of my life before I came here, and my time since I arrived in Cerion. Something shifts in the wards. Subtle. Silent. Careful. Like the pulling of a thread, unraveling the weave. I keep myself from jumping up to investigate. Instead, I rest back against the cushions and close my eyes like I'm sleeping, too. Try to focus on where and who. It doesn't take much. There's more than one. Three. Dusk imps. Hidden in the darkness. Pulling strings. Unraveling protections. My healed eye searches behind my eyelid. One near the pillared gate. One hidden on the cliff side just below the pyre. The third—

My pulse quickens. Slowly, secretly, I reach for my bandolier. Rest my right hand over it. With my left I poke at Twig, who's nestled in a crumpled veil beside the princess. He wakes up. I know he feels it, too. There's no way he couldn't.

"*Shush*," Twig pushes. "*Rian. A breach. They're here.*"

His silent announcement makes the unraveling pause. Rian taps Gaethon. The two stand up. Gaethon gestures to the other Mages. They stand, too. I don't have time to watch and see what they're going to do, or even to fasten my bandolier on. I draw two knives. Turn to the third imp. The one just beyond the wards, right behind the wall. The one with his sights on Margy. She wakes up just in time to see me slip away, out of sight. I pause at the wards. Check them. If I walk through, I won't break them. They won't fail. Good. I do. I step through, a knife in each hand.

The imp hovers just above the wall. Right beside the wards. His greedy eyes search the space where I just came through. He can't see me, though. I'm hidden.

"Can't see you, no," he hisses, "but can feel you, Tibreseli Nullen. The one who stole from us. Who tricked us. You thought we were after the princess? No. Our quarrel is with you."

I don't answer. I keep still. Silent. Raise my knives. I'm close enough, now. Close enough to slash at him. To end him.

"Yes, I feel your thirst for blood. Your desire to end me. I feel it, boy. But, you will not. Look to the south. Turn your attentions there. You will feel it. You will see it. The Dusk, poised. Ready. Cerion will burn. Innocents will die. Unless…"

My fingers grip the handles of my knives until my knuckles go white. I bite my tongue. Wait for him to finish.

"Give us back what was stolen, Tibreseli. What we rightfully earned. Your thievery was underhanded. Your actions will mar your journey. Your future will be cursed."

I feel a strange sensation, like the wind over dust. Like light stretching out over the land at dawn. A star breaking through thick clouds. The flap of a cloak. Protection. Valenor. The imp cowers.

I turn to the south and close my eyes. He's right. I feel them. Slinking in hidden places. Gathering in shadows. The Dusk and the enemies of Cerion, waiting. Dark places beside the points of light. Ready to strike. I'm not sure what's happening. Am I awake? Am I dreaming? I look back into the circle. Rian and the other Mages are on their feet. Mending the weaknesses in the wards. Being watchful. Margy is standing. Her hands are folded in front of her. Her head is bowed.

A figure enters the pillars. Cloaked. Hooded.

"You have less time than you think," the imp hisses behind me as I watch the figure kneel at the pyre. Fingers graze the stone before it. Rake through the ash. The assembly watches with mild interest. No Sorcerer could enter this sacred, protected place. At night, no outsider is permitted. Only a native of Cerion can come through the wards unaffected. There's no danger, no threat from this figure. The historians had explained that some would take some small collection of ashes. This is normal. It's expected. I tell myself all of these things, but I don't believe any of it. I would know her anywhere.

With my healed eye, I look through the cover of the hood. I'm greeted with a conniving, wicked smile.

Chapter Forty-Two

SPED SUMMONING

Celli

I make sure he sees me, just like Quenson said. Make sure he knows I'm the one who slipped past their wards. Blood of Cerion, Quenson said. They'd never see me coming. My master was right. My master knows all. His perfect plan had no chance of failing. He is a mastermind. He is everything. Brilliant. Infallible. Perfect.

With the king's ashes tight in my grip, I back to the wall beside the pyre. Someone murmurs at the benches.

"Son of the Prince. Ash of the father. No. Get her! Stop her!" he shouts. Rian. That Mage from the boy's house. The one who almost stopped us.

Tib takes off toward me. Across the circle. Fast, but not fast enough.

"It's too late," I laugh and spring up. Over the wall. Over the cliff. I start to plummet to the sea, but they catch my arms and legs. The Imps. The Dusk. Our allies. They grab me and yank me through space. Back to the keep. Back home, to Quenson. I fall at his feet. His perfect, handsome feet.

My fist is clutched to my chest. I feel my heart beat through it. Pounding from the excitement of what just happened. From the thrill of being close to my master again. He takes my wrist and holds a jar beneath it. I open my hand and let the king's ashes slip through my fingers into it.

"Quickly," the imps say, and then they're gone.

"Time," Quenson says with a whisper of excitement that sends a shiver through me. "You have bought us time, my dear. Weeks, with this acquirement. Weeks that won't be spent waiting. Come."

We weave through passages lit by torchlight. This time when others pass my master, they pause. They bow. They show the respect he deserves. They know he's winning. They know they'd better stay in his good graces. They know they were fools before, to ever ignore him. To ever doubt him. Even though they respect him now, I still hate them. I'll still jump at the chance to snuff their lives out. For him. For

Quenson. My master. My love.

"He saw you?" he asks me as we walk.

"Yes, Master" I reply. "I made sure of it."

"Then it is only a matter of time before he comes to seek you out," he says with a hint of triumph. "Subtlety, my dear, will tip the scales."

"The Mage, my lord," I say quietly. "He knew. When I took the ashes, he knew why."

"Good," says Quenson. "Then they shall be on alert. A challenge is always welcome, my dear. Otherwise, victory is dull. Don't you agree?"

He pushes the door open and Sybel looks up from her vigil at the dais where Eron lies. Beside her on the floor is the boy I stole, covered in a blanket. Nearly spent. Quenson raises the jar and Sybel's eyes light up. She looks at my master with a hunger that makes my blood boil.

"Ash of the father," she whispers with passion.

"Wait outside, Celli," he says to me. Reluctantly, I obey.

Chapter Forty-Three
KNOWLEDGE OF THE WELLSPRING

Azi

A fairy's mind is a strange, beautiful place. Flitt's had been filled with light, color, and song. Sapience's is similar, though the light is all gold, and the song is a hundred voices in harmony. Light and dark, good and wicked, pain and pleasure. The Wellspring. Through it, I can reach everyone. I can see everyone. Every link to every Mage. Every trail of magical power. Every reverent thought, and every selfish black tendril.

My understanding of how it works comes slowly, like the blossom of a morning glory unfurling in the first rays of the morning sun. I see everywhere the magic is. I know. The fae, of course, are the most present. Their use of the Wellspring is natural and lighthearted. Everything they do is allowed and needed. The coloring of spring buds, the shape of a snowflake, the pulse of sap through the trees, the red and gold design of an autumn leaf. Kythshire thrives on their magic. It needs it in order to go on. But the magic of their Wellspring stretches further. It reaches out in flowing jets carried through the Half-Realm. It streams across the leagues of mountains and fields to its many masters. Mages of Cerion's Academy, who have linked their learning to it. Mages who were attuned the moment they received the Mentor's print. The mark of a student, given by a mentor. The golden press of a thumbprint against a forehead, opening the link.

So vast is the power lent by such a small pool, that I can barely grasp the depth of it. Dozens of Masters, Mentors, and pupils, all governed by the Academy. All touched by a mentor and entrusted with this power. This sharing of energy is governed by the fae. We were right to treat it so sacredly. Cerion has been respectful of the gifts bestowed upon us by the fairies of Kythshire. My heart swells with pride.

But then, as always, there is the darkness. Members of the Academy and others who no longer associate themselves with Cerion. They have little respect or consideration for the Source. They desire only power, and concern themselves with their own gain and nothing else. The gold in their minds and in their hearts twists and taints. It turns black and blue like bruises of the mind and of the spirit. It prints on their skin to Mark them as wicked, selfish, and dangerous. A way for them to be identified to the Good. To the valorous, who would put a stop to them. These Mages— no, Sorcerers— are abominations. They twist the natural to their bidding. They waste and pillage and taint the magic until it's something different. They squander the gift of the fae until it becomes unrecognizable and fiendish.

Though I can follow the jets to dozens of Mages and Sorcerers alike, there is an end to my sight. Only those whose schooling started in Cerion, by the golden touch of Kythshire's Wellspring, can be tracked. I understand there other sources out there. Other Wellsprings, though it's difficult to see or track them. They are only very weakly linked. One has no way of knowing how the other is fairing without years of training, concentration, and attunement. A trail flows to some central point, but it's blocked. It ends, and for me there is no way to get to it.

My skin prickles at the realization that things were not always this way. Before Brindelier was closed, they were all tightly linked. Magic flowed freely from one place to another. There was no danger of one spring running dry, as almost happened in Sunteri two years ago. Restoring Brindelier will open the flow again, and will ensure that all Wellsprings everywhere will thrive. This isn't just about Dawn versus Dusk. This is about preserving the Source of all magic, everywhere. If the Dusk, if the Sorcerers, were to gain Brindelier, it would devastate all Wellsprings, everywhere. The lure would be too strong. They would never restrain themselves. I understand now, why Sapience has allowed me to see this. It's not just about my promise to Margy. It's about the preservation of the Wellsprings across the Known Lands.

While I'm coming to this realization I can feel him in my mind, a distance away. Sapience. He is watching everything. Pulling apart my deepest, most secret memories. Learning all about me. It doesn't feel at all like an imposition. This knowledge is his right, and it's my duty to allow him to see it. He looks into my lineage, far into my family's past. He shows me things about my mother and grandmother, and hers before her. Things I never knew. They lived here, the women of my past. On Kythshire's soil. Like so many others of my kind did before the Sorcerer King, they lived in harmony with the fairies here. This land was for human and fae alike. I feel it more than I see it: A connection to these lands. A calling home. I knew it on some level the first time I came to Kythshire to fight the shadow cyclones. I think, looking back, that Mum has known it all along. This is our homeland. Eron knew it, too. That was why he was so focused on gaining my allegiance before it was certain how loyal I'd be to my guild and to Cerion. He wanted to use me to get to Kythshire. He wanted the blood of my fairy homeland that flowed through me. My birthright.

"But why?" I ask into the memories. *"Why focus on that now? Eron is gone."*

I know the answer, though. He isn't gone, really. He's about to be returned. Our rivalry, our battle, is not yet over. His hatred for me runs thick in his blood, just as my desire for peace and light runs through mine. Eron is cursed as I am blessed, and now that they've mixed that with the darkest kind of magic, he will stop at nothing to claim the throne he believes is his. With an army of Sorcerers behind him, there will be no mercy. Cerion is threatened. Kythshire is threatened. We need a champion as righteous as he is wicked, as caring as he is cruel, as light as he is dark. Without that, there is no hope.

"Step into the pool," Sapience's answer is a thousand voices speaking as one.

"What?" I ask in disbelief.

"Step into the pool," the voices urge again. It's Flitt's though, Flitt's single, tiny voice in my ear from her place at my shoulder that truly convinces me.

I see everything. The memories, the Wellsprings, the Mages and Sorcerers. Cerion, Kythshire, fairies and humans. Moss-covered pebbles and the tip of my stone-like boot as it touches the golden surface. The liquid is warm and soothing as it flows to my toes. I enter the depths of the pool and it swirls around me, welcoming me. There's no way to describe how wonderful it feels. No words would do it justice, except one. Love. As the golden waters swirl around me, I feel as though I'm cradled in complete peace. Everything is still, warm, and safe. My skin tingles with euphoria as if every part of me is being kissed and held and adored. I think of Rian and his love, and my insides fill up with the same golden, perfect light that surrounds me from outside.

I tip my head back and feel the warmth of the pool as it caresses every follicle. I let the liquid seep over my face until only the tip of my nose is above it and then, as it, too, sinks into the gold, I hold my breath and surrender myself to the generosity of the Wellspring.

CONSEQUENCES

Tib

Something catches me by my boot. Fast. enormous. Its strong grip clamps below my knee and pulls me back over the wall. Away from the sea. Away from my chase.

"Fool kid!" Bryse growls as he tips me right-side-up and sets me on my feet. "What're you thinking, jumping off the wall like that?"

"It was her," I pull away from his grip on my shoulder and rush back to look, but she's gone. There's nothing there. Just the ocean and the wind blowing ash into it. "Celli. She's in league with them. The Dusk. The Sorcerers."

"Tib," Margy's voice is cautious from across the circle. It's the first time she's spoken since the Day of Silence. My name is her first word in her time of mourning. Something about that bolsters me. Calms me. I return to her side, and Rian and Master Gaethon gather close to us.

"Your Highness," Gaethon says with some authority, "I must advise you, with all due respect to the king, to move from this place into the shelter of the palace."

Margy shakes her head.

"I will not dishonor my father or my people by leaving the Rites, Master Gaethon," she says firmly.

"Princess, please. You must understand—"

"I fully understand the risk, Master Mage," she raises her chin, "but I will remain. I won't require it of anyone else, though." She turns to the rest of the mourners gathered. "If any of you should choose to leave, I won't hold it against you. Go, and be safe."

About half of them look a little hesitant, but go their way. I'm not at all surprised to notice that everyone who does go doesn't carry the princess's gift of light.

"Your Highness, we did not wish to frighten you before, but now I fear I must tell you. Your brother's body, it was stolen—"

"I know," Margy replies calmly, but Gaethon doesn't seem to hear her.

"Since then, it has come to light that his remains are in the possession of Sorcerers—"

"I know," Margy says again, and still he doesn't hear.

"We fear their intentions are most foul, most reprehensible, Your Highness. We fear—"

"Master Gaethon," Margy declares much more firmly, and Gaethon finally seems to hear her. "I *know.*"

"You...but, how could you? Your father swore us to secrecy. He said we shouldn't speak a word of it. Not to you or your mother. Not until we could be sure."

"Dreams," Margy says simply. "Nightmares. Portents. Friends."

She gestures to Twig and raises a finger, and he perches on it and offers Gaethon an apologetic shrug. Margy looks up. Into the city. "He's coming," she says. "They're all coming."

"When?" Gaethon whispers.

Margy doesn't reply. Instead, she raises her other hand and points toward the path. In the city beyond far to the south near the gates, pillars of smoke billow into the sky.

"They're trying to lure me away," she says, pursing her lips. "They're ruining Paba's memory."

I look around the circle. There are several mourners still here. A dozen commoners and five Mages including Rian and Gaethon. There's also Bryse, Lisabella, Benen, Mya, Brother Donal, and two generals of the Royal Guard. Some are watching the conversation; others glance nervously toward the city. One of the generals exchanges a glance with Margy, nods, and runs off down the path. The other one, Kristan, I think, commands the guardsmen lining the wall to be ready. They seem to stand taller in the sea of Twig's plumped-up bushes and flowers. Rian and Gaethon move to the gateway and prepare themselves to stop anyone who might try to breach the pyre.

"Be brave," I whisper to the princess and rest a hand on her shoulder.

"Your bandolier," she says, and points to the place where I left it in the pile of pillows and silks. I shrug into it and fasten the clasp over my white robes. I feel strange without my leather vest and bracers. Unprotected. Margy gives me a nod of reassurance and looks back toward the smoke. Then, to my shock, she settles back onto the pillows and closes her eyes.

"Watch over me," she murmurs, and her breath slows.

"No," I say through my teeth, "you can't, Margy."

"Keep me safe," she whispers almost silently.

I see them streak away. The cat, with Twig clinging to her black and orange fur.

"No," I growl, but it's too late. Zeze slips between Rian and Gaethon. Out of the wards. Down the path. Over the wall and gone, into the chaos of the city. I watch until I can't see her anymore. My teeth are clenched so hard they might crack. I pace around her sleeping form. Mya is the only one who seems to notice the odd sight of the princess, sound asleep in the face of such a threat. It only takes her a moment. Her face drains of color. She rushes to us and takes me by the shoulders.

"Is she?" she hisses a whisper. I nod.

"Zeze," I say. "I couldn't stop her."

"Who else knows?" she asks. Her green eyes flash with concern. Behind them, I can tell her thoughts are racing.

"I don't know," I reply. "Azi. I think I showed her. And she showed Rian some things."

"It's reckless," she sinks to her knees beside the princess and gazes out into the city. She reaches out to touch the princess but hesitates.

"What if we wake her?" I ask.

"You can't. She can only wake up on her own, when Zeze comes back."

"We can't force her?"

"Oh, no, that would be catastrophic," she whispers. "It would split her in two, in a way. It could kill her if she's not prepared for it."

"What if someone out there..." I start, and swallow. "What if Zeze—?"

"If Zeze is killed, Margy won't survive," she says. "They're one and the same." Her voice is so shaken it jars me. Mya is always confident, even in the face of danger. Her voice is her weapon. If she can barely speak, she must really be scared. "I can't believe no one knew about this. You should have told someone. We have to get her to come back."

"How, though?" I feel the blood drain from my face. My fingers are tingling. My ears are ringing. I should have told someone. She's right. Someone who could have protected her. Or talked her out of traveling as Zeze. If something happens to her, it'll be my fault. If Zeze is killed, or captured—

"I have an idea," Mya interrupts my thoughts, but then she doesn't say anything else. Or do anything. She just closes her eyes and starts humming some strange song. Even though she's right next to me, the sound of fighting in the city below drowns her out. It's moving closer. Louder. Not a fight or a skirmish. This is a war.

The elves swoop past us on their cygnets. Their bows are readied as they stand in their saddles and order the great birds to charge. I want to run to the wall and look into the city. I want to see if it's as bad as it seems. I can't, though. I swore to keep Margy safe. So I sit, helpless. Watching. Waiting. Mya goes quiet. Her head is bowed. Her lips move, but no sound comes out.

A commotion at the gate grabs my attention. Elliot. He announces himself, then rushes to Mya. To the princess. He doesn't say anything. He doesn't need to. He drops into the pillows and closes his eyes. The fox bursts from his chest and tears away. Back down the path. Back into the fight.

"He'll find her," Mya whispers. "Their kind can always find each other."

She still looks worried. Actually she looks more worried, now that her husband is at risk, too. She smoothes his shaggy red hair away from his face and sits waiting. Patiently.

I can't be patient. I can't just sit and have faith. I pace around them both. I watch and listen. I scan and reach out and try to feel. The wards around us are strong. The protections are thick. Outside of them more imps hover, watching. Waiting. Looking for weaknesses. I concentrate toward the city with my healed eye, but it's impossible to make anything out. It's all light and dark, and flames and smoke. Flashes of magic burst and clash. Rian looks to Shush, who nods. In a blink, he vanishes. I have no idea why. What I do know is that now, there are no fairies up here with us. I wonder if that makes any difference. I wonder how long it'll take for the fight to get to us, and what kind of shape Cerion will be in at that point. They've been peaceful for so many years. Do they even know how to fight a war?

The line of Royal Guard encircling the pyre tells me yes, they do. So does the sight of Bryse, Lisabella, and Benen, who move to stand shoulder to shoulder and shield to shield at the gateway as Rian and Gaethon back off. Their wards are as strong as they're going to be. They're saving the rest of their energy for what's to come. The pathway leading here is winding and narrow. The procession could only go two at a time, except for the litter-bearers. That means only two at a time will be able to get to us without risking a fall down the cliff side or having to climb steep, rocky terrain. I wonder whether the place was planned that way. How many ascending kings and queens have been challenged on this slab by armies of their enemies?

I hear it before I see it. The whoosh of an arrow from the rocky hillside to the northwest. Mya jumps up, turns toward the sound, and lets loose a scream that makes me clap my hands over my ears. Just before it would have pierced through the wards, the arrow slows and tumbles to the ground.

"Two! About! Shields!" General Kristan commands, and every other guard turns to face the outside. All of them raise their shields and stand their ground. They're inside the wards, so they don't move forward without direct orders. If they did, some of the wards would break, but there are so many that it wouldn't make a difference to lose a few. Same with the arrow. It might have broken a ward, but there'd still be two dozen left up. It was a stupid move. Whoever shot it had to have known that.

I look toward the source. What I see makes my skin prickle with chills.

Men. Twenty at least, stationed over the rocky hillside, hidden in the darkness. Half have bows. The other half stand with their hands raised, ready to cast. Their ranks are bolstered by imps. Dozens of them. Wicked little specks of darkness sprinkled like empty stars. I feel their intentions. Kill. Destroy. End the princess. Claim Cerion. Steal back what was stolen.

"Yes," their voices mix together like the wind, low and brutal. "Tibreseli Nullen. Dreamstalker, Steward of the Last, Knifethrower, Bearer of the Guardian, Slayer of Shadows, Liberator of Valenor, The Untouched, Key to the Skies. Give back what was taken," they say all together. Men and imps alike, talking all at once in an eerie chorus. "Or we will ravage this land. Give that and more, and we shall leave you in peace."

Everything goes quiet, from within the circle to the battle on the city streets. Silent. Waiting. Waiting for me, for my answer. I step closer to Margy and raise my blades defensively. Everyone inside the wards stares at me. My heart pounds so hard I can hear my pulse in my ears. I want to rush out. Charge them. Feel my blades drive through them. I want to make them hurt. Make them suffer. Show them they won't win. They'll never win. My hatred for them drives me. I take a step forward. I don't care about the wards. I don't care about anything but watching them all die.

Mya breaks the silence, humming a soft melody. At first I brush it off, but then I realize what she's doing. I know I need what she's offering. I let her voice affect me. Let it soothe and calm me. Rian turns. Slowly, he crosses to me and puts a hand on my shoulder. His eyes meet mine in a silent plea.

"What say you, Nullen?" the voices call. One of them stands out more than the rest. He spits my name like dragon fire. Quenson. I look up into the darkness. Into the crowd of shadows.

"I don't bargain with SORCERERS!" I shout. My voice echoes through the wards and up across the rocky hillside. I imagine it carrying everywhere. Down the path. Past the palace. Into the city. Across the hills.

The elves swoop overhead. A shower of arrows rains down as they streak past. Two of the Dusk archers are hit and drop to their knees. I take a step backward. Away from the Dusk. Closer to Margy. Something brushes my ankles. Zeze. She slinks among the pillows in the Half-Realm and burrows into the silks covering Margy. The princess sits up slowly. Reaches for my hand. I take it and feel the charge of her touch as I pull her to her feet. When I look at her I expect to see fear. Sorrow. Instead, her lips are a thin-set line. Her nostrils flared. Her eyes fiery with anger. Rian, Mya, and I close around her, protecting her. The guards outside the low wall stand their ground.

"Say it again, thief. Whelp. Refuse us and be witness to the might of the Dusk," the voices thunder together. "Deny us and watch Cerion fall."

"What is they want, boy?" General Kristan scans the hillside with his hand on the hilt of his sword. "Surely whatever it is is not worth the lives of innocent people."

"My people have courage, Kristan," the princess says with confidence. "They have rallied and they hold their own, even now, with my aid. We will not give in to their demands. We shall stand against them, and we will triumph."

Her voice carries over the pyre and beyond. I hear it echoing through the city, like the Sorcerers' did. Loud. Clear. Confident.

"You can't have it!" I yell as loud as I can. "You'll never win this!"

"So be it," the Dusk growls in unison, and poise themselves to attack. Sorcerers raise their hands. Bowmen nock their arrows.

The elves soar over again and the arrows fly, but this time, the Sorcerers are ready for them. A streak of red light bursts from the fingertips of an unfamiliar Sorceress and strikes a cygnet. Five arrows shoot past. Three destroy her wards. Two strike her in the neck and she falls. The victory is short, though. A healer rushes to put his hands on her. She stands up again as the injured cygnet's feathers flutter to the ground around her. Quenson plucks one out of the air. He whispers something to it and the same cygnet cries out again and plummets to the sea. His allies laugh. Like it's a game. Like they're just passing the time, amusing themselves until I give them what they want.

"*It's time, Twig*," Rian pushes to the fae.

"*Go, quickly*," Twig replies. "*The Dawn is prepared. We'll defend this place and the princess.*"

"What?" I whisper under my breath as Rian makes a quick gesture and fades away into the Half-Realm. From there, he vanishes. I can't believe he'd leave us now, right in the middle of all of this, but there's no time to wonder why.

At Margy's shoulder, Twig spreads his arms wide. He closes his eyes and brings his hands together, then stretches them up to the sky. The flowering bushes at the Royal Guards' feet begin to grow. Their strong roots crack the rock beneath them as they thicken into twisted brambles speckled with enormous flower buds, like a giant hedge between us and the outside. It grows taller and taller and stretches along the circle until we're completely enclosed in a dome of thorny vines and white blooms as large as my head. Rather than disturb the wards, the hedge dome seems to strengthen them. The buds bloom open and cast beams of light across the gathering of Dusk so that everyone inside can see their numbers. Seventy, maybe a hundred. Including the guards between the low wall and the hedge, we have only half that.

Until the fairies begin to come. They emerge slowly at first from the glow of the blossoms. Hesitantly. Dressed in armor of bark and stone. Earth fairies. Twig's charges, and then Shush's, too. A soft breeze blows, and more come. Feathered and winged. Protected by carapaces and insect shells that catch the light in colorful reflections. They bear swords and spears and arrows. With them are golems of wind and wood and stone.

Quenson's eyes glint with amusement.

"You expect us to be surprised?" he huffs and shakes his head. "You expect us to be intimidated by the fluttering of Light and flowers? You are all fools. Look, now. Behold the might of the Void. The power of obscurity. Death and darkness. Emptiness. Betrayal."

Behind us, the fire pops and crackles. My heart sinks as I catch the glint of triumph in Quenson's eyes. He looks past us to the pyre. Ash of the father. Son of the prince. I feel him before I can even turn to look. His presence at the pyre is strong, dark, and cruel. I take Margy's shoulders and push her behind me. Slowly, I shift my feet to get a view of the king's remains.

At the center of the pyre, a dark form swirls. The figure inside of it is barely visible. Black against black, silhouetted by fire. A cyclone of shadows, with tendrils that lash out from it like whips. The energy of the cyclone is mixed. Light and dark. Innocent and tainted. It spins violently, but it doesn't disturb the ashes or flames of the pyre. It doesn't affect the king's remains as it moves toward us onto the stone. General Kristan spins to face it, raising his sword boldly. The rest of the Elite close in around him, ready to join the fight, but the cyclone doesn't advance. It swirls around the form inside it, revealing it slowly. Head of curls, crowned with flames of magic. Proud black doublet flecked with swirls of gold and silver like Mage Mark. A sword to rival any other sword, made of shadow and tendrils of darkness. The cyclone swirls at his shoulders like a cloak of blackest night. Like dark, cold churning ocean. Like the void. The embodiment of nothing.

His sneer is noble and haughty. Eyes filled with hunger. Eyes like hers. Like Margy's. Her brother's eyes.

General Kristan's sword tip trembles. He drops to his knees. He bows his head. His weapon clatters to the ground. At first I'm furious with his disloyalty to the princess, but then I see the truth. Eron's power is impossible for him to resist. It flows from him so forcefully that it's overwhelming, even to me.

"I come to claim my throne. My birthright," says the prince. Slowly, he turns to Margy and raises his sword. "Stand aside, Sister."

Chapter Forty-Five
KYTHSHIRE'S GIFT

Azi

All the joys of my life, all the wonderful moments that warmed my heart are collected in this instance. The calm love of my mother, the courage and strength of my father, the friendship of the Elite. Rian's passion, Flitt's bright cheerfulness. They cloak me and bolster me. They nurture me and prepare me. They encourage and reassure me. They fold around me like the wings of a mother bird. *Wings. Wings. Wings.*

Whispers of a wish course through me excitedly. Like Midwinter's Feast Day. Mouli's sweet rolls. Gifts from my family, given and received. Every happiness, every delight. Every promise of victory. Every swing of my sword in the name of honor and right. Defend the princess. Defend the light. Defend all that is good. Save Cerion.

The magic of the Wellspring gathers around me, forcing me upward and away. Out of the pool. Out of the copse of trees and into the sky. Flying. As I reach the clouds, I feel no fear. The sensation is exhilarating. Freedom, pure and perfect. Nothing can hold me. No one can stop me. I have the blessing of Kythshire and the power of light within me. It radiates from me like a beacon of elation. *Joy. Joy. Joy.*

My wish, my hope, my right. Everyone's right. To be free. To be happy. To be safe.

I soar over treetops and ocean, beaming with such glee that I can't help but laugh. The moon is bright silvery blue. It casts its glittering light across the dark water, and I spin and dance and shoot away from it, to the east. Toward my people and my home, to do what I was meant to do. Bring light, have courage. Save Cerion.

Flitt giggles at my ear suddenly. Her voice is bright and amused. "Whoa, Azi! Look at you!" she squeaks. It takes me a moment to realize who she is, and that she's talking to me. Azi. I was so bathed in the glow of the Wellspring, I had forgotten myself. I grin at her as the ground blurs beneath us.

"Where are you going?" she asks.

"Home," I say.

"But you can just go through the Half-Realm," she darts around me as I climb and dive.

"This way is better," I reply.

"Why is it better?" she dives for my pauldron and takes hold.

"It's my turn for a question, if we're playing," I grin.

"Oh," Flitt groans. "No, we're not playing. Just answer."

"Just answer!" I raise a brow at her. "Since when do you shirk the rules?"

"Ha! You asked a question. Since now. So, answer me. Why is this way better?"

"Because," I reply, "this way, I can bring hope."

I do a barrel roll and then spread my arms wide. Something bright catches my eye and I turn to look over my shoulder.

"Are those?" I gasp.

"Uh huh," Flitt giggles. "Wings. Not real, of course, and not permanent. But yours, for when you need them. For times like now. Dark times. Times when you need to inspire. Made of light and magic from the Wellspring."

The mountains streak past far below me and I push myself faster toward the east. Rian, my family; my need to see them and be held by them speeds me.

"I don't want to be a fairy, Flitt," I say to her. "I like being human."

"Ha!" Flitt laughs into my ear. "You can't be a fairy, you oaf! Don't be ridiculous."

"Good, because—Oh no!" I yelp, and Flitt squeaks. "Saesa! I left her there!"

"You scared me!" she shoves at my face with her little hands. "Don't do that!"

"Flitt!"

"All right," she grumbles. "You get to Cerion. I'll go back to Kythshire and bring Saesa to you. But be careful. Oh, and Azi?"

"Hm?"

"The offering is in your belt pouch. Don't lose it!"

"I won't lose it, Flitt," I laugh and twirl and push my wings faster.

"You say that, but you lost my diamond—"

"That was two years ago, and it wasn't my fault!"

"Just be careful. See you in Cerion." She pecks my cheek with her tiny lips and vanishes, but the tingling sensation left behind by her kiss remains. It warms my cheeks, fills my heart to bursting, and propels me even faster than the wind. It lingers even after the pillars of smoke over Cerion emerge in the distance, and it lights my way even as the overcast sky goes dark and blots out the stars. I think of Mercy and my sword leaps to my hands as I bolt forward unflinchingly.

What I saw in the pool and what Rian and Tib showed me in Kythshire me culminate in my mind. Memories, visions, and portents. This battle was foreseen by many. This is a war that must be fought in order to win Brindelier for the Light. I push harder and fly faster, unafraid. Unwavering. Prepared for the battle ahead. Determined to face the enemy and secure my princess's kingdom. Ready for the victory that already swells through me, waiting to be claimed.

I can see the pyre as I near, at the highest point of land past the palace. The orange glow of His Majesty's flames makes my breath catch in my throat. I realize what it means. I've been gone too long. I missed the Day of Silence. I missed the procession and the viewing. My heart races with sudden regret, but I push it away. I was doing what I had to do for the princess. For Cerion and the Dawn. I was doing my duty as a Champion of Light, and with the king's blessing, I remind myself. I was ensuring the safety of the princess by securing the offering.

My wings fold around me as I spiral downward toward the city and glide over rooftops. In the streets, the common folk have armed themselves with everything they can. They charge side by side with the King's army against sentries like the ones we battled in Kythshire. Skeletons, animated by necromancy. Mages in Academy robes stand with the defenders, aiming spells at Sorcerers who lurk in shadows. Two Mages, three Sorcerers. One of them is so hidden I can only see him by Mercy's light. I dive at him before he notices me, and the light of my blade skewers him before he has a chance to react. A dozen skeletons crumple as their master's spell ends with his life. The battle pauses as everyone stares up at me.

"Keep fighting," I shout, "for Cerion!" I glide away, leaving our fallen enemies behind, proud to see that even without me Cerion has the upper hand.

The same is true throughout the city: Mages, guards, and commoners fighting Sorcerers, imps, and skeletons. Not only those. There is another enemy. A flag I haven't seen in years. Orange and red, just like Tib said. Redemption and the banished they've rallied from the Outlands flood through the streets. Their attacks are ruthless and filled with hate, but those loyal to Cerion don't back down. They fight, and as I fly past I feel them bolstered by the light of my wings and my sword. Their cheers rise up and drown out the horrid war cries of the Dusk. Margy's gift of light glows from many of those fighting, and my own light melds with theirs and gives them strength. Every battle I pass through pauses for just a moment, just long enough to give my allies the upper hand and the opportunity to cut down their enemies.

I soar toward the palace along the line of the cliffs, watching for other small battles to aid, but I find this area strangely quiet.

"*Azi*," Shush's voice rings through my mind. "*In here*." I slow my flight and look around, trying to get a sense of where he is, and I'm surprised to find myself right outside of the Academy. Strangely, the place is completely abandoned. "*Quickly!*"

His urgency and the eerie silence of the building make me pause. I lower myself slowly to the cobbles and try to get a sense of what I'm hearing in my mind and what I'm seeing. Is it really Shush, or a Sorcerer's trick? A warning seems to flare out from the walls of the school, telling me to run away. Commanding me to leave. I take a step back.

"It's really me!" he shouts from a window far above, and his voice is carried on a harsh wind that threatens to push me back. "Fight through the wards, I need you!"

His words force a change in my perspective. Of course. Wards. That's why the place is abandoned, to protect it. The mention of them brings them to my attention. The Academy is always lightly warded against outsiders, but tonight its protections are so strong they seem to be staving off even its own students from entry.

With a quick look over my shoulder, I push off from the stones and dart through the open window where Shush hovers waiting for me. My heart sinks in disappointment when I realize he's alone. I thought for certain if he was here, Rian would be, too.

"He's up at the pyre," he whispers to me, obviously noting the disappointment in my eyes. "He's safe, but something's happened up there. Eron."

"Eron?" I growl and tighten my grip on Mercy's hilt as I spin toward the window again.

"Azi, no, not yet. We need to—"

"The princess?"

"She's up there too, but no! Azi!" he darts in front of me and shouts, and the wind of his breath pushes me back into the room. "Twig, Rian, and Tib are all there. They have help. Mya and your parents are up there. They can hold their own. They'll protect her. We have other business to tend to," his voice fades to a whisper again toward the last of his words.

"What other business could possibly be more important— oh," I gasp as the light of the vials catches my eye. "Are those…?"

The sight of the two vials floating in midair at the center of the room dazzles me so much that I can't even finish my thought. One bottle is ash gray, filled with rose-gold liquid. The second is blood red and shines with pure gold. Both are scrawled with runes of protection that seem to crackle and spit at me the closer I get to them.

"We have three," Shush whispers. "We can open the gate now."

"How? And by ourselves? So soon? And in the middle of an attack?" I stare at the vials, unable to tear my gaze away even when a loud thump nearby should have drawn my attention.

"Focus, Azi!" Flitt chirps. She darts in front of me and claps her hands in my face.

"Oh, my lady," Saesa breathes. I turn toward her to find my squire kneeling with her fist to her chest and her head bowed.

"Saesa? Why are you kneeling? Get up," I say with a scowl. When she does and she looks at me, I see myself reflected in her eyes. It's me, but changed. I'm radiant with light. The luminous wings gifted by the Wellspring drape my shoulders like soft feathers. I take a step closer and feel myself tumbling into her green eyes, wanting to see more.

"Azi!" Flitt snaps her fingers in my eye. "There's no time for that right now. Listen. We have the three, and they know it. They're all looking for you, and for the vials. We have to get to the gate and present the offering before they reach us. Listen! Azi!"

I blink my eyes repeatedly and shake my head.

"What's happening to me, Flitt? Saesa, please stand up," I say to my squire, who has sunk to her knees again in awe of me. "I don't like this."

"It's just an aftereffect from the Source," Shush explains. "It'll fade. But Flitt's right. We have to open the gate. Quickly."

"How?" I ask as I reach for Saesa to pull her to her feet. "How do we find it, to open it?"

"Easy," Rian's voice sends a thrill of tingles through me. "Look outside." I whirl to face him and find him kneeling two paces away, his head bowed.

"You, too?" I exclaim and rush to him. When I reach to take his arm, his fingers crackle at his chest. "Rian!" I say firmly. "For all that's good in this world, will you *please* get up?"

"What did you do, Azi?" he whispers. His fingers spark and pop again as I move closer. He doesn't shy away from my touch, but he doesn't throw his arms around me, either, like he usually would.

"She went for a little dip, that's all," Flitt laughs. "Rian and Saesa, you're being ridiculous. She's still Azi. I'm surprised, Rian. Usually you'd be stuck to her face by now."

As I place a hand on Rian's shoulder, a surge of power sparks between us at my touch. When I pull it away in surprise, my fingers glow with magic. I feel the exchange between us. I've given him strength; he's given me love. Just as it always has been, but this time it's tangible.

Rian gazes up at me, as if the gesture was permission for him to do so. Our eyes lock and my perspective shifts instantly to his. I see myself standing before him, a beacon of light in the dim room. I feel the awe he feels when he looks at me. I look completely different, and yet the same. My braid, as golden as it has ever been, has unraveled, leaving my hair free to float around my head as though I'm under water. My armor shines with a light of its own, blue as it always is, but dipped in gold so that the light that catches it doesn't know what color to portray. It's a shift and a shimmer that's difficult to pin down. I try to make sense of it, but I can't. It makes me want to look away, but I don't. Instead, my eyes find my sword, which beams with light so bright that it obscures my hand and my arm up to my shoulder. My face, even as curious as I am now, is stern and kind all at once, like a warrior ready to rush in and defend the innocent. Then there are the wings. Not my wings, no. I won't call them mine. They're too mystical, too magical, to foreign to who I am. Yet they fit me. They suit my personality and what I stand for, just as Flitt's iridescent ones do her, Twig's sticks do him, and Shush's dragonfly wings do him.

"All that," Rian's voice forces me back to my own mind again, my own perspective, "and they couldn't make you just a smidge taller?" he chuckles and pulls me into his arms, and as I rest my head on his chest, and suddenly it's the same as it always has been between us. Perfect, safe, and right. When he holds me, I'm just Azi again, a young woman with a fervent need to defend her people and to make things right. Azaeli Hammerfel, daughter of the Elite. Fiancée to Rian Eldinae, loyal to the throne of Cerion. Ambassador of Kythshire. Knight. Paladin.

He raises my chin with a charged fingertip and kisses me, and when our lips meet the charge sparks warm and powerful, coursing through us both at once. I'm overwhelmed by the two sensations, his and mine, which clash and meld together so perfectly and completely. Light so bright there are no words for it. Love so pure it takes my breath away.

Our kiss is not just a kiss. The magic it holds manifests between us as an orb of light, of all of the colors of Dawn. I see it in the minds of the others in the room who are watching, but I don't pull away from Rian. His lips are too soft and sweet, his arms around me and his fingers through my hair are all I ever need. The light hovers at my waist and beckons to the offering. The other two vials are drawn to it, and glide across the room to join with it. The third vial slips from the pouch at my waist and joins the others.

"That's enough, you two," Flitt giggles.

Her words are barely heard. Rian and I are too entwined. I slip back to myself and let the moment take me. Just us, just he and I, our kiss, our love, our bodies pressed together. His hands slide to my shoulders and then to my back, and despite my armor I feel them leaving trails of warmth and goosebumps in their wake.

"Okay, it's getting gross now," Flitt tugs my ear. When I reluctantly open my eyes, I see that she's got her feet on Rian's cheek and she's actively trying to push him away from me. "Honestly, you two. Nobody wants to see that. I mean, Azi, you just bathed and now you have Stinky Mage smell all over you again."

Shush chuckles through his nose, and Saesa, dutifully as ever, has suddenly found the door to the east quite interesting to look through.

"Well, anyway, that's done," Flitt huffs, looking a little jilted. "Azi, take the orb and let's go."

"What?" I whisper in confusion as I open my hands and the orb containing the three offerings drifts into them.

"Don't be thick, Azi," Flitt says with an air of impatience. "Light and love go hand in hand, just like darkness and hatred do. You two just fused the offerings with your love, to claim them for the Dawn. This way, even if the Dusk did get their hands on the three we have, they wouldn't be able to use them to open the gate. Not right away, anyway. They'd have to break the bonds apart and claim them as their own, first. It's like extra protection. And now that you can fly, we can get to the gateway outside easily. It's a good thing, too, because you can't get there through the Half-Realm. It has to be in person. So you couldn't have just wished yourself there like you usually do. But you knew that part already, I think. So, ready?"

I nod slowly, still slightly confused by everything that has happened but too aware of the urgency of the situation to ask for further explanation.

"This way," Rian says. He takes my hand and leads the way through the Academy, up stairs and down hallways until we reach the observatory where the ceiling is open to the night sky. Smoke from the king's pyre to the north drifts up to the stars. At the base of it is a glowing dome of scattered white lights, and inside of that the king's fire still burns.

"There," Rian whispers, and points into the distance over the sea. Hovering high overhead, the black form silhouetted by moonlight is disturbing to look at. It's a mass of land like the one Tib showed me in his memory of the Dusk's fortress, but not the same mass. The formations of broken earth beneath it are different from the one he showed me. The stone is milky white like the cliffs of Cerion, not black and shale-like as the other one was.

Shush calls out something in elvish, and the wind picks up and carries his words away.

"Azi," he whispers as he bobs at Rian's shoulder. "You'll have to go on your own. Rian and Saesa will follow by cygnet."

"When I get there, what happens? What do I do?" I ask. The orb in my hands makes my fingertips tingle and pulls away from me as if desperate to get to the arch.

"Not sure," Flitt replies. "But don't worry. I'll be with you and the others won't be far behind."

"They're trying to go," I say as my hands are pulled toward the sky.

"Let's go, then," Flitt says excitedly, and tucks herself into my pauldron.

Rian and I exchange another quick kiss and Saesa stands looking hopefully into the starry sky as I push off, soar out of the observatory, and speed to the archway. Despite the sounds of battle ringing throughout Cerion, I don't meet with any resistance on my way to the arch. In the distance, I see the cygnets approaching. Over my shoulder, I watch them land on the rim of the observatory and I'm comforted knowing that Rian and Saesa won't be far behind me.

The archway grows larger as I near. It's a small piece of land covered in grass, and the arch is of carved stone. As I soar around it to assess it, I see that there is nothing else to it. It seems like I could fly straight through the arch to the other side if I wanted to. It stands on its own, the width of two men, possibly, and as tall as three. The stone is white, like the cliffs of Cerion and the broken earth beneath the island. Otherwise, the piece of land is eerily empty and unremarkable. If it wasn't floating in the sky, I doubt it would attract interest from anyone at all.

"So are you just going to fly around it for the rest of the night, or are you going to land eventually?" Flitt asks, laughing.

"I'm just looking first," I reply.

"It's an archway on a floating piece of land, Azi," Flitt chuckles. "Not much else to see. You've already circled it about ten times. Can we go?"

"Have I?" I ask, confused at first. Then I think back and realize she's right. I've been circling and hesitating. With Flitt's encouragement, I take a deep breath and fly closer, then land lightly on the grassy threshold of the gateway.

As soon as my feet touch the ground, everything shifts. Cerion and the surrounding area disappear. The ground spreads out from this point, ending in the distance at a thick forest. A fortified wall stretches from either side of the gate, and through the opening of the arch I catch glimpses of a fantastically built city before two solid stone doors slam shut, blocking my view. The figure of a knight emerges from the air. His silvery armor glints blue in the moonlight showing off the impressive intricate designs of strange flora and beasts etched into it. His hands rest at chest-height on top of his great shield, and his eyes are piercing as he glares unflinchingly through the slit of his helm at me.

"What is your intention, Knight?" he demands. "What reason do you have to approach this, the Gate of Brindelier?"

I stare at him, wide-eyed and tongue-tied. *Why, indeed?* I wonder to myself. The orb in my hands glows brighter, but the knight doesn't seem to notice it.

"We've come to waken the city," Flitt says. "And to revive the Great Source."

"You bring the petty battles of your people to our doorstep," his eyes narrow menacingly. "What right do you have?"

"Quite so! How audacious!" A high-pitched voice squeaks from inside the knight's hood. When I squint, I can barely make out a tiny face scowling out at me from beside the barrel helm. The glint of a wing tells me this knight has a fairy companion of his own. "What right?" he squawks.

"A suitor for the prince," Flitt pipes up proudly. "A way to claim Brindelier for the Dawn."

"This one?" the knight huffs, eyeing me. "She is too old. Too much a warrior. Brindelier seeks a peaceful ruler. Not one such as her."

"Not her," Flitt scoffs and pushes me away, wrinkling her nose. "Her name is Margary Plethore, Princess of Cerion."

"We haven't heard of her. Go away!" the voice inside the hood yelps.

"A princess?" the knight muses. "Plethore, you say? The same Plethore who cast down the Sorcerer Diovicus at the beginning of the Age of Slumber?"

"A descendant of his. Yes, sir," I explain.

The Knight takes a slight step forward. When he does, he seems to finally notice the offering in my hand and asks, "What is your name, Lady Knight, and what is it you have there?"

"My name is Azaeli Hammerfel, Knight of His Majesty's Elite of Cerion. Cerion's Ambassador to Kythshire, The Temperate, Pure of Heart, Reviver of Iren, The Great Protector, The Mentalist, The Paladin."

"*Oh, Azi,*" Flitt pushes to me as she covers her face with one hand, obviously embarrassed.

"Well, well," squeaks the voice inside the helmet. "Talk about presumptuous. Cocky, too, that one. Who goes around spouting off titles like that, eh? What pride! Don't let her in, Gustaven. You'd better not!"

"I didn't mean to—" I start, but the Knight interrupts me.

"You may pass, with proper payment," he declares.

I raise the orb of offerings to him and he looks at it dubiously and asks, "What is that?"

"It's..." I scowl and glance at Flitt. "It's our offering. The Dawn's. I was told we were supposed to bring it. Three offerings from three Wellsprings, to open the gate."

"Oh, yes, of course," the Knight mumbles. "To pass through the gate, that is what you need. But first you must pass through me, and in order to do so, you must offer payment."

"What kind of payment?" Flitt asks, exasperated.

"A coin," the voice inside of the helmet chirps.

"Gold? I have a few gold, I think," I say, and reach to rummage through my belt pouch.

"Not gold," says the Knight. "The Coin of Sky. If you had one in your possession, you would certainly know it, and so I will assume you do not.

"We do," Rian calls out from behind me. I turn to see him, Saesa, and Shush rushing toward us. He pats his robes and slumps his shoulders. "Well, not in our possession, but we can certainly get one. Tib has it," he groans at me. "I gave it back to him."

"Then that is what you must do," the Knight says with a curt nod, "Harbinger of Dawn."

"Oh! Another title for her to spout! That should please her pride!" the fairy inside the hood cackles. "Yes, go and get the coin, silly ninnies. Can't believe you came so far without it! What a laugh!"

"Go quickly," says the Knight, "I pray you return before the Dusk arrives with the same intent as yours. Brindelier is a great, pure city. Its people are lively, kind, and wise. They do not wish to live in Darkness, but they will have no choice. We must bend to the will of whomever comes bearing that which is required to lift the spell and wake them all."

"I'll go," I say to the others. "Hold this." I hand the orb to Rian.

"Be careful," he says to me, and with Flitt on my shoulder I shoot up into the sky, toward the stars.

Chapter Forty-Six

REINFORCEMENTS

Celli

"There are three entrances to the Catacombs," Sybel tells me as we run through the Sea Market. Everything is destroyed. Stalls on fire, wares scattered over the cobbles, groups of men fighting groups of Sorcerers while wives huddle in windows, watching. The lifts are all up and unmanned. The docks are abandoned. Nobody's leaving the city tonight by sea. "One through the palace courtyard, one through the High Court. The third way in is via the docks. A passage used to supply the prison beneath the city."

She pauses in the middle of her explanation and flicks her wrist lazily toward a group of six approaching soldiers. Her skeletons, which have been following us, march past and bear down on the enemies. Sybel looks almost bored as she whispers a spell and claps her hands and a jet of red light sears from her fingers and crashes into the soldiers. Three of them fall without even a chance to scream in pain. The skeletons take the remaining three, and Sybel whispers her spell and blows a kiss, and all six defeated soldiers stand up again. They mill around, looking blankly ahead, until she speaks.

"Follow and protect," she says, and the risen soldiers fall into line behind the skeletons, ready to serve the Sorceress.

"Foul and false and wicked," Osven's voice echoes over us on the sea breeze. "Your ways will catch up to you, Sybel."

"Shut it, jealous," Sybel sneers. "Celli. As I was saying, there are two entrances." She starts to walk toward the High Court. "I will cause the guards within to come to the surface entrances and face my legion. You will go to the third at the cliff side and make your way through the tunnels. You know what your task is, correct?"

"I do, Mistress," I use the title with a hint of distaste. I know what she did with my master behind closed doors and I hate her for it. Still, she made me attractive to him all that time ago, and if not for her he might have overlooked me. So I show her respect, for now, but my loyalty will always be to him. My thoughts wander to him, and what he must be doing now. I wonder if he's thinking of me, too. Quenson.

Quenson. He is. I just know it. He's thinking about me even now. Wishing for me as I'm wishing for him.

"Celli!" Sybel snaps her fingers in my face. "Pay attention! If you fail, you will never see your master again. Do you understand?"

Her threat terrifies me so much that I gasp for breath. My vision starts to close in. I feel the panic rising in me, ready to take me over. Then, Sybel's hands are on my shoulders, shaking me.

"He still needs you," she says, and her reassurance calms me in an instant. "Go and do what you were sent for. Down the cliff, through the passages. Number twelve."

"I won't fail you, or him," I say to her, and as she leads her battalion away, I pull my hood up over my head to hide me away, and I slink down the long carved staircase to the sea.

The entrance isn't hard to find. A thick wooden door, locked with a heavy bar and three padlocks.

"Fools," Osven utters in my mind. *"Sending a girl to do the work of a thief."*

"A girl is as good as anyone," I mutter to him as I work the first lock with the pick Quenson gave me. Beneath the wooden boardwalk, waves crash. My hands are steady holding his gift. I would never dream of dropping it. To lose this pick would be to lose my master's trust.

The lock clicks open and I pull it off and toss it into the waves. Two more to go. The second one is just as easy. I discard it, same as the first. The third takes longer. I have to force it, and when it finally clicks, a thick green liquid oozes from the hole and seeps over my gloves. Right away, the leather starts to smoke and burn. I grab the lock and fling it away and pull off my gloves and toss them to the boardwalk.

"Oh, very impressive indeed," the ghostly Sorcerer says, his tone dripping with sarcasm.

"Osven," I whisper to him as I slide the bar from the door, "I swear if you say another word, I'll toss this bracelet onto those gloves and enjoy watching it get eaten away."

"You wouldn't dare," he hisses. "What would your master say?"

"I'd tell him how insolent you were being, and he'd agree with my decision," I reply as I slink into the dark, damp passage. I pause and think. Leaving my gloves behind is foolish. Leave no evidence, Master told me. There's magic that could be used to track me, to see things I've seen while wearing them. But I can't carry them when they're covered in acid. I glance at Osven's apparition. Master hasn't had time to give me much training in order to tap into the ghost's powers, but he did tell me this. I can command him. Whatever I tell him to do, he must obey.

"Osven," I say cautiously. "You know a way to restore those, don't you? Answer me."

"Yes," he replies reluctantly.

"Show me," I say.

It doesn't take long at all for me to pick up his knowledge, to draw it through me and use it as my own. I move my hands the way he knows how to; I speak words that are foreign to me. The rush of it feels like it'll lift me up off the ground. The power. The ecstasy. I watch the acid crackle away. Watch the gloves restore themselves. Then I call them back to me and my insides tingle with the most delicious feeling as they drift through the air and back into my hands.

The thrill is so intense that I have to lean back against the carved stone to catch my breath. My eyelids are heavy with pleasure. I can't help but smile as I pull my repaired gloves back over my fingers. My eyes slide to Osven, who seems quite a bit dimmer after my efforts.

"You oughtn't take it from me," he says through a pout. "I don't have much to begin with. Those fools, they nearly stripped me completely."

"What happens if I do, and use you all up?" I ask. He stays silent. "Answer me, Osven."

"Then you'll lose me until I can come back again."

"Where will you go?"

"The Void."

"For how long?"

"I don't know, girl. I haven't been yet, have I?" his scowl is implied. I hate his tone. If he was solid, I'd punch him for daring to take that tone with me. I'm supposed to be his superior.

"If you continue to speak to me that way, you'll find out, Osven," I sneer.

"You're wasting time, Celli," he says sternly, but I sense a hint of fear in him anyway.

"Don't say another word unless you're spoken to," I command, taking a page from Quenson's book.

Osven's right about wasting time, though, I know. I close the door and bar it behind me, then start up the slick steps toward the catacombs. Two hundred steps at least, before I reach the first passage. I know the way. I'm guided by a strange magic. I can feel the anticipation of it. The muffled sounds of battle in the distance rumble through the stone. I get a thrill every time I pass by a guard unseen, and there are several, but not as many as usual. Just like my Master anticipated, a lot of the guards have gone to join the battle. Why should they need to stay here, to guard a bunch of spell-slept criminals? Still, there are enough guards that it would have been a problem if I didn't have my cloak. Every time I pass one, I thank Sybel for her gift. Right, left, left, right. Twelve. Twelve. Look for twelve. Eight. Ten. Twelve.

Silently, I draw out my pick again. I slip it into the keyhole without a sound, until I hear the click. My hand rests on the latch and I pause and listen. Rhythmic breathing. Sleeping men. Some snoring. I push the door open slowly, slip in, and close it behind me. There are four cots here. Four sleeping criminals. Dub is the farthest from the door, in the right corner. I slip past the other cots and stand over him, watching him sleep.

The potion my master gave me will wake him with four drops. I pluck it from my belt pouch, unscrew the cap, and look down at Dub. He isn't so intimidating this way. Sound asleep. His eye patch is gone. Probably taken by guards before they brought him in there. I lean over him, curious, and push his eyelid open. What's behind it isn't as grisly as I thought it would be. Just an empty space. There isn't even a scar on his eyelids. I pull my hand away and wipe it on my vest. Then, just because I can, I search him and come up with a few gold, a tiny blade the guards apparently missed in a secret pocket of his vest, and a tattered folded up piece of parchment. I open it up. It's a drawing of a woman. She's dressed in chain mail, and her hood shades her eyes, but they're still piercing as they look at me from the page. She's formidable. I can tell just by that look. A fighter. A good one. I fold up the parchment, shove my spoils into my vest, and drip the drops into Dub's open mouth.

Nothing happens at first, then after a moment of waiting, he licks his lips and swallows and sits up. He gets his bearings quicker than I would have expected.

"You have the other potions?" he asks me without a hint of a greeting. I nod.

"Good," he says, rubbing his eyes. "How's it looking up there?"

"Like war," I say.

"Right. We have work to do," he says and pushes himself up from the cot a little stiffly. "These three were part of the plan, so you can wake them. Then we'll work our way through the rest of the cells, explaining as we go. Instant allies. I'll wake that one," he says, pointing to the cot across from him. "He's jumpy."

We wake the four and move on to the next. Most are willing to come with us and fight. The ones who aren't we let go anyway. Some of them look like they're interested in stopping us, but think better of it when they see our numbers. Pretty soon, we don't have to sneak around. We outnumber the guards. We overpower the Mages.

"Twenty-six," Dub mutters over and over as he searches doors frantically. Finally, he finds the number he was searching for.

"Go on ahead," he says to the group. Three of the men from his room look him over a little suspiciously. "You remember where the arms lock was, right? We'll wake this level and meet you there."

I look from the group to Dub, unsure. Splitting up wasn't part of the plan. Something is off.

"Decide quick," Dub says to me as he unlocks the door with a key from the ring he took off a fallen guard.

I look from the backs of the men I don't know to Dub. I hate him. He's awful. But I know him. I don't know them.

"Master said..." I whisper, confused.

"He told you we were supposed to work together, right?" he says to me.

"Yes, but that was before..." I look at the others again. The last of them disappears around the corner.

"Get inside. You can change your mind later," he says, and pulls me in and shuts the door. This room only has two prisoners: a woman asleep on a single cot, and a giant hulk of a man lying across three cots shoved together. I recognize the woman right away, even before Dub wakes her. She's the one in the drawing.

Something shifts in him as he crouches at her side. He becomes gentler. Tender, even. He strokes her cheek with his thumb. Brushes the hair away from her temple.

"Stone," he whispers. "I'm here."

He drips the potion into her mouth and her eyes flutter open. She gets her bearings, shoves herself to her feet, and punches Dub hard.

"I deserved that," he says as he rubs his chin and opens his mouth to test his jaw. "You always could throw a punch, woman. Ow."

"Damn right you deserved that," she growls, and I think she's going to punch him again when she lunges at him, but this time she throws her arms around him and starts kissing him in the same spot she just punched him. "How long has it been?" she whispers passionately.

"Three months, two days. I had to gain their trust."

"Did you get it?" she asks him.

"Did I get it?" he huffs in disbelief, and she whoops and kisses him again.

"Get Muster, Celli," Dub murmurs in between Stone's kisses and tosses his head toward the sleeping giant.

Still confused by the greeting between Dub and Stone, I cross to the larger man and drip the potion into his mouth. Nothing happens at first, so I use a few more drops. The huge man blinks sleepily, rolls over, and goes back to snoring.

"Muster!" Stone breaks away from her embrace with Dub just long enough to bark.

"Maybe I need to use more," I say.

"Nah, he's lazy," Dub chuckles. "Just give him a shove."

My heart races as I do what Dub suggests and nudge the man's enormous shoulder.

"Wake up," I say, "it's time to fight."

"Fight!" Muster leaps from the cots, sending them scattering. He looks at Dub and Stone, and then at me, panting. "Where?"

"Up in the city," I reply. "The Dusk has released you."

"Ducks? Fighting?" Muster scratches his head and yawns. "Where's my club?"

"Dusk," I say. "They've freed you so you can fight for them."

"What are they payin'?" he asks me.

"Freedom," I say.

"Well, I got that already, now, don't I?" he smirks.

"That's only one option," Dub says quietly. With Stone still close in his arms, he crosses to us and keeps his voice low. "Fight for them, or get ourselves out of here. Start fresh. Hywilkin, maybe."

"Home?" Muster says.

"What are you talking about, Dub?" I feel my nostrils flare with anger. My lips press into a tight line. I glare at him. "We're supposed to go fight. My master—"

"Master?" Stone asks, her brow raised all the way up under her fringe of brown bangs. She looks from me to Dub. Dub doesn't say anything. He looks at Muster and jerks his head toward the door, and Muster goes to stand in front of it.

"She's blood bound," Dub says to Stone after Muster is in position. "Sorc got her. But she's a fair brawler, and just a kid. We could pay to have someone wash it out of her."

"What?" I whisper. My ears are pounding with blood. Panic starts to rise again in my chest, constricting me. He's talking about Quenson. About me. He wants to take me from my master. Sever our bond. Break us. I spin on my heel. Toward the door. The door Muster is blocking. I don't care. I won't let them take me from him. I'll fight. I do. I launch myself at the giant. Punch his stony chest. Claw at him. Kick him. He just stands there. Eventually, he lifts me up by my collar until my feet lift off the floor. I swing a punch and he stretches his arm out until he's too far for me to reach with my fist, but I don't care. I still fight. Still struggle.

"You sure?" Muster says to Dub. "I could just crush her. Might be easier."

"No, you can't crush her, Muster," Dub says. "Save the crushing for the enemy. She's just a kid."

"I'm for it," Stone says. "Hywilkin."

"No!" I scream. "You can't! Master!" I can't breathe. My throat is closing. My vision is clouding. I fight. I kick. I punch. His name pulses over and over in my blood. Screaming for him. Aching for him. Quenson Quenson. "Quenson," I screech in desperation.

"Someone'll hear, Dub," Stone says.

"Knock her out," Dub says, and everything goes black.

Chapter Forty-Seven
SPARKS AND PEBBLES

Tib

All around the circle, they kneel against their will. They bow their heads to the dark prince. They lower their weapons.

"Stop this," Margy says beside me. "I see how false you are. You're nothing to me. An abomination of Necromancy. My brother is dead."

Her voice echoes beneath the canopy of vines and flowers. It pulses with hope and reassurance. Some of those who bowed stand up. The Elite. The General. The fairies and their golems.

"Think, Sister," Eron urges. "Think of what we could accomplish. Two heirs. Two suitors. Side by side. We could rule Brindelier. We could rule all of it. The Dusk is strong, but so is the Dawn. Your side has gained that which the Dusk could not, but look at our power, sister. See the might of the Dusk. We cannot even be stopped by death itself." Like Margy's and Quenson's voices before, Eron's echoes through the cliffs and out over the city. It pulses with power. I feel its sway. This is my fault, I think. My fault for not stopping them from getting Errie. My heart pounds hard against my chest.

Eron holds his empty hand before his eyes and looks at it like it's the most amazing thing he's ever seen. Then he looks at Margy imploringly.

"We had dreams together, you and I. Dreams of places and adventures bigger than Cerion. Imaginings. Musings. We could delve into them as we always wanted to. You and me, Margy. Sister."

"No," Margy squares her shoulders. "You're not him. Don't you dare take what he knew and use it that way."

"I'm giving you a chance to see reason. We could easily destroy you, little girl," he threatens. His eyes flash with malice. He takes a step closer. In his other hand, his sword leaves an inky trail of black in the air as it moves.

"You dare threaten the princess, the rightful heir of Cerion?" Kristan barks. He raises his sword, but looks unsure. I feel Eron's power stretching over him. Keeping him back. The tendrils of his cloak and sword stretch closer to the general, winding around his arm, his blade. *Wait*, they're saying. *Wait just a moment longer.* Kristan is powerless to fight the suggestion. His eyes go dark and blank.

My fingers tighten around the hilts of my daggers. All around us, everyone is poised. Even the fairies and their golems. Ready to charge. Holding their breaths. Unaware of the shadows snaking closer, winding around them. Unaware, or unable to do anything about it. I'm not sure. They don't even bother coming closer to me. They know who I am. Instead, one of them stretches close to Mya, who stands guard on Margy's other side.

"What good is it, to be the heir of a fallen city?" Eron huffs. "Cerion will die, Margary. It will fall like our weak father did, and nothing will remain but embers and dust."

"My people are strong. Cerion will not fall," Margy raises her chin, "and I will never stand beside you. Never."

"I'm through with all this talking," I mutter. I half expect her to stop me, but Margy doesn't. Instead, she gives me a slight nod. Her permission is all I need. I throw my daggers, one, then the other. *Knifethrower*, I think to myself, focusing on my titles as I let go of the hilts. *Slayer of Shadows.*

One knife slices through the tendril that has crept to Mya. The shadows shrink away with a hiss. The other one severs one around the General's wrist, but his other hand is held, and a third shadow covers his face.

"Guards!" Kristan barks. "Face center! Advance!"

They do as he commands. Turn to face us. March forward, advancing on Eron. As they approach, though, the shadows wind toward them. When they raise their weapons, they're aimed directly at Margy. The Elite and our fairy allies struggle to face the guards and protect the princess, but they're held, too. The shadows are everywhere. Eron laughs. So do the Sorcerers poised outside of the vines.

"See the power of Dusk, sister?" he chuckles. "By the command of our shadows, they would end you now. Just a word is all it would take."

"It isn't too late, Nullen," Quenson calls from outside of the vines. "Turn the offering over to us, and we shall leave you to your burning city and defeated princess."

Across the platform, Master Gaethon pulls free of the shadows. He starts saying something in Mage-tongue. His words are sharp and quick. Light bursts from his fingertips, driving away the shadows.

"Get back to your stations," he barks at the guards. Then he turns to Kristan, growling, "You weak-minded fool." He snaps his fingers and the general collapses in a cloud of pink sleep.

"Irritable, Gaethon?" someone calls to us with a chuckle. The Sorcerer speaking isn't one I've seen before. His skin is black with the Mark, but flecked with gold. Mentalist. "I imagine you would be. So many years trying to warn these fools of the impending inevitable. So much effort put into your wards and protections, and yet you never expected this, did you? How could you foresee your traitorous prince resurrected? Called to the ashes of his father, despite your ridiculous efforts? You could not have imagined such atrocities. The fallen king who you failed to keep safe. So much failure on your part. So much wasted breath. And the others of your party. Your so-called guild. The Paladin, the warriors, the Bard, the healer. How often did they disregard your advice? How much breath was wasted falling on their deaf ears?"

As he speaks, the shadows creep in again. They wind closer to Gaethon. His eyes darken with every word. I draw my knives. I fling them at the threat and sever them. Gaethon blinks, but before he can clear his head fully more shadows rush in.

"He's right," he spins to the Elite, seething. "You never bothered to listen." He raises his hands to cast and Benen tackles him. Lisabella yelps in shock and dives at the both of them, trying to break up the scuffle between her husband and her brother. The shadows wind around all three of them as the chorus of Sorcerers outside laughs. It only takes the blink of an eye for them to get entangled, too. They stand and turn against Bryse and Donal, who back away unwilling to fight their companions.

"Advance," Gaethon shouts to the guards, and half of them do. The fairies dive in to fight them off. Eron stalks toward Margary with his sword raised. Twig bursts to human size beside her. I glance at Mya, but she's entangled again. Her mouth is bound by black tendrils. Her eyes are wide and shifty. She's trying hard to fight it.

The shadows are everywhere, though. It doesn't take long for everyone within the dome to be caught up in them. It happens too fast. There's no use trying to throw my knives. If I did, I'd have nothing to defend Margy with. Suddenly, that's all I can focus on. The swirling cyclone of darkness drives closer, reaching out for the princess, whipping and lashing and trying to grasp her. I slash at them with all of my strength and with all the speed I can muster.

The others bear down on us, too. It's just me, Margy, and Twig who haven't been overcome by the shadows. Mya doesn't attack us, but she's held and struggling to resist. I slash again and again at the tendrils, sending them curling and shrinking away, but for every one I slash, two spring up in its place.

Beside me, Margy and Twig fight, too. She doesn't say a word, but links arms with Twig, who towers above the two of us. Together, they send beams of light toward the shadows. Vines, like the tendrils of darkness that whip around us. The light twines with the shadow and casts it away. Just as it seems we might gain the upper hand, everyone pauses and everything goes silent. I sense the command before its sent, and my heart sinks.

"*Charge the wards,*" the shadows command, and the Royal guard is the first to obey. They crash through the wards surrounding and protecting us. They hack at Twig's vines. The barriers fall away, leaving us undefended.

The darkness from Eron's cloak and sword retreat to gather around him again, leaving the fairy defenders and the palace guards to pause in confusion over what just happened. He doesn't release the Elite, though. He uses the power he regained from releasing the others to bind them tighter and bend them to his will. They advance, eyes wild and dark, weapons raised. Lisabella, Benen, Bryse, Donal, Gaethon, all of them stalk closer to us, ready to strike. I take Margy by the shoulders and we back away into the wall with nowhere left to go.

Beyond them, the battle rages between Dusk and Dawn. Fairies charge forward with golems of wood and light and wind. Imps fight beside their own golems summoned from shadow and stone. I don't have time to see who has the upper hand. I'm too busy hacking and slicing tendrils away from the Elite and keeping them from hurting Margy. She and Twig try their light vine trick again, but it's too weak. Even with Twig's help, Margy isn't trained enough to fight against this sort of magic. She's worked long at hiding it, but not long enough to know how to use it.

Bryse looms over us, his eyes black with shadow, his stony fist raised in rage. He slams it down and Twig jumps in front of Margy to take the blow. Margy casts a ward, but it isn't quick enough or strong enough. Bryse's blow grazes Twig's shoulder. It's enough to make the fairy lose his footing. When he does, Bryse picks him up by the wing tips and flings him down onto the stone with an earsplitting roar. Benen follows with a sneer and kicks Twig while he's down.

"No!" Margy screams tearfully. "Stop! Please!" She dives to Twig and throws herself over him to shield him, but her presence doesn't make them stop. Lisabella raises her sword, ready to strike. Her expression is filled with hatred and malice. I arc my arm back to throw a dagger, but Donal blocks me with a thrust of his staff to my elbow. Pain sears all the way up to my shoulder and my arm goes limp. My dagger clatters to the ground. In a fit of rage, I throw my second one and strike him in the shoulder with it. Despite the blood that blooms from his shoulder, he doesn't even flinch.

"*Bring her to us*," the shadows whisper, and the rush of nothing that comes with the command helps me understand. Emptiness. Darkness. The shadows aren't commanded by Eron or that Sorcerer outside. They're commanded by the Void. The Dusk itself.

Bryse steps forward and swings his club-like hand toward Margy. He tries to scoop her up, but I grab her arm and pull her away before he can reach her. The princess thrusts her hands forward at the same time, and the shadowy tendrils retreat from the light of her spell, but not enough to release Bryse from their hold on him.

"Twig," she whimpers, and I spare a glance at him. His wings are snapped. He isn't moving.

"He's okay," I lie. "I'm sure he's okay."

There's no time to talk. Lisabella arcs her sword with a powerful swing, and Margy and I both have to duck to avoid being sliced in two. Behind her, a wood golem peppered with arrows splinters as it's hit by a bolt of purple energy cast by a Sorcerer. Lisabella doesn't even glance over her shoulder. Her eyes are completely black. She's empty. Gone. She starts to swing again, and Margy and I have no where left to go. We cower against the wall, holding each other, waiting for the blow.

It doesn't come. Everything goes silent, and then there's a blinding burst of light. It glares into every crevice of every crack in the stone. It washes over us like midday sun. Light and fresh. Peaceful and beautiful. Light so bright that squinting doesn't help me see. I gaze in the direction of it with my healed eye, and even that doesn't help me make sense of things. A human-sized fairy, carrying Azi's new sword. The light that floods the area is coming from her wings. Her hair and cloak swirl around her brightly, casting dancing beams of every color, like Flitt's hair.

"*Eron*," I sense Flitt's voice in the Half-Realm as she pushes it forth.

"*I see*," Azi says in reply.

Flitt darts to Twig and presses her hands to his forehead. Pink and purple light mixes with green and swirls around his face. His eyelids flutter. His wings straighten and heal. I glance at Margy for her reaction, but she's completely still. When I nudge her, she doesn't move. Everything Azi's light touches seems to be the same. Frozen in place and time. Unmoving and unchanging. Everything except Eron. He strides forward effortlessly. Raises his sword. Narrows his eyes and clenches his teeth in a threatening grimace.

They don't say a word. They simply advance on each other with furious speed. Azi's sword radiates with light as much as Eron's drips with darkness. When the two weapons clash together, the force of their strikes create sparks of light and darkness that spray out over them. Mercy sheds speckles of tiny stars that scatter across the ground. Eron's sword leaves a spray of pebbles so black the light can't touch them.

Azi drives Eron across the circle, all the way back to the pyre. With each strike of their swords, her light dims. The same is true with Eron. Every time their weapons meet, the darkness that drips from his blade seems to weaken. Their fight is fierce and merciless. Eron hacks at Azi, catching her waist with his blade. It slices between the scales of her armor with a sizzle. Azi screams and drives him back again. With a powerful slash, she carves a huge gash in the metal of his gauntlet. He almost drops his weapon then, but makes a quick fumble to save it. Azi takes the opportunity to swing again, and this time she adds a kick at the end that sends him stumbling into the pyre.

Eron screams in frustration and lunges himself at her. Azi spins to dodge him, but he catches her elbow and uses his momentum to throw her back behind him. She careens toward the pyre and throws her hands up to stop herself, and both her hands and her sword plunge into the red-hot embers. Eron gives a triumphant laugh, but it's short-lived. The fire doesn't seem to have hurt Azi. Her armor protects her from more than a weapon's blow. It has wards all over it. Sparks of magic embedded into the gold flecks, that redirect the heat.

"Forgive me, Majesty," she utters, staring horrified into the fire. She's so disturbed that she disturbed the king's ashes that she doesn't notice Eron creeping up.

"Azi, behind you!" I shout, and she whirls with her sword gripped in both hands. Her blade nearly meets its mark, but Eron parries. More dark pebbles scatter across the stone. More sparks fly from Azi's sword. One skitters to a stop at my feet, and I crouch to pick it up. It's not an ordinary spark. It doesn't burn me or fade in my hand. It pulses, like a chunk of pure light. It calls out to the fae: *Take me. Use me.* But all of the fairies and their golems are under the effects of the stilling spell. They don't see or hear. They hover in mid-battle, helpless and useless. All except Flitt, that is.

She flies up to my palm and takes the spark and goes back to Twig. Her color seems to brighten a little as she holds it, and Twig stirs as she places it on his lips. His eyes fly open and he looks at her, and she presses her hands to his lips and shakes her head. Frantically, Twig looks around. When he sees Margy, he shrinks back to fairy size and darts to her.

"*Margy!*" he pushes, but the princess still doesn't budge. "Help me, Tib," he whispers, and starts shoving her. I get the hint and take Margy carefully around the shoulders and pull her back, out of view of the fight. I wedge her beside me, between the back of the carved stone chair and the low wall. When I'm sure she's safely hidden, I peek out to keep watching.

Azi's wings have nearly gone now. Eron's cloak has stopped swirling. Their swords still glow with light and dark, but both are very weak.

"Look around you," Eron growls as the two opponents swing and slash and block and parry back and forth across the platform. "You will not win this, Azi. Your people are held fast by darkness. Sorcery has won. The Dusk will rule everything now, and with them, I will claim Brindelier and every land beyond this one. You have failed. Cerion is dying."

While he talks, he does something strange with his feet. Some sort of sword dance. Through the glow of her skin, I see Azi smirk.

"After all you've been through," she says, "you're still trying the same tired tricks, Eron?"

She crouches fast and sweeps her sword low, catching both his ankles in one swing. Eron lands hard on his back. His cloak slinks over him hungrily. Azi stands above him, her sword poised to strike. She raises it to thrust. One strike through his heart. One strike is all it would take. A single clap makes her pause. That one is followed by another, until the Mentalist-Sorcerer I spotted earlier steps forward from the frozen battle, applauding. Azi doesn't lower her sword. She keeps it ready to strike, but the Mentalist-Sorcerer has caught her attention.

"*End him,*" he pushes to her, "*and watch them all die.*"

With a flick of his wrist, he gestures to the other Sorcerers. His allies. They creep forward into the light. Their hands are all posed the same way: Palms up. Thumbs touching fourth fingers. Tendrils of the Void snake out from them. Three Sorcerers. Six tendrils. They slink along the ground, absorbing the black pebbles as they go. They wind around the Elite. Her mother and father. Her friends. They pull them up to hover in the air, and push them out over the wall so they dangle high over the rocky cliffs and the dark sea.

"You have something we need, Azaeli Hammerfel, Champion of Light. Something which was stolen from us. Give it to us now, and we might let them live."

A strange sensation distracts me from the scene. Something else, close by. A suggestion. A redirection. It's strong. Powerful. Dream Magic. Thoughts and wishes. It forces everything and everyone nearby to look away. Something somewhere else is much more interesting. I see it plainly. A diversion. A distraction.

"Tibreseli, Flitt, Twig," Valenor's whisper flicks across our ears. "Look over the wall."

"Oh," Flitt gasps as she drifts toward the sea. "Look."

I keep a hand on Margy and lean way over. With my healed eye, I peer down toward the sea. What I see makes my heart race. Sails and wings floating, held up over the water by great sacks of air. A ship, as fine as I've ever seen, hovering just out of view of those above. Ruben bobs just below me, waving excitedly from the crow's nest. At the ship's helm, Cort keeps the wheel steady. Raefe paces the forecastle, his hand on his hilt. Golems swarm around him, working the cranks and bellows, watching over the sides of the ship for attackers. Dozens of them. Forty or fifty, at least.

"Hide, Tib," Twig whispers.

"But, Margy," I mouth. Twig glances at Flitt, and she nods. She reaches into her belt pouch and pulls out her hand and sprinkles something that looks like gold powder into Margy's hair. The princess vanishes, but I can still feel her shoulder under my hand.

"Give me your coin," Flitt whispers, "and take her. You go with them, Twig. You're too weak. Hurry!"

Chapter Forty-Eight
TO THE VICTORS…

Azi

The air is tinged with smoke and shadow. His Majesty's pyre is dying out; its lingering smoke mixes with that of Cerion on fire. On the platform, everything is silent. The Sorcerers stand poised, holding my loved ones over the edge of the cliff, ready to drop them. Eron lies at my feet, the dark magic of his cloak lapping around him like black water. Mercy vibrates in my hands, pulsing with Light, waiting for my command to end the abomination that was once the prince.

"*I have it!*" Flitt yelps excitedly into my head. "*I have the coin!*"

I don't look away from Eron, whose eyes are black and impenetrable. Flitt shows me something else. A ship. It's there and gone again, but somehow I understand. She doesn't want to show me too much. Just enough that I understand what can be done, but not enough for the enemy to glean any information that could help them. I push to her, "*Bring it to the gate.*"

"*Without you?*" she asks. I nod, very slightly, and she darts off, hidden in the Half-Realm, unnoticed by my enemies.

"You're injured, Azaeli," the Mentalist hisses at me. His words seem to twist into the wound at my stomach where Eron's blade struck me. My breath catches. "Injured and alone." *Alone.*

Mercy pulses with a glow that seems to shove the Mentalist's intentions away from me.

"Who first, then?" the Mentalist murmurs. "The Paladin, I think. Her mother."

He points at one of the Sorcerers controlling the dark tendrils, and she drops her hands. Instantly, the tendrils break and Mum plummets out of sight.

"No!" I scream and plunge my sword downward with all my strength. I feel it meet with Eron's armor and go through to the stone beneath him. He snarls and writhes and his allies cry out in horror. Two of them lunge at me, breaking the tendrils that hold Bryse and Donal and my comrades fall away, disappearing beyond the cliff wall. Mya, Uncle, and Da are the only ones left now. They and the guards and the general are still frozen by the same spell that seemed to blanket this place as soon as I arrived.

The Sorcerers drive the shadows toward me and I lash out. Golden threads that whip at my enemies like arrows and plunge through them, forcing them back. My heart aches for those I failed to protect. I cling to the hope that'll somehow be saved by that ship, and I let their sudden absence fuel my need for victory. Narrowing my eyes, I guide the golden threads to bind each of those who face me. I imagine them thickening into ropes of gold which shine with the light of love and righteousness. I bind their wrists and necks. I force them to the ground to lie on their stomachs. I command the three who are still holding Mya, Da, and Uncle to pull my companions back to safety. I compel them to release their wicked tendrils. When they obey, I bind those Sorcerers, too.

Holding so many at once takes a great deal of concentration. I feel the power bestowed by the Wellspring slowly draining away. The wound at my stomach throbs, and I press my elbow into it to stop the bleeding. Eron moans and tries to get to his feet, but Mercy holds him. The Mentalist stands a safe distance away and watches the scene cautiously. When he speaks, his voice is both in my mind and outside of it. With every word, my head throbs painfully.

"At this point, one might imagine me offering you a different bargain, Azaeli. Your powers of Mentalism are stronger than I foresaw. One might expect me to offer you a place at my side. An apprenticeship, if you will. After all, it is not every day I am witness to a Mentalist of your skill and power." He raises his hand with a smirk. "But we both know such an offer would be a waste of breath, my dear. So instead, I beseech you. Release Eron. We would all agree that you are the victor in that match. Lower the magics you have placed on this fray. Allow it to play out. I have every confidence that the Dusk shall be victorious, but it would be quite a sight to see, would it not? Release my allies and your own from the Stilling. Let them have their battle."

I sense the urgency in his plea. His desperation shows me how important Eron is to their cause. Cautiously, with a firm hold on my sword, I look around at the fight that has been frozen in time, taking it in for the first time. Arrows have stopped in midair. Imps and fae hover in place with colorful blasts of magic puffed out from their fingertips, waiting to release their power. Guards stand encircling Margy's abandoned chair, their swords and spears pointed at a princess who is no longer there to cower from their assault. Golems of wood and wind lock together with shadow-beings in fierce, utterly still combat. It's like a painting or an arrangement of statues depicting a great fight, and according to the Mentalist, this is all my doing.

I glance at Eron, whose face is strangely highlighted by Mercy's golden pulse. No blood flows from his wound. No breath escapes his lips. He can't gasp or bleed to death. His dead eyes search mine as he struggles to free the blade from his chest.

I try to gauge who has the upper hand in the fight as I look over the scene of the king's pyre. It seems rather even, as long as the Mentalist stops forcing others to turn sides.

"I'll agree," I say, still unaware of how to release the spell, "as long as you agree not to force betrayal any longer. Let the Dawn fight for the Dawn, and not for you. If the Dusk's might is as strong as you insist, then you don't need petty tricks of the mind."

"A noble thought. I agree, Azaeli, Knight-Mentalist. And the victor of this battle shall claim the offerings. The one stolen by the Dawn, and the other two." The corners of his lips turn up in a wicked, blue-skinned smile. He flicks his wrist and Uncle's eyes clear of darkness. So do Mya and Da's. I try not to think about Mum or Bryse or Donal. I try to trust what Flitt showed me before she left. I push the thought out of my mind as tears sting my eyes. I blink them away and take a breath and try to remember what happened when I first arrived here to make the battle go still.

"*Azaeli, beware,*" the voice which echoes through my thoughts is melodic, yet commanding. The scene before me shifts and another scene transposes itself over it, like a sheer curtain over a window. The fairy queen, seated on her throne, smiles down at me. The light that shines from her makes me squint. "*Beware,*" she says, "*be ready. I am here. I shall aid you. Do not be afraid of what is yet to come.*"

Her warning bolsters me. I feel her with me. The light of the fae surrounds me and encases me. I gaze across at the Mentalist, and with a slight nod of my head, the spell I didn't even know I'd cast is lifted. The effect is immediate. Fae clash with imps. Sorcerers push their shadows at me. The guards, Mya, Da, and Uncle look confused for a moment, but quickly regain their senses and turn their attention to the battle. Every one of them seems enraged by the very idea that they had been used as tools for the Dusk, and together they unleash a mighty fury against the enemy. Half of the guards begin searching for the princess while the other half form a wide half-circle between the pyre and the oncoming attackers to protect His Majesty's remains.

The Sorcerers surge forward from the craggy hillside and let loose spells the likes of which I've never seen. Jets of purple haze that burns as it grazes my skin. Dark, seeping energy that makes my eyes and mouth prickle and itch. Mya sings and Uncle casts wards and the effects are diminished but not completely stopped. The fae order their golems to charge the source and together with them they surge forward bravely, but I notice their hair and skin going gray and their clothes withering. Some of them dive to the ground. They scoop up the chips of light which sprayed from my sword during my battle with Eron and nibble at them. The light chips rejuvenate them. The word of this healing spreads quickly, and for a moment it seems as though the Dawn might have the upper hand, but the Dusk imps catch on. They find the chips of darkness cast off by Eron's sword and restore themselves as well.

I gasp and cough within the poisonous purple and black fog. A shadow breaks through the barrier of fairies and soldiers and comes straight for me. Without thinking I pull Mercy free and slash at it, and it screams and fades. I realize my mistake too late. Something scuffles behind me and I turn and swing my sword hard. It meets with Eron's upper arm but he barely reacts to what should have been a bone-breaking blow. His black eyes seem to smoke with utter malice, and he dives at me bare-handed. I'm caught off-guard by his sudden attack and try to regain my footing but to no avail. I lose my grip on my sword and Mercy clatters across the stone several paces away as I fall hard onto my back. Eron's cold hands slip into my neck guard and close around my throat. He's strong. Much stronger than the former Eron had ever been. I try hard to push him off of me. I try to force my knee between us or to roll to one side. I try kicking and punching and pushing with all of my strength, but between the lack of air from choking and the effects of the Sorcerers' poisonous spells, I feel the hopelessness closing in. The pain of my stomach wound throbs. Pinpoints of darkness scatter across my vision. The bones of my neck crunch under Eron's inhumanly strong grip. My throat closes painfully. I fight to breathe as he stares down at me, his eyes empty and lifeless, and raises his fist.

Beyond him Mya's voice carries over the battle, clearing my mind of thoughts of despair. Her song shifts my outlook. Past the dark silhouette of Eron's head above me, through the narrow tunnel of my vision, I notice the sky growing brighter. The stars of night are fading. A soft glow on the horizon announces the pending arrival of the sun.

The Dawn.

"I already killed you once," Da growls over the din of battle. "Get off my daughter!"

His axe catches Eron in the side with a sickening thump and throws him through the air away from me. The force of Da's attack rolls me to my side, and the relief that courses through me as I cough and gasp for air is quickly blotted out by the head-spinning pain in my neck at even that small amount of movement. I struggle to get to my knees and try to help, but my throbbing neck isn't strong enough to hold my head up.

"Be still," Mya says as she drops to her knees beside me. Her hands are soft on my cheeks as they cradle my head. "Don't move." She begins singing a song of healing, and the magic of it soothes the burning in my eyes and mouth from the poison cloud that still hovers. It isn't strong enough to mend the damage Eron caused, though. I try to swallow and end up coughing instead as the pain sears through my throat. I try to push through it, to focus away from the pain and concentrate instead on the welcome sensation of breath filling my lungs. As tainted as it is, it's still a relief to breathe it in. Focusing on that, I watch Da stalk to Eron and strike him again. Eron fights fiercely, but Da is a seasoned fighter. I try to catch Eron with strings of Mentalism, but his mind is dead and empty and the strings don't take. Da doesn't need my help, anyway. Despite Eron's inhuman strength, Da finally bests him by throwing him over the cliff wall.

The loss of the prince causes an uproar of protests from the Dusk, who press their attack harder. Da comes to stand over us, his axe ready. Uncle holds his ground between us and our attackers and sends the blast of a fireball into the crowd of Dusk. Several imps and Sorcerers fall to the ground, screaming and burning. I try hard to lie still and allow Mya's song to heal me, but it's difficult. I yearn for Mercy and feel the sword heavy in my palm.

"Azi," Da warns. "Be patient or be lost."

"I can't be patient," I try to growl, but my throat is too sore and my voice cracks out at barely a whisper as tears slip from the corners of my eyes and roll into my ears. "I have to fight." I push against Mya's hold, but the pain is too much. In the distance, a Sorceress thrusts her hands forward, aiming her spell directly at us. I imagine the golden strings and they catch her hands and fling her away before she has a chance to cast.

"Healer!" Mya's shout rises over the battle and echoes across the hillside. Some of the fairies hear and come to hover close to me, but even with the sparks to rejuvenate them, their magic is too spent to do me much good.

"Here," comes a whisper out of nowhere. A flash of red fur streaks past my range of vision. Two hands graze my neck, and even as gentle as their touch is, it pains me until the prayer is whispered and the soft pink glow of healing floods my vision. The relief is immediate as healing magic weaves through my throat and neck, opening up my swollen airway and mending the crushed tissue and bone. When it fades, the face looking down at me shocks me.

"Dacva? How?"

"Elliot!" Mya cries. "You found him!"

"Long story." Dacva grins down at me. "Short version is, Redemption's back. Tried to force me to join up again, but I refused. Thanks to Elliot, I was able to get away."

"Thanks to you, I was alive to do so," Elliot says as he fires his bow into the fray with a quick, fluid motion. "Get down," he shouts and shoves Mya out of the way just in time to avoid a bolt of lightning from the group of Sorcerers that once held her. In front of us, Uncle throws up a ward just in time to block the surge of spells that scatter apart in a wash of color, missing us completely. Thanks to Dacva's healing, I jump to my feet to stand beside Uncle and face the attackers. A glance at Uncle shows him to be in bad shape. Blood drips from a gash at his cheek. His lips are pale, and I notice him clutching his side to cover a hole singed through his robes.

"Uncle," I whisper and step closer to him. When I do, a trio of arrows streaks past my ear. Mya screams and the sound of her voice seems to push them faster. Each arrow strikes a different Sorcerer with a force so hard that none of them have a chance. They fall over, defeated.

"I missed you," Mya's voice is much smoother this time. I know it's intended for Elliot, but the tone still sends a shiver of a thrill through me. Right away, I think of Rian waiting for me at the gate. I wonder what Flitt told him and why he hasn't come to see what's taking me so long.

My thoughts are cut short as three more arrows whiz past in quick succession, urged on by Mya's voice. Elliot is barely audible as he yawns back at her, "Missed you, too."

Dacva reaches past me and puts a hand on Uncle and the gash on his face closes. Uncle stands a little taller, squares his shoulders, and stretches his hands up to cast. His sights are set on the Mentalist.

409

Their eyes are locked. I see the effort between them. Uncle, trying hard to fight the mind-control, and the Mentalist working harder to force his will. I see the magic between them like ropes of energy, and I slash at them with Mercy, severing them.

"I should have expected you to go back on your word," I sneer at the Mentalist. As I stride toward him and the battle rages around us, I feel the sky lightening. The promise of morning bolsters me. The wings at my back grow bright and strong again. I feel the confidence I had when I arrived amplified. The Mentalist sees this in me, and for the first time I sense the fear in him. All around him, the bodies of his fallen allies lay crumpled and defeated. Only a few Sorcerers remain standing, and they have retreated to the hills again along with the imps who seem to see the approaching Dawn as a threat.

That's what I think at first, until I spare a glance at the shadow-strewn hillside beyond the wall. There, a Sorcerer has his hands raised to cast. I've seen him before, in the assassin's mind and in Tib's. Quenson. His spell summons darkness in a great, swirling black mass that bleeds with malice and evil. The Void. It's terrifying enough at first in its great formless mass, but then it starts to take a different shape: that of a serpent with sharp teeth which drip black like Eron's sword. The black creature seeps over the crags, dwarfing the hillside itself as it grows and sprouts wings from its scaly back. As it slinks forward, it absorbs Quenson into it. The agents of Dusk huddling in the craggy shadows follow him. They step into the darkness willingly, allowing it to draw them in, becoming one with it. With every new addition, the creature grows larger and more powerful.

"Return to me, Xantivus." The command is not a voice. It's everywhere. It resounds from every sliver of shadow and resonates like a dark and wicked thought through my mind.

To my shock, the Mentalist turns his back to us. He walks calmly away across the stone walk and straight into the mouth of the Void beast.

"Azaeli Hammerfel. Peons of Dawn," the beast hisses, "you are defeated." With every word, darkness drips from the creature's fangs and pools like sizzling tar on the stone before it. Its voice pierces through my ears like daggers, sending me to my knees. Around me, the Elite and the remaining Guard do the same, clapping their hands over their ears. I cover mine, too, but it does little to stop the torture. The fairies shrink away. Their golems vanish. His voice is too powerful. Too filled with agony and despair. "Your city burns. Your palace is taken. The sun will not rise. The Dawn has lost. Give us the offerings. Brindelier is ours to claim."

"*Stand now, my Champion,*" the fairy queen's voice drifts into my thoughts, soothing the pain, pushing away the fear. I see her clearly on her throne. She rises and glides down the stairs toward me with her wings slowly opening and closing. On the other side of the veil, the queen turns her back to me to face the Void. "Step into me, Azaeli," she says. As the first beams of sunlight break across the horizon, I step forward and, like the Agents of Dusk with the Void, she and I become one with the light.

Chapter Forty-Nine

MARGY'S CHOICE

Tib

We crowd into the crow's nest, as quiet as can be. Even though I want to whoop with excitement. Even though I could kiss Ruben and Raefe both for finishing it. For getting it going. I need to know how. I have so many questions. But, Margy. She's awake now. Dispelled from the strange trance that held her up at the pyre. She's angry, too. Pushing me. Crying. Fighting to get back to the Rites. I have trouble calming her. My elbow is still throbbing from Donal's attack. I try to use that arm, but it's too painful. I have to hold her with just one hand. For a princess, she's pretty strong.

"I can't be here. I can't leave him," she whimpers hysterically. "I can't dishonor him. Let me go!" She shoves me. Kicks. Claws herself away and climbs onto the rim of the basket.

"I'm sorry, Princess," Twig whispers. He opens his hand and a flower blooms from his palm. He blows the scent of it into Margy's face. She stops fighting. Her eyelids grow heavy. She slips down against the low wall of the nest.

"Did you just drug her?" I hiss at the fae.

Twig knits his brow apologetically. "She was going to hurt herself. We have to get her down from here."

"Keep a lookout, Rube," I say as Twig surveys the height of the nest and the narrow ratlines that lead up to it. Without a word, he pops up to human size, scoops Margy into his arms, and flies down to the deck.

The ship sinks lower and creeps closer to the cliff. It's almost like it has a mind of its own. Like it knows what to do, even though Cort is controlling it. I try to make sense of it as I pull a pink vial from my bandolier and drink it down. The bone knits back together and my arm tingles pleasantly. I breathe a sigh of relief as the pain goes away. It's not completely healed, but good enough that I can at least use it again. Climbing down the ratlines is painful, but doable. I reach the deck a little after Margy and Twig, grateful to be on solid footing again.

From the ship's helm, Cort gives me a wave. Behind him, golems that look like they're made of pure sky work the propellers and cranks. They remind me of the inside of Valenor's cloak: midnight blue and stars, but when they turn a certain way, blue sky. It's confusing to look at and try to make sense of. The sight of them makes me more aware. Valenor. He's all around us. Cloaking us. Protecting us. His magic encircles the entire ship. Gives it a consciousness, almost. I catch a glimpse of his face just beyond the starboard wall and I want to run to him, to ask him how it all happened, but Raefe rushes to me, interrupting my thoughts.

"Amazing idea, Tib. I can't believe it," he says with a grin, squeezing my shoulder. "A flying ship!" With a nervous glance up to the cliffs he asks, "Is Saesa...?"

"Saesa?" I scowl and glance at Twig, who's still holding Margy. I hadn't even thought of where Saesa could be. It's strange that Azi would show up without her squire.

"At the gate," Twig murmurs as he wafts another flower scent to Margy's nose. "She's with Rian, Shush, and Flitt. They're waiting for us. They need the Princess."

"How do you know that?" I ask.

"We have ways of knowing what's happening to each other," Twig explains, "especially when we're so close in proximity. Especially in times like this."

Margy's eyelids flutter open, and Twig smoothes her curls and whispers, "Ah, princess. I'm sorry." He brushes a kiss across her forehead. She smiles contentedly. My stomach twists in anger. I'm not sure why. Probably because he drugged her, and now she's gazing at him like he's the best thing in the world. He reaches to help her to stand, but I push between them and do it myself. Tears streak her cheeks and she wipes them away with the sleeve of her white robe.

"How could you take me away?" she narrows her eyes at me furiously. Her voice shakes with rage and betrayal. She pulls herself free from my arms and stalks away from us. "The vigil—"

"It's over, Princess," Twig says softly. He makes himself small again and drifts closer to her, opening his arms in a gesture of peace. She presses her lips in a tight, thin line. Her nostrils flare as she spins to face me.

"It's not over. It's defiled. Disrespected. Ru-ruined," she hiccups the last and takes a shuddering breath. Twig lands on her shoulder and strokes her hair. He whispers something to her, and again my heart thuds angrily in my chest. Margy shakes her head violently and Twig darts away from her whip-like hair. "Take me back to my father!" she screams at the two of us, her voice raised above the wind, her fists clenched at her sides.

"Shhh," Valenor's warning settles over us, but I can't help it.

"Ruined?" I shout. "You think your father's vigil is ruined *now*?" She cowers back against the bulwark as I stalk closer in my fury. "How about when his daughter is skewered by his own guards? What about then? You're not going back up there, Margy. Those Sorcerers, you're a threat to them. They turned your own guards against you. They want you dead, don't you see that?"

"Tib," Raefe takes my injured arm and pulls me away from her. The calmness of his voice only makes me angrier. "She's the princess. Show some respect."

"She's my friend, first," I tug away from him, growling at the pain that shoots through my elbow. I wasted that potion. You're supposed to rest, to let it work, and I didn't. I don't care. It doesn't matter. Margy ducks her head. Twig floats in the space between us, like he's defending her. I don't know from what. I don't want to hurt her. I'm trying to protect her. Trying to make her see. "What then, Margy? What happens after they kill you?" She winces at my question. "Who's left to rule your beloved Cerion, when you're d—?"

"Uh, Tib?" Ruben interrupts from above. He points up to the pyre, where three figures are being dangled over the cliff's edge by dark tendrils.

"Cast the nets!" Cort shouts.

"No time!" Twig cries. He flings his hands out, palms up, and tangle of vines shoots from his fingertips. They weave together to make a net of their own just in time to catch Lisabella, who's the first to be dropped. Azi's scream echoes from the top of the cliff. Soon after, the other two fall into the vine net. Twig, looking pale and tired, lowers the three of them to the deck. He bows his head like he's concentrating, and the vines spring back to him.

Margy gathers Twig close to her and whispers to him. I watch her give him her own energy. Watch him perk up a little. She's tired, though. They both are. She doesn't have much more to give. Watching the others warily, she creeps closer to me and clings to my arm. The bad one. It doesn't matter. I barely feel the pain as she comes to me for protection. My anger toward her fades. Having her so close, depending on me, sends a rush through me.

Silently, I position myself between her and our former allies, not knowing what to expect. I draw one knife from my bandolier. Beside me Raefe looks a little confused, but does the same with his rapier. We circle Lisabella, who's on her knees, hunched over her sword, trying to catch her breath. Bryse stands over her looking confused as he shakes his head and squeezes his eyes shut. Beside them, flat on his back, Brother Donal stares up at the stars. His hand drifts to his shoulder where I stabbed him. To my surprise, he doesn't heal it. Instead, he pushes himself to his feet with a little difficulty and steadies himself against the riggings.

Bryse is the first one to see Margy. His eyes flash with recognition. He strides closer to us and his heavy footsteps make the deck beneath us shudder and creak. I raise my knife, ready to throw it, knowing it'd do little against the giant of a man. I don't have to worry about that, though.

"Princess," he says, his voice heavy with grief. He drops to his knees. Thumps his fist to his chest. Bows his head. "Please forgive me. It was a spell. I would never…"

Lisabella and Donal approach, too. They do the same as Bryse. Kneel. Apologize.

I glance back at the princess and she nods. "I know," she says. Her voice is thick with pain and fear. "It's all right, Bryse. Sir Hammerfel. Brother Donal. I know it wasn't your doing. You'd never—" She interrupts herself with a scream as another figure hurtles over the side of the cliff and plummets toward the ship. Twig tries to catch it again with his net of vines, but he's too tired. Despite Margy's gift, his magic is spent. The figure hits the deck with a deafening crack that splinters the wood. At first, it doesn't move. Lisabella, Donal, and Bryse take a cautious step toward it. Margy ducks behind me and peers out cautiously. She grips my arm so tightly my fingertips go numb.

"You have lost, little sister," Eron's twisted, sinister voice is almost unrecognizable. He pushes himself to his hands and knees. His neck bends at an odd angle as he grins and looks to the top of the cliff. "The Void encroaches."

When he straightens to his full height, there's a collective gasp from all of us. His chestplate is pierced through, showing a wound that would have killed even the heartiest fighter.

"How is he not dead?" Lisabella whispers.

"Oh, but I am," Eron sneers and jerks his head to straighten his neck into place. "And soon you will be, too."

Bryse is the first to react. He's fast, for such a hulk. Even Eron doesn't see him coming. He clomps to him, raises his fist, and drives him like a nail all the way through the already cracked deck. Then he kicks some splinters of wood down into the hole that's left behind and grumbles, "That'll shut 'im up."

"Bryse!" Lisabella gasps in disbelief.

"Yeah," I scowl, "you put a hole in my deck!"

Cort scampers down from the ship's wheel and skids to a stop right before the hole. Together, he and Bryse peer into it.

"What's down there?" Bryse asks Cort.

"Barracks are up front, and storage," Cort replies. "Captain's and officers' quarters are at the stern."

They back away a little at the sounds of Eron's raging screams and thumps below.

"We should figure out a way to hold him," Lisabella says, looking plainly horrified. "And be respectful. He's still the princess's brother, after all."

"No," Margy whispers from behind me. "That thing is not my brother."

"She's right," Donal agrees quietly. He takes my arm and heals it the rest of the way with a graze of his fingertips. "Resurrection is Necromancy. That beast may seem like Eron, and look like him. It might even have Eron's knowledge, emotion, and memories. But it is a creature of darkness now. Immortal and changed forever. The butterfly can never again become a caterpillar." His voice is soft and calming. When he talks, it's like Lisabella's peace pulse. I let it soothe me and I realize it isn't magic. He's just got that sort of voice. He moves through the group of us, checking us over. Takes special care with Margy. Heals the small scratches on her. Gives Twig energy, too. When he's sure everyone else is healed, he finally heals himself of the knife wound in his shoulder.

"Sorry about that," I mumble sincerely.

"No need," he says with a dismissive wave. "You did what you had to in order to protect our princess and the throne."

Below deck, the crashing grows louder. Eron's angry howls give me chills. Lisabella and Cort exchange a glance.

"Are there iron chains on board?" Donal asks Cort.

"Aye," Cort nods.

"Those will hold him for now," Donal says, and Bryse and Cort agree to go and bind him up.

"How do we end him, Donal? Once and for all?" Lisabella asks quietly.

"This is one of those rare cases," Donal replies, "when healers and Mages must work together. It's like a stripping. Blood magic, Necromancy." He glances at Margy and looks away. "The life that was taken from another to be given to him…" he sighs and shakes his head, and my heart pangs for Errie. Donal rubs his eyes and strokes his palm over the bare skin on the top of his head. "It's complicated."

"Could the boy be saved?" I ask. "The one they used?"

Donal shakes his head mournfully. "What's done is done."

My stomach twists with guilt. If I hadn't been so bent on getting Dub, if I had just kept my temper, Eron wouldn't be here. This is all my fault. I pull away from Margy and go to the port side bulwark to look out over the sea. Between her outburst earlier and my own guilt, I need to be alone. She's got them now, anyway. She doesn't need me. Suddenly, I just want to be away from this. All of it. I stare at the horizon and imagine taking the ship and just flying away, forever. Valenor's face shifts before me. He doesn't say anything. Just shows me he's there. Shatters my daydream. Brings me back to the present.

As Cort and Bryse come back from below, a thundering voice from above grabs everyone's attention. I know it right away. The Void. Declaring victory. Claiming that it will own Brindelier. I forget my anger and guilt and whirl to face the others.

"We can't let that happen," Twig says. "Eron is the Dusk's claim to the throne. Where the princess is pure, just, and kind, Eron is her opposite: Corrupt. Wicked. Dangerous. The Dusk must not be allowed to bring him through the gates. He must be taken far from here until he can be destroyed."

"I know a place," Bryse says firmly. Cort glances up at him and nods. He seems to know just where Bryse means without him having to say it.

"If I can use the ship, we can be there in a day's time," he says to me.

"'Course you can use the ship," I say, a little disheartened by the reality that I won't be sailing off on my own any time soon.

"Whoa! Look at that!" Ruben shouts.

Above us at the pyre, a blinding light pulses. Bright as the sun. Warm. Perfect. It washes everything white. It pushes away the shadows and welcomes the Dawn.

"Azi!" Lisabella lets out a joyful gasp. I don't know how she knows, but she's right. I can't imagine who else would be able to do that.

"We have to go, quickly," Twig says. "Tib, you know where to go. Can you feel it?" I scowl at him, confused at first. Then I close my eyes. He's right. Out over the ocean, I can sense it. A magic unlike any other I've felt. It reminds me of the floating island near the Sorcerers' keep, but it's different. Brighter. Inviting.

I run to the helm. Take the wheel. Over my shoulder I call instructions to the golems working the cranks and bellows. The ship shudders and creaks. It teeters and rocks as it jolts forward. I spin the wheel hard away from the cliff and whoop as we list sharply to the side.

"Hey, hey, hey," Cort shouts as he takes the steps up to the helm two at a time. "Easy, easy. You have to be gentle. Treat her like a lady."

Beside him, Bryse grunts. "Like a lady, eh?"

"Quiet, oaf," Cort chuckles and guides my hand on the wheel, and we float higher into the sky. The wind catches the sails and puffs them out and we soar. The air sacs tied to the masts glow yellow and orange as they lift us higher. Fast. Faster. The ride is smooth. No waves to rock us side to side. No wake to cut through. Just ship and sky. Floating, like a dream. My dream. I forget about the impossible light. I leave The Void far behind. Ahead, the gate of Brindelier calls. As we race toward it, a figure on the forecastle catches my eye.

Margy stands at the rail. Her brown curls dance across her face as she looks into the distance. I follow her gaze to Cerion, growing smaller. Black smoke drifts up into the sky from all over the city. In the early morning light, flames glow at the base of the castle. Despite Lisabella and Donal talking nearby, she looks so alone, gazing across at her kingdom. I give into the overwhelming need to comfort her. I hand the wheel over to Cort and rush to her side. When I reach her, I don't know what to say or do, so I just put my hand on hers on the rail.

"How can I leave them, Tib?" she chokes. "My people? My kingdom? Look at it burn. Look what they've done to it. I can't turn my back. They need me."

I scan the city in the distance with my healed eye. See the truth of it. "It does look bad from here, Princess," I say. "All that smoke. But, look harder. Your light shines. All those people who accepted your gift, they're still there. Fighting. Helping. Look closer. See Azi's light by the pyre? She's still fighting. She's doing her part."

Margy moves closer to me. Pulls my arm around her. Keeps looking out to the city. My heart thumps in my chest. I tip my chin to her shoulder and my cheek brushes hers. Her skin is warm and soft and sweet-smelling, like flowers.

419

"He's right, Princess," Twig reassures her from his perch on her other shoulder. "Cerion's strong. They'll come through this. But if the Dusk claims Brindelier, all will be lost to darkness. Let them do what they must, so you can do what you must. Trust your people."

"You sound just like Paba," Margy sniffles, and her soft voice is carried off by the wind.

"Maybe so," Twig says. "Your father was a wise man."

Lisabella joins us and follows the princess's gaze. Her peace pulses over us. I straighten up, suddenly self-conscious, but Margy keeps a tight hold on my arms around her.

"Donal and I have decided to stay aboard with Cort and Bryse and see that creature safely into holding." Lisabella looks into the distance at the brilliant light beaming from the pyre platform. Worried. "Cerion is strong. They'll come through this." Her words echo Twig's and bolster the princess, who stands a little straighter. Her eyes flash with pride for her kingdom.

"You're right," says Margy, "Cerion will prevail."

"I'm staying aboard," Raefe says to me. "I've been learning about ships and navigation. They need me here more than Saesa does out there. Tell her not to worry. I'm safe."

I nod in agreement and chuckle to myself, knowing how Saesa would feel about Raefe tagging along into Brindelier. She'd be more worried about him coming along and being overbearing than staying behind and out of her hair.

The gateway isn't far away. We soar over the ocean and see it in the distance, still and dim. White stone covered by a patch of grass. Cort's got a masterful touch at the wheel. The ship seems to know just what he wants and respond. The golems turn cranks and pulleys. The propeller stops. The flames in the air sacs at the masts dim. Valenor's protection stays around the ship, hiding us from view. We glide up to the edge of the grass and dock so perfectly that there's barely a seam between the bulwark and the grass.

With a quick farewell to the others, Margy and I climb the few steps to the bulwark. Her foot touches the grass just as the sun breaks over the horizon. The ship vanishes from view the moment we leave it. In its place, a meadow of grass stretches out as far as we can see. It's just a few paces to the archway, where Rian is talking to a Knight in bright silver plate mail who seems to be guarding the only gateway into the city, set into a glittering stone wall. Beyond it, spires of towers stretch up into the sky. Rooftops glisten with morning dew. What I can see of the city is grand. Everything is highly decorated and interesting to look at. The towers are carved with figures and animals and brightly painted. Even the tiles of the roofs are adorned with intricate designs.

"I sing in the sunshine and the rain. I soothe in the summer. In winter I'm wicked again. What am I?" Rian asks as we near. His back is to us, and he doesn't seem to notice our approach.

"I know it! I know it!" a strange, high voice answers excitedly. Margy and I exchange an amused glance. The voice doesn't fit the Knight at all. She puts her hand up to stop me, and we pause to watch the scene.

"Answer, then, Stryker," a deeper voice booms.

"You answer," says Stryker. "I've already answered six. He's going to think you're dimwitted, Gus."

"Very well," the Knight shifts his stance and taps his barrel helm. "Sing in the sunshine..." he ponders.

"Oh, come now! It's wind! Wind! I'm right, aren't I?" Stryker yelps.

"Yes, that's right," Rian replies. In his hands he holds a glowing orb. A closer look with my healed eye reveals the three offerings inside it.

"What if Flitt held it, and I left to fetch her? I promise to come right back," Rian holds the orb out, and Flitt darts down to accept it.

"Your fancy Knight said she would return, and yet she never did! She sends a fae in her place. Trickery! They are trying to trick us, Gus! Be careful!" Stryker warns. The knight shifts slightly, like he's carefully considering the matter.

"I still don't understand why we can't enter." Rian says. "You've pretty much told us you want the Dawn to be the victors. Why are you holding us back? We have what you asked for. The three offerings, the coin. It's all here."

"It is not, and you do not!" Stryker squeaks. "You promised a suitor! They promised a suitor, Gus!"

"Calm down, Stryker," the knight booms. "We impressed upon the Lady Knight the importance of reaching us before the Dusk does. She is aware of the stakes. If she fails to deliver her promise, we can do nothing. Those are the rules, as you are well aware."

Beside Rian, Saesa stares off into the distance with a hopeful look. Searching for Azi. Obviously thinking she'll appear at any moment. She's the first to see us.

"Tib!" she shouts. "Princess!" She runs the short distance and gives Margy a hasty curtsy before flinging her arms around me. "How are you here? What happened? The vigil!"

Margy winces. Her eyes glisten with tears. She shakes her head.

"It's behind us," I explain. "What's important is that we're here now, and the Princess is ready to do what's needed."

Rian bends a knee to Margy as she approaches the Knight, who looks her over cautiously.

"Her Highness, Princess Margary Plethore, I presume?" he greets her with a much gentler tone than the one he used with Rian. Margy nods.

"Welcome to Brindelier, the Kingdom of Spires," he says with a bow. "We are aware of your intentions. You have all that is required to enter the gates. I will warn you, Princess, that though the city sleeps, it is not without peril. It would be wise for you to await your champion before you step within."

Rian groans. Flitt covers her face with her hand and shakes her head. Even Shush lets out an exasperated sigh and a gust of wind that sends the knight's cloak billowing out behind him.

"Sorry," the wind fairy mutters.

"I'll go get her," Rian says.

"Very well," says the knight. "With your princess here, we can be assured that your intentions are true. Go, Rian Eldinae. Go with haste."

Before the knight can even finish, Rian steps into the Half-Realm and   vanishes.

Chapter Fifty

DAWN VERSUS DUSK

Azi

The sensation is indescribable. I feel as though I'm in the Wellspring again, dipped in love and warmth, but this time it's more intense and complete. I am the Fairy Queen, and she is me, and we are Light and Dawn, Magic and Power. We know everything the light touches, and it is ours to command. The pyre of His Majesty's Rites fades from beneath us, and as we face the Void, we seem to float over nothing and everything all at once. The sensation is disorienting but not at all disconcerting. I have the Queen and the Light, and they have me. We're three: Her Majesty, me, and everything else that calls itself the Dawn. Together, we're safe and secure. My wounds are healed. I am strong and capable.

"Fighting is useless and primitive, Vorhadeniel," I say in unison with the queen. Her knowledge fills me with centuries worth of memories, of thousands of battles between Dawn and Dusk, most of which had been won by the Dawn. "You know this."

"Will you never cease this banter, Eljarenae? Does it not bore you as it bores me?" the Void echoes beyond our light. "The battle, the chaos, is my meat and marrow. *You* know *this.*"

"What you wish for can never be," we reply.

"Who do you deny it for, Elja? I know you wish it as well. A reprieve. A rest, if only for a decade or a century. Who does it benefit for you to be so stubborn? Your charges? Your champion?" The voice moves closer. Close enough to brush against the light. Close enough to touch, but it doesn't dare. The light quivers at its nearness. It stretches out slowly, longingly. Parts of it mingle with the Void in ways that only light can with shadow. Casting it, dancing within it, drawn to it and repelled by it all at once. It's beautiful, almost playful, until I realize the feeling behind it and understanding dawns on me. These two, the Dawn and the Dusk, are siblings. Brother and sister who share a rivalry as strong as their love for one another. She tries to placate him, but he won't hear her.

"Do not," we say. "Do not act under the guise that you have any concern at all for the Dawn, Vorhadeniel. What you call stubbornness, we call vigilance. We know what it is you wish. This time is no different from any other, and we will not stand down."

"You have seen my might, Sister. You have been witness to it. This time, I have been patient. I have grown strong. My numbers far surpass your own. Stand aside, and give us what was rightfully claimed by my agents, or you shall see a war to begin the Dusk of all time," the darkness laps toward us, threatening us. It takes the form of a great dragon, drawing all shadows to it, until its impressive wings stretch out from its back and it lifts from its feet.

Around myself and the queen, the light draws closer, the same way the shadows did with the Void. As we grow, we take a different form than the dragon: that of a winged centaur. We raise our hand and Mercy's light glows bright from it, driving the dark creature back.

"We will never yield to you, Vorhadeniel," we cry. Beneath our hooves, the rocky hillside crumbles as we drive the dragon back. "You cannot be trusted with the Great Source. You would claim it and waste it. You would destroy life and light and that which is pure and good. You would never accept the balance."

I slash Mercy down and strike the dragon's snout, and it howls and opens its mouth and spews a stream of shadow and darkness at us like a jet of pitch. It strikes us in the chest and pushes us back, then it flees over the hillside toward the city.

We give chase, pounding over the hillside, taking care not to trample the tiny people who dive away from our enormous hooves as we thunder after the dragon. It doesn't take flight. Instead it crashes past the palace and levels the forest park outside of its walls.

As we chase after the Void, I try hard not to be distracted by the state of the burning palace or the crushed and fallen trees where Rian and I once lay in secret in the grass, dreaming of our future together. Instead I focus on the beast that clambers away down the streets, paying no heed to the crowds of people fleeing. We pass the Elite complex and my breath catches in my throat. Half of its roofs are charred and melted. A thin line of smoke wafts up from my burnt bedroom, where an orange and red flag of Redemption flaps from my smashed and half-burnt window frame.

"No," I whisper, and my anguish takes the form of a gray stain that slashes across our pure white tabard.

"Our champion is strong," we shout ahead to the fleeing dragon. "She will not falter!" Our words strengthen me and push me faster.

Our hooves pound the cobbles as we gain ground. The Void streaks past the Academy, which is still pristine despite the ruins surrounding it. The dragon leaps from the sea wall and soars out over the ocean and we keep chase. The light of our wings flashes in the corners of my eyes as they propel us forward. I let my anger and sorrow fuel me, but the Queen's voice echoes in my mind.

"Bar the shadow from your heart. Let go of what you have seen. Do not allow darkness to stake its claim within your pure soul, Azaeli. Fight it. If you cannot, we must release you."

It's easier than I would have expected to follow the Queen's instructions and push away the hurt caused by the things I have seen. The result is a hollow feeling which fills quickly with light, much the same way a hole dug at the seashore quickly fills with water. The euphoria is similar to what I feel when I use Mentalism, and that gives me an idea. As the dragon pumps its wings faster over the surface of the ocean, we imagine golden ropes to hold it. With the help of the Queen and the Light, we make them chains, broad and thick. They stream away from us as we gallop across the air, and they catch the dragon around its neck and legs. It plunges into the sea, screaming and thrashing, and our small triumph causes the light around us to beam brighter.

"Kaso Viro," we call, and the serpent is there in a flash, streaking yellow and turquoise through the water. He strikes at the Void once, twice, three times, weakening and paralyzing it. Our golden chains constrict it as it sinks beneath the water's surface.

"To all the ends of these lands," we command, "we banish thee, darkness and shadow, Dusk and Void. We are the victors of this battle. Disperse, and wander in the night to dwell on the fatuity of your reckless and wanton depravity."

"*Strike it down, Azaeli,*" the Queen's voice in my head commands, and we plunge fearlessly into the water with Mercy raised and ready to thrust.

The moment my blade meets its black mark in the depths of the water, a scream unlike any I've heard screeches through the water around me. Fury, defeat, anger, rage, defiance, disbelief, darkness, shadow, hatred, death. All of these sensations barrage me at once as the shadows give under Mercy's attack and burst into thousands of shards of darkness. The dragon is defeated, the Void and its agents cast away with one mighty blow. The feeling of triumph overwhelms me as Kaso Viro pushes me to the surface and I gasp for breath. The light holds and protects me. It soothes and congratulates me. The elation of victory courses through me. The battle is won, for now. I close my eyes and drift to sleep, lulled by the ebb and flow of the ocean waves.

I wake some time later in the grass, utterly alone. Warm beams of midday sunshine splash across my face through the cover of the forest canopy. I test my arms and legs. I call Mercy to me and feel its hilt heavy in my palm. When I sit up, I find myself face-to-face with the veil. Beyond it, the queen smiles warmly at me.

"You fought well, my Champion of Light," she says gently. "And I and the Dawn thank you. But do not be quick to celebrate. There is still much to be done. Though the Dusk is dispersed, it is not defeated. Even now, its agents are waking and working to find each other. As you have seen, it shall not ever be ended. Not completely."

"I understand," I say, but my voice comes out only as a whisper. The grief of seeing and feeling her separate from myself overwhelms me. "Why did you split away from me?" I ask. "Why can't we be together as we were?"

"Though we are grateful for your aid," she explains, "we each have our own role to play. Eljarenae cannot leave the Light, Dear Azaeli. She is bound to it, as Kaso Viro is bound to the waters and Valenor is bound to Dreaming and Vorhadeniel is bound to shadow and darkness."

"I'm confused," I say, pushing myself to my feet. I reach out to her, and the soft, airy veil brushes my fingertips. "I thought you were Eljarenae."

"Eljarenae is the Muse of Light. She is an ally of the Dawn, as you and I are. She is a Muse of the Six, as Valenor and Kaso Viro are. Siblings of Vorahdeniel. Bound to their realms," she explains. "She and I are as separate as you and I are. Only in times of dire defense can we meld together."

"But if you're fae and she's light, why did you need me at all? Together, you have so much power."

"We have no dominion on the human plane, Azaeli. Certainly we can visit. We can grace these places, but your connection to Cerion and your loyalty to that land is what gave us the power to walk among humans, just as the Dusk had its own allies to allow them to do the same."

"You said Muse of the Six. Does that mean there are two more?" I ask.

"Yes. In due time, you shall learn of them. For now, you must carry out your vow to the Princess. Open the gates of Brindelier for the Dawn. Your task is nearly through." She looks past me and smiles again, her eyes glinting with happiness. "Do not be disheartened. You are not alone." She gestures behind me.

"Azi!" Rian calls as he runs toward me through the golden grass. "Azi!"

"Rian!" I take off toward him and we crash into each other's arms. The strength of his body against mine and his rough beard on my cheek brings tears to my eyes. All of the loneliness I felt being separated from the Light disappears in his embrace. His breath is warm and welcome as he tips my face toward his and kisses me hungrily. After a long, lingering moment, he holds me away and looks into my eyes.

"I was terrified," he says. "I couldn't find you anywhere. I thought..." his voice trails off and his fingertips crackle softly, tickling my cheeks.

"I was..." I say breathlessly and curl my fingers into his auburn hair. "I can't even explain it to you. Not now. Maybe she can," I say and turn to look behind me, but the veil is gone.

"You can show me," he whispers and brushes his lips across my cheek, "later. First, Brindelier. They're waiting."

He takes my hand and pulls me into the Half-Realm, and we tumble fast onto the grassy lawn of the gateway.

"Well, well," a squeaky voice rings out as soon as we stumble forward. "Took you long enough, Lady Too-Many-Titles!"

"Azi!" Flitt yelps and darts to kiss my cheek. I stroke her tiny arm gently with my fingertip and she shivers and giggles and settles into place at my pauldron. The others waiting echo my name, and I'm surprised and relieved to hear Margy's voice among them.

"Princess," I stride to her and dip to one knee, and she offers me her hand.

"What happened?" she asks. "Is Cerion safe?"

"I'll show you," I whisper, eager to share what I know with all of them. They gather around me as I cup my hands in front of me. Even the knight and his fairy companion lean over to get a view. I gaze into my palms and concentrate on the battle between Dusk and Dawn and my part in it, and the scenes play out across the gold-flecked palms of my gloves. Some things are difficult to show. They don't come through from my thoughts very clearly. My run through Cerion lingers too long on the burning palace and the Redemption flag in my window, and

Rian grips my shoulder reassuringly. When the battle is through, Margy looks away to the West, toward Cerion.

"We can rebuild, Princess," Rian says. "And quickly, with the aid of magic. Don't be discouraged. It can be restored in a matter of days, with the right provisions. It will be expensive, but it can be done."

"It did seem that our side had the upper hand," I offer reassuringly. "Especially since that dragon took much of the Dusk's forces away."

Margy nods slowly. With a glance at Tib, she takes a deep breath, squares her shoulders, and turns to the Knight. "I'm ready. We have all that is required, now."

Rian hands the coin to the Knight, who accepts it with a nod and tucks it into a dusty pouch at his belt. He then turns to the princess and salutes.

"I suppose there's nothing more to say than this," the knight says with a bob of his head. "Welcome to Brindelier, Princess Margary Plethore," he steps quickly aside, and the gates swing open.

"Welcome to you as well, Twiggish of Kythshire," Stryker peeps from his hood.

"Lady Knight," the knight nods at me as I escort Margary through the gates.

"Flitter, welcome!" Stryker says.

"Mentor Rian," the Knight says.

"And welcome, Shushing," says Stryker.

We pass through the gate to face another, larger gate of gilt filigree. Beyond it, the city of Brindelier shines with brilliant splashes of color that seem to adorn every surface. I gaze into the city, dazzled by the artistry of the carved stone walls and statues depicting everything from fish to birds and dancers to soldiers.

"Ho, wait a moment there, you two," the knight says, and I turn to see him straighten dubiously as he looks Tib and Saesa over. "You are unpaired."

"Oh, what now?" Rian murmurs under his breath.

"Unpaired?" Tib scowls. "What do you mean?"

"Saesa is my squire," I explain, reaching for her.

"That is acceptable," says the Knight, and Saesa slips past him to stand by me. He turns to Tib. "And you? Where is your Faedin?"

"My what?" Tib scowls.

"Your link. Your Ili'luvrie."

"I don't have one," Tib crosses his arms defiantly.

"He's lying!" Stryker gasps. "Why would he lie about his Faedin,

Gus? Deception! Danger!"

The Knight places a hand on his sword hilt for the first time since our arrival. "Why, indeed?" he asks with a warning tone.

"Wait," Rian says, stepping between the knight and Tib. "It's not a deception. Tib isn't lying. It's just a misunderstanding. Tib's Faedin is Mevyn of Sunteri. The Keeper of the Wellspring. His denial of their pairing is not a deception, but a protection."

Gus looks Tib over cautiously. "Is that so? Tib, is it?"

Tib glares at the knight, his arms still crossed, his fists clenched hard around the handles of the knives tucked in his bandoliers. His lips press into a thin line. He glances at Rian and huffs a single breath through flared nostrils. "Yeah," he finally admits through clenched teeth.

Still hidden in Gus's helm, Stryker sniffs loudly at Tib. "That's right," he declares.

"Enter, then, Tib. You are most welcome here," the knight says, and to my surprise, he bows to Tib in a gesture that is more reverent even than his treatment of the Princess herself.

The inner gate opens, and as we step through it I hear Stryker mutter to Gus, "What a motley bunch."

"Aye," says the knight as the gate creaks shut. "I wish them all the best."

"They'll need it!" Stryker's laughter is shut out as soon as the gate closes, leaving us in complete silence to stand in awe before the great city.

"Will you look at that?" Rian whispers. He takes my hand and gapes at the city streets that stretch out before us. Everything is brilliantly clean and shining. Even the roads are a smooth, solid stone like the polished floors of the palace in Cerion. Graceful statues of dancing children painted with bright colors line the entry to the city, and banners of every color flap in the soft breeze. The air is temperate, not too cold or hot, even when we step past the main archway into the sunny square beyond.

On the opposite side of the square from the gate, buildings of painted stone tower over a babbling fountain. The shape of them is strange, narrow on the bottom and wide at the top, and each one is uniquely decorated with carvings of flowers and fauna and depictions of people performing various tasks. Margy crosses the square, wide-eyed, and we follow in a close-knit group, scanning the area for any possible threat. The thought is practical, but it seems ridiculous. The city is eerily silent. No carts roll through the streets, no merchants call from their stands, no horses stomp their hooves, impatient for grain. If it wasn't so well kept-up, if things weren't so polished and cleaned, it might seem abandoned.

Margy pauses at the wide window of what seems to be a tailor. The clothes on display within are bright hues of blue, green, purple, and teal. Exquisite embroidered gowns sparkle blindingly, almost as though they've been enchanted with light. Beyond the shop mannequins, the figure of a woman lies stretched out on an ornate, heavily-pillowed chaise. Her hair is perfectly set in curls piled on top of her head. The ruffles of her gown drip from the edge of the chaise in a glittering cascade of teal and blue like a waterfall. Her painted red lips are parted slightly, and her thick lashes graze her pink cheeks as she sleeps. In her hand is an embroidery hoop stitched with bright red thread against a golden silk. It's tipped perfectly so that we can read the fine script that says, very plainly, "Welcome."

"She looks like a doll," Margy whispers. "A real, lady-sized doll."

She tears herself away from that window to the next, and the scene inside is just as enchanting. This window is highly decorated with cheerful ribbons that sway in the breeze as we approach. In the window, several groupings of wares are on display. There are finely crafted amulets, strangely shaped hats, boots with odd silver trinkets dangling from them, glass bottles of every shape and color, books with strange writing and bold, rich illustrations on the covers, wrist cuffs of gold and silver, fine daggers inlaid with rare gemstones, and so many more items that we all peer into the window, captivated by the scene.

"Uh," Tib tugs my cloak after a long while. "It's just a shop. Can we go?"

"Wait," Margy whispers and points to the window. Past the display, in the shop itself, a wizened old Mage with a long beard sits propped against the counter. His head rests on the counter top beside an enormous tome, and every once in a while, the pages are rustled by his breath. Along the counter's edge, silvery letters float aimlessly, spelling out a single word: Welcome. Two young apprentices lie curled up on the floor on fluffy cushions. Each has a fairy tucked in the crook of his arm. All that is visible is the glint of their wings as the apprentices' chests rise and fall. A long scroll is stretched out between them, and a single word is illuminated on the parchment, arranged so it faces us.

"Welcome," Margy reads. "See it?"

"It's like they've been waiting for us," Saesa says with wonder.

430

"It's almost as if," Rian says as he moves to the next shop window, "they knew they were going to be enchanted. They understood well in advance. Look how everything is decorated as if for a festival."

"To celebrating waking up," Flitt says as she presses her nose to the window and licks her pink lips. "Ohh, look at the sweets! Cubes and cakes, Azi! And look at those! Oh! They look like tiny rain drops!"

We gaze together into the window at the little cakes artfully arranged to form the word, "Welcome." Again we linger, taking in the array of colors and whispering about the slumbering shop keepers dressed in cheerful striped gowns and aprons and oddly shaped hats. Tib slinks away from us to the next shop while we ogle the tasty looking treats, our mouths watering. When we finally tear ourselves away and come to his side, Margy laughs.

"We're enthralled by sweets and magic, and this is where Tib finds his fancy," she giggles.

The display in this shop is cluttered with all sorts of metals and ropes. Wooden crates filled with gears and pikes and screws and nails are stacked to the ceiling precariously beside the window, as though they're about to tip. Tucked in the corner, looking rather grumpy, a red-nosed, round-faced merchant in a greasy leather apron sits with his arms crossed, snoring loudly. As we watch, his face starts to twitch. The long hairs of his mustache wind up around his nose. The shopkeeper sneezes so loudly that the crates in the window teeter dangerously. Giggles echo from the silence.

"Hey," Tib taps the glass, "stop that."

"Who are you—" I whisper, and clap my hands over my mouth as two fairies shimmer into view inside the shop. One tugs on the shopkeeper's mustache again, and the second perches on the nearly-tipping stack of crates. In unison, they wink at us through the window. The man sneezes, and the crates tip and smash through the window with a resounding crash, spraying us with shattered glass.

Rian throws up a shield before any of us can even think to duck, and the glass falls to the ground at our feet with a soft, chime-like tinkling. With another peal of giggles, the two fairies dash out of the broken window in blurs of gold and silver.

They dart around Tib, who raises his hands to swat them away. Before anyone can stop them, they unclasp his bandolier, pull it free, and tear off down the street with it, bubbling with laughter.

"Get back here! Give that back!" Tib bellow.

"Make us!" they squeal merrily in the distance. "Catch us!"

Rian whispers a quick spell that sends the crates and gears back through the window, stacked perfectly as they were before. Another spell sends the glass swirling into place, perfectly repaired. Margy and Tib are the first to dash off after the thieving fairies, with the rest of us not far behind.

Chapter Fifty-One
BRINDELIER

Tib

Red. Blue. Purple. Green. Yellow. Orange. With Margy's hand in mine, we race together through the streets of Brindelier after the two thieves who stole my bandolier. All the colors of the rainbow streak together along the walls of houses and shops as we chase after them. Running is liberating. I didn't realize how long it had been since I'd had a good, strong run. This city is doused with magic. It seeps through the stone walls. It hangs thick in the air. Creepy. Strange. Everyone else seems enthralled by this place and everything in it, but not me. I see it for what it is. An ancient place, frozen in time. Dipped and draped with strong enchantments to keep it still and perfect. To preserve it. Cakes and sweets that were baked a century ago? No, thank you. The way the others stood staring in windows, unable or unwilling to turn away, bothered me.

And now, this. Fairies. Not just mischievous but thieving. Stealing, trifling little sneaks. I pump my legs faster. To my surprise, Margy keeps up. Good thing. I'm so mad at those fairies I'd probably let go of her hand and leave her behind if she was too slow.

Up ahead, there's a fountain. A man on a horse, draped in flowers. The horse is rearing up. Water shoots from its mouth. The fairies glint and flash as they hover high above it, waiting. Margy and I skid to a stop just before the fountain's pool. The others aren't far behind us.

As soon as they're sure we're all together, the fairies start laughing again. They pull a purple vial from my bandolier and toss it down at us. Before it reaches the ground, it transforms into a butterfly. The butterfly turns into ten butterflies. They swarm around us, releasing golden dust that tickles my nose. Margy yawns and sways. Shush blows a puff of wind, and the butterflies tumble away.

"Go home!" the two cry in unison. "We'll pay you to leave!"

They throw another vial, this one yellow, and it bursts into a hundred golden coins that rain down on us and clatter on the polished stone of the street. As each coin falls, it multiplies into more coins until we can't take a step without losing our footing on them.

433

"You're wasting my vials!" I shout up at the pair. "Give that back!"

"Give that back!" the silver one mocks in a nasally, high-pitched voice. She tugs the bandolier from the golden one and tosses it onto the statue's raised sword.

"Get it yourself!" the gold one laughs. The two link arms and spin in place, and the silver one streaks down toward Azi. Flitt tucks the offering orb protectively into her belt pouch just in time. The gold fae plunges into Azi's chest plate and races off with her diamond before Azi can think to stop her.

"Flitt!" she shouts. "Your tether!"

Azi, Saesa, and Flitt rush off after the pair, who have already disappeared a safe distance down the street across from the statue.

"Here, Tib," Rian says hastily. He wriggles his fingers at the statue's sword and my bandolier floats down into my waiting hands.

"Thanks," I say as I buckle it back on.

"Let's go!" Rian says. He and I help the princess get her footing until she's past the coins, and together we race off after Azi, Flitt, and Saesa.

We find them in the midst of a sleeping parade route. Carriages decked in banners and streamers sit motionless along the main square, with people lying sound asleep both inside the carriages and on the street, draped in silks and propped on pillows. In the center of the square, a stage is set with yellow and green curtains. Dancers in gaudy costumes lay in a perfect formation on the stage, arranged to spell out the same word as in the windows: Welcome.

"Look," says Margy, "It's absolutely…" her voice trails off.

"Creepy," I finish for her with a mutter.

"Tib! No it isn't," she swats my arm as we watch Rian and Azi and Saesa pick their way through the sleeping crowd up to the stage, where Flitt's diamond glitters between the two hovering fairies perched in the curtains.

"Please," Azi calls up to them, "I don't understand why you're behaving this way. That diamond is precious to me. It means a great deal. May I have it back?"

"You don't think so?" I ask Margy. "How long have they been sleeping like this? A hundred years? Doesn't ever rain here? Don't they get burned by the sun? Or pecked at by birds? How are they not dead? When do they eat? When do they relieve themselves?"

"Tib!" Margy gasps, scandalized.

"What? It's a fair question."

"It's magic, Tib," Twig whispers.

"It's creepy. And why is everything all decorated for a festival?" I scowl. "It's very strange."

"It's wonderful," Margy says under her breath as Azi argues with the little thieves. "The kingdom knew they had to go to sleep, and they were so hopeful they'd be woken one day that they made ready for a grand celebration. They prepared for it. I think it's an amazing show of the sort of people they are."

"Look there," I say as the fairies toss the diamond back to Azi and dart off again. "Those hedges should have overgrown the entire place by now, and they're perfect. Who trims them? Who takes care of the sleeping city?"

Margy takes my hand and we run off after the others, back at the chase.

"Nobody does, Tib. It's magic," she says. "And it's remarkable."

I glance sidelong into her eyes, which are bright with wonder and hope. Innocence. Joy. She loves this. Even the part with the annoying little fae. She thinks it's an adventure. A story to be told one day. It makes me uneasy. This much magic, no matter why it's been used, is a danger. The fact that she doesn't see it and neither does anyone else, worries me. Even Azi and Rian are laughing ahead of us. The fae have taken something of Saesa's. Feat. Her sword. They disarmed her just like they disarmed me, and everyone thinks it's a game.

'How many circles are you, Magey-Mage?" the silver fairy calls down to the others, who are gathered below a painted statue of a herd of elk galloping across brook. Behind them is the grand stairway to a building so impressive it can only be the palace of Brindelier.

"Oh," Margy gasps in wonder at the sight of it. The face of the palace is made up of perfectly symmetrical webs of stone, like lace rosettes. Each one is lined inside with colored glass, so the entire front of it glitters and shimmers with reflections of the sky and the buildings around it. On the other side of the facade, there are dozens of spires that point up to the sky. They are all different heights, from two stories to probably twenty. Just like the rest of the city, every surface of every spire is carved with scenes and painted with bright colors.

The most disturbing part of the outside of the palace are the suits of armor lined up along the walk. They stand completely still. They don't even breathe. Still, I feel like they're watching us as Margy and I join the others. With my healed eye I look closely at them, but I can't tell if they're actual guards, or just enchanted suits of armor. The fact that I can't see either way puts me on edge.

"Yes, yes, how many Circles?" the gold fairy clicks his tongue at the silver one, and she tosses Feat to him. He catches it and swings it around aimlessly, which looks ridiculous because the sword is several times his size.

"Twenty," Rian answers warily.

"Twenty!" the silver one yelps.

"Twenty!" the gold one laughs. "How old are you?"

"Nineteen," Rian says. "Please return my Lady Knight's Squire's sword."

"Ooooh a Lady Knight and a Squire," the silver one chirps. "Which one is here to wake the twins, hm?"

"I am," Margy says, stepping forward. The gold fairy spies her, his eyes narrowed, and drops the sword. Rian flicks his wrist to slow it with a spell before it clatters to the ground, and Saesa rushes to retrieve it.

The gold fairy floats down slowly, looking over Margy in her plain, smudged white robes of mourning. He closes one eye, looks at her hand in mine, and sneers.

"Who's that?" he wrinkles his nose at me.

The silver fairy darts annoyingly around my head, and I swat her away.

"This is Tib," Margy says, and to my dismay, she lets go of my hand and takes a step away from me. "He's a friend."

"And who're you?" he asks. When he flies close to her, Rian, Azi, and Saesa take a protective step toward the princess.

"Margary Plethore, daughter of His Majesty, King Tirnon Plethore, grandson of His Majesty, King Asio Plethore, Princess and rightful heir of Cerion."

The two fairies dart around each other, whispering quickly.

"Pretty curls," golds says to silver.

"Dull brown eyes," the silver one shrugs. "And what is she wearing? Where is her crown if she's a princess? Do they all dress like that?"

"Don't know," shrugs the gold.

"What do you think?" whispers the silver. "Let her in?"

"Yes, let her in," the gold nods. "Let them decide."

"Come on, then, Princess. This way," the silver one chirps.

Margary takes a step, and the rest of us group up behind her.

"Oh, no, no, no," says the gold. "Just the princess."

"I'm not letting her out of my sight," I say sternly.

"Nor are we," Azi says, and I'm glad she sees things the way I do.

"Azi is her Champion," Rian explains to the fairies, who both hover with their arms crossed, looking dubious.

"We all go, or none of us goes," I say.

"All right, all right," says the silver. "You don't have to be such dudskuns. You can come in a little further."

"Dudskuns?" the gold one mutters to the silver, and they both giggle again as they lead the way through the palace doors and into the courtyard.

"Fillidinks?" the silver laughs.

"Sordiwumpuses," snorts the gold one.

"Gig-a-lum-kus-es," the silver gasps between each part of the word, trying to catch her breath from laughing so hard.

"Oh, that's a good one. Tell that one to Poe."

They pause in front of a set of steps across the courtyard. Here, we can look straight up and see the full height of the impressive spires. Even Rian stands with his neck craned back, gaping. Even I do, as annoyed as I am by this bold city and these stupid fae and their ridiculous games.

"You should really change," the gold one says to Margy. "What were you thinking coming in such a dull outfit?"

"Yeah, she's right," says the silver. "You'll never impress Poe looking that way."

"Poe?" Margy asks nervously.

"Yes, Poe. You know? Prince Poelkevren?"

"His name is Pole- kevrin?" I huff, and Margy quickly shushes me.

"Didn't you know that?" the silver one throws over her shoulder as she flutters away, leading us down a polished golden hallway. "You've come to offer your hand to someone and you don't even know his name?"

"How dare you," I utter under my breath and Rian catches me by the collar and tugs me back to keep me from snatching her right out of the air.

"Now," Azi says. She rests a reassuring hand on Margy's shoulder. "Wait a moment. We won't have you speak to our princess that way. She's been through many trials to get this far. We all have. And you've done nothing but make a game of all of us since we arrived here. You've insulted her clothes and her looks, and now you insult her intelligence. If you can't show her the respect she is due, then perhaps your prince isn't the right fit for our princess."

I look at Azi with admiration. She said exactly what I wanted to, but I never could have done it with that much respect and kindness. I'd much rather have wrung their tiny fairy necks.

The silver fairy stares at Azi, and the silence between them hangs heavy in the air. After a long exchange of awkward silence, the silver fairy sticks out her bottom lip in a tiny pout, shrugs her shoulders, and says, "Fair enough. But I really think she ought to at least change her gown."

"It's not a gown, you idiot," I shout, unable to control my anger any longer. "It's a robe of mourning! For her father! She left his Rites to come here, for you stupid people! She left him so she could save you before the Dusk gets here, you ungrateful little specks!"

"Specks!" the gold one yelps. "Specks!"

The others stare at me, horrified.

"I like it," says the silver one. "That's a good one. Look how angry he is. He's funny."

"Smart, too," says the gold. "Did you see that ship?"

"I saw it. Impressive," the silver one says coyly. "He's got a Keeper, too." She flits closer to me and I glare at her. "Oh, yes. We know about you."

"Yeah. We like you," says the gold. "You're spunky. Sparky."

"Sparky! Get it? Because he just bursts out unexpectedly?" The silver one pats the gold one on the back, and they turn from us to drift along the bright corridor. "Good one!"

"That's your nickname, then, Sunteri boy," the gold one says. "Sparky."

"No, it isn't," I grumble. "My name is Tib."

"The Knight can be Twinkles, because of her gold Mark."

"Twinkles, yes!"

"And the tall one is Lanky."

"Lanky!"

"And the—"

"No, the tall one is Rian," Flitt interrupts. "I call him Stinky, because you know, Mages." I can almost hear the eye-roll in her tone as she floats up alongside them.

"Stinky! That's great! What about you? What's your name? You have such pretty hair," the silver says to Flitt.

"Flitter. What's yours?"

"Aliandra," says the silver. "And this is my brother, Alexerin. We're

Earths-and-Light. You're pure Light, right?"

"Right," says Flitt.

The three fairies chatter together. As they us lead along the shining corridor, Margy slips her hand into mine again.

"*Should I fix them?*" she pushes to Twig. "*My robes?*"

"*No, Princess,*" Twig pushes back. "*Be yourself. Azi and Tib are right. Let them appreciate you for who you truly are. If they won't, then it's their own loss.*"

Inside of the palace is just as obnoxious as the outside. High ceilings that open to the blue sky. Walls of polished gold and silver in some places. In others, shining glass mosaics show scenes of kings and queens and Mages and fairies playing games, dancing, and singing. Chairs in the shapes of different animals and cushioned with patterns of stripes and spots are arranged in little groupings everywhere. Even in the hallways. Like the Royal Court of Brindelier can't bear to walk from one room to another without having to take a rest in between.

Some of the chairs have people sitting on them, all dressed in jewels and lace. Fairies curl in their laps or in the crook of their arms or on their shoulders. Asleep. All of them, asleep. I want to pull Margy away. Far from here. Fly away on my ship with her. This place doesn't suit her. She doesn't belong here. She doesn't need these riches. Even in her plain white robes, she's prettier than all of them.

She doesn't see it, though, my desperation to get her out of here. The look on her face is determined. Excited. Her eyes linger on the fairy companions as we pass by the sleeping subjects. This is a place she feels she can belong.

We follow the fairies up into an enormous tower, with a spiral staircase that goes up forever. I remember the tallest spires outside and imagine we must be climbing up into one of them. Finally, we stop before a set of tall doors that are arched to point. It's more of a gate than a door, gold and silver and bronze all twisted together like curling vines. Sunlight spills through them onto the floor in front of us, glaringly brightly. The shadows it casts on the polished marble swirl like Mage Mark. When we get close enough, Azi and Flitt's light cast the shadows away. The fairies turn to us and exchange an impressed glance. In awe, Margy steps closer.

The others can't feel it. I know they can't. The magic on the other side of that gate. Like a thousand spells, pulsing. Wards. Enchantments. Power. A Wellspring, much stronger than Sunteri's. Glowing. Breathing. Like a living creature.

"All right, Princess," the silver one, Aliandra, says as she darts around Margy.

"Do you have them?" asks Alexerin. "The offerings?"

"Oh! I do!" Flitt exclaims, and pulls the orb out of her tiny belt pouch. "Here!"

Suddenly, Aliandra and Alexerin grow hushed and reverent.

"Give it to the Princess," Alexerin says. Flitt does as she's told, and Margy takes the orb with her free hand, still clinging to mine.

"With that," Aliandra says, "you may enter. You, and the Champions of Light."

"But you said before..." Azi starts.

"That was a test. You showed us you were protective, and not stupid enough to leave your princess behind," Alexerin says.

"Yeah, we knew all along you were the Champions of Light, and she was the Suitor," Aliandra laughs. "And now, it's time to do what you came here to do."

Azi and Rian exchange a glance. Flitt puffs her chest out proudly. Shush bobs at Rian's shoulder. The four Champions' foreheads glow with a soft dot of white light.

"Very good," Alexerin says with a nod. "You four, then, and the Princess. And her Faedin, of course."

The gate swings open, and Margy starts to go in. I plant my feet. I squeeze her hand. She turns to me with a questioning gaze. I don't say anything.

"And Tib, of course, right?" Margy asks the fae. "And Saesa, Azi's squire?"

"Nope! Sorry, Princess. Rules are rules," Aliandra giggles. "They can wait out here."

Margy shifts uncomfortably and glances at Azi and Rian, and then at me.

"Come with us, Princess," says Alexerin, "or stay with Sparky."

Margy's deep brown eyes meet mine apologetically. Behind her, Azi puts a reassuring hand on her shoulder. I know already what she'll do. She'll make the choice she has to for her kingdom. She'll leave me behind. With a deep breath, she closes her eyes. Steps to me. Hugs me close.

"Thank you," she whispers. "I'll be right back. Promise."

I try to let her go, but I can't. She has to twist and tug her hand to free it from mine. She turns away, and I watch them disappear through the gate into the light.

"Don't worry, Tib," Saesa's gentle hand grazes my arm. "We'll wait together. My Lady Knight will watch over her. She'll be safe."

With the light of the Wellspring flashing in her bright red hair, Saesa seems different. Older. Smarter. Not a scrappy kid like she used to be. She has a calmness about her now. A loyalty. A reverence for her knight. She takes my hand, the same one Margy held, and smiles.

Her smile is different than the way she used to look at me. It's hesitant. Shy. Searching. Something about it thrills me and confuses me. My heart races, just like it does when Margy lets me hold her and I can smell the flowers in her hair. Strangely and suddenly, I remember all those days ago when Saesa fell into my arms at the apothecary booth. How she brushed her lips to mine. *I can't hide my feelings anymore,* she had said. I close my eyes and shake my head. Refuse to think about this right now. Not with whatever's happening on the other side of that gate. I blame it on the power that seeps from the very stones of this city and coats everything around us like dust. It's confusing me. Jumbling my thoughts and feelings. Saesa's green eyes gaze up, waiting. I close mine and turn away from her, and she drops my hand and goes to the gate to look through.

"I understand, Tib," she says with a hint of sadness. "It's like Nessa always says, 'The heart pays no mind to the mind.' Come on. We can watch from here."

"No," I say quietly. My heart is still thudding. I can't make sense of things. This ridiculous city is grating on me. The magic is suffocating. All the colors, all the grandeur. Everywhere I turn, there's no escaping it. Now this. Saesa. Margy. I can't stay here, knowing on the other side of that gate Margy is meeting her future…what? Husband? And Saesa, looking at me that way. I don't understand when things changed between us, but I hate it. I don't need this. I need to clear my head. Be alone. Hide away. Before I do something stupid. Before I hurt Saesa's feelings. "I'm leaving."

"What? You can't Tib, what about Margy?" Saesa steps away from the gate and reaches for me, but I back away. "You promised you'd wait."

"No, I didn't. She promised she'd be back. I didn't say I'd wait for her. I have to get out of here." I take another step backwards. The cobwebs brush my skin. I disappear into the Half-Realm. I turn to the stairs, and I run.

Chapter Fifty-Two
THE PACT
Azi

Despite the overwhelming feeling of welcome from within, I keep my guard up as the two fairies lead us through the gilded gate into the blinding sunlight of the gardens within. Unlike the rest of the palace and the city outside, the tower is full of life and sound. The rustle of leaves and chirping of birds tells me we're in a forest, though it's difficult to see anything at all in the brilliance of the silvery-gold light that beams from the open sky.

"This way," the fairies whisper, and I keep a firm hand on the princess's shoulder for fear of us wandering apart from each other as we stumble forward.

"It's so bright," Margy says. "But it sounds beautiful. I wish I could see it."

"Oh! That's our fault!" Aliandra giggles. "Tone it down, Alexerin."

The silver-gold light dims dramatically to reveal a living jungle surrounding a vast pool of glowing liquid. It swirls with the same light the two fairies cast: Silver and gold. Though it's surrounded by lush green fronds of fern and bright, enormous colorful blossoms, the pool is a perfect circle, like a bowl. It's filled only partway, and as we approach I notice there are six basins with spouts evenly placed around the rim of it tucked inside the greenery. Directly across from us, on the other side of the Wellspring, a pair of twin thrones overlooks the pool. Seated on the thrones are two children who don't look any older than thirteen or fourteen.

Each bears a crown: one silver, one gold. Each has shoulder-length hair so blond it's almost white, and sun-kissed golden skin. Each wears robes of silver under thick embroidered vests of gold. From the Princess's tale and the Fairy Queen's recounting, I know these are the Twin Heirs of Brindelier, and I know one is a Prince and the other a Princess, but their looks are completely identical, making it impossible to tell which is which. Even in sleep, they sit with their backs straight and their heads poised in a regal, commanding posture.

Aliandra flies to the one on the right and perches perfectly in the silver crown. Alexerin darts into the gold crown. Set in place, each looks as though they're part of the masterful jewel work that flashes with reflections of the Wellspring from below and the sunlight from above. The whole scene is brilliant, rich, and quite intimidating. Even the throne room itself in Cerion can't come close to comparing with the grandeur of this scene. Margy seems to agree. She shifts closer to me with the orb in hand, and Rian steps to her other side. To my surprise, he seems completely calm and collected despite how close he's standing to the Wellspring, which is easily double the size of Kythshire's and five times as deep. His hands are relaxed by his sides, and his fingertips aren't even crackling like they usually do in Kythshire.

"Present your offerings," the fairies say in unison. "Set them in their rightful place. Three to wake the heirs. Six to claim the city."

"Here," Rian says, and kneels beside Margy. He places a hand on the orb and nods for me to do the same. Flitt and Shush follow his lead.

My fingertips tingle with the rush of magic that's released as the orb fades to reveal the three bottles holding the offerings of Sunteri, Kythshire, and Haigh. Gently, carefully, Margy cradles them in her arms.

"What now?" she whispers.

"See there?" Twig answers quietly. "The basins. One bottle in each, Princess. Take one for yourself, and give one to Azi and the other to Rian."

"Does it matter who gets which?" she asks. Twig shakes his head. Margy takes Kythshire's teardrop-shaped offering for herself. She hands Sunteri's red, double-bulb-shaped vial to Rian, and Haigh's straight, pillar-shaped golden one to me.

"See how each bottle is shaped differently?" Twig asks in a hushed tone. "Find the basin that fits yours, and set it in place."

The broad green leaves framing the pool brush my shoulders as Flitt and I make our way around the wide circle and look into the basins. Inside each basin at the bottom, just as Twig explained, is a shape to match each bottle. Flitt and I find the one for Haigh to the left of the thrones.

"Together," Twig calls across the basin, and Flitt swoops in to stand beside the cutout that will hold the bottle. I reach in after her and hold it poised in place, then look across to Rian and Shush, who have found Sunteri's basin across the way from ours, and the Princess and Twig, who are on the other side of the thrones from us. "Three, two, one," Twig says, and Flitt and I push the bottle in place.

The bottle disappears beneath a flood of silvery liquid, and Flitt hops into the air just in time to avoid it touching her bare toes. She hovers over it and we watch the liquid pool upward, filling the basin until it spills over through the spout and trickles toward the pool below like a glittering silver fountain. Across the way, the red-gold offering of Sunteri spills over at the same time as Kythshire's multi-colored one. As the streams of offerings splash into the pool, a jet of light shoots up from the center and bursts in the sky in a dazzling display of fiery color. Sparks shoot off in every direction, out of view beyond the walls of the garden. Some of them drift slowly down to the thrones and settle on the shoulders of the prince and princess, whose eyelids flutter open.

In unison, they look straight ahead with piercing silver-blue eyes.

"We are Poelkevren and Pippaveletti Emhyrck. Rightful Heirs to the Throne of Brindelier. Faedin to Aliandra Silver and Alexerin Gold, Keepers of the Great Wellspring. The Allsource. Enchanted into slumber by The Muses of the Six, to await the Age of Awakening." The two rise to their feet, hand in hand, and survey the scene before them dreamily. "Step forward, Princess Margary Plethore, and with you, your Champions. Long have we awaited this moment. You are most welcome here."

Each of the twins makes a sweeping gesture, and the liquid in the Wellspring shifts and rises to form an ornate bridge which stretches from each of our spouts to the center of the Wellspring, and to the throne. With Twig at her shoulder, Margy takes a hesitant step onto the bridge. The light of the Wellspring shimmers over her plain white gown in a colorful array of silver, gold, blue, and red. Rian and I join her in the center, and together we walk across the pool to stand before the twins. Rian and I bow our heads to them, and the two greet Margy by joining hands with her. Both twins dip down into a bow or curtsy. It's still impossible to tell who is who.

"In whose name do you waken our city, Princess Margary of Plethore? The Dawn, or The Dusk?" the twins' voices echo together. Their movements are always in perfect unison. It's disconcerting, like a living mirror. Even more unnerving is the way their eyes stare forward blankly.

"The Dawn," Margy replies confidently. Her declaration seems to break the strange, dream-like state holding the twins. Another jet of magic bursts through the bridge and explodes into the sky above us.

This time, the shower of sparks is much brighter as it falls away.

The gold-crowned twin falls into Margy's arms, laughing with relief.

"Thank the stars," she lets out a long-held breath and hugs Margy tight.

"I told you it would be the Dawn, Pippa," the silver-crowned twin's voice is slightly huskier than his sister's.

"I know, Poe, but we could never be certain," Pippa whispers.

Poe grins and gathers his sister and Margy into his arms. He bends and kisses his sister's temple. "Oh," he clears his throat and steps away from Margy, then drops to his knee. "Forgive me for being so forward." He tugs on his sister's robes and she drops down, too.

"Yes, forgive us. We're just so pleased," she whispers, and bows her head to Margary.

"I am yours, Your Highness," Poe says formally. He stretches a hand to her, but keeps his head bowed respectfully. "Claim my hand and be my queen, and we shall rule Brindelier together."

"I-I..." Margy looks up at me, wide-eyed, then glances behind her at the far-away gate. Her eyes glint with tears as Poe risks a glance up. "I just..." she whispers.

"If you do not wish to rule beside me, then why have you come? What would possess one with beauty and talent such as yours to seek this place, if not to claim our throne?" Poe asks, puzzled.

"Please," Margy says after a shuddering breath. "Please, stand up. Both of you." She clasps her hands in front of herself and waits for them to do as she asks. "It isn't that I don't wish to join our kingdoms. It's just all very sudden, don't you think? Brindelier has been asleep for over a century. So much has changed in that long span. And Cerion has suffered in our efforts to reach you. My kingdom..." her voice trails off and she swallows back tears.

"What, Princess? What has happened to Cerion?" Poe asks with concern. Beside him, his sister looks equally grave.

Margy tries to explain, but her voice fails her each time. Finally, Twig speaks up.

"Sir Azaeli can show you," he says. "If you'll allow it."

Pippa looks up at me. Poe's eyes trace the golden Mark on my skin. I offer them both a kind smile.

"A Mentalist?" Pippa whispers in awe. "Truly?"

"They're probably quite common in this age, Pippa. Don't stare," Poe says with quiet reverence.

"They aren't!" Flitt pipes up. "They're very rare, actually! Azi is the only one in Cerion, that's for certain."

"All right, Flitt," I chuckle.

"Will you show us?" Poe asks hesitantly.

"Of course," I say.

The same way I did before at the gate, I open my palms and let my memories of the scenes of the battle and the important moments leading up to it play across my palms. The twins watch, entranced, until the moment we set the bottles into the basins. When the scene fades, the two of them blink. Pippa is the first to speak.

"Alex," she scolds, "you were very naughty."

"You too, Aliandra," Poe scowls.

The fairies in their crowns giggle and dart away, then splash down into the Wellspring.

"I apologize for them," Poe shakes his head, "they must have been very bored for rather a long time."

"It's no excuse," Pippa says, scowling into the pool.

"You're right," Poe says, and turns to Margy. "Your father," he steps closer to her and takes her hands in his. His eyes search hers, and Margy blinks back tears. "I'm so sorry. I understand now. You're in mourning. This is no time—"

"Splendid, splendid, a Princess for our Prince!" A hearty voice echoes through the courtyard from the gateway across the Wellspring. "The festival has begun, and this will be a day of great celebration. Poelkevrin, what a king you shall be!" A bald-headed man in an overly gaudy green-and gold vest and matching embroidered trousers rustles through the thick ferns and broad leaves and makes his way to the platform to join us. His smile shows a row of perfectly straight, shining white teeth, and when he reaches for Margy, I step closer to her. Mercy glints at my shoulder, and he glances at the hilt of it warily and back at the Princess again. He thinks the better of touching her, and instead leaves his hands at his sides where they belong.

"How lovely she is," he exclaims boisterously. "Your subjects are all in place, Your Highness. It shall be a wedding unlike any in the history of Brindelier. Oh, but you cannot be wed in such a drab frock, my dear. Come. We will make you a fitting bride."

"Thalin." Poe says sternly. "Thalin!" he calls again loudly, and the boisterous man turns and raises a brow at the prince.

"Your Highness?" he asks.

"There will be no wedding today," the Prince declares, and Thalin's face falls dramatically. A button of his vest pops out, and a fairy with fiery-red hair and bright yellow eyes peeks out at us through the button-hole.

"No wedding?" she squeaks.

"What?" Thalin asks weakly, obviously gravely disappointed. "But, Your Highness. The people...everything is ready... they expect..." his pleading turns to whimpering, and he wrings his hands nervously. "But...why?"

"The princess is in mourning," Poe explains. "She wishes to honor the Rites of her father. Her city is in ruins. As a gesture of gratitude to Cerion and the sacrifices her people have made to get here before the agents of Dusk, we shall offer them our assistance in rebuilding."

"To foster goodwill and strengthen our alliance," says Pippa.

"After which time, if she will agree, we shall have a proper courtship," Poe announces. He leans closer to Margary and looks her in the eye, "and you will be free to choose, Your Highness, without any pressure or obligation. Agreed?"

Margy looks up at him, her face flush with relief, and nods. "Thank you for your understanding."

"No wedding," Thalin mumbles, still quite agitated. "Well, then, a presentation, perhaps? Of the Champions and the Princess? We have to give them something, Your Highness."

Poe looks to Margy, and the princess nods her agreement.

"Very well," Pippa says.

"Excellent!" Thalin claps excitedly. "I shall make the preparations at once!" He rushes off in a blur of green and gold, and Poe sighs and shakes his head.

"You'll get used to Thalin," he says to her. "He's enthusiastic, but completely harmless. Come, let me show you around." He offers her his arm, and when she takes it, he leads her away with the rest of us following close behind.

Chapter Fifty-Three
RUINS AND RENOVATIONS

Azi

"Ugh, you said it wasn't so bad," Flitt sniffs at the soot-coated ribbons that once decorated her pitcher and wrinkles her nose. "It smells like smoke and charcoal, and burnt things that never should burn."

"I know," I sigh and pick through the fallen crumbled roof near what used to be my bed. The black rubble puffs ash with every step I take. This is the first time I've been allowed here since we returned from Brindelier. My bedroom seems to have suffered the most damage compared to the rest of the hall. Due partly to smoke damage and mostly to the Queen's favor, the Elite has been given rooms in the palace until we're able to clean up and rebuild. I've been here since this morning, combing through the rubble to see if there was anything I could salvage. From the looks of it, there isn't much.

The silver handle of my hairbrush glints in the sun and I crouch and pick it up. The bristles have burned away, but the rest of it can be saved. I wipe off the soot with the shredded remains of Redemption's flag and toss it into my rucksack.

"They're all just things, though," I say with a sigh. "And thankfully, the fire didn't reach far."

"Right!" Flitt chirps. "Good thing Mouli stayed safe. I'd be sad without her sweet rolls."

"And Luca, too," I nod in agreement.

"Yeah, him, too," she beams brightly. "Want to play?"

"Sure," I reply as I nudge aside a pile of burnt timber with my boot.

"Good!" she chirps, then scowls as she points at the torn banner in my hand. "Will they have their heads chopped, like Prince Creepy?"

"Most likely," I shove the rag into my pocket, gather an armload of charred masonry and roof tiles, and toss them out of the hole in my wall into the street below for the scavengers. "After the battle was won by Cerion, all of the banished members of Redemption were captured and sent to the dungeons. They say they recovered a good number of the escaped prisoners, as well. The elves were very helpful there. Eyes from the sky." I gather another load and toss it out. "So, what did you find out?" I ask. Ever since our return from Brindelier I've been keeping myself out of sight, worried that my involvement in the final battle would garner me too much fame to be able to walk the streets without being bombarded by people. I gave Saesa leave to help the Ganvents rebuild, so I'm grateful Flitt agreed to fly around and see what she could find out.

"Nobody knows it was you," she darts to my side, picks up a broken roof tile, and heaves it out of the hole. "They're all talking about it, of course, while they work. You should hear the chatter! I bet they'd get a lot more done if there wasn't so much gabbing. But you should see how much better things look already. Your uncle is doing a good job keeping his Mages busy."

"They aren't his Mages, Flitt," I laugh softly.

"Well, for all we're concerned, they are. I mean, Queen Naelle is doing all right as regent, but Gaethon is really the one in charge when it comes to rebuilding. He's keeping them in a good, straight line. And the Brindelier Mages are amazing. You should see them! Gaethon keeps having to tell them to tone it down, though. He doesn't want Cerion to look like Brindelier. I don't see why. Brindelier is so much prettier. And the regular people are working really hard when they don't even have to."

"It's our way, Flitt," I explain. "Cerion's craftsmen have always taken pride in their work, and for a long time, they didn't have jobs. His Majesty was too distracted by the trial to make time for new projects. Now, they can work at their crafts and get paid. It's almost like a rebirth for the city. In some ways, this is just what they needed."

"Anyway," Flitt says with a roll of her eyes. "To answer your question, everyone's talking about the black dragon and the winged centaur. Nobody knows you were inside of it, though. It must have felt unreal, Azi! Being one with Memi!" she gasps and twirls prettily, sending beams of rainbows scattering across my blackened ceiling. "Oh! I wish I had been there. Everyone says you were enormous. Taller than your house! I believe it. The Light is very powerful, and you had the actual Dawn on your side, too. Great timing, just at sunrise. But that wasn't an accident, I'm sure. Memi is smart. She was just biding her time for the sunshine. The fairies said you held your own pretty well before then. Your battle against Eron was impressive." She pauses to think of her question as she tosses another broken tile outside. "Have you heard from your mum today?"

"This morning," I reply quietly, my thoughts turning to my mother. Outside of my undamaged window, Da's hammer rings against his anvil. He's been working non-stop for two days now, since the battle ended, making trivial things: nails and door handles and tools for rebuilding. Keeping himself busy while Mum is away. "There was a bird to tell us she's safe. Rian's not going to attempt that journey again."

Flitt laughs, but I feel the color draining from my face at the memory of myself in his arms as we plummeted dangerously toward the ground on our first attempt to reach Mum. Apparently, traveling through the Half-Realm to a flying ship that we've never been on and don't know the exact location of is not a reliable way to reach someone.

"Luckily Rian kept his head, Flitt, or you would have had a flatcake for a Faedin." I shiver at the thought of it as I clear more of the rubble. Overcoming my fear of heights was short-lived. After my little adventure with Rian, I find I still have a hearty respect for heights. "So, we're sticking with birds for now. The old way. They're much safer for everyone. Once they arrive at the location, Rian and I will bring Uncle to meet them."

"And then what?" she asks.

"Ha! You lose!" I clap in triumph, sending a puff of soot dancing off into her beams of light. "It was my turn for a question."

"Oh!" she gasps and claps her hands over her mouth, leaving black fingerprints around her pink lips. She sneezes twice and then sniffles. "That's not fair!"

"It's fair," Rian appears in my doorway, grinning. "Looks like you're getting rusty at your own game, Flitt."

"Hmph," Flitt pouts. "I'll get you next time, Azi."

"Oh, I'm sure I'll regret it," I say with a laugh and turn to Rian. He's been hard at work with the other Mages, rebuilding and cleaning out, and yet his blue robes are perfectly neat and straight, and there is no hint of soot on his skin or pieces of rubble in his beard. A basket draped with a white cloth hangs on the crook of his elbow, and the aroma of fresh-baked bread and spices that wafts from it makes my stomach growl.

"Ready?" he asks me. I nod, and with a sweep of his hand, my clothing shifts from dingy gray pants and shirt to a soft white summer dress. My hair sweeps up on its own, my braid crowning my head. The soot and ash clear from my skin, leaving it soft, golden tan.

"Are you coming?" I ask Flitt as I pick my way across the room to join him.

"Not today," she replies. "It's dreadfully boring up there, and besides, Alex asked me to join him in the festival."

"Oh, it's Alex now, is it?" Rian wriggles his brow to tease her, and Flitt tosses her rainbow ponytails and raises her chin. Her cheeks go bright red, and her light pulses brightly. She doesn't say anything, she just shrugs.

"They sure know how to throw a party up there," I say, trying to steer the conversation away from the obviously embarrassing topic for her.

"Oh, yes!" Flitt exclaims. "It's been going strong since we left, with no signs of stopping. No wonder Princess Margy was eager to leave, considering."

"Right," says Rian. "Speaking of whom, we ought to be going."

"I'll see you tomorrow?" I ask Flitt, and she nods and gives me a sooty kiss on the cheek before darting off out of the gaping hole in my wall.

"I thought she'd never leave," Rian says, pulling me close. We fall into a long, lingering kiss, and then he takes my hand and leads me outside along the cobbled streets toward the palace.

We pause when we reach the forest park, where fallen trees trampled by the Void are being cleared away by horse and cart. The area is crowded with onlookers, mostly children, who have been gathered at the edge of the park since the work started here. They have come to watch the spectacle of fairies, friends of Twig, who meander through the splintered stumps and lavish their magic upon them, helping the wood to mend together and grow strong and tall once more. The park has always been beautiful, but now it is dazzlingly so. The breeze that rustles through the new leafy canopy is rich with magic and fairy song. This is one place where Uncle has allowed the fairies free reign with their magic, to do whatever they like. The result promises to be a park much more beautiful than the original; an enchanted piece of forest to mirror Kythshire itself.

We slip past the crowds after a short time watching and make our way along the Path of Rites alongside the palace. The line to the Pyre is quite long this evening, and many waiting to pay their respects whisper excitedly as they wait. Not only are they here to see the Princess, but word has spread throughout the city of the mysterious prince from a land like no other who has come to court her. I suspect that most of those waiting have come to catch a glimpse of him as he keeps vigil with Margy.

The line creeps forward, and Rian squeezes my hand as he gazes across the sea to the floating Gate of Brindelier. It hasn't changed since it first appeared. It still looks much the same: A mysterious stone archway set in the center of a small, floating piece of land. For now, while Cerion takes time to recover and Brindelier enjoys its Waking Celebration, it will remain out of reach of the common people. Eventually, when the Rites are over, the gateway will be open to anyone bearing a coin who swears fealty to the Dawn.

We reach the top eventually and pay our respects to the Pyre, and as soon as we turn to face her, Margy's eyes light up. Poe, the prince, smiles in greeting as Rian and I approach, and the two royals sit beneath their canopy of woven vines and flowers, the fine work of Twig. Both are dressed in robes of plain white, and both have set aside their crowns in mourning for the fallen King.

At the Princess's invitation, we sit beside them on cushions spread over the smooth, white stone. This area: the pyre, the wall, and benches were the first to be restored. There are no scorch marks left behind by our battle, no gouges in the stone where Mercy plunged through Eron and pinned him. The Circle of Rites is as pristine as it always has been.

Rian unwraps the sweet rolls and passes them around, and we eat together in silence as we greet the line of grievers that trickles in sporadically. The breeze blowing in from the ocean is cooler than it has been. Summer is waning, giving way to autumn. I lift my face to it and close my eyes as the sweet sugar icing of Mouli's sweet rolls melts on my tongue.

"Any word from Twig?" Rian asks the princess softly.

"Not yet," Margy replies. "And you? Have you heard from Shush?"

"I'm afraid not," Rian answers.

"Don't fret, Princess," Poe offers gently. "The fae are clever. They can search in places our kind can't. They'll find your friend."

Margy gives the prince a grateful smile. Though she was quick to accept Poe's offer of companionship through the rest of the Rites, I know the princess well. There is a sadness deep within her eyes when she looks away from the prince. Her concern for Tib, who has not been seen or heard from since he left the Great Source, is plain to see.

"You're right," she says, and leans back against her pillows. Her wistful gaze searches the skies past her father's pyre, out over the sea.

"They'll find him."

...to be continued in Book Four of the Keepers of the Wellsprings series.

CHARACTER GLOSSARY

Alexerin *(Ah-lex-AIR-in)* A light and earth fairy, Keeper of Brindelier's Wellspring, Poe's Faedin

Aliandra *(Ah-lee-AN-dra)* A light and earth fairy, Keeper of Brindelier's Wellspring, Pippa's Faedin

Amei Plethore *(Ay-mee)* Prince Eron's wife.

Asio Plethore *(Ah-zee-oh)* The first king in the Plethore Dynasty.

Aster *(AS-ter)* An enchanted wand, once in the possession of Kaso Viro.

Averie *(AY-ver-ree)* An apothecary merchant at the Sea Market.

Azaeli Hammerfel (Azi) *(A-zee, A-zay-lee)* *(Not OZZY)* A Knight of His Majesty's Elite, and Ambassador to Kythshire. Daughter of Lisabella and Benen.

Benen Hammerfel *(Ben-in)* Knight of His Majesty's Elite, Azi's father, and Lisabella's husband.

Bette *(Bet)* A cook at the Ganvent Manse.

Brother Donal Vincend *(DON-ol)* Healer of His Majesty's Elite.

Bryse Daborr *(Brice)* Shieldmaster of His Majesty's Elite, partner to Cort.

Cari *(Kaa-REE)* The bookbinder for the Academy.

Celli Deshtal *(CHEL-lee)* A street urchin from Cerion.

Cly Zhrel *(KLY zrell)* Warlord leading the attacks against the White Wall.

Cort Finzael *(Court)* Member of His Majesty's Elite. Swashbuckler and partner to Bryse.

Crocus *(Crow-cuss)* A plant fairy. Leader of the Ring at Kythshire, partner to Scree.

Dacva Archomyn *(Dock-Vuh)* Apprentice healer to Donal, Azi's former rival in training, former member of Redemption.

Dar Archomyn *(Dar)* A guard at the Sorcerers' Keep, a former member of Redemption.

Diovicus *(Dye-ah vik-us)* The Sorcerer King of legend, who nearly overtook Kythshire.

Dreiya *(DRAY-yuh)* A peasant from Redstone Row.

Dub (Wade Cordoven) *(Dub)* A hired assassin for the Dusk.

Dumfrey Pilsen *(DUM-free)* A bumbling Mage in the employ of the Royal Family of Cerion.

Elan *(Ee-LON)* A page at Cerion's castle.

Elliot Eldinae*(El-ee-oht)* Member of His Majesty's Elite. Husband to Mya, and Rian's Father.

Ember*(Ember)* A Fire fairy, and high-ranking member of the Ring in Kythshire.

Emmie Ganvent*(EM-mee)* The only officially adopted child in the Ganvent house.

Eron Plethore (Err-ohn) Son of Tirnon and Naelle. Prince and Heir of Cerion.

Errie Kreston*(AIR-ee)* Child of Maisie, a former resident at the Ganvent Manse. Illegitimate son of Eron.

Finn (Isaac Finnvale) *(Fin)* Princess Margary's personal guard.

Flit (Flitter) *(Flit (like bit))* A Light fairy who has befriended Azi and bonded to her.

Gaethon Ethari *(GAY-thon)* Headmaster of the Academy, Member of HME, Advisor to the throne, Azi's uncle, Rian's mentor.

Garsi Ganvent *(Gar-SEE)* A toddler, the youngest girl at the Ganvent Manse.

Gemma Vander *(JEM-muh)* A barmaid at Seabird's Swoop.

Giff *(Gif)* A friend of Celli's.

Gred *(Gred)* Guardian of the North of Sunteri's Wellspring

Gustaven Felior (Gus) *(Goos-tah-vin)* Gatekeeper of Brindelier - Cerion's archway

Haris Kenswen *(HAR-riss)* A Royal Guard stationed in Cerion's throne room.

Hett *(Het)* A new boy at the Ganvent Manse.

Hew Deshtal *(Hyoo)* Celli's baby brother.

Iren *(EYE-ren)* Guardian of the northern border of Kythshire, Spirit of the Shadow Crag.

Jin *(Jin)* A henchman at the Sorcerer's keep.

Julini Ensintia *(Joo-LEE-nee)* An elf archer, and member of the White Line.

Kasha Deshtal *(KA-sha)* Celli's mother.

Kaso Viro *(KAH-so VEE-roh)* A muse of the Six, a Master Mage bound to the sea.

Ki *(Ki (like eye))* Formerly Viala, an archer in the service of Iren, and Tib's sister.

Kristan Prew *(Kris-TAN)* A general of the Royal Guard.

Lilen Ganvent *(LILL-in)* A Mage Apprentice, the eldest girl at the Ganvent Manse.

Lisabella Hammerfel *(LIZ-uh-BELL-uh)* Knight of His Majesty's Elite, a Paladin, Azi's mother, married to Benen.

Luca Salvaneli *(LOO-kah)* Groundskeeper for His Majesty's Elite.

Maisie Kreston *(MAY-zee)* A former palace maid, mother to Errie. Lives in the Ganvent Manse.

Margary Plethore (Margy) *(MAR-jee)* The youngest princess of Cerion's Royal Family.

Anod Bental *(Ah-NOD BEN-tul)* High Master of the Academy, Mage-Advisor to the King of Cerion.

Mevyn *(MEV-in)* The last of the Sunteri fae.

Mikken *(MICK-ken)* A friend of Celli's.

Milvare (Sen Milvare) *(Mill-VARE)* A Mage-liason to Cerion's peasantry.

Mouli *(MOO-lee)* Housekeeper and cook for His Majesty's Elite. Married to Luca.

Muster *(MUSS-ter)* A half-giant thug for hire, worked with Dub in Call of Sunteri.

Mya *(MY-uh (not MEE-uh))* A bard. Leader of His Majesty's Elite. Rian's mother, and Elliot's wife.

Naelle Plethore *(Ny-ELLE)* Queen of Cerion.

Nan *(Nan (like Ann))* Tib's grandmother. A slave of the dye fields.

Nate *(Nate)* A page at Cerion's castle.

Nessa Ganvent *(NESS-uh)* Wife of Admiral Ganvent. Foster mother to Saesa, Raefe, and many others.

Old Ven *(Ven)* A resident of Redstone Row.

Oren *(OH-reh)* Plant fairies. The Guardians of the Eastern border of Kythshire.

Osven Chente *(OZZ-ven)* A Sorcerer for the Dusk.

Pearl *(Pearl)* Azi's Horse.

Pippaveletti Emhyrck (Pippa) *(Pip-uh-veh-LET-tee)* Princess of Brindelier

Poelkevrin Emhyrck (Poe) *(POLE-kev-rin)* Prince of Brindelier.

Polfe *(Polf)* Mikken's father

Prent *(Prent)* A healer for the Dusk.

Quenson Avenaire *(KWEN-sohn)* A Sorcerer for the Dusk.

Raefe Coltori *(RAFE)* A swashbuckling apprentice, Saesa's brother, lives in the Ganvent Manse.

Rian Eldinae *(RI-an)* Mage of His Majesty's Elite, Azi's childhood friend and love. Son of Mya and Elliot.

Ruben Ganvent *(ROO-bin)* An orphan living at the Ganvent Manse.

Saesa Coltori *(SAY-suh)* Azi's squire, a friend of Tib, lives in the Ganvent Manse.

Sapience *(SAY-pee-ense)* The Keeper of Kythshire's Wellspring

Sarabel Plethore *(SAY-ra-belle)* Princess of Cerion. Middle child, betrothed to Prince Vorance.

Scree *(SCREE)* Earth fairy. A rock, son of Iren, leader of the Ring.

Shoel Illinviesh *(SHOHL)* White Line, section leader

Shush *(SHUSH (like rush))* A Wind fairy, and high-ranking member of the Ring in Kythshire.

Stone *(STONE)* Leader of a band of thugs for hire, worked with Dub in Call of Sunteri.

Stryker *(STRIKE-er)* Gustaven's Faedin, Gatekeeper of Brindelier - Cerion's archway

Stubs *(STUBS)* An earth and plant elemental who lives in the Dreaming.

Sybel *(SIB-bel)* A Sorceress for the Dusk.

Thalin *(THAH-lin)* High Advisor to the Throne of Brindelier.

Tibreseli Nullen (Tib) *(TIB (like bib))* A slave to the dye fields who escaped to Cerion.

Tirie *(Tee-ree)* Margy's Nursemaid.

Tirnon Plethore *(TEER-non)* His Majesty, King of Cerion.

Tristan Ganvent *(GAN-vent)* Nessa Ganvent's husband, and Admiral of Cerion's Royal Navy.

Tru *Troo* Griff's father.

Twig *(Twig)* A plant fairy who has a special bond with Princess Margary.

Viala Nullen *(Vee-AH-lah)* A Sorceress who conspired with Prince Eron. Sister of Tib. Became Ki.

Victer Davesh *VICK-tur* A healer in Cerion.

Vorance Evresel *(Vore-ANS)* Prince of Sunteri, and Sarabel's suitor.

Wrett Oldsen *(Rett)* An archer assassin.

Xantivus Ucrin *(Zan-ti-vus)* A Mentalist-Sorcerer working for the Dusk.

Yorid Gauntry *(Yo-rid)* Mage General of Incarceration in Cerion.

Zevlain Esen *(Zev-LANE)* An Elf Knight and Cygnet Rider of the White Line.

Zeze *(ZEE-zee)* Tib's cat companion.

Zhilee Nullen *(ZI-lee)* Tib's younger sister, who was killed by Sorcerers.

Zilliandin *(Zil-lee-ANN-din)* The Fairy Queen's high advisor.

ACKNOWLEDGMENTS

As always, I'm so grateful to God for giving me the inspiration to write, and to everyone in my life who supports me in me creative endeavors. Thank you to my family, especially James and Wes, who live with me while I daydream of fairies.

Thanks to my mom, who reads every chapter as I write it. Mom, you are the snuffer of self-doubt, and I will always love you for it! To Jennifer, your beta reading enthusiasm is so very appreciated. I always look forward to our conversations. To all of my friends who lift me up and keep me going every day, I love you. You are the best.

Special thanks also to my online friends in SIA, especially: Ann, Christina, GG, Ray, VM, Dwayne, Chika, BB, and Riley for their constant encouragement and advice. Extra special thanks to Owen. Your thoughtful assessments were just the push I needed to keep going. I will always be grateful to each and every one of you. <3

ABOUT THE AUTHOR

Missy Sheldrake lives in Northern Virginia with her amazingly supportive husband, brilliant son, and very energetic dog. Aside from filling the role of mom and wife, Missy is a mural painter, sculptor, and illustrator. She has always had a fascination with fairies and a great love of fairy tales and fantasy stories.

FIND HER ON THE WEB:
Website: missysheldrake.com
Blog: Missyflits.wordpress.com
Goodreads: Missy Sheldrake
Facebook: MissySheldrake
Twitter: @MissySheldrake
Instagram: M_Sheldrake

Printed in Great
Britain
by Amazon